THE HEADMASTER'S LIST

ALSO BY MELISSA DE LA CRUZ

The Queen's Assassin
The Queen's Secret
Cinder & Glass
Jo & Laurie (with Margaret Stohl)
A Secret Princess (with Margaret Stohl)

The Alex & Eliza Trilogy
Alex & Eliza
Love & War
All for One

Because I Was a Girl: True Stories for Girls of All Ages
(Edited by Melissa de la Cruz)

The Never After Chronicles
The Thirteenth Fairy
The Stolen Slippers
The Broken Mirror

Disney Descendants Series
The Isle of the Lost
Return to the Isle of the Lost
Rise of the Isle of the Lost
Escape from the Isle of the Lost

THE HEADMASTER'S LIST

MELISSA DE LA CRUZ

ROARING BROOK PRESS
New York

For Mike and Mattie, always

Published by Roaring Brook Press
Roaring Brook Press is a division of Holtzbrinck Publishing Holdings
Limited Partnership
120 Broadway, New York, NY 10271 • fiercereads.com

Our books may be purchased in bulk for promotional, educational, or business
use. Please contact your local bookseller or the Macmillan Corporate and
Premium Sales Department at (800) 221-7945 ext. 5442 or by email at
MacmillanSpecialMarkets@macmillan.com.

Library of Congress Cataloging-in-Publication Data is available.

First edition, 2023
Book design by Aurora Parlagreco
Printed in the United States of America

ISBN 978-1-250-82738-8 (hardcover)
1 3 5 7 9 10 8 6 4 2

ISBN 978-1-250-89401-4 (international edition)
1 3 5 7 9 10 8 6 4 2

In the end,

one of them was dead,
one was in jail
one was in rehab
and only one graduated.

Eighteen, headstrong and stubborn.
Seventeen, and headed to play soccer for Michigan.
Sixteen, and just got their driver's license.
Fifteen, and just along for the ride.

One of them was driving.
One of them was high.
One of them screamed.
One of them died.

ONE

SPENCER COULDN'T TAKE HER EYES away from the officer's pen as it hovered over his report, patiently waiting. The cap of the pen had been chewed like a dog toy. Her head throbbed, pain all over. She blinked, realizing he'd asked her a question.

"What?"

Spencer's mother squeezed her hand and said, "Can't we do this some other time?"

"I understand that, Dr. Sandoval. I truly do. However, a child died. We take these things very seriously."

Spencer's gaze landed on his badge. Officer Potentas, no, *Detective* Potentas. He'd introduced himself earlier. Her brain was hazy around the edges, like a cloud. How much time had passed? A second? An hour? The drip of the IV was cool in her arm. Spencer could sink right through the hospital bed and onto the floor.

"Okay, Spencer, let's try again. What happened last night? Can you walk me through it?"

Scream. Float. Crash. An eternity in the blink of an eye. Who screamed? Did she?

"There was an accident," she said, and swallowed, her throat dry. Her teeth felt too big for her mouth, or maybe it was the other way around. He wrote as she spoke. "We were at a party . . . Before school starts. End of summer. In the hills."

End of summer. End of *Spencer*. Her heart pounded. Why was it so hard to breathe? She didn't feel real. She wasn't sure she was talking; in fact, she wasn't sure she had a mouth and she folded her lips over her front teeth. Drip-drip went the IV, away-away went the pain. Cloud nine.

"Do you remember who was in the vehicle with you?"

"My boyfr—Ethan."

"The driver."

Spencer's breath hitched. *Scream. Float. Crash. Pain. Ethan.*

"Do you remember what happened next?"

When she screwed up her face, remembering, the skin on her cheeks pinched. Stitches from her cheekbone to her jaw. Sewed together like a doll. Chewed up like the detective's pen cap. "No. I can't . . . think."

"She's on sedatives, Detective," her mother said. Her brown hair was so shiny, like a penny. Spencer wanted to reach out to touch it, but her other hand was in a cast and too heavy.

"I know this is difficult. But everyone's story checks out. I'll be in touch."

One minute the detective was sitting at the foot of her hospital bed, and the next he'd teleported to the door where

Spencer's father stood, holding Spencer's sister's hand while talking to a doctor. The detective said something to him, and her sister Hope looked at her and something inside Spencer snapped.

She cried, blinked, reliving it all over again. *Scream. Float. Crash.* She had to go. Run for help. Her mother held her down and called out, and a nurse rushed in and pushed a button on the IV. More cold snaked up her arm. Sink into the bed. Let it swallow her up. Sleep came over her like a wave crashing on shore.

"Shoo . . . shoo . . ." Her tongue felt like a worm trying to crawl out of her mouth.

"He's going, sweetie. He's leaving," her mother said, squeezing her hand.

Her lids were almost closed, going bye-bye. *Scream. Float. Crash.*

Bliss took her away.

Los Angeles Police Department
Crash Report Form

Crash Severity

Fatal / Injury / PDO

Time & Location Information

Date of Crash: 03/SEP/2021

Time of Crash: 2:30 A.M.

Time Officer Arrived: 2:34 A.M.

Weather Conditions: Clear

Road Hazards: None

At Intersection: Sunset Blvd & Benedict Canyon Dr

Number of Motor Vehicles: 1

Number Injured: 3

Number Fatal: 1

Section 1

Vehicle Year: 2019

Make: Porsche

Vehicle Type: Automobile

Use: Private Transportation

Airbag deployed: Yes

State: CA

Vehicle Identification Number: ███████

Vehicle Speed Est. 120 mph

Posted Speed: 45

Section 2

Name of Driver: Ethan Amoroso

Current Address: ███████████

Date of Birth: 12/NOV/2003

Driver License Number: ███████████

Injury Status: Minor injuries, declined transport

Drug & Alc. Test: Pending

Section 3

Please Fill Out for All Other Occupants Involved

Spencer Sandoval—18—F—Injuries requiring hospital transport

Tabby Hill—16—F—Minor injuries, declined transport

Christopher Moore—15—M—Fatal

Officer's Notes: Vehicle 1 collision—damage extensive—no fire. No immediate danger to first responders. Impact with tree (standing). Light conditions dark-lighted. Weather clear. Driver sitting on pavement next to Passenger 2 prone, unconscious. Driver suffered injuries to head and shoulder. Passenger 2 had substantial injuries to arm and face. Passenger 3 emotionally distressed on curb, visible facial injuries. Passenger 4 remained in vehicle, fatal status. Resuscitation unnecessary. EMS arrived at 2:45 A.M. Driver and Passenger 3 declined transport. Driver claims they were coming home from a party in the hills. No tire marking to indicate brakes were applied. Driver tested for alcohol and drugs on-site. Pending results.

Officer Diagram Attached

Case Status: Open

Get Salty: A True Crime Podcast with Peyton Salt

[Get Salty Intro Music]

Peyton Salt: Welcome and good listening, Salters. As always, I'm your host, Peyton Salt.

Sasha Firth: And I'm your cohost, Sasha. You're listening to *Get Salty*, now the twenty-fourth most downloaded true crime podcast on Earworm, the world's most popular podcast hosting network!

Peyton: Twenty-fourth! Incredible! Can you believe it? We love you all so much, Salters. Our fans are so supportive, and we look forward to getting some new merch available on our website as a special thank-you. Maybe some mugs or pins. We'll do a poll on our subreddit so people can decide! How does it feel, Sash?

Sasha: Unreal. I get to share my love of true crime with all of you!

Peyton: Oh, for sure! But this week, I've got a story for you, Sasha, that is as juicy—if not the juiciest yet, because this one is recent and hits close to home for me.

Sasha: Oh yeah? Tell me more!

[SFX: crickets, tires screeching, crash]

Peyton: In the early hours of September third, just a few days ago, a parent's worst nightmare—a phone call, informing them their child wouldn't be coming home. In a place like Los Angeles, the home of the rich and famous, one might be surprised to find themselves surrounded by death and tragedy. After a frantic nine-one-one call, EMTs arrived on the scene to find a black Porsche 911 Targa wrapped around a palm tree at the corner of Sunset Boulevard and Benedict Canyon, a scene of terrible carnage in the center of Beverly Hills's glitz and glamour. The driver and owner of the vehicle is Ethan Amoroso—

Sasha: How do I know that name?

Peyton: I'm so glad you asked! We covered a case a while back—

Sasha: Oh! The house party!

Peyton: Exactly. Episode one thirty-one, for anyone who wants to go back and listen. I know you Salters are already googling it furiously as I speak! [*laughs*] But for anyone who needs a refresher—the driver and owner of the vehicle is Ethan Amoroso, All-State athlete and millionaire's son and classmate of mine, the same Ethan Amoroso who two years ago was at the center of a huge scandal involving a serious accident at a party at his house in Brentwood, an incredibly affluent neighborhood in Los Angeles. Allegedly, the victim fell off a second-story balcony, suffering extensive injuries to the head, neck, and back, leaving the victim in a coma.

Sasha: That's awful!

Peyton: Usually we don't cover these kinds of cases, just because they're tragic if not common, but you can see why this one caught my interest. Star athlete, the Brentwood neighborhood, an obvious suspect.

Sasha: Now I know what you meant when you said this case was "juicy." Like OJ!

Peyton: [*laughs*] It's true, the murder of Nicole Brown Simpson did happen in Brentwood, but that's an entirely different case. We're not here to speculate, obviously, but you can see why I was so excited to share this! These kinds of things just don't happen in Brentwood. Ethan's involvement in one accident is a tragedy, but two accidents . . . let's say, my eyebrows are raised! Ethan hadn't been charged with anything before. Who knows what will happen now?

Sasha: What do you know so far?

Peyton: Ethan Amoroso and three others had been driving home from a party celebrating the end of summer, one last rager before school starts, in a residential development property called Highwood Estates in the hills when he crashed at high speed, shredding the car to ribbons. Only one person in the vehicle died. The victim, fifteen-year-old Chris Moore, was adored by just about everyone. He was about to start his sophomore year at a private school called Armstrong Prep.

Sasha: Ooh la la. Sounds fancy.

Peyton: [*laughs*] I know I risk doxing myself because I'm a junior at Armstrong, but I'd be doing a disservice to the community not talking about it. The tailored uniforms, the designer backpacks, daddy's money—definitely not my style, but it's the norm at Armstrong. Ranked top in the country in academics and athletics, Armstrong Prep is a private school for the rich and soon-to-be famous. Nestled among the meticulously green lawns of movie stars and tech moguls in the hills, it's the perfect spot for privilege to go unchecked, a sort of bubble from the real world. Ethan and all the others in the car are students there, one of them was even his girlfriend, I know them all personally and the incident has shaken me to my core. For sure, this is a tragic way to start the new school year.

Sasha: So the police don't think it was an accident?

Peyton: They want to charge Ethan for aggravated reckless driving and child endangerment, but they haven't arrested him yet. At the end of the day, I mean, it was an accident, but a senseless and selfish one.

Sasha: The cops sound real serious about this. Are they doing anything about it?

Peyton: Well yeah, an innocent kid died, Ethan put everyone in that car in danger. It could have been so much worse than it actually was. He could have hit another car even! Ethan had been going over one-hundred-and-twenty miles an hour before he crashed. I've got the police report right here.

Sasha: Drugs? Alcohol?

Peyton: It was a high school party in LA, of course there were drugs and alcohol. Duh. But the toxicology report on the driver hasn't come in yet. Since the case is so new, there's no other information to confirm, but it's safe to say that I won't be surprised if we find out he was drunk or high. He has a reputation after all.

Sasha: Horrible. What kind of person would do that?

Peyton: Someone who's not told *no* a whole lot. He actually just returned from a stint at a behavioral rehabilitation center—basically military school, but he came back to Armstrong Prep for his senior year. Could it be that he hasn't learned his lesson?

Sasha: Was Ethan the one hosting the party again? Like that accident before?

Peyton: No, for once. This party was thrown by the son of a multimillion-dollar housing developer, using the unfinished mansions like their own personal playground. Out in Mandeville Canyon, most of the houses are just skeletons of what their grandeur will soon be. Because they're empty and on winding streets up the mountain, with excellent views of the ocean by the way, it's the perfect location for a party to run wild. No neighbors to complain about the noise. No running water, no electricity, no rules. Rich kids just party different from the rest of us. Armstrong is like that.

Sasha: What makes the school so special?

Peyton: At Armstrong, there's this thing called the Headmaster's List. Only a few students are chosen every year, but everyone tries to make the cut since it's a surefire way to get into the best colleges. The Headmaster himself writes your recommendation. It's super competitive. Think of it as an honor roll but on steroids.

Sasha: Are you on it?

Peyton: No, sadly. I'd kill for a spot. But I'm too busy with this podcast anyway! Guess who is, though! None other than Ethan Amoroso. The crazy part is that everyone in that car was on the List too. The only one who wasn't was the victim, Chris Moore.

Sasha: That's crazy! I hope justice can be served, that Ethan will face the consequences of his actions.

Peyton: We'll see about that. His family is wealthy, like, absurdly wealthy. His parents are on what the school calls the "Headmaster's Circle," an exclusive club only for the richest donors to the school. It's easy for Armstrong to look the other way when you're in the Circle, especially when your family is helping to pay for a new stadium or the year's theater production. Is he on the Headmaster's List because of his daddy's money? Who knows. But I've been going to private school long enough to be cynical about these types of things. He's going to have a ton of resources on his side, but one can only hope that the case against him is strong. It's a shadowy reminder that privilege is a real problem. Being in Armstrong's good graces has shielded him from a lot of consequences. Affluenza is a disease! That's why I want to start a fundraiser

for the victim's family, so I'll set up a link on our Instagram page where you can donate in their time of mourning. Maybe we'll add a pin or T-shirts, showing support and getting the word out about the case. Justice for Chris!
I plan to keep you and all our Salters up to date on this case as it inevitably proceeds. But first, a word from our sponsors . . .

[End segment transcript]

Update from the Uploader:

BREAKING: Ethan Amoroso has been charged with felony manslaughter! Stay tuned for more episodes!

TWO

SPENCER WAS SECRETLY GRATEFUL THAT her parents had left her in peace for a couple minutes. If the doctors hadn't interfered, they would continue to fuss over her, constantly asking her every five minutes if she needed anything. Sleep. Lots of sleep. Maybe some more pain meds. A snack. And a book, something mindless. Her dad, chronically unable to sit still, went to the bookstore in the hospital lobby, no doubt picking up some reading material for them all, and her mom went to the cafeteria, hopefully grabbing Spencer as much cake and chocolate as her stomach could handle.

It was her younger sister Hope's first day of eighth grade at Santa Monica Middle School, so the lumpy chair she had draped herself in while flipping through channels on the television in the corner for the past week was empty. Things had been chaotic since the accident, but Spencer was starting to get into the rhythm of hospital life. Wake up, nurses make the rounds, a dietary aide asks her what she would like to eat for breakfast, eat breakfast that was unfortunately not sugary enough for her unquenchable sweet tooth, nap, check her pain levels, eat lunch, nap again, check her pain again, dinner, sleep, wake up with a nightmare, sleep, start over the next day.

Perhaps nightmare wasn't the right word. Night terror. Emphasis on the terror.

Scream. Float. Crash.

Memories of that night were still hazy, but the emotion was real. Her mind convinced her body that she was back in Ethan's Porsche, and she'd wake up in a cold sweat, screaming and crying, and the nurses would come running to make sure she wasn't being murdered. She couldn't help it. Flashbacks of the crash felt just the same as the real thing. Sometimes it would take a moment to realize where she was, but it would take hours for her heart to stop hammering in her chest and realize she wasn't actually dying.

It got bad enough that Spencer was afraid to close her eyes. She kept seeing the second before impact over and over again on a nonstop loop. They'd given her sleeping pills to help, but it could only do so much.

But being awake didn't solve her flashbacks, either. She couldn't stop it.

The doctors said she would need time.

While Spencer was alone for a glorious few minutes, she tried not to think about the crash and focused on counting the drop ceiling tiles. Two hundred six, if anyone asked. She was sick and tired of the daytime talk shows on every television channel in existence. Her phone had folded in half in the crash, completely destroyed, so she wasn't able to text anyone, hence her newfound interest in counting tiles.

Her phone had been such a fixture in her hand, sometimes she'd fumble around in the folds of the sheet trying to find it before she remembered that it was gone. She wanted to think about literally anything else other than the wreck that was her life.

Hospitals, in Spencer's opinion, were made for three things: sickness, death, and waiting, the last of which Spencer was extraordinarily familiar with. They'd kept her for a week for observation, and that meant Spencer didn't do much else but be confined to her hospital bed for the better part of a week, bored to tears. Already, the skin beneath the cast on her arm was starting to itch. The surgeon had done a good job, at least from what she could tell, putting the bones back into place inside her body where they belonged.

That meant Spencer would have to get used to this cast for the next four weeks at least, plus physical therapy to get back in shape enough for field hockey. She'd played field hockey year-round since she was fourteen, and she wasn't about to let a broken arm, wrist, and face stop her now. Even if she did have such a huge gash on her cheek it hurt to even smile.

Voices carried down the hall. They were muffled at first but got clearer as they grew closer.

"Oh, she's my sister, it's okay."

Before the baffled nurse could say anything more, Olivia's smile entered the room first, in her bubbly Olivia way, clutching a fistful of balloons in her hand. Olivia Santos definitely wasn't Spencer's sister, but they might as well have been. Ever since middle school, they had been next to each other on class attendance sheets, always had their lockers next to each other, and were practically joined at the hip. Muscles she didn't even know were tight loosened in Spencer's back when she saw her best friend in the whole world.

"Wow, you look terrible!" Olivia said with a grin, her cheerful face a welcome difference from the tired and professional expressions of the hospital staff.

"Hey, Liv."

Olivia snapped her gum between her teeth, dark eyebrows rising behind her round, gold-framed glasses. "Dang, you must be on some heavy-duty stuff. That's the best you can say to me?"

Dang. Olivia had the tongue of a sailor, more apt for a pirate with an eye patch and a peg leg. Even though she dressed like a woodland fairy when they weren't in their school uniforms and flitted into any room she entered because simply walking was too boring, she disarmed anyone who wasn't expecting it with her dirty mouth. She only censored herself when she was particularly upset, which was somehow more sobering than Spencer had anticipated.

Spencer hadn't looked at herself in the mirror since the crash, opting to avert her gaze whenever she hobbled to the en suite bathroom, like when she'd spook herself after playing a game of Bloody Mary at a sleepover and she was too afraid to look in the mirror and find out if the legend was true.

If it was as bad as it felt, Spencer didn't need to see.

Every time her fingers accidentally brushed over the stitches across her cheek to wipe away a stray hair, her thoughts immediately went to Frankenstein's monster. Children would see her in the street and scream and run for their lives. She couldn't blame them.

"It's not so bad . . . ," she said.

Spencer's eyes went to the IV bag, where more of the drugs were dripping through her veins. It was nice—the outside of her mind was soft and fuzzy, like the edges of a faded photograph.

"You look like you've lost about twenty IQ points. That stuff is making you dumber than you already are."

Their friendship was strong enough to consist of plenty insults-of-love, but Spencer didn't have the frame of mind to reply quickly. She felt like she would float away if not being held down by all these IV lines and weighted blankets.

"You better be bringing me coffee with that kind of roast," Spencer said, her lips lifting in a smile.

Olivia snorted and pulled out a Starbucks mocha-in-a-can from her purse, sweating with condensation and cool from the vending machine, and put it down with a flourish on Spencer's food tray, saying, "That better have not been a pun."

"I love you so much," Spencer said, cracking it open.

"Me, or the mocha?"

"It's not mutually exclusive." She always had a sweet tooth.

Olivia snorted and pulled up a chair to sit next to Spencer's bed. If Spencer hadn't gotten into the crash, she and

Olivia would be at the local café, Beans, right now—a ritual during their lunch break at school—and a privilege to go off campus grounds for the hour.

Olivia kicked her shoes off and rested her bare feet on Spencer's bed, as if she wasn't here because her friend had just suffered a traumatic car crash, but like she was lounging at the beach. Her blue toenail polish was chipped. Spencer wasn't sure why she focused on that detail—the painkillers made everything slow down, allowed her to hone her focus on the minor stuff, like seeing the detective's chewed pen cap that first night. She felt like her brain was processing information at half speed.

Spencer took a sip of her mocha and the sweetness of the chocolate instantly made her feel a thousand times better. She had been sick and tired of drinking apple juice out of the little plastic cups they gave her at mealtimes.

"For real, though," Olivia said, "how are you doing?"

"I'm okay. Surgery went well. No scissors left inside me, I'd call that a major win." She wiggled her fingers in her cast.

Olivia's eyes went to Spencer's cast. "I don't just mean your arm."

Spencer's lip twitched when she tried to smile. Blink. *Scream. Float. Crash.* The memory hit her just as quickly as the car hit the tree. She should never play poker; she wore her emotions on her face like a bright neon sign. "It's whatever."

That really was all she remembered of the crash.

Everything else was too out of her reach. Scrubbed clean. A blank slate.

Olivia's full lips were pressed into a thin line, but she didn't ask any more about it. From her purse, she pulled out a purple Sharpie. Olivia's bag was like Mary Poppins's, a nether realm of infinite space. Sometimes Spencer wondered what she *didn't* have in there—a severed and cursed human hand, a toboggan, the secrets of the universe? Olivia began absently drawing on Spencer's cast. She'd broken her left arm and shoulder in the crash, her dominant arm. Olivia decorating her cast would at least be an aesthetically pleasing temporary art piece in the meantime.

Olivia was a gifted artist, having won a series of art contests at Armstrong, her usual medium being charcoal, but her talent wasn't lost on the groove of Spencer's cast.

"Sorry I couldn't come see you earlier," Olivia said without looking up from her work. "They wouldn't let non-immediate family members in at first."

"I would have said you were my sister too, for the record."

"You better! We're practically twins."

"It's nice having you here. Things have been a little strict and all. Cops everywhere, trying to figure out what happened."

Olivia nodded soberly. "You really don't remember anything?"

"We talked to a neurologist, and a ton of doctors; they ran a bunch of tests. Apparently it's really common with head injuries after these kinds of accidents. I might get my memories back, I might not."

"Don't stress about it. Just don't hit your head anymore. You need all the brain cells you have left."

Spencer tugged on the end of Olivia's straight, platinum-dyed bob but let out a breathy laugh. Olivia swatted her hand away and stuck out her tongue.

"For real, though," she said, "do you remember that night?"

Spencer shook her head. "I remember the party. But, like, bits and pieces. I remember a fight with Ethan ..." Olivia raised her eyebrows ever so slightly at that, but Spencer didn't point it out. Olivia always had opinions about Ethan, but she had kept them to herself, resigning herself to only the language of her eyebrows to indicate any sort of feeling.

Olivia hadn't been at the party. Though they were best friends, they didn't do absolutely everything together. Olivia's definition of fun ended promptly at teenage she-nanigans and loud drunk people. Spencer simultaneously wished Olivia had been there, just so they could talk about it, but she also regretted that she hadn't decided to stay in with Olivia instead.

Spencer still couldn't wrap her head around the fact that Ethan had been charged for the crash. She'd heard police officers talking about it outside her hospital room a few days earlier. The tips of her ears burned at hearing his name. At one point not too long ago, her stomach swooshed with excitement hearing it. Now his name just left her feeling bitter.

"After that, I don't remember anything except, like, flashes. It's hard to explain. Like, I blink, and sometimes I remember it, the tree coming right at me. But the rest is just blank." *What with a literal gallon of painkillers coursing through my veins*, she thought.

"But you know about Chris, right?"

"Yeah. I know." The words felt like they took up a lot of space in her throat, and she had a hard time swallowing. She couldn't even take a sip of her mocha.

Chris Moore, everyone's little brother, had been pronounced dead at the scene. Killed instantly, was how everyone put it, taking away the implied edge of suffering. She didn't want to imagine the circumstances that would kill a person instantly, so she fought to keep that thought away.

It was hard for her to believe he was dead. Spencer could still see Chris's lopsided grin in her mind's eye. He was the son of one of her favorite teachers, Mr. Moore, and she'd seen the family resemblance from the start. Thinking he was dead now didn't feel right, like it was a fact she needed to disprove somehow because she'd just seen him the other day! He'd come to the Brain Freeze, the ice cream kiosk that she and Olivia worked at part time and on weekends, and he'd ordered a large chocolate-dipped cone, extra sprinkles.

He couldn't be gone, that just didn't happen to kids their age. And yet it was true; otherwise Ethan wouldn't be in so much trouble.

Oh, Ethan . . . Her stomach clenched wondering where he was now. It was a miracle he'd been able to walk away from the wreck with only a couple of scrapes, whiplash, and a broken nose. He was lucky. The bastard.

Spencer hadn't known Chris too well since he was younger than she was, but they mingled in the same circles, even though he was an AV kid glued to his computer.

"His funeral was today," Olivia said quietly, not looking up from her work on Spencer's cast.

There was nothing to say to that. Olivia cleared her throat and started coloring in the alien creature's face on Spencer's cast with crosshatch strokes.

No one expected Spencer to be at the funeral. She was still too injured to go anywhere except the five feet it took to get to the bathroom and back. The doctors were still concerned about her concussion and resulting memory loss. The last thing they wanted was for her to fall unconscious while in their care. The funeral was off-limits. She doubted Chris's parents would want to see her anyway. Seeing her might have been a bitter reminder of what their son wasn't—alive.

Olivia didn't mention Chris again the whole time she decorated Spencer's cast. Spencer had let a rerun episode of Steve Irwin's excitement over a venomous snake fill in the silence. In Olivia's own words, she didn't do well in the whole "expressing one's feelings" department; she'd rather put it on paper with charcoal. Spencer focused on her drink and finished it just as Olivia started sketching the outlines of a tentacled monster wrapping itself around Spencer's wrist.

In a mood to change the subject, Spencer asked, "How's the first week of school?"

Olivia rolled her eyes. "Typical. Spencer Sandoval gets into a freaking car crash and all she can think about is school and homework. Be normal, Miss Overachiever."

Spencer didn't deny it. Overachieving was in her DNA. "Please! It'll make me feel like everything's the way it used to be for a little bit." Spencer was one of the top students in her class, earning a coveted position on the Head-master's List—the alumni of which went on to become Pulitzer Prize–winning journalists, esteemed artists, even US senators vying for the presidency. She'd worked hard for it.

Olivia didn't put up a fight. Who could argue with a bruised and bloodied girl in a cast? "Well, Becca Thompson got that nose job she was talking about. We've got a sub for history since Mr. Moore, you know, because . . . And the whole school is talking about the crash, like it's the next . . . Maybe we shouldn't talk about it." She went back to her drawing.

"What are they saying?" Spencer knew from her tone that it wasn't going to be good.

Olivia looked hesitant.

"Come on, I've got no connection to the outside world. I need to know."

Olivia took a long second, cringed, and said, "Let's just say people are . . . *happy* to see Ethan get arrested. Like, almost rabid with excitement. There was this viral video that went around online of the cops taking him out in handcuffs and people made memes and stuff. I just think it's so crass. I mean, a kid died, why do we treat this like some reality TV show? I know we live in LA, but come on."

Spencer's stomach dropped as Olivia spoke. A chill streaked down her back and she suppressed a shiver. *Scream. Float. Crash.* All other details hazy, but she could relive those few seconds over and over again without any control. Breaking up with Ethan that night was still as raw as the gash in her cheek. She remembered that much, but only bits and pieces of their fight before the crash. Breaking up with Ethan had hurt deeper than any physical pain she'd experienced.

When she wasn't remembering the crash, she was remembering the way Ethan had broken her heart.

"That junior, Peyton Salt?" Olivia said. "The one with the podcast. She's all over the story like it's her own ticket to fame. She's milking what happened for her own credibility. It's gross. She's making it seem like it's this story, and . . . well, it's working. Ethan is a bad guy everyone can hate."

It had been an accident. Why were people acting like Ethan had meant to hurt anyone? Sure, he drove a little too fast sometimes, and he got a few tickets now and again, but he wasn't a monster. Spencer and Ethan dated for two years, even when he was sent away to a behavioral rehabilitation camp. Two years of movie nights, and Valentine's Day presents, and texts goodnight. He had always been wild, full of life, and had a way of sending a thrill down her spine, but did people really hate him that much?

Olivia sighed. "Sorry, I didn't mean to unload all of that on you." As if sensing the shadow looming over Spencer's head, Olivia tried to lighten the mood. "You'd be happy to know that I've got a metric ton of homework for you in my bag, so you've got something to do, you crazy person."

Spencer smiled ever so slightly.

THREE

SPENCER TURNED THE ORANGE PILL bottle over in her hands, worrying at the sticker label with her name on it with the edge of her nail. Vicodin was going to be her best friend for the next few months while she recovered. Earlier in the day, after passing all the discharge checks, she'd been cleared to go home and would start school tomorrow, Monday, a whole week late. Never did she think she'd be so eager to get back to normal.

"One or two tablets every four to six hours as needed," the doctor said while her mom packed Spencer's clothes and things away into a duffel bag she had brought along for the long stay. Spencer was finally going home, and she was more than ready to fall into her own bed and crawl under her own sheets. The doctor was sure to give her the rundown on what to do when not being looked after twenty-four seven. "Try not to take too much more than that if you can help it. Your clavicle will be sore for a long time since we can't splint it, so try not to move it too much."

"And that means no field hockey," her mom said.

The doctor nodded. "Especially no field hockey. Any sort of contact sport, really anything to do with your upper body, is off-limits. That means no carrying heavy things, like helping out with groceries, until we can make sure you're healing up right."

"What about school? I can barely hold a pen."

"I'll forward a note to your school. You'll probably have to have someone else take notes for you and carry your books until you're able to do it yourself. Spencer, need I remind you that you shattered several bones in your wrist? You need to take it easy and manage your pain until you can get back to your usual routine. You can't rush this."

Olivia had delivered Spencer's homework to her every day she couldn't attend, but her left arm was useless, and writing with her nondominant hand was harder than she'd thought. The idea that someone would need to take notes for her in class was more annoying than she wanted to admit. She had a very particular method of note-taking, and studying in general, that involved intense organization and color coordination. The person would need to be in all her classes, and be good at taking notes like she was, and be willing to tolerate her finely tuned strategies for maintaining her GPA. She couldn't afford to fall down on her grades, especially not now.

Her dream was to get into Caltech. She wanted to be an astrophysicist, even an astronaut if she could pass the tests, more than anything in the universe, and if she slipped up in even one subject, it could make or break her future. No one, nothing, especially not broken bones, was going to stand in her way.

"How long until I can play?" she asked. "Field hockey is

the only thing keeping me sane right now." Spencer didn't want to whine, but it hurt being told not to compete. She had been conditioning all summer long, running sprint drills in the park, footwork circuits with cones and jump ropes in her backyard, and going for hour-long runs before even the sun woke up. Being told to sit on the couch was about as easy as telling the sky not to be blue.

"Come back and see me in a couple of weeks when we get your cast off and then we can talk about physical therapy and getting you back onto the field. You want to have use of your hand again, don't you?"

"Yeah," Spencer said with a sigh. She knew field hockey wasn't everything, but a whole part of her life had been taken away in a single instant. Why couldn't she have broken the bones on the right side of her body? Even the surgeon had said he'd expected her right shoulder to have been broken instead, consistent with car crashes of this type, but of course she couldn't be that lucky. The important part was that she was expected to make a full recovery. That was what mattered.

The doctor went on, "I also want to help arrange a psychotherapist for your night terrors. PTSD isn't something that can heal as easily as broken bones, so you need a specialist who can help. Mrs. Sandoval—excuse me, Dr. Sandoval—I'll forward you a recommendation list so you can decide who is the best fit."

"Thank you." Mom and Dad were both veterinarians but still earned their titles as doctors. They were both from immigrant families, and Spencer and her sister were the first generation born in the States.

The doctor left, and her mom packed away the last of Spencer's things into her duffel bag before she held out a helping hand for her daughter to slide into a wheelchair, which Spencer thought was a bit overkill. Without delay, she wheeled Spencer out of the room, almost like she too was finally getting sick of the smell of antiseptic cleaner and soap.

The nurses bid her goodbye as they passed, which was definitely a nice touch on what Spencer could only summarize as being one of the most miserable times of her life, but she smiled and thanked them for their kindness.

In the elevator on the way down, Spencer twisted around to look at her mom. She wasn't wearing her usual green scrubs with a paw print embroidered on the breast. Sometimes it startled Spencer seeing both of her parents out of uniform, only because they were so often at the clinic. She didn't want to imagine how many hours they had to close its doors to take care of her.

Their vet clinic, a twenty-four seven emergency animal hospital called Paws Perfect in Culver City, was almost always busy. But Spencer had never seen dark circles as deep around her mom's eyes as they were now.

"I'm freaking out about school," Spencer said. "I can't miss any more days. The Caltech admissions office will probably look at my record and see a gap, and what if they don't care about what happened?"

Her mom only smiled in that tired but soft way that meant she understood it was Spencer's perfectionism getting the best of her. She squeezed Spencer's right shoulder assuredly.

"We'll figure everything out. Don't you worry. For now, there's someone special waiting for you at home."

The entire drive home, Spencer could barely open her eyes. She had them squeezed shut as she gripped the car door's armrest, willing herself not to panic. Every time her mom so much as tapped her foot on the gas, Spencer's stomach lurched like she was going to fall, and she gripped the armrest so hard, her fingers were numb and weak. Her hips were still bruised from where the seat belt in the Porsche had stopped her from flying through the windshield, and her sternum ached with the pressure the seat belt put on her chest now in her mom's Nissan Leaf.

"You okay, Spence?" her mom asked as they paused at a stoplight.

"Fine," she said through gritted teeth. "Just . . . go. Please?"

The light turned green, and Spencer braced herself. *Scream. Float. Crash.* Her throat was closing up and she tried not to go back to the crash, but it was easier said than done.

"We're almost home, sweetheart. Almost there." She eased the car forward once more.

Spencer was on the verge of tears but held her breath,

forcing herself not to cry. It burned in her chest. All she wanted was to fling the door open and throw herself out so she wouldn't have to endure it any longer.

She wondered if Tabby Hill, the other passenger who'd survived the crash, was feeling the same way about driving. Spencer knew Tabby, who was nonbinary, had just gotten their license. What if Tabby was too afraid to drive now? And Ethan . . . what was Ethan doing right now? Guilt was a monster roiling in her gut. If she'd been the one driving, what would have happened?

She wouldn't be deathly afraid of moving vehicles, that was for sure.

SPENCER! She heard Ethan's scream, echoing in her thoughts, a second before the crash. It was a new memory, one that punched her in the gut, and she remembered the terrified look in Ethan's eyes, the side of his face lit up as the headlights closed in on the tree before . . . His face was all wrong, all wrong, but she didn't know why.

Spencer covered her eyes with her hands and willed herself to breathe. She counted the seconds it took to inhale, and exhale, until her mom pulled them up to the driveway and turned the car off.

Their house, a cozy Craftsman-style two-story in West Los Angeles, was lit up in the bright blue afternoon sky. Spencer's car, a beat-up minivan (named "Gertie" because the van looked like a Gertie), which she'd bought off Craigslist when she got her license, would remain parked in the driveway for the foreseeable future. Hope and Dad were already home, waiting for them. She even spotted the flicker of the television through the living room window. Everything about the house seemed normal, and it occurred to Spencer that it was she herself who had changed.

Spencer tried to wiggle herself out of the passenger's seat, fumbling—thanks to her cast—with the lock on the seat belt. She couldn't get out of the car fast enough.

"Do you need any help, sweetheart?" Spencer's mother asked, a permanent furrow between her brows these days.

"I said I'm fine, Mom." Spencer unclipped her seat belt and opened the door. Her father had already opened the front door, waiting for them with a big grin.

Spencer's home was a much welcome change from the eggshell-colored walls of the hospital. The living room was the heart of the house, warm and vibrant with plush furniture and low-pile rugs that made one want to curl up with a book plucked from the wall of shelves. Her mom had put a mountain of candles inside the fireplace since they hardly used it. The couch in the living room looked like an awful good place to park herself after the arduous car ride.

Hope already had the right idea, sprawled on the couch with her phone playing a game. Usually she would be in the garage hammering away at her Rube Goldberg machine, but it seemed like she'd been called in to welcome Spencer home, though begrudgingly so. It was actually kind of a relief that twelve-year-old Hope hadn't changed a bit since Spencer's accident, being annoying as ever, because that meant some things could get back to normal. Her parents treated her like she was made of glass and might shatter at even the lightest touch.

"I already called dibs on naming her," Hope said, without looking up from the screen. Her phone dinged cheerily, as if mocking Spencer's confusion.

"Dibs? Naming her?" Spencer asked.

"Hopie . . . She already has one," Dad said. He kissed Mom on the cheek as she came into the house, carrying Spencer's things for her.

Mom threw Hope a withering look that didn't have any kind of heat behind it. To Spencer she said, "Your father and I—we talked with your doctors, and your father made some calls to get it fast-tracked. We had some old friends from school running a program out in Boulder."

"What are you talking about?"

"Why don't you go to your room and see for yourself?"

Spencer looked back and forth between her parents, whose faces were bright and excited, and she knew she wasn't going to get anything else out of them. Curiously, Spencer made her way upstairs, taking the steps carefully by holding on to the handrail for support, not intending to let her excitement put her back in the hospital, and headed toward her room at the end of the hall.

Her room, warm and inviting, the perfect place for her to throw herself down on the bed and stare up at the glow-in-the-dark stars above, glad that she didn't have drop ceiling tiles to count anymore. She had taken pride in decorating the room herself, in a soft robin's-egg blue peeking out behind all her band posters, and she'd even built her desk facing a large window of their quiet street, where she would gaze absently, ruminating over her essays or giving her eyes a break from staring at a screen for hours. She'd missed her room desperately and was glad to be back.

The newest and most unexpected addition to her room was waiting for her at the foot of her bed.

Small sounds of excited panting came from a large crate at the end of Spencer's four-poster bed and a copper-colored tail wagged through the metal bars. It was a fox-red Labrador, poking its snout through the slates of the crate, watching her with warm brown eyes.

"A dog?" Spencer asked, turning as she heard her dad come up behind her.

He leaned casually on the doorframe. "She's your service dog. She's going to be helping you through your recovery." He avoided saying the term "post-traumatic stress" like it was a curse word. Instead, her parents elected to use "recovery" and "struggles," as if it made what had happened to Spencer not as crippling as some might make it out to be. Her parents were trained medical professionals, but they were experts in the four-legged variety of medicine. They were trying to make Spencer feel better by lessening the impact of a word like "disorder."

"Are you sure?" Spencer asked. She'd never had a dog before. Even though they were vets, her parents were at the clinic most of the time, and with Spencer and Hope in school and doing almost every extracurricular offered, no one was home to take care of one. It was like the cobblers' kids having no shoes. No pets for vets.

Her dad moved toward the crate and put his palm flat against the bars, letting the dog lick his hand. "Of course we're sure! She's here to help. Our friend from school runs a charity in Colorado specifically training dogs to care for people with psychiatric needs. Like pressure therapy, disrupting emotional overload, reminding you to take your medicine, and even waking you up from nightmares, if you have them." He said *if*, but he really meant *when*. Spencer had already woken up every night from flashbacks so real, she'd start screaming in her bed loud enough that the nurses came running. Spencer could hardly contain the bubble of emotion swelling in her chest.

She wanted to feel grateful, but she couldn't help that instead she felt resentful, and she hated herself for it. It wasn't the dog's fault, or her parents', for that matter. But the dog was a reminder of what had happened. Not only would the evidence literally be on her face, but now she would have a dog at her side, broadcasting to the world that she was . . . broken. Everyone would treat her differently. Everyone would see just how badly her life had been ruined.

Dad unlatched the crate and the dog ambled out, heading straight for Spencer, tail wagging expectantly. The dog was already wearing a vest with patches sewn onto it specifically saying SERVICE DOG and DO NOT PET and I'M AT WORK. She licked Spencer's hand, then nudged it with her wet nose. Spencer wiped the drool on her jeans. Labs were always so slobbery; she'd seen her fair share at her parents' clinic, and the coldness of it jarred her.

Her mom appeared behind them, already having swapped out her contacts for her grandma glasses everyone so lovingly teased her about. "We still have to sort it out with the office at Armstrong, because you'll need to take her out at least once during the school day to do her business, but your doctors agreed, a service animal is a good idea."

"That's right, but remember, Spence," Dad added, "this isn't a pet. It's serious. She's a working dog, doing an important job. She's your friend, but she's also here to help you. She's to perform specific tasks and not play with your classmates. Understood?"

All manner of thoughts swirled in Spencer's head. She really wished that things could go back to normal, and a dog right now was feeling like a lot, on top of having to constantly be reminded about what Ethan had done every time she moved her shoulder wrong or caught her reflection in passing. Hesitantly, she asked, "Do I have to?"

"What's the matter?"

Spencer worried her lower lip with her teeth. "It's just another reason for people to stare."

Her parents glanced at each other before her mom said, "Sweetheart . . . It's for the best. Truly. Once you get used to it, you'll see."

"But what if I don't want to get used to it? What if I want things to be like they were? Normal?"

"This is normal. Lots of people have service dogs. There's

nothing to be ashamed of. This doesn't change who you are. You're still you, only now you're you with a little sidekick."

Dad said, "We'll feel better if you had some help when we're not around. You'll have more freedom too, especially at school."

Spencer dreaded the thought of school now. What would everyone at Armstrong think? *Poor little Spencer Sandoval needs special treatment, boo-hoo.* The dog looked up at her, eyes bright, tail wagging, waiting for a command. If things had been different, maybe Spencer would have been more excited about it, but pain in her shoulder was making her grumpy. It wasn't the dog's fault that she was in this mess. If this dog could help her focus on her schoolwork and get her back on track for Caltech, she guessed she could give it a shot.

Spencer took a deep breath and relented. "What's her name?"

"Ripley, like from *Alien*. Apparently, her handler was very into sci-fi movies. I think it suits her, though."

"Ripley, huh," Spencer said, testing it out. The dog's tongue snapped back into her mouth at the sound of her name, and Spencer smiled. It helped that Ripley was cute.

They would have a lot of work to do together.

FOUR

THAT NIGHT AT DINNER, RIPLEY sat under Spencer's chair at the dining room table, exactly as she was trained to do, while they all ate together as a family, a Sunday evening ritual that seemed more important than ever according to Mom. She'd ordered takeout from their favorite Thai restaurant—a special treat after all the hospital food everyone had been eating for the past two weeks—sure to add some desperately desired spice to Spencer's craving for flavor. The egg rolls smelled divine, and she almost swallowed them whole without chewing first. Even with a week's worth of practice, it was still hard using her right hand to eat. Chopsticks were impossible to manage, so a fork had to do.

No one spoke for a while, as if no one was sure what to say anymore. What else was left besides the treacherous topic of Spencer's ex-boyfriend having accidentally killed a kid?

Spencer was thankful that no one said much while they ate. She wasn't in the mood to talk about it, she was so tired, and she absently rubbed her foot on Ripley's back, raking her toes lengthwise down her spine. Ripley's leg thudded excitedly on the floor as Spencer hit just the right spot.

"What's this around Ripley's neck? It doesn't look like a normal collar." Spencer referred to a black band with a plastic rectangle on it, sitting above Ripley's leather one with her ID tag on it.

"Oh, it's just a GPS thing, all service dogs have them." Her dad shrugged.

"So when will you be normal again?" Hope demanded. She was using her chopsticks like two spears, one in each hand.

"There's nothing wrong with her," Dad said matter-of-factly. "Besides, it's not what we say about these kinds of things. There's nothing wrong with Spencer."

Hope ran her tongue over her braces and added, "Well, my friends at school are talking."

"Is it talking or is it just rumors, Hopie?" Mom said.

"What's the difference?"

"Rumors mean it's not true."

"They say Ethan was drunk or high, which means he's definitely guilty."

"Can we talk about something else?" Spencer interrupted, trying to put on a smile but failing. She hated how her heartbeat accelerated at the simple mention of his name.

Scream. SPENCER! Float. Crash. Pain.

She blinked furiously, scrubbing Ethan's terrified face out of her mind's eye. If she'd been holding wooden chopsticks, she was sure she would have snapped them in half, her grip was that tight.

"Okay," Hope said, and shrugged, eyeing the last egg roll on the plate. Spencer didn't blame her; she was at least saying what was on her mind rather than hiding behind a false sense of normalcy. The pain radiating from Spencer's shoulder gave her something to focus on. She needed another dose of Vicodin. The one she'd taken at the hospital was starting to wear off.

"How are you feeling about going to school tomorrow?" her mom asked. "You can stay home another week if you'd like . . . Get back into the swing of things slowly."

"No, I want to go. I need to. I don't want to be stuck in bed anymore."

"I can drive you," her dad offered, but Spencer shook her head. Usually she took Gertie the Van because she had field hockey after school, but she didn't want to be in a car again.

"I'll ride my bike. It'll be a nice workout before class at least."

"With Ripley?"

"She can run alongside. It's not *that* far to school," she said. They lived below Pico, whereas most kids who went to Armstrong Prep lived right by school in the tony neighborhood where it was located. "Right? I can't . . . I don't want to get into a car again. At least, not for a while."

Her parents glanced at each other. Mom tipped her head and murmured, "Riding home was rough for her today."

Dad looked at Spencer in a way that made her heart break, so she stared at her plate. "Sure, kiddo," he said. "Anything you need. Ripley will be with you the whole time, but if you ever feel like you need to come home early or if you're not feeling well—"

"I'm not made of glass, I swear, I'll be fine."

Her parents exchanged looks, but they didn't fight her—there was no winning against Spencer's determination.

Dad said, "The doctors mentioned that it will take a little while for you to adjust to everything, and we don't want you to push yourself too hard."

That used to be Spencer's every day. She had always needed to give everything of herself and more at work, school, and at field hockey practice. She'd enrolled in almost every club possible: debate, yearbook, chess, pi club, somehow able to fit everything into the day and still have time to work and eat and sleep. For her, taking it easy was not, in fact, easy. Some people might call her stubborn and hardheaded, and she was not used to asking for help.

With her broken arm now, though, she didn't want that to slow her down, although inevitably it would. She needed to focus on getting her applications done for college and she couldn't miss the deadline. Caltech wasn't going to wait for her. They wouldn't care if she broke her arm and was late on submission. Besides, Spencer hated being late, more so when others were late. Nothing else put her in a bad mood more than someone showing up later than they said they would.

Injured or not, she was going to get everything in on time.

"Weren't you guys the ones who said I needed to get into the best school?"

"That was before . . . ," Spencer's mother said.

"Before what, a debilitating car crash that killed a kid and almost killed me?"

Shocked silence.

After a moment, Mom barely managed to say, "It was an accident, Spencer. You need to go easy on yourself. It wasn't anyone else's fault but Ethan's. He's made some mistakes and now he's suffering the consequences. It's not up to you to decide what happens to him next. You need to focus on yourself and your future."

The way she said it made it sound like Ethan's future was already decided for him. Again, she saw his face, lit up in her memory, the surprise, the panic . . . He'd looked at her, right before impact, like he'd wanted to see her right before it all went dark. And something about it didn't feel right. She didn't know what, but she kept seeing his face every time she closed her eyes, like he'd been the one who died, and not Chris. His beautiful face was haunting her.

"May I be excused?" Spencer asked. "I need to get my stuff ready for school tomorrow."

Her parents exchanged another round of looks. She expected that would be happening a lot in her presence. Her attitude could use a check, but she had pity points she was willing to cash in. No one argued with her when she pushed back from the dining room table and Ripley moved out from underneath, following her up the stairs, taking the steps with her at her side. Only two years old and already so well trained, it was like Ripley knew what Spencer needed at all times.

When they made it back to her room, Ripley took up

a spot at the foot of Spencer's bed and watched as Spencer moved around her room, gathering her notebooks and supplies for her late start at Armstrong. Her uniform hung on a hanger, pressed and ready in her closet.

It was a nighttime ritual she looked forward to. She always put her things in her bag the night before school, sorted her books by smallest to largest to fit in the largest pocket, stowed her pencil case on top, and double-checked that her headphones were wrapped neatly in their case. Organizing everything the night before meant that it was one less thing she had to worry about in the morning. Even being five minutes early for something was considered late according to Spencer—a fact that Olivia liked to heckle her about. Olivia had a casual relationship with schedules. But Spencer was adamant. Her future was on the line.

In fact, when she'd taken the SATs just last month, Spencer got pulled over for running a stoplight, which forced her to have less time before the test to study, giving her only forty minutes when she'd planned on having a full hour. She didn't want to admit that it threw her off her rhythm. It'd be all her fault if she lost five hundred points on the test because of it.

Spencer wiggled her fingers in her cast, analyzing just how she would be able to put on the long-sleeved white blouse over her cast and decided it would be a problem for tomorrow. She turned to Ripley lying patiently on her bed, her head lowered between her front paws but watching Spencer with eyebrows raised, ready to jump into action at the first sign.

"What am I forgetting?" Spencer asked, mostly to herself but directed at Ripley. It was an attempt to jog her memory.

She moved to her closet, making sure she had everything for her uniform, and instead she found one of Ethan's hoodies, hanging on a hanger. Her stomach dropped at the sight of it. Evidence of him kept popping up, she couldn't escape him. In one move, she pulled the hoodie from the hanger and looked at it. Green, his favorite color, with a white stripe down both sleeves. She'd loved wearing it, especially at night when she could curl up in bed, pretending he was next to her. It still smelled like him, and she frowned.

Her parents hadn't approved of Spencer's relationship with Ethan, but they never stopped her from dating him. She knew they thought he was spoiled and irresponsible even though they never said it out loud. They had rules about people being over when they weren't around, as well as a keep-her-bedroom-door-open policy too, in case anything got too wild. They might have hoped that she would outgrow him, see that they just weren't compatible. At the end of the day, Spencer supposed they were right, but she would never admit it to them.

With a noise of disgust, she crumpled up the hoodie, threw it into a corner of her closet where it landed in a heap on the floor, and yanked the closet door shut, sealing her feelings away.

"I can't stop thinking about him, Ripley," Spencer said, keeping her voice low in case Hope had her ear pressed up against the closed door, which was an all-too-common occurrence in the house.

Ripley just looked at her, eyebrows moving as if trying to analyze the look on Spencer's face, trying to figure out if she needed help. Spencer wasn't sure this was the kind of thing Ripley would be able to help with. Everyone had said that the crash was an accident, but Spencer had the strangest feeling that things didn't happen the way everyone said they did.

Scream. SPENCER! Float. Tree. Ethan. Crash.

It was so strange. She remembered seeing the palm tree, lit up, brighter and brighter, as the headlights went careening toward it. Ethan's face, his eyes. The roar of the engine. Like an old VCR she could pause and rewind the memory.

She wasn't able to place a concrete reason as to why, but it felt like a pinprick in the back of her mind that something was wrong.

She still had no memory of the crash, or some of the hours leading up to it. The last part of that night she specifically remembered was breaking up with Ethan, screaming at each other, her back to the party raging behind them, Ethan's face slathered in guilt. His hands, the bounce of his hair as he shook his head, the dot of light in his dark eyes as he pleaded with her to forgive him, the way his cologne washed over him. It was a memory so real, she could touch it. But she couldn't remember getting into the car with him. Why had she gotten in his car if they were fighting?

Scream. Float. Crash.

And then the next thing she remembered was being in the hospital. It was like her brain was a thousand-piece puzzle and she was missing five hundred pieces and the box with the picture on it had been thrown away. No guide. There were so many questions that she needed answers to, and none of it made any sense.

"I know I'm probably overthinking this," she said to Ripley, knowing full well it wasn't any use talking to a dog, but it made her feel better saying the words out loud. "I just can't help but think it isn't right. I can see Ethan in my mind, but something is wrong. Something . . ." In her memory, he'd been wearing that hoodie in the crash. How could it be possible, though? Unless memories were overlapping one another, of driving with him before . . . Something else about his face was wrong, but she didn't know what. She couldn't trust her own mind anymore.

SPENCER! Crash.

Ripley tilted her head at Spencer, the folds of her ears raised curiously. Of course, she didn't know what Spencer was saying, but it was funny to think she did.

"You believe me, right, Rip? You don't think I'm crazy?"

Ripley's tongue lolled cheerfully.

"It's okay if you do. I think I'm crazy."

Ripley yawned and put her head on her paws, blinking drowsily. It was getting late.

So Spencer went to bed with Ripley warming her feet, staring at the glowing stars on her ceiling, seeing the lines of the tree and hearing Ethan's voice, until she fell asleep.

FIVE

SPENCER PARKED HER BIKE AT the rack in front of the east entrance at Armstrong Prep and caught her breath, wiping the sweat on her brow with the back of her wrist.

The school, a building in Romanesque Revival that exemplified the elite education that would be taking place inside its walls, sat on the edge of a hilltop surrounded by dense forest and gardens. It radiated excellence. Anyone who looked at it got a sense that this was an important place to be. To Spencer, it was just school.

Ripley waited patiently for Spencer to lock up her bike, panting after having jogged alongside Spencer the whole thirty-minute ride from her house to school.

She'd had to pedal fast to get there on time. Even though she had prepared for her return to Armstrong, she still scrambled to remember things before she could head out the door, like taking her medicine, and showering without getting her cast wet, and making time for her mom to help her with her braids because she couldn't do it with one hand. On top of that she couldn't find her favorite flats, the sparkly ones with bows, which Hope insisted she hadn't borrowed, which made Spencer have to settle for her old loafers. The medicine made everything soft, made her feel like she was losing track of everything.

She'd needed to figure out the safest route, avoiding the busiest streets and taking mostly neighborhood roads past the hedged estates and gated lawns, down the street where she worked at Brain Freeze, passing by St. Mary's with its marquee letter sign out front saying PRAY FOR JULIANNE, though groundskeepers were switching out the name with the beginnings of CHR, riding past the tents for homeless vets erected in the park, and taking a shortcut through the parking lot of the Brentwood Place Shopping Center. Admittedly, when she wasn't swerving out of the way of cars either oblivious to her presence or intentionally trying to get as close to her as possible to scare her, the ride itself was quite peaceful, what with the warm sea breeze slicing through the early morning sunlight that countered the dreamy haze of the morning's dose of painkillers. Spencer had quickly learned that the city was not designed for bikes. By the time she pulled up to school, she only had a couple minutes before the first bell.

Spencer cradled her cast to her chest as she fumbled with the bike lock's key in her right hand, trying to turn it but failing. This was one job Ripley couldn't do without opposable thumbs, but Spencer even had *those* and still struggled. She didn't want this one thing to fluster her, but she couldn't help the feeling of eyes watching her.

Before school, students often gathered on the front lawn,

sipping from their ventis and enjoying the last bits of the morning before the first bell ushered them into first period. Spencer was in the minority in riding her bike to school. It was more common to see BMWs and Teslas in the parking lot than her dad's old Schwinn on a bike rack, but that wasn't the reason people were staring at her now. She was capital *I* Involved in the crash that killed Chris Moore. Of course, she had prepared herself for this moment, ever since Olivia had said it was all the school talked about, but it didn't ease the tension that coiled in her gut when it was actually happening. Spencer tried to keep her head high, but no matter what, everyone knew. How was she supposed to get back to a normal life if she was forever labeled as That Girl from The Crash?

Even if they didn't know her name—which was wasn't likely since Armstrong's class sizes were small—they'd see it all over her face. The stitches in her cheek weren't going to be taken out for another week, but Spencer couldn't stand to miss out on any more school than she already had. It was her senior year, the most important to maintain her perfect GPA, and college application deadlines loomed. If she fell behind, even with her grade point average being one of the highest, she couldn't risk letting that be the deciding factor of her getting into Caltech or not.

She cursed under her breath when the key wouldn't twist in the lock. Would Caltech even want someone who failed at such a simple task as locking up a bike?

"Do you need some help?"

Without looking up, she said, "I got it." The key still wasn't turning. She wasn't going to be some damsel that needed Prince Charming to swoop in and save the day. Especially not Jackson Chen, Ethan's best friend.

"You sure?" Jackson's scuffed-up Vans appeared in her field of view as he stepped toward her. She lifted her eyes, squinting into the sunlight, landing on Jackson's gentle smile. Personality-wise, he was the polar opposite of Ethan. Whereas Ethan lived as if the runway was coming up short, Jackson's whole demeanor was more suited to the carefree surfer lifestyle. He had his skateboard tucked under his arm. Like Spencer, he'd opted to leave the car at home. He, however, lived closer to school than she did. He didn't look like he'd even broken a sweat.

"I'm fine." She wiggled the key, but it refused to budge. She thought about asking him how he was feeling, knowing his best friend wasn't coming to school, currently under house arrest, but she didn't quite know how to phrase it without sounding nosy. She settled on: "How are you?"

"Oh, you know. Here," he said with a shrug. Everyone knew that when a person said that, they were the opposite of *okay*. She knew that feeling all too well.

"Cute dog," he said about Ripley. Her tail slapped happily on the ground, as if she knew he was talking about her.

"Don't pet her. She's working." Spencer didn't mean to sound so clipped; her temper was shorter these days because everything wouldn't stop hurting.

"Of course. I can read, you know." He was referencing

the patches on Ripley's vest. "Doesn't change the fact that she's cute, but I'm not sure a service dog can turn a key. Are you sure you don't need a hand? Having two might work."

Spencer was about ready to kick her bike over in frustration before she took a deep breath. Riding her bike, especially so soon after the accident, may not have been such a great idea after all. Her legs already ached. But she'd never been in the habit of asking people for help. All her life, she'd been independent, getting a job scooping ice cream for some extra cash, picking up Hope after school in Gertie the Van, making dinner when their parents were working late. Asking for help was not in her user manual.

Before she could say anything else, Jackson kneeled down, setting his backpack and skateboard at his side, and pulled the chain tighter into the lock, allowing Spencer to twist the key.

"Thanks," Spencer said. She slipped it into the small pocket of her own backpack and picked up Ripley's leash.

"I get it. I broke my wrist skateboarding when I was ten. I don't think I have to tell you about the hassle of going to the bathroom . . ." The corner of his mouth quirked up, creating a little dimple in his tanned cheek. Unlike Ethan, he took a lot of the same AP courses that she did, but their schedules never lined up.

Spencer couldn't stop the smile that spread on her lips even though thinking about Ethan sent her stomach into knots. She'd known Jackson already for a few years, and seeing a friendly face eased her nerves.

Jackson was always the mild-mannered one whenever

Ethan would invite his friends over to swim in his pool, often the one to mellow out Ethan's high-octane energy with an easy laugh. He was on the soccer team with Ethan and was always over at his house. She had always thought he was cute, but seeing him now just reminded her of Ethan.

"Spencer!" Olivia's voice carried over the grounds. She was crossing the green lawn, waving her arm over her head.

Spencer thanked Jackson again before she and Ripley headed to the low wall where Olivia waited.

"And so she returns!" Olivia sang with a twinkle in her eye and together they headed into the building just as the first warning bell rang, giving them ten minutes to get to first period.

Coming back to Armstrong as a senior, Spencer expected much to stay the same. The long stretch of hallway branching off into classrooms lined with lockers painted burgundy to match school colors, the school crest in the tile underfoot, the posters broadcasting the upcoming homecoming dance and auditions for the school plays. School was back in session.

As Olivia guided her to where their new lockers would be for the year, Ripley made sure to keep the swell of students crowding through the halls at bay, a trained behavior that Spencer was more than a little thankful for. Obviously, people stared, both at Spencer and at the dog at her side. The crowd often parted like the Red Sea to get a better look. The flush on her cheeks stung. Her first day was already starting to be more overwhelming than she expected. The first thing she saw was a reminder of the crash.

A locker in the middle of the hall was covered in posters and flowers, messages left behind for Chris.

NEVER FORGOTTEN

MISS YOU FOREVER

LOVED YOUR SMILE

A group of sophomore girls stood in a circle close by, comforting another who was in tears, sobbing as mascara streaked down her cheeks. "I just m-miss him so m-much!" Her shoulders bounced with each hiccup.

Spencer kept her head low as she walked past. Chris's school photo was featured on a huge poster, smiling at her from the grave. He looked so young, especially for being only fifteen. It was a bitter reminder that he had just been a kid. Her stomach was threatening to rebel against her breakfast, but she kept walking. Everyone stared. She saw a couple of people wearing buttons with Chris's name on them. Voices carried, despite being hidden behind hands.

"—see her face?"

"Ethan's girlfriend—"

"Can't believe she's here . . ."

Spencer kept her focus firmly on the polished tile floors beneath her every footstep. Ripley bumped into her, encouraging her to keep going. Olivia eventually showed them to Spencer's new locker, conveniently right in front of the library entrance, and as expected, it was right next to Olivia's because of their last names. Spencer was grateful for the things that stayed the same today. No surprises.

Spencer gathered her things for homeroom. Per tradition,

Olivia and Spencer had synchronized their schedule, taking all the same classes, the only exception being homeroom—art for Olivia and study hour in the library for Spencer.

It took three tries doing her combination before Spencer got the locker open. She kept getting distracted by the unnerving feeling of stares on the back of her head.

"Just ignore them," Olivia murmured, gathering her acrylics from her decorated locker. This year's theme was apparently cottage core aesthetic, complete with a real daisy chain and pressed flowers on colorful construction paper collages taped to the back of the door. She always took the time to make her locker look pretty, saying it was a way to decompress in the middle of institutionalized academia designed to brainwash her into corporate life.

Spencer, however, liked the routine and schedule of school. Her binders were always color coordinated based on the subject, her notes meticulously organized and filed, and who didn't love a brand-new set of stationery at the beginning of the year? As words such as "anal-retentive" were thrown a lot whenever her name was brought up, Spencer preferred the term "chronically prepared."

Ripley pressed her body up against the back of Spencer's thighs, a gentle reminder that she was there, and Spencer nodded to Olivia, unable to find words that didn't make her feel like puking. She wanted to talk about the crash, about how it didn't feel right, but she didn't know where to begin. The bubble of anxiety in her chest was about to burst.

Before she could say anything, though, Olivia switched gears. "So, birthday."

Spencer was relieved for a subject change. She'd almost forgotten. "Right! Did you have anything in mind? How do you want to celebrate the big one-eight?" Olivia's birthday was at the end of October, but she liked planning for it ahead of time, for once taking a page out of Spencer's book.

"I'm thinking a huge party, maybe in Malibu? Vegan barbecue and a chocolate fountain, and a DJ. Maybe a bonfire? We can have them at Carillo Beach. I haven't decided yet."

Spencer let Olivia talk but tried not to show the twitch forming near her eye. The idea of a party right now, especially after what happened the night of the crash, set her teeth on edge. She couldn't tell Olivia no, though. Best friends don't *not* show up for a birthday party. It wasn't her party; she didn't get to decide what it would be. But she would be lying if she said she wasn't hoping to spend it as a night in with Olivia and a handful of friends ordering pizza and playing video games all night.

"Sounds great, Liv . . . ," Spencer said, hiding the edge in her voice as best she could. "I can't wait."

Olivia rolled her eyes, grinning. "I know, I should just lean into the whole Halloween thing and do costumes, but I want something new. Don't look at me like that. I know I'm being a cliché having my birthday on the beach. But I figure I only have so long to live out my dreams of kissing people by the ocean with a full moon high in the sky like in a high school rom-com!"

Just after the first bell, a voice came on over the sound system. "Good morning, Armstrong Eagles! Spencer Sandoval, please report to the headmaster's office. Spencer Sandoval."

"Uh-oh!" some guy called down the hall, jeering. "Someone's in *truh-bul*." A smattering of laughter followed.

Another voice called, "Your boyfriend better not've killed anyone else!"

Spencer went rigid, the muscles in her back seizing up. She closed her eyes and tried to quell the panic rising in her chest.

Scream. Float. Crash.

SPENCER!

Objectively she knew that wasn't why she had been called to see the headmaster. Her rational mind understood it was unlikely. But her body was trying to convince her that she was back in the car, going too fast, crashing. Sweat beaded on her forehead. Ripley tapped her cold nose on Spencer's palm, and it snapped her out of it long enough to remember to breathe.

"Shut up!" Olivia called at the heckler, which was only followed by more laughter. "Don't you have a bridge to live under, troll?"

"It's fine, Liv," Spencer said, slamming her locker shut. "I'll see you in physics."

SIX

IT GOT EASIER AND EASIER to make her way to the administrative office as people hurried to homeroom, clearing the path for her all the way to the west wing of the building.

Before she could open the door it swung away from her, and she nearly crashed into someone coming out. She took a faltering step back and said, "Hi, Tabby."

Tabby's expression morphed from startled to shocked to disgust in the fraction of a second upon seeing Spencer.

"Oh, it's you."

That was not the kind of greeting Spencer expected. Tabby Hill's face was a sickly shade of yellow, an attempt to cover the obvious bruise that remained from the crash, the makeup only hiding so much. Like their namesake, Tabby glared at Spencer through a sharp wing of cat-eye eyeliner.

Tabby looked down at Ripley with a scowl, then looked at Spencer like she was something unpleasant that had crawled out of a swamp. "See you're taken care of, huh. Must be nice."

The new kid at Armstrong, having enrolled mid-spring last year, Tabby was also on the Headmaster's List, an accomplishment in such a short amount of time, probably thanks to her parents being one of the biggest donors in the Headmaster's Circle. Like that podcast noted, money made things happen at Armstrong.

Tabby was in a different social circle from Spencer, usually hanging out with the emo and theater kids behind school near the emergency exit to vape and watch YouTube videos between classes. To be honest, Spencer didn't consider Tabby a friend, but rather they were friend*ly* toward each other. At least that's what Spencer always thought. Now she wasn't so sure. Tabby's attitude was frigid at best.

The way Tabby looked at Ripley made Spencer prickle, like Ripley was annoying or being a nuisance even though she was just standing there.

Spencer didn't know how to react. Did Tabby have some problem with her service dog? Her grip tightened instinctively on the leash.

Tabby didn't say anything else, just waited, staring Spencer down with a twist of the lips and folding their arms across their chest. At first, Spencer's mind went blank, processing what to do, until she decided to step aside. Apparently, that was what they had wanted all along.

Tabby pushed past Spencer and marched out of the administrative office, long black hair swinging. Spencer stared at the back of their head, wondering just what the problem was, but headed into the office.

The admin assistant, Mrs. Ross—a little old lady with round, Coke bottle glasses, barely tall enough to see over the counter where she sat—told Spencer that Dr. Diamond, the headmaster, was expecting her and that she could just "head on back there, okay, sweetie?"

When she did just that, Dr. Diamond, headmaster at Armstrong Prep for the past ten years, looked up from behind his grand oak desk, framed beneath a whole wall of books and accolades and awards from his tenure teaching at Oxford before taking up the task of molding the minds of future leaders in sunny California. His accent still had a hint of London in it when he spoke. He reminded Spencer of a chipmunk wearing a tweed coat, like something out of a children's picture book. He smiled at her and beckoned her to sit in one of the upholstered chairs in front of his desk.

Among his books were framed pictures of all the students on the List. It was a way for him to show off his best students, an academic humble brag of sorts, like a parent proud of their children. Spencer spotted a photo of herself in action, taken from field hockey state champs last year, mid-throw. If she could say so herself, she thought it was quite a good shot. She looked strong. The newest addition to the collection was Tabby's, with their acting headshot, looking as glamorous as an old Hollywood starlet.

Next, there was Jackson's photo. He was goalkeeper for the varsity soccer team, his gaze focused on a penalty kick coming from just out of frame, his gloved hands raised as he readied to leap. The shelf where one would normally see Ethan's photo celebrating a goal he'd just scored, clipped from the front page of the *Daily News*, was vacant.

"Good to see you're back on your feet, Miss Sandoval," Dr. Diamond said. Then he held up a finger as he paused, reared back, and sneezed loudly into the crook of his arm. It was so loud, Spencer actually flinched. She couldn't help it—loud noises had that effect on her these days.

"Excuse me," he said, sniffling.

Spencer hated that even the silliest thing like a sneeze could get her heart racing. Ripley rested her chin on Spencer's knee, grounding her back to reality. She was safe, everything was fine. She hoped he didn't notice how panicked she felt.

"I apologize," he said. He blew his nose into a tissue taken from a box on his desk. "I am terribly allergic to dogs."

Horrified, Spencer immediately moved to get up. "Oh, I'm—"

Dr. Diamond held up his hand. "Please, Miss Sandoval. It's no trouble at all. No trouble whatsoever. I understand your circumstance and support it fully. Ripley—is it?—is more than welcome in this building if it means your mental health is cared for. I'm afraid my own shortcomings are no fault of yours." He smiled but he sounded muffled, as his nose clogged up and his eyes watered.

Spencer smiled appreciatively, but she knew it came off as looking pained. The last thing she wanted was for someone's throat to close up because of her.

"How are you feeling being back at school?" he asked, swiping the tissue back and forth across his nose before throwing it into the wastebasket.

Spencer wanted to be honest, that being back at Armstrong was emotional to say the least, but she didn't want to admit to feeling like she was weak, or that she was seeking attention, or that she needed pity. She put on her best smile and said, "It's fine." She didn't want to think about Chris's decorated locker, or the girls crying in the hallway, or the stares that followed her wherever she went.

"If there's anything else I can do to accommodate for your condition, I'll be sure all the faculty know. No one should bother you about Ripley, either. Your doctor explained everything to me about your condition. If you need to step out of class at any time, take a break, as it were, feel free. Just don't go off campus or interrupt any other classes. Knowing you all these years, though, I don't imagine I have to worry about that." He sniffled and scrubbed his nose with pinched fingers, and it made a noise like a suction cup. "We want to keep our top student safe."

Spencer's cheeks grew warm. It was nice being reminded that all her hard work paid off.

"It's a terrible tragedy what happened to young Chris. I didn't know him that well, but he was a good boy. I know his family, his father is a fine teacher. He was a promising student, although he wasn't List material. Chris will be missed. Did you know him? Was he your friend?"

Spencer shifted in her chair. "Um, no. Not really." Chris was a freshman, and while she saw him around, she wouldn't go as far as to say they were friends.

"Ah. Well! So it goes." He sneezed again.

"*Gesundheit*," said Spencer.

When people found out that Chris was practically a stranger to her, it changed the narrative that many of them had formed about the crash in their heads. Questions swirled. Why was Chris in the car with Ethan anyway? Ethan was a popular senior; Chris wasn't at that level. It didn't make sense.

"Thank you." He blew his nose again but sounded too congested for anything to come out. "Even so, I'm not sure you've been made aware, but the school is hosting a small memorial service for Chris this Wednesday. A small garden has been built in his memory and we wanted you to say a few words at the candlelight vigil."

Spencer's stomach clenched. "I'm not sure I'm the best person to . . ." The thought of a hundred eyes on her, inevitably thinking the same things: that she had been in the car with Chris, that her boyfriend had gotten him killed, that she got to stand there now, alive, while Chris . . . It made her feel like crawling out of her skin.

Dr. Diamond continued, "Of course, we had discussed it, figuring since you were headed toward valedictorian status that you could take up the task. And we assumed since you were in the car with him that you were friends—"

"I'm sorry, Dr. Diamond. I don't know if I can handle doing something like that right now." Her voice wobbled like a plane in turbulence. She hadn't meant to cut him off so abruptly, but the walls were closing in on her.

She knew the school wanted to trot her out like they

always did. As one of the few brown kids at Armstrong, let alone a brown kid with one of the highest GPAs, Spencer was the face of their hastily put together DEIJ initiative. She never felt more like a scholarship student than when she saw her face plastered all over the banners that hung all over the school, or in every brochure. If you clicked on the school website, her picture was on the home page. Ethan used to joke she was Armstrong's only student.

Dr. Diamond watched her with sympathy, folding his lips together in resignation. "I see. That's disappointing. If you can't perform your duties as ambassador to student affairs, we can ask Hailey Reed instead. She's been eager to be more involved. It would only be natural for you to step down from the position. Though I don't imagine it would look too good on college applications if you did . . ."

Spencer clenched her jaw. Caltech would wonder why she couldn't handle basic extracurricular responsibilities. Holding that over her head felt like a low blow, especially after what happened, but she couldn't say anything. He knew he had her. Not only that, but for Hailey Reed to replace her in yet another realm of Spencer's life . . . She tried not to think about finding Hailey with Ethan that night of the crash, but a simmering heat had taken up a permanent place behind her sternum.

Dr. Diamond smiled and went on. "Either way, we would love for you to be in attendance. I'm sure his parents would appreciate it."

Spencer highly doubted that. If she was in their shoes,

she wasn't sure she'd ever want to get out of bed again. But she didn't say anything to contradict him. He was too busy honking into a handkerchief to notice the queasy look on her face.

He clicked his tongue behind his teeth. "It's been quite the start to our school year. One can only hope to move on for the better."

Spencer's gaze flicked up to the empty spot where Ethan's picture used to be. The headmaster too had written Ethan off. He was an embarrassment, a loser, no longer wanted. One mistake too many.

Dr. Diamond continued without noticing the sour look on her face. "I understand that you don't want to speak at the ceremony; however, we need some photographs of him for the stage. Our printing staff will need high-quality photos and his family has already approved the request. We just need someone to pick them up, and seeing as you live close by, I assumed it wouldn't be an issue for you to take up the task."

"You want me to go to his house?" Spencer asked.

"Yes, is that a problem?"

Spencer's whole life was defined by trying not to be a problem. She even felt bad that she had inconvenienced the nurses while she was in the hospital. But she also wasn't one to say no to figures of authority, especially to someone like Dr. Diamond. She'd already said no to public speaking, so she couldn't say no to going to the Moore house now. Why was she such a people pleaser?

If she continued to disappoint, her spot on the Head-master's List could be in jeopardy, and with college accep-tance on the line, she couldn't risk it, not when there were others like Hailey who were so eager to take her place.

But she had a history with the Moores. Not only was Mr. Moore her favorite teacher, but Chris's older brother Nick used to babysit her and Hope when they were little. She couldn't avoid them forever; she'd have to see them sometime. Better it be her than a complete stranger.

"Um, no, I mean, I can do it," she said. She hoped he could hear the discomfort in her tone, but he perked up and clapped his hands once.

"Excellent! You're one of the finest students at this school for a reason. Your strength and courage will be an inspiration to your classmates."

Spencer crinkled her nose. The last thing she wanted to be was an "inspiration." She wished he had chosen a differ-ent word.

"Is that all you wanted to talk about?" Spencer asked.

"No, actually, I wanted to let you know that as well as having Ripley at your side, I've also arranged for a student to chaperone you while you recover. Someone who can assist you with your studies until you're well enough to do so on your own. I had to make sure the right fit was in all the same classes that you were, make sure the schedules were lined up, so they had to be at the top of the List."

"Who?"

"Ah, Mister Chen, right on time."

Spencer twisted in her chair to see that Jackson had appeared in the doorway, his hand hovering on the doorframe, prepared to knock. He looked worried that he'd interrupted.

"Sorry," he said, "I was told to come in—"

"Yes, indeed. Not a problem! Miss Sandoval and I were just talking about you. She would likely appreciate your help getting to first period."

Jackson's cheeks pinked but he smiled at her.

Spencer thanked the headmaster for his time and stood up, leaving Dr. Diamond sneezing as she followed Jackson, who had offered to carry her backpack for her. They left the office and headed toward the library together.

"So!" Jackson said, bridging the gap of silence between them. Spencer was still chewing on her unsaid words to Dr. Diamond. "I guess we should get started then, right?"

She nodded, gnawing on her lip.

Jackson rubbed the back of his neck. "I know it's awkward. They asked me to and—"

"No, it's fine. Really. Thanks. I'm just getting used to a lot of things all at once."

Jackson let out a breath. "Yeah. I get it."

She knew he really did. "I have to grab something I forgot in my locker."

Jackson jutted his thumb over his shoulder, still carrying her bag. "Okay, I'll meet you in the library."

Spencer hurried to her locker, Ripley's nails clicking on the tile along her side, and threw the door open. She wasn't upset that she needed help from Jackson; in fact, she was grateful that he was paired with her, but she was upset that so much had changed in such a short amount of time. Her independence was slipping away from her bit by bit, like water from a leaky tap, and she just wanted things to go back to the way she had planned. She wasn't ready to let go of her old life just yet.

She uncapped the orange pill bottle and popped one of the painkillers in her mouth. Things were starting to hurt again.

SEVEN

SPENCER STRUGGLED ALL DAY, DESPITE Jackson and Olivia's help and all her meds.

She spent the whole first period in the library with Jackson, sitting diagonally across from each other at a workstation underneath the glass ceiling, her favorite spot in first period. While she caught up on her required reading for English, a slog through *Crime and Punishment*, Jackson finished his essay for AP psychology on his laptop, his keystrokes a soothing rhythm in the quiet of the library. He'd agreed to share all his notes with her, sparing her the arduous task of deciphering his "terrible, godawful, embarrassing handwriting" (his own words), which lightened the mood. He'd be sitting with her in every class, ready to add any notes that she felt necessary. Because first period went so well, she expected the rest of the day would go by just the same, sailing through second period physics class, getting into the swing of things with Ripley nearby.

In third period, history class, Spencer met their new teacher, Mrs. McNamara. She'd be replacing Mr. Moore. He would not be returning to teach for the remainder of the year.

"It's nice to finally meet you, Spencer," she said, smiling when Spencer walked in the door. Mrs. McNamara was much younger than Mr. Moore, probably in her twenties, but already had ribbons of gray streaking through her dark hair, tied back with a pin. She was strikingly pretty, which Spencer noticed immediately. "We'll get you up to speed in no time."

Spencer usually sat in the front, but Mrs. McNamara asked that she sit in the back with Jackson, so that they could coordinate their note-taking without distracting the other students. A fair request, Spencer agreed. She situated Ripley on the floor next to her chair while Jackson and Olivia sat next to her.

Faces turned to stare at Spencer, taking in the stitches and the bruises and her cast, seeing the echoes of the crash written all over her body.

One of those faces belonged to Hailey Reed. When their eyes met, Hailey moved to look away, but she gave one last look before turning to face the front of the classroom, writing in her notebook furiously, as if to give herself anything to do not to look Spencer in the eye.

Hailey Reed was a perky blond volleyball star, the always optimistic go-getter, a walking stereotype, a prime candidate to join the Headmaster's List now that Ethan had fallen off. Spencer had had no problem with Hailey before the night of the crash. In fact, they might've been friends. She'd been over to Hailey's house several times for birthday pool parties over the years, but now Spencer didn't even want to share the same breathing space as her. She knew she was being harsh, but she allowed herself to wallow in her hatred for a while.

Seeing Hailey here in class, after what Spencer had gone through that night before the crash, made Spencer's heart tighten. Heat burned her cheeks and it took everything in her power not to throw the desk across the room. Hailey had known that Spencer and Ethan were dating, so it wasn't some innocent mistake. And Spencer wanted to hate her for kissing Ethan, but she hated Ethan for kissing her back.

"Are you feeling okay?" Olivia whispered, leaning in so only Spencer could hear.

"Yeah, why?" she lied.

"You look pissed."

"I'm okay. Really."

Just then, a classmate, Brody Dixon, slammed his huge textbook down on his desk, obliviously laughing with his friends about something or other, it didn't matter. Spencer nearly burst into tears, her whole body as tense as a rubber band ready to snap. Olivia must have seen the flash of panic that slashed across Spencer's face. She was positive she was having a heart attack. All she wanted to do was run out of the room, get somewhere, anywhere, that felt safe.

Being her best friend, Olivia didn't need to see the silver tears lining the edges of Spencer's eyes to figure it out. Olivia reached across the aisle and squeezed her hand. Ripley too felt the panic vibrating through Spencer's body and put her paw on Spencer's lap. It helped somewhat, but it wasn't a permanent fix.

The bell rang, ending the break, and Mrs. McNamara called across the room. "Okay, folks, settle down. Let's get started!"

It took Spencer almost the entire class hour to calm down, wobbling on the verge of hysterics, and when she finally did calm down, she felt like she was constantly waiting for the worst to happen all over again. Her mind went to dark places, expecting more and more outlandish scenarios to happen, like an earthquake that crumbled the school into dust around her or an asteroid blowing up the earth. The longer she sat with her thoughts, the worse it got. It was just a matter of time before her brain went into panic mode, forced to repeat the crash, and that felt almost as bad as it happening for real.

Scream. Float. Crash.

It was embarrassing, being on the edge of a breakdown all the time, especially when her whole life she'd been in control, confident, strong. Her life had been perfect. A handsome boyfriend. A perfect GPA. Gunning for valedictorian.

Scream. SPENCER! Float. Tree. Ethan. Crash.

She knew people thought she looked crazy, especially crying in front of her classmates, who were just looking for any excuse to stare.

SPENCER! Crash.

She almost didn't notice when the bell rang at the end

of class and everyone started filing out to the hallway for lunch.

"Spencer," Jackson said, his voice overtaking Ethan's in her memory. His voice was gentle, helpful. He smiled at her kindly. She got the impression that he'd been saying her name a few times before she heard him.

She couldn't help it. The doctors could only sew up her body, not her thoughts. She was fraying at the seams.

"Tabby's probably just jealous, that's all," Olivia said before taking a bite out of a giant pretzel she'd bought at the stand parked outside of school.

Olivia and Spencer had decided to take their lunch outside, letting Ripley go to the bathroom and then lie down in the grass, soaking up the sun before having to head back into class. Spencer sat on the low wall looking out over the grass and took a sip of her sweet iced tea. She was grateful for a break from four walls bearing down on her. Olivia had a college brochure open in her lap, flipping through a giant stack of schools to choose from. Unlike Spencer, she hadn't yet decided where she wanted to go. She'd been trying to narrow down her options, but it felt like a never-ending list of choices. In a way, Spencer was a little envious of Olivia, just because Spencer was positive Olivia would flourish wherever she went.

Spencer had told Olivia all about her run-in with Tabby at the admin office and how awkward it was. Olivia and Tabby were familiar with each other, what with Olivia working on set decorations for the school play—this year's big production being *Beauty and the Beast*—and painting the stage murals while Tabby rehearsed for their big number as Belle.

"No—*duh*, who wouldn't want to have a dog at school?" Olivia added, talking around her mouthful of pretzel. "Tabby is just . . . Tabby. I wouldn't think about it more than that, honestly."

Spencer, whose appetite had disappeared over the course of the morning, sipped on her sweet iced tea and watched Ripley as she circled the grass a few times before choosing the best spot to pee. She didn't want having Ripley to look like special treatment, like Tabby had said. Ripley was here because Spencer constantly felt like she was teetering on the edge of panic at the slightest thing. It wasn't fun, or funny, or anything to be jealous about.

Ripley came back to Spencer's side and sat down on her loafer, keeping watch of the other students milling about the campus grounds in small groups. She'd done a good job so far of keeping watch on Spencer's needs, almost like she was reading her mind.

Her shoulder was starting to hurt again.

"How are you feeling?" Olivia asked, sensing Spencer's discomfort.

Spencer pushed her shoulders back as best she could, shifting painfully. "Managing." All she could think about was getting back to her locker to take some more Vicodin.

"I know you won't listen to me, but I say you should call

it a day. Truancy is a harmless endeavor. Go home early. No one will blame you."

"I can't. Besides, I've got practice. And I'm supposed to head to the Moore house later to pick up photos for the memorial."

Olivia cringed. "Are you sure you want to do that?"

"I said I'd go, can't really back out now. Dr. Diamond kind of dangled college in my face over it. It's fine."

"If you say so . . ." Olivia's gaze stretched out across the lawn, watching a few junior boys play a quick game of Frisbee, their blazers in heaps on the ground. A group of sophomore girls walked past, carrying paper bags from the burger place down the hill, and Spencer caught sight of a flash of a bright blue pin on each one of their lapels.

#justiceforchris

Stay Salty!

She'd seen those buttons earlier in the day but didn't realize what they were until now. The sophomores gave her lingering stares as they walked past, and not just because Ripley had rolled over onto her back at Spencer's feet, paws dangling in the air, rubbing herself in the freshly cut grass clippings.

"Are those the pins from Peyton's podcast?" Spencer asked, once they were out of earshot. She'd never listened to her podcast before, thinking it sounded more like gossip than journalism.

"Yeah, some sort of fundraising thing. They sold pins to help raise money for Chris's family. I've been seeing people wearing them all over town." Olivia flipped through the college booklet in her lap. "This one says it's got the largest recreation center in the nation, plus private training sessions and three different kinds of swimming pools. Don't know why you need three different kinds. Water is water, right?"

Talking about college was an attempt at normalcy, and Spencer was grateful for the diversion. She let Olivia go on about schools, debating which one had the better campus life based on the stock photos the school had provided, while Spencer finished off her iced tea. Ripley needed to burn off some energy, so Spencer took out a fresh tennis ball from her backpack, purchased specifically for Ripley, and waved it for her. Ripley immediately leaped up and Spencer tossed it across the lawn, awkwardly of course since it was her nondominant hand.

Playing with Ripley helped ease the tension in her shoulders. Ripley's joy was contagious. They did this for a while, with Ripley fetching the ball and bringing it back to Spencer's outstretched hand. Spencer had to admit, it was pretty fun.

"Uh-oh," Olivia said, making Spencer turn around.

"What?"

"Don't look now, but Peyton Salt is watching you."

Spencer froze, watching Olivia's gaze go past her shoulder to where Peyton was standing. "What does she want?"

"An interview probably," Olivia said. She hopped down from the low wall and looped her arm around Spencer's waist. "Let's get out of here."

Spencer let Olivia lead the way. "Come on, Rip." Ripley bounced after them, obediently coming to Spencer's other side. She knew she was imagining it, but she felt eyes on the back of her head and when she turned to look, she saw Peyton Salt gawking at her across the lawn, her phone clutched in her hand. She was a mousy girl with wavy brown hair, but her eyes were sharp behind her thick-framed glasses.

Spencer let out a breath, trying to loosen the knot in her chest. Of course, Peyton would want to know what happened. Spencer would be the perfect source.

Scream. Float. Crash.

She just wanted to be left alone, even though she herself wanted to know why she felt like she was missing crucial information about that night.

While they walked together before the end of the lunch break, Spencer figured she might as well ask Olivia what she'd been meaning to all morning. "Do you ever think that . . . maybe the crash didn't happen the way everyone says it did?"

"Why do you say that?" asked Olivia.

"I don't know. Just a feeling, I guess."

"Ethan was driving. He was speeding and he lost control of the car," Olivia said sharply. "End of story. Don't stress about it. You need to take care of yourself."

"Yeah, you're probably right."

EIGHT

FIELD HOCKEY PRACTICE WAS ONE of the few things Spencer looked forward to, especially with the mess that was her life trailing behind her. Nothing would make her happier than to get back out on the field, but because of Spencer's cast, she wasn't allowed to play.

"Sorry, Sandoval," Coach Fray said. "You know I can't let you."

"Can I at least stand with you? I don't want to miss anything."

Spencer'd gotten dressed in her usual practice gear, minus her shin guards and cleats, in a show of support. But Coach Fray's eyes went down to Ripley sitting obediently at Spencer's feet.

"Does the dog chase balls?" Field hockey balls were made of hard plastic, a perfect chew toy for any dog to nosh on, but Ripley wasn't just any dog.

"She won't," Spencer said. "She's well trained."

"Even so, I think it'd be better if you took a seat over on the bench. You'll be back on the field in no time, I promise."

Spencer glanced at her teammates, all of whom encouraged her to take it easy.

"It's okay, Captain!"

"Girl, we're good!"

"Feel better!"

Spencer tried to smile. Being forced to watch from the sidelines while everyone ran drills without her was a particular kind of torture, but she knew it was no use putting up a fight. Coach Fray, also her AP calculus teacher, said the team couldn't risk her breaking her wrist again; they needed her to fully recover to even hope to get back on the field. Spencer didn't want to feel jealous, but of course she couldn't help it.

While on the bench she fought the urge to open a book and study, so she perched her chin on her wrist and did her best to pay attention to the drills as Coach ran everyone through the gamut, barking about how the team hadn't been working out as they should have over the summer, and how state champs were going to be harder to go for if they didn't pick up the pace.

Because she had been absent the first week of school, she'd missed out on the news that the men's varsity soccer team and the women's field hockey team had to share the grass field. The soccer field's Astroturf needed repair after a pipe burst underground, turning the once perfect soccer field into a temporary swimming pool. Major renovations had to be done before the season started in full swing.

The men's soccer team was currently at the other end of the field doing passing drills, and Spencer tried to quash the boredom that was slowly seeping into her muscles. Everyone seemed to be doing something except for her.

Her painkillers mellowed her out, smoothing the edges of her mind. She'd taken more at the first sign of her shoulder and arm aching, and it made the world go all fuzzy in a way that comforted her. Among the haze, she could, at least for a moment, be at peace.

But she couldn't bear to watch practice from one spot, so she decided to take a small walk around the track circling the field with Ripley. Stretching her legs wasn't against the rules.

The soccer team had started running through corner kick set pieces. Spencer was only mildly aware of how the game was played, and not too familiar with the strategy despite dating the star striker. Watching Ethan from the stands was always fun. She'd gone to every one of his games.

The team, as always, looked strong and fast, moving for the ball and charging for the net as a unit while the coach yelled instructions. A rotation of goalies waiting for their turn had their hands looped through the net, yelling encouragement, and a player took a rocket of a shot at the goal that the keeper expertly punched clear over the net. The ball bounced all the way to Spencer at the track, and she stopped it with her foot.

Ripley's tail wagged as Jackson jogged over, his dark hair already plastered to his forehead with sweat. He'd been the one in goal; the way he'd moved sent chills down Spencer's spine. He threw himself from one end of the net to the other, like he was flying, the last line of defense. Like Ethan, he was good, as one should be on Armstrong's varsity team. Armstrong's program, both men's and women's, was legendary. Parents from all over the country enrolled their kids just so they could be on the team, hopefully getting looked at by college recruiters.

Ethan had already gotten offers from recruiters from the University of Michigan. Though, now with everything going on, Spencer wondered if that mattered anymore. A lump formed in her throat, but she swallowed it down.

Jackson beamed at Spencer when she kicked the ball toward him.

"Sorry to interrupt your walk," he said. "Thanks!" He flicked the ball up with his cleat and caught it, then lobbed it over his head back to his team. He didn't rejoin them right away, though; another goalie was already rotating it. Seeing him in his soccer outfit, a complete departure from his Armstrong uniform, was a welcome surprise. Heat rushed to her cheeks when she noticed how good his legs looked in shorts. Without his glasses too, he looked different, not better, but different, and it made Spencer feel dopey.

"Are you okay?" he asked. He let out a heavy breath, winded from the exercise.

"Define *okay*." She gestured vaguely to her team practicing without her, then to her face with a flourish.

"Stupid question, sorry."

Spencer tipped her head and the corner of her mouth lifted. "It's okay, I'm just being dramatic. Olivia rubs off on me in ways. Just trying to keep myself from going crazy."

Jackson relaxed too and returned the smile. Spencer's cheeks felt hot, as a knot loosened in her belly ever so slightly.

"I don't think you're crazy," he said.

"I don't know, sometimes I'll fool even myself."

"How come?"

Spencer wondered how much she should say. But Jackson had the kind of face that made her feel like she could tell him anything, open and honest and true. "I keep seeing flashbacks of the crash. Not just that, but things I remember don't really add up. Like, I keep seeing Ethan behind the wheel, specifically wearing his favorite green hoodie, but it's impossible because the hoodie was still in my closet from when I borrowed it from him. It's like my head is stuffed full of these images and it's all jumbled up, like memory puke."

He looked at her, his brow knit with concern, but he appeared to take her seriously. "That's awful. I'm sorry."

"Yeah, well . . ." She gestured casually. "I'm dealing with it. Thanks, by the way, for helping me today. You made it easier."

It was Jackson's turn to flush. He smiled and looked at his cleats. "No problem." When his eyes came up and met hers again, she realized she'd been staring and she cleared her throat, forcing herself to get it together. She blamed the painkillers for making her feel warm.

"I wish I could have done something," Jackson said. "I feel bad for not being there. Like, maybe I could have changed what happened."

"Right. I don't remember seeing you there. At the party."

Jackson nodded. "I was in Santa Barbara coaching

at a kids' overnight soccer camp when I heard the news. Drove all day to get back to be with Ethan, but . . . he won't see me."

That struck Spencer as odd. "Ethan won't talk to you?"

"No, I went to his house, and he turned me away at the door. He's not acting like himself. That's what's bothering me the most."

Spencer's heart broke for Ethan all over again. Sure, they broke up, but she couldn't help it. If he didn't even want to be with his best friend, he was hurting, and she felt bad for him. She wasn't some heartless witch.

Jackson continued. "He's got to be really torn up about Chris's death. He liked the kid, looked after him. Honestly, I think he's devastated. Like losing a little brother."

That was news to Spencer. "Really?" She hadn't put too much thought into why Chris had been in the car with them.

"Yeah," Jackson said. "Remember? Chris was his frosh buddy?"

"Oh, right." Last year, incoming freshmen were paired with upperclassmen, and Ethan had gone out of his way to make Chris feel welcome at Armstrong. Spencer felt a little guilty at that. She'd hardly paid any attention to her frosh buddy . . . Ella? Ellie? Spencer was too busy studying, she'd figured Ella or Ellie would figure out Armstrong soon enough.

"Anyway, Chris would come over and they'd work on Ethan's car together or just hang out, playing video games.

I think Ethan wanted to look out for him. So yeah . . . he's messed up. He won't talk to anyone; his parents say he just stays up in his room all day and night. I'm not even sure he's eating. You haven't talked to him yet, have you?"

"We broke up. I figured you'd have heard . . ."

Jackson's jaw dropped. "Oh. Sorry. No, I didn't."

"Well, glad to know some people know how to mind their own business, unlike everyone else in this town."

He flushed deeply.

"Sorry," she said. "I didn't mean for that to come off so harsh."

Jackson waved his hands. "No, not that. I just . . . I get it. I've been there."

How could she forget. His father. David Chen was a notorious fraudster, convicted a few years ago in New York City. Spencer didn't know the whole story, but it had been huge news. David Chen had been some kind of hedge fund manager. Spencer wasn't sure what that meant, but it sounded like he was making enough money. Apparently, it wasn't enough money, though, because he was caught siphoning funds from his clients into his personal bank account. As far as Spencer knew, he was still in prison. Jackson's mom, independently wealthy, moved across the country after that, and took advantage of her celebrity chef status to open a cookie café in downtown Los Angeles. But everyone knew about the Chens, even before they set foot in town. They were treated like outsiders from the start, every-one wondering just how much they knew or were complicit in the crime. People had opinions, and those opinions were hard to change. Spencer didn't think it was fair, though, to judge the family on what Jackson's father did, but the inner circle in Brentwood wasn't always as gracious.

She cringed. She hadn't meant to, but she'd picked at old scabs in Jackson's life. "Sorry," she said again. "I—Sorry." What else was there to say?

"It's fine, really." Jackson's eyes met hers and she didn't see any animosity there.

"I'm just not used to literally everyone knowing everything about me."

"Yeah," he said, managing a small smile. "I'm with you on that."

"Thanks. I just wish I had all the answers, you know? I hate not knowing what happened that night, even if it's nothing. I want the truth."

"What are you going to do?" he asked.

"What I do best—study. I want to document everything that happened that night, the crash, just so I can fill in the gaps in my memory and prove . . . Just so I know."

Jackson puffed out his cheeks as he let out a breath. "That sounds like a lot of work."

It would be. If she needed someone to help her with schoolwork, she'd need someone to help her with this. "Will you help me? Think of it like an extracurricular project," she said.

Amused, Jackson said, "Only you can sell it that well."

Spencer allowed herself to smile.

"But Ethan told the police what happened?" he asked.

"He was the one driving, and he was speeding. He ran the intersection. What more do you need to know?"

Spencer's gaze drifted across the field, as if a giant sign might have been erected in the past few minutes that would spell out the answers for her, but all she saw was everyone else getting on with their lives, playing sports, living, and Spencer felt like she was stuck in the past.

After a moment, Jackson asked, "Why do you think there's more to the story?"

Spencer twisted her lips, thinking. "I don't know, I just do . . ."

Why did she get in the car with him if they were fighting? They definitely broke up, she remembered that much. Why was Chris in the car with them? Or Tabby? She hardly knew either of those kids. It just didn't make sense.

"Tell me," he said. His voice was soft, and it gave her a little boost of bravery. If she could tell anyone, she could tell Jackson.

"I'm just not convinced Ethan's responsible for Chris's death."

Jackson's eyes widened, but he took it in stride. "Why, though? Do you think something happened that night that he's trying to hide?"

It sounded like there was a conspiracy to Spencer. She wasn't sure she liked the insinuation that something dark was hidden deep in the secrets of secluded parties in the multimillion-dollar housing developments, but if no one else was going to give her answers, she needed to go look for them herself.

"I know it's not a lot to go on, but that green hoodie . . . You just have to believe me that I feel like something is off. I want to know everything about the party."

A dimple appeared in Jackson's cheek as he thought about it. "If there's even a chance that we can prove he wasn't responsible, that he didn't cause it . . . That it really was just an accident . . ." He met her gaze solidly. "If we can clear his name, I'll help in any way I can."

Spencer smiled, relieved. "Thank you."

"For what?"

"For making me feel like I'm not crazy."

Jackson smiled, then said, "Ethan always talked about what a badass you are. Here it is in action."

Spencer had never been one to quit. Some people called it stubbornness, others called it hardheadedness. It was a benefit on and off the field, in her nature from the start. Once she set her mind to something, she never gave up. This was no exception.

"Some might say it's my best trait." She batted her eyelashes and smiled.

"I don't know about that," he said, rubbing the back of his neck.

She blushed too, realizing how flirtatious she was acting, and she bit her lip. Flirting with her ex's best friend felt like trespassing, even though she and Ethan were so over, but she hadn't meant to in the first place. She didn't want to get hurt again.

"Chen!" Jackson's coach hollered at him from the field,

hands on his hips. "Are you going to invite me to your little social gathering? Get back here!"

"I gotta go," Jackson said, walking backward. "But you should talk to Ethan. If he won't listen to me, maybe he'll listen to you. You might be able to shake some sense into him. I'll see you in the library tomorrow?"

"Yeah, tomorrow." It was one thing she could look forward to after what she still needed to do tonight at the Moore house.

"See ya later, Ripley!" Jackson said.

Ripley's tail wagged at Jackson's words as Spencer waved, watching him jog back to his practice. Still holding her hand aloft for a moment, she let what happened sink in. Someone believed her. She didn't feel so alone after all.

Get Salty: A True Crime Podcast with Peyton Salt

[Get Salty Intro Music]

[Transcription note: truncated for length]

Peyton Salt: Before we get into today's main story, I wanted to update our listeners about the Ethan Amoroso case from last episode.

Sasha Firth: Oh! Spill! I have been obsessed with this case since you first brought it up. Everyone at my school has been talking about it, too. Has anything new happened since he's been charged?

Peyton: No, unfortunately Ethan has kept a low profile since he returned home under house arrest, waiting to go in front of a judge.

Sasha: Oh, the horror, house arrest in a giant mansion. Gag.

Peyton: I guess now is as good a time as any to reveal to our listeners that this is the start of a new series we're calling *Lifestyles of the Rich and Reckless*. We'll be releasing an episode every week to shine a spotlight upon the toxic glitz and glamour of the privileged class. We've had an incredible outpouring of support about Chris Moore's tragic death, and we've gotten thousands of emails from you asking for more details about the fallout. Some big things are coming as we start to plan our episodes as the case unfolds, so be sure to subscribe, stay tuned, and don't forget to hit up our merch store. We've already sold out of our limited-edition buttons for the Chris Moore Memorial Fund, but we still have some other Get Salty swag that you can buy so you can help support the show.

Sasha: Maybe we can get some *Lifestyles of the Rich and Reckless* stickers up for sale soon!

Peyton: Oh, Sasha! Great idea. Rich kids like Ethan get it way easier than most people in his situation. I don't feel sorry for him in the least, especially not after I saw Spencer Sandoval, one of the passengers in the car, her first day back at school since the accident. You can see how violent the crash was on her face. It's horrible to look at. Everyone at Armstrong was buzzing. You couldn't walk down the hall without hearing her name on everyone's lips.

Spencer Sandoval is sporty and cute, her signature look being long brown braids that make her look like she's ready to spring into action at any moment. Like many victims, the ghosts of the past haunt her. She carries the burdens of her ex-boyfriend's actions on her shoulders. But she has some very special help from an adorable service animal and a surprising sidekick, Ethan Amoroso's best friend.

Jackson Chen is a strong but soft boy-next-door type. He hovers around Spencer, as protective of her well-being as Spencer's service dog, Ripley. He doesn't look like the kind of person who would want to be friends with the bad-boy Ethan Amoroso. With a face as easy on the eyes as his, one can't help but be reminded of a medieval knight, dedicating his life to chivalry and honor. To think the likes of the two of them could be friends with Ethan Amoroso is beyond me, but with Jackson Chen's family's history, I can't help but wonder . . . But that's for another episode.

Spencer was dodging me all day, declining to be interviewed, so I decided to ask what some of her peers were thinking about the whole ordeal.

[SFX: student chatter, slamming lockers, school bell ringing]

Luca Navarro (senior):

I always liked Spencer. She's nice, smart. She helped me pass my chem tests last year. I hope she gets better soon. It's really sad what happened. She's got a dog with her, though, it's really cool.

Grace Winkelman (sophomore):

Spencer Sandoval walked right by Chris's locker, didn't even stop at it. I was crying my eyes out all day, looking at his picture, and she didn't even look once. I was going to go to homecoming with Chris and . . . and now? It's not fair!

Valerie Lee (freshman):

It's so scary looking at her face. You just can't stop staring. Ethan really [*BEEP*]ed her up.

Tommy Fernandez (junior):

That girl? Spencer? So annoying. She's always so competitive. She's gotta be the best at everything and it's so irritating. And she's got her dog at school, too? Special treatment. Why can't I bring my dog to school? Oh yeah, cuz I'm not on the Headmaster's List.

Hailey Reed (senior):

I don't really want to talk about it. Spencer and Ethan are like . . . I don't want to say. I feel so bad. Sorry. I just . . . It's really hard to talk about it right now.

[SFX fade out]

Peyton:

I'll be doing my best to try to get an interview with Spencer and Tabby, the other passenger in the car that fateful night. I think it's super important that we let victims tell their own story, and I won't give up on an interview. And now, for our main story . . .

[End truncated transcript]

NINE

SPENCER LINGERED ON THE SIDEWALK, pacing back and forth, staring up at the Moore family's front door like she was staring down a minotaur. Damn her and her instinctual need to please figures of authority. Why couldn't she just tell Dr. Diamond she wasn't ready for this? He should have understood the mental torture she was going through. But it was too late now. They were relying on her to gather some photos for Chris's memorial. No one else would.

Ripley sat at her feet, watching her for a signal, her head tipped curiously to one side. At least Ripley didn't seem intimidated by this errand. Spencer took a breath and steeled herself, then made her way up the driveway, pushing her bike past a car covered in a tarp, and headed toward the bright red door, a week's worth of newspapers gathered on the welcome mat.

She'd never been to Mr. Moore's house before. He was her teacher, after all. She'd only seen him occasionally at the grocery store, where her parents used it as an opportunity to chat and have a small parent-teacher conference while Spencer tried not to be mortified talking to a teacher out in the wild. The Moores lived in a quieter part of Mid-City, off Santa Monica Boulevard. Their Spanish colonial house with its red roof and white walls stood out in the verdant brush that surrounded the property. It was a medium-sized house, definitely bigger than Spencer's, but it had a large yard, a novelty in the area, for sure.

She looked up at the dark windows on the second floor and wondered, morbidly, which one had been Chris's.

The porch light was on, and she could tell that someone was home, the telltale flicker of the television going on behind closed curtains. If she were a coward, she might have turned and headed home, pretending she had never come in the first place. But she was here now. No going back until she got what she came for.

Spencer tamped down the sudden urge to puke while she rested her bike on the lawn. It was now or never. She needed to do this.

She picked up a few newspapers on the grass that hadn't made it to the front porch and stacked the rest in her hand. When she rang the bell, her knees shook and she nearly forgot to breathe as the door opened. Instead of seeing either Mr. or Mrs. Moore on the other side, she was relieved to see Nick, Chris's older brother, home from college. He must be taking a break from UC Irvine.

He looked surprised when he saw her. "Spencer! What are you doing here?"

What *was* she doing here? This had been a bad idea, but she managed to say, "I've been assigned picture pickup."

"Right, the memorial." His eyes landed on the stack of newspapers in her hand, and she gave them over. "Thanks."

Nick's eyes were rimmed with red, clashing horribly with his auburn hair, but Spencer didn't want to stare. Both Moore boys had inherited their father's classic Irish coloring and freckles dotting their long noses. She used to have a crush on him, an innocent one-way affection, and her stomach twisted into knots seeing him this way.

"Come on in," he said, stepping back to let her into the darkened foyer.

"If it's a bad time I can . . ."

"Please. No trouble at all." He set the newspapers in a pile near the door.

He didn't question Ripley's presence and led the way toward the stairs. The Moore house smelled heavily like flowers, the source of which being almost an entire flower shop's worth of lilies erected in grand displays in the darkened dining room just to the left of the entry. The TV murmured quietly in the living room to Spencer's right, but there was no sign of Chris or Nick's parents anywhere. *Probably for the better*, she thought.

She didn't say a word as she followed Nick quietly up the carpeted steps. Usually she asked if she should take her shoes off when she entered someone's house, but in this case she wanted to be in and out as quickly as possible. The longer she stayed, the higher the chance that she would run into a grieving parent. And seeing his grieving brother was hard enough.

Up the stairs and down the hall, Nick led Spencer to

Chris's room. He flipped on the light and Spencer lingered outside the doorway, unsure if she should follow. The room felt off-limits. Nick meanwhile went right for Chris's desk, messy, untouched probably since the accident, and riffled through a shoebox full of photos.

Spencer couldn't help but look around at Chris's room, at the life he'd left behind. It was exactly how she expected a teenage boy's room to be, full of dreams and ambition, now marked by a gaping hole with his absence. His bed made and the sheets tucked in, never to be slept in again, his closet full of clothes he'd never wear, a memorial to his life on pause forever. He had obviously been into computers; the components of several were stacked in a corner of his room and an Xbox sat beneath a TV, a thin layer of dust gathering on top of it. He wouldn't ever again wake up and pull back the curtains at his window before he got ready for school, or tinker with his computer, or worry about what he was going to wear.

Spencer felt unmoored, like she was seeing the room through a television screen, rather than through her own eyes. This could easily have been her own bedroom, with her own parents grieving for her, with flowers from her own funeral sitting in the dark, leaving Hope to sort through photos for a school memorial. Ripley pressed her wet nose to the back of Spencer's hand, and it made Spencer jump, but she was grateful for the reminder to breathe.

"My mom used most of the good photos for the funeral, but these are a few more I thought would be nice. Some from his computer camp, this one of him with his friends . . . oh, here's one with me and Julie," he said sadly. Spencer vaguely remembered Nick was dating Julianne Greene, the girl who'd had that awful accident last year.

"How is she?" she asked.

Nick shrugged. "The same." She'd broken her back and fallen into a coma.

"I'm sorry," she told him. His girlfriend. Now his brother.

Nick didn't reply. Now he was holding out a small stack for her to take, and she did, with shaking fingers. The top photo was of Chris smiling wide at a tech convention, his vibrant red hair caught in the purple and red lights from a stage behind him.

Spencer's whole body felt cold. Guilt held her like a straitjacket. She knew she needed to say something, anything, but what could she possibly say that would make anything better?

"Nick, again, I'm so sorry . . ." She felt stupid for even trying.

He swallowed thickly and nodded. "Thanks, Spencer. If you need anything else . . ." An edge coated his voice, teetering on the breaking point.

That was her cue. "This is fine. I'll be going."

"Yeah."

Spencer turned to leave, and she distinctly heard Nick's muffled sobs coming from Chris's room. She pretended not to hear and left in a rush.

SNAPS

@tiny_neil:

#justiceforchris Catch and burn the one that did this!

@Resslersomemore:

It's crazy. Miss you man. @chmoore #justiceforchris

@norma.likes.drawing:

We can't rest until we get #justiceforchris. Look at this vid I found of Ethan's old parties. The guy was a maniac. Absolute moron.

@chockablock.marva:

He intended to do this! He didn't even brake at the intersection! Why aren't the lawyers getting on this? He's a sociopath.

@tiny_neil quote:

@chockablock.marva I heard Ethan Amoroso was talking about doing something like this a week before. He planned this!!!

@derikathedreamer002:

I don't want to throw around tea, but when it comes to Ethan Amoroso I have no limit to how much I can pour.

TEN

HOPE THREW HERSELF ONTO THE couch, which wouldn't have been a problem if Spencer hadn't already been stretched out, wearing her ice pack hat to quell the oncoming migraine that was threatening to ruin the rest of her night. Spencer yelled out as all of Hope's one hundred pounds fell on her legs, laughing all the while.

"Ouch! Hope!"

Spencer had been feeling too sick to even want to watch some of her favorite journaling and studying YouTube channels, an admittedly nerdy hobby of hers. Her eyeballs felt like they were going to explode out of her head, the migraine digging into her brain like an icepick.

"Move. You're in my spot," Hope said as she slapped her palms on Spencer's fuzzy socked feet, tapping out an annoying rhythm only baby sisters would know the beat to.

"No, I'm not. Your spot is on the lounger."

"Guess what, I want my spot to be here. I'm cold."

"Then go put on a hoodie."

"*You* go put on a hoodie."

"There's not enough room."

"I don't care."

It occurred to Spencer that this was a way for Hope to be closer to her. She couldn't imagine how scared Hope had been when she was in the hospital, so she didn't complain when Hope lifted Spencer's legs up and crawled underneath, draping them like a blanket.

Ripley had been dozing in her dog bed and opened one eye to see what the commotion was about, but she didn't move when the sisters settled down again. The TV droned on, and Spencer tried to ignore that Hope was fidgeting against her, tapping her foot to an unheard beat.

"Did you do your homework?" Spencer asked.

"Yeah, I did, *Mom*. Did you?"

"What I could." She had tried to read some of her assigned chapters in her AP English literature homework, but pain was starting to flare up again and she couldn't focus. Hence the ice pack hat. It was a bulky beanie, and Spencer thought she looked like Blossom, a character from a TV show her mom used to watch reruns of when she had a rare day off from taking care of sick animals. Both her parents were out of the house and weren't expected to be back until later. Pizza money had been left on the table by the door and the girls were, as usual, on their own for food.

Hope stole the remote from Spencer's grasp, which she didn't fight her for, and she flipped through channels, finally landing in the middle of a rerun of *Murder, She Wrote*, with Jessica Fletcher flirting with reformed jewel thief Dennis Stanton. Spencer closed her eyes and let their delightful banter lull her into a soft, cozy twilight doze. All she could do was wait for the Vicodin to make it all better.

"Why were you at that party?" Hope asked.

It was an unprompted question that seemingly came out of nowhere, but Spencer knew which party she was talking about. *That* party. Spencer squinted to look at her. Everything was too bright. "Because I thought it would be fun."

"You never want to have fun. You're too much of a dork."

Spencer didn't argue about that. "I went because I wanted to." And she knew Ethan would be there. She wished she hadn't. She wished she'd just gone home after work like she usually would have. Ethan making out with Hailey intruded on her thoughts and she huffed, "Why do you want to know?"

Hope shrugged a noncommittal shoulder. "Did you drink a lot?"

"I might have had one of those alcoholic seltzers, but . . ." She couldn't remember if she had more than that. She'd always favored the sweeter drinks. "I'm not sure."

Hope snapped, her voice rising an octave. "Yeah, well, that's really dumb of you! You shouldn't have done that! You shouldn't drink! You shouldn't have even been there."

Both of Spencer's eyes were open now. "Why are you so upset?"

Hope shrank into herself and folded her arms over her chest, pouting like she used to when she was five. It took her a moment to answer. "We had a drunk driving assembly at school today. They showed pictures and stuff, and it was really scary. I think they wanted to talk to us about . . . They had a mom talk to us about her daughter getting in an accident a couple years ago and dying and I . . ."

Hope picked at her fingernails as she spoke, unable to finish the words, not because she didn't know what to say, maybe, but because she didn't want to.

"Hey, it's okay—I'm okay," Spencer murmured. "I'm right here."

"I know, but what if you weren't?"

Spencer's heart dropped. Hope settled down in the space between Spencer and the couch, and even though it was uncomfortable, and her body weight pressed the air out of Spencer's chest, Spencer let her lie there until she started dozing off.

While the TV droned on, Spencer tried to wade through the memories, though her headache was making it particularly difficult. Things came back to her in pieces.

Rows of cars parked in a dirt lot.

A yellow Solo cup. Metallic tasting.

Music. But muffled, like it was in another room. Hazy, dreamy.

Kids sitting around the firepit, smoking.

It was coming together.

She was sure of one thing. She'd only had one drink that night. Why was it so hard to remember that night? Was her memory loss really from hitting her head in the crash?

"Please, wait. I can explain."

"What else is there to explain? You and Hailey deserve each other."

"Spencer!"

"Go to hell."

A hand on her wrist.

Then.

Engine roaring. Speed. Out of control.

Ethan in his green hoodie. No, wrong. Why?

Bright light. Eyes wide, terror.

The tree. The lines in the bark. Trapped in the headlights.

NO!

Pain. Darkness.

Cold hands on her face, wet, covered in blood. So much blood. She couldn't breathe. She was dead. Already dead. SPENCER! Crash. Float. Scream. Cold, wet hands cupping her face.

Wet nose, not hands. A wet nose, tongue. Ripley.

Ripley was on top of her, licking her face, waking her up, her body pressed against Spencer's chest. Her breath was hot on Spencer's face.

Spencer cried, sobs racking her whole body, rolling out of her in waves, thrashing in her bed. It had been another night terror. She hated feeling this way. Ripley buried her nose under Spencer's side, not giving up on her. *Get up, wake up!* Her rough paws felt like sandpaper on Spencer's arms. She tried to push Ripley away, she didn't want to be touched, yet Ripley refused to go. But Spencer actually did want to be touched, and she wrapped her arms around Ripley's neck and sobbed into her fur.

Her parents rushed into her room and flicked on the light, telling Hope to go back to bed as she lingered outside.

Spencer still felt like she was trapped in that memory, even when her parents assured her she was safe.

SPENCER! Tree. Scream. NO! Float. Crash. Darkness. Pain.

She needed to remember everything, even if it made her feel like dying.

WHAT I REMEMBER

*Highwood Estates
Cars parked
Unfinished mansions—scaffolding, dirt, no trees
Skateboards in an empty swimming pool
Yellow cup
Firepit
Music?—live or no??
Ethan—cheater
Hailey—backstabber
~~Green hoodie~~

WHAT I DON'T REMEMBER

Tabby
Chris
Between breakup and crash—totally blank
Why did I get in the car?

ELEVEN

SPENCER STARED AT WHAT SHE'D written in her journal, tapping her pen on the paper as she repeated the thought: *Why did I get in the car?*

Why didn't Ethan stop at the light?

Why were Chris and Tabby riding with us?

Her bullet journal was a complete mess. Using her right hand made her writing look like it was done by a second grader, and she could only write for so long before her hand cramped. But when she journaled, it helped calm the thoughts swirling in her head. Last night's night terror had shaken some things loose.

The moment she'd gotten to school, she went to the library and wrote down everything in an attempt to organize her brain while Ripley lay patiently under her chair. Even though she'd loaded up on painkillers, she was surprised by how much she did remember. She'd had to cross out green hoodie, because it wasn't possible that she remembered it, and her eyes skimmed over the other details. What else might she have misremembered? A part of her wished she could believe she didn't actually see Ethan and Hailey making out that night but . . . that was definitely real. So why did she get into the car with him?

She needed to talk to Ethan, but she didn't know how. It wasn't as simple as going to his house. Facing him again felt raw.

She'd already purged all their pictures together off her new phone, a gift from her parents. Each photo she deleted from the cloud felt like a paper cut, and after deleting the thousandth picture of them framed in a mirror, his arms wrapped around her shoulders, his chin resting on the top of her head with his devil-may-care smile as he grinned for the selfie, the emotional pain had started to rear its ugly head again. He'd hurt her too badly and too deeply for her to want to see him for a long time. There was baggage now, and she was tired of carrying it. She wanted to move on, hence the list. She needed to document everything, for her own sanity.

"Good morning," Jackson sang, appearing seemingly out of thin air. She almost jumped out of her skin. "Oh! Sorry. Didn't mean to scare you."

"It's okay." She forced her heart to settle back down. Ripley had perked up at Jackson's arrival, her tail thumping as he took a seat across from Spencer's side of the table. Spencer was glad to see a friendly face so early, too.

"Getting started on solving the mystery already?" he asked as he opened his backpack and brought out his laptop.

"Nothing major." Spencer shook out the cramp in her right hand. "I had a nightmare last night, needed to get some thoughts out."

"Are you okay?"

"I am now." Though the reality of her situation was becoming more concrete. A person didn't have a mental health service dog because they were going to get over their disability overnight. Ripley was in it for the long haul, and Spencer was coming to terms with the fact that she would be waking up with persistent nightmares and suffering from more panic attacks for the foreseeable future.

She had started picturing Ripley living with her in the dorm at Caltech, curled up at the foot of her bed to wake her up for early morning lab work. It didn't seem so scary now. More manageable. Even though it wasn't something she'd wish on anyone.

Jackson started to work on his laptop and pushed his glasses up his nose with his knuckle. She liked how good he looked in both his school and soccer uniforms. He kept his tie cinched neatly, compared to how Ethan always wore his loose, like he needed breathing room. With his glasses back on, Jackson reminded Spencer of Clark Kent and she caught herself staring.

Mercifully, Jackson didn't seem to notice and said, "So since I'm all caught up on my psych homework, I figured I'd get started on helping you remember that night. Maybe I'll start collecting some news articles for you and we can look them over together later."

"That sounds perfect, thanks." Spencer was grateful that he was taking her seriously. He didn't make her feel crazy. Doing this alone would have been impossible. "I've been meaning to ask, how do you play soccer without your glasses? Like, how do you see the ball?"

"Oh, I don't," he said dryly, still staring at his computer. "I fling myself in a random direction hoping to catch the ball. The secret is that I'm lucky." His gaze slid from his laptop and he cracked a grin. He was teasing her.

The laugh that came out of Spencer sounded like a bark, and she covered her mouth, remembering she was in the library and needed to be quiet. It felt nice to laugh like that again after so long. "That was pretty stupid of me, wasn't it?"

His dimple reappeared when he scrunched his nose, laughing. "Nah. To be fair, a field hockey ball is a lot smaller than a soccer ball when it's hurtling toward your face, a lot harder to see it coming. How you're not terrified of getting whacked in the face is beyond me."

"Occupational hazard. All my front teeth are fake," Spencer said, grinning. This time she was the one who was joking.

In the sunlight cast from the ceiling window, Jackson looked like he was glowing when he laughed, and Spencer made herself look away or else the flush on her face would be obvious. She looked down at her notes with the intent of focusing on something else, but she couldn't help smiling too, even though it tugged on the stitches in her cheek.

"Okay," she said, and chanced a glance his way to find him still smiling at her. "Shall we get started?"

At the memorial, Spencer and Olivia joined the throng of bodies in the courtyard as the sun was just starting to set.

Hardly anyone spoke, and if they did, it was kept to a hush. Even the bugs that usually came out at this time of night kept their buzzing to a low hum. She and Olivia, being part of the student union, had been recruited to help set up for the ceremony. With Spencer's injuries, she was delegated the task of handing out candles for the memorial.

When the box was empty, Spencer hovered in the back of the crowd, trying her best to blend in with the brickwork pattern of the rear wall of the building, waiting for the event to begin, holding on to Ripley's harness. The candle wax had already begun to drip onto the paper disk protecting her hand. The sea of heads in front of her were all turned to face the stage. Chris had been more popular than she thought. Tears glinted in the candlelight, and boxes of tissues were being passed around to people who needed them. A sound system and microphone had been set up on a small stage near the garden and they were playing a song by The Beatles, Chris's favorite.

The garden was small, big enough for only a single bench, but there was a small looping path so a person could disappear into the high foliage for a second. It looked nice, peaceful. Spencer wished it never had to be built in the first place.

The Moores had arrived only a few minutes earlier, shaking hands with some of the teachers. Mr. Moore looked grayer than she remembered as he firmly grasped Dr. Diamond's hand and they said some words to each other that were too quiet to hear.

Olivia emerged from the crowd and joined Spencer leaning against the wall. "Mrs. Moore looks as hot as ever. Why do all the heinously evil people always look like cliché stepmothers from a Disney movie?"

"Liv . . . we're at a memorial."

"I'm just stating a fact. Mrs. Moore tried to fine my parents because the grass in our front lawn was half an inch higher than the neighbor's just yesterday."

That definitely didn't sound like the actions of a grieving mother. But Catherine Moore was a classic Karen, determined to nose into everyone's business and generally difficult to be around. Mrs. Moore had famously—or rather infamously—as a city hall elected official, published an anti-homeless proposal regarding a gathering of tents outside the VA's office near the Brain Freeze, where Spencer's after-school job was. It was controversial to say the least. She'd also been one of the leaders of the silent blacklisting of the Chen family when they first moved here.

"Come on," Spencer said. "She just lost her son . . ."

Olivia sighed and folded her arms across her chest. She knew how to hold a grudge, but she didn't say anything else about it.

Mrs. Moore stepped up to the microphone. She was remarkably put together in Spencer's opinion, given the circumstances. Her honey-colored hair was pulled into a low bun at the base of her neck, not one sleek hair out of place. She looked down at her index card, tapping the edges into place with French-tipped manicured nails. The microphone whined with feedback as she leaned in, so she backed off and waited a moment before trying again.

"Thank you all for coming," she said. "My son Chris ... He would have loved to see all of you here today. Thank you to Dr. Diamond and the Parents' Association for this lovely memorial to my son's life. We also want to thank the student union for putting together such a lovely ceremony. Jonathan and I"—she glanced back at Mr. Moore, whose head was bowed low, he didn't notice—"are truly grateful for all the support the community has given us in ... in this trying time."

Mrs. Moore's voice sounded robotic, rehearsed, like she was a politician at a town hall meeting.

Spencer's heart felt like it was about ready to burst out of her sternum, like an alien exploding from her chest. She wanted to be anywhere but here, but if she left now, everyone would stare, and everyone would think she was being inconsiderate, so Spencer kept her feet rooted to the ground and rubbed Ripley's head rhythmically. All she could do was close her eyes and breathe. But she couldn't help the thoughts that swirled in her head like a tornado.

No matter how hard she tried to accept the official version of the crash—that Ethan was speeding, that he didn't brake, that he was most likely driving under the influence—she wanted to believe it was all just an accident. She wanted to believe that something like this couldn't be misunderstood, but the feeling that something was wrong wouldn't go away. It nagged at her, tugging at her insides, telling her that something wasn't right.

Scream. Float. Crash. Pain all the way down.

If she ever hoped to get any kind of peace about what happened, she needed to know all the details of that night. She needed to fill in the blank pieces in her mind; otherwise she would always wonder if she had done something differently, if she had said the right thing, maybe she could have changed how it had ended. She wouldn't be able to rest until she knew the truth, and journaling would only get her so far, as much as she hated to admit it.

It was Mr. Moore's turn to speak. He came up to the microphone, and he said, too far away from the mic so it sounded distant, a gentle thank-you, before turning and stepping down from the stage with his wife.

With a sinking feeling in her stomach, Spencer watched as Hailey Reed took the microphone next. She lowered the stand so it was level with her mouth. "We hereby dedicate this garden to Chris Moore, calling this area the Chris Moore Memorial Garden."

Spencer couldn't help the scowl that pulled on her lips. She couldn't even look at Hailey without wanting to scream.

The crowd clapped politely. Spencer joined in, half-heartedly, stopping just short of rolling her eyes. Her skin crawled and she had the sensation of someone watching her. Lo and behold, Tabby Hill was frowning at Spencer through the crowd. Spencer tore her eyes away, just as Hailey was replaced on stage by Harrison Ressler, with his long, dirty blond hair pulled back into a ponytail, holding his guitar.

When Spencer looked back at Tabby, Tabby was gone. Spencer got the distinct impression that Tabby had seen the scowl on her face and probably thought the worst of her. If Tabby didn't dislike Spencer before, they definitely did now.

Harrison had been the host of the party that night, but Spencer hadn't known before that he and Chris had been close. They must have known each other somehow, though, as Harrison's low, velvety voice carried over the crowd. "Thanks, Hailey. And thank you all for coming. I'm sure he would have been glad to see all your faces. I'm going to play a song to Chris's memory." He readied his hand on the neck of his guitar and turned his eyes to the sky. "You were taken from us too soon. This one's for you, man." As he began to play "Hey Jude," the crowd raised their candles high into the air, and Spencer took the chance to duck out.

It didn't feel right to sing along with everyone. Spencer quietly led Ripley down the sidewalk that wrapped around the school, pain rippling through her arm, determined to figure out everything that happened that night. She had too many questions that needed answering, but most of all, she had to prove to herself that she wasn't crazy.

It was time to see Ethan and find out what really happened that night.

TWELVE

THE CLARITY OF MIND SHE had when riding her bike from Chris's memorial felt incredible. The breeze cooling her skin, the sound of Ripley's claws scratching on the pavement as she cantered beside her, the sky turning a deepening shade of purple—all of it made Spencer feel surer than ever that it was time to see Ethan. It was long overdue that she got some type of closure or answers about what happened that night. She couldn't keep not knowing.

She needed to see him, even if it would be for the last time, but at least then she'd be able to take the first steps toward recovery.

The ride to Ethan's was a ten-minute coast down quiet Brentwood streets, the echoes of Harrison's rendition of "Hey Jude" at the memorial still echoing in her head. She only saw one or two cars on her way, which would have been a relaxing bike ride if not for the feeling that she was about to do something foolish.

The Amoroso home looked like a brick of cement, rectangular, with hard lines jutting out above tree cover. Typical of Californian modern architecture, it reminded Spencer more of a modern art museum than a house. Its many glass windows afforded plenty of sunlight, and some were lit up this time of night, meaning that someone was likely home.

The house sat behind a gate and a row of hedges, perfect for privacy. Spencer, however, still knew the code and punched it in before opening the gate just wide enough for her to slip her bike and Ripley through and shutting it behind her. How many times before had she sneaked out of the house to see Ethan past curfew, doing exactly this? The memory sat bitterly in her stomach.

She walked her bike up the drive, set it down on the front porch steps, and rang the bell. The moment she did it, she thought maybe she was being inconsiderate. It was just after nine in the evening, and maybe everyone was already getting to bed, but the foyer light came on and a shadow moved in the doorway window. The door unlocked and Ethan's father appeared in front of her. He had a phone held to his ear, but he put it to his shoulder when greeting her.

"Spencer," he said, surprised. Mr. Amoroso was a candy company executive, and he always had bowls of sweets and chocolates around the house, something that Spencer took full advantage of whenever she was visiting. Mr. Amoroso was the breadwinner of the family, or rather, Ethan liked to joke, he was the candy winner. This was the first time seeing him after the accident, and he took in her face with a graying expression. He looked like he'd been getting ready for bed, wearing plaid pajama pants and a T-shirt. "I'm just on the phone with Ethan's lawyers. Can I help you?"

"Hi, Mr. Amoroso, is Ethan home?" Dumb question, of course he was home. He was still under pretrial home confinement—aka house arrest—until he was brought to the courthouse for the first day in court. But she didn't care that she sounded stupid for asking.

"He's in the back," he said, tipping his head toward the backyard and stepping aside for her to enter the house. Inside, the house was much like the exterior, wide open and well structured, all lines and boxes, with everything in its place and a place for everything.

Mr. Amoroso went back to his conversation with the lawyer, talking about potential plea deals, leaving Spencer and Ripley to make their own way through the house. Perhaps he knew what she'd come here to do. She opened the sliding door leading to the yard and closed it behind her.

Just as his dad said, Ethan was in the backyard, laid out on a lounger by the glowing infinity pool. A small waterfall was the only sound as Spencer stepped forward, Ripley obediently at her side. As she got closer, she knew Ethan heard her coming, but he didn't stir. A few bottles of beer were open and empty on the ground next to him. A blunt rested in an ashtray half burned, and at first she thought Ethan was asleep, but his eyes followed her as she circled around the edge of the pool toward him. His lids were heavy, and he watched her approach without saying a word. They'd spent many days and nights here, swimming and playing and partying. *Kissing.* With a sudden flush to her cheeks, Spencer remembered the quiet night when they'd first started dating, sharing a kiss in the shallow end of the pool that literally stole the breath from her lungs. And then everything was ruined by another kiss.

Ethan was the type of guy whose wild and carefree aura made her feel like she could do anything, be anyone. He was charming and witty and a little reckless, but she wanted to be a part of that life, too. The money didn't hurt, either. With Ethan, they went everywhere—VIP tours at Disneyland, exclusive nightclubs on the Sunset Strip, his parents' private clubs where she'd see Harry Styles one day and Taylor Swift the next, and he hardly ever even looked at a bill. She'd felt different when she was with him. She felt important, like she mattered. She wasn't just some brown scholarship kid, a charity case. With Ethan, she felt like a movie star.

Then—Ethan's fingers twined in Hailey's golden hair, their mouths open wide like they wanted to swallow the other whole, Hailey's hand down the front of Ethan's jeans, and Ethan's eyes snapping open, then seeing Spencer standing there, her whole body freezing cold and boiling hot at the same time. While Hailey didn't even move her hand, she just smirked at Spencer. And somehow, Spencer knew—this wasn't the first time Hailey had kissed her boyfriend. That this thing between them wasn't new. It was just new to Spencer.

She clenched her jaw. Seeing Ethan again, in person, made the moment come back to her. She remembered that at least.

Was Hailey sleeping with Ethan? Because Spencer wouldn't?

It didn't matter. She still wanted to know everything. Still wanted to know what she couldn't remember.

"Hey, Ethan," she said quietly. Her throat felt constricted, and she was impressed she could even manage to say that much.

"What are you doing here?" His voice was gravelly low. She knew he'd ask that question, and yet she still didn't have an answer.

Spencer chewed on her lips for a moment and then took a seat on the chair next to his. He didn't stop her, instead taking a sip from the beer in his hand. She could smell it on him, the stale cloud of cheap brews hovering over his head like a storm. He must have been drinking all day, not caring that his parents were home, but then he never cared before. His face was shadowed, glowing blue from below, the light catching the slant of his nose in a way that made him look bruised. He didn't look at her now that she was close. She wanted him to, and maybe a little part of her wanted him to look at her the way he used to. But she was kidding herself—that wasn't going to happen anymore.

"I needed to see you," she said. He still wouldn't look at her. "How are you?"

He shrugged and hissed. "Great! Best time of my life. Going to jail instead of college!"

"Don't say that," she said.

"Why not? It's true," he replied.

Ripley sat on Spencer's shoe. Not protectively, more like she too was tired of his attitude.

"I found your hoodie," Spencer said. "Your green one."

"Keep it."

"I'll give it back."

"I don't want it. I gave it to you."

"Well, I don't want it, either. You can give it to Hailey."

He screwed up his face, as if that was the last thing he wanted her to say, and took another sip of his beer. He drained it empty and set it down with the others. "Did my dad let you in? I told him I wanted to be alone."

"Don't blame him. I came here on my own. I want to talk about what happened that night at the party."

Ethan rolled his head, exaggerating exasperation. "Of course you do! You're not here to see if I'm okay, you just want to find out all the details. Why am I not surprised?"

She let his anger slide. He was too wasted to even try to argue with. His T-shirt was wrinkled, and he was wearing old soccer shorts with paint stains on them. His ankle monitor blinked. From his spot on the floor, Ripley stared up at Spencer as she shifted in her seat. "Does your dad know you're out here drinking?"

"He doesn't care. It's the least of his problems right now."

"How about I get you some water."

Ethan sighed loudly. "Let me guess, Jackson put you up to this."

"No. But he is worried about you."

Ethan's smile cracked as he opened yet another beer. His gaze went skyward as he took a swig. "Why should he care? I'm a piece of shit. He's better off forgetting about me, same as you. You two might be perfect for each other, after all."

His self-loathing was getting tiresome, and she wanted to smack the beer out of his hand. "If you keep up that attitude, you're going to lose your case."

"Oh, I know I'm going to prison. I'm already packed, got my chinos and my toothbrush all ready to go." His attempt at a joke fell flat.

"No, you're not, stop talking like that. It was an accident!"

Ethan almost laughed but it came out like a wheeze. He still wasn't looking at her. The cut of his profile was something out of the history books. He looked like a timeless beauty, sculpted from marble and pure imagination. The shape of his cheekbones, cut against the dark sky, could send shivers down anyone's spine. If he wasn't so beautiful, she might have thought he wasn't real. How someone with a face like his could hate himself that much was beyond her understanding.

"Ethan . . ." She said it like a warning. His name was basically a warning on its own: caution, turn back, category 5. "It was an accident, wasn't it?" she prodded. "Or were you drunk?"

He snorted.

"The thing is, I know you, you wouldn't drive if you were drunk or high. You *wouldn't*." She firmly believed that. Ethan was wild and rich but he wasn't spoiled that way. He wouldn't deliberately put people in danger. Not when they lived in Los Angeles, where kids like him and his friends have been Uber-ing around since sixth grade. What was the point of driving drunk when you had Mommy's Uber Black account? "Did you?"

He stared her right in the eyes. "I didn't."

"So what happened?"

"You really don't remember?" He sounded genuinely surprised.

"No. I had a concussion. And lots of broken bones to remind me about it. The doctors say I might not ever remember the crash, and that makes it all the more important that I ask you."

"I was driving, I ran the intersection. I tried to brake, or I think I did, but the car didn't stop. So we crashed, what more is there?" he said with a shrug.

"That's it? There has to be more."

"Does it matter if there is?"

"It does. Because I say so."

Ethan actually cracked a smile, and he thumped the back of his head on the headrest, grinning up at the sky, still unable to look at her. "Well, there isn't, that's the whole story."

Spencer huffed, then said, "I don't care that you were cheating on me, just tell me the truth."

"For once in your life, will you just stop trying to find the right answer to everything? This isn't some test you need to ace, some perfect score at the top of your paper."

"Don't start with me, Ethan. I'm not here to fight with you. Why was Chris even in the car with us?"

Ethan shrugged. "I offered him a ride. He was totally out of it, he needed to get home. Maybe it was better that he was out cold. Couldn't feel a damn thing." He took another swig.

"Why though? He didn't seem like the party animal type."

"I don't know. Why does anyone do anything?"

"Jackson said you guys were close. I forgot he was your frosh buddy last year."

Ethan shrugged again. "He's a good kid." He caught himself and swallowed. "*Was* a good kid. All I ever do is muck everything up." He wiped beer from his lips with the back of his hand, just like he did after kissing Hailey. Wiping away the evidence.

"How long were you together?" she asked, keeping her tone level and strong, for her sake. "You and Hailey, I mean?"

Ethan wouldn't look at her.

"I just need to know . . . I need to know if we . . . if we were real," she said.

"We were real," he whispered. "But I was never good enough for you. Admit it. Miss Perfect with Mr. Fuck Up."

She grimaced. "And you and Hailey?"

He sighed. "We were fooling around for a year."

A whole year. Half their relationship, he was with another girl. "Were you sleeping together?" she asked.

Another long sigh. Then: "Yeah."

The pain she felt in her heart was harsher than in her body. She wanted to ask more questions, but she realized she didn't want to know the answers to them.

But it was Ethan's turn to ask a question. "Did you love me?"

Spencer clamped her mouth shut and sat back, shocked. She wasn't expecting him to ask her that. They had never said those words to each other. Did she love him? Was that why it hurt that much? She wasn't sure she could answer him. She folded her arms across her chest and sat properly on the lounger, legs crossed, back pressed into the recline.

She had been infatuated with him at first; like a lot of girls at Armstrong, she'd had a huge crush on him. But it had been more than that. She liked the way he smelled, the way he'd made her laugh, the way he always took care of her. And if she didn't love him, what was she doing here?

"I don't know," she said finally, because she didn't. "I thought I did."

Finally, she got her wish and he looked at her and she almost regretted it. Pain stretched across his features, his expression so hopelessly open. He took in the injuries on her face and it stole his breath away.

Slowly, he reached out and touched her cheek, tracing his thumb gently below her stitches. He'd done it so many times, a touch so effortless and true before.

Cold, wet hands cupping her face. So much blood. SPENCER!
She flinched at the memory.

Ethan's hand jolted back. His lip trembled, though he tried to hide it, and he turned away. He couldn't look at what had happened to her, what'd he done. "God, your face." He let out a small sob but sucked in his breath and held it. He was about to cry.

Spencer turned her head away from him too, just so he wouldn't have to see, and planted her gaze firmly on the waterfall burbling in the silence spanning between them.

Eventually, he said, his voice thick, "I don't even know what you see in me. All I do is hurt you."

Spencer couldn't argue with that, and she couldn't argue with someone who had five beers' worth of self-hatred churning in his belly.

"I just want all of this to make sense."

He snapped. "But there's nothing else to it! I killed Chris! I did it! I was driving too fast, like I always do. It's all my fault! There! Happy?"

"Don't say that! You didn't mean to, right?"

"You sound like my lawyer. Just because I didn't mean it, doesn't mean it didn't happen."

His outburst shocked Spencer enough, she closed her mouth.

"I'm not a good person, Spencer. I'm not like you. You've got a future, you've got dreams, you're going to do things. It's better if you just let me go. I'm only holding you back. This is how it's supposed to happen." His eyes looked like glass beads, dully reflecting the glow of the pool, but he wasn't really looking at it. It was like he was staring a million miles away and seeing absolutely nothing. "Everyone else knows it, when will you?"

Spencer didn't know what to say about that. She could say he was wrong, but he'd confessed. Everyone else in this town had given up on him, and so, it seemed, had Ethan.

Get Salty: A True Crime Podcast with Peyton Salt

Lifestyles of the Rich and Reckless Segment Transcription

[Get Salty Intro Music]

Peyton Salt: Ethan Amoroso had everything going for him, and like they say, the mighty fall hard. It's a long way down to the bottom.

The son of a prominent executive at Cooper Incorporated, the multibillion-dollar candy company based here in Los Angeles, Ethan grew up with a silver spoon in his mouth, constantly feeding him the sweeter things in life. Like so many of his ilk, the privilege of being rich and handsome meant doors opened for him, people gave him anything he could ever want—opportunities the likes of which you or me cannot even fathom were on the table.

Star striker of the Armstrong soccer team, Ethan had already been noticed by several college teams, with a professional career on the horizon so long as he didn't suffer serious injury preventing him from making it to the big leagues. Though, if we're telling all, even if his knee gave out, he'd still be able to fall back on being the sole heir to his family's immense fortune. Not exactly a bad backup plan.

Ethan's father, William, has his own fair share of controversies. A few years ago, he'd been caught sexting a subordinate, all while married to Ethan's stepmother, but the scandal was later swept under the rug, an all-too-familiar occurrence. Rumor has it that Ethan was cheating on Spencer Sandoval and she caught him red-handed the night of the crash. Like father, like son!

Ethan's fast-paced, carefree lifestyle paved the way for a recipe for disaster. After the incident with Julianne Greene, who attended a house party at Ethan's mansion and was left permanently paralyzed and in a coma, Ethan turned to drugs and alcohol.

The only two options were to send him to military school or to a behavioral rehabilitation program, and the elder Amoroso chose the latter. Ethan seemed to be far beyond what his father thought he could handle. A police report was filed because someone had set the house on fire when he returned home. The name was redacted on the report, but could Ethan have been trying to get back at his father for sending him away? Did his father get his name redacted in order to protect him, fearing it would cause greater embarrassment for the family name? Who knows at this point? We can only speculate.

As for us Salters, we can only look at the destruction caused by Ethan Amoroso and the hundreds of others just like him who see the world for the taking and will do nothing short of having it all for themselves. It doesn't matter who gets in the way—people like Ethan Amoroso are nothing but trouble.

THIRTEEN

THE FOLLOWING SATURDAY AFTERNOON, SPENCER expertly filled the ice cream cone, piling it with vanilla and chocolate swirl before dipping it into the melted chocolate and rolling it in sprinkles, then handed it to the man and his son waiting on the other side of the plexiglass barrier.

She'd worked at Brain Freeze since she was a freshman, and by now she was an ice cream aficionado.

The kiosk, built in the '50s, had been designed to look like a cup full of ice cream, the roof like a swirl on top, with large cartoon eyes. Last year, some vandals spray-painted the roof brown, making it look like a pile of poop. Since the kiosk was right on the edge of the Brentwood Sports Park, it was a popular place for a lot of kids her age to hang out, taking up some of the plastic seating and tables, shading themselves under the pinstripe umbrellas, and spending the rest of their day doing absolutely nothing.

Before, Ethan and his friends would come over while she was working, but at least Olivia still worked there with her. Spencer wiped the back of her hand on her forehead, brushing the stray hairs from her Dutch braids off her damp skin. Ripley couldn't physically fit inside the kiosk, it was that small, so she waited outside under the shade of a nearby tree where Spencer could keep an eye on her and refill a water bowl for her every thirty minutes.

"So when did you want to go dress shopping?" Olivia asked.

"Dress shop—" It took Spencer a moment to realize what she was talking about and then it clicked. "Oh! Homecoming. I totally forgot about it."

"Yeah! We're still going, right? I mean, since it's our last one and all, I figured we'd be stereotypical teenagers and do it this once to say we did it, and then maybe my parents will stop calling me antisocial, even though that's not what *antisocial* means . . . Soccer game got out," Olivia said, tipping her chin toward a minivan with a soccer bumper sticker on the back. A whole gaggle of kids poured out, their knees scraped up and dirty from the game. "Showtime." Olivia leaned on the counter, ready to take the orders and ring up the money.

Thinking about going to homecoming, especially without Ethan, felt like their breakup was real. He couldn't go, of course, even if he wanted to take Hailey. He was still under house arrest. But the thought of the two of them together still hurt. She wanted to move on from him, she knew she deserved that, but would she really be in the mood to dance the night away surrounded by everyone who'd been staring at her the past week since her return?

"I figured it'd be fun," Olivia said, punching in the orders of a scrambling mass of twelve-year-old soccer players resisting being wrangled by a mom who already looked like she was starting to regret mentioning coming here. "You know, get a dress, like a revenge dress like Princess Di, so when you post it online Ethan will see it and he'll feel like such a dumb-dumb for doing what he did, and then you and me, we can live it up and party like there's no tomorrow."

Spencer had to admit, that did sound fun. Like Princess Diana, she could make her first big appearance after the breakup looking like a million dollars. She thought about it, filling up a dozen ice cream cups with various toppings and mixing, moving quickly despite her sling so nothing melted too fast, and before long the throng of hungry kids were enjoying their well-earned desserts under the umbrellas.

"Can't we just stay in? Maybe take it easy?" Spencer asked. Simply thinking about loud noises and crowds was exhausting enough. And she wasn't sure she could stomach seeing happy couples dancing with each other. And it seemed wrong to go to a party when the Moores had just planned a funeral.

"You still have time. We can decide later."

Pain shot through Spencer's shoulder. It happened more frequently, especially if she was pushing herself too hard. She winced and said, "I might be over school dances."

Another customer stepped up to the kiosk and Olivia took their order. "Still," she said, turning back to Spencer as she made the strawberry cone. "It might help you get your mind off things. I want things to go back to the way they used to be . . ."

Spencer couldn't agree more. They worked the rest of their shift, hardly able to talk again with the rush of eager kids wanting a treat after their games. Before long, the garbage can was overflowing.

Spencer went out the back to take out the trash, heading through the parking lot, when she spotted two people standing near the dumpster by the community bathrooms. Tabby Hill and some person she didn't recognize were speaking about something that looked important, their heads leaning toward each other. The stranger looked shady, to say the least. He wore a hoodie, despite the heat, and his hair was a greasy, stringy flop that shadowed his eyes. He handed something to Tabby, who handed something back. Without another word, the stranger left, and Tabby put whatever it was in the front pocket of their jeans.

Spencer's and Tabby's eyes met for a fleeting moment, and Spencer pretended not to have been staring as she hauled the heavy garbage bag into the dumpster. Tabby hurried off, not giving Spencer another glance.

FOURTEEN

SPENCER HAD NEVER BEEN TO a police station, ever in her life. She'd had the privilege of not having to set foot through its doors to see the brown tiles or sit in the plastic-form chairs in the waiting area or smell the burnt coffee in the pot. When she walked in, naturally the eyes of people waiting in the waiting area and the uniformed officer sitting behind the desk fell on Ripley at her side, but no one said anything about it when they saw her face and the bruises still splattering up her skin like an ink spill. Her back was sweaty from the ride over, and she knew her hair looked like a rightful mess thanks to her helmet, but she didn't care. She was beyond caring about anything at this point.

"I'm here to speak to someone about an accident I was involved in," Spencer said.

"Was this recent?" The receptionist's eyes landed on the stitches on her cheek.

"No, my name is Spencer Sandoval. I'm here about the Ethan Amoroso case."

At the sound of Ethan's name, the officer's eyebrows rose. No need to elaborate. "Ah. I see. Then you're going to want to talk to Detective Potentas."

Right. Potentas. That was the detective who had visited her in the hospital after the accident. Spencer's memories of that day were still so hazy, but the moment she heard the name, she remembered.

"Please, have a seat," the officer said. "He's out getting lunch, but he'll be back any moment."

Spencer didn't have to wait long enough for the skin below her shorts to stick to the uncomfortable plastic seating before a man in a white button-down shirt and tie loose around his neck entered. She stood up and rushed over before he even had time to look up from the phone in his hand, his other clutching a Styrofoam to-go box that smelled like something fried. He looked tired and weary, which was understandable given his line of work.

"Detective Potentas, hello." Spencer's formality always came out when she was up against authority figures, especially ones who wore a gun on their hip. "My name is—"

"Spencer Sandoval, of course, I remember," he finished for her. "How can I help you? Is everything okay?"

"Yes, I just wanted to discuss the case I was involved in."

He glanced at the officer sitting behind the desk, who shrugged. "Okay, sure, let's talk in my office."

His office was more of a desk in the back corner of the open floor plan. Ripley padded along at Spencer's side while they walked down the aisle, listening to the furious typing of other detectives writing up reports behind their computers, or chatting with coworkers, or waiting for jobs in a copier to finish processing. It reminded Spencer more of a boring office setting than a hard-boiled headquarters for jaded police that she'd seen so much on television.

Detective Potentas fell into his chair at his desk and clicked away at his computer, typing in his login information, while Spencer took a seat in the stained chair next to his desk, awkwardly positioned in the aisle. Eventually, he leaned back in his chair, and it squeaked underneath him as he rocked. "What can I do you for, Miss Sandoval?"

"I was just wondering if I could look at the police report of the accident."

"Now why would you want to do that?"

Spencer wrung her hands around Ripley's leash as she lied. "School project." It was the best she could come up with.

At least Detective Potentas looked amused. "A school project . . ."

Lying to the police was a thing Spencer never expected to do, but she didn't know how else to ask for it. She tried to smile, but she knew it looked strained.

The detective sighed loudly, his nostrils whistling. "I'm afraid that's impossible. I can't share police reports for an active case." He must have read the disappointment on her face because he leaned forward, resting his elbow on the desk casually. "What's this really about?"

Spencer wasn't sure what to tell him. Would he believe her that she was certain something was wrong about that night? "I still don't remember what happened that night, and I want to know."

"I might be able to make a call to pull some strings, but this would have to happen after Mr. Amoroso's case is processed by the court. And by then, I'm not sure what good it will do you. I can tell you're looking for answers, but sometimes these kinds of things don't have answers."

"I spoke with Ethan, and something just didn't seem right. I think something else happened that night, I just need to know what."

"Miss Sandoval. I know you've been through quite a traumatic event, but it's better if you let us take it from here."

"Maybe if I saw even just a picture of the scene, I could start to remember, knock a memory loose."

Detective Potentas looked at his hands and took another breath. "I'm going to make an assumption here. You're a good student, right?"

"Yeah."

"I can see it, it's in your eyes. You're smart, you're driven, that's all good. This is probably the first time anything like this has happened to you, and I pray it'll be the last."

Spencer sank into the chair, feeling small. She knew where this was going.

"I'm going to say, for your own sanity, it might be better if you don't try to remember that night."

"I'm not here to ogle some dead body, Detective. There's nothing else you can share with me? Not even the written report?"

The detective looked resigned, and Spencer could tell, legally, his hands were tied.

"Sorry, Miss Sandoval. It's just not in my power to hand something like that over to you. I've already got enough to deal with, especially from some podcast that's been spamming my number for days on end . . ."

Spencer tried not to let the sinking feeling of failure weigh her down, but her options were getting smaller and smaller.

"Tell you what," he said. "Come back to me again after all this is over, once you've got some distance between yourself and the accident."

Spencer frowned. Another roadblock.

Detective Potentas took out a piece of gum from his desk drawer and offered a stick to her, but she refused. A first for everything. "I can tell you're a good kid," he said, popping the gum into his mouth. "You're not looking to start any trouble, but it's in my professional opinion to tell you that it's not worth it, getting hung up on this kind of thing. Crashes happen all the time, especially if the driver is under the influence."

"But we don't know that for sure," she said. "Ethan would never . . . he would never get behind the wheel if he was high. Maybe if he were alone, but not if he had other people in the car with him!"

"People make mistakes all the time," the detective sighed. "And once the toxicology reports come back, it'll prove that."

She chewed her lip. "But why can't I remember anything?"

"With crashes like these, head injuries are common."

"Could there be another explanation to my memory loss, though?"

Detective Potentas stared at her, analyzing. "Illicit drugs, maybe."

A yellow Solo cup, then the night being hazy after that. Spencer shivered. "I didn't take anything . . . At least, I don't remember."

"What can I tell you? We're living in a time where kids are taking fentanyl-laced pills," he said grimly. "They're all over the city. Check to see if the hospital ran any lab tests on you when you were admitted."

Spencer shivered again.

"Take care of yourself, Miss Sandoval."

FIFTEEN

THE FOLLOWING DAY AT BRAIN Freeze, Olivia was finishing up an order just as Spencer arrived for her shift. "Guess who was asking about you," Olivia said as Spencer walked in and Ripley flopped under a nearby tree, panting from the ride over.

"Who?"

"Peyton Salt."

Spencer frowned.

"She asked about an interview. I tried to run interference, but she's persistent. She gave me this card." Pinched between Olivia's index and middle fingers was a business card with the words GET SALTY on them.

Spencer sighed and snatched it from Olivia's fingers, crumpled it up, and then threw it in the trash under the counter.

"Figured as much," Olivia said. "Listen, I hate to do this to you, but I gotta split. Emergency on set. Someone decided to kick a hole in one of the castle walls during rehearsal last night, so I need to patch it before tomorrow. Think you can hold down the fort solo?"

Spencer gave Olivia a thumbs-up and she left, humming as she skipped to her car.

Unfortunately, soccer, baseball, and football games let out in overlapping intervals, which meant that the line at Brain Freeze was seemingly endless as Spencer worked hard to keep up with all the orders while also counting out correct change and making sure that everything was clean. Time flew in the blink of an eye. By the time the line had let up, Spencer rested her head on the cool countertop and took a breath. Her head wasn't hurting, but the rest of her was. What had Tabby been doing by the dumpster yesterday? What did the detective say? Illicit drugs were all over Los Angeles, and Spencer knew how easy it was to order them from the internet. Most kids she knew just DM'd a plug on Snapchat.

She heard someone step up to the kiosk and lifted her head to see a familiar face.

"Jackson, hi," Spencer said, finding herself smiling, not just because he wasn't Peyton.

"Tough day?"

"You have no idea."

"Oh, I can imagine." His cheeks and nose were pink from being in the sun, and he was wearing a warm-up jersey with COACH embroidered on his chest. "Coaching kids is like herding cats."

"What can I make for you?" Pain was already flaring up her back and down her arm, throbbing annoyingly, and Spencer had completely missed taking her usually scheduled painkiller break.

"Oh! Nothing. You looked like you need a morale boost. I just wanted to say hi. So, hi."

Spencer smiled. "Want to take a break with me?"

"Sure! I've got a second."

She planted a sign down on the counter that said STAY COOL! BE BACK SOON! "Give me five minutes and I'll meet you under the tree."

With two tall ice cream cups in hand, Spencer joined Jackson at the table under the pin-striped umbrella near the shady tree. Ripley's tail wagged wildly from her spot nearby. She clearly liked Jackson, but he was good about not petting her. Spencer took a seat across from him, sliding the ice cream over.

"Reese's, my favorite!" he said. "How did you know?"

"I remembered. That night at the fair a couple years back, you and Ethan had a pretend fight about what was better: peanut M&Ms or Reese's—"

"Right! The incident with the clown is the first thing that comes to my mind about that fair. Can't believe you remembered my evidence-based and accurate argument in favor of Reese's and that I won by a mile." Jackson's smile sloped upward and he dug the spoon in eagerly.

Spencer dug into her own ice cream, mixed with cookie dough.

"How do you like working at Brain Freeze?" he asked.

"It's not so bad. What about you, *Coach*?" She angled her gaze toward his jersey.

"It's fun. Kids that age cluster the ball like they're chasing a butterfly."

Spencer laughed, and Jackson's dimple reappeared when he smiled.

"How much do I owe you? For the ice cream?" he asked.

"On me."

"Really?"

"No problem. Don't mention it to my uncle, though, he owns the place. He'd kill me if he found out I was giving out ice cream. He may look like a surfer dude, but he's a real hard-ass."

"Secret is safe with me." He put his hand over his heart.

Now that she had some food in her belly, Spencer fished her painkillers out of her pocket and popped one. She washed it down with another spoonful of ice cream.

"How did it go at the police station?" Jackson asked, watching her.

"Not well, they think Ethan is definitely guilty."

"Did you talk to Ethan?"

"Yeah . . . he says he's guilty too, he doesn't even want to fight it. But I just . . . I just don't believe he'd deliberately do something like that, do you?"

Jackson shook his head. "No, of course not. If I did, I wouldn't be friends with him."

Spencer raised a scoopful of ice cream. *Cheers to that,* she thought.

He asked, "Have you been getting harassed by that podcaster following his case?"

"You mean Peyton Salt?" She thought about the crumpled-up card in the trash can.

"Yeah, her. She came to my house earlier and wouldn't leave. She kept throwing her phone in my face, saying she just wanted to ask some questions, how I felt about the charges against Ethan, but I didn't want to talk to her. I almost called the cops on her; she looked like she was going to camp out in the garden, but she left after a while."

"Yeah, she was just here. I've been dodging her, though. I don't think it's any of her business."

"Fair. Plus, once it's out there, it's hard to control what people think of the story. I'm worried I'd just make it worse, especially with his plea hearing coming up."

Spencer hummed in agreement. "I wonder how she's getting her sources. She seems like she's got a finger on the pulse, access to info we don't have."

"Like police reports?"

Spencer raised her eyebrows by way of an answer. "She might have a connection to the police somehow. In one of her earlier episodes, she said she had the police report in front of her."

"I didn't know you were a fan."

"I'm not," she said. "I was curious, read a few transcripts, and I don't recommend it."

"Believe me, I won't listen."

She regretted looking into Peyton's podcast in the first place. After reading a transcript about what other people had to say about her, she'd had to dose up on her painkillers as a migraine threatened to make her head explode.

She swirled the vanilla ice cream around her mouth for a while, savoring the cold, as her thoughts went back to Tabby. "Something else that the detective said, though, bothers me. I asked him about my memory loss and he said it could have been because of drugs. Like, serious drugs."

Jackson stared at her, wide eyed. "For real? You think you were dru—"

"It's not a fun thought, but . . . I remember only having one drink, and the rest of the night is a mess."

"That's fucked up."

"Yeah. It just got me thinking maybe Ethan was on something, too . . . but he didn't know it. I mean, he basically stopped partying since the accident at his house last year."

"Yeah, and he quit smoking pot since it would hurt his chances with Michigan."

Spencer nodded. She had been so proud of him when he went cold turkey.

"He used to get his weed from Brent Lang. Do you know if he was at the party?" Jackson asked.

"I think so. We should talk to him, for sure."

Brent was a self-proclaimed guru, touting the importance of meditation and healing through yoga and breath work. He had a group of devoted followers, mostly girls, who all embodied the New Age lifestyle, having started a yoga club during lunch period. In Spencer's opinion, he gave off "future cult leader" vibes. No matter the weather, he always wore a beanie, even at school where the dress code prohibited hats, and he wore crystals on leather ropes around his neck, claiming they cleared energy and opened his chakras. His mom was a pharmacist, but he'd constantly bash quote-unquote Big Pharma and how it was making people sick and that "natural remedies were the way, man." Would he really be capable of selling anything more hardcore?

Spencer and Jackson fell into a contemplative silence as they continued to eat their ice cream, though with less gusto now that the topic of Ethan possibly being high when he crashed loomed overhead like a storm cloud. Spencer could access her own medical records, so nothing was stopping her from finding out if she really did get her drink spiked. But somehow she didn't want to know; it was too terrifying to think someone would do that to her.

She asked, "Do you want to come over tomorrow? We can figure out our game plan then? Maybe sort through all the stuff we know?"

"Sure! I'd say 'sounds fun' but . . ."

Spencer allowed herself to smile. She appreciated his levity, even if it was short-lived. Having him around made her feel better.

But persistent questions hung heavy over her mind. Could she really have been drugged that night? She hadn't been paying attention to her drink, didn't even remember who handed her the cup in the first place.

SIXTEEN

AFTER SCHOOL, JACKSON ARRIVED AT her house, right on time, at five in the afternoon, after his soccer practice let out. Unfortunately, it had been Hope who had gotten to the door first.

"Spencer! A boy is here for you!" she hollered, her voice seemingly echoing through the whole house. Annoyingly, she sang it, too.

Spencer managed to get there only seconds later, bumping Hope out of the way with her hip. ("Hey!" she cried.) She definitely didn't need Hope blabbing to her parents that she had a boy over, let alone Ethan Amoroso's best friend, a double whammy of trouble in the making. He hadn't even gone home to change, evident because, when he arrived at her front door with his gym bag thrown over his shoulder, his hair was pushed back away from his forehead with sweat, thanks to the heat of the day.

"Sorry about my sister," Spencer said, flushed.

Jackson looked like he was trying not to laugh; his face was all screwed up but his eyes were bright. "It's all right. Hey, I'm Jackson," he said to Hope, who was thoroughly pouting.

"Hey yourself." To Spencer, Hope said, "Mom and Dad are going to freak if they find out you had a boy over when they weren't here."

"It's not like that," Spencer said, hoping that the heat wasn't showing in her cheeks. "This is a . . ." What was this exactly? She couldn't go around saying they were investigating when the police wouldn't.

"It's a project for school," Jackson said quickly.

"Right! A school project. So you don't need to go tattling to Mom or Dad about it."

Hope folded her arms over her chest. "What do I get for not telling?"

She was intent on being a pain in the ass today, but before Spencer could tell her off for it, Jackson asked, "Do you like video games?"

Hope's sneer softened, and she looked Jackson up and down, as if she was surprised a jock who looked like him was interested in that kind of thing. "Yeah. Depends though. Why?"

From his gym bag, he pulled out a Nintendo Switch. "See, I've got the new Zelda game and . . . well, let's say you can play it as much as you want, so long as you don't get Spencer in trouble."

Hope looked at Spencer and rolled her eyes, as if weighing her options and deciding which would be more fun: playing a video game or seeing Spencer get grounded for a few weeks. "Deal. You keep bringing Zelda, I keep my lips sealed."

Jackson smiled, the warmth of it reaching up to his eyes, and Hope scurried away to claim her usual spot on the couch, already firing up the system.

Spencer stepped back and let Jackson fully walk into the house. "Sorry about her. She can be such a brat."

"It's fine, really. With three younger brothers, I know the drill."

Spencer led the way down the hall, toward her warmly lit bedroom. "You can put your bag there," she said and pointed to the spot on the floor in front of her dresser, while she pulled an extra chair she had stolen from the dining room up to her desk. Jackson dropped his bag and looked around her room. Ripley's tail wagged on the bed upon seeing him.

"You're tidy," he said. "Hope you didn't clean on my accord."

"I like organizing. It keeps my mind at ease. I like it when things are neat."

"Clearly," he said, spotting her binders and color-coordinated folders on the shelf above her desk. One of the folders had a custom label she had designed: INVESTIGA-TION. "You're like a professional."

Putting a label on it helped remove the personal connection and made it feel like an assignment.

They both took a seat at her desk—Jackson insisting he take the dining room chair and Spencer take her swivel desk chair—and Spencer showed him what she had compiled so far. "I've sorted what documents I could gather into these three sections: The Party, The Accident, and Legal

Stuff. And then I typed up what I could to get us started." She flipped through, showing newspaper clippings of the accident, and she even drew her own map of the party and a line drawn toward the intersection at Canyon Drive.

Jackson's eyes flitted over the pages as she flipped through quickly. He looked at her, his smile filled with amusement. "You are such an overachiever."

"I know. Is that a problem?"

"Not even. What do we want to do first?"

"I figured we could go through the socials of everyone who might have been at the party. There's no cell reception up in the hills, so most people uploaded videos of the party when they got home and posted it to Facebook and Instagram."

Her heart pounded painfully in her chest. She hadn't gathered the courage yet to check her medical records to see if they'd given her a drug test when she was in the hospital. Part of her wanted to know what happened that night, but another part of her was afraid of what she might find out.

Plus, she didn't want to watch Ethan making out with Hailey all over again, as miniature in the grand scheme of things as it was.

Jackson seemed to sense this hesitancy, and he said, "How about I look through the videos and you start making a timeline of the party. Then we can start a short list of people we'd want to interview in person, maybe anyone who can confirm what happened, like Brent Lang and Harrison, and Tabby, too."

Spencer was grateful for his thoughtfulness and took out one of her gel pens from the bunch she kept in a cup on her desk and got to writing. Meanwhile, Jackson opened his laptop.

"Have you started to remember anything else about the party?" he asked.

"Some. The beginning of the night, I arrived at the party around ten. I hadn't planned on going in the first place and told Ethan so. He'd wanted me to come, but I'd just gotten off a shift at Brain Freeze, and I was tired, but I changed my mind. He didn't think I'd be there. I took a Lyft to the front of the neighborhood and walked. By the time I got there, the party was going hard. The firepit was lit, and people were skateboarding in empty swimming pools."

"Good, I mean—not *good*-good. But it's a start."

Spencer flipped to a new page in her notebook and drew a rough line down the middle of the page and started jotting down all the memories she could in her notebook, giving ample space to fill in the gaps. Her notes consisted of the following in her right-handed scrawl:

9:30PM—Brain Freeze shift ends
10PM—arrive at Highwood Estates
10:30ish—I buy a Diet Coke from the bar
10:45ish—I find Ethan and Hailey together
TIME?—Ethan and I break up
TIME?—we leave the party (me, Ethan, Tabby, Chris) in Ethan's car
TIME?—crash

Her pen stayed pressed on the paper after she finished the *h*. To think, if Spencer had just stayed home like she had originally wanted to, maybe everything could have turned out differently.

"Have you ever blacked out before?" she asked. "Not been able to remember a whole night?"

Jackson shook his head. "I bet it's scary, though."

"It is."

Jackson watched her thoughtfully. "Are you okay?"

"Just seeing it all laid out like this, it's surreal."

Jackson worried at a hangnail on his thumb with his index finger. "Is there anything I can do for you?"

"You being here is doing a lot more than you think." She smiled at him, and he smiled back, color brightening his cheeks. Her stomach swooped delightfully but she felt guilty. She shouldn't flirt with him. He was Ethan's best friend. It still felt off-limits, like she was somehow just as bad as Ethan—a cheater. Besides, Jackson was nice to everyone. Did she really think there was anything else there? She refocused by pushing stray hairs from her braid off her forehead and looked down at the page. "This is helping, though. It's bringing some memories back. Like, when I got to the party, I got a drink. They had a station on a tree stump with cups and snacks and everything, and I paid five dollars to get a cup."

"Five dollars, wow. Harrison must have made a killing that night. Remember when he used to charge five dollars just to get in the door and drinks were free?"

"No, I didn't go to parties freshman year," she told him.

"Oh," said Jackson.

"Anyway, we'd have to ask him, but yeah, everyone was pretty drunk and it was relatively early in the night." She massaged her temples, trying to remember. "People were playing corn hole, and there was a game of beer pong in a half-finished garage, and a few people were vaping on the lawn. I remember smelling cotton candy, from all the vapor. The details start to get a little hazy here . . . But I think I heard music." She flipped back to her notebook page about what she remembered. She still didn't know if it was live or a playlist on speakers.

Jackson already had an answer for her. "The Misstakes. They're tagged in this one video here. See?" He pointed to a recording of the band in front of a dozen people jumping to the beat. But Spencer didn't see anyone she recognized, including herself, in the video.

He typed The Misstakes into Google and pulled up their website. All the members went to Armstrong, like everyone else at the party. They did a lot of pop-punk covers that were a hit at those kinds of parties. Unfortunately, their website didn't have any footage of that night so Jackson went to their personal Facebook pages to find anything that might help.

As expected, there wasn't much to go on. The band had probably been too busy performing to take photos or videos during the party. Jackson let out a sigh that ruffled the bangs on his forehead. There was a lot of work ahead.

Spencer had an idea. "Do you want a snack? How about some popcorn?"

"That's . . . yeah, if it's no trouble."

"No problem! Be right back." He looked like he could use some calories after his practice. So Spencer went to the kitchen to grab a bag of popcorn from the pantry. Hope was still planted on the couch playing Jackson's Switch.

"Is he your new boyfriend?" Hope teased, without looking up from the screen. No need to elaborate.

"No." Spencer started the popcorn in the microwave and leaned on the countertop. While she was there, she spotted a fruit bowl with some grapes and nectarines, which she washed and put on a plate. "He's a friend."

"Yuh-huh," Hope said sarcastically. "Tell yourself that."

"You're twelve. What do you even know?"

"More than you."

Spencer scoffed and threw a grape from the fruit bowl at her sister's head. It landed somewhere on the couch and Hope retrieved it.

"Thanks!" Hope said, popping the grape in her mouth.

Honestly, little sisters.

Spencer returned to her bedroom and handed Jackson the fruit and popcorn, which he took with a smile. They shared the snack, quietly working side by side, and Spencer was satisfied knowing that this was exactly what friends did. There was nothing bigger happening between the two of them, both content with the ease with which they worked together as partners. Nothing more, she told herself.

"Spencer . . ."

The edge in Jackson's voice made her look up from her laptop. She'd joined in his efforts to do some more research, recording anything that might look like people were acting more drunk than usual.

Jackson pointed at his own laptop's screen of a paused video from Facebook, uploaded by Nea Varkaus, a junior at Armstrong. Nea was on the debate team, so Spencer didn't really know her that well, but she was a regular at Brain Freeze, and apparently had enough social standing with the kids on the Headmaster's List to be at the party.

It was hard to totally make out in the dark, and they weren't the focus of the video—Nea had been recording herself and her friends doing some sort of rehearsed dance for TikTok with the firepit in the background—but Spencer recognized her old bright white T-shirt, tossed in the trash long since the crash, and the back of Ethan's head. They were paused, both of them with their hands in the air, gesticulating wildly. It was hard to make out the details of her expression, but she remembered this moment clearly.

"Is this when . . . ?" Jackson started.

"Yeah, this was us breaking up."

Jackson didn't say anything, just awkwardly pinched his lips together. He took a moment but said, trying to lighten the mood, "It's lucky that someone caught it on camera, though."

"What are the chances, right? It's at least something. What's the time stamp?"

"1:45 A.M."

Spencer jotted that down, adding the time on the timeline. There were still so many gaps. "Is there any way we can track where we went from there?"

Jackson played the video, but the phone was too far away to pick up any audio of what was being said. Past-Spencer and Past-Ethan moved out of frame, Spencer throwing her arms up and stomping off and Ethan chasing, but the camera didn't follow.

"Maybe there's another angle?" Jackson suggested.

"Maybe . . ." She stared at her notebook, miles away in thought.

Jackson must have sensed the edge in her voice because he said softly, "Listen, if it's too hard to revisit all this, we can stop. We've been at it a while."

"No . . ." Spencer hated the idea of asking people about one of the most humiliating experiences of her life, but it was outweighed by her need to know everything. At least Jackson didn't seem to judge her.

"For what it's worth," he said, "Ethan's an idiot. Pretty sure I can certifiably confirm that fact. He doesn't even think Reese's is the superior candy."

Spencer's lips spread into an appreciative smile, and she glanced at him. She hadn't realized how close they had been sitting to each other as the hour slipped by.

Their heads were tipped so close together, nearly touching, she noticed that his eyes were a beautiful dark brown, with golden flecks toward the middle. She'd never noticed before how pretty they were, behind his glasses.

She cleared her throat and ordered herself to get it together. "We've got a pretty good start so far. But I still need to check my hospital records. I'll know for sure then if there was something in my system that messed with my memory."

"Okay," Jackson said, nodding, though he looked worried for her sake. "I guess it'd be one less mystery."

From: patientservices@mynsghospital.com

Subject: Patient Login Request

Thank you for using the Northshore General Hospital Patient Portal. Your login name or password has been successfully updated. Please click the link below to log in with your new credentials.

Patient Details

Patient Name: Spencer Sandoval

Date of Birth: 09/02/2003

Patient ID: SAN0982311-B

Status: Completed

Blood: B+

Most recent visit: 09/03/2021

Allergies: None

Quick-Click Documentation

Operative Report: SAN0982311-B-oprep.pdf

Drug/Alcohol Test Results: Pending

Upcoming Appointments

Cast removal–10/24–Send Email Reminder

Requesting prescription refill? Click here.

SEVENTEEN

SINCE ACCESSING HER MEDICAL RECORDS, Spencer had asked when any of her blood tests would come back, and the hospital explained it might take a few more days. She was still unnerved by the possibility that someone might have slipped something in her drink that caused her memory loss. The next day at school, Spencer and Jackson, with Ripley bounding along at her side, left the east wing of Armstrong when the lunch bell rang.

As expected, they found Brent Lang leading a yoga session near Chris's memorial garden. A couple of freshman girls moved through their poses on brightly colored vinyl mats. They were in the midst of doing an elaborate stretch that involved arms and legs wrapping around each other in a way that did not look entirely comfortable when Jackson and Spencer approached. Brent was wearing harem pants and his usual beanie, his legs wrapped around the back of his head like a human pretzel.

"Deep breaths, everyone," he said, with his eyes closed. "Release the worries of today. Exhale the bad, inhale the good."

He must have sensed the shadow passing across his face as Spencer stepped in front of the sun, looking down on him.

Brent opened one eye and looked at Spencer. "Can you not bring that dog over here? It's going to disrupt my aura's energy." Brent waved his hands through the air like he was scrubbing a window.

"Uh, sure," Spencer said, keeping Ripley at her side. "Listen, Brent? Do you have a second?"

"Can't you see I'm a little tied up at the moment?"

Jackson chuckled. "Good one."

Brent didn't look like he was trying to make a joke, though. Jackson's smile died quickly.

Spencer said, "We just wanted to ask you some questions about that night at the party."

Brent sighed when he realized that Spencer and Jackson were not going to go away anytime soon. He told his yoga students, "Move into Savasana and work on finding your breath. I'll be right back."

The students moved to lie on their backs, spread-eagle on the lawn, while Brent followed Spencer and Jackson so they could talk more in private. Brent always had a sleepy-eyed look, like he might curl up and take a nap under a desk at any moment at school. People at school were convinced he was on drugs, but Spencer had a sneaking suspicion that was just how he looked, perpetually calm and at ease with his place in the world.

Before Spencer or Jackson could say anything, Brent clapped his hands twice, closed his eyes, and breathed deeply. "I'm just clearing the air between us. Give me a moment."

Spencer and Jackson glanced at each other, and Jackson shrugged a shoulder. They waited until he was ready to speak.

"The spirits around you are very loud," he said. "It's distracting being around all that noise. Your aura is an oil spill, one big mess, and could really use a cleaning, you know."

Spencer wasn't sure what to say to that. "Uh, okay. Thanks?"

Jackson was trying not to laugh. Clearly, he didn't buy into the New Age lingo, either. The best course of attack, Spencer decided, was to just get straight into it. "We were wondering if we could ask you some questions about your, uh"—Spencer glanced at Jackson. "Side hustle. Selling some weed. The night of the end-of-summer party."

"God, it's crazy. Just remembering that night, what happened to Chris. Can't believe it."

"Do you remember much of the party? Anything unusual?"

Brent jutted out his lower lip. "Not really. Pretty run of the mill as far as Ressler's parties go. Ressler's definitely lost his touch, though; his parties used to be a lot more fun then. I think he's trying too hard. Charging too much."

"Do you remember seeing me at the party?" Spencer asked.

"Besides you freaking out on Ethan? Making a huge scene and all? Your aura was all spiky and red, such a buzz-kill. But not really. Why?"

Jackson jumped in. "What about anything else that might have been weird? Anyone who stood out to you? Something that didn't feel right?"

"Just the usual private school circuit. Kids from Armstrong, Westwood Prep, Oakhill. Can't say it was any different than you'd expect. It's just weird to think back on it now and realize it was Chris's last night . . . Hope he was happy." Brent's gaze drifted up as he thought about it. "Now that I mention it, I saw Chris over by the cars, actually."

That surprised Spencer. "You did? What was he doing?"

"I don't know. I didn't think anything of it until the crash. I think that was the last time I ever saw him alive . . . He looked like he was trying to find something. Like maybe he'd dropped something. He kept walking up and down where the cars were parked. I wasn't paying too much attention, though. Didn't seem like something to pay much attention to, you know? Why bother."

"Did anyone else see him at that time?"

"Yeah, my girlfriend Alison was there with me. She'll tell you the same thing. We were . . . ahem, *occupied* in the bushes."

"Right . . . ," Spencer said, catching the hint.

Jackson was furiously taking notes in his notebook. She saw him write down Alison's name. Spencer had the same thought about asking her about that night too, just to make sure it was accurate. But Brent seemed like he was sure he'd seen Chris before the accident.

"Do you know around what time specifically?" she asked.

Brent shrugged a shoulder and shook his head. "Nah,

I wasn't really keeping an eye on the clock, you see. It'd be kind of rude. Besides, time is a construct invented to further capitalist agenda."

"Listen, dude, did you hook up Ethan that night?" Jackson asked. "Edibles, pre-rolls?"

"Ethan?" Brent asked. "No, man, you know he's been sober for a year now. If he was high that night he didn't get it from me." Then his face shifted and a shadow passed over his eyes. "But people keep saying he was high the night he crashed. Is that true?"

"We don't know." Spencer faced Brent directly. "Were you selling other stuff at the party?"

"What are you looking for?" Brent asked, suddenly shifting into business mode. "I don't have any on me right now, but I can get it to you later. You want to get a body high or are you trying to get more in touch with your ancestors and see God?"

"No, this isn't for us, no," Spencer said hurriedly. "We wanted to figure out who was selling drugs at the party that might have made me forget stuff."

"*Marijuana* is not a *drug*, she's a plant of the earth. Nature is all around us. Making a plant illegal is just another extension of the Man. They just want to keep us oppressed. We're all slaves to the patriarchy."

Spencer stopped him before the inevitable rant she could sense coming. "I get that, but did you happen to know about any other drugs being passed around at the party that night? Anything a little more . . . mind altering?"

"I only sell weed and shrooms. I don't do the harder

stuff. Won't touch anything that's been in a lab. But yeah. There was probably some Molly being passed around."

"From who?"

"Junior. I think the name is Tabby Hill? Tammy maybe?"

Spencer looked at Jackson. "It's Tabby. You were right the first time."

Jackson's eyebrows were raised sky-high. "Tabby's a plug?"

Brent went on. "Yeah, man. Sells a lot of 'scrip. You should ask them. Say, what's with the pat down? You guys snitches? Working for the cops or something?" Brent asked, looking back and forth between the two of them.

"Brent, we've been in school together since sixth grade," Jackson said with a small smile.

"Oh right." He blinked lazily.

Jackson glanced at Spencer, as if to say, *Can you believe this guy?*

Spencer asked, "What does Tabby sell?"

Brent's smile slipped wider. "Ooh, does Little Miss Four-Point-Oh Spencer Sandoval use some performance-enhancing drugs to ace all her tests?"

Spencer's face felt hot. "No, of course not." *And by the way, I have a 4.9*, she wanted to add. Brent had probably never calculated a weighted GPA in his life.

Brent held up his hands, defensively. "Just saying! I wouldn't be the first to think it."

Spencer didn't want to argue with him; she didn't come

here for him to start anything. She just needed answers. "You said Tabby sells 'scrips."

"Adderall, Ritalin, Xanax, Percocet . . . Don't tell anyone I told you, because it skeeves me out, but I heard they'd gotten their hands on some dark shit. Like, stuff that could land a person in jail, no doubt. Plus, there's a lot of dummy Xannys and Addys laced with fentanyl on the market right now. It's Russian roulette out there. But lots of their clients are people who want to focus up during the day and then decompress at night. So yeah, there were probably pills floating around. I mean, it's LA, man."

"Right," Jackson said. Spencer was feeling simultaneously nauseous and exhilarated. If someone had slipped her something at the party, that would explain her memory loss. It was their first lead, and she could barely keep her breakfast down.

Brent looked over his shoulder and licked his lips. "Look, you didn't hear this from me, but I heard that Tabby got expelled from their last school for some crazy shit. Their family covered it all up, but things leak. Heard they were selling coke, heroin, meth even. Whatever it is, you should be careful. Tabby has all this bad energy. You never know with folks from Arizona."

"Noted," Jackson said flatly. It appeared that his opinion of Brent was waning alongside Spencer's. He didn't sound like he believed Brent in the slightest.

"Look, I really gotta go," Brent said. "My students will fall asleep if I'm not back. Do you need anything else?"

Spencer said they didn't, and Brent returned to his group of yoga acolytes.

"Heroin? Meth? You think Tabby was selling that stuff?" Jackson scoffed. "Maybe coke, but come on. It's all a bit extreme. What is this, a show on HBO?"

"We can't rule anything out," Spencer said. "The best we can do is talk to Tabby."

"If they'll even talk to us."

"We have to try."

"Tabby called in sick from school today. We'll have to wait until they're back to talk, then." Jackson clicked his pen thoughtfully a few times before putting it between the pages of his notebook. He had a habit of clicking his pen when he was particularly flustered.

Hearing that Tabby might have had a hand in Spencer's memory loss was frightening to say the least. If Brent's suspicions were right, Tabby wasn't someone to take lightly. But Spencer wasn't in the habit of listening to rumors.

Spencer bent down to scratch Ripley's back and Ripley looked up at her, mouth open in a wide smile. Spencer felt like even the dog understood that they were on to something. It was a step, even if it felt like a baby step, toward piecing together what happened that night.

EIGHTEEN

OUTSIDE IN THE BACKYARD, SPENCER focused the telescope, then pulled back to look at the moon with her own eyes. Living in Los Angeles, Spencer hardly ever saw more than three stars, two if the moon was full. The light pollution and smog always made the sky hazy and impossible to see through. One of her dream trips would be a visit to the Cosmic Campground in New Mexico, located in the Gila National Forest. She could camp and watch the night sky, getting as many photos as she possibly could with the astro-photography camera she'd been saving up for all summer. Hike and cook on an open fire all day, and sleep under the stars at night.

But for now, she was stuck at home, until she was finally able to sit in a car again.

The moon was full and bright, a rarity in the city, and Spencer had set up her telescope on the deck, Ripley watching curiously from the grass. The crickets were out, the air was warm, and Spencer finally got to have some time to herself. She had lit some candles to see by and could blow them out when she needed to. For now, she had some time.

"Hey."

She turned to see Jackson, emerging from her living room, sliding the glass door behind him and smiling, as always.

"Hey!" she said cheerfully. "You made it."

She had invited Jackson over for a study session for their AP psych exam. Her parents were out at work, so it shouldn't be a problem. Besides, they were doing things for school. Why would she get in trouble for that? But she had something else in mind before they got to work.

"Hope let me in," he explained. "What are you doing?"

"Come see," she said, tipping her head to the telescope.

When he approached, she could smell him. Whatever he used when he showered, she liked it, a pleasant combination of cedar and rosemary. It reminded her of a forest trail on the northern coast. She was thankful for the dark, concealing the heat in her cheeks.

He leaned down and peered through the eyepiece. "Whoa," he said, completely—for lack of a better word—starstruck. "It's so clear."

"She's beautiful, right?"

"Totally." Jackson pulled back from the telescope and smiled at her; then he looked through the eyepiece again. "It's—wow, amazing! You can almost see the ranges in the mountains. Everything is . . . wow!" Spencer smiled. She too sounded lost for words the first time she saw the moon with a telescope. By making the moon so large, one can really feel so small. It had the opposite effect of being alone in an empty room. Instead, it made her feel closer to the cosmos. Like she could reach out and touch it. If she were at a dark sky park, she imagined the night sky full of stars could open up and swallow her whole. Someday she'd get there.

Jackson looked up at her. "Is this what you do most nights when you're not studying?"

Spencer smiled. "As if I couldn't be any more of a nerd."

"Not like that's a bad thing. I think sometimes we see the moon so much, sometimes we take it for granted."

He had a point. "I'm curious, though. What do you see in the moon?"

"What do you mean?"

"Like, when you look at the moon, what looks back?"

He looked through the eyepiece and said, "I think I see a man. The eyes, and the mouth, making it look like he's surprised." He tilted his head up again. "Is this some kind of Rorschach test? Did I pass?"

Spencer lowered her voice and stroked her face, as if she had a long beard. "Ah yes, you see a man in the moon, therefore you are at war with your conscious and unconscious mind." She laughed and dropped the act. "I'm joking. It's just fun to ask what people see. Everyone sees something different. It's called lunar pareidolia. What people see in the light or dark spots of the moon." The dark craters of the moon could form the impression of handprints, or the profile of a dog howling; some people saw the face of a man, others saw a woman with an updo. People could argue for decades about which was correct, but in the end, no one would be right. The only truth was that people saw patterns in random shapes as a result of asteroids hitting the surface with no atmosphere. And Spencer found comfort in the idea that there was an inherent need in people to see patterns and faces in randomness. Everyone was always looking for answers.

"Really?" he said. "I always thought it was pretty standard across the board."

She nodded. "You'd be surprised. Tons of people around the world see different things. I see a rabbit. The ears, the little tail."

Jackson looked back through the eyepiece and *ooh'd*. "Now I see it! But I can't see the man anymore. That's wild." He kept looking through the telescope, completely drawn in. Spencer stood by, holding herself and smiling as she looked at the sky, too. A plane flew overhead, its wingtip lights blinking.

Spencer glanced at the time on her phone. It was almost time.

"This is amazing. I've never seen the moon like this before . . . What are you doing?"

Spencer blew out the candles and counted down the seconds on her phone. "You don't think I wanted you here just to look at the moon, did you?" she asked with a grin. "Look again. Three, two, one . . ."

Jackson lowered his gaze to the telescope and after a second, he tensed up. "What is—it's moving! What is that? It's so fast!"

Spencer smiled wider. "Right on time. Perfectly predictable."

Jackson looked at her, his expression tight. "Aliens."

Spencer laughed. "I wish! No, that was the International Space Station. Pretty cool, right?"

"For real?" Jackson moved back to the telescope, but it would have been long gone by now.

"Four-point-seven-six miles per second. That's how fast it's falling. Can you imagine that? Weightlessness? Zero gravity?"

"No, I really can't. I've never even been on a roller coaster. Freaks me out too much. Heights? No thank you. That's way too intense for me. But still, this was so cool. Thanks for showing me."

"I'm glad you could see it! The conditions have to be perfect; fortunately we didn't have any cloud cover. Sometimes things just work out when you need them to."

Spencer half-heartedly kicked a rock down the sidewalk. It rolled down the pavement a few steps away, for Spencer to kick it again. They had taken a break from their AP psych notes to take Ripley for a walk. The conversation turned back toward Ethan and the case.

The first day of his trial was coming up next weekend. Inevitably, it stirred up excitement for people who were paying attention to the case.

"It's awful reading what people are saying about him online," Spencer said. The phone lit up her face in the dim light of the fading evening. "Reddit is the worst. And everyone's private stories on Snap."

"Yeah, it's brutal, they all say he's guilty."

"Spencer?" Jackson asked.

"Yeah?"

"What if he is?"

Spencer put her phone away. "He can't be. He wouldn't. Even Brent said Ethan was sober."

"But he doesn't know if he was sober *that night*. And you don't remember."

"I just—I just don't want to believe it's true."

Jackson put his hands in the pockets of his hoodie. "Yeah."

"The faster we figure all this out, maybe the faster we can prove people wrong," she said.

Jackson pushed his glasses up his nose and took a breath. "You really think when faced with the truth, people will change their minds?"

Spencer didn't want to think about the alternative, that even with all the facts, people have already found Ethan guilty and there was no going back. She didn't answer his question and turned Ripley down the corner, making sure she didn't stick her nose in the lawns with the warning signs about spraying pesticides in the grass. In a way, going online these days felt like she was sticking her own nose in poison.

It was surreal to think that everyone had an opinion about Ethan's case.

After the fifth celebrity tweeting about how they wanted #justiceforchris, Spencer couldn't take it anymore. Truth was discovered in split-second decisions, posted online for all to see, no going back.

"Any luck finding more videos from the party?" she asked.

"We've collected most of what I could track down. I think we've got a pretty good timeline of events."

The streetlights overhead crackled on, one by one down the street, lighting up the road in a pale orange hue, and Jackson's glasses caught the glint of a passing car, their high beams on bright. The flashback hit her head-on.

Ethan's face. Lit up. Shadows cast across his cheeks. Crash.

Spencer took a steadying breath and gripped Ripley's leash tighter.

"What do you know about Tabby Hill?" she asked.

Jackson bowed his elbows out, maintaining his hands in his pockets while shrugging his shoulders. "Nothing really. They seem aloof and we've never had a chance to talk. What Brent said about them makes me think that there's a lot we don't know. But how do we get them to talk to us?"

Spencer explained seeing Tabby while at work the other day, and how suspiciously they were acting when Spencer even tried to look in their direction.

"Weird," Jackson said. "But are we being just like these strangers on the internet, trying to accuse people of things before we even have all the facts?"

"We're not doing this for fun. This is real. Tabby should

be able to tell us more about that night. The only way to know is if we ask."

But that was easier said than done.

All week at school, Spencer continued organizing the events of that night. She pretended to be listening in class, even going so far as to use her large textbook to block Mrs. McNamara from seeing that she was really watching videos from that night and recording her thoughts in her notebook. She'd gotten in deep with the investigation, tracking down all the videos that she could, sometimes even cornering people in the hall to get them to give up any videos or photos of that night. She kept all of it in a small black notebook, which she could tuck easily into her bag and whip out at a moment's notice.

The whole time, Tabby almost made a point to avoid Spencer at all costs, ducking out of sight whenever Spencer and Jackson drew near. It was like trying to catch a cloud.

Once, by random encounter, Spencer managed to find Tabby in the bathroom right next to the cafeteria. When Spencer opened her mouth to speak, Tabby shot her the coldest look Spencer had ever seen. It actually stopped Spencer in her tracks.

"Tabby, I—"

"I'm keeping my mouth shut. Same as you."

Spencer didn't know what to say, let alone try to stop Tabby as they pushed past her to leave, looking over their shoulder only once, glowering at Spencer like she was the filth of the earth.

Get Salty: A True Crime Podcast with Peyton Salt

Lifestyles of the Rich and Reckless Segment Transcription

[Get Salty Intro Music]

Peyton Salt: I wanted to get a bigger picture about Ethan after several of you have flooded our inbox about this story. (Don't forget to hit us up online, even just to say hi! We love hearing from our fans!)

Tabby Hill, the acclaimed child star you might recognize from those cookie commercials, continues to decline any chance at an interview. We've been trying our best to get their side of the story, but it would appear there's nothing else to say about the matter, otherwise they would want to talk to us, right, Sasha?

Sasha Firth: That's right. We want victims to have the chance to tell their story, but we also want to make sure we get the full picture about Ethan. I have to admit, like so many others, I'm obsessed. This case has taken over my brain.

Peyton: [*laughs*] I too can't give up. I need to know why Ethan did what he did. Since I have almost exclusive access, I interviewed several people about him from Armstrong and beyond, including those directly affected by his reckless behavior, to get behind the psychology of the rich and reckless.

[SFX: school bell rings, voices in a crowd, lockers closing]

Harrison Ressler (senior):

Ethan's a cool guy. He used to throw the biggest parties. I learned a lot from him, but he's a bit of a hothead. Makes him good at soccer, though. Bet he could have made the national team. His dad's got enough money to buy it for him if he doesn't anyway. [*laughs*]

Tracey Pujolaso (junior):

I nearly got run over by Ethan in the parking lot at school last year. He came peeling into an empty parking space, nearly killed me. Oh my gosh. Do you think maybe he tried to?

Abigail Brak (sophomore):

Everyone said he was the hottest guy in school. I still do. I mean, he's a piece of [*BEEP*] but it doesn't make him any less hot.

Nick Moore (victim Chris Moore's older brother):

Ethan needs to be locked up for a long time. He got my brother killed, my girlfriend's in a coma because of him . . . The world would be a better place if he wasn't in it.

Patrick Hackett (senior):

I heard he got shipped off to military school or whatever, total maniac. They do that to seriously messed-up people, right? I also heard his parents were sick of him, too. I'm not surprised he's going to jail.

Alejandro Rojas (junior):

Dude's loaded. He just didn't care he was driving fast. If he got a ticket, he could just pay it off or whatever. A two-hundred dollar ticket is chump change. With people like him, it's either get out of the way or get flattened, simple as that.

Teresa Ferrera (senior):
> I heard a rumor he had a stalker, but isn't that what all scumbag guys say about girlfriends? "That chick was crazy." I don't buy it for one second.

Daphne Deargacha (freshman):
> I don't really know him, but he's been all over the news. If everyone's saying all that stuff about him, it's true, right? Why else would people hate him?

NINETEEN

THE DAY OF ETHAN'S FIRST appearance in court, Spencer went to the garage, following the sound of the metal hammering coming from inside.

While Spencer always thought she was smart and got good grades because she worked hard for it, Hope was a real genius. It never bothered Spencer that Hope was naturally talented at all things engineering and invention. Math and physics came to her as easily as breathing came to most people. When she was four, she built her first robot. At ten, she made a solar-powered automata out of pinewood.

Her current obsession was Rube Goldberg machines. She used various mechanics, like bowling balls as weights, pulleys, and springs. A few times the neighbors complained to the homeowners' association about a raccoon infestation, but it had just been Hope scrounging around in their garbage for anything she could use to make her machine bigger and better.

Her current project was huge, spanning the entirety of the garage, so much so that both family cars had to be parked in the driveway because there was no room to fit either one.

Hope had entered a contest for young engineers and needed to submit a video for the judges showing her work in progress. She was in the midst of recording a video, testing the machine. The grand prize was four thousand dollars and an article about the winner written in a magazine. Hope had been working on her project all summer, spending most of her days and some nights in the garage, finessing every detail and planning out each stage in a stack of notebooks. If there was any doubt they were related, Spencer and Hope's love for notebooks was a dead giveaway.

Spencer kept to the edge of the garage, staying out of frame of the camera as Hope's machine had run its course, the final domino falling over. Hope got started setting up for another run.

Spencer asked, "Did you steal my shoes?"

"Which shoes do you refer to, oh great and terrible queen?"

Annoyed, Spencer said, "My flats, the dark blue ones."

"Oh, those. No, why?"

"I can't find them. I haven't seen them for ages." The last time she'd worn them was . . . Spencer couldn't remember, but it bothered her. She liked knowing where all her things were and that things were in their rightful place.

Hope shook her head. "Why would I take them?"

"Because you've taken my stuff for your projects before." Spencer glanced at their mom's old bra being used in the machine as an elastic slingshot.

"I told you, I didn't take them. Maybe Olivia did," Hope said, focusing intently on balancing the dominoes.

Spencer sighed. Hope was many things: a genius, an annoying little sister, and a total nerd, but she wasn't a liar.

"Need help resetting it?" Spencer asked, about to reach for a bobbing bird garden decoration when Hope barked.

"Don't—touch that."

Spencer held up her hands innocently and backed up. "Did you get this from Mrs. Piripi's yard?"

"I didn't steal it. I'm simply . . . borrowing it."

"Hope."

"I left a note. I needed something to flip the coin." She referred to the tail of the bird that would flip a coin into a bowl of water. The whole setup was extraordinarily elaborate. Hope had said she wanted to build roller coasters when she grew up, and based on the expanse of the Rube Goldberg machine, Spencer didn't doubt it for a second.

"Where are you going anyway?" Hope asked.

"Ethan's court appearance."

"Oh. Do me a favor and grab those dominoes for me." Hope pointed to a bucket near Spencer's elbow, resting on top of an old carpenter's workstation. Spencer got the dominoes, and Hope took out some more blocks.

"How's it coming along?" Spencer asked.

"Fine," Hope said with a sigh. Spencer noticed how much older she looked these days. What happened to her baby sister? She was becoming a grown-up faster and faster. She sighed like their mom did. "I still have more work to do. But I feel like it's missing something. Some pizzazz." She waved her hands in the air, as best she could with one fist full of dominoes, doing jazz fingers.

"Maybe add some lights? LEDs or something that changes color?"

"Maybe . . ." Hope's gaze followed the track of the Rube Goldberg machine, watching it execute its function in her mind's eye. "It's not very good, is it?"

"What are you talking about? It looks great."

Hope shrugged a shoulder and twisted her lips, looking bashful. "Flip that switch over there. No, not—yeah, that one."

Spencer did as she was told and stood back with Hope as they admired her work. The machine started up beautifully. A series of ball bearings rolled down zigzag ramps, growing larger and larger in size, intending to get all the way to a bowling ball at the end, moved through a series of falls, rolling down tracks, spinning through tunnels, all the way to a wooden train set that flew off the tracks and fell to the floor with a plastic clatter.

"It's not finished . . . ," Hope said, almost like she was embarrassed. "I feel like something is missing. I can't get this one stage to transition into another. It's like . . ."

"A gap."

"Yeah," Hope said, folding her arms over her chest.

"Courtroom number two," said the security guard at the Santa Monica courthouse as Spencer walked through the metal detector. Then he noticed Ripley. "Is this a medical service animal?"

"Mental health," Spencer corrected. She picked up her backpack as it left the X-ray machine, thankful they didn't make a fuss about the painkillers inside.

"Fine. But be aware that Judge Patel might request that you take the dog out if it causes any distractions."

Spencer doubted that it would be a problem, but she understood why. If anyone was allergic to the dog, like Dr. Diamond at school, she didn't want to be the one standing between Ethan's fair trial and justice. How would she feel if she was the one who got Ethan in trouble because the judge might be in a bad mood?

As she approached the courtroom, she recognized some people waiting in the hall: The Moores were talking with the lawyer in red-soled Louboutins near the coffee machine; a couple of fellow students from Armstrong had come wearing #justiceforchris badges; even Detective Potentas was there, standing by the staircase and talking on his phone. Spencer had come to the trial without her parents. They didn't think it was a good idea, but she was determined to show her face at the trial. She wanted to be there, make sure that no one thought she was hiding. It was a terrible crash, but she needed to be there. She needed to see it through to the end.

But she couldn't help the nagging pull in her belly, telling her to go home. She was embarrassed, and anxious, and a little lonely. She'd tried to dress appropriately, but she couldn't help but feel like no matter what she wore, she would stand out in the courtroom.

That was when she spotted Jackson leaning against the wall near the water fountain, folding and refolding the end of his tie nervously, head lowered, lost in thought. His dark hair was slicked back from his forehead, and he wore a white long-sleeved shirt and slacks. If he didn't already look like Clark Kent, he did now. She could only imagine the worry he must be feeling for Ethan.

She sidled up next to him, standing at the wall too, watching the parade of people in suits filling the hall. She knew that he knew she was there, but they didn't say anything to each other for a moment, simply standing in silence and taking a breath before the inevitable chaos that would be the first day of Ethan's trial. She had no idea what to expect. She'd only seen trials on TV and she didn't think it could be like that, could it?

Jackson was one of the few people she wanted to be with at that moment, and it helped calm her nerves a little bit.

Spencer ran the tip of her thumbnail through the groove on Ripley's handhold on her vest. It helped ground her into the moment, feeling like she was real. She liked the way the cement wall cooled the sweat on the skin of her back, and she wiggled her toes in her shoes. She was alive, she was here, and she could get through this. But even then, it still didn't stop the flashback from happening in the span of time it took her to blink, and she let out a shudder of a breath.

SPENCER! Cold, wet hands on her face. Engine roaring. Crash. Float.

Images and sounds rushed through her head, out of order. She'd had to take a double dose of her pain pills today. It helped take the edge off.

"This sucks," Jackson said finally. He blew out a sigh that ruffled a stray curl on his forehead.

She glanced at him, noticing that he had turned his attention to the crowd of lawyers and stenographers and general employees of the courthouse as they went about their business, moving from one office to the next, just doing their day jobs and thinking about other things, and definitely not worrying about this one case because it was just another sheet in a pile on their desk, and they just wanted to get home to their families. Spencer had an instinct to tell him everything was going to be okay, but would she have believed herself if she was in his shoes?

"Yeah." That was all Spencer needed to say.

The courtroom doors opened, and the bailiff let everyone inside.

It was time.

She and Jackson found Ethan instantly—he was already sitting with his lawyer, Ray Cardona, at a table on the right side of the courtroom. Mr. Cardona looked a lot different than he did on the commercials running on TV; his teeth weren't as bright and his hair wasn't as shiny, but he wore a very expensive suit that fit him well, and his shiny gold watch caught the harsh lights from above. He and Ethan had their heads tipped toward each other, no doubt discussing some last-minute advice before the judge arrived. Ethan's jaw was clenched, but he nodded every so often. He was wearing a suit and tie too, his best foot forward.

Spencer and Jackson chose to sit in the back where she

and Ripley could cause the least disturbance. A few glances here and there, especially at Ripley, was the extent of what Spencer could handle while her stomach wanted to protest.

Ethan turned around in his chair, perhaps looking for a friendly face in the crowd to give him some courage. The bruising on his face had subsided significantly, now just a shadow of the accident remaining. Their gazes met and Spencer tried to give some sort of sign of support, the slightest smile, but he clamped his lips shut and turned away from her, facing the front of the courtroom once more.

Spencer couldn't help but think he looked guilty.

Why was she even here? She should hate Ethan's guts. No one would be angry with her for not showing up. He'd hurt her, in more ways than one that night, so what was she even doing sitting here on his side of the courtroom? Her gaze fell to Ripley at her feet, and she clenched her fist tightly.

The judge entered the courtroom from a side door, obviously the judge's chambers, and everyone stood up respectfully. Judge Patel was an older Indian woman with gray hair and gold-rimmed glasses. She looked serious, no nonsense. Spencer couldn't help thinking that didn't look good for Ethan. She didn't seem like the type to go easy on reckless teenagers who lived their lives thinking they were invincible.

When everyone took their seats again, Spencer was surprised that everything was a lot different from what she saw on TV. In courtroom shows, it was a lot more dramatic and tense, but the atmosphere in the courtroom was clinical, businesslike, and—frankly—boring. The lawyers listed off various technical terms noted by the judge and Spencer couldn't help but zone out. It wasn't just because the painkillers were taking effect, it was because trials were unexpectedly so mundane.

While the proceedings started, Spencer's attention landed on the Moores. They were seated together; Spencer was only able to see the backs of their heads. They were holding hands, but Spencer couldn't help but notice that Mrs. Moore's fingers were tapping impatiently on the table in front of them, her manicure making a noticeable rhythm on the wood. It was almost as if she was impatient, waiting to do something more important with her time. Spencer furrowed her brows and tried not to read into it, but it struck her as somewhat odd. They were suing the one responsible for their son's death. What could possibly be more important than that?

The judge looked up over the top of her glasses. Her voice was firm, like a strict schoolteacher's. "I'd like to remind everyone that no recording devices are allowed in my courtroom and that I expect everyone to behave accordingly, otherwise you may be removed at any time."

Spencer noticed she was speaking in the direction of a person sitting a few rows ahead of Spencer on the other side of the aisle. Peyton Salt. She lowered her phone when she noticed the judge was speaking about her. She blushed and pocketed her phone.

Spencer tasted something bitter in the back of her mouth as she glared at Peyton. All the terrible things she'd said about Ethan, about the crash . . . Spencer forced herself to look away, otherwise she was afraid she would scream. At what point did journalism turn into exploitation?

The Moores' lawyer went up first, the one with the red-soled Louboutins Spencer had noticed earlier. Spencer got the impression that she was good at her job and had the fancy heels to prove it. She introduced herself as Thora Barancewicz to the judge, submitting her case documents to the court and stating the charges pressed against Ethan. All the while, Spencer kept watching the back of Ethan's head. He sat motionless, watching the lawyer present her case, and barely flinched when the lawyer gestured in his direction. Jackson too watched quietly, powerless to do or say anything.

Ripley put her head in Spencer's lap, and Spencer realized that while the prosecution was describing the events of the crash, her breathing had become ragged and shallow. Ripley reminded her that she was okay, that she wasn't alone. Spencer realized just how important Ripley had become in her life. She might not have been able to sit there if it wasn't for her.

"The events of that night could have been prevented," the prosecution said. "Ethan Amoroso, known in the community for driving without care, for racing, for partying, for inconsideration for his neighbors and fellow students. His pattern of reckless behavior is an unfortunate result of carelessness, callousness, and a lack of empathy for others. Your Honor, this case is solid. When will the community finally be able to rest?"

Ethan didn't even move. Spencer couldn't take her eyes off him. To hear the lawyer say it so plainly, it put everything that had happened into a perspective that Spencer hadn't been prepared to deal with. Ethan was in deep trouble. He'd accidentally killed someone. It wasn't just a matter of blaming it all on a freak accident. He wouldn't be able to pick himself up and move on. This was big.

Jackson fidgeted beside her, picking at a hangnail on his thumb, worrying at the flap of it so much it had started to bleed, but he didn't notice. He must have been so scared for Ethan. She could see it in his eyes, and in his jaw, too. She was tempted to reach out and hold his hand to stop him from further hurting himself, but she didn't want to cross a line and ruin their friendship, so she clasped her own hands together instead.

"Mr. Ethan Amoroso," the judge said, pausing a moment for his lawyer to gesture for him to rise. "You have been charged with aggravated reckless driving, child endangerment, and felony manslaughter. How do you plead?"

But instead of answering, his lawyer stood up. "Your honor, I have in my hand Ethan Amoroso's toxicology report from the night in question."

There was a murmur from the crowd.

"May I approach the bench?"

The judge nodded.

Ethan's lawyer handed the report to the judge, who studied it, face impassive.

The lawyer turned to the courtroom. "As you can see, Your Honor, Ethan Amoroso was not driving under the influence. His blood alcohol limit was 0.06 percent. He was well within the legal boundaries of the State of California to get behind the wheel. The crash occurred at a blind intersection where there have been many complaints filed to the city to put in a traffic signal instead of a mere stop sign. What happened to Christopher Moore was tragic, but it was not done with a wanton disregard for human life. It was an accident. Ethan Amoroso is innocent. We would like to file for dismissal."

The courtroom exploded with whispers and shocked gasps. The Moores looked downright furious. Mr. Moore looked like he was about to stand up and throw something, while Mrs. Moore looked like she was plotting his demise.

Spencer couldn't breathe.

She was right!

Ethan wasn't high!

He was innocent!

The judge ordered a recess, and when everyone filed back in, the tension was palpable in the air. Would the case be dismissed? Would Ethan go free? It was too much for Spencer, whose head was throbbing. She fished around in her backpack for her orange pill bottle. Before opening the cap, she tried to remember how many she'd taken already that day.

She knew she took some with breakfast, and again between taking Ripley for a long walk and Olivia coming over to swap notes for a group project for AP Spanish. But she hurt, and decided to take another, just to get her pain under control.

She noticed Jackson beside, her, gripping the edges of his seat, his knuckles white.

The judge returned, and everyone rose.

After everyone was seated once more, the judge addressed the court. "I have studied the evidence and the new information, and consulted with lawyers for the prosecution and defense. Although it's been proven that Mr. Amoroso was not driving under the influence, the state's charges of aggravated reckless driving, child endangerment, and felony manslaughter still apply. Mr. Amoroso, you have been charged. How do you plead?"

Ethan stood up and faced the judge. "Not guilty."

After the opening statements, the trial was over for the day. Spencer tried to catch Ethan's eye before he left, but he wasn't looking her way.

"Fuck," Jackson whispered. "I thought it was over."

"Yeah, me too," said Spencer. It was too much to hope, but the prosecution made the argument that even if Ethan hadn't been drunk, the facts remained that he was speeding and hadn't stopped at the intersection and had caused the death of a human being.

A voice carried down the hall, over the din of people chatting. Curt and courteous. "Spencer."

"Detective Potentas!" Spencer put her pill bottle back in her backpack as he walked over, looking somewhat distracted, as if he was thinking about someplace else he wanted to be.

"I'm not surprised I keep seeing you around. Don't you have school? Extracurriculars?"

"Why shouldn't I be here? I was in the crash." Spencer wasn't sure why she felt so defensive, but she couldn't help it.

Detective Potentas put his hands in his pockets and looked around. "You're still trying to find information on your boyfriend's case?"

"Yeah," she said.

"You should leave the investigation to the police. You're only causing more trouble."

Surprised, Spencer raised her eyebrows. "Why? Has someone complained about me?" Her mind immediately began filing through all the names of the people she had interviewed.

Detective Potentas rubbed his chin and sighed. He looked beyond her, warring with himself over his words. That was when Spencer saw Mrs. Moore standing behind him, halfway down the hall, but she was glaring in Spencer's direction. Her dark red lipstick was nearly gone, she was pinching her lips together so tightly in disapproval. Nick, Chris's brother, was standing next to her, rubbing her shoulder in an attempt to calm her down.

"Your name has been brought up," Detective Potentas said finally. "You're not exactly being subtle about it."

"I'm not trying to do anything but fill the gaps in my memory, and until I find out what happened that night, I'm not quitting."

Why was she with Ethan if she had broken up with him?

Why was she in the car?

Why was Tabby with them?

And Chris?

It just didn't make sense.

"I knew you'd say that. It's not just that, though; you're causing more pain for yourself. Take my word for it: There's nothing to this case. I haven't seen an easier case closed in a long time. We have our guy. You heard the judge, even if he had nothing in his system, he was still speeding. Going 120 miles an hour in a residential zone. He lost control of the vehicle and killed that kid. You're not a detective. There's nothing to detect. Move on from all this, believe me. It's for the best."

"What if I say no?" There were two Spencers, one Before, and one After the crash. If the Before Spencer had heard the way she was talking to a cop, she would have been shocked. The Spencer who had come out of that crash had a sharper tongue, especially with the pain radiating through her body, reminding her of everything she'd lost. Girls with her skin color didn't have too many good experiences with police.

But Detective Potentas just sighed, like he was talking to a petulant child who refused to eat her greens. "Take care of yourself, Miss Sandoval. Don't go looking for relief at the bottom of a bottle, either."

When Detective Potentas walked away, Jackson returned. His cheeks were shiny, she suspected as a result of him splashing water on his face in the restroom, and he lent her the smallest smile, but his face fell when he spotted Peyton Salt lingering halfway down the hall.

Spencer frowned when she noticed her, too.

"Come on," she said. "Let's get some air." She wanted to get as far away from Peyton as she could. Jackson didn't argue. He carried her backpack for her as they left.

Spencer wasn't like Peyton. Peyton treated the crash like a story, but this was Spencer's life. Didn't she deserve to know what really happened that night? She'd been living with the direct consequences. Her life had been upended, not to the same degree as the Moore family, but she was nevertheless changed.

But where would investigation end and invasion of privacy begin? She wanted to believe that she and Peyton were different on all fronts, but would she be able to stop if she started hurting people in the process of discovering the truth? She felt sick just thinking about it.

Would she discover some secrets worth keeping hidden?

TWENTY

THE NEXT DAY, A SUNDAY, Spencer got her cast off. It was a relief too, couldn't have come any sooner. She might have been able to be happy about it, though, had it not been for what Detective Potentas had said at the courthouse. A part of her knew that he was right, that she was just digging up dirt that muddied the water. Ethan's confession was crystal clear, solid. It was Ethan's car. Ethan was driving. Was she just making it more difficult for the other victims to move on? How would Tabby feel knowing that Spencer was refusing to let the case be closed once and for all?

Spencer tried going about her day, taking full advantage of the time Uncle Martin had given her off from Brain Freeze for her arm, and focusing her attention elsewhere, but her thoughts always circled back to the crash, like water going down a drain.

When night came, Spencer tried to enjoy sitting on the couch with Hope, but she wasn't even registering what they were watching, a *Murder, She Wrote* rerun she'd seen a dozen times. Hope wasn't even watching, either. She was on her phone playing a game.

Spencer's mood had turned inward and before she knew it, she was lost in thought, staring at the empty, used plates where peanut butter and jelly sandwiches had sat on the coffee table in front of them. Spencer hadn't had the energy to make anything fancier for dinner. Hope didn't seem to mind; it seemed like she could tell Spencer was having an off day.

It was in the police's best interest to close cases as quickly as possible. The quickest way was a confession, and with Ethan's case, it was open and shut. He had admitted to being behind the wheel that night. He was driving and it was his fault. What more could anyone ask for? Wasn't it the perfect case? The job had already been done for them. There was nothing more to see, nothing else to look for but secrets that would complicate the matter. Ethan's fate had been sealed the minute he confessed.

Ripley pawed at the door to ring a row of bells hanging from the doorknob to the backyard, as she was trained to do whenever she needed to go out.

It was unnecessary, but Hope kicked Spencer's leg, nudging her to get up. Spencer was already moving by the time she made contact and Spencer swiped at the air above Hope's foot, half-heartedly, and Hope settled back in for more gaming.

It had been dark for a few hours now, pitch black on the other side of the sliding glass door. Because of it, it looked like a mirror. Spencer looked like a ghost moving through the reflection as Ripley waited patiently for Spencer to arrive. She felt like a ghost, too.

"Okay, let's go potty," Spencer said as she opened the door. The motion-sensor light on the back porch turned on as Ripley cut down the deck and into the grass. Spencer followed, closing the door behind herself, and hugged her hoodie closer to her body as she watched Ripley—nose down, tail up—make the usual lap around the backyard before relieving herself.

The crickets were loud that night and Spencer tipped her head back, breathing in the crisp night air, catching remnant whiffs of a neighbor's barbecue somewhere close by, and waiting for Ripley to do her business. A dog barked somewhere in the distance, but Ripley paid no mind and trotted back up the stairs of the deck toward Spencer.

"Good girl," she said, but before Ripley came within arm's reach, she stopped and turned around, staring into the dark of the yard.

Spencer hadn't noticed it before, but there was a dark shape just out of the light from the porch, a shape that shouldn't belong there.

The little hairs on the back of Spencer's neck stood on end. The shadow was vaguely human shaped, but unmoving. Spencer froze, straining her eyes to make out any details, trying to see through the dark. Had Hope left something in the yard from her Rube Goldberg project? Was it some yard equipment her dad had been using earlier in the week? She would have thought nothing of it, chalked it up to just a trick of the eye, searching to make out random shapes like lunar pareidolia, but the hackles rose on Ripley's back and she let out a low growl. Whatever it was, Ripley saw it, too.

"Hello?" Spencer asked.

It was unmistakable. The figure moved.

Someone was in her yard.

Head, shoulders, distinctly there, but no way to make out any details.

Had they been looking in through their window? They hadn't drawn their curtains. Spencer and Hope had been sitting on the couch, in full view, illuminated on the inside, visible to anyone outside in the safety of darkness. Static rage snapped everything into focus.

Spencer took a step forward, heart hammering. Ripley backed up, though, shielding Spencer, but Spencer moved around her.

Spencer blinked, and in that fraction of a second the shadow took off into the deeper dark, and Spencer jumped down the steps, rounding the house, blood rushing in her ears and drowning out all sensibility to go back inside, Ripley hot on her heels.

Spencer sprinted over grass slick with water from the sprinkler. But by the time she rounded the corner, coming through the alley between her house and the neighbor's, the shadow was already around the corner. Spencer stopped in the front yard, panting, scanning the hedges and fences for any sign, but the street was darker. With the adrenaline hot in her head, she couldn't see or hear anything. Whoever it was, they were gone.

Ripley came up to Spencer's side and pressed her body against her legs, whining. Spencer took an extra second to see if she could spot the shadow, but it was no use. They had vanished.

Spencer looked over her shoulder as she brought Ripley back inside, but the street remained dark, and she tried to shake the feeling that she was still being watched as she locked the door behind her.

TWENTY-ONE

THE LIBRARY IN THE MORNINGS at school was one of Spencer's favorite places to be. The skylights overhead filtered in the warm morning light, draping the desks in a comforting haze of dust floating in the air. The librarian, Mrs. Patton, with her beaded glasses chain, always greeted her while she was reshelving books, never bothering to check up on her frequently, knowing full well that Spencer was hard at work studying. She would usually sit alone during her free period, catching up on homework or rewriting her notes in neater script, using different colored pens to draw attention to important details, which was what she was currently doing with her right hand.

Even though she'd gotten the cast removed yesterday, her left wrist felt stiff, and she had to keep stopping to rest, opting to use her right hand so as not to break her flow of concentration.

She was shaking out her wrist and rereading her notes when Jackson took his usual seat across from her at the table.

"Hey!" she said, smiling. "Good morning."

"Morning! Your cast is off!" He put his backpack on the table and took out his textbooks and notebooks.

"Yeah, yesterday. It feels so weird. I'm getting used to having my hand back. When they took the cast off, my hand was all gray and wrinkly, like an old sock."

Jackson scrunched his nose and laughed, amused and disgusted at the same time. "Gross! I didn't want to picture that so early in the morning. Thanks." Seeing him was a breath of fresh air.

Spencer found herself smiling more easily, especially with Jackson around. She bit her lip, guilty of this newfound warmth in her belly, and lowered her gaze to her notebook. Ethan used to make her happy. Sometimes. His spirit infected Spencer's rigid habits, broke her down to bare desire. She'd wanted to date the hottest boy in school, and she did for a while. Did that make her truly happy, though? She wasn't sure.

Jackson busied himself with his laptop, tugging at his lower lip with his thumb and index finger, lost in thought, as his eyes flicked back and forth on his screen. She watched him for a quiet moment, admiring the lip-pulling habit of his. Was he even aware of it, or was it just as natural as breathing to him? He looked at her, and she lowered her gaze, feeling like a creep for staring so long. If he noticed, he didn't say anything.

"So, it took me forever, but I mapped out the entire night's events at the party. Almost down to the minute."

"Really? Great job!"

"Thanks! I mean, it's not really groundbreaking stuff.

Mostly drunk kids making out with one another and doing keg stands and stuff, but yeah. It's all done."

"What'd you find?"

"It occurred to me that maybe we've been focusing so much on recording your movement through the party, it'd be worth a shot looking for anyone else from the car. And . . . I found something that you might be interested in."

He spun the laptop around and Spencer saw a video pulled up.

"It took me a few viewings to catch it, but . . . here." He pressed the space bar and the video started. The video had been uploaded by Ed Hughes, a sophomore, featuring himself and his friends chugging cans of beer in record time in the unfinished kitchen of the housing development. The camera was shaking so hard that Spencer could barely make anything out except for the faraway looks of sophomore boys who were too drunk to realize they were basically walking blurs of bad decision-making. But Jackson pointed to a few frames when the camera swirled around to the crowd of people dancing in the yard. He pressed the space bar again and said, "Is that who I think it is?"

"Chris . . . ," Spencer said, eyes wide, jaw dropped. He was slumped on the ground, draped over a tree stump littered with what looked like red Solo cups, but the image was too blurry to make out for sure. There was no mistaking it, though, that was Chris. Spencer's stomach dropped, thinking that a couple hours after this footage was taken, he'd be dead.

"He looks wasted, right?" Jackson asked.

"Yeah, pretty par for the course at the party."

"Exactly. Which got me thinking. I went back through the night, working backward through all the videos in my timeline, to see if I could follow him, track his movements. I tried seeing how many beers he'd gone through, but . . ."

"Let me guess, only one."

Jackson nodded grimly.

"Harrison had it set up that you got different colored cups for what drinks you paid for, with little tally marks for how many you drank. Red was for beer. Every video I saw, Chris only had the one red cup with one red slash."

"So if he was drunk enough to be slumped over like that . . . you think he was drugged?"

"It's not out of the realm of possibility, is it?"

"But who would do something like that?"

"My thoughts exactly, until I found this video. It took me a while, but . . ." Jackson spun the laptop back to himself and used the track pad to pull up something else, before turning the screen back to Spencer. She couldn't help but lean in, like she would fall right through the screen and into the past.

It was a different video, uploaded by someone named Johnny Larchick, a name she didn't recognize. This time it was an Instagram video of a group of kids lip-syncing a song the band was playing behind them. They were acting like they were at a rock concert, and dressed for it too, singing along and throwing their hands over each other's shoulders, leaning against one another like they would topple over at any second, but Spencer could tell it was earlier in the night. People's hair and makeup were mostly intact, inevitably getting messier as the night wore on. Spencer unconsciously clenched and unclenched her left fist, stretching the sore muscles in her broken arm, as if she was ready to spring into action.

Jackson pressed pause again, and it was hard to see in the dark, but Chris's auburn hair was unmistakable, his white UC Irvine hoodie standing out from the crowd. His hand was outstretched, his face smiling, as a red Solo cup was being handed to him by none other than the new kid at school and Spencer's latest nemesis, Tabby Hill.

"No way."

"That's what I said."

Spencer couldn't believe it. "Why would Tabby want to drug Chris?"

"Guess we should ask Tabby."

Spencer twirled her pen expertly between her fingers, a trick that she did whenever she was trying to keep her thoughts from going a million miles per hour. "Could Tabby have been in my yard last night?"

Jackson paused, then did a double take, blinking hard, processing what she just said. "Wait, someone was in your yard?"

Spencer shifted in her chair, making the wooden legs creak beneath her. She was worried he'd react this way, but she couldn't keep it from him. "Yeah, but I chased them off."

"You chased—Spencer! Did you call the police?"

"It was no big deal. The person ran away. Not like the cops would do anything about it anyway." There had been a Peeping Tom in the neighborhood a few years back, several reports of people seeing a pale face looking in on them through a dark window, nightmare fuel. But the most the cops did at the time was tell people to close their curtains at night and not to change clothes near the window. Spencer never found out what happened to the Peeping Tom after that; for all she knew, he was still out there. What happened then didn't seem to match what happened last night. If it was Tabby, they must have been a track-and-field sprinter to get away that fast from Spencer.

"No big deal? Spencer, that's . . . really creepy." He shivered visibly. "Why would someone do that?"

"I don't know. But . . . something tells me it's not a random incident. I think it means that we're on to something with Ethan's case."

Jackson's brow twisted with worry. "You mean someone is trying to stop you from asking questions?"

"Let's talk to Tabby as soon as possible."

TWENTY-TWO

"TABBY!" SPENCER BELLOWED ACROSS THE lawn, Jackson hustling right at her side.

Tabby whirled around, hair flipping expertly over their shoulder like a shampoo commercial. Their eyes narrowed after realizing who it was. Immediately, Tabby glowered at Ripley.

Spencer could hardly wait to talk to Tabby, but there wasn't a good opportunity during class sessions, or any time when Tabby didn't disappear like a ghost in the wind. Lunch was the only chance they had. Mostly everyone was out grabbing food, meaning students who had permission could leave campus to eat at any of the nearby restaurants or go home to have their private chefs whip up something before they had to be back in time for fourth period. It was unusual for a junior like Tabby to get permission to go off campus, but being on the Headmaster's List came with specific perks that other students in their class didn't get. They were headed to their car, a perky little VW bug, and Spencer and Jackson had only managed to catch up in the parking lot just in time.

"What do you want?" Tabby asked, barely repressing a

sneer. They glanced over Jackson, curiously, before settling a level gaze on Spencer. They folded their arms hastily across their body, or—Spencer thought—made an unconscious move to put up a barrier between them.

"We wanted to ask you some questions about the party the night of the crash," Spencer said.

"Not without backup, I see."

Obviously, they were talking about Jackson, who lowered his brows at the accusation that he was here because Spencer couldn't do it on her own.

"We just want some answers," Jackson said. "Saw something pretty interesting that we wanted to get your side of the story on."

Tabby's face went white, all the color draining away. They swallowed. "I don't know what we have to talk about."

Spencer watched Ripley at her feet. Ripley didn't react to Tabby at all, no sign of raised hackles or growls. In fact, Ripley seemed at ease. Maybe Tabby hadn't been the one standing outside her house watching from the shadows.

"We have video of you giving Chris a drink that night," Spencer said.

"So?"

"Pretty soon after that he started acting drunk, way more than he should be. We heard that you might know more about that."

"I don't know what you're—"

Jackson stepped forward. "Come on, Tabby. Enough lying. Did you put something in Chris's drink?"

Spencer glanced at the other students walking by. Some turned their heads toward them at the name Chris, but none stayed to eavesdrop any longer. A sheen of sweat had appeared on Tabby's forehead. Their eyes darted back and forth, cornered.

Spencer was about to worry that Jackson had come on a little strong and was about to try to convince Tabby everything was fine, but Jackson's tactic ended up working.

"Okay," Tabby said, sneering. "Not here, though. Let's go somewhere private."

"I didn't roofie Chris, if that's what you're thinking."

Tabby sat on the upper row of bleachers at the soccer field, Spencer and Jackson one row below. There was no one within earshot, save for the groundskeeper drawing new paint lines on the field with a spray can attached to a cart, but that was way too far for anyone to overhear.

"But I wanted to, I was planning to," they told them.

"You were going to roofie him?" Jackson asked. Spencer was grateful that he asked; she was too busy trying to figure everything out to be able to form words at the moment. She absently patted Ripley's side.

Tabby shrugged. "Yeah. He was blackmailing me."

Spencer's eyebrows shot up, same as Jackson's, and they both looked at each other before Spencer asked, "What are you talking about! Why would Chris Moore—one of the nicest guys at Armstrong—blackmail you?"

Tabby sighed, their shoulders slumping, and looked out

over the field, trying to find the words. "It's so dumb, I'm honestly so embarrassed about it. Don't know how he found out."

"It's okay, Tabby, you can tell us," Jackson said. His words were soothing, and the look on his face was encouraging but open. Even Spencer felt like she could tell him anything. He had that way with people.

Tabby worried their bottom lip, spinning the rings around their fingers. They looked like whatever they wanted to say, it was something worth keeping a secret for.

"We promise, we won't tell anyone. This doesn't have to leave here," Spencer said. Jackson gave an encouraging nod.

Tabby sighed. "Fine. I got expelled from my old school because I was caught selling Addy to some students."

"Adderall?"

Tabby nodded. "Back in Arizona, the school was kind of like Armstrong, and there was a lot of pressure for kids to get good grades, just like here. I have ADHD and figured I could make some extra cash on the side. The school found out and expelled me."

Spencer frowned. "Aren't you rich or something? Why do you need money?"

"My *parents* are rich. And strict. I barely have an allowance. But once I started selling extra pills from my prescription, I couldn't stop. It was . . . it was a high, making my own money. So I knew a plug who could get me some more, but not just that, he could also get other stuff, shrooms, Molly, coke, whatever. Then Harry—Harrison Ressler—asked me to make the party more fun; he knew I could get some of the good stuff."

"Coke? Molly?" Jackson asked.

Tabby nodded. "Don't look at me like that. Listen, I'm not a bad person. I mostly sold Addy, but if someone asked for some other stuff, I didn't care so long as I got paid. People can do whatever they want with it. I'm not going to ask questions."

Spencer didn't agree with that moral justification, but she didn't press it. She needed Tabby to keep talking.

"You sold roofies at the party?" Spencer asked.

"No, I only had one on me. I was planning on using it on Chris."

Spencer saw Jackson's reproachful look, but he didn't say anything about it, either. He looked just as judgmental as she felt.

"Why though?" he repeated.

"My parents donated an insane amount of money to Armstrong's sports program to get me in and keep my record sealed. And it was enough to get me on the Headmaster's List, too. Somehow Chris found out about it. I don't know how, but that doesn't matter anymore. He cornered me one day, said he'd use it against me, said that he would tell everyone at school that I was a drug addict if I didn't pay him money every month to keep his mouth shut."

Spencer's jaw dropped. Everyone's little brother really knew how to play.

Jackson asked, "How much money?"

"Two hundred dollars at first, but over the summer he came to me asking for more, three hundred now and he wanted it every two weeks. I was sick and tired of being yanked around, so I wanted to scare him. I wanted to show that I wasn't someone he could mess with. So at the party I thought I'd spike his drink."

Spencer and Jackson shared another look. "But you didn't?" Spencer asked.

"No, man, you know what was in that cup he was drinking? It wasn't beer. He was drinking straight vodka. Like almost an entire bottle of vodka in one of those cups. Sixteen ounces of vodka in, like, twenty minutes on an empty stomach. I was handing him a cup of water so he could sober up! He was drunk as fuck because he was drunk as fuck. A total mess. It was too pathetic so I figured I'd get my revenge another day. Then he was all over me, and I just wanted to get away from him. I saw you and Ethan heading home and asked Ethan for a ride, figured it was time for me to go home anyway. I was kind of high and out of it, too. We carried Chris to his car. Ethan was worried about him, asked him if he was okay. He cared about him . . . He was in the middle of the fight with you. Don't you remember any of this?"

"No," Spencer said, shifting uncomfortably. She felt disconnected from her past self; hearing about it from someone else made it seem like they were talking about someone else. "So if you didn't use the roofie on Chris, did you use it on me?"

Tabby looked appalled. "You! No! Of course not. Why would I do something like that?"

If they were lying, they were exceptionally good at it. Tabby looked more disgusted about the accusation than anything, which actually worked in their favor for Spencer to believe it.

"What happened next?"

"I got into the back seat with Chris—he was lying down on the seat—and I waited for you and Ethan to stop fighting. You two were really going at it. You've got some pipes, girl. I bet the whole Westside heard you yelling at him. Hailey Reed, huh."

Spencer couldn't help the flush in her cheeks.

"Around what time did Ethan get in the car?" Jackson asked.

"I don't know. I fell asleep waiting, you guys took so long. You were so dramatic. 'How could you do this to me?' 'You betrayed me!' 'I trusted you!' You know the drill. I'd pay an admission fee to watch if I wasn't so high myself. Next thing I knew, I smashed my face into the back of the passenger's seat when we crashed. And Chris ... well ..." Tabby gestured with their hand, leaving the rest unsaid.

Spencer sighed.

Tabby seemed disconnected from the accident, as if they had nothing to do with any of it. Sure, Tabby hadn't caused the accident, but did they have to be so blasé about it?

"I feel bad about what happened to Chris, I really do," Tabby said, "but to be honest, I'm kind of relieved, too. He wasn't the nice guy everyone thought he was. He was dirty. I feel like I can finally breathe again."

But he was only fifteen, just a kid, Spencer thought, remembering the hollow eyes of Chris's parents.

"You won't tell anyone about any of this, right?" asked Tabby. Their dark eyes flashed, a hint of a threat peeking its head out from the cat-eye eyeliner. "About me I mean."

"No, your secret is still safe." Spencer kept her voice flat, emphasizing her disapproval. It was tempting to call in an anonymous tip to the police about Tabby's illicit activities. What if someone else got hurt because of what they were dealing? But Spencer had a feeling that Tabby would get caught on their own one of these days. Besides, Tabby was planning to hurt Chris to protect themselves. Would Spencer want to risk Tabby's wrath by calling the cops? Even though Tabby was innocent with regard to the accident, did Spencer want to push Tabby's boundaries of what they were capable of in moments of desperation?

Ripley watched all of this, her head raised, as if she knew what everyone was talking about. She was one of the biggest clues about what happened last night with the stranger. She had acted instinctively to protect Spencer then, putting herself between her and potential danger. If Tabby was stalking her, threatening her, Spencer needed to know.

Spencer had one more question. "Where were you last night?"

Tabby answered easily. "Rehearsal for *Beauty and the*

Beast. I was in the auditorium until eleven or so. Why? Did you want to buy anything?"

Jackson scoffed in disbelief.

If they were at the play, starring as the lead in the musical, there were obviously witnesses who could account for her whereabouts, meaning Tabby was unlikely the person who had been standing outside Spencer's house. Spencer wasn't sure if that made her feel better or worse, knowing that Tabby wasn't some criminal mastermind. Even though it was a relief, whoever had been watching her from the shadows, trying to scare her, was still an unknown, and that made her skin crawl.

Spencer was getting tired of Tabby. They had clearly thought they weren't in the wrong and didn't contribute to Chris's death in any way. Of course, they'd been trying to do the right thing in getting him home safely, right? Tabby's hands were clean, relatively speaking. At least, they thought so.

If Chris hadn't wound up in that car, if he'd been buckled safely into his seat, maybe he would still be alive today.

"I can get you more Addy. Best price in town," Tabby said.

"No," Spencer said coolly. "I don't do drugs."

"You'd have me fooled. I see how many pills you've been popping," Tabby said, with a careful eyebrow raise. "Better keep your habit in check there, girl."

Spencer's face felt hot. "I'm not—"

But Tabby perked up and waved, signaling to a group

of friends who were calling toward them. The three of them had been talking for so long, they'd completely blown through the lunch period. "I gotta go," Tabby said, and without waiting for anything more to be said, left.

Jackson watched Tabby step down the bleachers and disappear with their friends, shaking his head. "I can't believe Chris would be capable of blackmailing Tabby . . . He struck me as the harmless type."

Jackson's thoughts had been in line with Spencer's. She was trying to put all the pieces together, staring distantly, putting the events of the night into context.

Was Chris really such an angel? Everyone seemed to think he was, but what else didn't people know about him? If he was capable of blackmailing Tabby, could he be capable of blackmailing more people? Maybe someone else who had a grudge? There was more to Chris than she thought.

"Is Tabby right, though?" Jackson asked. "About your medicine?"

"I don't have a problem. I'm not an addict." Spencer thought of people with addictions as having an uncontrollable urge to repeat destructive behaviors, couldn't help that they were doing it. Spencer could stop taking her pills any time she wanted to, couldn't she?

Jackson's face pulled tight with worry, but he didn't say anything. Polite as ever. "What do you want to do next?"

"I think we have a lot more work to do than I thought."

TWENTY-THREE

SPENCER SET HER PEN DOWN on the page and massaged her eyes, which ached deeper than any late night cram session she'd done before. The lead with Tabby was a bust, but it opened a whole new can of worms about Chris. Why would everyone's little brother resort to blackmail?

Looking into Chris's past felt like she was digging up dirt from his grave, but she needed to know more. She learned that he'd been talented with computers, with dreams of starting his own software company when he was out of college, dreams that now would never be realized. With someone as good with computers as he had been, it made sense that he could find records about people's past.

Then she found it. It was nothing—a throwaway comment Ethan had made a while back—about how some kids he knew were getting into poker online. Spencer knew the site Ethan used and with a little help from Hope, she found the jackpot.

Chris was one of the top players on the site. He was a gambler. He was blackmailing Tabby to feed his addiction. Money made people do nasty things. She had no way of knowing if there was anyone else Chris had been black-mailing, but it raised some ugly questions about the crash. What if Tabby wasn't the only one who might have wanted to get back at Chris for something that he had done?

She took a chance and emailed Nick Moore, asking if he had any other information for her, maybe mysterious behavior or an influx of cash. He'd responded with no more information, just that Chris had been to a computer sum-mer camp that July, but he didn't know about any other side hustles he might have been working on.

If you have any other questions, let me know, Nick wrote in the email. *Don't hesitate to ask. I understand it's hard to move on, but I want to help.*

She appreciated the offer, but she was in too deep. The puzzle seemed to be getting more complicated the longer she looked into things. She was becoming an expert in every-thing about Ethan's case, inside and out, and she had hand-written nearly all her notes, compiling them into her binder. The binder was thick and heavy enough that she could slam it into the library's study table and probably break it in half.

She'd barely gotten more than two hours of sleep last night, despite Ripley's best efforts to calm her down, but admittedly the case was wearing on her. And every time she closed her eyes, she saw legal words floating behind her eyelids. If she didn't find answers soon, she wasn't sure how much longer her body could take it.

Jackson appeared from between the aisles of bookcases holding two to-go cups of coffee.

"Caffeine time," he said cheerily. Instead of wearing the Armstrong uniform, he was wearing his warm-up sweats for soccer, a burgundy getup that all the teams wore on game days. It made them stand out from the blazer uniforms but was still an acceptable outfit for the dress code. A small pang pinched behind her heart as she remembered she'd have to sit out her field hockey games this season.

Jackson handed her the coffee, and she took off the lid. The whipped cream had deflated a little on top of her latte, but she was grateful that he'd thought of her.

"I owe you one," she said, taking a sip. The whipped cream tickled her upper lip and she wiped it away with the back of her wrist. "Big-time."

Jackson took a seat across from her. "You deserve it. I'm the one that owes you. Look at all this! You are really thorough." He gestured to the binder, eyebrows raised, impressed.

"I had some free time."

"Some free time? I don't even want to know what you're capable of if you did this as a career. You're kind of scary. I mean, you found Chris's dirty secret in what, a day?" Jackson hadn't been surprised when she'd told him about the poker addiction. He said he was just surprised it wasn't bitcoin trading.

"Does that intimidate you?" Spencer asked, teasingly sticking her tongue out of the corner of her mouth.

"A little, yeah! In a good way, though."

Spencer laughed easily and was surprised by the warmth in her belly at his smile.

"So what did you find?" he asked.

Spencer took another sip of her coffee. "Let me show you!"

"You've got some, uh . . ."

He reached over, his finger crooked gently, moving toward her face.

Spencer's heart beat once, then twice, as Jackson too froze, arm outstretched, before realizing what he was doing.

"Um." Jackson pulled back and brushed his fingers on his own nose. "You've got a little whipped cream there."

Spencer scrubbed at the tip of her nose and wiped it clean. Jackson's light eyes caught a ray from the sunlight overhead and he bowed his head sheepishly, his ears flushing a soft pink.

What had just happened?

"Thanks," she mumbled.

Spencer tried not to let the heat fully consume her face as she returned to the screen in front of her. "So, anyway, I was looking into this camp that Ethan went to."

"Right. Camp." Jackson cleared his throat. Back to work.

"He attended one of their longer sessions offered, a two-month trip into the Chihuahuan Desert in New Mexico. I managed to do some digging and found a ton of stuff about the camp, some of it really shocking."

Jackson pinched his lips together with concern. "Like what?"

"So the reviews on the site itself say that it's all about promoting personal responsibility, character building, and reforming the lives of troubled youth, with hundreds of testimonies from graduates who went through the course. But there's a darker side. I found some reports of abuse, mental and emotional mostly, where some kids were punished, often going without food, if they weren't able to do certain survival techniques or didn't participate in 'camp' activities."

"Yikes."

"I cross-referenced a few names from Ethan's followers list with names from his camp, and figured out who his friends were. He follows them on Instagram."

"Ethan's never on Insta."

"Not anymore, but he used to be. His profile is still up." Spencer pulled up a page and spun the laptop around for Jackson to see. "This is what I found. Look at this picture and all the comments below it."

Ethan only put up one photo, but there were two dozen comments underneath it, most of them from the same person.

"'Dreamy Dayz'? Creative," Jackson said with a wince.

"The posts are dated after he got back from camp, which means they most likely met there. Look."

All the messages were from over the summer, mostly during August and at all hours of the day.

Jackson read the messages aloud. "'Can't stop thinking about you!' 'Call me when you get a chance.' 'Why are you ignoring me?' 'We need to talk.' Jeez. Whoever this person is, they sound obsessed."

"Keep going," Spencer said.

Jackson cleared his throat again. "'I'm warning you.' 'Don't make me do this.' 'You'll pay for this.'"

Jackson shifted uncomfortably in his chair. Spencer too felt queasy reading those messages. Whoever had sent them was definitely unhinged.

"So Ethan had a stalker," Jackson said.

"Yeah, check his tagged photos."

Jackson did as Spencer said and the muscles in his face tightened. "Oh."

The photo was graphic, to say the least. It was of Ethan's face, photoshopped onto a dead pig with his eyes scratched out with black *X*s. It had been uploaded by the Dreamy profile.

Jackson closed the laptop. He actually looked green, like he was ready to puke.

When Spencer had seen that photo too, she almost did. If she wasn't already a vegetarian, that photo definitely would make her want to be.

"That's just . . . sick," Jackson said.

"I'm sorry. I didn't want to keep this from you."

"No, it's fine. Really. I just wasn't expecting things to get that serious, you know? At first, I thought this was just an accident but . . . a lot of people didn't like Ethan, did they?"

"No. No, they didn't."

Neither of them spoke for a long moment. The library, quiet as always, felt particularly full with all the unsaid things that rushed through Spencer's head. What if someone had actually wanted to hurt Ethan? He kept saying he'd tried desperately to brake that night, but the car didn't stop—so what if—what if someone had messed with his car to make it look like an accident? The thought alone sounded like something out of a conspiracy movie adapted from a book she might read in the airport: fantastical. But could it really be out of the realm of possibility?

She'd heard of people, spurned by lovers, seeking revenge for less. Spencer liked to believe that people were generally good-natured at heart, but it would be foolish to deny that there weren't some real messed-up people walking the same earth she did.

Spencer remembered a specific case from the 1950s involving a housewife. Spencer didn't remember the name, but the woman had killed four of her husbands with rat poison and staged it to look like they were dying of a disease. They only caught her when the fifth husband went to the hospital on his own complaining about stomach cramps. She'd been using a fake name and identity for decades, avoiding suspicion before that. Who could ever suspect a poor, weak housewife of committing such heinous crimes?

"Do you think this person might have really wanted to hurt Ethan somehow?" Jackson asked.

"It's definitely worth looking into."

"That's crazy. Do you think he knows about this?"

"Like you said, he doesn't go on Insta anymore. Otherwise, he might have deleted these comments."

Jackson let out a low breath and leaned back in his

chair. He folded his arms across his chest and shook his head. "Should we tell him?"

Spencer chewed on the inside of her cheek. "You know him better than I do. How do you think he'd take it?"

"Not great! I mean, who would see something like this and laugh it off? I definitely wouldn't . . . But he deserves to know, right?"

"Yeah. I'd totally be locking my doors at night and constantly be looking over my shoulder."

"He might even be able to shine some light on it. Tell us who it could be. For all we know, it could be some practical joke."

"Not sure what kinds of friends would pull these kinds of pranks, though. Doesn't sound like anyone I would want to hang out with."

"Yeah, me neither . . . It doesn't feel right." Jackson's mouth dropped open. He looked like he'd seen a ghost, his skin went so pale. "Spencer, you don't think . . . Whoever wrote those comments knew that you two were dating?"

Spencer's stomach dropped. "Maybe. It's not like it was a secret. I'm not on Instagram either, and I don't think Ethan talked about our relationship online, but we were tagged in a few photos together. They might have been jealous."

"Do you think that they might have been the one at your house that night?"

A chill raked down Spencer's spine. She shivered violently and held her hands up in the air in forfeit. She needed a minute to process the idea that she might be in danger.

Was this person trying to intimidate her into giving up on Ethan so they could have a chance with him instead? Or give up on trying to look deeper into the crash so that Ethan was sent to jail? It was confusing. There were so many weak threads everywhere.

Was this even worth it?

As the detective had told her, even if Ethan wasn't under the influence, he was still driving recklessly. He was speeding way above the limit. The year before his party had gotten out of control, and a girl was in a coma. This time, he was reckless and someone died. Why did she keep thinking there was more to the story?

"I'm sorry," Jackson said, waving his hands apologetically. "This is just getting weirder by the day, and I want to make sure nothing happens to you. Maybe we should just drop it. He has a good lawyer, you know."

It was as if Jackson could read her mind. But she just didn't want to give up yet.

"Besides, my mom thinks it's crazy they're trying him as an adult. He's only seventeen. She thinks the case will be dismissed still."

"Wow, really?" Spencer asked.

"It happens. Anyway, you haven't seen them again since, right? The shadow person?"

"No, no sign. I wonder if me chasing them off might have scared them, too."

"Just don't do it again, okay? Next time, call the cops."

Heat spread on Spencer's cheeks again. She liked that

he cared so much. "Adrenaline is a hell of a drug. Besides, with you and Ripley at my side, I feel braver."

Jackson smiled sweetly at her. He looked down at Ripley and lifted his chin. "What do you think, Rip? You keeping her safe?"

Ripley's tail *thwapped* against the floor as she wagged it excitedly.

Jackson smiled, a big toothy grin, and looked at Spencer. When he smiled, truly smiled, his nose scrunched up and his eyes sparkled behind his glasses. Spencer diverted her gaze back to her computer. She felt rude for looking at him like that. He was Ethan's best friend. It felt as if she was toeing a line that instinct warned her not to cross, even though what she had with Ethan was long over. Besides, weren't there some sort of unspoken bro rules about this type of thing?

She also felt stupid for worrying about it. Ethan's whole future depended on her finding out the truth of that night. Complicated feelings couldn't get in the way.

Spencer pretended to focus on the screen, but she felt cross-eyed. "I'll have to do some more research, maybe find out who this is, or if they went to camp together and have a reason they'd want to hurt Ethan."

TWENTY-FOUR

SPENCER CAME HOME THAT DAY to find a letter in the mail for her. It wasn't from Caltech, which immediately calmed her beating heart. It was from Ethan's lawyer, Ray Cardona, asking if she would be a character witness for Ethan's case.

They wanted people to take the stand to defend Ethan's character and potentially help with his defense that the crash was merely an accident. Spencer read through the letter a few times, thinking about it all night. She texted Jackson about it.

Spencer: Did you get a letter too?

Jackson: Yeah. I found it taped to my door. At first I thought it was junk, from Peyton Salt again, but . . . I should do it right?

Spencer nodded, reading his text, tucked in bed. She had her feet under the covers, and under Ripley, wiggling her toes as Ripley dozed peacefully. She couldn't help the queasiness churning in her stomach. As usual, the concept of public speaking made her want to crawl into a cave. And to speak about the crash, in front of a whole courtroom—it made her want to implode. She could already imagine the faces staring at her, judging her, even though she wasn't the one on trial.

Jackson: You don't have to if you don't want to. I get it. He'd get it.

"He," being Ethan.

Everything always circled back to Ethan. He was a black hole, whose gravity was so strong, nothing could escape his pull, not even light, not even someone as strong as Spencer. How she hated not being able to escape him. No one would blame her for wanting to hate him. She wanted to hate him. But she couldn't really ever hate anyone. Even him. Deep down, she knew she couldn't.

Spencer had every reason not to want to take the stand to defend Ethan's character. But she felt like it was the right thing to do. She needed to tell her story, tell her side of things, take back some control. Maybe then it would help her figure out a piece of the puzzle that would get her closer to closure.

I'll do it too. An idea struck her. She continued to type. *Maybe we can prep each other? We can ask each other some questions a lawyer might, just so we're ready.*

Jackson: Sure! Just say the word, I'll be there.

Interview with Jackson Chen, Ethan's Best Friend—
Recorded on Spencer's Laptop

[*muffled adjustment of microphone*]

Spencer: Okay, you can talk normally.

Jackson: Is this fine?

Spencer: Yeah, perfect. Okay, you ready?

Jackson: Where do you want me to start?

Spencer: How do you know Ethan?

Jackson: Well, we're best friends . . . Sorry, I
                can't help but feel like I sound stupid.

Spencer: It helps if you don't look at the screen.
                Just look at me, talk to me like I'm a
                friend.

Jackson: Aren't you?

Spencer: What.

Jackson: A friend?

Spencer: Yeah. [*laughs*] Sorry.

Jackson: It's just weird because, you already
                know all this, so I'm not sure what else
                there is to say.

Spencer: Okay. Yeah, I know. I didn't want to make
                you write it all down for me. But I had
                to get a good biography of Ethan somehow
                for our notes. My notes on him feel
                incomplete. I know who Ethan is to me,

but I want to know who Ethan is to you. Plus, sometimes just saying it out loud puts things into perspective. [*pause*] How about this, how did you two meet?

Jackson: Well, I met Ethan when we were in middle school, sixth grade. It's funny, I remember the exact date–February first.

Spencer: Why do you remember the date?

Jackson: It's my birthday. See, these other kids in our grade picked on me. I wasn't exactly the toughest kid on the playground, and I was a bit of a crybaby. Still am!

Spencer: No judgment! I love a good ugly cry now and then.

Jackson: [*laughs*] Anyway, my mom packed me this birthday lunch, with homemade cupcakes, and I was supposed to hand them out to my friends. They had sprinkles, and buttermilk frosting, my favorite. But before I could pass them out, one of the bullies–I won't dox him, it's not important–the bully saw this Tupperware container full of cupcakes and couldn't resist. He smacked the whole thing out of my hands. Right up into the air and onto the floor. *Blam.* Frosting everywhere, all over my shirt, in my hair, up my nose. Huge mess. I was embarrassed more than anything and didn't even know what to do. I stood there, covered in frosting, and before I knew it, Ethan comes flying out of nowhere and starts whaling on the guy.

Spencer: Oh wow.

Jackson: It wasn't really a fight. We were just kids. Ethan was way smaller than him anyway. We were in sixth grade, those kids were in eighth, and Ethan didn't stand a chance. Plus, you know the way kids fight, it was mostly just windmilling, no one actually got hurt. But it scared the bullies off. Then Ethan took the shirt off his back and gave it to me to wear.

Spencer: I didn't know that.

Jackson: Really? I mean, it's not like we talk about it every day, but it kind of cemented our friendship. But yeah . . . The rest of the day he wore his soccer uniform from his locker. We started playing on the same team the next season. Him being striker, me in the net. He actually got in trouble for fighting that day, but he never regretted it. Those bullies didn't bother me again and, me and Ethan, we've been friends ever since. He's always been there for me. If I could describe him in one word, though, it would be complicated. He rubbed a lot of people the wrong way.

Spencer: Do you think Ethan had a hard time making friends?

Jackson: Not really. He's the kind of guy that might throw you off, because you expect one thing from him, but then he comes out of left field, totally taking you by surprise. He got into trouble a lot at school, and at home. Maybe it was because his parents split up when he was younger? I'm not a psychologist, but that would mess anyone up. You remember, he got sent to that rehab camp.

Spencer: Right, the behavioral rehabilitation camp for minors.

Jackson: He hated that place. That summer before junior year was practically torture. He basically said so, but he wouldn't talk about what happened. Even when he was off this summer, he sent me letters.

Spencer: So you know about Ethan's camp experience? He barely talked about it with me.

Jackson: I wouldn't call it camp. It was more like juvie wearing summer-camp clothing.

Spencer: Right. They called it . . . what was the name?

Jackson: Camp Ervo. I think it's an acronym, but I don't know for what. It's where a lot of parents send kids when they get too much to handle. I don't know, I think it's just easier to send a kid away rather than deal with the fact that they might be going through some stuff.

Spencer: Going through some stuff, you mean . . . ?

Jackson: He never got over what happened at that party when Julianne fell. It wasn't his fault that everyone was crowded out on the roof. He wasn't even up there when it happened. He was with me by the pool when we heard the screaming. It was horrible—when we found her there in the grass, all splayed out. We all thought she was dead. Ethan still beats himself up about it, blames himself for not keeping people from going up there. Of course, no one pressed charges, it was an accident. But he started smoking weed to deal with his feelings about it, drinking, too. His parents thought that to toughen him up he needed to go away to "camp" to learn his lesson. And when he was back he was sober, straight-edge.

Spencer: His parents, his dad and stepmom, were they cool with what happened at the camp? He lost a ton of weight; when he came back he looked like a skeleton. He sent me a few letters, too. He didn't sound like he was having a fun time.

Jackson: From what I could tell, they were censoring his letters, too. Sometimes I'd find a page missing, like a sentence would cut off on one page and then it would start up on another with a totally different subject.

Spencer: Right, I've got a few of them here. They're in the drawer by your elbow. You don't have to go searching for it, but I remember reading those letters and thinking he didn't sound like himself. Like he was writing about things that he

	knew he was allowed to say. Do you think he'd try to censor himself? In case he said something he didn't want to get out? Like a girlfriend? Would it really be so out of character for him to cheat on me with someone while he was at camp?
Jackson:	I know Ethan. If he said nothing happened then, nothing happened. He wouldn't lie about it. Oh, wait. Did he lie about cheating that night on you?
Spencer:	Well, I mean he couldn't lie, I caught him. But I guess he had been lying to me since it turned out he'd been seeing Hailey almost the entire time we were together.
Jackson:	While I know Ethan's not a saint, it's not like he's some criminal mastermind, either.
Spencer:	Do you think what happened to us that night was an accident?
Jackson:	[*pause*] Look, I'm not saying I know all the facts. Ethan has a ton of speeding tickets on his license; honestly, I'm surprised it took this long for someone to get hurt in his car. I'm sorry, but that's the truth. He was driving, and someone died. Maybe we just have to accept that. We both love him, but we can't be blind to his faults.
Spencer:	But come on, can you think of any reason why Ethan would be—Mom!

TWENTY-FIVE

SPENCER BOLTED TO HER FEET, as if she'd been electrified. Standing in the doorway to Spencer's bedroom, still wearing her scrubs from work, was her mother. The expression on her face, stony and immovable, as she stared at Jackson was enough to send Spencer's heart hurtling into her stomach.

"Hi, Dr. Sandoval," Jackson said, already on his feet, too.

"Jackson." No smile, no lift of her voice, nothing.

Jackson was closing his laptop and moving for his bag. "I should get home," he said. Spencer could see the flush on the back of his neck, bright red.

"Yes, I think you should," was her mother's reply.

"We weren't doing anything," Spencer said.

"Of course not." Her mom was not in a good mood. The energy emanating off her body felt radioactive.

"Bye, Spencer. See you tomorrow. It was nice seeing you, Dr. Sandoval." Jackson disappeared down the hallway, showing himself the door. Her mom let him pass without moving a muscle. She simply looked at Spencer with a raised eyebrow.

If there was a good time to crawl under the bed, now would be it.

Dinner with the family was a tense affair after her mom had caught Jackson in her bedroom. Spencer sat at the table, fork hovering over her pasta, watching her parents silently pass dishes to each other, spooning piles of greens onto Hope's plate; her sister had already begun eating greedily. Spencer was waiting for someone to make the first move, say something so she wouldn't have to, but they were keeping quiet. Her dad impishly smiled at her mom, knowing that she was dragging out the torture of the silent treatment. What for? Spencer didn't have anything to be ashamed of.

"You're home early from work," Spencer said, trying to lighten the mood.

"We had a cancellation," her dad said. "What's this about a boy being over?"

Spencer shrugged. "No big deal. Can you pass the salt?"

Her attempt at deflecting was caught by her mom, who was an expert at detecting such tactics. "It wasn't 'no big deal.' I was just surprised seeing a new boy so soon."

"I promise, we weren't doing anything but working. It's not like that with him."

"Mom, they were totally making out. Eating each other's faces," Hope said, grinning.

"We were not! She's making that up! Don't listen to her!"

"Hopie, don't start trouble," her dad said with a look.

"He's helping me with school. He's nice, I promise."

"Then what were you doing?"

Spencer wasn't sure she wanted to tell them that she was turning into a private investigator, looking into Ethan's case. If they knew that she was obsessively compiling any information she could get her hands on about the case, she imagined they wouldn't react to it well, maybe even have her visit the doctor again. "Research for a project," she said. It was true at least.

"Yeah, anatomy," Hope said.

Spencer kicked her underneath the table. Hope let out a yelp.

"We weren't doing anything, I swear! The door was open the whole time. Mom, you saw."

Her mom just kept her mouth in a line, not saying anything. Even before the crash, her mom had been strict about a keep-the-door-open policy. If Ethan was over, there was to be no "canoodling" in her house. That was why it was more fun to go over to Ethan's anyway. His parents didn't seem to mind what he did with his girlfriends.

Spencer didn't mind the door-open policy. She respected it. The whole time they were dating, she hadn't gone all the way with Ethan. He definitely wanted to, but she kept wanting to wait. The timing never felt right. She felt the same bitterness about Hailey boiling up to the surface.

"Who is this Jackson boy anyway?" her dad asked with a curious lift of his eyebrow.

"He goes to Armstrong with me. He's on the soccer team."

Mom said, "You said his last name is Chen. Is he related to David Chen, that criminal?"

Spencer sank her shoulders. "Yeah, that's his dad."

Mom tipped her head back, looked down her nose, and made a noise halfway between a noncommittal grunt and a huff of interest. "I'd be interested to know what kind of person you become when your father is a criminal."

"Hey, now Gabby," her dad said. "Don't go making assumptions. Your father was a mailman. I don't see you handing out letters. Just because your parents do one thing doesn't mean you have to."

Mom threw up her hands. "I know, I know. Fair point. I'm just being protective of our daughter. You can see why I'm wary."

Spencer added, "He's not like his dad. He's sweet." She found herself thinking about his smile and the way he used his knuckles to push his glasses up his nose when they slipped down. Something must have crossed her face, because Hope noticed it.

"We should have him over for dinner," Hope said, eyebrows raised high, as if taunting Spencer with the prospect of introducing him to their parents.

"That sounds like a wonderful idea," her dad said, brightening.

Spencer glared at Hope, clenching her teeth, but she took a bite of her pasta to stop herself from saying anything. She didn't have to hide Jackson. She was being honest about there being nothing more to their relationship. He was just a friend. She agreed that she'd ask him if he was available sometime soon.

"How's school otherwise? Homework all done?"

"Mostly," Spencer said. "Just need to catch up on some reading."

"Good. Anything in the mail from universities?"

"Nothing yet."

"Well, that's the most important thing. Focus on school, then you can think about boys. You know what, I change my mind," Dad said with a teasing grin. "Nix that. No thinking about boys. Ever. In fact, no thinking about girls, either. No dating until you're married."

That got her mom to smile, too. "Ah yes, because that worked out so well for us."

"It did!" Her dad cheerily took a bite of his pasta.

Hope crinkled her nose as their parents nuzzled noses. "Ew. I'm going to the garage." And she hurried out of the dining room.

"Jackson and I are going to be character witnesses for Ethan's trial," Spencer said matter-of-factly. "We're helping each other get ready for it."

Her mom and dad gave each other looks, this time with less unspoken volume behind the eyes, and then Mom said, "Just remember to keep the door open."

Jackson had a second chance at redemption with her parents and that was more than Ethan ever got.

TWENTY-SIX

THE MOMENT SPENCER STEPPED UP to the stand as a character witness, she felt like her knees were going to give out. Just like Jackson, who sat at the back of the courtroom, she'd taken a half day off from school. Now, sitting in front of the courtroom with Ripley at her feet, she twisted the hem of her skirt between her fingers as the lawyers went through all the usual legal proceedings, which mostly went over her head. The noise became a dull drone as anxiety took hold. She focused on the hairs on Ripley's back, attempting to count them to try to calm down, when Thora Barancewicz stood up and approached the bench.

"Spencer Sandoval, Ethan's ex-girlfriend, and victim," the prosecutor said in an accusatory tone.

Spencer's eye twitched at the word *victim*.

"Thank you so much for taking the time to tell your story. I can imagine how difficult it must be, sitting here, facing the one who did this to you."

Spencer absentmindedly traced the scar on her face. The doctors said it would heal, and in time, a good plastic surgeon could render it invisible.

Ethan was at his table, staring at the wooden surface, unable to look at her. Spencer blinked a few times. "Yeah."

"Can you tell us a little bit about your relationship with Ethan? How would you define it?"

Spencer thought about it a moment, careful with her words. The Vicodin was making things feel slow again. She'd had to take some to feel better. Even though her cast was off, everything still hurt. "Fun."

"Fun!" Ms. Barancewicz repeated, smiling. "I definitely know that feeling! Young love, first love?"

Spencer found herself nodding.

"And what about your relationship at the end? What made it all come crashing down?"

Spencer took a steadying breath and kept petting Ripley. "He cheated on me."

Ms. Barancewicz rolled her eyes. "Boys, am I right?" She was playing the "best friends type," trying to make Spencer feel like they weren't in the middle of a courtroom right now. Ms. Barancewicz continued. "What kind of person would cheat on a catch like you? You're attractive, you're smart, you've got a personality. You're the total package, wouldn't you agree? Straight-A student, Headmaster's List, Field Hockey Captain."

Spencer wanted to disagree, but the painkillers were making it difficult. "It's not my fault he cheated."

"No, it's not! And it's not your fault you got in that car with him that night. So why did you?"

"I still don't remember."

Ms. Barancewicz said, "Let me remind the court that Miss Sandoval suffered a major traumatic brain injury as a result of Ethan Amoroso's actions."

His lawyer protested the accusation and there was a bit of an argument between the lawyers and the judge, but Spencer wasn't paying attention. She was holding on to Ripley, afraid she was going to topple over the bench. Ripley was doing a great job putting pressure on her legs.

Ms. Barancewicz was able to continue. "Only someone whose moral character is a bit on the wonky side would cheat on you, right?"

Spencer shook her head. "Maybe."

"I don't know, Miss Sandoval. If I found my boyfriend cheating on me, I'm pretty sure I'd be furious."

"I was angry. No doubt. But him cheating on me has nothing to do with what happened."

Ms. Barancewicz sighed. "Maybe Ethan was ashamed about what he'd done to you. Maybe he wanted to apologize. Maybe he was distracted, emotional. We have some eyewitness reports from the party that you two were having a major argument right before, isn't that right?"

"I don't know! I don't remember!" Spencer yelled.

If only she could. If only she could piece together what happened, maybe they wouldn't be sitting in this courtroom right now.

"Regardless, he drove the car into that tree. His actions had consequences. A family was broken apart because of him. He could have broken yours too, if he hadn't already broken your heart."

Spencer's gaze landed on Ethan. He stared firmly at the table in front of him, refusing to look at her still. Then, as if drawn by a string, she found Jackson's eyes. He gave her the slightest nod of encouragement, and for a split second, she wondered what could have been, if she had been dating Jackson instead, and guilt spiked in her chest.

Ms. Barancewicz was done. She turned and took her seat with the Moores.

Ethan's lawyer, Ray Cardona, stepped forward. Spencer second-guessed everything she had said. Had she answered everything the way she wanted to? Could anything be misconstrued? Did she just screw up Ethan's case?

Ethan's lawyer only had one question for her, and he asked it, giving her a steady look. He got straight to the point. "Has Mr. Amoroso ever before shown reckless behavior or self-destructive tendencies that might have worried you?"

Spencer couldn't help the memory that rushed into her head.

"Careful, Ethan!" Spencer said, despite laughing.

Ethan surprised her with a drive to the mountains, making her squeal with delight as he took turns so fast they sent her stomach every which way. He blasted his music with the windows rolled down, and Spencer coasted her hand through the air, melting on good vibes and the beach air, singing along badly without a care. The bass thumped the whole car. She liked the Targa, how the leather seat seemed to hug her body, the purr of the engine vibrating beneath her sneakers, the hot metal smell of the car baking in the sun.

He took her down to the coast, weaving through traffic, the other cars turning into blurs as Ethan never let up on the gas. Spencer didn't care that her hair was coming out of her braids. The wind whipping through the car and the music blaring from the speakers made her ears hurt too, but she was young. And alive. With Ethan.

He took her to the mountains where they got out and walked on the dirt path, winding like a snake above Malibu.

Ethan jumped down from the rock ledge and scooped Spencer up in a kiss, pulling her hips toward his. Her smile pressed into his lips and she pushed him away playfully.

"Ew. You're all sweaty and gross," she said and stuck out her tongue.

"I thought you liked it when I was sweaty and gross." He raised a suggestive eyebrow and she punched him in the arm. His smile reminded her of her first taste of champagne: sweet and bubbly. She wanted more of it.

She kissed him again, for real, and he sighed into her lips.

When he took her hand, he leaned in and said, "Come on. We're almost there."

Together they jogged up the crest of the hill, coming upon a flat spot where a small bench sat beneath a tilting oak tree teetering over the edge of the cliff overlooking one of the best views of the city Spencer had ever seen.

For once the smog that usually hung over the landscape had been swept away in the wind, leaving the sky blue and unblemished without a cloud to ruin it. The ocean, a strip of blue in the distance, nestled up against the rest of the city. Ethan scuffed his sneakers in the dirt. There wasn't much to say except to enjoy the feeling of being very small in that moment.

Ethan balanced on the rock face, his arms outstretched for balance, as he showed off his athleticism. He always did that, showing off, climbing walls or dangling from trees, putting his muscles to good use, performing for the world at all times. He was so carefree and wild, down to the waves in his hair, which was still in the awkward growing-out phase after his head had been shaved for camp. Ethan walked right up to the edge of the rocky cliff and looked down. Spencer didn't have to know it was a straight drop down, not to mention, far. If he slipped, he could get seriously hurt. Or worse. But Ethan always had to look down. Spencer's nerves twisted in her belly. She sensed something that she couldn't quite put her finger on. He was always toeing the line. Ethan, never the coward, always had to look down and see for himself.

But Spencer didn't say anything. She held her elbows tightly, squinting in the sunlight. The sun burned on the top of her brown hair, and she had wished she hadn't left her baseball cap in the car.

"It's so weird, isn't it?"

She almost didn't hear him. He was talking away from her, his voice carried by the wind.

"What?"

"All this. Life. Living one minute, and the next . . . it's gone."

She didn't know what he was talking about, at least not at the time. Looking back at this memory, she knew he was hurting a lot. He never showed it, never talked about it, at least not with her. All she could do was stare at the back of his head, at the hair growing in slowly, returning to how it used to be but never quite the same. The shape of his cheekbones set against the bright blue sky, turned away, still.

His voice was clear now. "One step. That's all it would take. One." Ethan stared at his shoes. The wind kicked up, the gust buffeting Spencer's hair from her braids. The Santa Ana winds were strong.

Maybe she did know, somewhere deep down, that he was in pain, and Spencer instinctively reached out and grabbed the back of Ethan's shirt as Ethan spread his arms wide. But he didn't jump. He just breathed deeply and tipped his head back, as if embracing the sky.

The wind cut all around them, spraying dust and dirt into Spencer's eyes. She turned away, but Ethan didn't. He was flying.

The courtroom waited, all eyes trained on Spencer.

"Miss Sandoval?" Ray Cardona had been waiting patiently. "Please answer the question."

"I'm sorry, could you repeat it?" Spencer's mouth had gone awfully dry and she swallowed.

"Has Mr. Amoroso ever displayed self-destructive behavior or any other pattern of thinking that might signal intent to harm himself or anyone else?"

Spencer squeezed Ripley's harness handle for support.

"No," she lied. "Never."

Ethan, finally, looked up and stared at her. She didn't look away, determinedly setting her jaw.

"Thank you, Miss Sandoval," Mr. Cardona said. "That's all for now."

Only after she left the courtroom did Spencer feel like she could breathe again. The judge had called for a lunch recess, and everyone exited the courtroom.

The floor beneath Spencer's feet felt uneven and she needed to take a seat on a bench in the hallway. She felt unmoored, untethered, and the Vicodin was a riptide pulling her into the deep, dark ocean, where it was peaceful and quiet.

Ripley placed herself on Spencer's lap, the whole half of her body weighing down on her, and Spencer almost didn't notice the shadow that had stepped in front of her. She looked up to see it was Ethan.

"Why did you lie?" Ethan asked, keeping his voice low.

"I didn't."

"Spencer . . ." He licked his lips and shifted his weight to his other foot. His gaze landed somewhere above her head. He knew she was lying, even now, but he didn't want to broadcast it in front of everyone. He glanced behind himself, at his father, stepmother, and lawyer talking to one another. "Don't make this worse."

Spencer's brain was taking a second too long to rev up. She couldn't find the words.

"Where's Jackson?" Ethan asked.

He didn't have to look any further. Jackson had appeared around the corner holding two paper cups of water. He saw Ethan and stopped. They stared at each other for a moment, then Jackson nodded.

Ethan bowed his head. He finally looked at Spencer with a deep understanding, one that Spencer wasn't even able to admit to herself. "It's better this way. I promise."

He looked at her with a sadness that twisted her insides, then left without letting her say another word.

TWENTY-SEVEN

THE REST OF THE DAY went by in a haze, and then—just like that—it was over. Spencer barely registered that Jackson had answered the lawyers' questions. The painkillers had wrapped her in a safe cocoon and she spent most of the time watching Jackson, admiring his poise, distantly drifting off into a pain-free daze. The Vicodin started to wear off by the time the judge dismissed the court for the day.

She met Jackson outside where he was shrugging off his Armstrong jacket and undoing his tie. His white undershirt made him practically glow in the sun. He saw her coming and his jaw relaxed, as if the mere sight of her made him feel more at ease.

"How are you feeling?" she asked.

"Okay. How about you?"

"Better now." She still felt loose, but it was better than the throbbing pain in her shoulder.

Jackson managed a small smile. "Do you want a ride back to school?"

"No, thanks. I rode my bike. Maybe I should start a petition to the city to get bike lanes. I feel like that frog in that one video game."

"Frogger. A classic. You're heading home?"

"I guess. I don't really want to, though."

"You're sure you don't want a ride? It might be safer, especially with it getting dark soon and all."

Spencer waved her hand. "I've had enough of cars for one lifetime, I think."

Jackson nodded and mussed up his long bangs. He looked more like himself again. "Fair. It was worth asking. I don't really want to go home, either. I was just going to sit in an In-N-Out and stare at the wall. Today has been a lot . . ."

"How about we go for a walk? Ripley needs to stretch her legs."

Jackson smiled. "Anything for Ripley."

Together, they headed toward the pier, not intending to go anywhere in particular, just *away*. Jackson walked alongside Spencer, Ripley between them, as the sun started to sink in the sky. Someone gave Ripley a milk bone. Ripley had done a good job today, keeping Spencer calm during the proceedings. She deserved all the milk bones in the world.

"I felt bad, talking about the times I've been in the car when Ethan was driving. But I couldn't lie." Jackson crumpled up his napkin and threw it in the trash can.

Spencer shuddered. She had. She had lied. Jackson was a better person than she was.

They walked along the boardwalk, their footsteps thumping hollowly on the wooden boards beneath them, and Spencer watched the white crests of the sea where some surfers were catching a few waves. "He's off the List, you know," Jackson said with a sigh.

"Yeah." It was expected. Couldn't have a murderer on the Headmaster's List, could you? "Maybe Ethan is guilty. I don't know. It's kind of beside the point for me right now. I just want to know the truth."

"Maybe we'll never know," said Jackson.

"If we can at least prove with physical evidence that it wasn't his fault, it should help his case . . ." She was starting to have the shape of an idea.

They hadn't had a chance to go to Highwood Estates yet. With everything going on, getting ready for today, they hadn't had a chance to spend the day searching for clues like the Scooby Gang. They already had a dog; they just needed a VW bus to make the trip complete.

Jackson leaned on the metal railing, his face turned toward the sunset.

"I think a person can be good and still do bad things," Jackson said. He looked out over the ocean without really seeing it. His thoughts were elsewhere. She couldn't help but get the impression that he wasn't just talking about Ethan.

"Your dad?" she asked.

Jackson nodded.

"You don't have to talk about it if you don't want to."

"I guess I thought I was done with courtrooms. But that smell . . ."

Spencer knew that smell was the closest sense tied to memory. Any time she smelled exhaust, when the air was still, she was back in Ethan's car again, dying. It stood to reason that being in court would stir up a lot of emotions that Jackson had been trying to juggle all at once. Just like her, he was going through it and trying to pretend like everything was fine.

"He's a criminal but he's still my dad," Jackson said. "Sometimes the people closest to us can disappoint us the most."

Out of the corner of her eye, Spencer caught a flash of light, a reflection, and she looked over to see Peyton Salt lowering her phone, obviously having just taken a picture. A picture of her and Jackson standing together.

"Not now," Jackson said with a groan.

"Do you mind?" Spencer called, throwing her arms wide.

Peyton took that as an opportunity to walk over. Her #justiceforchris pin proudly glinted on the lapel of her Armstrong blazer, sparkling almost as much as her teeth. "You two make quite the pair. What are your thoughts on Ethan Amoroso?"

"Did you follow us?" Spencer asked. They had easily walked a mile after leaving the courthouse. Spencer tried not to think about how creepy that was. "I would really appreciate it if you didn't take photos without our permission for your show."

"Please delete whatever pictures you took," Jackson said. "It's not cool."

"What's the matter? It would look great on our website.

Especially if there was an exclusive interview to go along with it . . ." Her voice lifted to go along with her smile.

Spencer just scowled.

"I've been trying to reach you for a while now. I spotted you at the courthouse; you're a hard face to miss in the crowd, Spencer! In case you haven't been getting my messages, here's my card." She flipped it to Spencer, who robotically took it, operating on autopilot. "I think you'll find there's some mutual benefit to us connecting. Lots to talk about, lots to discuss. My live tweets about the case are already going viral. This is going to be huge."

Spencer's lunch was threatening to make a reappearance. Jackson huffed and turned his back on Peyton.

"Now's really not the time," Jackson said. He was trying to be polite, but Spencer could see his hands were shaking.

"Oh, for sure. I know it's been a troubling time, to say the least. But it'll be over soon!"

"Why do you want to talk to us anyway?" Spencer asked.

"Everyone wants to know everything about you, even what you had for breakfast. Trust me. You're a big deal. DM me whenever you're ready! I've got friends in a lot of high places around here. Just say the word, and I can get you anything you want, but you need to play ball with me, too. Don't be shy. I'm here to help."

With that, Peyton Salt turned and walked away. Spencer watched her go, dumbfounded. That was not at all how she expected the conversation to go.

She spun around to face the ocean with Jackson, turning

the card over and over in her fingers. They didn't speak again for a long while. Spencer wasn't even sure why she was still holding the card. She didn't plan on calling Peyton Salt anytime soon, but something she said made her continue flipping the card end over end through her fingers. *I can get you anything you want.*

"Do you think she could get us the police photos from the scene?" Spencer asked.

Jackson looked at her, surprised. "You really want to do that?"

"I asked Detective Potentas and he said no. But maybe someone with her influence can do what we can't."

Jackson tipped his head. "I guess, sure, but . . . it feels like asking a favor of the devil. Who knows what it'll cost in the end?"

"Yeah, maybe you're right . . ." She folded up the card and threw it into the cigarette bin nearby. Both of them were quiet for a moment again, listening to the waves hitting the legs of the pier underfoot, the caw of seagulls flying overhead looking for an easy snack, the cry of children wanting some cotton candy. If things were different, she might have been able to convince herself she was having a nice night. The breeze was warm, the surf was clear—it could have been a perfect day.

She thought about the disturbing photo that someone from Ethan's behavior camp had sent him. The one with the dead pig with his face on it. Before they had started dating, Ethan had been a player—someone who broke hearts wantonly, recklessly. He broke hearts like he was accused of driving—recklessly.

Which made her think of someone else. Someone else's heart he must have broken, was breaking. Hailey Reed.

She and Ethan had been secretly hooking up for a year, Ethan had admitted. What did that do to a girl? And what if . . .

What if Hailey had snapped, seeing Ethan leave with Spencer that night? Even after Spencer had caught him cheating?

What if . . . ?

"What do we do now?" Jackson asked.

Spencer dug her thumbnail into the groove of Ripley's leash, and Ripley looked up at her as if asking that exact same question. She felt like she was being pulled in several directions at once, but Ripley and Jackson were pointing her toward the right one. There was something they needed to do. She would look into Ethan's stalker later, and talk to Hailey even later than that. For now . . .

"It's time we go to Highwood Estates."

TWENTY-EIGHT

SPENCER STILL HAD TO PICK up the things she had dropped off at school before going to the courthouse. She had a lot of things on her mind, including working on her college applications. She and Jackson had parted ways at the courthouse parking lot, and she rode all the way back to school, arriving just as the streetlights were coming on.

No matter how many times she stayed late at school, doing homework in the library, or dropping off something in her locker after practice, or roaming the halls during a school dance to get some air, she thought school after dark was creepy.

The absence of people crushing into the hallway, their voices carrying, the sound of lockers closing, the smell of deodorant—it made the school feel like it was missing a vital organ.

She moved around as courteously as she could, to avoid the freshly mopped spot the custodian Mr. Burnham was washing in the hallway. He waved at her with a smile while his headphones blared jazz loudly as he worked. They were both common figures to be seen after hours, and Spencer always said hello to him whenever she could. He looked busy, though, so she didn't bother him.

At her locker, she let Ripley sit so she could gather her things, and she was so busy thinking about what she wanted to eat for dinner that night, she almost didn't notice a piece of paper fall to her feet. She stooped down and picked it up, almost not opening it until she saw handwriting in red letters that definitely wasn't hers. In big, blocky script, it said something that made Spencer's heart pound.

Stop looking into the crash
Or else

She looked up and down the empty hallway, but the only person she could see was Mr. Burnham swaying his hips to the music while he worked, oblivious to the panic quickly consuming her.

The note obviously wasn't signed—who would sign a threatening letter?—and she didn't recognize the handwriting. Tamping down the bile determined to lurch out of her throat, Spencer scrunched up the paper and shoved it into the pocket of her backpack. All thoughts of her college applications vanished.

Ripley's eyes, amber and pensive, watched her expectantly, aware that something was wrong but unable to react to it. This was not in her training regimen.

Spencer slammed her locker shut and hurried out of the building as quickly as possible, continuously looking over her shoulder, wondering who might be watching her leave.

Wondering if the person who'd sent the note was watching her right now.

Jackson's brow was furrowed as he read the threatening letter.

Spencer had rushed over to his house, riding as quickly as she could, him being the first person she wanted to talk to about it.

When he opened the door, he looked as if he'd just gotten out of the shower. He was already in his pajamas, a plain white T-shirt and sweats, but his hair was damp and sticking to his forehead. He had been slipping his glasses on when he opened the door. The first thing out of his mouth was to ask her if she was all right, immediately seeing the excitement in her eyes. He let her in the house without hesitation.

His house was near the coast, up a winding hill with sweeping views of the Santa Monica coastline. His neighbors included several Hollywood stars, famous musicians, and models, looking for their own slice of heaven in the hills.

His mom, a celebrity chef, was filming a competitive cooking show downtown, so the house was mostly empty, save for one of Jackson's younger brothers in his room playing video games with some friends.

Jackson brought Spencer to his bedroom where they could talk in private.

She might have been embarrassed that they were in his

bedroom, but she was too amped up to dwell on it. She paced in his room, Ripley sitting obediently at Jackson's feet while he read the note.

Spencer kept looking out the window, stepping away and then returning, pushing back the curtains, wondering if there was someone watching from the shadows like before.

"I hate this so much," he said finally. He tossed the paper onto his desk and leaned back in his chair, massaging his temples. "Maybe you should tell someone about this, someone who can help."

"Don't you see? This is a good thing."

Jackson looked at her like she was speaking Klingon. "Excuse me?"

"That letter is proof that we're on to something."

"Spencer. You're amazing and everything, but I fail to see how that makes sense. This is scary. If I got a letter like this, I'm pretty sure I'd shit myself."

"Don't get me wrong, I'm so freaked out. But this is just the tip of the iceberg. Why would someone go through the effort of warning me to stay away if Ethan wasn't really at fault? What if it wasn't an accident?"

Jackson paused, staring at her, and blinked. "What are you saying? You think someone *made* Ethan crash?"

Spencer nodded. "Why else write that note? Not only that, but I think whoever wrote it is getting desperate. They just showed their hand."

"How?"

"How did they know that my locker is *my* locker? That I'm looking into Ethan's case?"

Jackson pursed his lips. If she wasn't so amped up, she might have noted how cute he looked. But her heart was racing, her adrenaline pumping so fast, that she didn't have time.

"You think it's a student," Jackson said, vocalizing her thoughts for her.

"Maybe a classmate. Maybe someone—"

"Who was at the party that night," Jackson finished for her. Their thoughts were in sync. Jackson was standing now, his eyes bright with newfound energy.

Someone at the end-of-summer party up in the hills, someone who wanted Spencer to keep quiet, someone who might very well be in one of the videos they'd been combing through for the past few weeks, someone who could have inadvertently opened up a new part of this case that Spencer hadn't considered.

One thing was clear. Spencer's memory was the key. And someone didn't want it opened.

TWENTY-NINE

THE TRIP TO HIGHWOOD ESTATES had been long overdue. The threatening note was proof of that.

That Saturday, Spencer rode her bike all the way from her house to the new development, Ripley—as ever—jogging at her side, keeping pace with Spencer's pedal strokes. She and Jackson had decided they would go to the scene of the party early that morning.

Spencer had gotten used to riding around town, even though she felt guilty leaving Gertie the Van gathering dust in the driveway. She wasn't sure when she would willingly get into a car again, maybe not ever.

A fine sheen of sweat had already pooled at the small of her back, pressed up against her backpack, by the time they reached the start of the Mandeville Canyon trail.

Ripley led the way down the dirt path. Spencer, despite conditioning all summer for the field hockey season, huffed and puffed, appreciating all the downhill slopes as she scaled the dirt trail heading toward the location of the party. Dried shrubs and gnarly-looking bushes threatened to scratch Spencer's ankles and jam into the spokes of her wheels, but it was a relatively pleasant ride through the hiking trails and toward the neighborhood that would soon be called Highwood Estates. Harrison's dad, a huge developer of the area, was in charge of overseeing twenty houses on two-acre plots of hillside. The construction crews in charge of building the houses hadn't started their day yet, so hardly anyone was around, even as the sun started to lighten the sky from gray to a pale hazy pink.

She had arrived before Jackson and took a water break with Ripley (who happily lapped at a foldable bowl Spencer had brought along) under the shade of a tree by a clean-smelling port-o-potty. A couple of minutes later Jackson pulled up in his black Tesla.

He waved at her through the windshield before he parked and got out of the car with two to-go cups of coffee.

Spencer's smile went wide.

"Mochas, I got you some extra whipped cream, too. Hope that's okay," he said, handing her the cup.

"That's perfect, thanks!"

She appreciated the forethought of having some caffeine in them for the start of their investigation. Together, with Ripley leading the way, tail held high, they started to search for any clues about the party. Even though dawn was approaching, it was still too dark to find anything that might be too small or hidden in the shrubs, so Jackson used a flashlight to scan the area.

Remnants of the party had mostly vanished, either blown by the wind or scavenged by animals. What little evidence there was left of a party ever having been there was a large firepit, with some ashy, chopped logs and a single Solo cup still wedged underneath the teepee formation, and trash underneath some nearby brush. From atop the mountain, there was an incredible view of the entire city. If it wasn't so hazy with smog, Spencer guessed she might have been able to see all the way to the beach from here, reminding her of the date with Ethan atop the mountain.

"Looks like the party was a real rager . . ." Jackson said, using his foot to flip over a flat piece of rock, spooking a lizard from its nap and sending it scurrying into the dirt.

A twig snapped, making Spencer whip around. The sound had come from behind a small hill, out of sight.

Was it the shadow person who had been in her yard?

Jackson held out his arm in front of Spencer, instinctually, and stepped forward. Ripley's tail was up, alert, but when Jackson pushed back the brush, he saw who it was.

"Brent Lang?"

It was indeed the "future cult leader" Spencer had interviewed a while back. He wasn't alone. There were about two dozen other people, scattered about the terrain, using sticks with pokes on the end, picking up trash and putting it into bins attached like backpacks over their shoulders.

"What's going on here?" Spencer asked, though she could guess for herself.

"Collective action. After no one came out to clean the place after the party, we decided to do it ourselves. We're the Green Initiative." Everyone was wearing green shirts with SAVE THE PLANET on them or HUG A TREE on bandannas wrapped around their heads. It definitely looked like a uniform. "I sent out the word online to help clean this place up after the mess. You wouldn't believe the number of pounds of trash we've collected."

Spencer quickly got over her shock about seeing him here at this hour and asked, "Did you find anything that might have been out of place for the party? Anything at all?"

Brent looked confused at first, and asked, "Out of place?"

Jackson jumped in. "I know, it's a weird question to ask, but if you've found anything you might have noticed that wouldn't look like usual party trash."

"Me personally, no. But you're welcome to look through our bags if you want." He gestured to the backpacks filled with trash that the team had already collected.

Spencer huffed. Digging through the trash was not exactly on the top of the list of things she wanted to do this morning, but if they really had picked up all the trash from the party, what other choice did they have? She glanced at Jackson, who shrugged, seemingly on board.

"Okay. Do you have any spare gloves?"

"Incoming."

Spencer stood up and stepped back as Jackson dumped another bag of trash into the already heaping pile. She had to turn her head away, sparing herself an eyeful of dust. The stench alone was something Spencer was all too familiar with when taking out the garbage at Brain Freeze, a combination of sickly-sweet decomposing food waste in dozens of pizza boxes with discarded leftovers and the acrid stench of stale beer. Empty Juul cartridges, dozens of empty liquor bottles, broken beer bottles, smashed beer cans, open condom wrappers . . . *Yuck*. Spencer had been using a trash picker to move things around, having thought of bringing along seemingly everything in her backpack except for a pair of gloves. Brent and his team didn't have any extras. Jackson, a little more courageous than she, had picked up some of the cleaner looking bits with his bare hands.

"Is that the last of it?" Spencer asked, referring to the now empty bag in Jackson's hands.

"Yeah. Find anything?"

"No. Not unless you think someone leaving their retainer wrapped in a napkin is interesting."

Jackson scrunched his nose. "Not particularly."

Brent watched them with a bemused expression from afar. "You guys are going to pick all that up again, right?" he asked, calling from atop a nearby hillside. He and his group had moved on down the hill.

Jackson assured him they would, while Spencer stared at the mess they had made. The sun was almost entirely overhead now, close to noon, and all Spencer had to show for her efforts was an aching back, and she was stinking like garbage.

She wasn't sure what she expected to find here, and she felt a little foolish thinking she could find a clue like they do on television. Did she really think she was Sherlock

Holmes, analyzing footprints with a magnifying glass and smoking a pipe? She took a seat on the ground, arms resting on her knees, and Jackson plopped down next to her. Ripley, being the only wise one of the group, had sought the shade of a nearby tree, waiting for them to realize that they'd wasted the whole morning for nothing.

If she looked anything like Jackson, Spencer looked tired and sweaty and ready to call it a day.

She offered Jackson a granola bar and he waved her off. "I've got garbage stinking up my nose. I doubt I'll be able to eat for a week."

She couldn't blame him, but she was too tired to care as she ate her granola bar and sulked. With this much garbage littering the landscape, she was starting to lose faith in humanity.

"Well," she said, grunting. "Guess that was all for nothing."

As if taunting her, the wind kicked up and garbage rolled away in the breeze.

Jackson and Spencer both swore and gave chase, catching what they could, stomping on flyaway cups and fluttering napkins. But it felt like with every piece of garbage they caught, two more would go flying past.

"Go that way!" Spencer called to Jackson, pointing to trash that spread out down the hill. Meanwhile, she went for the garbage that had scattered across every flat space nearby. Shrubs snagged the lighter pieces and, thankfully, the wind died down enough for Spencer to put everything safely away into a large garbage bag.

She sighed at the task ahead of her, but she spared no time in collecting what she could. It was only after she picked up a napkin from the snares of a bush that she realized this place had been used as the parking lot during the party. Seeing it in daylight, and not through grainy, underexposed footage from phones, was different, but she was certain this had been where Ethan and everyone else parked their cars that night. She spotted the telltale tire treads of dozens of vehicles having sat in the soft dirt. Dozens of shoe prints showed just how many people had come through the area. No wonder there was so much trash left behind.

So much, in fact, that the volunteers had missed some hidden beneath some of the underbrush. Spencer got on all fours and found some glass bottles and even a sneaker. *Who just loses a sneaker and doesn't go looking for it?* The sight of the lone sneaker shook her memory—it reminded her of something, but she couldn't remember what exactly. She shook her head. She was just about to return to Jackson when something peculiar stood out to her.

At first, she thought it was just a broken branch; no wonder people missed it. But on second glance, it was too straight to be anything found in nature. She had to stretch far beneath the shrub to get it, but when she did, she realized what it was.

"Jackson!" she called.

He must have heard the excitement in her voice, because a few seconds later he came running over.

"What's wrong?" he asked.

"I think I found something."

She handed it to him: It was a pair of wire cutters, the handles dirty from being in the sand for a few days. But otherwise they looked like they'd just been left there.

"Where did you find them?" he asked, looking them over curiously. When she pointed to the bushes, he said, "Weird. How do you know they're not just junk?"

"There's no rust on the metal. They haven't been out here long enough."

"Unless they were left over by the construction workers, but . . ." His eyes widened when he realized she was right. "Oh my God, do you think . . ." Suddenly, as if he'd been shocked, he pinched the handle with just his index finger and thumb, holding it out like it might bite him. "What if it has fingerprints on it?"

"Only one way to find out."

THIRTY

DETECTIVE POTENTAS'S EYEBROW REMAINED RAISED as he stared at the hastily wrapped pair of wire cutters, the only clean place to put them being in an unused dog poop bag, courtesy of Ripley.

Jackson and Spencer had rushed over from the mountains to the police station as quickly as they could. She knew she smelled like a locker room, but she didn't care. She hadn't spent the day looking through garbage to stop now.

"What am I supposed to be looking at?" Potentas asked.

"Isn't it suspicious?" Spencer sounded breathless, even to herself. It was tempting to get into Jackson's car to get to the station faster, but she still opted to ride her bike. She probably looked like a mad woman storming into the precinct, helmet hair definitely not the most fashion-forward style.

"Walk me through your theory." He looked tired. Dark circles bruised around his eyes, and the wrinkles around his mouth looked deeper. He took a long, deep swig from a hand-painted coffee mug, glancing at the door. He appeared as if he wanted to be anywhere but talking to a couple of teenagers who had just been shoving trash under his nose first thing on his shift, but he indulged his curiosity.

"Someone *wanted* Ethan to crash, someone tried to kill him," Spencer said. "Did you check the car? See if anything was wrong with it?"

Detective Potentas pulled his lips tight, having taken another sip of coffee. "The car was a hunk of twisted metal, kid. There was nothing left *to* check. Besides, Ethan Amoroso confessed at the scene that he was driving. Nothing else to it. Otherwise, we'd be wasting manpower when we had everything we already needed right in front of us."

Spencer's mouth could barely keep up with her brain. "But it can't be a coincidence, not after I got this threatening letter about me looking into this case . . ."

"You got a what?"

Spencer flapped her hand. "Let me finish, hold on. But it got me thinking: How would the person know I was looking into it, let alone which locker was mine? They all look identical, unless the person knows it's mine because they go to school with us." She gestured to Jackson, and Detective Potentas's attention flicked toward Jackson and then back to her. He still looked confused.

Jackson continued for her. "So we figured, maybe the person who wrote the letter was at the party. Almost everyone was there that night."

"Ethan said that he tried to stop but that the brakes weren't working. Because the brakes were cut. With these." Spencer held up the tool.

"You really think someone sabotaged Ethan's car?" Potentas screwed up his face in a way that made him look like he was trying not to laugh.

"Don't you think Spencer getting a threatening letter is reason to think something weird is going on?" Jackson asked. Spencer was thankful he was at her side.

"Not really. Do you have the letter as proof?"

"No, it's at home."

"Right. So it could be nothing."

"Or you're wrong and it's everything!" Jackson said, his voice rising.

A few officers nearby looked up from their lunches, and Potentas waved them off. "Who are you again?" he asked.

Jackson settled his gaze. "Jackson Chen."

"Chen. As in Ethan's best friend? As in David Chen? That New York banker?"

Jackson's ears flushed red. "Yeah . . ."

Potentas seemed like he had all the ammunition he needed though, and he set his mouth in a thin smile. "You two really think you have uncovered some sort of conspiracy, haven't you?"

"Isn't it kind of weird that we found wire cutters at the scene of a huge party?"

"That is a huge stretch, Miss Sandoval. What you've found is essentially garbage."

"Can't you just run the prints? There might be something on there that's suspicious."

"Look, kid." Spencer bristled at being called *kid*, but she didn't have a chance to say anything as he went on. "It's not like what you see on TV. I can't just 'run prints' whenever. There are always prints that need to be run. There's a huge backlog in cases, and it could take weeks to even get it to the lab, if anything is worth salvaging. I would need to file a literal metric ton of paperwork, because the case has already gone to trial. But that's beside the facts. This. Isn't. A. Conspiracy."

He emphasized each word to make a point, and Spencer pinched her lips tightly together to stop herself from saying anything she might later regret.

"Your boyfriend was driving like a fool."

"Ex-boyfriend," she corrected automatically.

"Right. Ex. Which means it's probably in your best interest to remember why that is. Why are you so determined to keep doing this?"

Spencer didn't have a good answer. But she knew she wasn't going to get anywhere with Detective Potentas anymore. He was never on her side, never had been. She was always going to be a victim in his eyes, always looking for answers to a tragedy she had been helpless to stop.

But she had to know.

Ethan had been sober for a year. He wasn't drunk and he wasn't high. The toxicology report confirmed that. He wouldn't deliberately put people in danger. Maybe himself—he hated himself that much, but other people? After how badly he felt about what happened to Julianne? She just couldn't believe it. He had been her boyfriend for two years. Sure, he was cheating on her. He wasn't perfect. But he wasn't . . . he wasn't . . . he couldn't . . .

There was something wrong here. She just had to remember!

"So you're not going to help me?" Spencer asked. She hated that her voice cracked. Heat bloomed behind her eyes, a mixture of frustration and anger threatening to bring on the tears, but she refused to show it.

"No," Detective Potentas said. "I'm sorry. I'm not. Be my guest to look at the car in the impound lot, but take some advice. Leave it alone."

She shoved the wire cutters into her pocket, spun on her heels, and marched out of the precinct, Jackson hurrying after her.

Spencer still refused to cry, even when she got to the parking lot. Ripley looked up at her, her eyes soft, as if to say she was sorry too, and Spencer put her hand on top of her dog's head appreciatively. Jackson slid up next to her, standing just far enough that it wasn't uncomfortable but close enough that she felt reassured he was there.

She sighed loudly, wiping furiously at her eyes. She didn't want him to see. If he noticed, he didn't say anything. They stood together, watching the rows of police cars in the parking lot, not saying anything for a long while before Jackson broke the silence.

"I know why you're so determined to help Ethan," Jackson said, as if answering Detective Potentas's question.

Spencer smiled sardonically. "You do?"

"Yeah. You care, even when it's easier not to. You want justice in the world. You want to see the best in people. It's what I always liked about you."

Spencer let his words hang in the air a moment. *Liked me?* She figured it was just a slip-up, but Jackson's ears were still red. She chose not to bring attention to it even though her stomach was doing cartwheels.

"I don't care what Potentas says. I think we're on to something," she said. "Ethan loved that car. He would get it fixed if he knew the brakes were busted—it just doesn't make sense."

Jackson was silent.

Spencer's stomach went icy cold as another idea came to her. "I don't want to sound like a conspiracy theorist or anything but . . . everyone at the party was either on the Headmaster's List or vying for a top spot, right?"

"Yeah."

"What if . . ." Spencer swallowed. She knew what it would sound like and still she said it anyway. "I've been thinking of Ethan's stalker, and maybe even Hailey."

"Hailey? What's Hailey got to do with it?"

"Maybe she wanted revenge on him for being with me. I don't know. But now I'm wondering . . . what if someone was trying to clear the board? What if someone cut the brakes so a spot at the top would open up?"

She felt queasy saying it and Jackson looked like he was going to throw up, too. He let out a shaky breath. "That's . . .

super messed up. I mean, come on, the Headmaster's List isn't that big a deal, is it?"

"Isn't it? Everyone at Armstrong is obsessed with getting on it."

"Yeah, but come on . . ." He shrugged. "Half the kids at Armstrong don't need to go to college, they're all trust fund kids, they don't need to work a day in their lives."

"That's not the point—remember the Varsity Blues case? All those kids came from rich families, from families that didn't need their kids to go to Yale or Stanford or USC. One of those kids was already making a million a year as an influencer. She didn't need to go to USC! But all those parents still cheated. Still wanted the prestige of an elite school. And that's all people care about here. Prestige. Status. They'll cheat to get it. You know that."

Jackson looked stung.

She flushed.

He sighed. "You're right. People are crazy about stuff like that."

"I don't want to jump to conclusions, but we need to keep digging, right?"

"Yeah, but now I'm starting to get a little freaked out."

"That makes two of us." She took a deep, steadying breath and clenched her fist around the plastic bag holding the wire cutters. Scared or not, she wasn't going to give up.

ETHAN AMOROSO CASE FILES
Updated by Detective Potentas

Our records indicate the Amoroso family filed a restraining order against a young woman named Jessica Summers. She'd made several threats against Ethan's life, both online and in person, suffering delusions and episodes of psychosis involving a believed relationship with Ethan after they both attended Camp Ervo, a behavioral rehabilitation program for troubled youths. After Camp Ervo, she repeatedly made attempts to get Ethan Amoroso's attention, escalating to a point when she went to Ethan's house, climbed the property fence, and set a garbage can on fire that was next to the house. It didn't leave any permanent damage, but it was enough for us to step in. She was later arrested, but the family didn't press charges, insisting she receive medical assistance instead.

For the past two months, she has been receiving mental health treatment at a facility in Henderson, Nevada, called Calm Springs Ranch. Round-the-clock supervision there means all patients are kept under close watch to ensure they do not hurt themselves while receiving care, and Jessica Summers has not left the campus since she was admitted.

It is complete conjecture that she had something to do with the crash. There is no evidence to indicate she was anywhere near the area on the night in question.

THIRTY-ONE

"THAT'S THE CAR?" JACKSON ASKED, nonplussed.

Spencer could hardly believe that a sports car could be so small when it was compacted into a cube.

The foreman at the impound lot just shrugged his shoulder. "Not sure what else to tell ya. That's the Targa. Shame. Real nice car, too."

Spencer's whole world felt like it had narrowed down to a pinpoint. Their one piece of physical evidence had been turned into a two-foot-by-two-foot cube of twisted metal and plastic. She could just barely make out the shattered glass of one of the side mirrors. Ripley sniffed at the cube curiously and sat in the dirt, as if confirming Spencer's worst fears. This was a dead end.

The foreman flipped through some papers on a clipboard and said, "We only got confirmation to strip it and then compact it a few days ago. The cops had already done everything they needed with it and, well, there you have it. Was there something important in there?"

There would be no way to tell if the brakes had been cut on the car. Not unless she had a time machine.

"Not anymore," Spencer said. She turned and headed down the aisle walled on either side by stacked, wrecked cars ready to be compacted next.

Jackson thanked the foreman and hustled after her, jogging to her side. Spencer's pace was breakneck. She needed to think of another plan, and quick. She was running out of time to prove Ethan wasn't at fault.

"Potentas knew the car was going to be destroyed. He could have told us. I'm so stupid."

"Don't be so hard on yourself."

"Just let me be hard on myself for a second. It makes me feel better," Spencer said. She didn't mean to snap, but she was getting frustrated. "I guess I have no choice, I'm going on that podcast."

"Come on, are you serious? She's a nut. We're not talking to Peyton Salt."

"I know, I know it sucks. But what if she has something that will help?" From what she had gleaned from overhearing conversations in the hallway, Peyton had the scoop on things that only Ethan's lawyers should have access to. Jackson had to admit, even though Peyton Salt was annoying, she had information they needed.

"Fine." He finally agreed. "But don't be surprised if I end up punching her."

Peyton Salt's smug smile instantly made Spencer question whether or not this was a good idea, but it was too late to turn back now.

They'd used Spencer's account and contacted her through the DMs of her podcast's official Instagram page (with an astounding 1.4 million followers), and Peyton replied so quickly Spencer almost thought she was waiting for them to reach out. They set up a time to meet later in the week at Beans at noon during their lunch break off campus.

Peyton Salt arrived late, only by five minutes, but it was already enough to put Spencer in a sour mood. She waved at them cheerily before she ordered the biggest cappuccino on the menu, which made her even later, then sat down across from them at a small table toward the restrooms. By the time she'd unpacked her things, Spencer had already finished her mocha and even the sugariness of the whipped cream wasn't enough to sweeten her mood. Peyton's #justiceforchris pin on her Armstrong jacket caught Spencer's eye.

"My fans will go absolutely rabid the minute they get your side of the story," Peyton said breathily. Ripley regarded her with an air of reproach that Spencer might have found funny if Spencer wasn't feeling so low as to reach out to someone like Peyton Salt for help.

"I was wondering when you'd reach out," she said, tapping her fingers pensively on the laptop sitting on the coffee table separating them. "You two make quite the dynamic duo, so cute in your matching uniforms." Peyton pointed her fingers at them. "The victim, the best friend, tragic connection, working together to solve a mystery. It's all very dramatic and I'm living for it."

Peyton liked to hear herself talk, so it would seem. She

barely paused long enough for either Spencer or Jackson to get a word in edgewise.

Jackson sat beside Spencer, his back rigid and his coffee untouched, but he didn't respond. Spencer knew this was only going to get worse from here on out. Peyton Salt—the podcaster, wannabe Pulitzer Prize winner—had the pictures from the scene of the crime. How else was she able to describe them so clearly on her podcast?

"You're finally ready for an interview?" Peyton asked, but Spencer shook her head no.

"Not just yet. We were hoping you could help us first."

Peyton Salt's eyebrow arched up. Curiosity lifted the corner of her mouth. "Oh? And what might that be?"

"How are you getting all the details for Ethan's case?" Jackson asked.

Peyton bobbed her shoulders playfully. "I have my sources. But a good journalist never reveals them."

"Come on, Peyton," Spencer said. "We know you've got an in with the case somehow. You have information and we need it, too."

"Like what?"

"Police report, crime scene photos . . . whatever you're using for your podcast," said Jackson.

"Morbid curiosity?"

Spencer tapped her finger on the table. "You could say that."

Peyton shivered with the excitement of it all. "I might be able to find a way to get you what you want, but I have something I want, too. I can't just give these kinds of things away for free."

"What do you want?" Spencer asked, although she already knew.

"An exclusive interview. Nothing more."

Spencer glanced at Jackson, asking for silent approval. He bobbed his head once.

"Fine," she said. "If we agree to that much, will you be able to get it to us quickly?"

"Depends. Why do you want to know about it so much anyway? It's nothing everyone doesn't already know."

"I need to see it for myself. I . . . I need proof." Spencer wasn't sure how much she should reveal, so she skirted saying it outright. "We just want to make sure everything is normal."

Peyton took a sip of her cappuccino and smirked. "I'm not sure what else you're looking for. You of all people should know it's a pretty open-and-shut case. He was speeding, lost control, and crashed the car."

"We're not asking for much, just information that the police aren't willing to hand over so easily."

"Not asking for much? Girl, don't you see? This is asking for everything. It'll take me a few days to compile it for you, and even then, I'm not sure why you want to see that kind of thing in the first place."

Jackson spoke up. "We don't care how long it takes, right?" He added the last part, looking at Spencer, who nodded.

"Don't be surprised if by the time I get it to you, Ethan's already convicted." She shrugged, saying it as if it was a casual conversation about the weather.

Spencer furrowed her brow. "Aren't you always saying you're a journalist? Shouldn't you be impartial? Don't you want to know if there's more to it than that?"

"Listen, hun." Peyton leaned on the coffee table, resting her elbows on the top and linking her fingers together under her chin. "My listeners want to feel things. Everyone does. The root of my show is based entirely around emotion. A villain, a victim; a hero, a loser. It gets the heart pumping, gets the mind racing, gets people talking. The more people care, the more people engage. Everything doesn't have to fit into its own neat little box to be a good story. Once you tap into the heart of a story, you tap into the hearts of millions. Studios have already reached out to me, and it's going to be big. Like Netflix docuseries big. People want this."

"So you admit to sensationalizing Ethan's story," Jackson said, failing to hide his disgust. Spencer, too, seethed. Peyton was making money in the wake of her tragedy. No one asked her if she ever wanted to be a part of this.

"If people don't want to listen to me, they can just shut me off. Simple as that. But they don't. They love being mad, they love to hate, and—sorry, not sorry—but they love to hate Ethan. I just give them what they want."

Jackson let out a snort of a laugh and looked away, staring out the window. It was the best he could do to keep from storming out of the place, Spencer was sure of that.

She could barely control her own voice when she spoke next.

"So you want to use us, too."

"Use you? I see it as mutual promotion. You're the perfect victim, a tragic figure in this whole mess. Deceived by an unscrupulous, conniving prince, a woefully doe-eyed angel who has been caught up in Hurricane Ethan."

Spencer cringed. She didn't think she was perfect, far from it, and to hear that other people might think otherwise set her teeth on edge. Peyton seemed to sense that, leaned in, and touched Spencer's hand. Her fingers were cold.

"People are rooting for you, Spencer. They want you to win."

Spencer doubted there was any winning in this scenario, but it would be pointless arguing about that. Spencer plastered on her best smile and said, "I want to win, too."

At least it was partially true. Winning meant proving her sanity. Winning meant showing everyone she wasn't going to ignore her gut. Winning meant she had to play ball.

"Go ahead. Ask away."

Get Salty: A True Crime Podcast with Peyton Salt

Get Salty Exclusive Interview Episode Transcript

[Intro Music]

Peyton Salt [*voice-over*]:

Wow. Wow-wow-wow. Y'all. Do I have a treat for all you lucky listeners. It must be fate because, lo and behold, I was fortunate enough to be contacted by two people directly affected by Ethan Amoroso's case— our newest deep dive into the scandals of rich and privileged Los Angeles life. Be sure to catch up on all our episodes. I met with Spencer Sandoval, Ethan's ex-girlfriend and passenger injured in the crash, along with Jackson Chen, Ethan's best friend, for an exclusive interview about how Ethan's case has affected their lives and rocked a small community to its core.

When yours truly arrived at the coffee shop, I had no idea what to expect from the interview, and definitely didn't expect to uncover a lot more than what I intended.

A little background—Spencer and Jackson have been investigating Ethan's case independently, determined to find truths where there appear to be none, caught up in the concept of innocent until proven guilty, despite Ethan's case being closed any day now with the judge expected to make her decision once proceedings are over. It's pretty clear what happened: He was speeding, he didn't brake, he killed Chris Moore. He's a reckless, arrogant brat. End of story. But maybe there's more to it than that, since two of those nearest and dearest to him are trying desperately to search for answers among the rubble.

Pictures from the interview will be made available on our Instagram page, including a transcript of the interview within the next few days.

What could these two possibly be doing to heal from this case? What kind of relationship do they have? A couple, thrown together by tragedy such as theirs, is bound to be looking for comfort. I myself have seen them spending a lot of time together around school, united in a shared cause, which has everyone talking. They agreed to sit down with me to have a one-on-one chat.

[SFX: chairs scraping on pavement and the hum of cars passing down the street, a bell chimes as a door opens and closes]

Peyton [*voice-over continues*]:
We sat outside a local coffee shop to hear their side of the story.

Peyton: Thank you both for being here. Spencer, can you tell me a little bit more about yourself?

Spencer Sandoval:
I'm Spencer, I'm a senior at Armstrong Prep, I play field hockey, and I plan to go to Caltech next year.

Peyton: And you, Jackson?

Jackson Chen:

Yeah, uh, I'm Jackson, Ethan's best friend. I also play soccer with him on the school team at Armstrong.

Peyton: So let's jump right into it. How does it feel to be at ground zero of America's latest true crime sensation?

Spencer: It's . . . It's a lot.

Peyton: Let's talk more about the incident. What was it like, the moments leading up to the crash?

Spencer: Ethan and I broke up that night. I was furious at him, but I don't remember most of the night. I have memory loss. This far out, I'm not sure I'll ever remember. I have no idea what happened in the car. I woke up in the hospital.

Peyton: Horrible! And your face, scarred . . . Do you regret getting in the car?

Spencer: Of course I do. But I can't change that. I wish no one had gotten in that car in the first place.

Peyton: And Jackson, do you regret not being there for your friend? You were at some overnight soccer camp?

Jackson: Yeah, I wish I was there, maybe I would have stopped him from driving. I still have nightmares about it, that maybe if I was there it wouldn't have happened.

Spencer: You never told me about that.

Jackson: Well . . . when compared to you, it feels minuscule. Like, why should I have nightmares? I wasn't even there. How can I have nightmares about something that happened to someone else?

Spencer: You should have said something . . .

Jackson: I didn't want to bother you. You're going through it as it is.

Peyton [*voice-over*]: Spencer and Jackson can hardly take their eyes off each other. They find solace in each other's eyes. It's almost like I'm not even there.

Peyton: Have you two gotten close since the accident?

Jackson: Close? I mean, we were already friends before.

Spencer: Yeah, it's true, we do hang out more. Looking into Ethan's case and everything. But no, it's not a big deal.

Peyton: Does Ethan know?

Spencer: Know what?

Peyton: About you two? I imagine his ex-girlfriend and best friend getting together would be a source of some emotion. Has your friendship with Ethan changed over the course of your investigation?

Jackson: No. He says it was an accident, and we believe him.

Peyton: And nothing more has become of it?

Spencer: It's not like that. We're friends. We're not together.

Jackson: Why do you think we're together?

Peyton: Just a little hunch. Call it intuition.

Spencer: We have nothing to hide. But Jackson and I are doing this because we care about Ethan's case. We want to make sure everything sees the light of truth in the end.

Peyton: Of course you do! There's that Armstrong Preparatory School spirit. Which reminds me— you both attend Armstrong. Spencer, you've been on the Headmaster's List for a while now, and Jackson, you just got on, didn't you?

Spencer: Oh! You did? Congrats, Jackson, that's great.

Jackson: Thanks. It's a hard thing to celebrate, honestly.

Peyton: Everyone wants to be on the List, don't they?

Jackson: I wouldn't go that far again. Some people make it out to be a big deal, but it's really not like that.

Peyton: I find that hard to believe. Armstrong is pretty cutthroat. The Headmaster's List is a shortcut to the Ivies and Stanford. It's a pretty big deal.

Peyton: Do you think Ethan deserved to be on the List? Isn't it meant for future leaders of America, after all?

Jackson: That's not for me to judge.

Peyton: Spencer? What about you? Do you think

	Ethan deserved to be on the List? His grades weren't near what yours are, or Jackson's.
Spencer:	Of course he deserved it.
Peyton:	Did he? But it's common knowledge that if your parents write a big enough check, you can buy your way onto the List. Doesn't that make you mad, Spencer? That other people might be using other means to get what you've worked so hard for?
Spencer:	It would make me mad if they cheated, but—
Peyton:	Ethan is a cheater. Perhaps in more aspects of life than one! Shouldn't he be punished?
Spencer:	Are we done here?

SNAPS

@chockablock.marva:
Jackson is so quiet and awkward. Is he hiding
something? Getting weird vibes from him. Red
flags everywhere. Anyone find more info on him?
#SaltyInterview

@Turkiwi:
Jackson seems so fake, it's not even funny. Why wasn't
Ethan's so-called best friend at the party with him? He
might just be looking for attention. I bet they hardly
know each other IRL. #cloutchaser

@OctoPuddle09:
#SaltyInterview They are dating. Obviously.

@Awolfe04:
No mention of Chris? They don't even care about
the real victim. Sketchy as hell. #justiceforchris
#SaltyInterview

@norma.likes.drawing:
Jackson Chen is just like his dad, except instead of
stealing cash he's stealing Ethan's girl! lolololololol

@itslilylom:
Who names their kid Spencer? I thought it was the dude
at first!

@Nidusrez2000:
They're totally hooking up. #goodforher #SaltyInterview

@Muhd_adLinsey:
LOL why is this chick even bothering? Waste of time.
THE DUDE WAS DRIVING. Guilty as sin.

@laterhaterz:
Team Spencer! Ethan is scum. #SaltyInterview #menaretrash

@anniehallcrocodile:
Jackson Chen is so cute, I want to scream. Why can't I get a hot guy to help me solve a mystery? #foreversingle #SaltyInterview

@petrichordreams:
More of these interviews please! @GetSaltyPod You did such a good job! Congrats on the Netflix deal!

@AskAWalrus:
It's finally time trash like Ethan pay for what he's done. #justiceforchris #burninhell

@leprecorn:
Hot take—maybe we should all cool it? Doesn't anyone else think it's weird that we're creeping on the lives of private people? Those paparazzi style pics of Spencer and Jackson? Kind of weird. We all want #justiceforchris but this feels like harassment.

@Morgen0girl:
Does this mean Ethan is still single? Asking for a friend. #SaltyInterview

THIRTY-TWO

ANOTHER DAY OF THE TRIAL, and Spencer took her usual seat in the rear of the courtroom. Ripley obediently lay at her feet, her warm fur brushing up ever so slightly against her bare calves. Jackson was next to her, his hands clenched between his knees, stopping himself from picking his nails until they bled. He had an unconscious habit of picking at his nails when he was worried. Spencer was worried, too. Ethan was taking the stand today.

Spencer had an instinct to reach out and hold Jackson's hand so he wouldn't hurt himself, but she stopped herself. It wouldn't be appropriate. Especially now that Ethan had been called up, and already sworn on the Bible, waiting for the lawyers to finish preparing for questions.

"Mister Amoroso," Thora Barancewicz, the Moores' lawyer, said, pausing for dramatic effect. Spencer took a short, shuddering breath.

Ethan looked paler than usual, sickly even. House arrest had not been kind to him. It wasn't just lying around the house and doing nothing, it was lying around in the house and worrying. The usual cut of his cheekbones had a sharpness that veered into gauntness, and his eyes had a hollow look to them that wasn't just the remnants of bruising from the accident. She could tell he was self-soothing, rubbing his hands together under the stand, and he stopped himself after realizing it was making him look guilty.

"Please state your name for the record," Ms. Barancewicz said.

"Ethan Alexander Amoroso."

"Thank you, Mister Amoroso. You're a longtime resident of the area, right?"

"Yes, my family moved here from London when I was two. I've lived here practically my whole life."

"And your parents, who are they?"

"My father works as an executive and my stepmother is in marketing."

"What of your birth mother?"

"She's still in London. I don't see her a lot."

Ms. Barancewicz rested her elbow casually on the witness stand, as if she was chatting with someone while out on the town. "Would you say you had a happy childhood?"

Ethan shrugged a shoulder but agreed.

"A privileged childhood, to be sure." Ethan nodded. Ms. Barancewicz walked back to her table and flipped open a folder, but she spoke too quickly to have read anything. She already knew the fact that she was pretending to look for. "It says your family is worth an estimated one hundred million dollars. That's definitely a lot more money than most people in this courtroom can even dream about."

Spencer had always known that Ethan's family was rich, it wasn't a secret. Sometimes it bothered her, simply because she felt intimidated inviting him over to her house. Her whole house could fit into his backyard. A lot of people cared about the money the Amorosos made; rumors that they'd made it illicitly were not uncommon when it was a slow news week.

"Having that kind of money, you probably weren't in want of too many things. Perhaps the word 'no' wasn't in the vocabulary."

"I'm not sure what—"

Ms. Barancewicz didn't let him finish. "It's no secret then that your family sometimes had trouble disciplining you. Records show you attended a behavioral rehabilitation camp, Camp Ervo, just this past summer, before the accident. A camp intended to reform troubled youth. Can you tell us more about that?"

The skin on Ethan's face got tight. "There's not much to say. We camped in the desert for two months. It . . . wasn't fun."

"Why not? A privileged kid like you, not used to living it up in the wild?"

Spencer could see Ethan's whole body seize up. He'd probably been dreading this topic. From what she and Jackson knew, the camp had a firm hand when it came to reform, sometimes letting the kids go hungry if they weren't able to build the fires correctly or sleep in the cold when the inevitable desert night came around. It was supposed to

build character, but Spencer considered it more like punishment.

"It's not my definition of a vacation," Ethan said. Spencer could hear the edge in his voice.

But what else was Ethan supposed to say? Lie? Tell
everyone it was the best thing ever? How would he defend
himself in this situation?

"What is your definition of a vacation? A getaway to
the Alps? Jet setting in the tropics?"

"I hated it," Ethan said. "Two guys showed up at my
house in the middle of the night, put me in the back of a van,
and drove me to the desert until morning. They didn't tell
me where we were going. I thought I was being kidnapped."

"If your parents resorted to sending you to a camp, it's
a pretty good indicator that even they didn't know what to
do with you." She said it with an unintended wink, like she
was making a point that nailed his coffin closed.

Ethan's eyes went to his parents sitting on his side of the
room. From Spencer's vantage point, she saw Mrs. Amoroso's shoulders bouncing up and down, silently sobbing. Did
she feel guilty for sending Ethan to that camp? Mr. Amoroso sat rigidly still, as if his spine had been glued straight.

Spencer never had seen any evidence that his parents
physically abused Ethan, but what kind of parents would
send their kid away to a camp like that? Parents who might
have thought they were doing the right thing . . . but Spencer
didn't imagine she could ever send any future children she
had away like that.

Ms. Barancewicz went on. "I understand that you're no stranger to this kind of environment, is that correct?"

"Y-Yes." He licked his lips. Spencer could see how dry his lips were from her seat all the way in the back.

"You've had your fair share of run-ins with the law. Tell us more about that."

"I . . . I drive too fast sometimes. I guess it's a bad habit."

"A habit, Mister Amoroso, is biting your nails, or grinding your teeth, or fidgeting. I wouldn't call driving recklessly, speeding into the triple digits, participating in drag races and such, as being a habit but rather active choices, choices that you are able to control."

Ethan had nothing to say to that.

"This is not an interrogation, Mister Amoroso," the lawyer went on.

Really looks like it, though, Spencer thought.

"This is an analysis of your character, and your previous history with accidents happening a lot around you."

"If this is about what happened to Julie—"

"Does that not reflect your moral character? A selfishness and lack of empathy for those around you?"

"Objection, Your Honor." Ethan's lawyer stood in a half crouch. "My client is not on trial for a case that has already been resolved as an accidental fall. How is this relevant to the case at hand?"

Judge Patel made a note with a flourish of her pen and said, "Overruled. This better be going somewhere, Ms. Barancewicz."

"It is, Your Honor. Two years ago, Ethan Amoroso threw a house party big enough that it made the headlines, is that correct?"

Ethan looked at his lawyer, his lips pressed in a thin line. The lawyer bobbed his head and Ethan took a breath. "Yes."

"Tell us more about that. What happened at your party?"

"There were about a hundred of us, mostly kids from my school—"

"Armstrong Preparatory School. One of the most exclusive private schools in Los Angeles, if not the best."

"Right. Yeah. A few friends came over for some fun, and I admit, it got a little out of hand."

"Out of hand? There are several police reports from your neighbors about noise complaints, underage drinking and smoking marijuana, and drag racing in a residential zone."

Ethan's cheeks pinked and he leaned forward into the microphone. "Haven't you ever thrown a party when you were a kid my age?" Spencer wanted to tell him to calm down; she could see the frustration bubbling up his throat. He couldn't snap, or look angry—the jury wouldn't like that at all. But all Spencer could do was sigh and hold Ripley's leash in her lap.

"I'm not the one on trial here, Mr. Amoroso," Ms. Barancewicz said. She spun around and walked back to the prosecution table, absently pushing papers on the desk. It drew everyone's eyes naturally to the Moores, sitting there, glaring at Ethan.

"When Julianne Greene fell off the roof, where were you?"

"In the pool house. With some friends. We were . . . playing beer pong."

"Playing beer pong while an innocent teenager fell from your roof, breaking her back on the lawn. Let the record show that Mr. Amoroso nodded his head. Next time it'd be helpful if you verbalized your answers."

Ethan looked like if he opened his mouth he would puke.

Ms. Barancewicz didn't seem to care. "What did you do when you found out?"

"Called for an ambulance."

"After five minutes."

"We panicked. We all thought she was dead."

"But she wasn't dead. And if you had acted sooner, maybe she could have regained consciousness."

Ethan's chest heaved. He was getting more flustered by the minute.

"Your Honor," Ethan's lawyer said as he stood up again, half raised from his chair. "What does this have to do with this current case?"

"I'm getting there, Your Honor. I promise."

The judge looked unamused but gestured for Ms. Barancewicz to continue.

"Whose car was it when you crashed that night?"

"The Targa is mine."

"That your father paid for."

"Yes, but he didn't drive it."

"Certainly. He gifted it to you, is that correct?"

"For my sixteenth birthday."

"Interesting. Every boy's dream! And you imply that you have a complicated relationship with your parents. What kind of parents would send you away to a behavioral rehabilitation center, when only the year before, they gifted you an expensive sports car? Do you feel like the car was used as a tool to try to control you?"

Ethan stammered. "What? No!"

"Do you act out to get attention from them?"

"No!"

"Were you planning to wreck the vehicle to get back at your father?"

"No! I wasn't—" Ethan stopped himself short and clamped his mouth shut. For a millisecond, his eyes turned to the people in the courtroom, locking gazes with Spencer. Her heart seized up and she forgot to breathe. Ethan looked back at the lawyer, his calm demeanor returned. "No. It was an accident."

Ms. Barancewicz seemed content with what she had gotten out of him. She turned back to the court and said, "One accident is just that, an accident. Two accidents, though . . . This pattern of reckless behavior, of his admitted habit of speeding, instigated by a privileged youth who has evaded justice from the law time and again, emphasizes the lack of moral character we are all witness to here today. Ethan says he panicked when they found Julianne Greene fighting for her life on his lawn. Strange how he can only think quickly when he's behind the wheel of a fast-moving vehicle. It was only inevitable that it come to this. That is all, Your Honor."

THIRTY-THREE

SPENCER HATED TO ADMIT IT, but she desperately needed a break.

She'd been working basically two jobs, one at Brain Freeze and one surrounding Ethan's case, plus school and field hockey practice (granted, she was still on the bench) and physical therapy, all while trying to keep on top of her pain, visit with her PTSD specialist, Dr. Alex, as usual, and still have time to sleep at the end of the day. It was starting to weigh on her.

She massaged her eyes after pausing a YouTube video she'd been watching about bullet journal spreads on her phone. Seeing how other people organized their thoughts and put them on the page eased her worries. She also got some ideas about how she wanted to organize her planner, now that she had her hand back, even though it was still sore and continued to cramp when she tried to hold a pen. She wondered if that would ever go away.

She and Jackson had been working on Ethan's case for the better part of a month. Time had flown by so quickly, she barely had time to register that Halloween decorations had already been put up—artificial cobwebs and plastic pumpkins galore. The school library had turned into a haunted mansion.

"How's it going?" Jackson asked, looking up from his own work.

"I'm okay. Thanks."

Jackson went back to his worksheet, filling out the questions in his usual scrawl.

He'd been working hard, too. Having to take notes for her, on top of all his other responsibilities was a lot. She had to repay him somehow.

"Hey, um . . . ," she started to say, and Jackson looked at her. "How would you like to go see a movie with me? I think the newest Marvel movie is out. My treat, for all your help with school and everything."

Jackson's cheeks flushed bright red. "You really don't have to do that. It's no trouble, really."

"Please, it's the least I can do for you, especially since you won't let me pay you any other way. Without you, I would have been so screwed this year."

Jackson smiled and dipped his head as he rubbed the back of his neck. "That sounds great."

"How's seven o'clock? Tonight?"

"I'll be there, for sure." His smile was so warm, and when he looked at her with those brown eyes, Spencer's stomach did a happy little flip.

With Ripley at her side, Spencer rode her bike to the movie theater, a restored classic building called The Pix, and locked it up near the 7-Eleven parking lot across the street. She was pleased to find Jackson already there, waiting for her under the brightly lit marquee. He was standing with his hands in the pockets of his jeans, his shoulders scrunched up toward his ears in the chill of the night despite his zip-up hoodie, but he relaxed and smiled when he saw her. Spencer had planned it out so they had plenty of time to get their tickets, get some snacks, and find their seats.

The Pix was her favorite movie theater to go to, ever since she was little, and she went almost every weekend with Olivia last year. She liked the old-Hollywood look of the theater, reminding her of a time long since gone. Her favorite piece of decor was the replica Hollywood sign being eaten by the *T. rex* from *Jurassic Park* in the ticket lobby. The theater often showed a lot of classic movies, but it also had some new ones, and Spencer wasn't too picky on what she wanted to see, so long as it would be at The Pix.

But when she went to buy their tickets, her heart dropped into her stomach. Just as another couple moved out of the ticket line and into the theater, Spencer saw, behind the counter, none other than Hailey Reed. Like every other employee at the theater, she wore a bellhop uniform complete with a hat on top of her head. If Spencer had to wear an outfit like that, she would have felt ridiculous; Hailey, though, made it look like the latest front-page fashion. Spencer had completely forgotten that Hailey worked at The Pix, and she wanted to turn and run before Hailey noticed her, but it was too late. Hailey's eyes widened ever so slightly when she spotted Spencer.

Jackson stepped up to Hailey's counter and Spencer forced herself to do the same. She automatically asked for two tickets, and Hailey looked at Spencer, then at Jackson, doing some mental calculations and assumptions in her head, but Spencer was trying to keep the wasps swarming in her throat from coming out and stinging everyone with all the words she wanted to say.

She clamped her mouth shut, trying not to remember the way Hailey's tongue slipped in and out of Ethan's mouth, and her lips went numb because she pinched them between her teeth so hard. Hailey didn't look at Spencer, which made Spencer feel a little better. *Good, let her feel ashamed*, Spencer thought.

Though she almost wanted Hailey to look at her, make her see the rage burning in Spencer's eyes. A punctuation mark on the events of that night.

But she didn't want to fight over a boy. She wasn't that type of girl, even though a petty part of herself wanted to be. She could imagine herself getting a good punch to Hailey's perfect nose, but Spencer knew it wasn't worth it in the end. She would just feel worse.

Hailey was about to ring them up when she gave a weary look at Ripley.

"You can't have pets in the theater," she said, her voice tinny through the speaker system through the plexiglass barrier.

Spencer had anticipated this kind of reaction. "She's not a pet. She's a service dog."

"I don't think my manager will let you, though."

"Come on, Hailey," Jackson said. "She won't make any noise. We promise. We'll leave if it becomes a problem."

"No," Hailey said. "It's against the rules."

"Are you serious?" Spencer demanded.

"I don't make the rules." Hailey turned away.

Spencer banged on the glass.

"What?"

"Are we going to talk about it?" Spencer demanded.

"Talk about what?"

"The fact that you were sleeping with my boyfriend for a year?"

Hailey came out of the booth, her cheeks red and her arms crossed. She looked at Spencer with utter disgust. "What's there to talk about?"

"I thought we were friends."

Hailey barked a laugh. "Friends?"

"Weren't we?"

"No."

"But I thought . . ."

"You thought just because we're in the same AP classes and all that crap that we're friends. You might even think we're alike. But no, Spencer, I'm not like you. Unlike you, I'm not deserving of certain privileges, even though we have the same GPA and I have even more extracurriculars than you do. No, I'm just another white girl in LA. But you— you're *special*." Hailey's eyes flashed with so much resentment, Spencer had to take a step back.

"My sister put herself through State, but her

roommates—both of them were minorities, so they didn't have to. My sister worked three jobs because our step-father wouldn't pay for college. She couldn't get financial aid, she had no help from anyone."

Spencer shook her head. "That's not my fault . . ."

"Yeah, but I didn't make the Headmaster's List and you did, and we all know why," Hailey bit.

Spencer did know. She was the happy brown successful face of Armstrong, and to be honest, she was happy enough to play that part when it suited her. But then again, there were a ton of kids on the Headmaster's List who got on because their parents were big donors or had some kind of connection to the school. She fit a certain bucket, but then, so did the other kids. But it was always easier to blame the brown kid for taking a spot, wasn't it?

"You know why Ethan didn't break up with you? Why he was with me but never made it public?"

Hailey didn't wait for Spencer to answer.

"It wasn't because he felt sorry for you. It was because he was *scared*. He thought people would think less of him for dumping sweet perfect Spencer Sandoval. That people might think he was racist for breaking up with you and dating me. Even though I was better for him in every way. I loved him. You didn't even know him. He was with me for a year and you hardly even cared that he wasn't around. You didn't even notice."

Hailey sneered, then looked down at Ripley. "Fine, whatever, take your stupid dog inside."

With that, Hailey went back into the ticket booth.

Jackson jogged over with Cokes and popcorn.

Spencer had tears in her eyes.

"Hey, are you okay?" he asked. He looked at Hailey in the ticket booth. "Did she say something to you?"

"I'm fine, it's nothing," she sniffed. "Come on, movie's going to start."

With Ripley safely beneath Spencer's legs and Jackson sitting warmly at her side, their elbows almost touching, Spencer finally allowed herself to breathe.

She didn't notice Jackson watching her carefully, but she did notice Ripley shifting under her legs, the warm fur of her back brushing against the back of Spencer's calves. She tried to focus on that, but everything felt so loud, even the rush of blood in her ears as panic held her captive. She felt glued to her seat, unable to move, unable to think or focus on anything else except what was happening. Her memories of the past crashed into the present. The walls were closing in. All the air was sucked out of the theater.

She closed her eyes before she could see it happen on screen. All she heard was the scrape and crunch of metal, the oddly quiet moment when the car was in the air, spinning, the thump of the body thrashing around in the cabin, the shattering glass.

Scream. Float. Crash. Pain.

A whimper escaped her lips, and she squeezed her eyes tight.

Engine roaring. Cold, wet hands on her face. SPENCER!

Twisting metal. Float. SPENCER! Tree bark. Ethan's face. Ethan! I CAN'T—! Cold. SPENCER!

Pain. Nothing else.

Don't, please don't, not here, she told herself, in an attempt to stop her memories from flooding her brain like a failing dam. She didn't want to make a scene, she didn't want to draw attention to herself. But she wanted to run. She felt like she was dying.

"Spencer." Jackson's hand was warm on top of her own. Shocked, she opened her eyes, saw his own in the flickering lights of the screen, and knew what he meant. She rose to her feet.

He didn't question it. He held her hand as she stood, Ripley at her side, and they all quietly exited the theater.

"I didn't know there'd be a car crash in the movie," she said. "This was all my fault. I should have known going in, should have seen reviews or something. This is so embarrassing, I'm so sorry. I ruined everything."

Jackson waved his hand. "You didn't ruin anything. It's not your fault you got triggered. I'm not disappointed, I promise. Don't worry."

Spencer couldn't help but worry. That was all she did these days. She blew into the tissues and rubbed the top of Ripley's head. She sat on the curb, and the dog rested her chin on Spencer's lap and looked at her with those golden amber eyes, as if telling her it was all going to be okay.

Spencer took a breath and all she could do was wait for the panic to subside. The muscles in her back ached from crying so hard. She drew in a deep breath, forcing air into her lungs, and she realized that Jackson's hoodie was draped over her shoulders. He was sitting next to her in just his T-shirt. When he'd done that for her, she didn't know.

"Are you sure you—" She tugged at the sleeve, moving to take it off.

"No, it's fine. You take it. You need it more than I do."

"Thanks," she said, blushing.

Her gaze snagged on Jackson's mouth, at the gentle curve of his lips as he smiled. They looked soft, and she wondered, for a brief moment, what it would feel like to kiss him. The remnants of her panic flitted on the outskirts of her mind, still threatening to rage like a storm once more, but having him next to her made it feel less like she was drowning.

Jackson noticed where her eyes had landed and a flush went up his cheeks. He went very still as he watched her, shoulders tense like he was holding his breath, and she wondered if he wanted to kiss her back. His eyes were round and full in the marquee lights from the theater, and her stomach did a delightful cartwheel, but something held her back.

What would she be risking if she went for it? They were friends, but what if he just wanted to be friends? What if she was reading into everything? But her eyes landed on his lips again and a bubble expanded in her chest.

Ripley broke the moment by shoving her snout into Spencer's face, digging her cold, wet nose into Spencer's cheek, eager for attention, making both of them laugh.

Jealous, much? Spencer thought, amused.

If Jackson was disappointed, he didn't show it. He cleared his throat and rubbed his lips together, as if applying ChapStick. She wondered if maybe she had been wrong after all and let the moment pass. It felt safer this way.

"Anyway," Spencer said. "I should really be going."

"Tonight was fun, all things considered."

"All things considered," she repeated.

His eyes were still bright in the lights from the theater, and he smiled as he pulled his gaze away.

She couldn't help but smile, too. With him, it felt good.

By the time she got home, she realized she was still wearing Jackson's hoodie. It smelled like him, cedar and rosemary.

But she couldn't forget Hailey's icy gaze.

You didn't even know him, Hailey had told her. *I loved him. You hardly cared that he wasn't around. You didn't even notice.*

At least one mystery was solved.

Hailey cared about Ethan. She wasn't the one who caused him to crash.

THIRTY-FOUR

SPENCER USED TO BE A morning person, but ever since the crash, it got harder and harder to wake up. She used to be able to jump out of bed, get dressed in her running gear, queue up her running playlist, and go for a half hour–long jog through the neighborhood, taking a break halfway through to do some more stretches and calisthenics in the park before heading home, about three miles total on an average day. For school, she'd been chipper and refreshed, ready to take on the day. She liked the routine of it, the predictability in a schedule, and it was a comfort especially when midterms and finals made a valiant effort to hack away at her spirit.

Ripley had been trained to jump onto her bed and lick her, nudging her face with her wet nose, once Spencer's alarm went ignored. Spencer could not ignore an enthusiastic dog weaponizing her cold nose before the sun was up.

"I'm up, I'm up," Spencer said, gently pushing Ripley's head away. Her hot, stinky dog breath could wake the dead. But Spencer was still so tired. She'd woken up in the night, as usual, but she felt like she hadn't slept at all.

She tipped a few of her pain pills into her palm so they would be working by the time she made it to school. However, there wouldn't be any school today. It was a scheduled in-service day for faculty, so students had the day off. Normally, Spencer would use it as an opportunity to catch up on homework (although it was likely she was all caught up) or use it as an opportunity to jumpstart on any essays or projects she knew were coming up, thanks to her bullet journal. But that wasn't going to be happening.

The temptation to take her medicine and go back to bed was powerful. It seemed to call to her, luring her back under the sheets, like a siren at sea. *You don't want to move. Stay here. It's safe. You don't want to do anything.*

If it wasn't for Ripley, she might have done just that, pulled the blanket up to her chin and gone back to bed. But Ripley was very good at her job.

Bed-headed and bleary, Spencer got up, threw on her bathrobe and slippers, and shuffled to the kitchen where she could let Ripley out into the back.

Her parents were, unsurprisingly, gone already. They'd left the kitchen with some cereal set out and ready for Spencer to have a bowl. Hope was already enjoying hers on the couch watching cartoons. Unlike Spencer, she had school today, but Spencer didn't have the energy to tell her to stop watching cartoons and get ready.

Spencer hugged her robe around herself as she let Ripley make a few laps around the yard, nose pressed down toward the grass, on the trail of whatever animal had made a journey through it in the night, while Spencer tried to wake up. A combination of sleep deprivation, obsession over Ethan's case, and the side effects of her medication was making everything feel like it was moving through molasses.

"Your phone has been going nuts all night," Hope said matter-of-factly.

Spencer had left it on the kitchen table when she got home after leaving the movie with Jackson, to prevent herself from getting distracted from her work reading over Ethan's case transcripts. It was dull work, but she couldn't let the phone tempt her from it.

She was curious, though, as to why her phone would be "going nuts" and Spencer picked it up off the table. Three missed calls, eleven unanswered texts. All from Olivia. With a sinking feeling, Spencer read through each one.

> 6:30pm–Hey! Don't forget to bring your sunblock. We are NOT having another Aloe Vera Incident.
> 6:54pm–Where you at?
> Missed call from Olivia Santos at 7:01
> 7:02pm–Are you coming? People are here.
> 7:04pm–Cake is here! Strawberry and chocolate for miles!
> Missed call from Olivia Santos at 7:22
> 7:49pm–Is everything okay?
> 8:04pm–Spencerrrrrrrrr
> 8:10pm–I'm eating this whole cake without you!
> 8:59pm–You could have at least said you weren't coming.

9:12pm–People are asking about you.

10:07pm–Are you mad at me or something?

Missed call from Olivia Santos at 11:27

11:28pm–Don't bother coming.

Spencer had completely forgotten about Olivia's birthday party.

She immediately tried to call Olivia, but it rang once and then went straight to voicemail. Olivia wasn't just mad, no—she was hell-fire furious.

Spencer swore several times and tried again. It went straight to voicemail again. "Hi!" Olivia's cutesy voice said. "If you're not in immediate mortal danger, you know it's better to text me. If you're a spam caller, I look forward to blocking you!" *Beep.*

"Olivia!" said Spencer. "I'm so, so sorry. I can't believe I missed your party. I'm so . . . Please call me back."

She hung up and Hope was staring at her. While she had been going to a movie with Jackson, she had completely forgotten about her best friend.

"Am I a bad person?" Spencer asked.

Hope pouted her lips thoughtfully. "I'd say you're probably not great."

Spencer let out a groan and called Ripley inside.

"I feel so bad," Spencer said, leaning on the counter of Paws Perfect. She often visited her parents at their work, but usually they were too busy for it to be anything but a quick hello and dropping off a couple scones from the bakery next door.

"Don't be so hard on yourself," Dad said, typing away at the computer at the front desk. "These things happen. I'm sure Olivia will forgive you."

It was Halloween. As per tradition, kids in the neighborhood would visit various shops and businesses on the street for trick-or-treating, so he was dressed up and ready with a bowl of candy, which Spencer had already helped herself to. Even chocolate couldn't make her feel better.

He was busy working the front desk, scheduling and managing appointments, while Mom was in the back giving a terrier puppy his shots while dressed like a ketchup bottle. Dad didn't seem as bothered by what happened as Spencer was.

"You two have been friends for forever. It's not like one little thing can get in the way of that."

"Yeah, but she's so mad. She won't answer the phone or respond to my texts."

"Give her time. She'll come around," he said.

"I can't take you seriously with that outfit on."

"What? The mustard? You don't *relish* my costume?"

"Funny."

The next school day, Olivia hardly paid any attention to Spencer, even when they sat next to each other in history class. While Mrs. McNamara was busy teaching a lesson about fur-collar crime after the Hundred Years' War, Spencer slid a note over to Olivia. Olivia pretended not to notice, continuing to take notes, and Spencer nudged it closer to her. Olivia sighed dramatically and took the note.

Spencer had written: *I'm sorry. Please talk to me.*

After Olivia read it over, she didn't even look at Spencer. She crumpled the note up and stuffed it under her notebook. She put her hand up to her eye, blocking Spencer from view, as she kept writing. Spencer's chest tightened. She knew she had messed up, but Olivia was a grade A grudge holder, and the fact that she wasn't even letting Spencer explain herself had Spencer's insides churning up like they were in a blender.

Spencer, too, tried to focus on class, but Mrs. McNamara's voice faded into the background as Spencer's blood rushed through her ears.

After class let out, Olivia tried to rush out, but Spencer caught up to her and pulled her to the side, out of the way of their classmates heading toward next period.

"Liv, please. I'm sorry," Spencer said. "I'll make it up to you."

She narrowed her eyes. "I think it's too late for that."

"When will you talk to me?"

"I don't know, Spencer. When were you going to tell me that instead of coming to my birthday, you were on a date with Jackson Chen?"

"How did you know that?"

"*Everyone* knows that. Snap Map? Duh! You forgot to ghost your avatar. Anyway, it's all anyone's been talking about. Maybe if you got your head out of your ass, you'd be able to hear them."

Spencer's eyes stung. She didn't want to get angry, but she could feel pain creeping up her throat. She tried to swallow it down and said, "I lost track of the days. I didn't mean—"

"No, I get it. Ever since the crash, you've changed. You're not yourself."

"Obviously, Olivia!" Her voice had risen loud enough that people started to stare. "Can you blame me?"

"You barely acknowledge my existence! All you do is hang out with Jackson and talk about Ethan, how he didn't do it, when it's obvious to everyone but you that he did! I know Chris died, but you didn't!" Her eyes were glassy and her voice wobbled. She was barely keeping it together, too.

Spencer got the feeling that this was bigger than missing a birthday party, but the rational side of her brain had been overtaken by wildfire. The pain in her shoulder flared. "I'm trying to help Ethan!"

"Are you really? Or are you just using it as an excuse?"

"An excuse for what?"

Ripley leaned into Spencer's legs and Olivia scoffed. People were full-on staring at them now.

"You coming to my birthday meant a lot to me, and I know it's just a stupid party, but you're my best friend! I wanted you there!"

"How many times do I have to say I'm sorry?"

"You don't get it," Olivia said, snarling. "You're obsessed and it feels like you don't even know it."

"Not everything is about you!" Spencer roared. She regretted saying it the moment it came out, but her anger burned hot on her cheeks. In that moment, she knew she had royally screwed up, and what was worse was that Olivia didn't say anything back that had nearly as much heat.

Hurt, Olivia took a step back. She flashed a pained smile. "Right, of course it's not. Because everything is about *you*. How silly of me to want a little attention from my best friend on my birthday," she said softly. "Bye, Spencer." And with that, she walked away.

When Spencer arrived home one day, mid-November, she found an unmarked manila envelope sitting on top of the pile of the rest of the uncollected mail. Spencer dumped the junk mail and catalogs onto the kitchen counter and tore open the envelope. She didn't need to know who it was from.

Peyton Salt had come through. Her and Jackson's interview had paid off. Inside was a stack of large photographs of the crash, a sticky note attached to the front photo.

Thank me later!

Love–P.S.

Spencer shut herself away in her room so no one could see what she was doing and try to stop her.

Looking at the photos, she expected that it would unlock some part of her memory, immediately put her back to the event and everything would click into place. She desperately, now more than anything, wanted things to get back to normal. She wanted to be a better friend to Olivia, a better sister to Hope, a better . . . *whatever* with Jackson. But looking at the photos now, it felt like she was looking at something in a textbook. The warped metal and plastic, broken glass, unrecognizable pieces of lives shattered in an instant. But it felt as if it had happened to some other person, a distant tragedy that hadn't affected Spencer as deeply as she knew it had.

She didn't remember any of this, how the car had wrapped itself sideways around the palm tree. Ethan had tried to turn the car, avoiding the inevitable, but the car folded in half like a cheap piece of paper. The photos, of course, were taken at night, the flash of the camera illuminating the polished black hood of the car, making everything else in the frame expand with a long shadow stretching over the street. No one else was in the frame. The photographer had moved around the car, taking in the scene as completely as possible before moving on to the details of the car, the driver's seat, too destroyed to . . .

Bile churned uncomfortably in her gut, and Spencer already tasted the bitterness in the back of her throat.

Her heart thudded painfully in her chest as she flipped through the photos, waiting for the inevitability that was sure to come. Brace for impact.

The next photo was of the driver's side, of the mangled steering wheel, chaos of the footwell now more bent metal than anything recognizable, broken glass everywhere, the seat almost flush with the steering wheel, the airbag deflated like a limp ghost. She remembered learning to drive manual transmission in that car.

The memory came back to her so suddenly, it almost

took her breath away for a different reason: a flash of the sun on her face, the smell of pavement baking in the heat, Ethan's laugh as she stalled the car once again. It had been in the school parking lot on a weekend in spring. The garden in front of the school had just been planted. She could still smell the flowers. Flowers, like a funeral. Chris's funeral. And just as quickly as it came, the memory left and she felt so hollow. She thought it had been a happy memory. She'd been with Ethan, she'd learned how to drive stick, they'd been so wild and free. All that, for this. Clinical, unemotional police photos of the result of a wreck. Shambles.

Spencer knew it was coming, she could feel it. Each photo moved her closer and closer to evidence of Chris's mortality, captured on flimsy photo paper. Her whole body went cold when she saw the distinct tuft of auburn hair. That was all she needed to see.

Oh God.

Ripley, sensing her mood, planted her body against Spencer's legs.

Spencer's vision darkened on the edges, and she reeled. The world was tipping underneath her. She tried to remember how to breathe, but she choked. She willed herself to move on to the next photo, and a limp and bloody hand greeted her. It was too much.

Spencer dropped the photos and dashed to the bathroom. She barely lifted the toilet lid in time before she puked deep into the bowl, her whole body purging what she'd just seen the only way it knew how. Her eyes watered as she gagged, her stomach twisting with each heave.

Ripley barked outside the door.

She regretted seeing the photos, but she knew she had to. It was the only way she could remember. And now it felt like it had been a fool's errand. It didn't unlock some deep memory or give her the final clue she'd been missing. Instead, she saw something she couldn't unsee. For what? What did she hope to prove?

She clenched the cool porcelain edges of the toilet bowl and heaved, but nothing else came up. All she was able to do was kneel down, wipe her mouth, and rest her forehead against her arm.

If she had any hope of facing what happened that night, she needed to be able to see those photos like a detective would. She needed to see the scene for what it was, rather than how it felt, removing the emotion from the situation. It was easier said than done, to divide a part of herself from that night, but she had to try. For herself. For Ethan. For Chris. Didn't they deserve closure, too?

She needed to prove she wasn't crazy, that she wasn't looking at the evidence and stirring the pot for nothing. If she didn't believe in herself, no one would.

She pulled herself up to her feet, rinsed out her mouth, and spit the acrid remnants of her lunch down the drain. The girl that stared back at her in the mirror was almost a stranger. The scar on her face was still healing, still pink, though the stitches had been removed long ago. Her skin looked dull, her hair flat, her eyes sunken. She splashed water on her face, the coolness shocking some nerve into her spirit, and took another breath.

What had happened, happened. Chris was dead. Looking into the case wouldn't change that. The photos didn't change that. That thought didn't make it feel any more real, but it did invite a new feeling of determination that swelled in her chest. Olivia could stay mad at her for it, for all she cared.

But she had to know what she couldn't remember. She couldn't let it go. She was going to do this. She needed to do this.

THIRTY-FIVE

SATURDAY NIGHT, SPENCER AND OLIVIA closed up the kiosk.
The air between them was as cold as the ice cream they
served.

Spencer wiped down the plexiglass divider as Olivia
picked the music to zone out by. It was a soft, bedroom pop
playlist that she'd been obsessed with lately, making it easier
to get into a cleaning rhythm. They had just had a huge
rush of customers after a nearby baseball game had started
at the sports complex, the whole time spending it without
speaking to each other unless they needed to.

Every inch of Spencer was sticky. Her fingers were like
glue, a result from seemingly the millionth chocolate shell
cone she'd served up, having to fight the urge to lick her
fingers clean. It was hard work, but it helped her focus on
something that wasn't her crumbling life.

She was sad about the fight with Olivia, and not only
that, but everything that had been happening lately bore
down on top of her, like a mountain of weights pressing on
her chest, squeezing the air from her lungs with each breath
she tried to take. The podcast, the shadow person in her

yard, the unending mountain of homework that awaited her at the end of every day. And she wasn't able to talk to anyone about it since it felt like it was all her own doing.

Her pain was particularly bad, too. Even though the cuts on her face had all healed, the reminder of the stitches in her cheek formed a faded stripe of darkening skin that she was sure would never go away, and the pain in the rest of her body never seemed to fade. She'd wake up in the night, feeling like she'd been trampled by a stampede and need to take another dose of Vicodin just to be able to fall back asleep, which would be lucky for her if she wasn't stuck staring up at the glowing stars on her ceiling, thinking about everything that was happening with Ethan and Jackson, and feeling like she was going to puke. Then she'd have to properly get out of bed and get ready for school to start the day all over again.

She knew she looked miserable; she hardly recognized the face she saw in the mirror every morning. These days in particular, she almost jumped out of her skin when she caught her reflection.

Olivia and Spencer finished up the closing down routine and locked the kiosk on the way out.

Spencer kept her bike locked up at the bike racks, as usual, by the baseball diamond. Olivia's voice made her turn around.

"You sure you don't want a ride?" she asked softly. It was the most she'd said to Spencer all day.

Even though they were fighting, it was sweet that she

still offered, but Spencer shook her head. "Thanks, but ..."
She couldn't finish the thought.

Olivia bobbed her head but said nothing else. Spencer
ached for things to be better between them, and it was all
Spencer's fault.

They parted ways, and Spencer and Ripley walked
along the sidewalk looping around the parking lot. Spencer
wished she could get Olivia to understand. It was harder
and harder to remember things lately. No matter what she
wrote in her bullet journal, some things slipped through
the cracks. But it was still her fault. What kind of friend
was she?

The bike rack, situated underneath the streetlamp, was
in clear view of the street. Being a girl, naturally Spencer
kept her wits about her when walking anywhere alone at
night, especially near a parking lot. Now with the thoughts
of some creepy Peeping Tom watching her from the shadows of her own backyard, she was extra aware of her surroundings. But Ripley didn't seem to be perturbed, and no
one was lurking in the parking lot as far as she could tell. A
baseball game was going on nearby, which also put Spencer
at ease a little bit, listening to the crack of the bat and the
cheer of the crowd in the stands.

She got her bike lock key from her backpack and put
her helmet on and got to work unlocking her bike from the
rack. Behind her, a car pulled up to the curb, its headlights
blinding her a little bit, and she turned her back to it to
see her bike lock better. Black dots from the light lingered

in her vision for a second, but she got her bike unlocked and readied herself to go. She didn't think anything of the car whose headlights were blaring behind her, throwing her shadow in a long stripe across the pavement. When she turned to look at it, wondering if it was Olivia making sure she was okay, she couldn't get a good look at the car at all. It could have been black or red, it was hard to tell in the dark. The engine idled, its purr a low rumble. A lone person sat in the driver's side, indistinguishable in the dark. Maybe they were waiting for someone at the baseball game, ready to pick them up, so Spencer didn't worry too much.

Calculating, but still ever cautious, Spencer wheeled her bike off the sidewalk, Ripley taking a moment to scratch herself before trotting to Spencer's side.

Always be aware of what's around you, her mother would often warn. *You never want to be unprepared. Make a scene if you have to, apologize later.*

She couldn't explain how she knew it, she just felt it, an intuition that was as mysterious as it was real, a warning prickling on the back of her neck to tell her that someone was watching her. She wanted to think that she was just being paranoid, already jumpy and looking for killers wherever she went, but she couldn't shake the twist in her gut telling her that something was off.

She glanced at the baseball field, flooded in bright lights, and wondered if she should go there, where there could be more witnesses, or even help if she needed it. But would she be overreacting?

The logical, rational side of her brain told her that she was being silly, start riding, and she would see soon enough that she was just being paranoid. So she did just that. She took a breath and left the parking lot, Ripley jogging happily nearby. But the car followed.

The headlights washed over her as it turned, inching behind her down the street, getting closer.

She tried to tamp down the panic that was bubbling up in her throat. If this was Olivia, playing some sick joke on her, or to get back at her for missing her birthday, Spencer was going to lose it.

The car engine revved behind her. Cold fear gripped her. *Please go around. Please go around*, she thought.

The car felt like it was right on her back wheel. The engine was so close, and she could almost feel the heat radiating off it.

Instincts that she had been so determined to ignore were practically screaming at her. Her whole body was tight. She tightened her grip on the handlebars.

Then she took off.

The car wheels screeched after her, accelerating.

She stood up on her bike, pedaling as hard as she could as she took a turn down the street. Ripley kept up, galloping in stride, and still the car was right on her.

She didn't have time to think about how she should have stayed at the field, maybe waited for her mom or taken that ride with Olivia. She just had to get out of there fast. Her heart pounded, her breathing hard. She pushed herself fast, but the car, of course, was faster.

It was so close, the headlights were so bright, but she kept going. She couldn't stop. If she did, she'd meet the hood of the car in an instant. The engine was screaming at her, drowning out all other noise. Her legs burned with the effort, but fear had taken over.

Help, please help me! Anyone!

Something told her to jump, and she did. The instant she flung herself off her bike and into the bushes, the car clipped her bike with a horrible crunch, and took off down the street, its red taillights disappearing as it sped away.

For a moment, all Spencer could hear was the hollow pulse of her heartbeat raging in her ears and the dull echo of Ripley's barks as she lay in the bushes, the branches painfully stabbing her in every part of her body. But she was safe.

The pain was immediate and constant, but Spencer pulled herself out of the bushes. Ripley was barking furiously at the car, unhurt but frightened, and then she immediately went to Spencer's side. It took a moment for reality to set in.

Spencer had almost been run over, narrowly avoiding a direct hit.

Someone was trying to kill her.

THIRTY-SIX

SPENCER CAME HOME TO FIND Mom and Hope on the couch, curled up watching an old rerun of *Murder, She Wrote*, a fitting and somewhat ironic thing, given Spencer's current circumstance. Spencer could hear Dad in the shower. She was still dazed, not quite sure what had just happened.

Mom leapt to her feet when she laid eyes on Spencer. "What happened to you?"

Spencer inspected herself. The scrapes and bruises on her knees and elbows were clear in the light of the house now, and her mom rushed to her, fussing.

She pulled a leaf from Spencer's hair. "What is this? Are you hurt?"

"I'm fine, Mom. Really." The bike, not so much. To avoid any more cars, Spencer had cut through a few alleys (in hindsight, not the wisest decision, either) and climbed over a few neighbors' fences so as to stay out of sight of whoever had tried to run her down.

But she told her mom everything, and without hesitation, her mother immediately rushed to the couch and grabbed her phone. Hope sat by, looking at Spencer with shock.

"What are you doing?" Spencer asked.

"Calling the police."

Spencer groaned. "Mom, don't."

"Why not? Someone needs to look into this." She held up the phone to her ear. Spencer could hear the line ringing on the other end. It was already so late, she didn't expect that too many officers would be available to take a call to the non-emergency line.

"Seriously, it was probably just a drunk driver." Spencer doubted her own words, but her mom didn't need to know. It felt like an attack.

"That's worse, Spencer. They could hurt someone else. This town has enough drunk drivers as it is . . ." She probably hadn't meant to say it, but her eyes widened when she realized that Spencer was putting two and two together. Ethan. Of course, Ethan. "I didn't mean . . ." But it was too late.

"It's not worth it," Spencer said. "I'm fine. Ripley's fine. I just want to go to bed."

"Are you hurt? Do you need to go to the hospital?"

The last place Spencer wanted to be was inside another car, and she shook her head.

Mom wasn't through with the interrogation. "Well, did you see who did it? The car?"

"I didn't get a good enough look, just the taillights as it sped off. It'd be impossible to find them."

The lines around her mom's mouth deepened as she frowned. She wrapped Spencer in a tight hug, which made

Spencer wince in pain, but she didn't pull away. Finally, someone on the other end of the phone picked up.

Mom stepped away. "Yes, hi, hello," she said. "I'd like to speak to a Detective Potentas—Yes, I understand he'd be at home, can you leave him a message? It's about my daughter, Spencer Sandoval."

Spencer didn't hear the rest. She went to her room and called the person she wanted to see most right now.

"Wait, wait, back up. You almost got run over? Are you okay?" Jackson's voice was nearly drowned out by the sound of one of his younger brothers playing some kind of shooting video game and yelling taunts at the other team. Jackson moved away from the ruckus and closed a door, probably to his room. It was quieter now, and she heard the squeak of a mattress as he sat down.

"I'm fine," she said, nodding, assuring herself. "Can I send you a picture?"

"Is it a photo of the driver?"

"No." Spencer flipped open to a blank page of her bullet journal and started sketching. "I didn't get a good look at the car, or who was driving, but I did get a look at the taillights. Do you recognize this shape?" She took a photo with her phone and sent it, waiting a moment for Jackson to see it.

She wasn't an artist, but she was able to sketch the general outline of the long, rectangular-shaped taillight, broken up by what looked like a series of lines like a cage.

But Jackson sighed. "Sorry, I don't. I'm not really a car guy. But I know someone who is."

Ethan did not look happy to see them. "What are you two doing here? It's almost midnight." He glanced at his watch.

"We just had to ask you a question, it'll be really quick, I promise," Spencer said. She'd slipped out of the house, forgoing her bike until she could get it fixed, and ran to meet Jackson in front of Ethan's house right then.

"If this is about . . . God, Spence, please, just go home. You too, Jax. You shouldn't be here." He moved to close the door, but Spencer kicked out her foot and it jammed on her sneaker. Ethan looked shocked, but he didn't try to push her away.

"I just need your expertise, please. It's one question."

Ethan sighed, his lips pressed together. Then he glanced at Jackson.

"Please, man," Jackson said. Whether he meant to or not, Jackson flashed the best puppy-dog eyes in the world, and Ethan's shoulders dropped, relenting.

"Fine, what."

Spencer handed him the paper with her drawing on it. "Do you know what kind of car would have this taillight?"

Ethan scrubbed his chin thoughtfully, then said, "That's an old-school Dodge Charger. Probably R/T 440. I'm guessing from 1968 or so. That kind of car is super hard to find, you've got to restore it. I don't know anyone who has one. What's all this about?"

Spencer's heart pounded. "You're sure? You're positive that this is a Charger?"

"Well yeah, they have a really distinctive rear light."

"They couldn't be confused with any other type?" Jackson asked.

"No, like I said, they're pretty unique. Why are you asking me this?"

Spencer looked at Jackson, her eyes bright, his too. It was their first real break.

But Jackson's phone rang in his pocket, and he answered it, stepping away. "Hey, Mikey. What's up?" Spencer could hear one of his younger brothers' voices on the other end. "Yeah," Jackson said. "I'll be back in a few minutes." He hung up and looked at both Ethan and Spencer. "I left my brothers at home, and I shouldn't leave them alone too much longer or they'll set up a booby trap for the Wet Bandits. I need to go."

"I'll explain everything," Spencer said.

Jackson tapped his phone in his palm. He clearly looked like he wanted to stay, but other responsibilities were pulling him back. "You'll tell me if you figure anything else out?"

"Absolutely."

"What is going on?" Ethan asked as Jackson waved and crossed the lawn to his car parked in the driveway.

Spencer let Ripley walk first into Ethan's house and she followed after. He didn't argue. There was no sign of his dad or his stepmom, but Spencer didn't care if anyone overheard. She wasn't planning on staying long anyway. She took a seat on the couch in the living room, overcome with exhaustion. "Someone tried to run me off the road. I didn't see the car except the taillights."

Ethan looked horrified. "What? Oh my God, are you okay?"

"I wouldn't be here right now if I wasn't. Do you know anyone who drives that car?"

Ethan put his hand on the top of his head, in shock. "No. Why would someone do that?"

"I think whoever it is, is trying to scare me."

"Why?"

"Because I'm looking into what happened, finding the truth, about the crash."

Ethan groaned and threw his head back. "Why am I not surprised."

"I need to know, Ethan!"

"I told you what happened!"

"But . . ."

"And now you're almost run over by some lunatic. What if they don't miss next time?"

Spencer clamped her mouth shut and glared at him. Being angry with him was easy, but she had more pressing things to worry about. "I found wire cutters at the party. I think the brakes on the Targa were cut."

Ethan actually laughed. "That would explain a lot."

"Do you know of anyone who might want to do that? Maybe your stalker?"

"She's not involved in this."

"How do you know?"

"I just know, okay? She's getting help. She wouldn't do that."

Based on the firmness in his voice, she knew he was telling the truth. She didn't have the full picture, but Ethan did, and he seemed convinced enough. She took a breath. "Fine. I just can't help feeling like I'm so close to figuring it all out. I got a threatening letter in my locker, and someone's been lurking outside my house—"

"Fuck, Spencer!"

"You can see why I'm a little freaked out! The police don't believe me, so Jackson's been helping me figure out what made you crash. I think whoever is behind this is afraid of the truth coming out."

Ethan sighed and took a seat on the floor across from her, his elbows on his knees. He looked wary, not from lack of sleep, but a deeper kind of tired that made him look older somehow. "Do you believe me?" she asked softly.

"I *believe* you and Jackson make a good pair. You two seem to be getting cozy with each other," Ethan said, smirking.

Spencer huffed. "You've been listening to too much of the *Get Salty* podcast."

Ethan put his hand to his chest mockingly. "You wound me." But then he smiled, and her heart fluttered with excitement. She hated how his smile still had that effect on her.

Ethan's smile fell and he looked at her, concern furrowing his brow. "Come on, Spence. None of this is worth it. Leave it alone."

"You know I can't."

"I'm begging you," Ethan said, eyes shining. "Please. If not for me, then for Jackson."

"Why?"

Ethan paused before answering. "What if that nut job tries to go after him next?"

Spencer's stomach dropped. She hadn't thought about that. The whole time, she'd been so selfish, caught up in her own world.

Ethan continued. "Come on, if someone is trying to hurt you because of me, wouldn't they go after him, too? And if they succeed . . . I won't be able to live with myself."

A chill raked down her spine. *If they succeed* . . . She shook her head. "I've come too far to give up now."

Ethan pressed his lips together and sighed. "I knew you'd say that. I figured I might as well try."

Guilt wrapped a cold hand around her stomach. If Ethan was right and whoever was trying to intimidate her tried to hurt Jackson, she'd feel responsible. Her crusade for truth could get other people hurt and it'd be all her fault. She looked at Ripley, who looked back at her, eyebrows raised expectantly. After a beat, she took a steadying breath and looked at Ethan. She couldn't let whoever was behind this win.

"What does your lawyer say? About the verdict? What are your chances?"

"Because I wasn't driving under the influence, it's harder to prove 'wanton disregard for life,' especially in a blind intersection like that. Even if I was speeding, there's still a chance it wasn't my fault. So the onus is on the prosecution to prove my character. That I'm the type of guy who would do this, who would willingly speed without thinking about the consequences."

Spencer nodded. "And . . . ?"

"He thinks my chances are fifty-fifty."

"I'm sorry, Ethan."

"Yeah," he said, resigned. "I'm sorry, too."

THIRTY-SEVEN

"I KNOW WHAT I SIGNED up for," Jackson said the next morning. Spencer had told him everything that she talked about with Ethan as they walked together toward the police station, Ripley panting happily at her side. "I can't give up on him. Or you."

"You're not afraid?"

"Oh, I'm terrified. But it's too important to me now to see this through."

She was glad he was as stubborn as she was, but a prickling sensation of worry creeped along the back of her neck. She hoped she wasn't dragging him into a mess that was quickly growing out of control. Having him with her as they walked inside the station was like a lifeline at sea, and she was grateful he had been with her throughout everything so far. She didn't want to lose him, too.

Detective Potentas didn't try to hide the groan that came out of his mouth when he saw them come in.

There wasn't any time to call him out for it. She needed to speak, or else she felt like she was going to explode. She could barely sleep the night before and couldn't wait to show him what she'd found. "Detective, I have something you might want to look at—"

"Not another piece of garbage . . ." He tried to move around them, carrying his mug of coffee for a refill, but Spencer and Jackson followed. It looked like he'd been there all night, or he'd never gone home.

"It's not! I almost got hit by a car last night—"

"Yes, I got your mother's message."

"Then you know I've been targeted by some maniac on the road. The car they're driving is a Dodge Charger from 1968. We need to be on the lookout for anyone who has one, who might know Ethan and would have a reason to want to hurt him."

Potentas rolled his eyes. "This is a separate, unrelated incident. Please file your report to the receptionist and we'll get right on it."

"Yeah, right," Jackson said, rolling his eyes.

Potentas shot him a look, then to her he said, "Miss Sandoval, I have tried being polite, tried being open-minded, but I'm at my wit's end. I can't help you anymore. I just can't. I have more cases that I need to worry about, and this isn't something I can help you with."

"She's being threatened, Detective," Jackson said.

"By whom? Exactly? A mysterious stalker? I've been in my line of work for fifteen years, and I've never had one single case with circumstances as outlandish as yours. For all I know, you could have written this so-called letter yourself, seeking some sort of attention."

"You don't believe her?" Jackson asked. Anger coated his voice.

"Frankly, Mr. Chen, I've got too much of a caseload. I'm not in the business of humoring a couple of teenagers looking to play Scooby Doo."

Spencer was desperate. "Someone tried to run me over, Detective! Don't you care if they're actually successful next time?"

Potentas sighed. "I wish I could tell you what you want to hear. But I'm sorry. Don't come back here."

Jackson and Spencer sat on the steps of school, the first bell having long since rung. The lawn was empty, everyone already having gone to class. After the police station, neither Jackson nor Spencer felt like sitting in the library for an hour. Ripley dozed on the grass, her ears twitching now and again, as if she was lost in some dream.

Spencer hugged her knees to her chest, feeling the need to hold herself for fear that she might crumble to pieces otherwise. It was over. Detective Potentas was not going to do anything.

"Why won't they listen?" Spencer asked. "I did everything. I gave them more evidence, more things to consider, and they look at me like I'm wasting my breath."

Jackson let out a small laugh.

"What's so funny?"

"Nothing you said, it's just . . . I used to want to be a police officer when I was little. I used to believe that the world could be just, that the good guys would always catch the bad guys. Like in the movies. But after everything with my dad, with Ethan, now you go to them asking for help and . . . Is this what growing up feels like?"

Spencer rested her cheek on her arm, watching him as he spoke. He was looking toward the horizon, the morning softening his face with warm colors despite the sadness in his eyes.

Spencer hesitated, but thought it was only polite to reciprocate. He had offered a shoulder for her to lean on; the least she could do was offer the same. "Do you want to talk about it?"

Jackson shrugged, but he didn't get angry at her or defensive when she asked. "What else is there to say? With my dad, I . . . I looked up to him for my whole life, and then like that, it was gone. Like it was nothing. Something like that changes you, especially when you're a kid. There was me before, and then there's me after. And no matter how much the world changes around me, I don't want it to change me where it counts."

She'd felt the exact same way about the accident. They didn't talk again for a long beat. Spencer wished she had taken the time to get to know Jackson earlier. She couldn't do anything like this with Ethan, something as boring as sitting on the steps at school and talking. There always had to be movement, action with Ethan, never a moment to breathe. But with Jackson, time slowed to a comfortable pace, a pace that Spencer could feel the edges of and hold on to.

Jackson snapped her out of her thought spiral when he asked, "What about you? What did you want to be when you grew up?"

"An astronaut," she said. "Always have. I want to be the first person to land on Mars."

"And come back to Earth after that, I hope!" Jackson said with a laugh.

"How else would I get all that fame and fortune I so desperately desire?" Spencer said dryly with a wave of her hand, which made Jackson laugh harder. She smiled too, basking in her ability to cheer Jackson up even just a little. "Don't tell anybody, but I actually wanted to be an astronaut *princess* when I was little. What will NASA think?" Jackson snorted and nudged her with his elbow. Spencer let the good air hang for a moment before continuing. "All my life I've been working toward my dreams; then this one thing happened and it put everything into perspective. I don't want anything else to get in my way."

"You'll make it."

Jackson was looking at her now, with a level gaze and a proud smile. He said it so assuredly, it almost took her aback.

"That's one thing I'm sure of in this world now," he said. "Once you've set your mind on something, God help us, Spencer—you're unstoppable."

Spencer smiled and her cheeks felt hot. They'd been doing that an awful lot lately whenever Jackson was around.

He rubbed his thighs nervously, smoothing out invisible

lines in his slacks, and cleared his throat. "Sorry, I'm just grateful for everything you've done so far. Without you, I might never have done nearly as much to help Ethan. I don't think I've ever properly thanked you for it, either. So thank you."

"So much good it's done for him now, though."

"Maybe there's something we missed. We can keep trying."

Spencer wanted to believe him, and the way he was looking at her made it easier. "I wish we'd gotten to know each other at school before this whole thing."

Jackson's voice was soft. "Yeah, same. But to be honest, I've always liked you, Spencer. I've had a crush on you forever."

Spencer blinked, surprised. "Really?"

Jackson nodded. "Ethan beat me to it. He's always faster than me. Faster to act, faster to do things that might scare me, faster to go for what he wants. I always felt guilty, though, for liking you. It felt wrong after he asked you out. But I couldn't help it."

"Jackson, I . . ." The words felt full in her mouth.

The blush was bright on his cheeks. "You don't have to say anything. I've been waiting to tell you for a long time, so . . . now you know."

"Yeah, the thing is, I . . . I feel the same way."

Jackson's eyes were round behind his glasses, his lips slightly parted in shock.

She liked Jackson. She couldn't deny it now. She really *liked* him. She liked the way he worried his fingers over his lower lip when he was deep in study, she liked the way his nose crinkled when he laughed, she liked that he cared about her and propped her up, helping her take one step forward, together. She had thought she had her whole life mapped out, and still it found ways of surprising her. Jackson was helping her in so many different ways.

Her heart galloped wildly in her chest as she leaned toward him, and he leaned toward her. She felt like she could fly. They were close enough now that Spencer noticed a small scar below his right eyebrow, more pronounced now that his eyes were closed.

All she had to do was close the gap; their lips were already a hair's breadth away. She could feel his breath on her skin, tickling the small hairs on her cheeks. His lips looked so soft. All she yearned for was to close her eyes and lose herself in his touch. She'd never felt like this about anyone before, including Ethan. She wanted to kiss him more than anything.

But something held her back. It tugged at the back of her thoughts, and she pushed against it, but deep down, she understood. She couldn't do this yet.

"Jackson . . . ," she whispered. It was like a magic spell had been lifted.

Jackson pulled back and smiled softly. He knew it wasn't right, too.

Spencer touched her fingers to her lips and took a breath. Her heart felt so heavy. She was holding herself back because of Ethan, again.

Jackson ran his hands through his hair bashfully. "I'm so sorry. I—"

They talked over each other. "I wish we could but . . ."

"I'm Ethan's best friend. I can't do this to him. What am I doing?"

"It's not that. Ethan and I are so over, but I need more time. I want to kiss you. I don't think you know how much I do."

"Really?"

"Yeah," she said, smiling. "Really. I need some time to . . . heal? It sounds dumb but—"

"No, I totally get it. No pressure."

Jackson's expression softened. When he looked at her, she felt real. His smile melted her heart, but she could feel the distance spanning between them growing further. She wanted to move on from Ethan, but everywhere she looked, all she could think about was him. In a way, she hated Ethan for that. She couldn't move on because of what he'd done. It had affected all three of them so deeply; Spencer needed even more time to shake off the debris so she wouldn't get hurt again.

Jackson looked over his shoulder to the empty hallway. "We should get going. Second period will start soon."

THIRTY-EIGHT

THE DAYS PASSED, AND THEIR investigation into the crash had come to a screeching halt. They had nothing else to work with, now that the police had shut the door on both of them. Ethan's case was drawing to an inevitable end, and it was only a matter of time before his fate was sealed. They were running out of options, but there was no place left to turn to. They had run out of leads.

That morning, Spencer was at her locker, gathering her books while Ripley sat at attention behind her, and she thought about everything that had happened. Olivia still wasn't speaking to Spencer. She avoided her at every turn, never being at her locker when Spencer was there, and it made most mornings lonely. Her absence was an ever-present ache.

Everyone else at Armstrong went about their morning, laughing and chatting, like it was any other day, but Spencer felt like she had blinders on, only able to focus on the task in front of her. Her world had narrowed to a singular point, and guilt pressed at her from all sides. She wished she had all the answers, that she could fix everything, but she couldn't, and it felt awful.

With a sigh, she closed her locker and moved toward the library to meet Jackson as usual, but instead, she saw Jackson coming toward her, looking like he'd swallowed something nasty, his skin waxy and pale. He gave her one look, and she knew. Something was wrong.

"Are you okay?" she asked.

He nodded stiffly. It was obvious he was lying.

"Jackson."

Whatever it was, he didn't want to say it aloud. He reached into his pocket and pulled out a folded piece of paper and handed it to her. It was in the same handwriting as the note that had been shoved into her locker.

Stop playing Watson

Or Spencer Sandoval will pay

"It was on my porch this morning," he said, his voice thick.

Spencer felt like she'd been punched in the head; her ears were ringing. Ripley pressed herself up against Spencer's thigh, worried she might fall over. Ethan had been right.

Spencer grabbed Jackson by the hand and walked him down the hall. "Let's get out of here," she said.

Jackson looked small, his shoulders hunched, as he picked at the grass underneath his crossed legs. Spencer and Ripley sat next to him.

"They must be listening to the *Get Salty* podcast," he said. "How else would they know I'm helping you with Ethan's case?"

She didn't want to spiral down that rabbit hole. It felt like she was standing on the edge of a bottomless pit and Jackson was right there with her.

But the person who wrote that note knew where Jackson lived, and Spencer worried about his younger brothers, and his mom. What if they got caught up in the crossfire?

Spencer held Jackson's hand, finding his skin dry but smooth. His fingers wrapped around hers and a shine in his eyes broke her heart. His shoulders dropped and he hung his head low, but he didn't let go of her hand.

With a sigh, she said, "You need to take a break from this case."

His head snapped up. "What? Spencer, no."

"If you respect me at all, you'll take a step back. It's not worth it for you anymore. There's too much at stake."

"Spencer, I—" He saw the hardness in her eyes, and he clammed up. "Come on, we're a team."

"Ethan was right. I dragged you into this. It's my fault."

"You didn't drag me into anything."

"Okay, then I'm dragging you out."

"Spencer . . ."

"Please. Just for a little while."

Asking this of him looked like she was asking him to saw off his own arm. "I can't let you do this alone."

"I'll be okay." She hated the idea that whoever was writing these notes was getting exactly what they wanted. She was afraid, not only for herself, but now for Jackson, and the threats were working. "I'll be fine."

"Will you?" He looked at her, and she wished he hadn't. But he knew she was too stubborn to admit how she was feeling. She needed to be strong, for his sake.

He let go of her hand and stood. Ripley raised her head, watching him go. She let out a small whine, confused and sad that he was leaving without saying goodbye.

Spencer wanted to call out to him, tell him something that would make everything better, but she didn't. She should have known that it would get messy. Regret made her queasy.

Her phone buzzed in her blazer pocket and, for a hopeful split second, she thought it was a text from Jackson, but her heart lurched when she realized it wasn't a text, but a new email alert.

It was from the Admissions office at Caltech.

She opened her inbox with trembling hands and clicked on the email. She managed to read the first sentence, and then read it again, to make sure she had understood it correctly. Her body went cold the third time she read it. Ripley watched her patiently, sensing something was up.

"I didn't get in," Spencer said. "Look, Rip—it says—'we regret to inform you that we cannot offer you admission at this time.'" She dropped her phone into her lap and held her head in her hands. Ripley nudged her nose under Spencer's armpit, but Spencer refused to budge.

Spencer wanted to put on a brave face, but the well of tears shining in her eyes gave her away. Her voice cracked. "I didn't get into Caltech." She could barely say it, it felt like fiction. "I didn't get in . . ." She held her breath, trying to keep it all down deep, the sob burning hot behind her sternum.

This was her worst nightmare.

She'd been so optimistic and determined, all the essays and interviews, and all those extracurriculars, all that work to get on the lauded Headmaster's List.

And they said no.

She held in the tears so furiously, they burned like fire in her eyes. She didn't want to look any more pathetic than she already felt, didn't want to show how much it hurt.

Spencer heard the door to her bedroom creak open. From the sound of the floorboards, and on account of the fact that Hope usually barreled into her room like a bull charging a red cape, Spencer knew it was her mom. Hope must have told them when they got home what had happened, otherwise Mom wouldn't be walking in like she was there to defuse a bomb.

Spencer had been crying furiously into her pillow for hours, the kinds of sobs that racked her whole body, painfully seizing every muscle with each breath. Ripley had tried lying on top of her, but Spencer still wouldn't stop. Everything was terrible. Nothing was happening the way it was supposed to. Her life was in shambles, and it only now felt real. First field hockey, then Olivia, now college. Hadn't she worked hard enough? Hadn't she done everything everyone had told her to do to be successful? Wasn't this part of the deal: get good grades, get into a good school, start the future out on the right foot?

She felt so stupid for getting her hopes up about getting into Caltech. Of course, even though she had done everything she was supposed to do, it still wasn't enough.

The mattress depressed beside her and her mom lay down next to her, pulling up the comforter around them both. Ripley's hot breath remained on Spencer's back.

"It's okay to cry," her mom said softly. Giving her permission to cry only made it feel like she was a complete loser, which made Spencer cry harder. She went on like that for a long time, until finally there was nothing left, and exhaustion replaced the hollow hole in her chest. Mom let Spencer cry for a long time, until Spencer was sure she'd run out of tears, and it only came out in dry heaves. What had she done wrong? Was she not smart enough? Had she not joined enough clubs? Had she not participated in the right after-school activities? Did she not commit hard enough on the field? Wasn't being at the top of the Headmaster's List worth anything? Why wasn't she good enough?

Her pillow was damp with snot and tears, but she didn't care. All she wanted was to wallow in self-pity and defeat. Her entire future had felt so real and full, like she could hold it in her hands, but in an instant, it crumbled to dust between her fingers and no matter how hard she scrambled to keep hold of it, it blew away into the wind.

"It's not your fault," her mom said, rubbing soothing circles on her back with her palm. "It's not your fault."

Spencer rolled over; her face felt puffy and hot. Ripley

readjusted and hopped down to the floor. The spot where she'd once been felt cold. "You say that, but it is! I'm a failure!"

Her mom shushed her. "That's not true. One rejection doesn't make you a failure."

"Yes, it does!"

"Spencer Rose Sandoval, you stop it right now. You're being too hard on yourself."

"I don't know what else I'm supposed to do!"

"That school puts so much pressure on you kids, honestly . . . Always a competition. The Headmaster's List isn't everything, sweetheart. These parents in LA just think it is."

"I'm never going to be hired by NASA. Who would want me?"

Her mom didn't say anything, just let her cry it out some more. There was no use trying to reason with her. All her pain and regret bubbled up her throat like bile, and the best way to get rid of it was for Spencer to purge. She cried into her pillow a little more before it slipped into silent hiccups.

She must have dozed off, because the next thing she knew, her bed was empty except for Ripley snoring at her feet. Her mom had left some time ago. A plate of home-made fish tacos was waiting for her on her desk, already cold, and she scarfed them down, staring out the darkened window to the street below. Making the Headmaster's List had been a huge waste of time. What was the point any-more? All of it, for nothing.

All she had left was Ethan's case.

* * *

If not for Jackson's text, she might have remained in bed forever. Her phone buzzed, reeling her brain out of a slog of Vicodin-induced haze. She'd stayed up most of the night, feeling sorry for herself and pouring over Ethan's case, reviewing the photos from the crash until she felt like she had gone cross-eyed, before the painkillers started to make her sleepy.

She fumbled on her nightstand for her phone. It was a text from Jackson. Her heart fluttered a little just seeing his name.

Jackson: Thanks for doing all you could.

Spencer sat up to reply, her whole body electrified. *What happened?*

Get Salty: A True Crime Podcast with Peyton Salt

[Intro Music]

Peyton Salt: Before we get into our main story, we've got an update on the Ethan Amoroso trial, Salters. You're going to want to find some place to park, because I know you listeners love to tune in on your commute, and if you're not driving, you're going to want to pop open a bottle of champagne!

Drumroll, please!

On the counts of aggravated reckless driving, child endangerment, and felony manslaughter, Ethan Amoroso has been found . . . Guilty!

[marching band celebratory music playing]

It's been a wild ride, for sure. I have to say, I'm surprised it unfolded the way it did. Usually, people of Ethan's pedigree get a slight slap on the wrist. Maybe from now on we'll be seeing more kids like him get their comeuppance. It only took the court two hours to come to a consensus, and boy, oh, boy, are we glad that they did. Just in time for the holidays!

Obviously our thoughts are with the Moore family, and me and everyone here in the studio hope they feel a sense of justice now that Ethan Amoroso will be facing his punishment. So far, the Moore family fund is over one hundred thousand dollars, thanks to our generous community. There's still some time to buy our merch. All proceeds go toward the Moore family fund, so get yours now before they sell out! And now, a word from our sponsors.

THIRTY-NINE

IT WAS OVER.

All over.

With Jackson gone, Spencer felt like a part of her was missing. He had been a fixture at her side, looking into this case with her, getting deeper into the weeds together. Not having him there to talk things through hurt more than she had realized.

She didn't blame him for his decision. She blamed everyone else for pushing them to their limits.

Detective Potentas, Peyton Salt, even Dr. Diamond for putting so much pressure on them as the best students in school. They all ignored Spencer, made her feel crazy and alone, and maybe, with Jackson now taking a step away from the case, she really was.

Maybe she had truly lost it.

Like most nights, she spent it in her room, looking through every conceivable source of information because it might be the one thing she'd been missing this whole time, and if she could only find it, maybe then she could rest.

But Ethan's case was over. It was all for nothing.

She lost track of how many pills she'd taken during the last few days. It felt like she was taking more and more, just to get by without feeling like her skin was melting off from the pain. She popped one after another, because her whole body ached, probably because she was hunched in her desk chair, her posture turning into an old crone's hunch as she stooped over her laptop, scrolling, scrolling, scrolling. Definitely not taking too many. Definitely not.

She barely focused on her appearance anymore. Usually at school, she'd have her hair up in braids, but these days all she could manage was running her fingers through the tangles and letting her waves hang loose over her shoulders. She didn't even bother with makeup anymore. What was the point? Everyone saw what they wanted to see anyway. She was unraveling at the seams; once having been the chewed-up doll stitched back together, her stuffing was now coming out.

Perfect little Spencer, perfect little mess.

Ripley whined at the door, needing to go out, but Spencer didn't hear her. She'd rung the bell a few times already. Spencer's mind was elsewhere, blankly staring at the screen.

She also didn't hear it when her dad came in, saying her name a few times until he put his hand on her shoulder, making her jump.

"Hey, Ripley needs you," he said.

"Just one more minute," Spencer said, returning to stare at the screen.

"Spencer . . . she needs to go outside. She's your responsibility."

"I said one more minute! God!"

He stood up straighter, shocked at her outburst, but Spencer didn't notice. She was too honed in on the words on the page, even after they'd turned into a blur and she couldn't read them anymore; her focus slipped and she stared at nothing. The search for Ethan's appeal was getting farther away. It barely registered that she didn't sound like herself anymore. Without saying a word, her dad opened the back door for Ripley to go out into the backyard.

Jackson, Olivia, Ripley . . . Background noise. Spencer was on her own. One more pill. Just one more. She didn't want it, but she needed it. Just to get through the day. One more.

Weeks passed in a blur of monotony.

Homework piled up on her desk, forgotten. Messy mountains of trash overflowed on her desk, dirty plates and crumpled-up napkins. Bedsheets kicked to the foot of her bed. Spencer's room had become a sty.

All she could manage to do was sleep. Wake up in the night, crying. Ripley on her chest. Wake up. School. Start over. Numb.

Ethan's case was over.

She'd failed.

In class, Jackson and Olivia noticed how distant she seemed, retreated into herself, consumed whole by echoes of the past, and they shared worried glances. The nightmares didn't stop, the flashbacks during the day made her flinch and ask to be excused from class to walk with Ripley around campus, not caring about anything at all. She needed to move, she couldn't focus, she didn't feel like she was real anymore. Pain was constant.

Nobody understood what she was going through. Nobody could help her.

Scream. Float. Crash.

She was trapped in a time loop, repeating the same terror over and over again, and she just wanted out. She wanted to escape, one more pill, that was all. Then she'd be better. Then she'd be stronger, back in control.

On the periphery, she knew people were talking about her, hiding their words behind their hands, behind closed doors.

What do we do about Spencer?

Spencer hadn't heard Jackson come up behind her. She was at her locker, putting away her books when she felt a presence behind her, aside from Ripley. She whipped around, heart in her throat, and rammed her back up against the locker, making the door slam wider with a horrible clang. Jackson held his hands up, startled, eyes wide. He was in his soccer gear, his duffel over his shoulder, ready for practice.

"Spencer, I—"

"Don't do that!" Just as the words came out, she regretted saying them. She sounded feral, so unlike herself, and she noticed the hurt in his eyes. Her heart felt lodged in her throat and she swallowed it down. "Sorry," she said. Ripley put her nose on Spencer's hand and heat rose in her cheeks.

She hated that for a split second, she thought he'd been the person who had written the threatening notes, coming to fulfill their promise when her back was turned. Paranoia was getting the best of her.

"I called your name," Jackson said. "I thought you were ignoring me."

"I wouldn't ignore you on purpose."

Jackson let out a slow breath, watching her with a line drawn between his brows. "I wanted to check up on you. Since I'm not . . . you know, since you don't want my help anymore."

"It's all under control," she said. "This is for the best."

"Olivia and I have been worried about you."

"I'm fine. You two can rest easy."

Jackson didn't rise to the heat in her tone. She didn't want to snap at him, but she couldn't seem to stop herself. It was like there was a different Spencer controlling her tongue. Jackson, though, didn't take it to heart. He said, "I don't want you to feel alone, so I wondered if you wanted to go get some ice cream with me tonight. No pressure, just ice cream."

The way he looked at her disarmed the acid in her stomach. Something as simple as ice cream wouldn't fix her problems, but it wasn't about ice cream at all. She knew he cared about her, but she couldn't even care about herself. She was a mess, and it was difficult to wade through the wreckage. She had a hard time living with herself, and the ugly part of her had been winning for a long time, pushing everyone away when it was the exact opposite thing she wanted. It would have been easy for the people around her to walk away, leave her to her own destruction, but there Jackson stood.

"That would be nice . . . Yeah," she said. "I'd like that a lot."

"How about eight? Don't be late?"

Spencer managed a smile. "Wouldn't dream of it."

FORTY

THEIR PARENTS HAD A LATE night in the clinic again. A
Pomeranian puppy had gotten into an entire bag of Valentine's Day chocolate and needed an emergency stomach
pump, so that left Spencer and Hope to fend for themselves
on food. Spencer, too tired to make anything and definitely
not in the mood to think about what she was hungry for,
ordered a pizza from Little Italy's Pizzeria, and they ate
their large mushroom and olive pizza on the couch. Spencer's headache had returned, so she sat on the couch with her
icepack hat on and draped her arm over her eyes to cover
the flickering light of the TV as Hope sat curled up in the
reading chair watching another old rerun of *Murder, She
Wrote*. Even Angela Lansbury's delightfully mid-Atlantic
accent wasn't enough to soothe Spencer's throbbing head.

Ripley lay curled up at Spencer's feet, keeping her
warm, and she wiggled her toes appreciatively. Midterms
were coming up at school, some of the last tests Spencer
would ever have to take as a senior, and the pressure was on
to ace them all. Studying all afternoon, now that she didn't
have Ethan's case to worry about or field hockey practice

to attend anymore, was all she did these days. All the stress was what probably triggered her current headache. She knew she needed to rest, even for a little bit, because if she was remotely fatigued, it could be the determining factor between a 100 and a 99 percent, a fraction of a mistake she couldn't afford to make.

"Hey, Hope?" Spencer asked, without removing her arm from her eyes. She knew Hope was still there; she could hear her tapping away on her phone.

"What?"

"Can you do me a favor and grab my pills for me? They're by my bed ..."

Hope sighed but got up anyway and padded to Spencer's room. A minute later, she came back, shaking the pill bottle in Spencer's face. Spencer took it, again without looking, and thanked her.

"Need anything else, m'lady?" Hope asked sarcastically. Spencer could practically hear her rolling her eyes.

"No, I'm fine." She didn't rise to Hope's level, too tired to say anything snarky back, which must have disarmed Hope because Spencer felt the couch compress near her knees as Hope took a seat.

"Jackson hasn't been around lately ... ," she said, trailing off. "Have you two split up?"

"We weren't dating."

"Could have fooled me."

Spencer managed a smile. She finally twisted open the pill bottle and poured a dose into her palm and swallowed it without water, embracing the bitter taste. She hadn't needed to wash down her medicine for a while now.

"Is something the matter?" Hope continued.

"No, everything's fine. We're actually supposed to meet up for ice cream in . . ." She glanced at the clock on the wall, always keeping an eye on the time. "Forty-five minutes."

Hope crawled over Spencer's knees and squeezed herself onto the couch, sandwiched between Ripley and Spencer. Hope always liked to fit herself into tight spaces; it reminded Spencer of a bird in a nest. She felt safer when she was surrounded in warmth.

Hope said, "I think he's nice."

"He is nice. We're just taking it slow, that's all."

"You guys are confusing."

Spencer smiled.

They went quiet again as the episode continued playing. Spencer dozed off a little as the pills took their hold on her. She knew she needed to get up, but she was so tired. She just needed to rest her eyes for a minute.

"Hospitals in TV shows always look so much better than they do in real life," Hope said, referring to the television. She watched as the character Jessica Fletcher bantered with doctors.

"It's like that for most things," Spencer said. "Things are always better on TV. It's all fantasy."

"Yeah, that night in the hospital after the accident . . . Definitely not what they'd put on TV. I was there when you woke up. Mom and Dad didn't want me to see, because you were so out of it; they didn't want to scare me. You were freaking out on the nurses and they had to hold you down. You were screaming at everyone."

Spencer didn't say anything. It sounded like someone possessed, not her.

Hope laughed nervously. "You were shooing everyone out, like they were stray cats who had wandered in. I think you were hallucinating."

Spencer got very still.

Shoo. Shoo . . . , she'd told Detective Potentas when they first met.

"Hope," Spencer said slowly, and Hope looked at her. "What specifically did I say? The exact words?"

"Shoo! Just like Grandma used to shout when she was scaring off the squirrels hanging on to her bird feeder." Hope laughed at the absurdity of it all, but Spencer felt like the world had fallen out from underneath her.

She sat up so quickly, it startled both Ripley and Hope. "Watch it!" she cried, but Spencer was already tearing off her ice pack hat and hurrying to her bedroom.

She didn't bother closing the door behind her as she pulled Ethan's case binder from the drawer in her desk and flipped it open to the police photos of the accident, courtesy of Peyton Salt. Her heart raced as she scanned the pages, her stomach churning in knots, but she found what she was looking for.

She landed on the photo of the driver's side. Anyone looking at it would hardly believe anyone could have made it out of the seat as uninjured as Ethan had. But that wasn't important. She was looking for one thing, and she found it.

There, buried in the depths of the driver's-side footwell, hidden among the debris and chaos, was her missing flat. The sparkly ones she'd been trying to find for months, her favorite pair that she just assumed Hope had borrowed all this time. But the telltale bow lay there in the photo, and the truth buzzed loudly in her head, like a hornet's nest.

She remembered. She remembered everything.

Ethan wasn't guilty.

Because she was.

Spencer was driving the car that night.

FORTY-ONE

SPENCER DIDN'T SCREAM. DIDN'T GASP. Didn't cry. She barely felt real in that moment as she stared at the photograph, everything coming into place in her mind, lining up the facts of that night like puzzle pieces finally nestling into place. It all made sense now. Clarity. Mystery solved.

The proof was right there, staring at her through the debris, looking like the rest of the car, all twisted and bent. But it was unmistakable, evidence that only she would know.

She collapsed onto her bed, eyes squeezed shut, as the memories rushed in.

The party, in full swing by the time she'd arrived. She could smell the smoke from the firepit, hear the band harmonizing, see the familiar faces of her classmates grinning and laughing as the last part of the summer felt it could never end.

A yellow Solo cup full of Diet Coke. She hadn't been drugged at all. *Where's Ethan? Have you seen Ethan?* Brent Lang saying he saw him behind the house. Skateboards in an empty swimming pool. Ethan and Hailey sitting on the edge, making out. Wipe away the evidence. Spencer feeling hollow.

Ethan chasing after Spencer, catching up to her in the

front yard, where kids were gathered around the firepit. He could explain. Yelling, rage making her vision all red, and Ethan saying it was a mistake. Trying to calm her down.

Spencer hated him then. She hated him so much. *Take me home!* She demanded. *I want to leave right now!*

Tabby underneath Chris, who was slobbering all over her, and Tabby asking Ethan, with dazed eyes, *Hey, can we get a ride?*

Sure. He okay?

He'll be fine. Just drunk off his fucking ass. Tabby and Chris piling into the car, asleep immediately. No seatbelt. No one remembered to put it on him.

I'm driving! Spencer had yelled. She was so angry, she wanted to be in control. Didn't want to give him anything. Didn't want to give him the satisfaction.

How much have you had? Ethan asked.

Nothing! She'd shrieked. *I'm fully sober!*

He had the keys in his palm and she snatched them out of his grasp. *Give them to me! I told you, I'm driving!*

Fast. Too fast. She was yelling at Ethan, about how he broke her heart, and how could he do this to her, and her shoe wedged between the floor and the gas pedal. The car roared forward. She got the shoe out, but she still can't stop. Can't brake. She tries. The pedal goes to the floor.

I can't! There's no brakes!

Ethan looking at her. The right side of his face lit up as the headlights reflected back as the tree loomed. That's why her memories were so wrong; the shadows on his face weren't right. Him looking at her now from the passenger's seat, the truth laid bare. But she can't stop. The tree.

SPENCER!

They are going too fast.

No—

Scream.

The car jumping the curb.

Float.

Breaking glass, breaking bones.

Crash.

Pain. Pain. Pain. Pain. Pain. Pain.

Her shoe was pinned underneath the gas pedal, the sparkling rhinestones easily mistaken for broken glass. But it was there. Clear as day. It couldn't have gotten there any other way.

She had been driving the car when it crashed at one hundred twenty miles per hour into a palm tree. It was her fault that Chris had died.

She hadn't been saying "shoo" in the hospital. She'd been saying "shoe."

She had tried to tell them what happened, but she was so drugged out, she wasn't able to articulate. Everyone thought she was in shock; no one listened. Why would they? Ethan had admitted to causing the accident. He'd said he'd been driving. But why?

It didn't matter now.

Her injuries had revealed the same truth. She'd broken her left clavicle—the driver's-side seat belt crossed her chest from left shoulder to right hip. The facts were plain as day on her body, and everyone wanted to ignore it because of Ethan. *Ethan.*

He was going to prison for her. He was protecting her and her perfect future.

She needed to confess.

It was the only thing she could do now.

She grabbed her phone, pulled on a hoodie, and hurried out of the house. Hope asked where she was going as Ripley bounded from the couch and rushed after Spencer. But Spencer didn't answer Hope's question as she hurried to the front yard and got on her bike. Her dad had been able to fix it after it got run over. She needed it now more than ever. She took off down the street, pedaling hard, Ripley galloping after her.

She needed to tell the truth about that night. All of it. And she needed to tell the Moores before it was too late.

FORTY-TWO

IT TOOK RECORD TIME TO reach the Moore house, but Spencer was running on adrenaline and barely out of breath when she dumped her bike on the front lawn and pounded on the door, each knock as frantic and hurried as her racing heartbeat.

She desperately needed to tell the Moores what had happened. They deserved to know first. Once they knew the truth, all of them including Spencer could go to the police and sort everything out. She was the only one responsible for Chris's death, not Ethan, and they could all figure out what to do next. But they needed to know. She knew it would hurt to say it, but it had to happen.

And when the front door of the house opened, it wasn't Mr. or Mrs. Moore who answered, but Nick, Chris's older brother, still home from college.

"Spencer?" he asked, confusion written all over his face.

She barely had time to take a breath as it all came spilling out. "It was me! I did it. It was all my fault. It was me!"

"What? What are you talking about?"

Spencer swallowed, let out a ragged breath, and said,

"Are your parents home? I need to talk to them. It's important."

"No, they're out but . . . what's wrong? What happened? Tell me."

She did. She told him everything, holding nothing back. It flooded out of her, and once she started, she couldn't stop.

"I was the one who crashed. Tabby was trying to get rid of Chris and asked Ethan for a ride, but I was so angry at him that I insisted I drive, so I did it. I started driving, and I was so angry with Ethan, shouting at him, I didn't notice that my shoe got stuck under the gas pedal, the car was so fast. Too fast. I couldn't stop. I—I crashed. I did it. I killed Chris. It was an accident. Ethan is innocent. It was me." She gasped, her breath hitched, and her heart felt like it was going to explode as she watched Nick.

Nick listened patiently as she talked, his face set like stone and his pale skin growing whiter under his freckles. The reality of what happened that night was setting in. Now no one could blame Ethan. It had been Spencer all along. She had tried to do the right thing, tried to get everyone home safely even though she was so furious and had every reason not to. She could have just turned around and told Ethan to figure it out for himself. But she hadn't. She was trying to be a good person, and Chris died because of it.

Nick didn't say anything as he stared at her, frozen, an unreadable look on his face.

"We need to go to the police, tell them the truth," she said. "I need to clear Ethan's name. I need to turn myself in."

He nodded stiffly. "Give me a moment to grab my coat," he said and disappeared into the house.

Spencer paced on the front porch, barely managing to contain her shaking limbs. Ripley watched her from the lawn, head tilted, carefully following her with her eyes. Spencer was amazed she wasn't hysterical by now, but finally telling someone the truth of that night was validation that she wasn't crazy after all. She had been right the whole time. But she never would have thought she had been the one to do it.

It had really been an accident after all. But they pinned it on the wrong person. Spencer needed to see it through to the end this time, for sure.

Nick returned with his coat on and his keys in his hand. "Let's go," he said. "I'll drive you."

Spencer hadn't gotten into a car since her mother drove her home from the hospital. Her stomach nearly dropped to her shoes at the thought of getting inside one again. But Nick opened the back door of the car parked in the driveway and waited for her, allowing Ripley to jump in first.

Fear spiked hot through her bloodstream, making her feel somehow both freezing and boiling hot at the same time, and she took a faltering step back. It felt like an eternity, but it was probably only a couple of seconds to steady her nerves.

She needed to get over her fear. This wasn't about her anymore.

She took a breath, mustered up the courage, and got into the back seat.

Ripley put her head on Spencer's shoulder, doing her best to calm Spencer's nerves, as Nick drove them east toward the police station, but Spencer held tightly onto Ripley's collar and the ceiling handle as if her life depended on it. She didn't want to look too crazy. Nick wouldn't understand what she was going through, and she didn't want to show just how vulnerable she was, reliving the most painful experience of her life over and over again in her head. So she clamped her lips together and closed her eyes.

Ripley's happy panting against her shoulder helped a little bit.

"How are you doing over there?" Nick asked. His green eyes caught the lights from oncoming traffic as he checked the rearview mirror.

"I'm fine," she said. "Just trying not to have a panic attack."

"It'll be over soon. I promise."

She nodded. "I'm sorry it took me so long to remember. I wish I had been able to sooner."

"It's okay. I don't blame you for what happened. I really don't. And I'm not sure you're in your right mind right now," Nick said.

Spencer swallowed; words were difficult now as her throat closed up with the guilt of what she'd done. She put her hand on her forehead and forced herself to breathe. She focused on the interior of the car. It was a classic. Ethan would have liked it, and it smelled like exhaust and polished leather.

Scream. Float. Crash.

Ethan's hands, carrying her out of the car. "Spencer, oh God, Spencer! Not like this. Please, Spencer, wake up." Blood on her face. Ethan blocking out the night, hovering over her, his eyes wide and afraid. Afraid for her. His nose bleeding, he was hurt too, but all he cared about was her.

He'd taken the fall for her. To protect her. Because no matter what, he'd loved her.

Her stomach lurched when Nick took a turn, and she fell forward, almost hitting her nose on the back of the front passenger seat. She stared at the tape deck, a relic, and wondered what kind of car still had a tape deck these days. Her gaze slid over to Nick's grip on the steering wheel, his knuckles pale in the dark. Taking note of her surroundings helped ground her. She just wanted all of this to be over.

"Sorry," she said, gasping. "I still have a fear of driving. I know I'm being ridiculous."

Then she looked at where he was driving. They weren't going to the police station at all.

"Nick—where are we going?"

"I called your mom earlier, when I was getting my stuff. She's meeting me at the hospital. You're hysterical. I told her what you just told me, that you were confessing to a crime. I told her you were having an episode. It's normal for brain trauma victims to be confused."

"What? Nick! No! I'm not confused. I'm totally lucid."

Nick glared at her.

"Why—why are you doing this?" she demanded. "I'm telling the truth!"

"I told you to stop looking into the case, Spencer," he said grimly. "But you just wouldn't listen. I tried to warn you."

The letter in her locker. Somehow he'd gotten the number, probably asked someone who didn't even think twice about it. He might have even gotten it by using his father's login information as a teacher to get into the school's database and look up her profile.

"This doesn't sound like you, Nick," she said. She thought maybe trying to reason with him would get him to let her go. She kept her voice as level as possible. "Come on, let's go to the police and talk all this through—"

"NO!" he screamed. "STOP IT!"

Spencer cringed away from him when she noticed the car's logo on the steering wheel. It was a Dodge. Nick was driving a Dodge Charger. The car that ran her off the road.

"You were the one standing outside my house," she said. She licked her lips; they'd gone desert dry. "You tried running me over! You almost killed me."

"Because you WOULDN'T STOP." He turned around to her and the anguish in his eyes was hard to look at. "They found him guilty! You could have just walked away, let that rich smug asshole kid go to jail! He deserved what he got! Everyone says so! He's a worthless pile of trash! But Spencer Sandoval doesn't know when to quit."

"Why do you hate him so much?" she whispered.

"What do you think? Julianne was my girlfriend. Even if she wakes up, she'll never walk again. Ethan took that all away. Ethan was there when she fell. He didn't do anything. I was there that night, but I was too late. But I saw him. He just stood by and left her lying there, gasping for breath, back broken. It was Ethan's party; it was his fault people were up on the roof, he was always making people do stupid, dangerous things."

Spencer didn't argue with him. She just let him talk. The words spilled out of him like acid, making him sick until it all came out.

"After that, he strutted around the school like it didn't matter. Everyone forgot about Julie. But I didn't. And now Chris, too. He killed my brother. You say you were driving, but I don't believe you. It was Ethan, Ethan has to pay."

"It was me! Chris died because I couldn't stop!"

Nick snarled. "Chris died because of Ethan! Ethan killed him, whether or not he was driving!" It didn't make sense, but there was no reasoning with him. His warped, twisted view of what he'd done was justified in his mind and in the minds of everyone who already assumed Ethan was guilty.

Spencer's heart beat furiously, she couldn't help the anger that had risen in her chest. "Ethan looked after Chris! He saw that he needed help getting home that night. He felt terrible for what happened to Julie and treated Chris like a brother. He cared about him! You didn't see any of that!"

Nick didn't reply, just kept driving.

"You cut the brakes on his car," she said dully.

"Brakes? What are you talking about?"

That was when Spencer realized they were at her parents' animal hospital. Nick hadn't lied. He was taking her to her mom.

Nick's face was pale. "What are you saying?"

"You didn't—you didn't cut the brakes on Ethan's car?" she asked.

"No, why would I do a thing like that?"

"You just don't want me to tell the truth—so that Ethan rots in jail, is that it?" she asked.

"The case is closed, Spencer," Nick said. "Let it go."

Spencer saw her mom walk out to the parking lot. But she couldn't talk to her mom right now. She needed to find someone who would believe her.

FORTY-THREE

JACKSON CHEN'S HOUSE WAS LIKE a French château landed in Bel-Air. When she arrived, it took a while for the butler to bring him down.

"Spencer, what's going on?"

She told him what she remembered about the crash, and that Nick had confessed to stalking her, sending those letters and trying to get her to stop looking into the case. But she remembered everything that happened that night now. It was all coming back to her. She was driving. It was her.

"Does anyone else know what you just told me?" Jackson asked.

"Just Nick, but he doesn't want to believe me. He wants Ethan to pay for what happened to Julie and Chris. I didn't even tell my family where I was going."

"Okay, good. We'll get this sorted out."

Jackson drove, and the two of them sat in silence. Then she realized, like Nick, he wasn't driving to the police station. He was driving somewhere else.

"Um . . . isn't the station that way?"

"No, this is a shortcut." He coughed.

Spencer was so confused. First she remembered the

crash, confessed to Nick, and then Nick confessed to his own actions. And now ... now ... Jackson was acting weird. But he hadn't said anything since they got into the car.

A million thoughts rushed through Spencer's head at once as she tried not to panic.

There had to be an explanation. Jackson couldn't mean to hurt her. She couldn't be getting kidnapped. That wasn't possible.

The rational part of her brain tried to tell her that she was being silly; of course, it had to be some misunderstanding. Maybe this was a shortcut ... Getting kidnapped just didn't happen. Especially by someone she trusted.

Still ... why were they driving so far out of the city? And turning up to the hills?

A small part of her tried to believe it wasn't true. She wasn't even sure it was real. It didn't feel real.

She'd always thought being kidnapped was a lot more dramatic, a furious battle with screaming and kicking and clawing for freedom, and there she was sitting quietly in the passenger's seat, too frightened to move. To an outsider seeing her expression, she might look like she was carsick instead of being taken somewhere against her will.

She reached into the pocket of her hoodie, but just as her fingers wrapped around her phone, something shiny and black flashed in Jackson's other hand as he pulled something out of his pocket.

He leveled a gun at her. She didn't know what it looked like, or what kind it was. Her brain only registered *gun*, and she froze.

"Don't," he said. His voice was low and gravelly. He was not messing around. This was not a joke. This was real. And Spencer was terrified.

Spencer held up her empty hands, heart in her throat. She'd never even seen a gun in real life before, let alone had one pointed at her. She didn't know what else to do. Crying wasn't even an option.

Jackson kept his eyes on the road, driving her God-knew-where, but he didn't put the gun away. Ripley, oblivious to the situation, watched the world go by out the window, leaning with the momentum of the car as Jackson paused at a red light at an intersection.

Spencer had half a thought to jump out of the car and make a run for it. But then she would be leaving Ripley behind, and she couldn't do that.

He must have seen her eyes dart to the door handle because Jackson said, "I wouldn't do that if I were you."

Spencer was so afraid, she couldn't move. All she could focus on was the gun aimed at her. "Are you going to shoot me?"

Jackson didn't reply. The light had turned green, and the car started moving again. No one in any nearby cars, even if they glanced her way, would have seen the gun in Jackson's hand. No one knew where she was. No one knew she had gone to Jackson's house.

No one would know what happened to her. No one would know she'd gotten into his car. No one would know.

She was going to be the next great mystery.

FORTY-FOUR

JACKSON HAD DRIVEN THEM IN silence all the way through the city, until Spencer saw the sign for the canyon up ahead. He'd taken her to Highwood Estates, the neighborhood under construction.

She tried not to panic as he pulled the car down a dirt trail through the woods, darker under tree cover. Her heartbeat was thumping so loudly, she was certain he could hear it, but he didn't say anything to her all the while until he parked in the flat space near the spot where the party had been, the party that started all of this. The houses, unfinished and unused, stood out like bleached skulls in the night.

Jackson turned off the engine but kept the headlights on.

"Get out," he said.

It took Spencer a second to process that he was speaking and did as she was told. The air was crisp and cool, unusual for LA, but she hardly noticed. She fumbled with her phone in her pocket, but it was useless. There was no cell signal out here. She had missed her chance to call for help. She needed to think fast if she wanted to get out of this alive. So she pressed another button on her phone and shoved it into her pocket as Jackson rounded the car, aiming the barrel of the gun at her even when he let Ripley out of the car.

"Sit," he said, pointing to the dirt.

She didn't argue with him, and she sat hard on the ground. Ripley immediately went to her side. She sensed Spencer's panic, and she put her nose under Spencer's armpit, but Spencer didn't move to pet her.

"Why are you doing this?" she asked Jackson. "What's going on?"

"You said you remembered everything from that night," he said.

She blinked. She did remember . . . What was Jackson getting at? Then she remembered. Like a flash. "You were there. The night of the party. I saw you."

"You weren't supposed to see me. I had an alibi."

"You told everyone you were at an overnight soccer camp, but you were there. I saw you by the cars. In a soccer hoodie." The same soccer hoodie that Chris wore. All the soccer guys were so interchangeable in the dark. But she had seen him there. "Why?"

Jackson shrugged.

"He was your best friend."

"I never asked him to be," said Jackson. "But he was just—so insistent. I could have fought off those bullies in sixth grade on my own. But no—he had to. He had to be a hero! And it was always all about him."

He was always faster than me.

He always got what he wanted.

I liked you first.

"But why? Why cut the brakes?"

"I didn't think anyone would get hurt . . . He was always driving too fast, always endangering the lives of anyone else on the road. He never thought about anyone else but himself. He needed to be taught a lesson. I just wanted him to fuck up."

"So you could get his spot on the Headmaster's List. So you could prove you weren't like your family. That you were better." Spencer couldn't believe it. "Your dad . . ."

"Shamed us, no one would talk to us. Especially not the Moores, and Ethan, oh, it was just another of his hero moments to stand up to everyone and befriend a guy like me."

"But Ethan wasn't driving. It was me."

Jackson actually smiled, but it was distorted and strained, robotic. "I admit, I didn't expect you would be behind the wheel."

"Didn't you care about us crashing into anyone on the road?"

Jackson shrugged.

He didn't care. He had pretended to help her, so he could keep an eye on her. Because she was the only one who knew the truth.

Resentment was a disease. That's all it was. Everything that had happened these past few months was because of pure resentment. So many people got hurt to get it. It was so simple, and it left destruction in its wake. She felt sorry for him, even though he was aiming a gun at her. He was hurting, but he was dangerous. His eyes were cold. Spencer tried to talk to the Jackson she had known these past few months.

"You wouldn't do this. You're not a killer."

"Yes, I am," Jackson said with a laugh. It was high-pitched, unhinged. "I already killed Chris, didn't I? What's one more?" He tightened his grip on the gun.

He was going to kill her.

FORTY-FIVE

SPENCER'S BODY WENT COLD. SHE held out her hands, the only thing she could do.

"Don't, Jackson."

She waited for the gunshot, but it never came. Jackson looked at her, his face screwed up like a demented mask, and Spencer wondered if he saw the girl he'd been spending all this time with, unarmed and defenseless in the dirt with her service dog pathetically trying to get her attention. She needed more time, she needed to get him talking.

"We can figure this out," she said. "We can get you some help. It'll be okay."

"SHUT UP," he screamed. Spencer's eyes never left the gun. She stared down the barrel. How a person could get this deep in their own grief, she understood too well. But to do something like this . . . Her heart pounded in her throat.

"I get it, Jackson. I do. But let's just take a breath—"

"It's too late, you always tell the truth, you'll tell them," he said, cutting her off. He adjusted his weight, shifting on his feet, antsy, and Spencer worried he'd squeeze too tightly and shoot. "But it doesn't have to hurt. We can make this painless." He licked his lips, his eyes dancing wildly. "I know you're taking medicine for your pain. Finish your whole bottle right now. It'll be just like falling asleep."

It would look like a suicide.

Someone would notice—her parents, Hope, Olivia—that Spencer was missing and call the police. Maybe it would take a few days, maybe more, but they'd find her body, sitting beneath the spindly tree, Ripley curled by her side, refusing to leave her alone. It would look like an accident, just like the crash. They'd have a funeral for her, with the same flowers they used at Chris's ceremony, pose her to look like she was sleeping in her casket, peaceful. Ripley'd refuse to leave her casket, choosing to stay curled up on the floor, perhaps hoping that she might wake up. People might say a few nice words about her, maybe shed a few tears, assume that she couldn't take the guilt of the crash any longer. Maybe it would come out that she was really the one behind the wheel, maybe someone would figure it out, maybe not. No one would look into her death. No one would have any reason to.

Tears burned the edges of her eyes. Instead of getting scared, she got mad. What Jackson wanted her to do made her insides turn to fire. When she got mad, it consumed her.

She stood up, hands clenched into fists at her side.

"Sit down," Jackson said, pointing the gun in the direction he wanted her to go.

"No." She lifted her chin defiantly.

Jackson worked his jaw back and forth, annoyed, as if

she was the one inconveniencing him. His finger twitched on the trigger. One small move, and it'd be over for her. But she was so angry, she didn't care. She almost wanted him to shoot her, because then there'd be an investigation and the truth would come out.

"You don't want to do this, Jackson," she said. She took a step closer. He took a step back.

"What are you doing? Stay where you are." He was the one who sounded scared now.

Anger had overridden her fear. She raised her voice. "You don't want to hurt me, Jackson. We're friends!" *I was falling in love with you* . . .

"No! You don't get it. My family's gone through enough."

"I get it. If something happened to my sister, God, I don't know what I would do. But if you kill me, you'll be ruining her life too, just like what happened to you. Do you want anyone else to feel that way?" Thinking of Hope made her voice quake, but she couldn't explode. Not yet.

Jackson's hand shook, but he braced himself with two hands on the gun. She took another step forward. She was not going to let him get away with another death.

"Shut up," he said. His lips pulled back into a snarl.

"You don't want to do this. There's another way. You can get help."

"No one can help me."

"Yes, they can. You just need to lower the gun . . ." He lifted it higher, pointed it at her face. She flinched. Would she even have time to realize he had pulled the trigger?

Jackson was beyond talking to, but she had to try.

Ripley put herself between Jackson and Spencer, shielding Spencer as best she could. She didn't know what was going on, but she knew something was wrong.

Ripley was trying so hard to help. That was all she ever tried to do. Spencer couldn't imagine her life without her. It was hard to believe she had been so hardheaded at first to think she could do anything without her help.

If anything happened to Ripley . . .

"Please," Spencer said, looking at Jackson as her voice cracked. "Don't hurt my dog."

She didn't realize what she was planning to do until she was already doing it.

When Jackson's eyes moved to Ripley, that's when Spencer tackled him. Head down, she dived straight for his chest, wrapping her arms around his body and knocking them both to the ground. No thoughts, pure adrenaline. The wind got knocked out of her lungs when she hit the dirt, but she fought through it. Jackson was taller, and stronger, but Spencer was not going down without a fight.

She grabbed for the gun, but he batted her away, writhing. They fought, kicking up a cloud of dust, but Spencer didn't give up.

Lights burst in her vision as something smashed over her head, the butt of the gun hitting her skull with a tremendous *CRACK*, and the world tipped sideways. Something warm trickled down the side of her head but Spencer was too stunned to do anything else.

Jackson let out an earsplitting scream as Ripley bit down hard on his arm holding the gun, her teeth breaking through the skin. The sound of fabric tearing, Jackson's cries, and Ripley's growls as she dragged Jackson away from Spencer.

Ripley shook her head furiously, not letting go, even though Jackson hit her repeatedly in the face, trying to get her to break free. Spencer tasted dirt and blood, and tried to get up, but her limbs weren't working.

Ripley was trying to save her.

She let out a yelp as Jackson hit her one more time, and the next moment Jackson was running away back to his car. The engine roared and dirt kicked up over Spencer. She tried to move, but it felt like her arms were made of lead. Something wet and warm dripped over her eyes, blinding her.

Ripley barked furiously at the car, each sound cutting through Spencer's head like a hammer on a gong.

As the car disappeared down the dirt road, Spencer puked, the world still spinning. Ripley came to Spencer's side, nuzzling up against her.

Jackson had gotten away.

But Spencer wasn't done.

She slipped her hand into her hoodie pocket and checked the screen of her phone. The audio recorder app was still going, and she ended it with a tap. Blood from her fingers streaked across the screen. She had captured Jackson's whole confession on audio, but the world was going dark.

She couldn't send the file to anyone. She still had no

signal. All she could do was lie on her back, feel the tickle of blood pooling under her head, and stare at the stars. They arced across the sky, like a long-exposure photo, getting bigger and bigger, swallowing her whole. She was floating, spinning in space, away, away. Spencer was going to throw up again.

Ripley whined, nudging Spencer's face with her wet nose, but Spencer was losing the fight against unconsciousness. Her head felt like it'd been cleaved in two.

The world became less and less real, the ground falling away from her as she ascended into the warm abyss of nothingness.

The last thing Spencer saw before the world slipped away was the blinking green light on Ripley's collar.

FORTY-SIX

A VOICE.

Spencer!

Spencer!

Oh God, Spencer, please!

Olivia's face appeared above her, blocking out the stars. Spencer wanted to stay awake, to say goodbye, but it was getting harder. Lead weights were pulling her eyelids shut.

She's over here! she called to someone behind them. A girl's voice called back.

Hope? Spencer wasn't sure she said it out loud.

Red and blue lights illuminating her face. Sirens in the distance.

Tires crunching on the dirt. Barking incessantly. Ripley.

Spencer, I'm here. It's okay. Olivia's face took up her entire vision.

Then darkness took over.

FORTY-SEVEN

HEAVEN SOUNDED AN AWFUL LOT like a hospital room.

Spencer heard the steady beep of a morphine drip machine, the distant murmur of doctors talking in the hallway, a TV soap opera with volume set to low.

Opening her eyes was a chore, but she managed to do it.

She was indeed in a hospital room, very much not in heaven. The dull reminder of a throbbing headache made sure of that. The bandage around her head was proof that she lived.

"Dang! She lives!" Olivia stood frozen in the doorway, her eyes shining with silver tears.

Spencer immediately started crying with joy. She couldn't help it. She had missed her best friend so much; it hurt deeper than discovering Jackson had been playing her for a fool all along.

Olivia ran at Spencer and threw herself on the hospital bed, holding her so tightly it snatched the breath from her lungs. But Spencer didn't care. She just wanted Olivia back.

"I'm so sorry," Spencer cried through her tears. "For everything. For not being there. For all of it."

"I know, I know!" Olivia sobbed.

They held each other for a long time, crying and saying how sorry they were to each other, like broken records. But Spencer felt like she could give herself back to Olivia, who hadn't deserved everything that had happened between them. Spencer had been a terrible friend, but Olivia would forgive her.

"How did I . . . ?" She wanted to gesture to the room, but her arms felt too heavy. "What happened? How did you guys find me?"

"Hope. It was all Hope. She had your mom call Nick, who told us you'd run off, and when you weren't answering your phone, they activated the GPS in Ripley's collar."

Ripley, the best girl, lay curled on a cracked leather arm-chair in the corner of the room, peacefully asleep. If it wasn't for her, Spencer wouldn't be here now.

"It was Jackson. Jackson Chen. He was there the night of the party. He cut the brakes in Ethan's car."

Olivia looked pale but nodded. "I know. The recording was on your phone. Your parents gave it to the cops. Hope you didn't mind. How did you solve it?"

Spencer didn't hold anything back as she explained everything leading up to her kidnapping, how it was really she who had been driving and how Ethan had covered for her, how she'd seen the proof in the police photos, how Nick had wanted her to stay silent, and how Jackson had let a toxic resentment build to murder.

"Ethan's innocent," she said. And so was she. She had been driving, but she hadn't caused this.

Jackson had cut the brakes.

Olivia let Spencer's parents into the room, and Hope followed but immediately went to Ripley's chair to give her a good smooch on the head.

Spencer allowed them to fuss over her, she was so relieved to see them. To think she might not have ever held them again was unbearable. They freaked out, rightfully so, about what had happened, but Spencer didn't care. She was just happy to see their faces again.

***Get Salty*: A True Crime Podcast with Peyton Salt**

[Intro Music]

Peyton Salt: I'm not sure what else I can say, Salters . . . But I'll try! In a twist of fate, we have an update on the absolute last case that I thought I'd be covering today. The one and only case of Ethan Amoroso, a fan favorite.

Turns out, there's been some new information that sheds some light on his case that may overturn his conviction in a new trial.

Thanks to the tireless efforts of Spencer Sandoval, it was uncovered that Jackson Chen was the one behind the tragedy. Early this morning, as I was recording this episode, police caught Jackson Chen trying to cross county lines. Ethan Amoroso may be innocent in all of this, after all. I am one to admit that sometimes I get it wrong, and this time, folks, I was very wrong. The details are hazy for me now as I'm waiting on my sources to confirm, but what I gather is that Spencer Sandoval uncovered the truth not long before being kidnapped and attacked by Jackson Chen to cover up his crimes. Needless to say, this case has worked its way into being one of the most compelling stories we've covered on this show. We've seen a lot of criminals get put away for less, so we can expect Jackson Chen's journey to be a long but certain one behind bars. Like father, like son!

FORTY-EIGHT

ONCE SPENCER MADE A FAST recovery after a few days, suffering only a minor head wound that needed stitches, she was transferred to the rehabilitation wing. Doctors said she had been taking too much Vicodin, and they needed to monitor her as she cut back on her doses. They didn't say the word *rehab* lightly.

Everyone in school knew what had happened. Word spread fast. Both amateur and professional news outlets ran the story about Spencer's confrontation with Jackson Chen. Detective Potentas reinterviewed Ethan and he admitted that he lied about who was driving that night. He wanted to protect Spencer, so he took the fall after pulling her out of the car. A judge was going to review his sentence. He wasn't going to get away scot-free—he did lie to police, after all—but now that Spencer's testimony broke the case wide open, Ethan would likely be free in a few weeks. Chris's death could finally be solved.

One bright day, Ethan called her from home. He still wasn't allowed to leave his house until everything was sorted out, but it was nice hearing his voice after everything. She sat at the window on one of the two lounge chairs in her room, looking out across the hospital's quad, picturing him standing there just like old times out her bedroom window. Her heart galloped hearing his voice. The first words that came out of his mouth were "Thank you."

Heat rushed to her face. "You were willing to go to jail for me?"

"Yeah, well . . . It would have been worth it. People say I do stupid things all the time."

"Maybe you should stop being stupid, then."

He laughed easily, and she couldn't help but smile, too.

"All this time, I thought I was protecting you," he said. "But turns out you were protecting me. You never gave up. Think we can start over? Think we can try again—being us?"

She knew what he meant. Starting their relationship anew, with everything they'd done for each other, felt like a fantasy. And she wasn't sure if it was even possible. He'd still broken her heart. She wasn't sure she could ever recover from that. "Us? I think I need some time being me again." Without all the painkillers, she was starting to remember what that felt like. She read tons of books, and studied, and journaled under the careful eye of nurses and doctors, but she was feeling better already. Just like her old self: different, but better. "I'd like it if we can start over being friends," she added.

She could almost hear his smile. "Yeah. Friends."

"Congrats on CAL," he said. "I know it's not CalTech, but CAL's a great school."

"I think that's a double congrats, isn't it?" She smiled, because she knew Ethan had gotten in, too.

She'd gotten the acceptance letter at her second-choice school while she was in the hospital. It was close to home and had a great astrophysics department.

"I hear you and Hailey broke up," she said.

"Yeah," he said.

"I'm glad. You deserve better," Spencer told him, and meant it. "Take care of yourself, okay?"

"You first." Typical Ethan.

She hung up, still smiling as Olivia laid out a stack of papers on the table near the window.

"All good?" she asked.

"All good."

Ripley looked up at Olivia from her spot next to Spencer's chair. Spencer's trauma from the accident on top of what happened in the Highwood Estates wasn't going to fade anytime soon, and Ripley was fulfilling her duties most admirably. She was truly the best partner anyone could ask for.

"So . . ." Olivia said, staring at all their papers stretched out on the table, grinning despite the sheer amount of it all. They used to do this together all the time. She'd missed that.

"So," Spencer said, eyes shining bright with the prospect of homework. "Let's get started."

ACKNOWLEDGMENTS

HUGE THANKS ALWAYS TO MY amazing team at Macmillan: my incredible editor, Kate Meltzer; my fabulous publisher, Jennifer Besser; and everyone who made this book shine. Thank you to my agents, Richard Abate and Ellen Goldsmith-Vein. Thank you to my awesome beta readers for such helpful feedback. Thank you to my friends and family. Thank you to my loyal readers. Thank you to Mike and Mattie always, top of my list in every book.

A TREASURY OF
Sea
Stories

A TREASURY OF
Sea Stories

Compiled by

GORDON C. AYMAR

Illustrated by

ROCKWELL KENT

A. S. BARNES & COMPANY

NEW YORK

8310
Manufactured in the United States of America

To My Wife, PEGGY AYMAR

ACKNOWLEDGMENTS

The editor is indebted to the following people for suggestions of sources of material or for confirmation in selections already made: Theodore Bolton, Librarian of the Century Association; Urana Clarke; Linton and Theodora Foster; Frederick Gade; Elinor Hughes, Librarian of the Darien Library, Darien, Connecticut; John Jamison; Frank Jones; Rockwell Kent; Wallace N. Long, Curator of the Nantucket Whaling Museum, Nantucket, Mass.; Alfred Loomis; Wirt M. Mitchell; J. Lowell Pratt; Lorimer Slocum; Edward Stackpole; Alfred Stanford; William H. Tripp, Curator of the Old Dartmouth Historical Society and Whaling Museum of New Bedford, Mass.; and Richmond Weed.

The editor also wishes to acknowledge the constructive criticism he has received from his entire family, parents, children and sons-in-law, in that fine, free-swinging style which is the prerogative as well as the duty of families. But above all, the editor wishes to thank his wife, Peggy Aymar, for the genuine service she performed in reading the vast amount of literature which was a necessary preliminary to making the final selections.

By great good fortune, this book is being illustrated by Rockwell Kent, who brings not only great distinction to its physical appearance, but has himself experienced the sea under difficult circumstances in small boats and thus adds a genuinely salty flavor to the whole enterprise.

Noroton, Connecticut

CONTENTS

Contents

INTRODUCTION

The origin of the sea is shrouded in the mists of antiquity. Quite literally so, if we are to believe the theory that it sprang from the condensation of global clouds which are presumed to have hung above the gradually cooling molten mass called Earth.

Whatever its origin, the sea has today arrived at a point in its development where it can be measured with a practical degree of accuracy. Its boundaries have been traced, its currents plotted, its depth sounded, its salinity calculated. It is common knowledge that almost three quarters of the Earth's surface is immersed in water and that if all the continents with their towering mountain ranges were hurled into the sea they would disappear beneath an average depth of two miles of water.

But this is not what concerns the seafaring man. It is his own personal relationship to it. The sea is an alien element. If he falls into it, it will uphold him only so long as there is air in his lungs and strength in his limbs. If it wets him in winter, he freezes; if it wets him in summer and the wind blows, he is cold. If fog collects over it, he is lost. If it penetrates his ship, he is drowned. If the wind blows hard enough, it ceases to be the highway which is its greatest use to man. Those who give their lives to it are separated from the rest of mankind for long periods and if they die and are buried at sea, they go to rest in an unmarked spot enveloped in all that primitive instincts recoil from—the cold, the wet, the dark, the solitary. It is, therefore, little wonder that the literature of the sea concerns itself to a large extent with its grim aspects.

There is, however, the other side of the picture. There are the respites between storms when the wind has abated and there comes a sense of relief and well-being which is all the more poignant by contrast.

There are rewards in the solitude that comes with life at sea. It is difficult for those who live and work in cities to remember what healing there is in being alone in an immensity of surrounding space. Those who operated Aircraft Warning Stations in the suburbs during the war experienced an odd phenomenon. Instead of it being difficult to fill the night watches with those who had worked all day in the city, it was a relatively easy matter. For not only did the watchers have a feeling of contributing their share to the work, but there was a definite answering of a deep human need in standing watch with a congenial companion in the silence and the peace of night with the sky as the only focus of interest.

Again, there is a common bond between shipmates which is duplicated in few other places. What happens to the ship is of paramount concern to all aboard and as such cuts through the disparities of caste, character and personal idiosyncrasy.

For those who live and work ashore there is an appalling monotony which is startling when looked at in retrospect. But with the life of ships, there is a voyage to be planned, begun, experienced and ended.

In spite of all that is forbidding about the sea, the love of it and longing for it run deep. This is not a pose. It is a fact. A friend of mine told me that in his younger days he was forced by circumstances beyond his control to live for a period of four years far from any water. At last, one fine summer day, he returned to Cape Cod. On his first night home he dined with a friend whose house was situated near the water. At sight of it, he obeyed an irresistible impulse. He ran straight into it until he was completely submerged. He had not had a drink. He was, and is, a stable, conservative New Englander. He admitted the act with confusion, being unable to explain the power that motivated him.

The Navy can tell you something about the strong influence that the sea exerts. It is true that re-enlistments in normal times may be due in large measure to a man's feeling so out of step with life ashore that he gravitates back to that way of life with which he is familiar. Nevertheless, part of the reason for his return, and a part he would be the last to admit, is the elemental fascination of a life of adventure on an unpredictable element.

The stories which follow run the gamut of man's activity upon the sea—his explorations, battles, mutinies, shipwrecks, rescues, his efforts at survival when adrift, his struggle for trade, and even his racing and cruising for pleasure. They were chosen because they are authentic—a valid reflection of life at sea untarnished by sentimentality. Those who have been to sea will not tolerate the fake or the sham. If the tale is true, they respect it. If it is an invention, it must carry the stamp of truth gained from experience.

In one respect the lot of an editor is not a happy one. He reads and enjoys and wants all to enjoy with him the full measure of what he reads. Yet what is a fragment of Moby Dick? One piece of scrimshaw in a whaling museum. And how can the sustained and carefully planned blocking of Zeebrugge be more than hinted at in one chapter from the book? How can the protracted agony of hunger and thirst on a ditched plane's raft be understood when days and weeks of it are omitted? It is hoped that the reader of these excerpts will be moved to read the entire books from which they have come.

The selections have been arranged roughly in chronological order, beginning with the tales of today and reaching back into antiquity, allowing a certain latitude for stories not specifically dated. This has seemed the simplest solution and one which, it is hoped, implies the timelessness of the struggle with the sea. The wind blew with the same strength upon Columbus' little flotilla as it roars into a carefully plotted "low" on a weather chart today. The water was just as wet, the sea as deep, and the sky as high.

When Fred Fenger in 1911 sailed his canoe past Les Saintes in the Caribbean, he experienced the same freshening of the trades at a certain hour in the day, that enabled Rodney at that same spot and the same hour to break through the French fleet under De Grasse in 1782.

The sea was just as salty and undrinkable when Lieutenant Bligh made his trip of over three thousand miles in an open boat as when Bomber Pilot Dixon crossed a thousand miles of water in the same ocean on a rubber raft a century and a half later.

Those particular parts of the books have been chosen which add to a seaman's understanding and experience of the sea. For example, anyone who has been to sea has probably rehearsed to himself as he lay in his bunk what motions he would go through in abandoning ship. The passages from the Bird of Dawning and Gallions Reach recount two such experiences. If he has been in the Navy he is curious about the fighters of other times. Hornblower and Nelson and Carpenter are here for him to call on. He has imagined himself rescuing others from drowning. Commander Ellsberg tells in his own words how it was done. He is eager to know how others handle boats in emergencies so that he may not fail when the need arises. He reads Captain Slocum's adventures in a small sloop and how Alfred Loomis' skipper in a racing schooner takes aboard survivors from a wreck in a heavy sea.

These are the things that matter to men—how to do things, how to measure up.

⚓

THE LANDING ON KURALEI

⚓

THE LANDING ON KURALEI

James A. Michener

⚓ *It may seem odd to begin a collection of sea stories with one which deals so largely with a land action, but that is one of those straws in the wind which has more than a passing significance. From time immemorial, one of the main functions of a navy has been the delivery of troops to attack and hold territory. After centuries of great tribulation in which it was almost axiomatic that a ship could not shoot it out with land fortifications, along comes the air arm and helps make such action possible.*

The following story, however, needs no justification. It can stand by itself. It rings true. It has that unmistakable imprint of authenticity. Mitchener has earned his Pulitzer prize.

WE WOULD have captured Kuralei according to plan if it had not been for Lt. Col. Kenjuro Hyaichi. An honor graduate from California Tech, he was a likely choice for the job the Japs gave him.

As soon as our bombers started to soften up Konora, where we built the airstrip, the Jap commander on Kuralei gave Hyaichi his instructions: "Imagine that you are an American admiral. You are going to invade this island. What would you do?"

Hyaichi climbed into a plane and had the pilot take him up 12,000 feet. Below him Kuralei was like a big cashew nut. The inside bend faced north, and in its arms were two fine sandy bays. They were the likely places to land. You could see that even from the air.

But there was a small promontory protruding due south from the outside bend. From the air Hyaichi studied that promontory with great care.

3

"Maybe they know we have the two bays fortified. Maybe they will try that promontory."

The colonel had his pilot drop to three thousand feet and then to five hundred. He flew far out to sea in the direction from which our search planes came. He roared in six times to see if he could see what an American pilot, scared and in a hurry, would think he saw.

Then he studied the island from a small boat. Had it photographed from all altitudes and angles. He studied the photographs for many days. He had two Jap spies shipped in one night from Truk. They crept ashore at various points. "What did you see?" he asked them. "Did you think the bay was defended? What about that promontory?"

He had two trained observers flown over from Palau. They had never seen Kuralei before. When their plane started to descend, they were blindfolded. "The bays?" Hyaichi asked. "And that promontory? Did you think there was sand in the two small beaches there? Did you see the cliffs?"

Jap intelligence officers brought the colonel sixty-page and seventy-page reports of interrogations of American prisoners. They showed him detailed studies of every American landing from Guadalcanal to Konora. They had a complete book on Admiral Kester, an analysis of each action the admiral had ever commanded. At the end of his study Lt. Col. Hyaichi ruled out the possibility of our landing at the promontory. "It couldn't be done," he said. "That coral shelf sticking out two hundred yards would stop anything they have."

But before the colonel submitted his recommendation that all available Jap power be concentrated at the northern bays, a workman in Detroit had a beer. After his beer this workman talked with a shoe salesman from St. Louis, who told a brother-in-law, who passed the word on to a man heading for Texas, where the news was relayed to Mexico and thence to Tokyo and Kuralei that "General Motors is building a boat that can climb over the damnedest stuff you ever saw."

Lt. Col. Hyaichi tore up his notes. He told his superiors: "The Americans will land on either side of the promontory." "How can they?" he was asked. "They have new weapons," he replied. "Amphibious tanks with treads for crossing coral." Almost a year before, Admiral Nimitz had decided that when we hit Kuralei we would not land at the two bays. "We will hit the promontory. We will surprise them."

Fortunately for us, Lt. Col. Hyaichi's superiors were able to ignore his conclusions. It would be folly, they said, to move defenses from the natural northern landing spots. All they would agree to was that Hyaichi might take whatever material he could find and set up secondary defenses at the promontory. How well he did his job you will see

At 0527 our first amphibs hit the coral shelf which protruded under water from the shore. It was high tide, and they half rode, half crawled toward land. They had reached a point twenty feet from the beach, when all hell ripped loose. Lt. Col. Hyaichi's fixed guns blasted our amphibs right out of the water. Our men died in the air before they fell back into the shallow water on the coral shelf. At low tide their bodies would be found, gently wallowing in still pools of water. A few men reached shore. They walked the last twenty feet through a haze of bullets.

At 0536 our second wave reached the imaginary line twenty feet from shore. The Jap five-inch guns ripped loose. Of nine craft going in, five were sunk. Of the three hundred men in those five amphibs, more than one hundred were killed outright. Another hundred died wading to shore. But some reached shore. They formed a company, the first on Kuralei.

It was now dawn. The LCS-108 had nosed in toward the coral reef to report the landings. We sent word to the flagship. Admiral Kester started to sweat at his wrists. "Call off all landing attempts for eighteen minutes," he said.

At 0544 our ships laid down a gigantic barrage. How had they missed those five-inch guns before? How had anything lived through our previous bombardment? Many Japs didn't. But those hiding in Lt. Col. Hyaichi's special pillboxes did. And they lived through this bombardment, too.

On the small beach to the west of the promontory 118 men huddled together as the shells ripped overhead. Our code for this beach was Green, for the one to the east, Red. The lone walkie-talkie on Green Beach got the orders: "Wait till the bombardment ends. Proceed to the first line of coconut trees." Before the signalman could answer, one of our short shells landed among the men. The survivors re-formed, but they had no walkie-talkie.

At 0602 the third wave of amphibs set out for the beach. The vast bombardment rode over their heads until they were onto the coral shelf. Then a shattering silence followed. It was full morning. The sun was rising. Our amphibs waddled over the coral. At the fatal twenty-foot line some Japs opened up on the amphibs. Three were destroyed. But eight got through and deposited their men ashore. Jap machine gunners and snipers tied into tall trees took a heavy toll. But our men formed and set out for the first line of coconut trees.

They were halfway to the jagged stumps when the Japs opened fire from carefully dug trenches behind the trees. Our men tried to outfight the bullets but could not. They retreated to the beach. The coconut grove was lined with fixed positions, a trench behind each row of trees.

As our men withdrew they watched a hapless amphib broach to on the coral. It hung suspended, turning slowly. A Jap shell hit it full in the middle. It rose in the air. Bodies danced violently against the rising sun

5

and fell back dead upon the coral. "Them poor guys," the Marines on the beach said.

At 0631 American planes appeared. F6F's. They strafed the first trench until no man but a Jap could live. They bombed. They ripped Green Beach for twelve minutes. Then the next wave of amphibs went in. The first two craft broached to and were blown to shreds of steaming metal. "How can those Japs live?" the man at my side said. In the next wave four more amphibs were sunk.

So at 0710 the big ships opened up again. They fired for twenty-eight minutes this time, concentrating their shells about sixty yards inland from the first row of coconut stumps. When they stopped, our men tried again. This time they reached the trees, but were again repulsed. Almost four hundred men were ashore now. They formed in tight circles along the edge of the beach.

At 0748 we heard the news from Red Beach, on the other side of the promontory. "Repulsed four times. First men now safely ashore!" Four times! we said to ourselves. Why, that's worse than here! It couldn't be! Yet it was, and when the tide started going out on Red Beach, the Japs pushed our men back onto the coral.

This was fantastic! When you looked at Alligator back in Noumea you knew it was going to be tough. But not like this! There were nine rows of coconut trees. Then a cacao grove. The edge of that grove was Line Albany. We had to reach the cacao by night. We knew that an immense blockhouse of sod and stone and concrete and coconut trees would have to be reduced there before night. We were expected to start storming the blockhouse by 1045. That was the schedule.

At 1400 our men were still huddled on the beach. Kester would not withdraw them. I don't think they would have come back had he ordered them to do so. They hung on, tried to cut westward but were stopped by the cliffs, tried to cut eastward but were stopped by fixed guns on the promontory.

At 1422 Admiral Kester put into operation his alternative plan. While slim beachheads were maintained at Red and Green all available shock troops were ordered to hit the rugged western side of the promontory. We did not know if landing craft could get ashore. All we knew was that if they could land, and if they could establish a beach, and if they could cut a path for men and tanks down through the promontory, we might flank each of the present beachheads and have a chance of reaching the cacaos by dark.

At 1425 we got our orders. "LCS-108. All hands to Objective 66." The men winked at one another. They climbed into the landing barges. The man whose wife had a baby girl. The young boy who slept through his leave in Frisco. They went into the barges. The sun was starting to sink westward as they set out for shore.

Lt. Col. Hyaichi's men waited. Then two fixed guns whose sole purpose was to wait for such a landing fired. Shells ripped through the barges. One with men from 108 turned in the air and crushed its men to death. They flung their arms outward and tried to fly free, but the barge caught them all. A few swam out from under. They could not touch bottom, so they swam for the shore, as they had been trained to do. Snipers shot at them. Of the few, a few reached shore. One man shook himself like a dog and started into the jungle. Another made it and cried out to a friend. "Red Beach! Green Beach! Sonova Beach!" You can see that in the official reports. "At 1430 elements from LCS-108 and the transport *Julius Kennedy* started operations at Sonova Beach."

The hidden guns on the promontory continued firing. Kester sent eight F6F's after them. They dived the emplacements and silenced one of the guns. I remember one F6F that seemed to hang for minutes over a Jap gun, pouring lead. It was uncanny. Then the plane exploded! It burst into a violent puff of red and black. Its pieces were strewn over a wide area, but they hurt no one. They were too small.

At 1448 a rear-admiral reported to Kester, "Men securely ashore at Objective 66." The admiral diverted all available barges there. Sonova Beach was invaded. We lost three hundred men there, but it was invaded. Barges and men turned in the air and died alike with hot steel in their guts, but the promontory was invaded. Not all our planes nor all our ships could silence those damned Jap gunners, but Sonova Beach, that strip of bleeding coral, it was invaded.

At 1502 Admiral Kester sent four tanks ashore at Sonova with orders to penetrate the promontory and to support whichever beach seemed most promising. Two hundred men went along with axes and shovels. I watched the lumbering tanks crawl ashore and hit their first banyan trees. There was a crunching sound. I could hear it above the battle. The tanks disappeared among the trees.

At 1514 came the Jap's only airborne attack that day. About thirty bombers accompanied by forty fighters swept in from Truk. They tried for our heavy ships. The fleet threw up a wilderness of flak. Every ship in the task force opened up with its five-inchers, Bofors, Oerlikons, three-inchers and .50 calibers. The air was heavy with lead. Some Jap planes spun into the sea. I watched a bomber spouting flames along her port wing. She dived to put them out. But a second shell hit her amidships. The plane exploded and fell into the ocean in four pieces. The engine, badly afire, hit the water at an angle and ricocheted five times before it sank in hissing rage.

One of our transports was destroyed by a Jap bomb. It burst into lurid flame as it went down. Near by, a Jap plane plunged into the sea. Then, far aloft an F6F came screaming down in a mortal dive. "Jump!" a thousand voices urged. But the pilot never did. The plane crashed into the sea right behind the Jap bomber and burned.

A Jap fighter, driven low, dived at the 108 and began to strafe. I heard dull spats of lead, the firing of our own guns, and a cry. The Jap flashed past, unscathed. Men on the 108 cursed. The young skipper looked ashen with rage and hurried aft to see who had been hit.

The Japs were being driven off. As a last gesture a fighter dived into the bridge of one of our destroyers. There were four explosions. The superstructure was blown away with three dozen men and four officers. Two other fighters tried the same trick. One zoomed over the deck of a cruiser and bounced three times into a boiling sea. The other came down in a screaming vertical spin and crashed deep into the water not far from where I stood. There were underwater explosions and a violent geyser spurting high in the air.

Our planes harried the remaining Japs to death, far out at sea. Our pilots, their fuel exhausted, went into the sea themselves. Some died horribly of thirst, days later. Others were picked up almost immediately and had chicken for dinner.

While the Jap suicide planes were crashing into the midst of the fleet, a Jap shore battery opened up and hit an ammunition ship. It disintegrated in a terrible, gasping sound. Almost before the last fragments of that ship had fallen into the water, our big guns found the shore battery and destroyed it.

Meanwhile power had been building up on Green Beach. At 1544, with the sun dropping lower toward the ocean, they tried the first row of coconut trees again. They were driven back. This time, however, not quite to the coral. They held onto some good positions fifteen or twenty yards inland.

At 1557 Admiral Kester pulled them back onto the coral. For the last time that day. He sent the planes in to rout out that first trench. This time, with noses almost in the coconut stumps, our fliers roared up and down the trenches. They kept their powerful .50's aimed at the narrow slits like a woman guiding a sewing machine along a pre-determined line. But the .50's stitched death.

At 1607 the planes withdrew. At a signal, every man on that beach, every one, rose and dashed for the first trench. The Japs knew they were coming, and met them with an enfilading fire. But the Green Beach boys piled on. Some fell wounded. Others died standing up and took a ghostly step toward the trench. Some dropped from fright and lay like dead men.

But most went on, grunting as they met the Japs with bayonets. There was a muddled fight in the trench. Then things were quiet. Some Americans started crawling back to pick up their wounded. That meant our side had won.

Japs from the second trench tried to lead a charge against the exhausted Americans. But some foolhardy gunners from a cruiser laid down a pin-point barrage of heavy shells. Just beyond the first trench. It was dangerous, but it worked. The Japs were blown into small pieces. Our men had time to reorganize. They were no longer on coral. They were inland. On Kuralei's earth.

At 1618 Admiral Kester made his decision. Green Beach was our main chance. To hell with Red. Hang on, Red! But everything we had was thrown at Green. It was our main chance. "Any word from the tanks?" "Beating down the peninsula, sir." It was no use banging the table. If the tanks could get through, they would.

At 1629 about a hundred amphibs sped for Green Beach. They were accompanied by a tremendous barrage that raked the western end of the beach toward the cliffs. Thirty planes strafed the Jap part of the promontory. A man beside me started yelling frantically. A Jap gun, hidden somewhere in that wreckage, was raking our amphibs. "Get that gun!" he shouted. "It's right over there!" He jumped up and down and had to urinate against the bulkhead. "Get that gun!" Two amphibs were destroyed by the gun. But more than ninety made the beach. Now, no matter how many Japs counter-attacked, we had a chance to hold the first trench.

"A tank!" our lookout shouted. I looked, but saw none. Then, yes! There was a tank! But it was a Jap tank. Three of them! The Jap general had finally conceded Lt. Col. Hyaichi's point. He was rushing all moveable gear to the promontory. And our own tanks were still bogged down in the jungle.

"LCS-108! Beach yourself and use rockets!" The order came from the flagship. With crisp command the young skipper got up as much speed as possible. He drove his small craft as near the battle lines as the sea would take it. We braced ourselves and soon felt a grinding shock as we hit coral. We were beached, and our bow was pointed at the Jap tanks.

Our first round of rockets went off with a low swish and headed for the tanks. "Too high!" the skipper groaned. The barrage shot into the cacao trees. The Jap tanks bore down on our men in the first ditch. Our next round of rockets gave a long hissss. The first tank exploded loudly and blocked the way of the second Jap.

At this moment a Jap five-incher hit the 108. We heeled over to port. The men at the rocket-launching ramps raised their sights and let go with another volley. The second tank exploded. Japs climbed out of the

9

manhole. Two of them dived into the cacaos. Two others were hit by rifle fire and hung head downward across the burning tank.

The third Jap tank stopped firing at our men in the first trench and started lobbing shells at LCS-108. Two hit us, and we lay far over on the coral. The same foolhardy gunners on the cruiser again ignored our men in the first trench. Accurately they plastered the third tank. We breathed deeply. The Japs probably had more tanks coming, but the first three were taken care of.

Our skipper surveyed his ship. It was lost. It would either be hauled off the reef and sunk or left there to rot. He felt strange. His first command! What kind of war was this? You bring a ship all the way from Norfolk to stop two tanks. On land. You purposely run your ship on a coral reef. It's crazy. He damned himself when he thought of that Jap plane flashing by. It had killed two of his men. Not one of our bullets hit that plane. It all happened so fast. "So fast!" he muttered. "This is a hell of a war!"

At 1655 the Marines in trench one, fortified by new strength from the amphibs, unpredictably dashed from the far western end of their trench and overwhelmed the Japs in the opposite part of trench two. Then ensued a terrible, hidden battle as the Marines stolidly swept down the Jap trench. We could see arms swinging above the trench, and bayonets. Finally, the men in the eastern end of trench one could stand the suspense no longer. Against the bitterest kind of enemy fire, they rushed past the second row of coconut stumps and joined their comrades. Not one Jap survived that brutal, silent, hidden struggle. Trench two was ours.

At 1659 more than a thousand Jap reinforcements arrived in the area. Not yet certain that we had committed all our strength to Green Beach, about half the Japs were sent to Red. Lt. Col. Hyaichi, tight-lipped and sweating, properly evaluated our plan. He begged his commanding officer to leave only a token force at Red Beach and to throw every ounce of man and steel against Green. This was done. But as the reserves moved through the coconut grove, the skipper of the LCS-108 poured five rounds of rockets right into their middle. Results passed belief. Our men in trench two stared in frank astonishment at what the rockets accomplished. Then, shouting, they swamped the third Jap trench before it could be reinforced.

At 1722, when the sun was beginning to eat into the treetops of Kuralei, our tanks broke loose along the shore of the promontory. Sixty sweating footslogging axmen dragged themselves after the tanks. But ahead lay an unsurmountable barrier of rock. The commanding officer of the tanks appraised the situation correctly. He led his ménage back into the jungle. The Japs also foresaw what would happen next. They moved tank destroyers up. Ship fire destroyed them. We heard firing in the jungle.

At 1740 our position looked very uncertain. We were still six rows from

Line Albany. And the Japs had their blockhouse right at the edge of the cacaos. Our chances of attaining a reasonably safe position seemed slight when a fine shout went up. One of our tanks had broken through! Alone, it dashed right for the heart of the Jap position. Two enemy tanks, hidden up to now, swept out from coconut emplacements and engaged our tank. Bracketed by shells from each side, our tank exploded. Not one man escaped.

But we soon forgot the first tank. For slowly crawling out of the jungle came the other three. Their treads were damaged. But they struggled on. When the gloating Jap tanks saw them coming, they hesitated. Then, perceiving the damage we had suffered, the Japs charged. Our tanks stood fast and fired fast. The Japs were ripped up and down. One quit the fight. Its occupants fled. The other came on to its doom. Converging fire from our three tanks caught it. Still it came. Then, with a fiery gasp, it burned up. Its crew did not even try to escape.

At 1742 eleven more of our tanks landed on Sonova Beach. You would have thought their day was just beginning. But the sun was on their tails as they grunted into the jungle like wild pigs hunting food.

An endless stream of barges hit Green Beach. How changed things were! On one wave not a single shot from shore molested them. Eight hundred Yanks on Kuralei without a casualty. How different that was! We got Admiral Kester's message: "Forty-eight minutes of daylight. A supreme effort."

At 1749 the Japs launched their big counter-attack. They swept from their blockhouse in wild assault. Our rockets sped among them, but did not stop them. It was the men in trench three that stopped them.

How they did so, I don't know. Japs swarmed upon them, screaming madly. With grenades and bayonets the banzai boys did devilish work. Eighty of our men died in that grim assault. Twelve had their heads completely severed.

But in the midst of the melee, two of our three tanks broke away from the burning Jap tanks and rumbled down between trench three and trench four. Up and down that tight areaway they growled. A Jap suicide squad stopped one by setting it afire. Their torches were their own gasoline-soaked bodies. Our tankmen, caught in an inferno, tried to escape. From trench three, fifty men leaped voluntarily to help them. Our men surrounded the flaming tank. The crewmen leaped to safety. In confusion, they ran not to our lines but into trench four. Our men, seeing them cut down, went mad. They raged into trench four and killed every Jap. In a wild spontaneous sweep they swamped trench five as well!

Aboard the LCS-108 we could not believe what we had seen. For in their rear were at least a hundred and twenty Japs still fighting. At this moment reinforcements from the amphibs arrived. The Japs were caught between heavy fire. Not a man escaped. The banzai charge from the blockhouse had ended in complete rout.

At 1803 Admiral Kester sent his message: "You can do it. Twenty-seven minutes to Line Albany!" We were then four rows from the blockhouse. But we were sure that beyond trench seven no trenches had been dug. But we also knew that trenches six and seven were tougher than anything we had yet tackled. So for the last time Admiral Kester sent his beloved planes in to soften up the trenches. In the glowering dusk they roared up and down between the charred trees, hiccupping vitriol. The grim, terrible planes withdrew. There was a moment of waiting. We waited for our next assault. We waited for new tanks to stumble out of the promontory. We waited in itching dismay for that tropic night. We were so far from the blockhouse! The sun was almost sunk into the sea.

What we waited for did not come. Something else did. From our left flank, toward the cliffs, a large concentration of Jap reinforcements broke from heavy cover and attacked the space between trenches one and two. It was seen in a flash that we had inadequate troops at that point. LCS-108 and several other ships made an instantaneous decision. We threw all our fire power at the point of invasion. Rockets, five-inchers, eight-inchers and intermediate fire hit the Japs. They were stopped cold. Our lines held.

But I can still see one flight of rockets we launched that day at dusk. When the men in trench two saw the surprise attack coming on their flank, they turned sideways to face the new threat. Three Americans nearest the Japs never hesitated. Without waiting for a command to duty they leaped out of their trench to meet the enemy head on. Our rockets crashed into the advancing Japs. The three voluntary fighters were killed. By their own friends.

There was no possible escape from this tragedy. To be saved, all those men needed was less courage. It was nobody's fault but their own. Like war, rockets once launched cannot be stopped.

It was 1807. The sun was gone. The giant clouds hanging over Kuralei turned gold and crimson. Night birds started coming into the cacao grove. New Japs reported to the blockhouse for a last stand. Our own reinforcements shuddered as they stepped on dead Japs. Night hurried on.

At 1809, with guns spluttering, eight of our tanks from Sonova Beach burst out of the jungle. Four of them headed for the blockhouse. Four tore right down the alleyway between trenches five and six. These took a Jap reinforcement party head on. The fight was foul and unequal. Three Japs set fire to themselves and tried to immolate the tank crews. They were actually shot into pieces. The tanks rumbled on.

At the blockhouse it was a different story. Tank traps had been well built in that area. Our heavies could not get close to the walls. They stood off and hammered the resilient structure with shells.

"Move in the flame-throwers. Everything you have. Get the blockhouse." The orders were crisp. They reached the Marines in trench five just as the evening star became visible. Eight husky young men with nearly a hundred pounds of gear apiece climbed out of the trench. Making an exceptional target, they blazed their way across six and seven with hundreds of protectors. They drew a slanting hailstorm of enemy fire. But if one man was killed, somebody else grabbed the cumbersome machinery. In the gathering darkness they made a weird procession.

A sergeant threw up his hands and jumped. "No trenches after row seven!" A tank whirled on its right tread and rumbled over. Now, with tanks on their right and riflemen on their left, the flame-throwers advanced. From every position shells hit the blockhouse. It stood. But its defenders were driven momentarily away from the portholes. This was the moment!

With hoarse cries our flame-throwers rushed forward. Some died and fell into their own conflagration. But three flame-throwers reached the portholes. There they held their spuming fire. They burned away the oxygen of the blockhouse. They seared eyes, lips, and more than lungs. When they stepped back from the portholes, the blockhouse was ours.

Now it was night! From all sides Japs tried to infiltrate our lines. When they were successful, our men died. We would find them in the morning with their throats cut. When you found them so, all thought of sorrow for the Japs burned alive in the blockhouse was erased. They were the enemy, the cruel, remorseless, bitter enemy. And they would remain so, every man of them, until their own red sun sank like the tired sun of Kuralei.

Field headquarters were set up that night on Green Beach. I went ashore in the dark. It was strange to think that so many men had died there. In the wan moonlight the earth was white like the hair of an old woman who has seen much life. But in spots it was red, too. Even in the moonlight.

Unit leaders reported. "Colonel, that schedule for building the airstrip is busted wide open. Transport carrying LARU-8 hit. Heavy casualties." I grabbed the man's arm.

"Was that the transport that took a direct hit?" I asked.

"Yes," he said, still dazed. "Right in the belly."

"What happened?" I rattled off the names of my friends in that unit. Benoway, in the leg. The cook, dead. The old skipper, dead. "What happened to Harbison?" I asked.

The man looked up at me in the yellow light. "Are you kidding, sir?"

"No! I know the guy."

"*You* know him? Hmmm. I guess you don't! You haven't heard?" His eyes were excited.

"No."

"Harbison pulled out four days before we came north. All the time we were on Efate he couldn't talk about anything but war. 'Hold me back, fellows. I want to get at them!' But when our orders came through he got white in the face. Arranged it by airmail through his wife's father. Right now he's back in New Mexico. Rest and rehabilitation leave."

"That little Jewish photographic officer you had?" I asked, sick at the stomach.

"He's dead," the man shouted. He jumped up. "The old man's dead. The cook's dead. But Harbison is back in New Mexico." He shouted and started to cry.

"Knock it off!" a Marine colonel cried.

"The man's a shock case," I said. The colonel came over.

"Yeah. He's the guy from the transport. Fished him out of the drink. Give him some morphine. But for Christ's sake shut him up. Now where the hell *is* that extra .50 caliber ammo?"

The reports dragged in. We were exactly where Alligator said we should be. Everything according to plan. That is, all but one detail. Casualties were far above estimate. It was that bastard Hyaichi. We hadn't figured on him. We hadn't expected a Cal Tech honors graduate to be waiting for us on the very beach we wanted.

"We'll have to appoint a new beachmaster," a young officer reported to the Colonel.

"Ours get it?" the colonel asked.

"Yessir. He went inland with the troops."

"Goddam it!" the colonel shouted. "I told Fry a hundred times . . ."

"It wasn't his fault, sir. Came when the Japs made that surprise attack on the flank."

There was sound of furious firing to the west. The colonel looked up.

"Well," he said. "We lost a damned good beachmaster. You take over tomorrow. And get that ammo in and up."

I grabbed the new beachmaster by the arm. "What did you say?" I whispered.

"Fry got his."

"Tony Fry?"

"Yes. You know him?"

"Yes," I said weakly. "How?"

"If you know him, you can guess." The young officer wiped his face. "His job on the beach was done. No more craft coming in. We were attacking the blockhouse. Fry followed us in. Our captain said, 'Better stay back there, lieutenant. This is Marines' work.' Fry laughed and turned back. That was when the Japs hit from the cliffs. Our own rockets wiped out some of our men. Fry grabbed a carbine. But the Japs got him right away. Two slugs in the belly. He kept plugging along. Finally fell over. Didn't even fire the carbine once."

I felt sick. "Thanks," I said.

The colonel came over to look at the man from LARU-8. He grabbed my arm. "What's the matter, son? You better take a shot of that sleeping stuff yourself," he said.

"I'm all right," I said. "I was thinking about a couple of guys."

"We all are," the colonel said. He had the sad, tired look that old men wear when they have sent young men to die.

Looking at him, I suddenly realized that I didn't give a damn about Bill Harbison. I was mad for Tony Fry. That free, kind, independent man. In my bitterness I dimly perceived what battle means. In civilian life I was ashamed until I went into uniform. In the States I was uncomfortable while others were overseas. At Noumea I thought, "The guys on Guadal! They're the heroes!" But when I reached Guadal I found that all the heroes were somewhere farther up the line. And while I sat in safety aboard the LCS-108 I knew where the heroes were. They were on Kuralei. Yet, on the beach itself only a few men ever really fought the Japs. I suddenly realized that from the farms, and towns, and cities all over America an unbroken line ran straight to the few who storm the blockhouses. No matter where along that line you stood, if you were not the man at the end of it, the ultimate man with his sweating hands upon the blockhouse, you didn't know what war was. You had only an intimation, as of a bugle blown far in the distance. You might have flashing insights, but you did not know. By the grace of God you would never know.

Alone, a stranger from these men who had hit the beaches, I went out to dig a place to sleep. Two men in a foxhole were talking. Eager for some kind of companionship, I listened in the darkness.

"Don't give me that stuff," one was saying. "Europe is twice as tough as this!"

"You talk like nuts," a younger voice retaliated. "These yellows is the toughest fighters in the world."

"I tell you not to give me that crap!" the older man repeated. "My brother was in Africa. He hit Sicily. He says the Krauts is the best all round men in uniform!"

"Lend me your lighter." There was a pause as the younger man used the flameless lighter.

"Keep your damned head down," his friend warned.

"If the Japs is such poor stuff, why worry?"

"Like I said," the other reasoned. "Where did you see any artillery barrage today? Now if this was the Germans, that bay would of been filled with shells."

"I think I saw a lot of barges get hell," the young man argued.

"You ain't seen nothing! You mark my words. Wait till we try to hit France! I doubt we get a ship ashore. Them Krauts is plenty tough. They got mechanized, that's what they got!"

"You read too many papers!" the second Marine argued. "You think when they write up this war they won't say the Jap was the toughest soldier we ever met?"

"Look! I tell you a thousand times. We ain't met the Jap yet. Mark my words. When we finally tangle with him in some place like the Philippines . . ."

"What were we doin' today? Who was them little yellow fellows? Snow White and the Seven Dwarfs? Well, where the hell was Snow White?"

"Now wait! Now wait just a minute! Answer me one question. Just one question! Will you answer me one question?"

"Shoot!"

"No *ifs* and *ands* and *buts*?"

"Shoot!"

"All right! Now answer me one question. Was it as tough as you thought it would be?"

There was a long moment of silence. These were the men who had landed in the first wave. The young man carefully considered the facts. "No," he said.

"See what I mean?" his heckler reasoned.

"But it wasn't no pushover, neither," the young man defended himself.

"No, I didn't say it was. But it's a fact that the Nips wasn't as tough as they said. We got ashore. We got to the blockhouse. Little while ago I hear we made just about where we was expected to make."

"But on the other hand," the young Marine said, "it wasn't no picnic. Maybe it *was* as tough as I thought last night!"

"Don't give me that stuff! Last night we told each other what we thought. And it wasn't half that bad. Was it? Just a good tough tussle. I don't think these Japs is such hot stuff. Honest to God I don't!"

"You think the way the Germans surrendered in Africa makes them tougher?"

"Listen, listen. I tell you a hundred times. They was pushed to the wall. But wait till we hit France. I doubt we get a boat ashore. That's one party I sure want to miss."

There was a moment of silence. Then the young man spoke again.

"Burke?" he asked. "About last night. Do you really think he'll run for a fourth term?"

"Listen! I tell you a hundred times! The American public won't stand for it. Mark my words. They won't stand for it. I thought we settled that last night!"

"But I heard Colonel Hendricks saying . . ."

"Please, Eddie! You ain't quotin' that fathead as an authority, are you?"

"He didn't do so bad gettin' us on this beach, did he?"

"Yeah, but look how he done it. A slaughter!"

"You just said it was easier than you expected."

"I was thinkin' of over there," Burke said. "Them other guys at Red Beach. Poor bastards. We did all right. But this knuckle-brain Hendricks. You know, Eddie, honest to God, if I had a full bladder I wouldn't let that guy lead me to a bathroom!"

"Yeah, may be you're right. He's so dumb he's a colonel. That's all. A full colonel."

"Please, Eddie! We been through all that before. I got a brother wet the bed till he was eleven. He's a captain in the Army. So what? He's so dumb I wouldn't let him make change in my store. Now he's a captain! So I'm supposed to be impressed with a guy that's a colonel! He's a butcher, that's what he is. Like I tell you a hundred times, the guy don't understand tactics."

This time there was a long silence. Then Eddie spoke, enthusiastically. "Oh, boy! When I get back to Bakersfield!" Burke made no comment. Then Eddie asked, "Tell me one thing, Burke."

"Shoot."

"Do you think they softened this beach up enough before we landed?"

Burke considered a long time. Then he gave his opinion: "It's like I tell you back in Noumea. They got to learn."

"But you don't think they softened it up enough, do you, Burke?"

"Well, we could of used a few more big ones in there where the Japs had their guns. We could of used a few more in there."

Silence again. Then: "Burke, I was scared when we hit the beach."

"Just a rough tussle!" the older man assured him. "You thank your lucky stars you ain't goin' up against the Krauts. That's big league stuff!"

Silence and then another question: "But if the Japs is such pushovers, why you want me to stand guard tonight while you sleep?"

Burke's patience and tolerance could stand no more. "Goddammit," he muttered. "It's war. If we was fighting the Eyetalians, we'd still stand guard! Plain common sense! Call me at midnight. I'll let you get some sleep."

⚓

THE ROOMMATES

⚓

THE ROOMMATES
Thomas Heggen

⚓ This chapter from "Mister Roberts" has been included because it is in recognition of one phase of life at sea which has seldom been considered worth writing about, but which is as real as the ship itself. That is the abrasive effect of one human being on another due to closeness of quarters and monotonous routine.

LIEUTENANT CARNEY, the first division officer, and Lieutenant (jg) Billings, the communicator, had a fight one day. It wasn't a fight, really—more of a spat than anything else—but even so aborted a difference between the two was an event of genuineness. Until this particular day they had roomed together for fifteen months without so much as a sharp word. While the other officers fretted and cursed and complained, Carney and Billings had made a separate peace with each other and with the ship. While the other officers prowled the ship and plotted against the Captain and wore themselves out seeking diversion, these two lay in their bunks and wrestled such conflicts as whether to get up now or wait half an hour until noon. Carney and Billings had reduced life in stateroom number nine to the ultimate simplicity, and were working constantly to push it beyond that point. All the needs of man were right there: the room owned a private head and twenty steps down the passageway was the wardroom with its food and coffee Silex and acey-deucey board. What more could a man want? Billings hadn't been out of the amidships house in two months, since the time he got lost looking for the paint locker.

They lived a little idyll in stateroom number nine. Billings, who stood no watches, slept every day until noon, but one day out of four Carney had to get up at eight. The process of arising at noon and greeting the not-very-new day was always the same: Billings, who occupied the top bunk, would dangle an arm or a leg over the side; Carney would command fiercely, 'Get back in there where you belong'; Billings would comply and say meekly: 'I'm sorry'; and Carney would finish off, 'And stay there!' This happened three days out of four, and every day—sometimes two and three times a day—another little ritual would be acted out. One would say to the other: 'Feel like getting your ass whipped?'; to which the reply was: 'Think you're man enough?': and the reply to that was: 'Yes, I think so.' Then the two would march to the wardroom, for this was the invitation to acey-deucey combat.

These sequences were the fixed points of the day, the clichés, the rituals, and like all rituals they were performed automatically, unconsciously, and without awareness of repetition. The plan for the rest of the day was fixed too, but it allowed some small room for improvisation. There were at least two ways in which the afternoon could be spent. Carney was from Osceola, Iowa, where he operated his father's shoe store; Billings was from Minnesota, where he ran a dairy farm. Many afternoons slipped by in thoughtful talk, Carney picturing for Billings the romance of the shoe business, Billings pointing out the grievously neglected fascination of animal husbandry. Other happy afternoons would be devoted to what might be called (if the word did not imply the contrasting present of a gainful occupation) avocations. Carney painted in water colors. He started out on landscapes: he painted a simple pastoral scene, animals grazing in a field, but perspective gave him unexpected trouble, and the cows seemed to be suspended in air over the pigs. He decided he wasn't ready for landscapes. Next he did from a photograph a portrait of his wife, but it was unfortunate too. One eye was larger than the other and focused in another direction, the nose was crooked and the mouth was pulled up as though with paralysis. Carney decided he wasn't ready for portraits either, and painted from life a red and yellow-striped thermos bottle which was more successful.

Billings's hobby was socialism. He had acquired it unexpectedly by reading Upton Sinclair, and been confirmed in it by the pamphlets of Norman Thomas and the essays of Bertrand Russell. He had placed himself on the mailing list of twelve Socialist organs and three Communist, and these of an afternoon he would read aloud to Carney at his painting. Billings tried earnestly to bring Carney to his persuasion, but, although Carney always listened politely, it was clear that he would not become a convert during Billings's lifetime. In the room, though, they lived a quite definite communal life. When the laundry was late, Carney wore Billings's scivvies, and Billings Carney's shirts. Whichever toothpaste happened to be out was the one used. Books had no ownership at all. Through an unuttered agreement

Billings supplied cigarettes and soap for the room, while Carney provided Coca-Cola, which he had bought from a merchant ship. Everything in stateroom nine was organized like that; every problem that life could throw up was absorbed, smothered, controlled. Carney and Billings had made an approach to Nirvana equaled by few in our time. It was strange, then, that they should have this quarrel.

It happened while the ship was unloading again at Apathy island. It was a wretched place, flat and rank and bilious green; bad enough to look at and worse to smell. Great fat swollen flies with a sting like a bee's swarmed out from the island and infested the ship. Long, vicious mosquitoes came out too. Eight- and ten-foot sharks patrolled the ship to prevent swimming. There wasn't a thing over on the beach; not an officers' club, not even a single bottle of beer. And hot!—all day long the sun pounded down through the breathless air, and all day the porous jungle absorbed and stored the heat. And then at night, when the sun had set and the cool time should begin, the jungle exhaled in a foul, steaming breath, the day's accumulation of heated air. It was a maddening place; everyone got on the nerves of everyone else; there were five fist-fights while the ship was there. Still, you had a right to expect Carney and Billings to be impervious to all this.

The quarrel began in the morning and gathered momentum through the day. It began when it became too hot even to sleep, when both Carney and Billings awoke at the unheard-of hour of nine. For a while they lay in their bunks and didn't move and didn't talk. From the top bunk Billings could look out the porthole and see the glaring water and the seedy island. Carney couldn't see them from the bottom bunk, but he knew they were there. Then Billings dangled a foot over the edge of the bunk. 'Get back in there,' Carney said listlessly, out of old habit. Billings's answer was unexpected and startling: 'Cut it out,' he said sharply.

For a moment, after it was said, it was very quiet in there. Neither said any more and after a little Billings sat up and crawled down from his bunk. He was sweating and he plodded to the head to take a shower. He came out cursing: the water was off: it was outside of water hours. Angrily, he put on his shoes and started dressing. He couldn't find his shirt right away. 'Where's my goddamn shirt?' he grumbled, more to himself than to Carney. It didn't require an answer, but Carney, smarting under Billings's testiness of a few minutes back, gave him one. 'How the hell should I know?' he snapped.

If Billings had said something then, if perhaps they had exchanged a few words, they might have removed the whole matter from their chests. But Billings turned his back and didn't say a word. He went down to the wardroom for a cup of coffee and he was sore. He was sore and simmering when he went into the wardroom, but when there was no coffee on the Silex he

23

flared into anger. That son-of-a-bitch, he thought: and curiously enough he wasn't designating the steward's mate who had neglected the coffee, he was thinking of Carney.

Within the next half-hour a combination of several things set his nasty temper like plaster. Upon investigation he found that tonight's movie was a dreary, stupid musical which had already been shown once on the ship and which he had seen in the States three years ago. That took the last bit of hope from the day right there. Then the Captain called him up and ate his ass out for the way the signalmen were keeping the flying bridge. After that Billings sat down and broke a message which ordered the ship, upon completing discharge, right back to the place it had left, a place almost as sorry as this. And, finally, he learned that the unloading was going very slowly, so slowly that they wouldn't be out of here for a week anyway. Everyone had counted on getting out in four days at the most.

That did it, the last piece of news did it. A little later Billings went down to the room. Carney was up now, sitting at the desk in his shorts writing a letter. His clothes were thrown across Billings's bunk. Billings exploded: 'Get your goddamn crap off my bed!' He flung the clothes onto the bottom bunk.

Carney didn't look up from his letter. 'Screw you, you silly bastard,' he said coldly.

'Right through the nose,' Billings replied and went out. The thing was declared then; it was out in the open. From then on, it mounted steadily. Noon chow, consisting of a New England boiled dinner despised by all, eaten in collaboration with a hundred arrogant flies, didn't help matters. After lunch Carney got into the room first and into the shower first. That was at twelve-thirty; the water went off promptly at one. Billings wanted very much to take a shower. He sat around the room quite obviously waiting to do so. At one minute to one Carney, singing happily, stepped out of the shower.

'You're pretty goddamn smart, aren't you?' Billings snarled.

'I think so,' said Carney blandly.

'Jesus!' Billings said disgustedly. He stalked out and the heat of his anger climbed higher and higher. 'Jesus,' he fumed, 'what a cheap son-of-a-bitch!' As the afternoon wore on, he thought furiously and obsessionally of his roommate, and the more he thought, the angrier he got. And, curiously, the angrier he got, the thirstier he got. By three o'clock he craved a drink, specifically a Coca-Cola, more than anything in the world. Every afternoon at three he and Carney would drink a Coca-Cola cooled with ice from the wardroom refrigerator. It had become an addiction for both, and Billings had to have his now. It was, of course, out of the question to ask that son-of-a-bitch Carney for one, so Billings decided to steal it. But when he went down to the room to accomplish this, Carney was there, sitting at the desk, approximately the size of life. He was painting what seemed to be a native outrigger canoe, and on the desk beside him was a frosty glass of Coca-Cola. Billings went out without a word. Craftily he went to the wardroom and seated himself so that he could watch the door. It wasn't long until Carney came out and went down the passageway. It wasn't long then until Billings streaked for the room. The cokes, he well knew, were at the bottom of Carney's closet. He was delighted with himself, exhilaratingly revenged, elated, until he tried the closet door. It was locked.

To Billings's credit, it must be said that he took this in stride. He did the only thing possible under the circumstances. He collected all of the cigarettes, all the matches, all the soap, even tiny slivers from the trays, and locked them in his drawer. It wasn't enough, but it was the only thing he could do. He went out and when it was time to wash up for evening chow, he returned to the room. Carney was still there. Without a word Billings unlocked his drawer, took out the soap and washed himself. Then he locked up the soap again.

Carney watched, smiling superiorly. 'My,' he said, 'aren't we smart?'

'I think so,' said Billings. He knew that Carney was burned up.

That was the penultimate round. The climax came after the movie. The picture turned out poor as everyone knew, and some of the crew didn't even wait for the finish. Billings and the amiable Ensign Pulver left early and were sitting talking in stateroom nine when Carney came in. Pulver, who was ignorant of the day's tension, greeted Carney cheerily: 'Hi, Louie,' he said. 'Sit down and let's have one of your cokes.'

Carney replied with a geniality that sharply excluded Billings. 'Frank,' he said, 'I think that's a fine idea. Let's you and I have one.'

Pulver thought it was some kind of game. 'Ain't you going to give old Alfy here one?' he said thoughtlessly.

Carney snorted. 'Hell, no! Let the son-of-a-bitch buy his own!'

Billings said immediately: 'Who the hell wants your cokes, you silly bastard?'

'Who wants them?' Carney said sweetly. 'You do. You'd give your left leg for a coke right now.'

'The hell I would.' Billings turned to Pulver, who was sitting very much surprised at this sharp and sincere exchange. He had never known the two to talk like this. 'Jesus,' said Billings scornfully, 'did you ever hear such a petty son-of-a-bitch? He's got his cokes locked up in that closet! Afraid somebody's going to get one of them!'

'I'm not afraid *you're* going to get any,' Carney sneered. 'That's for sure.'

Billings continued to address the bewildered Pulver. 'That is the cheapest son-of-a-bitch I ever knew. You could count on your fingers all the money he's spent since he's been on this ship. Mooch!—all the bastard does is mooch. He hasn't bought a cigarette since he's been on here. He's the penny-pinchingest, moochingest bastard I ever knew!'

'Wouldn't you like a coke?' Carney taunted, but his face by this time was flushed red.

'Jesus, what an ass!' Billings was saying. 'What a petty no-good bastard! Sits on his ass all day and does these stupid paintings. Have you ever seen any of his paintings?—a five-year-old moron could do better!'

Carney couldn't keep the anger out of his voice now. 'Look who's talking! The sack-king himself! That son-of-a-bitch spends so much time in there he gets sores on his back. Actually!' he turned to Billings. 'Why don't you get up in your sack where you belong?' he sneered.

'Why don't you put me there?'

'I think that's a good idea!'

'I'd like to see it!'

It was a bad moment. Both roommates were on their feet ready to swing. Ensign Pulver, normally a rather ineffective young man, suddenly arose to greatness. He got between them and he made it a joke. 'Boys, boys, boys,' he soothed. 'Take it easy or Stupid'll be running down here.' He pushed Carney down in the chair and then he got Billings to sit down again on the bunk. For a moment they sat glowering at each other. Then Carney picked up the quarrel.

'Talk about petty,' he said to Pulver. 'Do you know what that guy did today? Actually did? He locked up little tiny slivers of soap so I couldn't use them! So small you could hardly see them, and he locked them up!' Carney shook his head. 'Boy, that beats me.'

'Nothing beats you,' Billings shot back, 'when it comes to pettiness. You're the world's champ!'

'And not only that,' Carney went on to Pulver, 'but the other day he was up banging ears with the Old Man again. He tells us he hates him and every chance he gets he sneaks up there and bangs ears. That's a nice guy to have around!'

'You wish you could get up there yourself, don't you, you son-of-a-bitch!'

Carney swung around in the chair. 'Better watch your language,' he said tightly.

'Why should I?' Billings challenged. 'Can you tell me why?'

Pulver stepped into the breach again. 'All right, goddamit,' he said sternly. 'Knock it off. It's too hot for such crap. Now knock it off, both of you.' Pulver probably surprised himself, but he was certainly effective.

Billings stood up and stretched elaborately. 'Yeah,' he said, 'you're right, Frank. It's getting boring in here. Let's you and I get out.'

'That's a fine idea,' said Carney. 'Not you, Frank,' he added.

Billings ignored this. 'Yeah, let's go visit our friends,' he said. 'The company's getting stupid in here.' He threw an arm around Pulver and led him toward the door.

'Yeah, go visit your friends,' Carney sneered. 'Billings has so many of them.'

Billings nodded knowingly to Pulver. 'Come on,' he said. Pulver hesitated in the doorway, obviously glad enough of an excuse to get out. 'I'll see you later, Louie,' he said impartially to Carney. Then he and Billings went out.

That was all, then; the thing was over. Billings sat for three hours with Pulver in the wardroom playing acey-deucey, and he lost every game but two. Ordinarily Pulver couldn't take a game from him, but tonight Billings was so gorged with anger that he couldn't see straight. His mind wasn't on the game, his mind was trying to figure some way to get at Carney, but he couldn't think of a thing. Finally at midnight they quit, Billings went in to go to bed. The room was dark, and Carney was already in bed. So, in the process of undressing, Billings turned all the lights on and slammed the door to the head as loudly as he could. Then he climbed into his bunk. He was just about asleep when all the lights flashed on and the head door slammed like an explosion. It was Carney retaliating.

That night it rained, and all night long it rained. Next morning it was still raining, a chill, shifting, continuous tropical rain. Both Carney and Billings awoke at eight, felt the rain, pulled a sheet about them, and went snugly back to sleep. At eleven, in co-ordination, they awoke again, and both felt fine. A lovely cool breeze was coming in the porthole, and outside the rain was smoking on the water, so dense that Billings, looking out, couldn't even see the hated island. He yawned, stretched happily, and carelessly dropped an arm over the side of the bunk. Before he remembered and caught himself, Carney almost told him to get back in there. After a while Billings got up and dressed. 'Jesus,' he said, 'rain.' He said it with just the right impersonal inflection, that didn't necessarily invite a reply. 'Yeah,' said Carney. He said it just right, too; not too coldly, not too cordially; just right. That was all the conversation until noon.

All the officers were in good spirits at lunch. The rain made them feel good, and besides, there was the news that an extra stevedore gang was being assigned the ship, which meant they'd be out of here in four days after all. Not only that, but there was a good movie—Rita Hayworth—scheduled for tonight, and it was only six months old.

Billings felt so good that he went up to the radio shack and did some work. As he worked, his glow of general and diffused mellowness concentrated itself into a beam of good feeling directed at Carney. He thought what a good roommate Carney was. He thought over the events of the previous day and how foolish, really, the quarrel had been. He resolved to go down and start patching things up.

In the room Carney was painting at the desk again. Billings went over to the washbasin and scrubbed his hands and scrupulously examined his teeth. Then, as he started out the door he said informatively, casually, and as though it had just occurred to him: 'Oh, say, the exec was looking for you.' Carney looked up and said politely: 'Yeah, thanks, I saw him.' Billings went back to the shack then and finished his work. He felt that they were ready now for a full reconciliation. It was about three o'clock, Coca-Cola time, when he returned to the room.

He stood peering attentively over Carney's shoulder. The work in progress was that of a red stone building of an architecture possible only for a court-house or a schoolhouse, set in the center of a public square. The square had a lawn of bluish tint, and there were several improbable-looking trees scattered about. Atop the building was what was evidently intended for a cupola, but with its upcurved corners looked more like a pagoda.

'Where is that?' Billings asked respectfully.

Carney looked up and smiled. 'That's Osceola,' he said. 'The courthouse at Osceola, the county seat of Clark County.'

Billings continued to study the picture seriously. 'What's that?' he said, pointing to the pagoda-like structure.

'That's the cupola,' Carney said. He cocked his head at the picture and grinned. 'Those curves represent the Chinese influence on my work.'

Billings stroked his chin and with a perfectly dead-pan face he asked: 'Are you sure they don't represent the Asiatic influence?'

And then both of them were laughing easily together, and Carney, still laughing, was waving his hand and saying carelessly: 'Get the ice.'

Over the cokes, they sat back and examined the work critically. 'I think it's my best work,' Carney said. 'What do you think?'

'I think it is,' Billings agreed. He turned his head this way and that. 'You're getting good on sidewalks,' he noted.

'Yeah,' said Carney. 'I'm good on sidewalks. Those are pretty good trees, too, don't you think?'

Billings nodded. 'Fine trees,' he said positively.

They finished the cokes and Carney leaned back in his chair and yawned and stretched. 'Well,' he said. 'I've done enough work for today. I think I'll knock off.'

Billings yawned and stretched, too. He scratched his head. Very casually he said: 'Feel like getting your ass whipped?'

Carney cocked an eyebrow at him. 'Think you're man enough?'

'I think so,' Billings said.

'Okay.' They stood up and Carney led the way to the wardroom.

⚓

THE BATTLE OFF SAMAR

⚓

THE BATTLE OFF SAMAR

Robert L. Johnson, Jr.

⚓ *World War II was every man's war. It was a long way from the token battles of David and Goliath, the heroes of Greece and Rome, or the decorous strife of the Knights of the Round Table. The men of those days were symbols whose mighty deeds formed the nucleus around which revolved the literature of their respective nations.*

Today, the countless multitudes of contestants, the very mass and bulk of deeds of extraordinary bravery tend to obliterate the individual prowess of the leaders.

Therefore, it is not the classic saga that is significant. It is the fragmentary experience of the average G.I. Reach down into a bag of V-Mail and take out a letter at random. There you have the story of this war.

Lt. Johnson was Anti-Submarine Warfare Officer on the "U. S. S. Raymond" (DE 341, one of the first 5"-class DE's in the Pacific. Their armament was two 5", two 40 mm. antiaircraft, a few machine guns, depth charges and, to the loud amusement of all destroyer men, a triple torpedo mount.

The following letter was written with no thought of publication. It is a letter recording the kind of experience through which many passed. It is one man's view of the Battle of the Baby Flat Tops, which took place on D day plus 5.

SALLY darling: Just came down from a fairly dull 12-16, and since I'm not on again till the 4-8, maybe I can make this a real letter for a change. I'm writing this in the wardroom because George has his recognition stuff spread all over my bunk for inventory or something; and if the table here

Reprinted by permission of the author.

doesn't come loose on some overenthusiastic roll to port (as it does on occasions) and land in my lap, I'll manage all right until the evening's bridge game gets under way.

An AlNav has just come out relaxing the censorship rules on anything over a month old; so let me tell you about a little run-in we had with the Japs last fall, not long after that stalwart son of ours was born—before I knew about it, in fact.

When we left Pearl last August, we headed south at a leisurely pace and by devious ways finally wound up at Manus, in the Admiralties, a hot, wet little island, mostly jungle and rusting beer cans. We operated out of there for a while, going through tactical maneuvers with a bunch of CVE's (small carriers) until somebody decided that we knew the job all right. Then we shoved off for Morotai. The landing there was the first real operation we took part in; but from where we sat, all tense and expectant at first but soon enough all limp and bored, it was just another shakedown cruise—except that we got more sleep. So presently back we went to Manus and lay at anchor and discovered a new officers' club—one with a door elaborately labeled "Women" painted on one wall, and some rum to supplement the waxy-tasting beer.

Little by little the harbor filled up with heavy stuff; battle wagons, cruisers and carriers (big ones); and then one day the word got around ashore that we were going to invade the Philippines pretty soon—a couple of months earlier than scheduled. That evening the old man told us to get our departments ready for sea. Three days later we got under way.

And this time when we pulled out of Manus, everybody was pretty sure that we were finally due to see some action. After four months of waiting, the idea wasn't unwelcome—particularly to men who'd never been shot at, and that included most of us. The run up was uneventful, and we took our position east of Samar Island on D minus four, the northernmost of three almost identical groups of baby flattops on hand to soften up the beachheads and supply air cover for our troops until Army planes could use the strips inland. Our Unit was made up of six CVE's, with a seven-ship screen—three cans and four of us 5″-class DE's. Enough to handle any subs that might happen along, probably, and to put up a fair amount of AA, if need be. Not a lot, you understand, but some. We weren't supposed to run into anything tougher.

That first morning we were all naturally pretty much on edge: we really expected some sort of trouble—enemy planes at least. But our carriers launched their strikes without interference. There wasn't a sign of a Jap anywhere, though we knew there were plenty of them on Leyte, a bare fifty miles southwest of us. It was ludicrously anticlimactic. Somehow we felt cheated.

The days passed and still nothing happened to disturb the routine of steaming up and down our patrol area, launching planes before dawn and three or four times during the day, standing watches, going to General Quarters morning and evening as a routine precaution, wondering why the Japs didn't come out and fight.

D-day, H-hour rolled around. We knew our assault troops were hitting the beaches on Leyte. General Mac was returning. But nobody seemed to know or care about us. The torpedo planes and fighters flew their strikes and came back to roost, to rearm and take off again. They at least were seeing action. Less than thirty miles away, we on the escorts didn't even hear about it. You probably knew more about what was going on than we did. I'm sure you couldn't have felt more remote from the fighting. So the big day came—and went; and beyond our normal GQ's we didn't even have an alert. Some war!

A couple of days later, on October 24th, I came down to the wardroom after an uneventful 16-2000 watch and found Jack (still Exec then, of course) and some of the others clustered around a large-scale chart of the area, picking out the positions of two Jap task forces that our subs had reported in the vicinity, moving in from the southwest. We knew our Seventh Fleet had heavy stuff guarding the approaches down there; so we probably wouldn't see anything ourselves, but at least it did look as if the Japs were finally going to bring their navy into the fight. The thought gave us a pleasant tingle of vicarious excitement, and I stayed and speculated with the others for a while before hitting the sack.

At 0330 the next morning the bridge messenger woke me for my watch and I climbed out covered with sleep, threw some water in my face, dressed in the dark and, trailing a life belt in one hand, groped my way up to the wardroom for coffee. Doug and Bill joined me there in the murky red light presently; and we decided that I'd stand this one in the coding room, since my foot was still pretty sore after that accident.

Sunrise was about six o'clock; so at 0530 Doug passed the word from the bridge, "Now all hands . . . man your battle stations for morning alert," pausing in the middle the way he always does. I left my decoding and went topside with the customary feeling of resigned boredom. Up there in the pre-dawn dark the usual morning launchings were in progress. We could look across and see the red truck lights of the carriers involved winking vaguely, and the white and amber lights on the escorts giving the pilots their bearings. We'd hear the sputter and then the roar of each plane as it left the flight deck, and the blue-white flame of its exhaust would flicker briefly before its wing-tip lights blinked out and it was off for the beaches with a cargo of light bombs and fifty caliber machine gun slugs. Everything went like clockwork.

At six a watery sun came up through the uninspiring grey overcast, revealing the formation to our starboard, with the screen in an interrupted circle around the carriers. Samar showed indistinctly to the southwest. Intermittent squalls hung about, trailing heavily from the clouds. At about six-thirty we secured from GQ and set the normal war cruising watch. It looked like just another day.

On my way back down to the coding room, Dick called my attention to a funny thing. Off to port, in the far distance, was something that might have been AA fire—except that it couldn't be, because we knew there wasn't another outfit that close to us. Still, I showed it to the captain, wondering whether he'd bring us back to GQ in an excess of caution; but it faded away shortly and nothing more was said about it. Instead he came into the coding room with me and looked over a long secret dispatch that I'd almost finished breaking. Then he went out; and I started in on it again with only a line or two to go, glad that the watch was almost over.

Almost immediately the loudspeaker outside started to crackle. There was a sort of breathless pause; then the old man's voice came over all in a rush: "A Jap force of four battleships, six cruisers and ten destroyers has been reported twenty miles astern of us, heading this way." He'd hardly stopped before the strident, impatient clanging of the general alarm started feet pounding outside. I felt suddenly as if someone had kicked me in the stomach, and my heart was thudding in my throat as I typed out two more words, to see if I still could. Burns, the radioman, stuck his head in the door and said, "GQ, Mr. Johnson." I said, "Thanks," and picked up my life belt. As I started for the door, the captain's voice came over again, with no hesitation this time: "We're under fire."

In about three seconds I was up the ladder and on the bridge, buckling my belt around me, picking up a battle helmet. The captain looked anxious, a little harassed. Talkers were putting on their telephone headsets. I looked around quickly for the enemy but couldn't see them. The horizon was indistinct, and it had evidently been raining. There was no wind to speak of, and the sea was dead flat.

Then all at once I saw a salvo land over on the other side of the formation, a neat little row of geysers like poplar trees along a French country road. But no sound of their impact reached us; everything was very quiet. Stan stopped talking to his gun crews long enough to remark that they looked like 14- or 16-inch stuff; and from the tone of his ex-professor's voice he might have been remarking on the weather. As he spoke, another line of tall splashes materialized and collapsed; then another—and another. I stopped counting.

Soon the salvoes began coming closer, landing with a sudden, oddly quiet *thwuck*, like a very short roll on a muffled drum. They weren't exploding on impact, which meant they were armor piercing—not that there was any armor to pierce in our outfit! So far they weren't hitting anybody, just feeling out the range; but it was only a matter of time.

The Admiral's voice rasped over the TBS voice radio, telling us to "make smoke." We called the engine room to give us stack smoke, and the chemical generators on our fantail began to trail dense white clouds astern. In another minute all the ships were making smoke, the escorts cutting in and out to put it between the enemy and ourselves.

All this happened much faster than I tell it. At the same time we'd gone to flank speed, racing to reorient the screen after the carriers had wheeled around into the wind to get their planes off those precarious flight decks and into the air. It's a mad scramble, planes clawing their way out helter-skelter and no time to rearm with torpedoes. The few that are armed carry small fragmentation bombs or depth charges, plus their guns; many, just back from the beaches, aren't armed at all. Too late now: the launching course is taking us straight at the Japs.

We all keep sweeping the vague horizon with our glasses and finally I make out a battleship hull down in the distance. George gets a quick look at it, but it disappears in the mist and rain and smoke before he can identify it.

Suddenly, without warning, the quiet is blasted by a crashing roar from ahead. The destroyer on our starboard bow has a target off on the formation's port quarter and has opened fire with her after battery, shooting over us at about maximum five-inch range. With that maddening calm of his, Stan trains our guns around and asks the captain's permission to open fire. In no time all the escorts have taken up the refrain and the air is alive with the crash of our guns. Most of the time we can bring even our forward gun to bear and, trained aft, it throws waves of deafening heat back onto the bridge, sprays us with particles of smoldering cork. Beneath our feet, the ship jumps to the recoil of each salvo.

Further reports of the enemy have brought the cruiser estimate up to seven or eight—some heavy, some light; and we plot them as coming in at about thirty-five knots. Eighteen is the best our unit can make, though we DE's are doing almost twenty-five and the cans, of course, better than that. Still, we have to stick to the carriers. We're all pretty scared, I guess. None of us see any way out of this spot. It's a foregone conclusion that they'll sink every one of us inside twenty minutes.

Their salvoes are coming faster now, and landing closer. A couple of heavy cruisers have started up each flank, and their eight-inch guns are rapid-firing. Those diabolically neat little rows of white water are springing up all through the formation. They're still about five hundred yards short of us, but coming closer to the flattops. The Japs are using dye-loaded shells that burst green and red and milky white on impact, each ship using a distinguishing color, so they'll know which bursts are whose and can correct their aim. We're cutting for land, the formation tacking along in shallow reaches, to spoil the enemy's fire control problem, individual ships maneuvering at will within the general pattern—chasing salvoes, firing over our shoulders. It's a wild game of trying to outguess the other guy. The *Raymond's* making more speed that I'd thought possible, twisting, turning, using full rudder all the time, weaving a tangled trail of black and white smoke, firing continuously, and still keeping more or less on station. But for all our efforts the Jap shells are coming nearer each time. Again and again he'll walk salvoes right up to us and then, just when the next one is due to hit us squarely, he'll shift targets for no apparent reason. Then it happens: one of the flattops is hit, the *Gambier Bay.*

The bridge speaker crackles again. Admiral Sprague orders his "big boys" (destroyers, and not very big when you're thinking in terms of cruisers and battlewagons) to form for a torpedo attack—"little boys" to stand by for a second attack. And that, by all that's awful, means us! The picture of a DE making a run on a battleship or even a cruiser is really rather terrible—running in under 8-, 14- and 16-inch guns with no armor and not enough speed. But there's no time to worry about it.

The destroyers pull out of formation. One cuts across our bow, knifing through the water on her way in, black smoke streaming from her stacks, forward guns blazing. No one on our bridge says anything, but we're cheering her in our hearts. It looks like plain suicide, even for a can—a gallant, futile, foredoomed gesture. "Give 'em hell!"

Then it's our turn. We cut back through our own smoke, heading for the nearest cruiser. Number Two gun is masked now, but Number One keeps pounding. George and I look at each other, smile and shrug. The smile says, "So long, fella;" the shrug says, "It can't be helped." (It's queer how quickly you accept the idea of dying, though I thought about you, darling, and wanted very much to live.)

Meanwhile the range is closing fast. Suddenly there's a splintering, tearing crack overhead, like a big tree abruptly split in two. It's an air burst. They're trying to clear our decks and bridge with shrapnel. Salvoes are hitting close around us now, too. Still we keep going.

We train our tubes out to starboard and wait for the range to get down to ten thousand yards. More AA shells are ripping apart overhead, spraying the forecastle with chunks of twisted steel. There's a kind of screaming whistle, and a salvo lands close astern. That's bad. Up to now he's overestimated our speed, but now he's reaching out. Another salvo splashes abeam to port, perhaps a hundred yards out—too close. Another rips the water to starboard: we're bracketed. The cruiser ahead seems huge and close; actually it's still just a little too far for a decent chance.

But our patch of water's getting awfully hot. Maybe better fire those fish while we still can, even at long range. A salvo lands ahead of us and to starboard. It's unbelievable that we haven't been hit a dozen times. The skipper looks around quickly. Nobody astern of us to port. To the talker, "Stand by torpedoes." Then, "Left full rudder." The ship heels over sharply as we turn to unmask our tubes, then straightens up. "Fire when ready." *Bang . . . swish.* Twice, three times. I see them hit the water clean and straight and hot. We continue our turn and double back on our wake. Number Two gun takes up where Number One left off, hammering away at the Jap as we twist and turn, dodging salvoes, trying to outguess the cruiser's guns. We keep looking back at her, to see whether any of our fish get home, but we can't tell. Our own smoke's too thick.

So we rejoin the formation. Somehow, miraculously, we've made our run, fired our fish, and come back. We've steamed into the enemy's guns and we're still afloat. We begin to hope again. If only our heavy stuff will come up in time! Where in God's name *are* they? Where's Halsey? He *must* be on his way, just over the horizon, maybe. If we can just hold out for another half-hour!

It's 0830 now. We've been under fire for an hour and a half, and the flat seas are still torn with Jap salvoes. An hour and a half is a long time of hell —a hell of a long time. The gun crews are splendid, but tired. Two men have passed out from exhaustion in the forward handling room. Those shells are heavy, and the guns have been eating them fast. The repair parties pitch in and keep the ammunition coming.

Suddenly the port lookout points wildly and shouts. "Torpedo!" Sure enough, right there, coming straight at our port bow, tearing along just below the surface, broaching viciously, spraying water as it breaks the surface. "Left full rudder . . . shift your rudder. Steady." It passes close across our bow, foaming, silent, deadly. Almost instantly the cry comes again: "Torpedo." This one races down our port side and passes clear astern. Another, deeper, passes beneath our screws. We hold our breath and strain our eyes, but no more follow.

Looking around, I can see only five flattops. The *Gambier Bay* has been left behind, crippled. And there are only four escorts in sight—one can, three DE's. No one has seen the *Johnston,* the *Hoel* or the *Roberts* since our torpedo attack. We reform what's left of the screen around the remaining CVE's and continue our limping dash for Samar.

The Japs are still closing in. Their flanking forces are nearly abeam now, pinching tighter around us. And the enemy's fire is beginning to tell. Time and again one ship or another shudders under the impact of a hit. One of the DE's takes a shell forward. A flattop rocks back under a raking salvo. The only remaining can is hit below the waterline. One by one, all are hit except the *Butler* and ourselves. The leading cruiser on our side of the formation is coming in at a sharper angle now, for the kill. The range goes down to 12,000. Every time she fires I want instinctively to duck. And she's firing steadily, the *thwuck* of her salvoes a monotonous counterpoint to the crash of our guns. Her fire is murderous. Soon all her salvoes will be hitting. It looks pretty bad.

Then comes the order, "Small boys on port quarter, intercept leading cruiser." We don't have to look to know that we're the only "small boy" in that position. Below in the radar plotting room, Jack acknowledges: "Wilco. Out." Without batting an eye, the captain leans forward to the voice tube. "Left standard rudder." About then the idea starts to penetrate—*we've* been ordered to intercept a heavy cruiser!

We come to a collision course, keeping her a little on our port bow, closing to engage at point-blank range. Seeing our maneuver, she concentrates her fire on us, and the sea around us churns and leaps under her shells. The range is down to 10,000. This is where we turned away last time; but not now—we stick to our course.

Through my glasses I can see the big Rising Sun flag at her forepeak. And I can see our salvoes landing around her, hitting in her superstructure. Our firing is beautiful. But five-inch shells won't sink a cruiser. There's a sudden, split-second whine. "Hit the deck." A wall of water hides our target momentarily as the salvo lands just short. We twist and turn but keep going. The range is 9,000 yards.

Time and again we're bracketed—one salvo short, the next over. Our world is full of noise and tumult, angry white water, and pounding guns. AA bursts rip open overhead, spattering the sea around us, tearing our eardrums with their splintering crack. We're still pounding in, the decks quivering to the overload on the shafts and bucking under the steady fire of our forward gun. We're still putting shells in her upperworks too, hurting her some. The range is down to 8,000!

Nothing is important any more except the flame of the cruiser's guns and the answering roar of our own, the scream of shells passing low overhead, the rending crack of airbursts, the vibration of the deck, and the swiftly closing range. The little bridge is our whole world. Now and then, above the roll of the enemy's guns, between our salvoes, I can hear the captain's constant orders to the helmsman, weaving us between pillars of water, twisting and dodging, holding her steady for brief seconds, then turning sharply, running the gauntlet. Each time the cruiser's guns flash, we brace ourselves for a hit. The range is 7,000!

Crack! A shell bursts low and close on our port side; there's a brief, high whine, and a chunk of steel sizzles across the bridge at head level, striking the water close aboard to starboard with a little puff of spray. Too close for comfort. A near miss sprays the forecastle; we turn sharply to starboard, then straighten up, as the next salvo lands astern and to port. We risk a steady course. The sea churns up dead ahead—right on in deflection, but short. We swerve back to port, and the next salvo lands close along our starboard side, a neat row of splashes. The range is 6,000 yards. A short, snarling whine, and we all duck as a salvo straddles us amidships, two shells kicking up water to starboard, three to port—right across us. The closest splash is a couple of yards to port; water sprays the bridge.

Short of ramming him, there's no point going in any further, so the skipper brings us around broadside to, paralleling the Jap; and both guns go into local control, rapid fire. We can't miss at this range, and we don't. Even without my glasses I can see our shells bursting around her bridge and along her side. One of her turrets stops firing, and the others seem to be slowing down. Somehow, we must have got in a telling hit or two somewhere.

For a couple of eternal minutes we slug it out on this course, then turn away slightly and start back toward our formation, still firing steadily with both guns. The cruiser follows along, though; and the range even closes a little. Then, abruptly and to our amazement, she swings slowly away from us. For the first time the range begins to open. We stare at each other, dumfounded.

We couldn't believe it. In another ten minutes the whole Jap force was out of five-inch range. We ceased firing. Pretty soon only their upperworks showed over the horizon. Then nothing. They'd gone. The battle was over. The captain took off his helmet, lit a cigarette with not-quite-steady fingers. It seemed deafeningly quiet. Kelly, the signalman, turned to me. "I guess God was sure taking care of us, Mr. Johnson," he said.

And that (said John) was that. What's more, the bridge game is getting noisy, with Chris and Julian arguing about how the last hand should have been played; so I'm off to see if George has put away that mess on my bunk.

We'll be back in port pretty soon, and I'm looking forward to more news of you and the baby. Wish I could see him.

All my love,
Bob

⚓

THE CRASH
and
LAND

⚓

THE CRASH and LAND

Robert Trumbull

⚓ *In a booklet published by the Aviation Training Division of the United States Navy there is a list of over one hundred items to be found aboard the kind of raft that serves several men after their plane has crashed in the sea. But things seldom go according to plan—to borrow a phrase from the German General Staff.*

What did Dixon and his two companions have?

    1 *police whistle*
    1 *mirror (small)*
    2 *pairs of pliers (one of which broke immediately)*
    1 *pocket knife*
    1 *can rubber cement*
    1 *piece patching material*
    1 *.45 caliber pistol*
    3 *clips ammunition*
    2 *life jackets*

No food, no water, no instruments . . . for 34 days.

God, there must be some new word for hero! Some word not tainted with sentimentality and cant to be mouthed by politicians. Something clean and strong and new. Something big enough to fit a man.

THE plane struck the surface of the sea with a sound like the slap of a giant hand on the water. A great splash of water instantly covered the glass in front of me, momentarily shutting out my vision. Two sharp bumps, and the plane settled quietly back on the long, slow swells. I had made a good landing.

As I rose from my seat in quick concern for Gene, Tony, the raft, and a multitude of things that competed for my attention in this crowded moment, I was conscious that the plane was bobbing gently up and down, but that at any second a wave might pull a wing, and we'd be gone. The sea that had looked so flat and solid from the air was now a reaching, greedy thing that shook its prey before devouring it.

I knew that our small three-man scout bomber would not float long. It is no great trick to set a land plane down on water, but these heavily armored war jobs are not intended to float. I had no idea of staying with it very long.

I jumped as quickly as I could onto the left wing to receive the raft from Tony Pastula, my bomber, and he was right there to hand it to me without an instant's delay. Gene Aldrich, my radioman and gunner, was raising himself from the rear cockpit and was busy with his gear. I was already trying to open the raft's gas valve, which seemed to stick.

Suddenly there was no airplane. The next thing I knew I was hanging in my life jacket, kicking the water.

The sinking of that plane was like a magician's trick. It was there, and then it was gone, and there was nothing left in our big, wet, darkening world but the three of us and a piece of rubber that was not yet a raft.

Of course the plane took with it everything the two boys in their well-disciplined haste had pulled together from emergency stores and equipment. I was soon to discover that what fight we were to make for our lives must depend upon the "junk" in our pockets, tools attached to the raft, which were so negligible in value as to be almost frivolous, and the uses we could make of the clothes upon our backs. All these things were to stand us well until they were wrested from our grasp, one by one, by the great unseeable enemy we fought, and then our only weapon was the mind, until this too began to go in the particular corrosion to which it is susceptible.

Finally I got the raft blown up, but the thing inflated itself upside down. Fortunately there was a handrail around it, of half-inch manila line. As soon as the raft expanded to its full size we had grabbed hold of this. I was at the bow, and struggled to twist the raft right side up, with the boys holding on so that we were fighting each other's weight as well as the clumsy vessel. After I struggled for fifteen or twenty minutes, with the sea banging me in the face and filling my mouth with salt water, I did get the raft turned over once. I can't remember for sure whether I tried to climb onto it, or not. The only thing I recall is that the raft flopped over, and I was mighty anxious to get on it.

The handrail ran along the side, and the boys, across from me, had a grip on it. The raft weighed only forty pounds, and their weight tipped it right over again on top of them. My work had been for nothing.

By this time we had been floundering and coughing in the water for quite

I asked the boys to hold me upright.

a while, and were all exhausted. So then we calmed down and hung onto the handrail to rest.

It was quite dark now, but our eyes were becoming accustomed to it and we could see quite well, as anyone can after a few minutes in what at first seems to be pitch blackness.

Gene spoke first.

"There's a way to get this thing over," he said, still a little short of breath.

Those deliberate words, spoken in a slow Missouri drawl with no more or less concern than if he were laboring over a recalcitrant mowing machine on his father's farm, brought our problem back to matter-of-factness.

"We've got to stop and dope us out a scheme," I said.

Tony chimed in.

"All right," he said, blowing sea water from his lips, "how about we take off our blouses, tie 'em together, tie one end to the line on one side of the boat, throw that up across the bottom of the boat, then we all go to the other side and pull, and see if we can't turn her over that way."

The minute he said it, I knew that was the right answer, and I was chagrined that I hadn't thought of it myself.

So we tied the blouses together as Tony had suggested, worked around to the other side and pulled, and boom!—over she came, with a homely thwack on the water.

"You stay here and hold her down, while I get aboard on the other side," I said.

In the raft, I pulled the boys aboard by the wrists one at a time, and for the moment our troubles were over. I looked around and reflected that it was swell to be alive, though why I should have thought that then I don't know.

As we huddled together in the darkness trying to keep warm while the wind held our clammy clothes against us, we were not downhearted. I had confidence in the raft's ability to stay afloat, and the boys were sure we would be rescued in the morning. There was much complaining over the loss of our cigarettes and matches, which had of course been ruined in our long immersion. I too would have liked a cigarette, but most of all I wanted a cup of hot coffee.

We settled down to rest as best we could until dawn, but we soon learned that we could not sleep. The raft was only four feet long by eight feet wide. With its sides inflated like tires, it resembled an oblong doughnut. The dimensions inside were eighty inches by forty inches. We discovered almost at once that it was impossible for three men to dispose this space so that any one of us would be comfortable.

Tony lay most of the night in the bottom of the boat, his spirits seeming to rise and fall like the sea beneath us. Sometimes he would talk cheerfully, almost gaily, and then he would lapse into a depressing silence, in which

45

his gloomy thoughts could be felt by Gene and me, as we felt the darkness of the night.

Gene perched on the gunwale, occasionally moving restlessly. He had been brought up in a rural community, and chafed at confinement. He stood up to stretch occasionally, but found it hard to keep his balance with his feet pushing that thin rubber floor against the sea beneath as into a cushion

We passed a long night, it seemed. Our conversation, when we talked, consisted mostly of reassurance, repeated and repeated, that a plane or ship would find us in the morning. I hoped so, and pretended confidence.

Day approached imperceptibly until suddenly it was dawn, in the abrupt way of the tropics. All at once the sea appeared, a leaden gray; then little white tongues of fire danced on the waves, and the east became a conflagration that resolved itself into a pleasant, rising ball, the sun. Before this, as soon as the sky had taken misty form, we three were straining our eyes for sight of a rescue ship or plane.

The boys discussed every possibility with cheerful eagerness. They were confident that many ships were scouring every square mile of this area to find us. If we weren't found today, they agreed, help would surely come tomorrow.

But I was not so sure. I was an old head in this business, and I knew that our admiral could not risk his entire force in a doubtful attempt to rescue three men. After all, we were at war. We were in the vicinity of known enemy positions and naval forces. There would be one quick look, and then we must be given up for lost.

This would be a bitter pill for the boys to swallow. But it was only simple, military logic.

My thoughts were not gloomy, but they were hard, and I kept them to myself.

A moment came when I thought the boys were right and I was wrong, to my great relief.

I judged it to be about 8:00 or 8:30 A.M. when we sighted the plane. At first I thought it was a bird, but far away as it was we could see that it was steady on its course, and in a few minutes we heard the faint sound of motors.

We jumped to our feet in our excitement, and almost tipped over the raft.

"Hey, take it easy, there," I ordered sternly. "We've still got plenty of time to drown!"

I didn't have to issue a second warning. We sat down carefully, keeping our eyes on the plane. She was from our own forces, all right.

We looked at our watches, but they had all stopped at 7:40, evidently the moment our plane dropped from under us and we went into the water.

I opened the face of my watch and lifted out the works. They were already corroded beyond repair.

It was plain that we were being hunted. The plane approached on an easterly course at about 140 knots, never deviating from her line of flight. As she came nearer, we began to wave our arms, but there was no sign that we were seen.

Then Gene and Tony began to shout. I wished we had been able to save one of the parachutes. I would have opened it now and let it billow on the water. I made one quick search of the raft. There was not a single thing that we could use as a signaling device, except our shirts. Gene and Tony already had theirs off and were waving them wildly. Their voices were becoming hoarse from shouting.

Evidently our tiny raft, being orange-yellow in color, was invisible in the silver path of the morning sun on the sea. The plane came closer, and closer, until she was within a half mile of us.

Finally it was clear that we had not been seen. The plane was going away now, the sound of her motors dwindling to the southward like the last note of a dirge.

I sank down upon the forward thwart. Gene and Tony were leaning by their hands on the sides, still waving halfheartedly, and staring as if their thoughts could bring him back.

Now the plane was a speck in the sky, and the only sound was the lapping of the waves against the raft. Then the speck was gone, and we felt terribly alone in the immensity of sky and sea, and sun.

The boys sank down, their faces expressionless.

I have been sorry that I said what I did then; it was automatic, I guess, and I didn't even remember until Tony recalled it later, bitterly:

"Boys, there goes our one and only chance."

⚓　　⚓　　⚓

LAND

W E PASSED a night of misery in the brewing hurricane. Without an anchor we were at the mercy of the wind, and it blew viciously. Many times we just missed tipping over again, by maneuvering our weight to shift the boat's center of gravity when the mountainous waves knocked us off balance. High combers kept breaking into the boat, half filling it every time. We scooped the water out with our twisted garments, although we thought we would freeze, naked in the cold, slashing rain.

Toward morning the gale slackened, but the sea still boiled. As dawn approached and I was able to see a few feet around, I marveled that we were still afloat among those giant wind-whipped swells. When full daylight came I saw that our world had closed around us. We were in the center of a small circle of agitated green water, under a dome of gray mist. We could not see far in any direction. Everywhere we looked the sea was in frenzied motion, countless white-topped peaks appearing, rolling, and bursting in a gush of foam.

When we stopped shipping water, we sat in the boat with our backs hunched against the rain and wind. We were still drifting to the northeast, making fast time away from where we wished to go.

We said very little to each other. We were hungry and disheartened.

Toward the middle of the morning we took the jacket, on which I had drawn our chart, and held it over our three heads to give a little protection from the chilling rain.

"Hold it careful, boys," I said. "If we lose this, we don't know where we are."

The canvas chart kept the rain off us a little bit, but our clothes were soaked and clammy, and plastered to our skin. I would have been glad to see the sun again, and wondered if I ever would.

"There's your albatross," Tony said.

I looked up, and saw the old gray bird sailing along above us, his wings

48

spread wide, apparently oblivious to the rain and wind. I watched him for a while until my eyes began to hurt. I lowered my head, relaxing, and my beard scraped the sunburned triangle below my throat.

Something thumped me on the head. I sat still, and felt a heavy weight settling on the top of my skull. It moved slightly, and after a tense moment I realized what had happened.

The albatross had alighted on my head. He was pluming his bedraggled feathers there.

I sat very still, figuring what to do. The boys hadn't seen him yet. I considered whether to make a grab for him myself, or let one of the others try.

The chart's being over my head rather complicated matters. There was a chance that as I grabbed for the albatross my hand would become entangled in the canvas.

I studied the situation carefully, and decided to chance it.

Silently, I slid my right hand outward, gauged my aim as best I could since I was unable to see my quarry, and snatched quickly.

The albatross must have been squatting down as I reached for him, because my hand struck him in the breast. The blow knocked him backward into the water.

He floundered for an instant, righted himself indignantly, and rose above the water with a flap of his mightly wings. He flew away, high, then circled back as if to reconnoiter us.

"Jeez, you almost got him, though," Tony said.

I was feeling very glum, and bitter at my failure in this heaven-sent opportunity to obtain food that we all needed so badly. I was sorry I had not let one of the boys try to grab the bird. They could have seen him, whereas I could not.

"Well, I'm afraid he's gone," I said disconsolately.

"Cheer up, chief, it was a good try," Tony said.

"Wonder if we can't find a little more room in here?" Gene asked.

"Any change would help," Tony said. "I'm getting pretty stiff."

I myself was sore all over. We shifted our positions so that two of us sat with our backs against the forward thwart, while the third huddled among our knees.

"We'd be better off in a telephone booth," Tony said. "It'd be dry."

Gene and I mustered a feeble laugh at Tony's witticism. Then we sat silent a few moments as the rain beat on the chart we held over our heads, and the water ran down our necks in cold rivulets.

Tony spoke again.

"That damned albatross is getting familiar again," he said. "Look to starboard, chief."

I turned quietly, and there was our friend, sitting right alongside me in the water. He was feeding.

"Oh, God, one more chance," I said softly, not in supplication but in gratitude.

The huge bird drifted to within three feet of the boat, and ducked his head under the water. He held his beak and eyes submerged for all of ten seconds. It was as if he were inviting me to grab him.

I thought: If he keeps his head down that long, I'll wait until he does it again, and give myself more time.

I sat still until he came up for air. He looked about him in the water, but didn't move his body. He seemed to find what he wanted, and jabbed his bill back into the water.

Without waiting longer than it took to gather my muscles for the effort, I dived over the side, my hands outstretched to grab the bird.

But I never finished the dive. My feet, instead of driving me forward, pushed the boat behind me. The next thing I knew, I was lying full length, face down. The whole front of me smarted from the smash against the water.

In my surprise and disappointment I couldn't think but I instinctively dropped my feet and spread my arms to keep myself afloat. My long body was being lifted by the choppy waves, and the boat was already several feet away. As I lunged for the raft I couldn't help looking for the albatross, who had escaped me for the second time in a way that was humiliating, and worse. The bird was fluttering away—taking his time about it, too— and I swear that if birds can laugh, the gray albatross was hooting at me.

Tony grabbed me by an arm, and I was quickly in the boat.

"Where's the chart?" I demanded immediately.

"It went over the side with you, chief."

I turned, but instantly I abandoned whatever idea I might have had of diving to retrieve the chart. In that sea, it was gone.

We were now without a single article of any use to us, except our anchor line, one water rag (badly tattered), a pair of pliers, and the pocketknife. We were without protection of any kind against the weather, except the sparse clothing on our backs.

I decided to strip off the useless oar pocket to make a covering for our heads. This I did. The piece of fabric thus obtained was almost square, twenty inches long by sixteen inches wide. It served us better than nothing.

It rained steadily all morning. Shortly after noon we hit a heavy squall, with high winds and a terrifying sea, and we tipped over again.

How we got back into the raft against the waves I don't know. When we did, we found that all our gear was gone—knife, pliers, our newly obtained head covering, the unsuccessful sea anchor, and our last rag.

Now we had nothing to protect ourselves, nothing for bailing, nothing for catching food.

Our courage almost failed. This had been a day of horrible disaster.

Tony Pastula, bless his game soul, spoke up at last.

"Well, fellows," he said wryly, "it has all happened now, it looks like. What do you say we shake hands all around and start all over again?"

Gene and I instantly agreed. Crouching in the wobbling rubber tub, with the wind blowing icy rain at us in fire-hose gusts, we exchanged handshakes and declared to each other that this would be a new beginning.

Evening of the thirty-second day we got a shift of wind to the north. Night fell ominously. The sky was dark and threatening; the sea turned from gray to black. As we tumbled along uneasily, our way was lit by long, jagged streaks of lightning, each flash followed by a rolling thunder clap like cannon fire. The air was heavy and stirred sluggishly in the fitful breeze. The waves had lost their frenzy, but still rose high in powerful surges of slowly expanding force.

In the weird twilight, the sky was an awesome spectacle foreboding ill. I called it to the attention of the boys.

There were several layers of clouds, and each layer seemed to be traveling in a different direction. This was beyond the experience of any of us, and we could not imagine what it portended.

"Whatever it means," Tony said, speaking for us all, "it don't mean nothing good."

In my twenty-two years in the navy I had never seen a sky or sea like this, and I didn't like the look of things a bit.

"Better rest while we can," I advised the boys. "Any minute we'll have to bail."

We lay down in the bottom of the raft. The spray that broke on us was cold, and we squeezed ourselves together to keep the warmth of our bodies.

It rained often during the night. Each time we got up to bail and wring out our clothes again.

Tonight we talked more than usual, trying to cheer each other. We all realized, I think, that our spirits occasionally dropped near the danger point of lowness, and it became a game to see who could do the most to lift us out of our despondency. We made little jokes, forced and desperate.

We didn't mind the bailing. Our hips and shoulders were so numb and sore from lying wedged in the bottom of the raft that we actually welcomed the opportunity to get up and move our stiffened muscles. We suffered from lack of circulation. We had so little flesh that our veins were drawn across our bones. When we sat up, our blood would move, but this exposed

51

us to the wind and spray. We chilled easily, so that after a moment we would be forced to lie down again in search of warmth.

Thus we passed the night. It seemed a long time until daylight came.

With morning, we saw that the sky was almost solidly overcast. We waited in vain for the sun to come out and warm us. Everything was gray, except our yellow raft. Its giddy color on the muttering, gloomy sea accentuated its incongruity.

The wind now had shifted to the northeast again, and was driving us along at a lively clip. This was more to our desire, but we couldn't be sure where we were, and couldn't have done anything about it if we had known. The only chart we had was in my head.

About eleven o'clock in the morning we hit a shower, heavy and as cold as ice water. The raft held water over our ankles when it ended.

We had lost the last of our rags in the last tip-over, so we took off all our clothes, mopped the bottom of the boat and wrung over the side, repeating until the raft was dry.

As we finished this tiresome chore the sun appeared, for the first time that day. In our chilled condition the rays felt good.

"Let's take a sun bath before we put our clothes on," I suggested.

The boys assented readily, and we lay against the sides to rest, for we were tired as well as cold. We stretched our clothes across the thwarts to dry.

After a while Tony spoke up nervously.

"Don't you think we'd better put on our clothes?"

I wasn't looking forward to it. They were damp.

"Well, it's pretty rough, you know," Tony argued. "The boat's liable to go over on us again."

The wind had risen and the waves were coming to a boil. The raft was bobbling like an orange rind.

I hesitated for a few seconds, and was just about to agree with Tony when a big comber caught us.

We were lifted high, the raft on such a slant that we had to grab the sides and thwarts to keep from falling out. As we started to slide down the long, sheer trough of the wave, the breaking crest gave us an extra push upward on one side. The wind caught beneath the rounded air chamber. There was a wild scramble of arms and legs, mad grasping, and a confusion of shouts.

"The clothes! The clothes!" I yelled frantically as I went through the air. The scornful wind snatched the words, and a great wave engulfed me.

My head was out of the water again, and somehow my hand was on the raft. Gene, it appeared, had never let go, and was hanging on desperately. Tony had fallen almost on us. I grabbed him by an arm.

The waves were flinging us about, pulling at our legs as if with hands. The raft was upside down.

Never letting go our handholds, we grouped ourselves together and at an unspoken signal heaved the raft upward, trying to keep our grasp on the upended gunwale at the same time. A comber thundered down and almost tore it from our grip.

Quickly, before the next wave came, we pushed upward again. The light raft went over this time, and I worked my way to the opposite side to hold it down while the boys climbed in.

For a few minutes we rested, panting, each with an arm locked across a thwart in case we tipped again. The blood was pounding in my temples. I couldn't breathe without pain.

My chest and torso ached, and, as I have explained before, I was perpetually half numb from the hips down. With a supreme effort of will I raised my head and rolled my body over so that I faced upward across the raft. The boys were lying still, heads down, twisted, inert, like dead men except for their loud and broken gasps for air.

I noted automatically that our weight was not all on one side, which seemed to be our greatest peril. The raft was riding evenly; although it pitched and swerved in continual jerky motion, the bottom was holding to the water. So I sank my head upon my breast and rested.

How long we lay this way I don't remember. I know that we were not in full possession of our minds. When I myself began to think again, it frightened me to realize how easily I slipped away.

I found myself as if awakened by a noise I half remembered from a dream. The boys were sitting up, revived but not disposed to talk. I tried to straighten on my haunches, and then the situation struck me like a blow.

All our clothes were lost—every thread and stitch, except, ridiculously, a police whistle that hung by a cord around my neck.

Now on this day, our thirty-third in the raft, our position was desperate. Since we had lost even my last inadequate makeshift sea anchor, we had no means whatever of controlling our progress. From now on we would go where the wind sent us, and that might mean that we would float until the rubber boat finally rotted and burst. We had lost all our rags, so had no way of catching drinking water beyond what might lie in the bottom of the raft. We had nothing for bailing except our hands. We had one shoe-paddle left, two wallets which had somehow become wedged in the front of the raft, and my police whistle. I did not see how we could make any use of these.

The worst blow of all was the loss of all our clothes, and the piece of fabric we had been using to shade our heads. From now on we were entirely unprotected against the equatorial sun, and it was midsummer. We knew, too well, what the sun was going to do to us.

We thought we were in the vicinity of islands, but with no charts and no navigation instruments we could not be positive as to our position. As far as we could be sure, we might still be a thousand miles from land. Now we would never know where we were unless we actually sighted an island.

This was the one time during the entire trip that I was truly disheartened. In fact, I was just about ready to give up. I knew that the end of our voyage was very near; we must make an island in a day or two, or die.

Tony shared my gloom. He considered going over the side; it would be a quick death, without the torture that the sun had in store. But he changed his mind.

"We've come this far," he argued, "and by God we'll go on!"

Sitting glumly about the boat, discouraged, the three of us considered all the possibilities.

Loss of our clothes, our only shelter, seemed like a mighty hard blow for us to take at this stage of the game, after we had worked and schemed for so long to save ourselves.

The thought of what we had already gone through—that clinched the argument. We all agreed that neither this nor any other disaster which could overtake us now was sufficient reason for giving up the fight we had been making. Again we shook hands all around, and vowed we'd go on.

It was another night of chilling showers. We huddled together in the bottom of the raft, and talked a great deal to keep up our spirits, pursuing any subject that came into our minds.

After every shower we scooped out most of the water with our hands, and lay down again to keep warm. It took just about all our courage to stay cheerful. We knew that the end of our voyage was coming soon, one way or the other.

We were glad to see daylight in the morning. Although we knew we were going to be badly burned when the sun came overhead, we were anxious to warm ourselves. I tried to keep from thinking about what the sun was going to do to us later in the day. I preferred to let that worry come when it must.

The sun did not emerge from behind the clouds until about 8:30 o'clock in the morning. When it did, I stretched out on the forward thwart to warm myself and rest. Tony lay in the bottom, while Aldrich sat up, watching.

By this time, I thought, the navy must have given us up for dead. I learned later that this was true. I would have preferred another end, but this morning I let the sailor's fatalism have its play. I got to thinking over my past life. I had left home at the age of seventeen, worked my way around the country for a year at various jobs, then joined the navy. My older brother had been in the navy during the First World War, as they call it now.

I envied my older brother. I had been reared in a typical midwestern farm family, and the adventure of going to far places in uniform appealed to me. I tried several times to enlist, but first I was too young, then too thin, to make the grade. As I grew I put on weight, and finally got in at nineteen. I had no idea then of making the navy my career; I just wanted to serve a "hitch" for the experience.

That was twenty-two years ago. The navy had been good to me, and I was glad to die in the service, the warsman's way, if die I must.

I scooped up a bit of the indigo sea in my palm, and drank it. Toward the end I could stand a bit of sea water; my system seemed to be in need of salt. I blamed the sun for this.

I had shed two sets of skin prior to the time we lost our clothes. I was in the process of building a new set now, and the tender underskin was still exposed. Lying there entirely unprotected, I began to smart all over my body. My loins and midriff, which had never been sunburned before in all my life, turned scarlet in a half hour. Before the day was over this part of me looked as if it had been seared with a red-hot iron. The rest of my body, which had been protected somewhat by my rotting clothes, burned almost as severely.

The boys were in the same state. The scalding torture we had felt on our faces, hands, and arms now covered our bodies, every inch. The clouds had rolled away and the sea threw back the glare, so that everywhere we turned there was solid heat. I shifted my position frequently to take all advantage I could of the shade of my own body, and to try to keep from exposing the same area too long, but this did little good. The sun hit us practically all over, all of the time. I felt as if I were on fire. My body will always bear the scars of that cooking.

"Good Lord!" Gene said. "Look at that shark!"

I shaded my aching eyes against the sun, and saw a great black dorsal fin cutting the water a few yards from the boat. It was the largest shark I had ever seen.

He came close to the surface, and I whistled soundlessly when I made out the size of that sinuous, powerful body. I estimate that he was not less than fifteen feet long, and must have weighed upward of a thousand pounds.

"If he hits the boat, it's good-by," Gene said.

"Don't attract his attention," I whispered.

He cruised about the boat for about twenty minutes, then went away.

The sun began to hit Tony.

He was lying in the bottom of the raft, the back of his hand lying across his eyes. Suddenly he took his hand away, and sat up, listening. He seemed to be looking far off. He smiled slightly.

"Hey, chief," he said softly. "I hear music."

Humor him, and maybe he'll snap out of it, I thought.

"What kind of music, Tony?" I asked casually.

"Beautiful—like a choir of angels!"

He slid back into the bottom of the raft and closed his eyes again, still smiling.

Although we had divided our days into two-hour watches, I was up and vigilant myself most of the time until my eyes began to fail. Now, because of that and my general physical condition, I was forced to let the man on watch take full responsibility for the boat while I conserved my dwindling energy for my own two-hour shift. Thus I lay on the forward thwart this thirty-fourth morning, turning uneasily under the sun so that my body would burn evenly and I would not suffer unnecessarily from overexposure of any one area more than another. Gene was on watch; Tony was lying in the bottom trying to shade his face—his delirium when he heard the music seemed to have passed.

It was about ten o'clock. The sky was hot and clear as a blue flame. The wind was steady, and the boat was rising and falling slowly on long, gentle swells. The sun was just now approaching the fullness of its anger.

We topped a wave, and in that brief instant while we seemed to hang suspended before the long downward slide began, Gene spoke for the first time since taking the watch.

"Chief," he said, "I see a beautiful field of corn."

I didn't even look up. I thought sadly that the boy's mind had finally gone, and I wished he had taken my advice to cover his head when we first went into the raft.

Without moving, I cast my eyes about the sea, but we were in the trough and I saw only the rumpled carpet of waves. It was possible, I said to myself, that Gene was seeing a mirage: the sun does play tricks on you sometimes. At any rate I was not surprised that Gene was affected. There was nothing I could do for him, so I paid no more attention.

After a few minutes, when we had risen to the next crest, he spoke again insistently: "Sure enough, chief!—I see something green in the distance!"

With this statement, so rationally put in his Missouri drawl, it dawned upon me suddenly that perhaps he did see something. I looked hard, but could still see nothing in the tumbling sea. Tony was looking too, but had not spoken. I tried to stand up, and found I couldn't balance on my cramped and crooked legs. I asked the boys to hold me upright.

We stood, the three of us, in the center of the boat, the boys each with one hand against the side and an arm around my waist, holding me erect with their shoulders while I steadied myself with arms around their necks.

We came to the summit of the next large swell. Sure enough, in the distance I could see something green. As Gene had said, it was beautiful. I instantly recognized it as an island, one of the low, verdant atolls of the far South Sea. I let out a hoarse whoop and turned to Gene, tightening my arm about his neck.

"Boy," I said exultantly, "you have won yourself a dinner!"

Tony took a deep breath, and let it go out noisily, trying to repress his joy.

"Well," he said, "thank God—and it's about time."

We were still far off. The island appeared as a low shelf of green— coconut trees, I guessed, and I was right. Chartless, we had no idea what the island was, whether it was inhabited, or whether it was in friend or enemy's hands.

The wind had risen strongly, making long and prominent streaks on the water, which gave me an excellent gauge of the exact wind direction. I took a bearing on the island, compared it with the wind direction, and found that our course of drift was carrying us about ten degrees to the right of the island.

We realized, of course, that this was our God-given chance for refuge, so, weak as we were, we saw nothing for it but to row. I took the port side of the raft, using our one remaining shoe-paddle. Gene and Tony paddled together on the starboard side, using their hands only.

We turned to with a will, rowing across the wind to make up for the distance by which the wind would cause us to miss the island if we simply drifted. In this manner we were able to make about one knot across the wind while we were being driven about five knots downwind.

It was fortunate indeed that we were able to see the island from such a distance. If we had been much closer when we began to row, the wind would have taken us past it because we would not have been able, by our feeble paddling, to compensate sufficiently for the drift.

We rowed all day, exactly across wind at 90 degrees to our sailing direction. I kept watching the island at intervals. We found it better to row facing the stern of the raft, pushing the water behind the boat with a forward sweep of our arms, so I had to stop rowing occasionally and turn to keep my bearing.

At first we thought there was only one island, but as we approached we saw that there were two, with a wide gap of water between. It was easy to make a choice. We took the nearer island.

By one o'clock our progress was visible. The waves were longer and crested in knifelike ridges that curled and broke in a thunderous gush of white foam. There was danger of our tipping over any time one of these breakers got behind us, but, while they were in front, the spray blowing backward enabled me to judge the wind exactly.

Suddenly Tony let out a screech. His hand flew out of the water and over his head as if jerked by a string. He half turned, holding the hand tenderly.

"Chief, a shark hit my hand," he yelled, his voice shaking slightly.

Gene and I hardly hesitated in our rowing.

"Did it bite you?" I asked.

"No," he said, looking and testing his fingers.

"Then to hell with it," I said. "Let's go on rowing!"

Without another second's hesitation he jabbed his hand back into the water, deep, and we went on rowing.

As we came up on the island, I thought it couldn't possibly be anything but a desert atoll, although it was a lovely green and apparently stuck up pretty well out of the water. When we came within six or eight miles I saw what I thought was a ledge of rocks above the white beach. I figured then that it must be a volcanic island, and we might find shelter in a cavern. This would also mean that the island was marked on the map, and might be visited—by our own or friendly forces, I hoped. There was still the uncertainty that this might be in the Japanese mandate, and if that was so I could see our doom. However, as long as we were determined to get there, I preferred to think that it was uninhabited.

The closer we approached, the better the island looked to me. I could see two or three especially tall trees that towered above the others. We wondered if they might be coconut trees, but that seemed too much to hope. Until I was close enough to identify them honestly as palms, I didn't dare believe they were.

I was sure, at any rate, that there would be lots of birds on the island, which meant eggs and possibly young birds that we could capture. I thought too that there might be mussels, and possibly fish in abundance that we would rig spears to catch.

Aldrich's eyes were still in good condition. As we came in closer, perhaps within three miles of the curving beach, he turned and took a long look. We had seen by this time that the island was not so high as we had thought at first.

"Chief," Gene said, "those aren't rocks on the beach. They're shacks."

I looked again, and again I decided they were rocks.

"Wishful thinking, Gene," I said. "If they were shacks it would mean that the island is inhabited. They still look like rocks to me."

Tony had his revenge.

"Hell with the rocks," he said. "Row!"

The waves were very high, and we could see the island only when we came to a crest; when we dipped to the valley of the waves, the island sank from sight. The buoyant raft rode the roughening sea so easily that it appeared as if the island and not we were rising and falling steeply in an even rhythm, while the raft lay perfectly still.

When we were about a mile from the island I saw from the wind streaks and blowing foam that we were directly upwind, and that the stiff breeze would land us at the center of the beach without assistance.

"Okay, boys," I said. "We can knock off the rowing."

We stopped and turned about, to watch our progress. We were completely exhausted, I know now. We had been rowing all day on will power alone, but we were so intent on reaching this island that we didn't realize our terrible weakness, and rose above it.

"Well," Gene said joyfully, "are they shacks or rocks?"

He was right. They were shacks.

From now on it was just a matter of drifting in the wind. I kept a close eye on the bearings by the wind streaks, to be sure that we hit the beach.

We became conscious of a steady, sullen thunder that seemed to grow in volume. I realized after a moment that it was surf breaking over a barrier reef, and I feared we were in for a little trouble. As we drifted closer I was able to see, and immediately gave the order to square away for a possible tip-over.

I had seen natives bring outrigger canoes over heavy surf in Hawaii, but those breakers were not nearly so murderous as these appeared. The nearer we approached the reef, the larger the breakers looked. I soon saw that our eyes were not deceiving us. These waves were building up characteristically in rows one behind the other, each coming to its turn as leader of the irresistible flow to shore.

The leading wave gained swiftly in height and speed as the wall of coral dammed the powerful tide that pushed against it, and the rushing tons of water found their only outlet upward. When the wave reached the reef it was about thirty feet high. The crest began to curl dangerously, seemed to hesitate the merest fraction of a second, then fell forward over the natural dam. There was a roar like a cannon shot as the mass of water smashed, and a great burst of foam spewed forward in a straight line of boiling white which diminished in size but held its form until it washed high on the beach, far ahead.

These rows of waves were building behind us now. Our only hope was to paddle over the reef ahead of the breaker—that is, in the interval between two waves.

We were fortunate enough to pass over the reef at the one brief instant when the surf was not breaking. We could have been dashed against the rocky bottom, or the ledge itself, if we had been caught in that wild churning of forces when the breaker crashes from its great height. As it was, we did not come out unscathed.

The breaker caught the raft behind. The heavy blow of the rushing foam against the stern sped us up the sloping rear of the smaller, shoreward-speeding wave ahead. Instead of sliding down its front, we shot straight out into the air.

The raft turned a complete flip-flop. When we saw it next it was speeding landward like a chip before the surf. The three of us were in the water.

I can remember spinning head over heels three or four times, and raking along the floor of the sea. Whether it was sand or rock I don't know, but afterward I discovered that a patch of skin about six inches in diameter had been scraped from the center of my back. Gene and Tony, I learned, were going through exactly the same thing. Tony said this was the first time he had ever had his eyes open underwater.

"Everything was green and pretty," he said.

After a threshing by the water that left me only half conscious, I found myself sitting on a flat ledge of coral rock. The raft, I saw, was upside down again and was heading for the beach about a hundred yards away from me. Gene and I were close together, and we still had about three hundred yards to go to reach solid ground. Tony was about fifty yards behind us.

None of us was able to stand. I tried to raise myself on my feet, but couldn't get my balance. Then I found that the current was skidding me along on my bottom. Gene, even with me and to my right, also let himself drift and we kept abreast.

I heard a call for help, and looked back. It was Tony. Being unable to swim, he thought he was going to drown. When I waved and yelled, he realized he was out of danger, and thenceforth scooted along like Gene and me. I imagine things had happened so fast that when Tony got into shallow water he didn't realize it, and possibly he was hollering as a nervous reaction from the terrific beating his shrunken body had taken in the surf.

We caught the boat at the very edge of the beach, and grabbed the anchor line. Crawling on all fours, we dragged ourselves from the last persistent clutch of the sea, and somehow hauled the raft behind us.

We tried to stand upon our feet, but couldn't. We were terribly dizzy from exhaustion; the whole world seemed to be spinning around us. We lay on the beach together, faintly conscious of the broken coral that was cutting our flaming, sunburned flesh as our bodies jerked in the effort to breathe.

When I was able to look about, the sun was low.

A short distance away several rotting piles had been driven into the sand, evidently placed there by someone for tying up boats. The three of us took hold of the anchor line, dragging the raft with one hand while with the other we pulled ourselves painfully, inch by inch, over the jagged coral to the row of wooden stakes. I felt each of these ancient poles, selecting the one that was most solid. We tied the boat to that.

There were several thatched huts a few yards from where we lay.

Grasping one of the pilings with both hands, I pulled myself to my knees.

"Boys," I said, "you know there may be Japs here waiting for us."

They raised their heads and nodded.

I looked at each one closely. They were gazing steadily into my eyes. Tony gestured toward the police whistle, still on a cord about my neck.

"If we have to scatter," he suggested calmly, "two blasts on the whistle will be the signal to meet wherever you are."

It was agreed.

We were too weak to try to find food, so we decided to rest for the night in one of the shacks.

I chose three long pieces of driftwood lying about that were best suited to my purpose, and handed one to each.

"If there are Japs on this island," I said, "they'll not see an American sailor crawl. We'll stand, and march, and make them shoot us down, like men-o'-warsmen."

Using the sticks of driftwood as canes to support us, we got on our feet. Three abreast then, myself in the middle, we walked to the nearest hut and went in.

⚓

RESCUE

⚓

RESCUE

Commander Edward Ellsberg

⚓ *I believe Commander Ellsberg will become a legendary character. There is something about him which symbolizes indomitable man fighting singlehanded against all the forces of stupidity, cupidity, inefficiency and sloth.*

If I were God, and had a particularly tough dragon to cope with, I would say, "Ellsberg, take this worn out shield, this helmet that won't fit, these outmoded greaves and broken sword. Bring me the dragon's head in ten days." On the evening of the third day I would be hunting for a place to bury a dragon's head. Read the whole book and you will understand.

The selection which follows relates an incident which took place during the raising of one of the Italian dry docks at Massawa.

ON SUNDAY, September 13, the starboard side of the dry dock floated up, exposing all the deck hatches. I brought aboard the barnacled deck some small 3-inch gasoline-driven pumps, with which we then swiftly pumped free of water all the storage and machinery compartments in the upper part of that side wall, thus floating it up further till about three feet of the starboard side wall was completely out of water.

All the deck hatches in the starboard side wall deck leading downward to these upper compartments we found worthless for water-tightness, as their gaskets were all rotted away from long submergence. As we were unable to close these hatches therefore to retain compressed air, and the next deck down was leaking air so badly the compressors were unable to gain further on the water in the lower holds, it became necessary to get into these freshly pumped-out upper compartments and work inside them to plug leaks in the steelwork below.

For that purpose, I brought over from the big Italian dock a small gang of ironworkers composed of Armstrong, riveter; Larsen, welder; and Jones, shipfitter. Armstrong and Larsen were Americans; Jones was a very tall, very thin Englishman, one of the mechanics just through with the cruiser *Euryalus* repair job on the Persian dock near by.

With hand tools, this small crew started forward inside the newly exposed and pumped-out upper compartments of the starboard side wall, plugging all the air leaks they could find, and gradually worked their way aft.

Meanwhile, the air compressors, which had been running night and day in much hotter weather even than we had had in mid-May when we raised the first dock, were having troubles. This was particularly true of the big low-pressure Sutorbilt compressor, which, never designed for service under any such conditions, was running with its compressor main bearings smoking hot all the time, literally so hot it would have been simple to have broiled steaks on them. We used the best hard grease available for lubricating those bearings, but it always melted swiftly and ran out like water, to fry odoriferously on the hot metal, giving to all the surrounding atmosphere a smell of cooking going on on a major scale. That odor of frying grease, mingled with the smell of rotting mussels on the now exposed starboard wall of the dry dock, gave an unforgettable aroma to the whole salvage operation.

But as well as we could we kept both our compressors going and kept the air going down. I was holding the water level steady in the afloat starboard side and sending most of the compressed air through the cross connecting mains to the port side, hoping soon to get buoyancy enough on that side to float it also off the bottom.

In this situation, the dry dock was on a considerable slant to port, with its port side still resting in the mud on the bottom of the harbor and nine feet of water over its port side deck, while the starboard side was afloat, about three to four feet out of water along its whole length from bow to stern.

What I was working for was to get an even amount of buoyancy all along the port side so it would finally float up evenly, bow and stern together, with no trim. Of course this could not be assured for there was no way of telling whether the side still in the mud was more firmly stuck to the bottom at one end than at the other; also the only set of air pressure gauges we had or could get was none too reliable in showing how far down the water had gone inside any port side compartment.

All Sunday and Sunday night, and on into Monday, we kept on plugging leaks and pumping air. My three ironworkers finally arrived by the middle of Monday afternoon at the after compartment in the afloat starboard side in their quest for leaks, and there they found a very bad one. They sent Jones, the English shipfitter, for me to look it over.

I followed Jones, who very much resembled a bean-pole in build, aft along the barnacle-encrusted deck to that stern compartment. While all the other hatches in the deck were on low horizontal coamings, the hatch to this after compartment was different. It was a booby hatch; that is, it was a vertical steel structure rising above the deck to the height of a man nearly, with a rather small vertical steel door opening on its forward side to give access to a steep ladder going below from just inside that door.

Jones had to duck his lanky figure considerably to get through the opened door; then he descended the steep steel ladder inside. Even I had to duck a bit to avoid bumping my head on the steel door frame above; then I followed him down the ladder to find myself in an elongated water-tight compartment, steaming hot inside, with no openings for ventilation except that booby hatch at the forward end by which I had entered.

Lighted only by my flashlight, I followed Jones through the water-logged rubbish of what perhaps had once been used as an Eytie storeroom, some forty feet aft to the very after end of that compartment. There was Larsen alongside Horace Armstrong, who in the cramped space overhead was futilely trying to get a decent swing with a hammer on his caulking chisel.

Armstrong paused to indicate to me the trouble. A strong stream of compressed air from the still-submerged dry dock section below was whistling out past an atrociously driven rivet in the top bounding bar of the after bulkhead. It wasn't just a little air leak; it was a big one. The rivet, very loose, came nowhere near filling its hole; evidently the Eytie riveters, in originally driving that rivet, had had difficulty getting at it and had left the job badly botched.

Armstrong, Jones, Larsen, and I held a conference on that rivet. It was finally agreed to accept Armstrong's solution—give him time and he felt sure he could get that rivet point sufficiently caulked to stop the leak. It would be a slow job since he could hardly find space overhead amidst the cramped steel bracing for a fair swing with a hammer, but he felt he could do it. So, leaving Larsen and Jones to hold the light for him and spell him on the caulking, I left them fairly cooking in the hot vapor surrounding them and, with difficulty, threaded my way forward through the inside wreckage to the ladder, climbed up it, and squeezed out the booby hatch door to the deck.

When I first went down that booby hatch, dressed only in a khaki shirt, khaki shorts, and some old shoes, I had already been thoroughly soaked with sweat; when I came out, however, I was positively dripping. I felt sorry for the men below.

It was several hours after lunch and everybody was hard at work. As I went slowly forward along the starboard scaffolding reading the pressure gauges, I noted that the Eritreans were as busy as usual, scraping away from floats alongside at the barnacled side wall of the dock. Back aft was the thirty foot boat which we had fitted up with a small compressor for diving. Doc Kimble, fully encased in his diving rig, was descending the ladder over the stern of the boat to caulk some underwater leak, while Al Watson, in bathing trunks only, and Lew Whitaker were acting as his tenders.

Bill Reed, salvage master, was in the boat with them to receive whatever reports Doc had to make over the diving telephone from below. On deck the dock itself below me, Lloyd Williams was working with various mechanics engaged in trying to make watertight and airtight the ruined gaskets on the deck hatches and on some other hatches which needed bracing to hold the air pressure below them.

When I finally came amidships, Jim Buzbee, pump mechanic, who was standing watch on the air compressors, called to me to come down off the scaffolding and take a look at our big twin-engined air compressor; it looked to him as if we were in for serious trouble soon.

I clambered down off the scaffolding; went by the air valve manifold, an intricate array of valves by which the flow of compressed air was directed from our Sutorbilt compressor to various parts of the submerged dry dock; and then crawled down the vertical ladder on the outboard side of the dry dock to the barge on which the throbbing Sutorbilt compressor stood.

It was certainly a huge array of machinery. The two massive Waukesha engines, side by side, which furnished the power, were far too big ever to dream of starting by hand cranking. Instead, in between them stood a small gasoline engine whose sole purpose was to start the big ones. After they were both unclutched from the compressor, the little gasoline engine was started by hand cranking, then clutched in to the big engines one at a time to start them; then, when both the big engines were running, they were clutched in on the compressor to carry the heavy compressor load. It was quite a slow and complicated arrangement, but workable; by hand alone, no one could ever get the rig going.

However, it wasn't the engines that were bothering Buzbee; they were doing all right in spite of the heat. It was the compressor itself. Specifically, he called my attention to the main bearings at each end of the compressor casing—they were smoking as never before.

"Cap'n," complained Buzbee, "I was just about to go looking for you. If we don't shut this machine down quick, she'll shut herself down. I've never seen those bearings so hot before. I've been shooting grease steadily into 'em, but it's no use. She's running hotter'n blazes, and why that bearing metal hasn't wiped out already, I don't know. Better let me shut her down right now so she can cool off, or we won't have any compressor left!"

I looked at the bearing housings. The iron had a peculiar gray tinge I hadn't seen before. Buzbee was certainly right; they were far too hot to continue operation. It wasn't any use to try feeling the bearings to test whether they were too hot or not; I should only get a seared hand from that. I would have to go by sight alone and by the odor of that sizzling grease as it ran from the bearings, smoking as if it were on the point of spontaneous combustion.

"O.K., Jim, you're right. Shut her down. Only give me a few minutes to get up at that air valve manifold to close off the valves to this machine when you stop her, or the compressed air from inside the dock'll blow back through this compressor and run it in reverse."

I climbed hurriedly up to the valve manifold above and stood by to shut off both the four-inch valves there. As soon as I was set, I waved to Buzbee below me, who promptly unclutched the compressor and shut down both engines while I hurriedly, with both hands, screwed shut the air valves to prevent blowing back and losing the valuable compressed air we already had pumped into the dry dock.

Immediately, a strange silence fell over the dock, now the roar of those two huge engines was stilled, broken only by the comparatively trifling exhaust from the smaller Ingersoll-Rand compressor still running across the water in its barge outboard of the submerged port side of the dock.

I sighed regretfully. We had lost about 80 per cent of our air supply; it was doubtful if the Ingersoll-Rand by itself could even make good the leakage from all over the dock. I could now expect the afloat starboard side of the dry dock to start to sink slowly as the air leaked out from below. To minimize that, I set the air valves to throw all the air from our remaining compressor over to starboard to make good leakage there and hold the starboard side up as well as possible till the Sutorbilt compressor had cooled enough to hold grease in its bearings and make it safe to start it up again.

Hardly had I finished setting valves, when I felt a tremor in the dock beneath my feet. Startled, I looked up, to see that the wood scaffolding atop the submerged port side wall of the dry dock had lifted higher above the water!

The sunken port side of the dry dock was coming up, and at no slow speed either! Swiftly my eye ran along the hundred yard length of that scaffolding to port of me, to note to my dismay that it wasn't coming up evenly fore and aft; that whatever the reasons, it had already risen farther at the stern than at the bow, and that that already bad situation was getting worse as she rose.

I gazed in agony. At this moment of all moments when I had just lost my big air compressor and with it all chance of controlling the movements of that dock, the port side with no air at all going into it any longer, had broken free of the mud at last and was on its way up, stern first instead of evenly, throwing the whole dry dock out of balance and heading for possible catastrophe!

By now the port side had risen three or four feet, easily visible to everyone anywhere on or near the dock. All around I heard men begin to cheer at the sight, but to me it was nothing to cheer over. In anguish, I sang out to Buzbee below me to starboard, just beginning to inspect the dead compressor.

"For God's sake, Jim, start that compressor up again! Never mind if we ruin it now! START IT UP!"

Buzbee, masked by the starboard outboard side of dry dock near him from any view of what was going on to port, couldn't understand my sudden reversal of his orders, but like the faithful helper I had always found him, asked no questions and dashed for the little starting engine to crank that up first and get things going, while I stood by the compressor air manifold valves to twirl them open the moment the big compressor started to roll over, and shoot all the compressed air I could get forward into the starboard bow of the dry dock to hold that up. We were going to need it there.

For already I could see that the starboard bow of the dry dock was trimming lower into the water as the port side rose, high by the stern. A few seconds more and the stern on the port side broke above the surface while the starboard bow directly ahead of me, previously three feet or more out of water, slowly sank lower and I could see the ocean gradually rising toward the deck.

Below me to starboard, Buzbee was frantically working to start up the compressor engines, but it was an involved and a slow job. I looked to port. The whole deck of the port side wall was now above water, still stern high, with the entire skeleton of that eleven foot high scaffolding standing on it completely exposed.

But now I could see also that on the depressed starboard bow the ocean was already lapping aft along the deck and water was starting to pour down the forward hatches into the bow compartments of the dry dock. For me, that spelled the end. Even if I got air now from the compressor, it was too late. Nothing could save the entire dock, now all afloat, from swiftly sinking again as those bow compartments flooded and the water ran swiftly aft to flood other compartments in succession.

There was no longer any hope of keeping the dock afloat. All I could do was to see no one was trapped inside when it went down. I left my useless station at the air manifold to run aft along the scaffolding shouting for all hands below to get up on deck. Whether Jim Buzbee ever got that air compressor started then, I don't know yet. It made no difference any more.

Long before I got near the stern along that stretch of starboard side scaffolding, the whole dry dock had submerged again, both sides. Nothing of it was visible any more except a foot or two of the tops of the scaffoldings which a moment or two before had all been completely above water. All about, swimming in the turbulent sea, were the men who had been working before on deck the starboard side, and, I fervently hoped, those who had been working below decks. The broken water all about, badly disturbed by the sudden rising and the even more sudden sinking of the dry dock, was a mass of foam in which heads were bobbing about, striking out for the scaffoldings or the boats for support.

I had only one worry—had everybody got clear from below? Hurriedly I looked about me, but with mainly only unrecognizable heads dotting the foaming sea, there wasn't any way of taking an immediate muster.

But one thing I knew—whether anyone else had been below when the trouble started, Armstrong, Larsen, and Jones certainly had been. They had all been far aft inside the very compartment at the stern now submerged beneath my feet, into which I could see a flood of water must be pouring through the invisible booby hatch leading down to it, marked at that instant by a swirling vortex of water going down and of air bubbling up. Had those three men got out before the dock submerged aft, the last part of it to vanish?

In agony I looked about. I saw nothing of any of them on the scaffolding, in the few boats or floats near by. They might indeed be among the swimmers I couldn't recognize; that I couldn't tell.

My eyes fell on Lloyd Williams on the scaffolding near me. He had been on deck the dock near that booby hatch when the dock started to submerge. He might have seen whether those men had escaped or not.

"Lloyd!" I shouted. "Where's Armstrong and his mates? Did they get clear?"

"Don't know, Captain. I didn't see 'em get out. All I think I saw was a hand waving out that booby hatch when she went down, but I can't swear to it!"

So probably they hadn't escaped; they were trapped below by the inrushing water. If we would save them, we must act swiftly. Close by me at the stern now was my diving boat. In it, still fully dressed in a diving rig except for his diving helmet and his partly unbolted breastplate, sat Doc

Kimble, apparently up from his last dive and being undressed when catastrophe struck. Near him in the boat were Captain Reed, with Al Watson and Lew Whitaker who had been undressing Kimble.

"Bill!" I shouted to Reed. "Clap Doc's helmet back on him again and get him overboard! There're three men trapped in the stern here!"

"No use, Cap'n," shouted back Reed. "It'll take five minutes to get Doc dressed again. They'll all be drowned by then!"

Reed was right. That couldn't be done swiftly enough to matter. But alongside Kimble was Watson, a fine swimmer and an expert diver in a face mask, which would take him only a moment to slip on and go overboard.

"Al!" I shrieked. "Get on your face mask and get overboard to help those men!"

Watson took a look at that veritable maelstrom of water and air over the booby hatch, then answered briefly.

"Can't be done, Cap'n. Anybody going in there now'll only be sucked through and killed himself!"

My heart turned to lead. There was no absolute certainty that those three men were trapped below, but they probably were. And if they were and we waited either for Doc to get dressed or the water to calm enough for an expert swimmer like Al to dare that whirlpool in a face mask, it would be too late. I wasn't much of a swimmer myself, but those were my men trapped inside that submerged dry dock and I was responsible for them. They couldn't be allowed to die without at least an effort, poor as it might be, being made to save them. I plunged overboard from the scaffolding into the boiling vortex marking the booby hatch.

It was nine feet down through the water to that booby hatch and the instant I submerged, I could no longer see anything—just a mass of swirling water, milky with air bubbles, impossible to see through even an inch. Fortunately, my plunge took me straight down where I wanted to go; possibly the inward rush of water helped suck me to the right spot.

At any rate, completely blinded, I still by feel spotted myself in front of the booby hatch, over toward the latch side. I turned right side up, felt the door was open a bit, not much, and grabbed its edge with one hand to hold myself down while I felt round the steel door with the other. My fumbling fingers came across something soft, an arm, jammed between the door and its frame. There was somebody still down there! One man at least!

I tried to swing the steel door open but still there was some pressure of water pouring through to hold it closed. Frenziedly I braced both my legs somehow against the unseen barnacle-encrusted booby hatch, clinging to that arm with one hand lest I lose it in the rush of water when the door opened, while with the other I heaved with all the strength I had against that steel door. It swung back.

With both hands then, I got a good grip on the shoulder of the arm I had and dragged a completely limp body out of the hatch, though still I could see nothing of it. Gripping that body tightly now, with one arm and both legs, I pawed my way up through the sea to the surface.

Immediately I came up, gasping for air, a dozen arms reached down to grip me and my burden. I was alongside a boat which apparently had got there while I was below. Willy-nilly, I was dragged up into that boat, still clinging to whoever I had in my arms. In the process, the whole right half of my khaki shirt was torn from my back by someone heaving on me. The next moment, I was inside the boat, half strangled, gasping for breath and looking down at Horace Armstrong unconscious at my feet.

If Armstrong had been caught below, the two others with him probably still were there.

"Give 'im first aid, quick!" I mumbled, and then went overboard again.

Once more I brought up alongside the booby hatch, to grip it with both legs while I felt about in the milky swirl inside the now opened door. My hands came across another body, just as limp as Armstrong's, jammed in the upper part of the booby hatch against its curving steel back. With a strong tug, I dragged it clear, and shoved off for the surface again with whoever it was clutched tightly against my breast.

I saw it was Lloyd Williams who dragged me into the boat this time, while others helped. I dropped my lifeless burden on the floor boards, looked at it. It was Larsen. A little aft in the boat several men were already working on Armstrong. Only Jones could be left now. I jumped overboard a third time to get him.

For the third time I went down. The water around that booby hatch door was quieter now but as impenetrable to sight as ever. I felt through the door. My clawing fingers touched nothing. I jammed a whole arm and part of my body inside, clinging somehow with my legs to the framework of the booby hatch to keep from going through into what must now be that wholly flooded compartment, and thank God, my fingers closed on another body in the upper part of that booby hatch, apparently as lifeless as both the others. This must be Jones; there were only three men there.

With considerably more trouble than before, I managed to drag Jones' limp figure out through the little door into the clear and start up with him through the sea.

For the third and last time my head popped through the surface, there finally to be dragged into the boat to stay. Exhausted, I sank down on a thwart, while others began first aid on Jones, when to their surprise he opened his eyes languidly and looked around. The other two, who had been brought up first, were completely out, perhaps dead, but Jones, who had been down longer than either, was semiconscious! The only way I could ever explain that was that being so very tall, his nose may have come into a little pocket of air in the top of that booby hatch above the door frame, allowing him to get at least a few whiffs of air while the others, completely engulfed in water, strangled.

But there was no time for speculation. Hurriedly all three men were put in separate boats where they could all conveniently be worked over at once, and first aid for drowning proceeded on all of them.

In a few minutes, Glen Galvin and my boat, which had raced ashore for the surgeon, was back with Lieutenant Salmeri (who had lately relieved Captain Plummer as our surgeon), together with several Army hospital corpsmen and their pulmotor equipment. Out in open boats over the now wholly sunken dry dock, they went to work.

Jones was speedily restored to full consciousness. Within an hour Larsen also had been brought to, was breathing regularly, and was out of danger. Only Horace Armstrong, the first man I had brought up, still was not revived, though Dr. Salmeri thought that he could detect a faint heartbeat in his stethoscope. They would keep on working on Armstrong.

With a heavy heart and my prayers following him, I watched Horace Armstrong, still limp, still steadily being worked on with a pulmotor, taken ashore in my boat (together with the now revived Larsen and Jones), there to have resuscitation methods continued in the sickbay.

For the first time, now that the three men were gone from out in the harbor, I took a look at myself. I was a mess. I had on only half a shirt, the left half; the right half of my shirt, together with the gold-striped shoulder mark that belonged there, was gone completely. But what surprised me was that the left leg of my khaki shorts was cut wide open, and my left leg inside from knee to groin was a mass of gashes, looking as if a razor had slashed deeply into it vertically at least a dozen times. And I hadn't even noticed it before! Apparently at some point below while I was gripping that booby hatch between my legs to hold myself, the barnacles encrusting it had gone to work on me.

Lew Whitaker had in his diving boat a bottle of some special antiseptic he had brought from Los Angeles, used by the fishermen around Catalina Island to avoid infection from cuts on fish. We had found it helpful in Massawa. A good part of the liquid in that bottle went on my leg into all those gashes; then Doc Kimble (who actually was an M.D. but preferred diving for a change) bandaged up the whole inside of my leg and I was ready to go to work again.

It was around 5 P.M. Still out on the scaffoldings or in boats near by were all my men (except the three Dr. Salmeri had taken ashore) gazing mournfully at what little of the scaffoldings still showed above water. So far as I could judge, nothing of our air main setup or of the scaffoldings supporting it had been injured during the wild gyrations of the dry dock in rising and sinking again.

My men were still all more or less in a state of shock over what had just occurred; when they got over it, what their reactions might be to continued work on that unfortunate dry dock would be difficult to estimate. But at the moment, all were too numbed to do much thinking, so before their wounds could stiffen, so to speak, and slow them up, I started all hands immediately on the re-raising of that dry dock.

The bearings on the Sutorbilt compressor had cooled somewhat; we packed them with fresh grease and started it up, sending all its air down to the sunken starboard side. That done, I busied all hands in getting out from shore and from the big Eytie dry dock another set of gasoline-driven 3-inch pumps to replace the ones now on the submerged dock beneath us, which would be waterlogged and useless even when they emerged once more from the sea.

At 10 P.M. that Monday night, lighted only by the stars and the glimmer of a few electric lights, the starboard side of the dry dock floated up again. All hands turned to with the new pumps to dry out for the second time all the upper compartments, including the after one where stood that now innocuous-looking barnacle-covered booby hatch in which our three shipmates had been trapped.

There was no cessation of work, even in the darkness. Once the starboard side upper compartments were pumped dry and that side again as high out of water as it originally had been before our accident, I swung most of the compressed air over to the port side.

We had one thing in our favor. Now at least it was night, and hot though it was, we were spared the radiant heat of the sun playing on our big compressors. If only I could get the port side up again while still I had that big Sutorbilt compressor running, I would be all right. Hour after hour, I kept pouring compressed air into the port side, praying for action before dawn, while yet we had the night to favor us.

At 3:30 A.M. the port side showed signs of movement, then began to float up as before somewhat by the stern. Instantly, with Bill Reed helping me twirl valves, we shut off air from the port side, shot everything we had in the way of compressed air from both compressors forward into the bow compartment on the starboard side to hold it up in spite of the tendency of the rising stern to trim it down into the sea again.

It worked. This time the bow never went under as the port side broke surface and then after bobbing about in a mass of broken water settled down with the whole dry dock on a fairly even keel.

Savagely, in the darkness the salvage crew shifted our 3-inch pumps across the water over to the port side, hurriedly to pump out the now exposed upper compartments there and ensure enough buoyancy to avoid that side's sinking again. Meanwhile, to help the same end, I redistributed the flow of compressed air all over the dry dock to hold it as level as possible.

When dawn came not long afterwards and the flaming sun went to work on us again, we had won. Both sides of the dry dock were high out of water, all danger past, and rising rapidly from all the compressed air now being poured in. The salvage task was over. In sixteen days, by September 15, with somewhat less than half the men used to raise the large dry dock in nine days, Captain Reed and his little crew had salvaged its smaller sister, just as badly blasted by bombs.

But the dawn brought us no feeling or triumph as we gazed on our handiwork. For Horace Armstrong was dead. At midnight my boat had brought out to us the sad news. At 11 P.M., after seven hours of continuous first aid in resuscitation, at first by hand in the boat, later by pulmotor ashore, whatever faint signs of life Armstrong had manifested had vanished completely, and Dr. Salmeri sadly had to admit there was no longer any hope of revival. Our shipmate was gone. As I remembered Horace Armstrong, swinging a huge sledge hammer under the stern of *H.M.S. Dido*, together with his comrade Bill Cunningham, showing the Middle East what an American could do when it was necessary, I wept when I heard that he was dead.

⚓

MIRACLE AT DUNKIRK

⚓

MIRACLE AT DUNKIRK

Arthur D. Divine

⚓ *As long as there is a library standing, as long as there is anyone left who can speak or write, the great glory of Dunkirk will live in the hearts of men. I say their hearts. Men's minds and hands worked at Dunkirk, to be sure, but the miracle was wrought with their bare hearts.*

I AM still amazed about the whole Dunkirk affair. There was from first to last a queer, medieval sense of miracle about it. You remember the old quotation about the miracle that crushed the Spanish Armada, "God sent a wind." This time "God withheld the wind." Had we had one onshore breeze of any strength at all, in the first days, we would have lost a hundred thousand men.

The pier at Dunkirk was the unceasing target of bombs and shellfire throughout, yet it never was hit. Two hundred and fifty thousand men embarked from that pier. Had it been blasted. . .

The whole thing from first to last was covered with that same strange feeling of something supernatural. We muddled, we quarreled, everybody swore and was bad-tempered and made the wildest accusations of inefficiency and worse in high places. Boats were badly handled and broke down, arrangements went wrong.

And yet out of all that mess we beat the experts, we defied the law and the prophets, and where the Government and the Board of Admiralty had hoped to bring away 30,000 men, we brought away 335,000. If that was not a miracle, there are no miracles left.

When I heard that small boats of all sorts were to be used at Dunkirk, I volunteered at once, having no vast opinion of the navy as small-boat handlers. I had been playing with the navy off and on since the beginning of the year, mine sweeping and submarine hunting, convoying, and so on. So friends of mine at the Admiralty passed me through without formalities, and within two hours of my first telephone call I was on my way to Sheerness. From Sheerness I acted as navigator for a party of small boats round to Ramsgate, and at Ramsgate we started work. The evacuation went on for something over a week, but to me the most exciting time was the night before the last.

I was given a motorboat about as long as my drawing room at home, 30 feet. She had one cabin forward and the rest was open, but she had twin engines and was fairly fast. For crew we had one sub-lieutenant, one stoker and one gunner. For armament we had two Bren guns—one my own particular pet which I had stolen—and rifles. In command of our boat we had a real live Admiral—Taylor, Admiral in charge of small boats.

We first went out to French fishing boats gathered off Ramsgate, boats from Caen and Le Havre, bright little vessels with lovely names—*Ciel de France, Ave Maria, Gratia Plena, Jeanne Antoine.* They had helped at Calais and Boulogne and in the preceding days at Dunkirk, and the men were very tired, but when we passed them new orders they set out again for Dunkirk.

They went as the leaders of the procession, for they were slow. With them went a handful of Dutch *schouts,* stumpy little coasting vessels commandeered at the collapse of Holland, each flying the white ensign of the Royal Navy, sparkling new, and each fitted out with a Lewis gun. Next went coasters, colliers, paddle steamers that in time of peace had taken trippers around the harbor for a shilling, tugs towing mud scows with brave names like *Gallions Reach* and *Queen's Channel.*

There was a car ferry, surely on its first trip in the open sea. There were yachts; one the *Skylark*—what a name for such a mission! There were dockyard tugs, towing barges. There were sloops, mine sweepers, trawlers, destroyers. There were Thames fire floats, Belgian drifters, lifeboats from all around the coast, lifeboats from sunken ships. I saw the boats of the old *Dunbar Castle,* sunk eight months before. Rolling and pitching in a cloud of spray were open speedboats, wholly unsuited for the Channel chop.

There was the old *Brighton Belle* that carried holiday crowds in the days before the Boer War. She swept mines in the Great War, and she swept mines in this war through all the fury of last winter. I know; I sailed with her then. Coming back from her second trip to Dunkirk, she struck the wreck of a ship sunk by a magnetic mine and slowly sank. Her captain, a Conservative party agent in civil life, got 400 men safely off and at the last even saved his dog.

There was never such a fleet went to war before, I think. As I went round the western arm of the harbor near sunset, passing out orders, it brought my heart into my throat to watch them leave. They were so small! Little boats like those you see in the bight of Sandy Hook fishing on a fine afternoon. Some were frowsy, with old motorcar tires for fenders, and some of them were bright with paint and chromium—little white boats that were soon lost to view across the ruffled water. And as they went there came round from the foreland a line of fishing boats—shrimp catchers and what not, from the east coast—to join the parade.

When this armada of oddments was under way, we followed with the faster boats—Royal Air Force rescue launches, picket boats and the like—and with us went an X-lighter, a flatboat, kerosene-powered built for landing troops at Gallipoli and a veteran of *that* evacuation more than 20 years ago.

It was the queerest, most nondescript flotilla that ever was, and it was manned by every kind of Englishman, never more than two men, often only one, to each small boat. There were bankers and dentists, taxi drivers and yachtsmen, longshoremen, boys, engineers, fishermen and civil servants. There were bright-faced Sea Scouts and old men whose skins looked fiery red against their white hair. Many were poor; they had no coats, but made out with old jerseys and sweaters. They wore cracked rubber boots. They were wet, chilled to the bone, hungry; they were unarmed and unprotected, and they sailed toward the pillars of smoke and fire and the thunder of the guns, into waters already slick with the oil of sunken boats, knowing perfectly well the special kind of hell ahead. Still, they went, plugging gamely along.

I had a feeling, then and after, that this was something bigger than organization, something bigger than the mere requisitioning of boats. In a sense it was the naval spirit that has always been the foundation of England's greatness, flowering again and flowering superbly. I believe 887 was the official figure for the total of boats that took part over the ten days of the evacuation. But I think there were more than a thousand craft in all. I myself know of fishermen who never registered, waited for no orders, but, all unofficial, went and brought back soldiers. Quietly, like that.

It was dark before we were well clear of the English coast. It wasn't rough, but there was a little chop on, sufficient to make it very wet, and we soaked the Admiral to the skin. Soon, in the dark, the big boats began to overtake us. We were in a sort of dark traffic lane, full of strange ghosts and weird, unaccountable waves from the wash of the larger vessels. When destroyers went by, full tilt, the wash was a serious matter to us little fellows. We could only spin the wheel to try to head into the waves, hang on, and hope for the best.

Mere navigation was dangerous in the dark. Clouds hung low and blotted out the stars. We carried no lights, we had no signals, no means of recognition of friend or foe. Before we were halfway across we began to meet the first of the returning stream. We dodged white, glimmering bow waves of vessels that had passed astern, only to fall into the way of half-seen shapes ahead. There were shouts in the darkness, but only occasionally the indignant stutter of a horn. We went "by guess and by God."

From the halfway mark, too, there were destroyers on patrol crossing our line of passage, weaving a fantastic warp of foam through the web of our progress. There were collisions, of course. Dover for days was full of destroyers with bows stove in, coasting vessels with great gashes amidships, ships battered, scraped and scarred. The miracle is that there were not ten for every one that happened.

Even before it was fully dark we had picked up the glow of the Dunkirk flames, and now as we drew nearer the sailing got better, for we could steer by them and see silhouetted the shapes of other ships, of boats coming home already loaded, and of low dark shadows that might be the enemy motor torpedo boats.

Then aircraft started dropping parachute flares. We saw them hanging all about us in the night, like young moons. The sound of the firing and the bombing was with us always, growing steadily louder as we got nearer and nearer. The flames grew, too. From a glow they rose up to enormous plumes of fire that roared high into the everlasting pall of smoke. As we approached Dunkirk there was an air attack on the destroyers and for a little the night was brilliant with bursting bombs and the fountain sprays of tracer bullets.

The beach, black with men, illumined by the fires, seemed a perfect target, but no doubt the thick clouds of smoke were a useful screen.

When we got to the neighborhood of the mole there was a lull. The aircraft had dispersed and apparently had done no damage, for there was nothing sinking. They had been there before, however, and the place was a shambles of old wrecks, British and French, and all kinds of odds and ends. The breakwaters and lighthouse were magnificently silhouetted against the flames of burning oil tanks—enormous flames that licked high above the town. Further inshore and to the east of the docks the town itself was burning furiously, but down near the beach where we were going there was no fire and we could see rows of houses standing silent and apparently empty.

We had just got to the eastward of the pier when shelling started up. There was one battery of 5.9's down between La Panne and Nieuport that our people simply could not find and its shooting was uncannily accurate. Our place was in the corner of the beach at the mole and as they were shelling the mole, the firing was right over our heads. Nothing, however, came near us in the first spell.

The picture will always remain sharp-etched in my memory—the lines of men wearily and sleepily staggering across the beach from the dunes to the shallows, falling into little boats, great columns of men thrust out into the water among bomb and shell splashes. The foremost ranks were shoulder deep, moving forward under the command of young subalterns, themselves with their heads just above the little waves that rode in to the sand. As the front ranks were dragged aboard the boats, the rear ranks moved up, from ankle deep to knee deep, from knee deep to waist deep, until they, too, came to shoulder depth and their turn.

Some of the big boats pushed in until they were almost aground, taking appalling risks with the falling tide. The men scrambled up the sides on rope nets, or climbed hundreds of ladders, made God knows where out of new, raw wood and hurried aboard the ships in England.

The little boats that ferried from the beach to the big ships in deep water listed drunkenly with the weight of men. The big ships slowly took on lists of their own with the enormous numbers crowded aboard. And always down the dunes and across the beach came new hordes of men, new columns, new lines.

On the beach was a destroyer, bombed and burned. At the water's edge were ambulances, abandoned when their last load had been discharged.

There was always the red background, the red of Dunkirk burning. There was no water to check the fires and there were no men to be spared to fight them. Red, too, were the shell bursts, the flash of guns, the fountains of tracer bullets.

The din was infernal. The 5.9 batteries shelled ceaselessly and brilliantly. To the whistle of shells overhead was added the scream of falling bombs. Even the sky was full of noise—anti-aircraft shells, machine-gun fire, the snarl of falling planes, the angry hornet noise of dive bombers. One could not speak normally at any time against the roar of it and the noise of our own engines. We all developed "Dunkirk throat," a sore hoarseness that was the hallmark of those who had been there.

Yet through all the noise I will always remember the voices of the young subalterns as they sent their men aboard, and I will remember, too, the astonishing discipline of the men. They had fought through three weeks of retreat, always falling back, often without orders, often without support. Transport had failed. They had gone sleepless. They had been without food and water. Yet they kept ranks as they came down the beaches, and they obeyed commands.

Veterans of Gallipoli and of Mons agreed this was the hottest spot they had ever been in, yet morale held. I was told stories of French troops that rushed the boats at first so that stern measures had to be taken, but I saw nothing like that. The Frenchmen I brought off were of the rear guard, fine soldiers, still fighting fit.

Having the Admiral on board, we were not actually working the beaches but were in control of operations. We moved about as necessary, and after we had spent some time putting small boats in touch with their towing boats, the 5.9 battery off Nieuport way began to drop shells on us. It seemed pure spite. The nearest salvo was about 20 yards astern, which was close enough.

We stayed there until everybody else had been sent back, and then went pottering about looking for stragglers. While we were doing that, a salvo of shells got one of our troopships alongside the mole. She was hit clean in the boilers and exploded in one terrific crash. There were then, I suppose, about 1000 Frenchmen on the mole. We had seen them crowding along its narrow crest, outlined against the flames. They had gone out under shellfire to board the boat, and now they had to go back again, still being shelled. It was quite the most tragic thing I ever have seen in my life. We could do nothing with our little park dinghy.

While they were still filing back to the beach and the dawn was breaking with uncomfortable brilliance, we found one of our stragglers—a navy whaler. We told her people to come aboard, but they said that there was a motorboat aground and they would have to fetch off her crew. They went in, and we waited. It was my longest wait, ever. For various reasons they were terribly slow. When they found the captain of the motorboat, they stood and argued with him and he wouldn't come off anyway. Damned plucky chap. He and his men lay quiet until the tide floated them later in the day. Then they made a dash for it, and got away.

We waited for them until the sun was up before we got clear of the mole. By then, the fighting was heavy inshore, on the outskirts of the town, and actually in some of the streets.

Going home, the Jerry dive bombers came over us five times, but somehow left us alone though three times they took up an attacking position. A little down the coast, towards Gravelines, we picked up a boatload of Frenchmen rowing off. We took them aboard. They were very much bothered as to where our "ship" was, said quite flatly that it was impossible to go to England in a thing like ours. Too, too horribly dangerous!

One of the rare touches of comedy at Dunkirk was the fear of the sea among French poilus from inland towns. They were desperately afraid to forfeit solid land for the unknown perils of a little boat. When, on the last nights of the evacuation, the little boats got to the mole many refused to jump in, despite the hell of shells and bombs behind them. I saw young sub-lieutenants grab poilus by the collar and the seat of the pants and rush them overside into waiting launches.

There was comedy of a sort, too, in the misadventures of the boats. The yachting season hadn't begun and most of the pleasure boats had been at their winter moorings when the call came; their engines had not been serviced and they broke down in the awkwardest places. The water supply at Dunkirk had been bombed out of use in the first days, and the navy ferried water across to keep the troops alive. Some of the water went in proper water cans, but most of it was put into two-gallon gasoline tins. *Of course* some of these tins got into the gasoline dumps, with lamentable results. I ran out of gasoline myself in the angle between Dunkirk mole and the beach, with heavy shelling going on and an Admiral on board. He never even said "damn." But we were lucky. A *schout* with spare fuel was lying a mile or so from the beach, near a buoy. I got to her with my last drop of reserve.

Then, for grim humor, there is the tale of the young sub-lieutenant, no more than a boy, whom I saw from time to time on one side of the Channel or the other. He was sent in the early days of the show to the beach east of Gravelines, where he was told there was a pocket of English troops cut off. He landed at the beach with only a revolver and walked off into the sand dunes to hunt for them. In the darkness he suddenly saw two faint shapes moving, and called out, "Here we are, boys, come to take you off."

There was silence, and then a guttural, *"Lieber Gott!"*

"So," the boy told me, "I shot them and came away."

He had walked right into the German army.

One of the greatest surprises of the whole operation was the failure of the German E-boats—motor torpedo boats. We crossed by a path that was well lit by light buoys, spread clean across from Goodwins to Dunkirk Roads. Well-handled E-boats could have got among us in the dark and played havoc—either in the Channel or in Dunkirk Roads.

I had stopped once off one of the light buoys when a division of destroyers passed me. They could see me only as a small dark shape on the water, if at all, and had I had torpedoes I could have picked off the leaders. I might have been a German motorboat, and if the German navy had any real fighting spirit I ought to have been a German motorboat. They did send a few boats in, and I believe they claimed one of our destroyers somewhere off La Panne, but they never pressed the attack home, never came in force against our motley armada off the beaches. The German navy lost a great chance.

Germany, in fact, failed in three ways at Dunkirk. Against a routed army she failed on land to drive home her advantage, though she had strategic and numerical superiority. She failed in the air, though with half a million men narrowed into one small semi-circle, she should have been able—if air power ever could be decisive—to secure decisive victory. And at sea, her motorboats were so lamentably handled that we almost disregarded them. For long hours on end we were sheep for the slaughtering, but we got back to Ramsgate safely each time. There we watched the debarkations, two and three hundred men from each of the larger boats marching in an endless brown stream down the narrow curve of the east harbor wall. Among each load would be five or six wounded. The hospital ships went in to Dover; at Ramsgate we saw mainly the pitiful survivors of ships bombed on the way over—men with their skin flayed by oil burns, torn by bomb splinters, or wounded by machine-gun fire from the air. Most of them were unbandaged and almost untended. They were put ashore just as they were pulled from the water, the most pitiful wrecks of men. Yet they were surprisingly few.

Well, that's the story of Dunkirk, as I saw the show. Just afterward, I volunteered for a new picnic farther down the coast. Our 51st Division had got cut off with a portion of the French army in the new battle which had developed from the Somme downward, and our job was to try to get it away.

I was given a Brighton Beach boat as warship this time, one of those things that takes trippers for a cruise around the bay. We left before dawn on a Wednesday morning and made the first half of the crossing in fog. We headed for Dieppe at first, but Dieppe had already fallen, and we veered toward St. Valery-en-Caux, a little down the coast. I knew the place well, having been there two or three days before the war broke out. We sighted the French coast in the early afternoon and closed to within about five miles of it. Our destroyer escort never turned up, though we heard it having a bright little scrap on its own just below the horizon to the southwest.

About the middle of the afternoon, we sighted two boats rowing toward us and picked them up. They were full of French seamen who said that they were the last survivors of St. Valery. They had fought the Germans from their ship with machine guns until she sank under them, and then had rowed out of the harbor. They were very badly shot about, many of them dead and a large number wounded. I was called onto the tug to give first aid. We stowed them on two of our faster boats and sent the wounded off.

The German planes were buzzing around most of the time, but high up. Just as I got back to my own boat we got the signal to scatter. Three Heinkels had come over to deal with us.

My engine wouldn't start, as I had not been on board to see that it was warmed up, and the boat ahead of me was out of action with a fouled propeller. Neither of us could move, so we had to sit and watch the attack. The bombing was pretty good, but not good enough. For a long time it looked as if bombs from the first Heinkel were falling absolutely straight at us, tiny black specks that grew most horribly. They fell about 15 or 20 yards clear, and though they blew us sideways over the water they did us no harm.

Then the second bomber dived and dropped eight bombs, and again they fell just clear. While the third was maneuvering, my engineer got the engine going. I threw a towline to the other fellow, and we got under way. I had the flight of the bombs pretty well judged by then, and we worked clear of the third attack.

We started out for England. The bombers, having used up all their bombs, left us and we had a spell of quiet. However, big fighters came out to have another smack. We were far from the rest of the fleet and going along lamely. They attacked the others from a height, but when they came to us—thinking we were helpless, I suppose—they dived low and machine-gunned us heavily.

I was standing at the tiller, steering, and there was no sort of cover. One of the bullets got me through the middle. It felt like the kick of a mule, and knocked me away from the tiller to the bottom boards. However, there was not much real pain then, and I got up and examined myself. From the looks of the hole, I didn't think I had much of a chance. I told them to put me on the bottom boards, forward, and gave my gunner the course for the English coast. The tug picked us up after a time, and we were towed to New Haven, arriving about six next morning.

I was weak from loss of blood and wasn't betting too heavily on my chances of survival. However, I was operated on within an hour of landing, and it was found that I had been amazingly lucky. The bullet had done no serious damage.

I went to a hospital at Brighton. After three weeks the Admiralty moved me to a country hospital so that I could have a quiet rest. I didn't. We had 28 siren warnings in 20 days, and were bombed one night.

I am now back in town. The Admiralty offers me a commission, as a reward of virtue, I suppose, but the medical examiners say that I cannot go to sea. I don't want a shore job, so I have turned down the offer. I shall be a good boy and sit in an office awhile until the wound is better. Then I shall wangle my way to sea. I think I know how.

Meanwhile we are all right here. Germany is not starving us out; she is not going to invade us out; and she isn't going to air-raid us out. If I can't quite see yet how we are going to win—the method and so on—I certainly can't see how we are going to be defeated.

Twenty miles of sea is still twenty miles of sea, and the Straits of Dover are the best tank trap the world has ever devised.

⚓

PROFESSIONAL AID

⚓

PROFESSIONAL AID

Alfred F. Loomis

⚓ *A book of stories of the sea without an acknowledgement of the part that racing has played would be a most incomplete collection.*

Racing, from time immemorial, has been the life-blood of seamen. In the very beginning, with the launching of "Dugout Canoe II", there was laid the foundation of the first yacht club. Those two canoes were raced and the crowd on the shore were no less noisy and partisan than the crowd that watches the sixty foot, eight-oared college shells today.

Down through the centuries history-making races have taken place, in every conceivable kind of floating contraption. Perhaps the most notable were the clipper ship races. To be sure, they were not quite Cornithian, but pride of the ship and her handling was a major element, nevertheless.

Today we have ocean racing, the noblest sport in the world, where man not only contends with his rivals but with wind and sea as well. It is one thing to take to the sea for a livelihood, in ships built to withstand any storm. It is quite another to take the grilling the sea can give, just for the love of it, in boats built primarily for speed. The record made in World War II by ocean racing men is evidence of the initiative, courage and powers of leadership engendered by this sport.

Alfred Loomis, who wrote "Professional Aid", served in the Navy in both World Wars. He is a seasoned ocean racer. What he writes is authentic to the last reef knot.

THE eighth day of a transoceanic yacht race frowned on a sea rising in long, crest-tortured rollers, sinking in foam-flecked hollows. The sky, a gray ceiling of nimbus, darkened here and there over falling showers of rain; and the sea, reflecting the hue of the clouds, ineffectually attempted independence with its flashing whitecaps. The wind, ever the tormentor of sky and sea, pressed heavily from the west, ironically belying its force by the delicate tracery of its invisible fingers on the breasts of the waves.

At about the forty-fifth meridian of longitude and the fortieth parallel of latitude—an intersection discernible only to the human imagination—a small schooner of low freeboard drove across the tumbling confusion of the waves. There were men aboard her, and by that token the schooner was superior to the chaotic triune of wind, sky, and sea—she alone having definite form and pursuing a definite course. And these were men indeed, as could be told from the sail the schooner carried. It was not in the reefed mainsail that they asserted superiority. The two tucks in that expanse of canvas, bellying outboard to starboard, were, in fact, a concession to the pressure of the wind. But the number three spinnaker, its four-inch pole flexing like a willow wand, its thin canvas straining at the seams! That impertinent kite showed invincibility of mind.

And yet the men aboard the 54-foot over-all schooner, half of them sitting in the cockpit while the other half slept below, saw nothing magnificent in their audacious defiance. Those on watch—except the captain-helmsman, who occupied himself otherwise—looked steadily at the whipping spinnaker pole, at the frail triangle of cotton interposed before the rushing strength of the hard westerly. They would have said—had said, in fact—that if the Lord objected He could easily blow it away. Failing divine interference, if the spinnaker drove the schooner so fast that the sea sucked aboard her stern, the sail could readily be handed and passed below. While it preserved its integrity against the wind it added three knots to the schooner's speed and steadied her helm in the lifting, overtaking seas. There was appreciation in the eyes of the three idlers of the watch on deck, an amused quirking of the lips as they regarded the spinnaker and reflected that under ordinary circumstances a yacht like theirs would have been hove to. But they were racing.

The captain, who was also the owner and at the moment the helmsman of the schooner *Thetis,* looked only occasionally at the racing sail, and then only when the heave of a swell rolled the little ship to port and he wanted visual assurance that the spinnaker pole would not jab the wave crests. He steered with an automatic coördination of muscle and sense, a coördination so perfect that it almost defies division into its separate elements.

The helmsman's hands on the wheel, for instance, now lax and now suddenly white-knuckled, kept the schooner as true as might be on her easterly course—and it was the touch of the wheel which largely told him when to apply strength to right or left. So swift, so instinctive, was the reaction that the sensory impulses short-circuited direct to the muscles and even transcended instantaneity, to the end that for long periods of time the schooner hung immovable on her course, no more than a finger's strength sufficing on one spoke or another to keep her so.

Yet the little black-hulled schooner, presenting her stern to the onward drive of the rolling seas, was potentially able to outdo the strength of two men if more than an instant's inattention gave her charge. She could broach—that is the word of awful significance—and bury her nose and be pressed down by the weight of the wind in her sails while the sea threw high her stern and rolled her over. And then what of the men in her cockpit and those four below who had done their trick and had reposed their lives in the keeping of the helmsman?

But it was not by the delicacy of his strong hands alone that the captain steered. His eyes, clear, now snapping with enjoyment, now soft with content, watched intermittently the compass needle in the binnacle before him. That noiselessly oscillating magic of immovability gave the base course, the steering ideal. The hands, deceived by a groove in the sea when the yacht rode even-keeled and true, might have departed from the ideal by a point or more. But the needle, transmitting its immutability to the eyes and thence to the hands, brought her back again. Nor did the eyes linger in self-hypnosis on the compass card. They looked out ahead to see that the course was clear; they sought every minute the telltale whipping forward from the mainmast-head; they watched the tumble of the seas near and far, and ranged often the sails and rigging. Each glance of the clear blue eyes conveyed to the captain's brain a message of reassurance, each constituted an addition to his overflowing cup of timely knowledge.

With all going well, the sense of hearing was not called upon to aid the steerman's other senses. His ears picked up but let go the spasmodic conversation of his watchmates, and the overtone of the wind in the rigging. They were attuned only to the sibilant susurrus of the schooner's rush through the water, the rhythm of the waves overtaking.

In this art which the captain practised, the sense of touch informed him by another means. The wind, ruffling the short hairs of his neck, was a truer guide even than the masthead telltale. The eyes must impart many messages to the brain, but the skin has only to feel the direction of the wind. If the skin of the cheek as well as that at the back of the neck feels the draft, then the wind has shifted and some change must be made in steering. If, however, the cheek warms again, then it was only a temporary flaw and the course may remain the same.

Blending with all these sense impressions which made steering possible in that hard-pressed sea was the authority given by still another sense— the captain's sense of balance. At intervals the ship rose to a wave and for an instant hung. Then occurred a transition so slight as to be indefinable— so slight that not the compass card could detect it, not even the trained responsiveness of the hands on the wheel. But the helmsman's body as a whole felt the infinitesimal change in balance, and the anticipatory message was telegraphed to the wheel. Sliding off the crest of the wave, the yacht drove fast and true.

All this complicated human mechanism of steering was accomplished without fettering the imagination of the helmsman. His conscious brain forged ahead to possible eventualities, reflected back to past experiences on such stormy days at sea. His judgment hovered in a state of delicate equilibrium, ready to interpret an unusual sound in the schooner's rigging or to seize a portent from the sea. On a moment when the *Thetis* lifted high on a greedy, disappointed wave, he looked ahead and saw a patch of weeds in the course. Instantly a ferment started in his cup of knowledge.

II

The schooner had cruised for days the axis of the Stream, where Gulf weed floats in long brown disrupted banners. She had plowed through it, and her men, leaning over the side, had scooped up handfuls of the growth to examine it for crustacean life. Gulf weed had been a commonplace of the voyage. But, the Stream curving northeast while the yacht continued east, its distinctive weed had thinned. This patch ahead lacked the suggestion of buoyancy and mobility. Better, then, not to sail through it, but to give it a berth and watch it as it went by. At the next wave crest the patch was dead ahead and a hundred yards away. Tenderly the helmsman altered course to starboard and prepared to look overboard to port. The weed flashed by, and a wave in the schooner's wake broke over it.

The helmsman spoke: "Boys, did you see that? The stump of a spar with moss growing on it. Three feet in diameter and twenty feet long —end on."

The three in the cockpit jumped up and looked astern. They sat down. One of them spoke: "Hmph. Good thing you saw it, Charley. It would have gone clean through us."

"Good thing it wasn't night," said another. "Bye-bye, *Thetis.*"

The spell of silence having been broken, the captain, shifting slightly on the wheel box, asked one of his shipmates for a cigarette. When it had been thrust, ready lighted, between his lips, he puffed and offered comment. "Good going, this. Wonder how the boys on the sloop *Alcazar* are making it?"

"I dare say they're carrying on," said the first speaker in the cockpit; but added admiringly, "I never saw a boat pushed like this one, Charley."

The captain shifted position again. "A grand rag, that small spinnaker. I don't see why it stays with us." Thus he disclaimed personal merit. Of his skill as a helmsman, no thought entered his consciousness. A clock struck in the cabin, its quick double notes faintly covering the rush of wind and water. "Read the log, somebody," continued Charley. "We're making knots."

One of the three rose and half climbed, half walked, around the helm to the low taffrail. He leaned over, his bare toes hooked over the mainsheet traveler, supporting and steadying himself on knees and elbows. Astern the white cotton log line spun dizzily and whipped the water in long, serpentine billows. The revolving wheel of the log stopped reluctantly as the sailor bent his hands from the wrists and brought the moisture-beaded dial into range of his vision. "Twelve point eight," said he. "That's—let me see—ten and a half miles since five. A tenth less than the previous hour. I wonder if the wind's letting up, Skipper."

The captain stole a second from his employment and cast a glance around the heavens. "Maybe," he conceded. "But as long as we're doing better than ten we'll carry on with this short rig. No use running risks."

"Oh, I wasn't criticizing!" exclaimed the sailor, steadying himself with a hand on the captain's shoulder as he stepped back into the cockpit. "If I were in command I'd have been hove to all night."

"Yes, you would," jeered one of his watchmates. "You'd be blowing away topsails, ten every hour."

The first sailor and the captain grinned. "You're a sail-carrying crew," observed the latter happily. "And look at the smile on the face of Chris."

The paid cook had emerged from the galley hatch and stood by the fore shrouds, reacquainting himself with the appearance of a stormy sky and sea. He looked aft and caught his employer's eye. "Where we go now?" he shouted. "To hell maybe?"

"Speak for yourself, Chris," returned the captain. "We're all pure daft here. How do you like ocean racing, Chris?"

The cook nodded his head in enjoyment and admiration. "You fellers sure know how to sail!" he exclaimed. "I'll get you a good hot breakfast."

A murmur of appreciation rose from the cockpit. "Good man, that," said one. "The first pro I've ever seen that wasn't sick or scared in an ocean race. But he positively likes it."

Chris, with one foot down his hatchway, took a look around. He pointed suddenly to northward. "Look!" he shouted. "Schooner in distress!"

"The *Alcazar,* I hope," said the captain, skeptically.

"No. Honest. A coal hooker or something. Mainmast gone and sails carried away. See the shirt in the fore rigging?"

Everybody jumped up, and one sprang to the weather main shrouds. "Yes," he confirmed. "Her hull's practically awash, and I see men waving from her quarter-deck. What do we do, Charley?"

"Get that spinnaker in quick. We'll have a look."

There was instant concerted action. The man in the rigging jumped down and ran to the lee pinrail, from which he upset the spinnaker halliard to the deck. Another jumped to the foremast, and the third, at the word of command, cast off the after spinnaker guy. The outer end of the spinnaker pole swept forward, spilling the wind out of the sail. The man by the foremast jumped the jaw of the pole clear and staggered aft with it. The man at the halliard cast off, but kept the line within the circle of his arms as he hauled down the shaking spinnaker and smothered it. As the racing sail came in, Chris, acting spontaneously, shot the staysail up.

"Snappy work, boys!" called the skipper. "Set the jib too, cast off the boom tackle, and then come aft on the main sheet."

III

For the moment interest in the discovered wreck was in abeyance, and even when the *Thetis* on her new course plunged toward it the crew were concerned with their own change of circumstance. Instead of flying smoothly (however dangerously) before the wind, they were now jammed hard upon it. Two men from the watch below, finding themselves thrown from their weather bunks to the cabin floor, came up, rubbing sleepy eyes. A vicious burst of spray doused them from head to waist, and they descended with howls of protest. The *Thetis* became a leaning, laboring thing, her decks and booms dripping and her bow rising and falling with a force that jarred. Instead of slipping quietly by, waves now broke against her port side, and the wind which whined evilly in the rigging threw the crests high.

"There's weight behind this breeze!" exclaimed Charley, whose helmsmanship was now concerned only with meeting the onrushing waves to best advantage. "Glad we haven't had this for the last eight days."

A shout from below preceded the eruption of four men from the cabin. They were all clad for heavy weather, and they scrambled to places in the crowded cockpit with expectancy in their faces.

"What's the big idea?" asked their leader, amateur mate of the amateur crew. He was large, his bulk accentuated by the close fit of the borrowed oilskin jacket into which he had thrust himself. The straining sleeves stopped short of his wrists and the button and buttonhole at the throat came not within three inches of meeting. With the first dash of spray his bare head glistened, while drops streamed from his rugged face and coursed unregarded down the strong column of his throat.

Charley glanced at this tower of strength affectionately. "Glad you came up, Hank," said he. "We've sighted a shipwrecked schooner, and we'll need your moral support."

"Not one of our compet—— No, I see her. Golly, she *is* wrecked. Say, Charley, it's been blowing out here."

"And still is. We've got all we can stand under this rig, but I need both headsails for maneuvering."

"Right. What'll you do? Come up under the schooner's lee?"

"Yes, but they'll have to jump. We can't go alongside."

"We-ll," the mate drawled in disagreement, and then changed his mind "I guess you're right. We've still got the race to think of. Hope they can swim."

Each corkscrew heave of the *Thetis* brought her nearer to the wreck, which was now seen to be heeled to an appalling angle. Five men clung to the weather rail of the slanting poop deck, and their calls for help came thinly down the wind. Charley, on his feet now, sized up the situation. He knew little of merchant schooners and could not guess the life expectancy of this one. She might float for an hour or a month. His problem was how to approach her. There might be—there was—wreckage to leeward. He must not go too close. And yet he must not expect her crew to swim far. Perhaps they were on the edge of exhaustion. Nor could he throw his own vessel into the wind and let her lie there indefinitely, her sails spilling. Slatting about, they would blow to pieces.

"Boys," he suddenly said, "her stern's pretty much up in the wind, and we'll pass under the bow and come about to weather. I'll luff past as close as I dare, and we'll tell 'em what to do as we go by. Then we'll have to work fast. As soon as I get room I'll run off, jibe over——"

"Jibe, in this?" someone asked incredulously.

"The boom will be hauled flat. She'll stand it. We'll jibe, shoot up, and lose headway abreast her stern. Hank, you tend jib sheets; Chris, stand by to back the jumbo; and the rest of you heave lines and haul the men aboard. Somebody fetch the megaphone now, and stand by to come about."

They passed close to leeward of the wreck. Her mainmast, with its smaller spars and shreds of sail trailed in the water, still held by the starboard shrouds, which on the instant snatched the sticks back to punch hollowly against her. Of her decks all but the poop and forecastle were under water, and the sea tumbled over her weather bulwark to resurge convulsively over her waist. The foremast and the bowsprit, still upthrust, seemed to lean despairingly from the wind's blast. A sound of the groaning of tortured wood and wire came to the *Thetis* as she punched by.

Now the *Thetis* tacked to weather of the wreck, and the crew saw how her main chain plates had been torn away, opening up her port side and letting the mast go by the board. This side was high out of water—at least, as the breaking waves fell away from it—and all the opened seams of its black planks wept rivulets.

A leaping sea threw the *Thetis* bodily so that scarce twenty feet of open water kept her from the sullen hulk, and a voice which carried upwind arose from her poop. "Sheer off, you fools! You can't do anything to weather of us!"

Charley smiled as his crew watched him anxiously. He raised his megaphone. "Pipe down and take instructions. Can you all swim?"

"All but one. What's the matter with your dory?"

"It won't live in this sea. I'll round up to loo'ard. Jump as you see your chance. We can handle you all at once."

Hank added a postscript. "Here's a lifebuoy with a rope. Give it to the one that can't swim." He swung his powerful arm and a white ring bounced over the ship's rail. A grasping hand caught the attached rope and Hank let go its end. The *Thetis* passed astern.

Instantly Charley brought up his helm and paid her head off. Her jibs, from curved, straining boards, became gently shaking cloth. The spray dropped and the motion eased, but now the mainsail, feeling the wind on its leech, began jumping and pulling intermittently at its taut sheet. "Jibe oh!" cried the captain. "Weather jib sheet! Hold on!" With a sudden shift from port to starboard the main boom swept rebelliously through its narrow arc, and for the instant that the *Thetis* swung broadside to the wind she lay over on her starboard beam ends. Then, rudder and pressure of wind assisting her, she whisked around, presented her bowsprit to the eye of the wind, righted, and lost headway. She lay where her captain wanted her, no more than a long jump from the hulk, smooth water between.

"Your only chance, men!" he shouted through his megaphone. "I might crock up next time."

They slid, scrambled, and fell down the sloping deck and plunged, heads thrown back, into the water. Three swam independently and reached the *Thetis's* side in ten strokes and were hauled aboard. The fourth wore the white life ring beneath his arms, and the fifth paddled with the end of the rope in his fist. He passed it up to reaching hands, and turned back to his helpless comrade. But impatient voices restrained him. "We've got him, all right. Come within reach. We can't lie here all day."

To these persuasions Charley added his. "We're gathering sternway, boys. If we get meshed in those spars and rigging we'll never get out. Now! I've got to let her fill away. Back that jumbo, Chris."

"Heave ho!" cried Hank, hauling in the port jib sheet, but watching the rescue operations over his shoulder. "There are five aboard us, Charley. Is that all, Cap?"

"That's all—and damn glad to be here. Where are you bound?"

"Never mind that now," answered Charley. "I'm jibing again." His heart thumped with the exultation of a dangerous job well done. His eyes shone. "Somebody write up the log and get their names and facts. Oh, and the patent log. Did that foul anything?"

"No. It was taken in."

"Fine. Stream it, and—jibe oh!"

Again the close-hauled mainsail thundered over, and now, as its sheet was slacked out, the *Thetis* resumed the long rushing roar of her former gait. The derelict dwindled rapidly over her port quarter.

"I guess you can set that spinnaker again. No. Wind's moderated a lot. Make it the size larger. . . . Well, men, you're welcome to what hospitality we have."

IV

To the crew of the *Thetis* these five shipwrecked mariners who lay exhausted on the schooner's deck were Titans of the sea. They belonged to that unfathomable, almost mythical order of beings who keep to the sea in all seasons to wrest a scanty living from it; who, with inadequate equipment and in insufficient numbers, drive ponderous schooners through winter gales, and arrive, overdue, unconscious of their heroism. These five, who had suffered shipwreck and stared death in the face, who had accepted rescue without visible emotion, were objects of special admiration. Under their eyes, and particularly under the eyes of their captain, who had shown his contempt of amateurs in the moment before his rescue, the Thetans must sail with every ounce of smartness at their command.

As was to be expected, the story of the mariners' privations was simply told. In a hard blow seven days previously the schooner *Maribella's* cargo had shifted. To top that, the main chain plates had pulled out of timbers which had long been rotting, and the mast had given way. A week of pumping had been in vain. The stores were wet and the fresh water was gone. The end had been in sight when the *Thetis* came up. Luck had been with them, and now where were they bound?

Hank brought brandy, and Chris fresh water and biscuits, and promised hot food within the hour. Feeling the stimulant, the shipwrecked ones sat up and looked about them in amazement.

Their captain, who gave his name as Duggan, voiced their wonder.

"What the hell is this little peanut shell doing here with no harbor to run to? Racing? Where? To England from New York? What for? For the *sport* of it? Could anybody be so crazy as to look for sport in midocean in a thing like this?"

These questions prodded the pride of the Thetans. Their schooner was a staunch little ship, designed especially for ocean cruising. They raced her because there was no sport like it—no other sport in which man pitted his wits against the elements while in competition with his fellows.

It was Duggan's opinion, candidly expressed, that if they wanted to live to race another day they'd better be jogging along under foresail and wung-out jumbo.

"But what about the other birds?" asked Charley, who had been relieved of the wheel. "There are four of them back there who won't be jogging along. They'll be carrying on."

"What! More of them doing the same?" asked Duggan, his wonderment increasing. "Well, if there were any professional seamen in the lot they'd be riding easy under square sails."

Professionals. The Thetans had small opinion of such as ship aboard yachts, looking for soft berths and generally finding them; and these shipwrecked mariners had been excluded from that category. But here was the classification out of Duggan's own mouth—if they had the wisdom of professionals they'd be playing safe under square sails.

"If any of our adversaries are carrying square sails," said Charley, "you don't have to ask why they're behind us. This number two spinnaker of ours makes us know we're racing."

"So that's what you call that balloon, eh? I was wondering what it was. Looks to me like a man-killer." Duggan cast his glance aloft. "Look at your spars buckling. And look at that damn slender preventer stay. It isn't heavy enough to seize a clew to a boom, and if that lets go you'll be like we were a week ago."

"That's a chance we have to take," said Charley; "and I hope you won't feel you've jumped out of the frying pan into the fire."

"Who, me? Race your fool heads off for all of me. But suppose the ship does break up beneath your feet and you have to take to the small boats. Where'd you be in that dory, even without the five of us?"

The crew of the *Thetis,* attending to this conversation with interest and a sense of disillusionment, glanced at the dory lashed bottom up on deck and grinned. It was intended for ferrying men to shore in quiet harbors. Five was its maximum capacity in still water. There were now fourteen souls aboard. The dory situation was one of the inherent humors of ocean racing. It never had seemed more laughable than at the present moment.

"We'd have to swim ashore," said Charley; and the conversation lapsed.

Around midday, by which time the rescued mariners had fed and had fallen into a heavy sleep below decks, the wind moderated still more, and changes were made in the schooner's sail spread. The reefs in the main were shaken out and the whole sail hoisted. The spinnaker was taken in. The balloon jib and balloon staysail were set, and the course was slightly altered so that these swollen acres of canvas would fill and draw to top advantage. By these changes the schooner's speed was maintained despite the softened wind.

As Duggan came topside in the afternoon his eye lighted to see blue between the scurrying wefts of cloud. But his square, unshaven jaw dropped as he looked forward and observed the schooner's mountain of canvas. Speechless, he walked gingerly to the foremast and with his tough fingers felt the texture of the balloon staysail. It was thin, like the cloth of a much-laundered shirt. He returned aft and sat down. Like a man in the zoo he inspected one by one those of the Thetans who were on deck, seeming to see rare specimens in which indications of rampant madness were all too evident. But he remained silent, neither displaying interest in the badinage which flashed back and forth between the lighthearted watchmates nor offering to help them in the minor details of ship's work which engaged their hands.

Three of Duggan's shipmates dribbled up, refreshed, and grouped themselves compactly near him. They were clad in an odd assortment of flannel trousers and varsity sweaters with the initials turned in. In response to questions they declared that they had never felt better; but they too seemed disinclined to talk or mingle with their rescuers. They exchanged words among themselves, but these were monosyllabic. They touched cleats and rope ends and such other small objects as lay within their reach—touched them wonderingly, as one will a baby's hand, or a tiny bird's egg.

At supper time the commander of this incomprehensible craft came up from a berth which he had fashioned for himself on the cabin floor. He inspected carefully the stand and trim of the sails and climbed aloft to look for signs of chafe. Satisfied, he came down and for some minutes watched in silence the run of the sea and the appearance of clouds and westering sun. At length he gave the result of his deliberations.

"I think we'll have a good night, eh, Hank? Certainly no reason for shortening before sundown."

"Everything's as slick as hair oil. We batted off 240 between afternoon sights, yesterday and to-day. And that's going."

Captain Duggan stirred and spoke. "'Scuse, me, Cap'n, but you ain't thinking of carrying this light stuff all night, are you?"

"Why, yes. Every mile we make in this westerly weather is good for two miles at the other end. Play your luck while it lasts, or it won't last."

"I was just wondering. S'pose there was some other derelict like the *Maribella* on your course at night. What then?"

Charley shrugged his shoulders. "I've also heard," said he, "of icebergs, and ships struck by meteors. We take those chances."

"At least you keep a proper lookout?"

"I've been thinking of that. You noticed, I suppose, that we have places in the two cabins for only six to sleep at one time. Your cook has gone forward to help Chris, and there's a spare berth for him in the fo'c'sle. So that leaves just a dozen of us aft. Now, I don't want to make you work, as we have a full crew without you; but I'm afraid you'll have to stand watches with the rest of us, so there'll be room to sleep. If you and your men care to do lookout duty, it would be a first-rate solution of the difficulty."

"That's fine. Men, we'll keep the regular watch order, and I'll stand with the captain here. And, Cap, don't think we don't want to work. Anything we can do, or any advice my mate and I can give, we'll be glad to."

V

No doubt it was the memory of his almost fatal shipwreck which warped Duggan's weather judgment in the continuing days of fine westerly weather. This, and his deep-rooted conviction that a yacht less than sixty feet long was a rich man's toy, fit only for harbor sailing. The advice which he contributed with less and less reserve was always on the side of caution. Fair-weather clouds, when robbed of the lingering luminosity of the setting sun, became the forerunners of black squalls. Minor fluctuations of the barometer aroused his concern.

Once, calling upon his years of experience to back up his dicta, Duggan persuaded Charley to take in his kites on the advent of a midnight squall. But his acceptability as a weather prophet terminated when with the lapse of two hours of expectant waiting nothing happened.

Duggan's men, ever suspicious of the amateur's sailing ability, but faithful to their duties as lookouts, met their Waterloo on the day when, the fine weather ending, the *Thetis* crashed into an easterly. This was in the Chops of the Channel, where the ocean shoals and the waves are steep. The Thetans could and did make allowances, for they had been unmercifully shaken up the day after the start. They knew, too, that a man who is immune in big ships or even in ships of moderate size may succumb to the violence of a small yacht lying on her ear in a short head sea.

So on this revealing occasion the Thetans said nothing, and did not even exchange meaning glances among themselves. But the distressed mariners, more distressed now than they had been in a lifetime of sailing, dropped their heads in mortification. Lookout duty might have seemed to them a supererogation when each tortured, sea-whipped lurch of the frail *Thetis* promised to be her last. They huddled wet and miserable during their tours on deck, and one of them expressed the sentiments of all when he said, "We knew we were going to drown on the *Maribella* schooner, but this damn being half drowned and half bounced to death is what gets me."

When the strong clear easterly gave way to a thick southwesterly and the *Thetis* once more laid her course, her captain showed first signs of worriment. He was now, after more than two weeks of unlimited sea room, running fast on a lee shore, and a reliable fix was as important as the need for making every minute count. But here luck intervened. At noon the sun showed itself long enough for an accurate shot for latitude, and two hours later two coasters crossed the *Thetis's* bow—one bound north and the other south.

At sight of them the worried frown left Charley's face. "Boys," said he, bringing a folded chart up on deck, "here's where we are. Latitude by observation, forty-nine, fifty-two; longitude, a line drawn close to westward of Wolf Rock. See? That's where those coasters are going—one south out of the Irish Sea, having rounded the Longships and given the Wolf a berth, and the other on the reverse course." He gave the helmsman a steering order that, allowing for tides, would take them close past the Lizard.

But Duggan interposed his last objection. "I want to say, Cap, that in the last nine days I've changed my mind about yachts and gentlemen sailors. I take off my hat to you for making a schooner go. But going it blind on a day as thick as this ain't seamanship."

"How do you mean, 'going it blind'?" asked Charley. "My latitude was good; and what could be better than longitude gained from those two coasters? Don't they know their way?"

"Yes, they know it; but you don't. They might be going anywhere but where you say."

"But where?" Would they be running onto the rocks of the Scillies? Or full bore into Mount's Bay? And we can't be as far east as Plymouth. You'll find I'm right, Duggan. I've cruised this region."

"That's all right, but if this were my ship coming onto a foreign coast I'd feel my way. You'll pile her up, and then what will the underwriters say? Were you taking it easy? Did you run a line of soundings?"

"I'm not insured. So what do you say, boys?" And Charley put it up to his men.

"I say I'm with you until the keel rises up through the deck," said Hank. "That bad spell of easterly weather let the sloop *Alcazar* and probably a couple other windward workers slip through us. At least we don't want to finish last."

So the final hundred miles were run in an atmosphere brittle as icicles. The Thetans felt intuitively that if ever they had held the ascendancy over their rivals they had lost it in the head winds. The Maribellans knew that they would yet have to swim for their lives, holding to the gunwales of that ridiculous dory. And the quartering sea roared, and invisible steamers

bound down Channel shaved them as darkness came in, and every man
jack stayed up to see the finish.

The siren of the Lizard boomed too close as they flashed by it in a thin
fog. But it sounded when and where the captain of the *Thetis* wanted it.
And four hours later—but it seemed like fifteen minutes—they clocked
their time of rounding Plymouth breakwater and brought up in the
anchorage. No committee came to greet them, and until morning there was
no way telling whether they were first boat in or last. This gave to the
transoceanic its final fillip of excitement.

There were people at home fully as anxious for news of the finish
of the race as the crew of the *Thetis,* and they had only another day to
wait for it. It ran, from the facile pen of a shore correspondent:

At 12:15 Monday morning the yacht *Thetis* won the transoceanic
race in the remarkable time of seventeen days and seven hours, setting
up a record for small yachts that may stand for many years. She
defeated her nearest competitor, the sloop *Alcazar,* by twenty-three
hours and forty minutes. On the harrowing voyage the *Thetis* figured
in the thrilling rescue of the captain and four men of the merchant
schooner *Maribella,* abandoned in mid-Atlantic. While there is no
inclination here to belittle the sterling performance of the amateur crew
of the *Thetis,* it is believed in shipping circles that they could not have
won such an overwhelming victory without the superior ability of the
professional seamen from the *Maribella.* If this is true, the race must
take its place among the stirring romances of the sea. In return for
their lives, Captain Thomas Duggan and his men from the *Maribella*
showed the amateur sailors the way to the winning post. . . .

There was more in this vein, but a little should suffice.

⚓

THE FIRST LEG

⚓

THE FIRST LEG

Rockwell Kent

⚓ *The inclusion in this collection of a part of "N by E" is not simply a gesture to Rockwell Kent. The choice was made before he consented to illustrate this book.*

It was made because Mr. Kent's writing and experiences are valid reasons quite apart from his gift as an artist. His imagination and vigor are applied alike to his writing, to his drawings and to his life.

To start for Greenland in a 33 foot cutter is an indication of an adventurous spirit and when you combine that with the eyes of an artist, the result is worth listening to as an antidote for the blind ways and timid, humdrum life into which most of us slip.

I

THE boat lay nearly built when Arthur Allen bought her; he took her finishing in hand. All that was good he bettered—and the best he doubled. And when the three ton iron shoe was bolted to her oaken keel we thought God help the rocks she hits! Then she was launched and named.

There was to me something forbidding about her name, ominous I could not then have said; however, subsequent events incline me now to read such meaning into it. The name, a proclamation of man's will, was an encroachment on the special and sole virtue of the Gods. *Seem* to be carefree, light of heart and gay—the very elements will love you. Call your ship Daisy or Bouncing Bess—and the sun of life will sparkle on that course where fair winds drive her laughingly along. "There is," said

Arthur Allen, "one most essential thing a man must have in life, DIREC-
TION. That's what we'll call the boat."

And now *Direction* with her name in golden letters on her stern flanks
lies moored in the broad river. The bright sunshine of early May glistens
on varnished spars and polished brass. Her tawny sails flap idly in the
breeze. All is on board—not stowed as yet, but there. And as Arthur Allen
had given his care to the ship, so had I lavishly provisioned her.

For economy of space in stowing the provisions the bulk of them were
in a raw state; we carried dried milk, fruit, beans, peas and other vegetables
in preference to canned articles, though of these we had a small supply
for use in such rough weather as might prohibit cooking. Of eggs we had
twenty-four dozen, gathered fresh-laid from the countryside and preserved
in waterglass. Potatoes, onions and cabbages we had in quantity; oranges,
a crate; and sweets for luxury. We carried wood and coal for fuel, and
kerosene for light; tobacco and cigarettes—no, these arrived too late. We
loaded them in Nova Scotia.

So now for Nova Scotia the *Direction* sails. There we're to join her,
Skipper Sam and I; there we're to recondition her, from there set sail.
And yet this first departure was for Arthur Allen an event, a touching one.
Few men in all their lives are moved to give so much to any enterprise
as he had given here. The boat at last was his achievement—for his son.
And it was above all in tribute to himself that Arthur Allen's friends stood
around him there that day to see his boat depart.

The mate and two men are in charge. They cast off. The water widens
in their wake. The mate goes below.

"Goodbye, goodbye!" cries everyone.

Suddenly the mate pops up again. "Say," he bawls, "where in hell are
those cigarettes?"

II

Paris to New York   *New York to Baddeck*

Our crew, as Captain Sam at last made it, was to consist of three: him,
me and one called Cupid. Cupid was in Paris. "Oh, well," he wrote his
friend, "I'll go with you this once." And he bestirred himself at last and
came. He was a big fellow, huge. His vast muscles were encased in fat.
He had curly golden hair, a face like his name, and the expression of a
petulant potato. He was an experienced and competent sailor. He would
discourse on navigation with a familiarity that was disconcerting, and so
bewildering a technical vocabulary that, amateur navigator as I had presumed to be, I could only stammer my incomprehension. And I was
brought to wonder then why Sam, who knew his friend's accomplish-
ments so well, had chosen me to be his navigator. Cupid, as the mate,

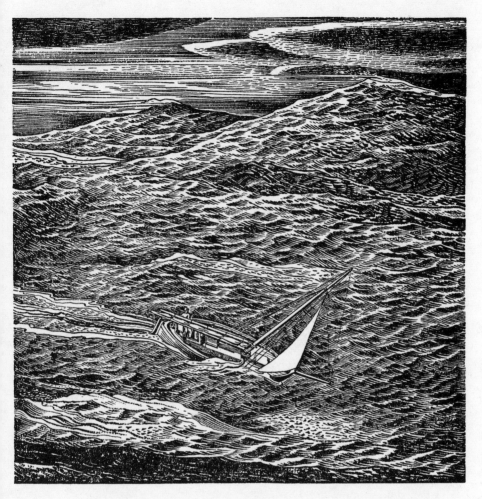

At ten o'clock we shorten sail and are hove to under staysail.

proved grand; humanly he was offensive; while financially he was a disappointment and, at last, a liability.

We have left *Direction* following, at Cupid's whim, her nose to Nova Scotia. First she stuck it into a barge in the passage of Hell Gate and broke it; then she nosed into Westport for a few days' jamboree, into Provincetown for local color and to whine again for cigarettes, into Halifax that the mate might gild the lily of his navigation under the guidance of a local master; and at last, two days before us, she arrived in the Bradore lakes and anchored at Baddeck.

There for a week we worked. *Direction* was hauled out, repaired and scraped and painted. The skipper worked on the hull and rigging; I made shelves and racks for stores, and stowed provisions; my fair wife scrubbed and polished; and the mate heavily betook himself from one berth to the other, at request, and smoked. Inertness can infuriate as nothing else; not only were we daily confronted and hampered by that heavy presence, but the very disorder and dirt and the filthy utensils that we contended with were themselves the accumulation of a full month's slothfulness. Of slothfulness the ravaged stores were evidence: half of the eggs had been consumed and most of the canned goods; while perishable supplies had been left soaking in the water of the bilge.

The skipper showed himself temperamentally disinclined to meddle with ship's discipline even when riot and mutiny were imminent. They were. Here at the outset of an enterprise on which three men must live for weeks in the confinement of a little boat, to be day in and out each other's world of human kind, one man had proved so gross a shirker of responsibility and work as to endanger the morale of the expedition. If we could only sail, I thought, things may be different; and with the thought of removing at once the thorn that festered in my disposition and the mountain that obstructed our movements, I demanded that while I was on the boat the mate should stay off. Off he stayed. Now we could work!—and sing about it.

Clothes were washed and hung to dry. Bedding was aired. The soaked food was spread in the sun to dry, and packed again in tins, and stowed. We improved the conveniences of the main cabin and so remodeled the narrow dreary forecastle that was to be my quarters that only *Direction's* last convulsions could disturb the order of its shelves.

Too often is a boat's *inside* neglected although the value of living is conditional upon how. It is essential but hardly enough that a house roof be tight. We assume that, and proceed to the establishing of conveniences and comforts within, knowing well how closely they concern our happiness. Fundamentals are important—but they are merely what we build upon, and of themselves of little value. Of what use is it to build your house foundation on a rock if you don't build a house on the foundation; if you don't make a home of the house; lure a woman to the home, beget children and establish a line of archangels that will go on and on forever? What use in merely being safe at sea? Rear on that restless element your structure of non-fundamental all essential comfort so that you may at least occasionally *think* without a world of dishes, food and what-nots crashing on your head.

So, using the little time and the few tools and materials I had to the utmost, I did, during the hours of the mate's exclusion from the cabin, build myself so secure and comfortable a little retreat in the cramped fore-castle of the boat that I could thereafter withdraw from his dull presence at every leisure moment, day and night, that came to me. And did.

III

Lat. 46° 08′ 00″N.   *Long.* 60° 30′ 00″W.

At four-thirty in the afternoon of June 17th we sailed. The exasperating delay that had put off our sailing until that date, and on that date until that hour, the misgivings I had felt about the mate, all were forgotten in that moment of leave taking. The bright sun shone upon us; the lake was blue under the westerly breeze, and luminous, how luminous! the whole far world of our imagination. How like a colored lens the colored present! through it we see the forward vista of our lives. Here, in the measure that the water widened in our wake and heart strings stretched to almost breaking, the golden future neared us and enfolded us, made us at last—how soon!—oblivious to all things but the glamour of adventure. And while one world diminished, narrowed and then disappeared, before us a new world unrolled and neared us to display itself. Who can deny the human soul its everlasting need to make the unknown known; not for the sake of knowing, not to inform itself or be informed or wise, but for the need to exercise the need to know? What is that need but the imagination's hunger for the new and raw materials of its creative trade? Of things and facts assured to us and known we've got to make the best, and live with it. That humdrum is the price of living. We *live* for those fantastic and unreal moments of beauty which our thoughts may build upon the passing panorama of experience.

Soon all that we had ever seen before was left behind and a new land of fields and farms, pastures and meadows, woods and open lands and rolling hills was streaming by, all in the mellow splendor of late afternoon in June, all green and clean and beautiful. We stripped and plunged ahead into the blue water; and catching hold of a rope as it swept by, trailed in the wake. It was so warm—the water and the early summer air. So we shall live all summer naked, and get brown and magnificent!

I cooked supper: hot baking-powder biscuit and—I don't remember what. "You're a wonderful cook!" said everyone. So I washed the dishes and put the cabin in order.

"Oh," thought I, "people are nice! the world is grand! I'm happy! God is good!"

IV

June 17th, 1929   *Cabot Strait*

Twilight, the ocean, eight o'clock have come; I take the helm on my watch. The wind has risen, the horizon is dark against a livid sky. It's cold. Never again for months to come do my thoughts run to nakedness. Nor do I see green fields, nor thriving homesteads, nor people long enough except to part from them; nor—though it's June—the summer; not for a thousand miles. And as it darkens and the stars come out, and the black sea appears unbroken everywhere save for the restless turbulence of its own plain, as the lights are extinguished in the cabin,—then I am suddenly alone. And almost terror grips me for I now *feel* the solitude; under the keel and overhead the depths,—and me, enveloped in immensity.

How strange to be here in a little boat!—and not by accident, not cast adrift here from a wreck, but purposely! What purpose, whose? And if I call to mind how I have read of Greenland and for years have longed to go there, how I have read and read again the Iceland sagas and been stirred by them, how I've been moved by the strange story of the Greenland settlements and their tragic end, by all the glamour and the mystery of those adventures, how I have followed in the wake of Leif and found America, and how by all of that I've come to need to know those countries, tread their soil, to touch the ancient stones of their enclosures, sail their seas to think myself a Viking like themselves,—then I may boast that *purpose* and *my* will have brought me here. And yet this very moment is the contradiction of it. The darkness and the wind! the imponderable immensity of space and elements! My frail hands grip the tiller; my eyes stare hypnotically at the stars beyond the tossing masthead or watch the bow wave as we part the seas. I hold the course. I have no thought or will, no power, to alter it.

So midnight comes; I rouse the captain. Chilled to the bone I go below, make coffee, wash up and turn in. Cold, but more tired, I sleep.

V

Cabot Strait   *Course N. by E.*

I came from my dim forecastle into a cabin illuminated by the morning sun. Beyond the open hatch, braced at the tiller, sat the mate, his yellow oilskins glistening under flying spray. Breakfast! "How about coffee?" and I reach out a cup to the mate.

"Just a moment," says the mate in strangely muffled, hasty tones, and he leans suddenly over the side. "Good," says he a moment later, wiping his mouth as he sits up again, "Now let's have the coffee." And he drinks it up.

The mound of blankets in the captain's berth resolves itself into the captain; devours, still sleeping, a hearty breakfast; draws the blankets over itself again, and again is mound. Even so must do the dead into whose tombs their friends with loving care put food and wine. Even so may do we all and call it life—but I no way believe it. It is eight o'clock and I relieve the mate on watch. Whew! what a cold north wind and white capped sea! Dream? here is reality so real it nips the bone.

We're in the midst of a stampeding myriad of white-maned beasts of Neptune, rearing their crests and backs against the sky, rushing upon us to overwhelm us, tossing us. We ride them, we hold our course close hauled for Channel. The wind is rising and we ought to reef. At ten o'clock we shorten sail and are hove to under staysail. So we ride out the hours of my watch.

VI

Lat. 55° 45′ 20″ *N.*   *Long.* 59° 45′ 0″ *W.*

It is five minutes before noon when the captain relieves me. I go below. With tremors that I will not show I carefully, bracing myself against the violent tossing of the boat, open a square varnished wooden case and, letting no fingers touch its silver arc, lift out my beautiful and precious sextant.

Inside, on the lid of the box, is secured a card; its heading reads:

THE NATIONAL PHYSICAL LABORATORY
CERTIFICATE OF EXAMINATION
CLASS A

and after various preliminary statements of fact about the instrument, including that "The shades and mirrors are good," informs the reader that it has no error.

I have had this instrument for years and never used it. Never known how. Its mere possession moved me. Often I have opened its case and looked at it—so beautifully contrived and made, and its bright arc so cleanly and minutely graduated. And once I found that someone had laid hands on it, for there, oxidized upon the silver, was a great thumb print. But not even to cleanse it of that would I touch it, for a stain can less obscure the graduations of that arc than the erosion of polishing.

And now at last, at noon of the 18th of June in the year nineteen twenty-nine, having for nearly forty-seven years knocked about the world East, West, North and South, in high places and in low, and been more or less finger printed and soiled but—pray God!—not too much polished off, I propose to take my sextant in hand, cautiously creep along the pitching, tossing, rolling desk of my small ship, mount to the highest place against the mast, twist my legs around the halyards, brace my shoulders between them, and, resting one eye as it were on that fixed point of the absolute, the sun, and the other on the immutable horizon of this earth, find by triangulation where I am. And if, after combining with my calculations on that sextant reading every mitigating factor the equation calls for, I choose to publish the result in the cryptic terms of degrees and minutes, it may be understood that I am not too proud of where I found myself.

I was, we were, I figured it, in lat. 45° 55′ 20″ N. And for being about sixty miles wrong in my result I can only plead that I had never figured a sight before.

Now plain work-a-day navigation is not a difficult science. It can easily be mastered by a reasonably logical mind. And yet that reasonable logic is enough to bar anyone from acquiring the least glimmering of navigation from the average routine navigator. How many times have I not, with bridge privileges at sea, tried to learn something about his art from the second officer or captain. The most that I could get was such an arbitrary rule of thumb as could prove only exasperating to one who needed to know *why*. And when once without a rule of text-book I had of myself contrived a system so that a child might have comprehended it, a captain dismissed it because it was unorthodox and set me down as a hopeless sinner. And because captains are all like that, and all text-books have been made by captains, I might have finally despaired of myself—but that I knew a poet who happened to be a mate and, more than that, a Dane. And words were images to him, and stars were playthings of this thoughts. He taught me for a day. And all I know of navigation stems from there. All that I know is little. I can find my latitude and my longitude; I can cross them and know the spot I'm standing on. I can plot my great circle course and, allowing for the deviation and the error of my compass, lay it. And that's all. But I've seen men who, with all the systems of the universe at their finger-tips, knew less.

"Why don't you try your Sumner line, or Saint Hilaire's?" said I to the mate of the *Direction*.

"Why?" he answered and turned over.

VII

Wind N. by W.   *Barometer* 29.9

All day the wind continued; the barometer was falling. At four o'clock we set a double reefed mainsail; we were getting nowhere. Below, in the cabin, the inadequacy of the standard equipment of racks and drawers was displaying itself in the growing confusion of the place. Nature and human nature were at odds; chaos versus order, wind and water, gravity and centrifugal force versus the frail fabric of the human disposition. And against such odds we had not merely to contain ourselves but to create, build up, more flesh and blood and bone and nerves against the ravages of the moment and the erosion of passing time. We hungered and we ate. And if ever I am challenged at the bar of heaven to account for my stewardship on earth I'll say: "Remember, Lord, that when you most harassed me, when you set pandemonium loose on my appointed task, when you put out my fires, suffocated me with smoke, poured red hot coals upon my feet, upset my kettles scalding me with boiling soup; when, not content with this, you kicked and struck me, knocked me down and rubbed my nose in all of it—there, then and always without fail, on time—I served hot meals, and good ones."

And, if there is heavenly justice, and if the mate by any chance passes the outer police courts of eternity, judgment will read: "You ate the eggs and canned goods on Long Island Sound."

VIII

Cabot Strait   *June 18th,* 1929

If anything, the wind and sea increased that night. Motionless in the narrow cockpit, drenched by the flying spray of icy seas, chilled by the wind, four hours seemed eternity. A liner passed us to the westward bound for Sydney, a slowly pitching carnival of light; passed and was lost again over the black rim of the world. How dark it is!

A low light is burning in the cabin; and in the binnacle a feeble lamp. Squalls strike us; the lamp flickers and goes almost out. There are no stars. You watch the compass card; and all the rest of the universe is sound and feeling. Feeling of wind and wet and cold, feeling of lifting seas and steep descents, of rolling over as the wind gusts hit; and sound?—of wind in the shrouds, of hard spray flung on drum-tight canvas, of rushing water at the scuppers, of the gale shearing a tormented sea.

Midnight; the skipper takes the deck. The stove is out. It's a cold forecastle and damp that is my room, and water has leaked through the hatch into my blankets; all nothing to a tired man. My blankets are of magic stuff; drawing them over me I'm wrapped in sleep.

Soon after midnight the light at Cape Ray was sighted. The headwind had already put us miles to the eastward of our course to clear the cape, and in the hours elapsing till we neared the land we made more leeway.

The choice was then of making port or of coming about on a long westward tack to sea. The wind by now amounted to a gale.

Youth's judgment sets the stage for its own courage; we kept at sea. And when I took my watch at eight, there, astern and off our starboard beam, lay Newfoundland.

Not Newfoundland as I had first seen it here at sunrise years ago, a brown and golden land with the sun glistening from its mountain faces and from the spires of Channel, but a grim land shrouded in scud, steel gray against the low dark ceiling of the sky. No threatening sky; it made its promise good. The norther raged, lashing the mountain seas, beating their crests and whipping them to vapor. And every hour increased its fury. Slow work and hard to beat to windward in a gale like this! Slow work and useless as the outcome proved.

There was no comfort on board and nobody cared. On duty you hung to the tiller and took what came. Off duty you went to bed. Water dripped through on everything and when the boat rolled over bilge water flooded the shelves above the cabin berths. And roll she did! Roll till her running lights rolled under; sailed with them there. And you hung on and wondered—wondered—if she'd right herself again. And pitch! How she would lift and ride those short, steep seas! climb to their tops till, over-balanced there, she'd pitch head foremost to the trough with the resounding smash of her broad cheeks and thirteen tons on water. And from my forecastle I thought: "The keel is an iron casting weighing three tons. It is secured to the boat by vertical iron bolts. On the end of these are nuts screwed upon slender threads. It is these threads that hold that iron to the boat. God, is that all!"

Long before noon, having put Cape Ray so far to the eastward of us that there appeared some hope that we could weather it, we came about; and by the hours that followed proved that in such wind and sea *Direction,* with every brave appearance of sailing a northerly course, could go exactly east and west; no more. And so much for a name.

But the ocean is of three dimensions; and if we could negotiate but one of them the wonder is that we were spared the third. Stripped to a double-reefed mainsail, *Direction* fought; she took her beating and her knock-downs and came back for more; and, as that evening we tacked into the little port of Channel, the low sun broke through the clouds to greet us and display us clothed in glory to the wondering crowd.

⚓

BORN TO BE HANGED

⚓

BORN TO BE HANGED

William McFee

⚓ *Somehow or other most of the tales of the sea have come from the deck force. Perhaps this is because when the potential young authors signed on they wanted a berth aboard from which they could take a look around. When a man with a writer's imagination deliberately chooses to be a member of the black gang, take notice, for something very special is bound to take place. Imagination combined with discipline is well nigh unbeatable.*

THE steamer *Rotherfield* lay rolling in the open roadstead at Port Nolloth, South-West Africa. She had almost completed loading five thousand tons of reduced copper ore for Swansea. Port Nolloth lay behind an enormous barrier reef that runs for many miles along that desolate coast. There was a passage for lighters and small boats. A bell-buoy made a doleful sound. There was nothing to break the momentum of the antartic rollers crashing upon the savage ledges of the reef. On the calmest day ships rolled deep as they lay at anchor. Often they rolled idle, when the surf was too bad for the lighters to go out.

It had been fine for a week. The captain and chief were ashore. The *Chatfield,* the sister-ship, on arriving that morning, had drawn her fires. The ships lay rolling gently in the green immensity of the Atlantic.

The tug that came for the lighters brought the captain and the engineer. As they came alongside the lighters, which were plunging like wounded leviathans in the mighty swell, the two men prepared to get on board. They resembled two elderly lunatics as they suddenly sprang on the upward-rushing craft and clung to the bollards. They were not very friendly really, but they seemed to have an insane affection for each other as their heads came together. We watched them from the deck without emotion.

Steam was up on one boiler and we lit the fires of the other. The hatches were going on as fast as the carpenter could hammer home the wedges. The shore signals were flying 'Come in at once.' The Bushman labourers poured into the lighters and they drew away behind the tug. The wind was from the north-west.

About dusk it blew harder. Down in the engine-room, where we were warming the main engines as fast as we could, as we passed beneath a ventilator we would become aware of a great roaring noise, a boom as of disaster on the wing, a terror coming over the sea. The ship, with her cargo very heavy in the bottom of each hold, swung with a vicious jerk that sent wrenches and oil-feeders clattering across the floorplates. At the levers the second engineer, who had been on an all-night drunk with rum sold to him by the steward, was talking to the engines and trying, it seemed, to goad them into activity. The steam roared through the drains into the bilges. As he wrenched the starting-valve levers up and down, the engines groaned as though in agony and moved a little. Hot water fell on us as the ship rolled to starboard. The water in the bilges seethed through the flames. The lamp flared on the bulkhead. We watched the steam pressure rising.

Up on deck men moved about holding on to what came handy. The poop awning had blown away. The chief stood by the scuttle, sheltered from the wind, stroking his military moustache. Across the wave tops he could see the *Chatfield* moving out to sea. She had lighted her fires again and had raised steam quickly. Her engines were warm.

Suddenly a man in oilskins and sou'wester rushed round the corner and brought up against the chief.

'The old man says the anchor's gone! You've got to get way on her, he says!' he shouted. The chief dived into the engine-room. He came down among us on the starting platform, looking stern. He knew the second had been drunk. He took the manoeuvring valve, opened it slightly and started the reversing engine. It gave a loud report and suddenly jammed. The chief stopped and felt for the drain. It was shut. He looked at the second and then made a desperate attempt to pull the wheel over by hand. The telegraph clanged and the pointer moved over to 'Full Astern.'

'Pull!' said the chief. 'All of you, pull!' He knew that something had broken inside the reversing engine, but he also knew that the steam valve, like most of them on the ship, was leaking because he tried to keep repairs down. We would have to pull the reversing gear over to astern against the pressure of steam.

It was awful. We called in the firemen, and anyone looking down from above would have seen us like madmen, piled on that four-foot flywheel. The telegraph clang-clanged 'Full Astern!' and the engines did not move. We sweated and yelled at each other to pull. The chief slipped and fell against the manoeuvring valve, cutting his head in a long gash. The telegraph clanged. The second engineer let out a stream of obscenity. We leapt upon the wheel and slowly bore it round. A figure in oilskins came down the ladder backwards, his head over his shoulder, his face red and wet as though he had been weeping.

'The skipper says, if you don't get her astern she'll be on the reef in five minutes, he says.'

'Oh, for Christ's sake get to hell out of it!' said the second, and the man ran up the ladder very fast.

'Don't say I didn't tell you!' he shouted and disappeared high up among the gratings.

We leapt upon the wheel and bore it round. 'Now!' screamed the chief, 'Now!' He opened the manoeuvring valve. There was a loud noise of water hammering in the cylinders, a grunt and the engines gathered way. They were moving astern. The telegraph banged like a brazen lunatic. FULL—FULL ASTERN! The engines gathered more way. The fire-doors slammed as the men got back to their work. The chief stood looking at the gauges, breathing in great gasps, blood running down his face and over his chest where his singlet was torn. It had clotted on his moustache and his eyebrow. A handkerchief was tied around his head, smeared with grease and blood. It seemed a long time before the order came to go slow ahead. And the rolling had ceased. She pitched slowly as the old man headed her to the north-west into the terrible wind. Afterwards we learned how he had watched the ship drifting upon the reef while we were struggling with the broken reversing engine. She shuddered as the oncoming seas struck her on the bows.

Down below we were too busy to notice the weather. It was ten o'clock when the chief told me to go and turn in. My watch was at midnight. I had been down there for eleven hours. I washed my hands and ran up the ladder.

The sea was washing about the after well-deck. Our quarters were under the poop. It was very dark. Over-side the teeth of the wave tops showed white. I had to get along. I jumped down and ran as far as number three winch, when the ship went forward and the shock and stumble as she took it green on the foredeck made me pause. Then I let go of the winch and ran. The sea came along at fifty miles an hour. I remember a thundering noise, as of a vast herd stampeding behind me. I was caught up, and in a sort of trance I seemed to float away out of the world.

There remains no memory of fear or conscious peril during that moment. Only an elemental curiosity and a faint embarrassment at the unexpected novelty of extinction. There came, as I lay face downward in the subsiding water pouring off the poop, where I had been carried, a dull, familiar vibration. As though a man, passing through a dark purgatory, should hear a clock ticking. The beat of the propeller came up the tunnel ventilator.

Blessed sound! I was alive. Lying there in sodden immobility, the thought of being alive became unimportant. The drag of heavy dirty clothes soaking with sea water reminded me that my bed-place would be flooded. The ventilator, which I had turned that morning to keep the stench of the captain's hen-house from my cabin, would swallow that sea wide-mouthed. I could see, without being there, my shoes and carpet washing to and fro on the floor, my blankets dripping, my pillow and mattress repulsive pieces of sludge. Curiously that became enlarged in the mind: I could not face it. For a moment there was blended with the wonder of my experience a revulsion from the misery of the next two hours. And then came an insistent desire to make a renewed contact with humanity. For all the rest of them knew, I was gone overboard. Through the darkness, by the faint glow from the galley window, I saw one of the lifeboats lying on the deck, stove in. I saw strange serpentine forms on the deck below me, which were the rails and steampipes torn into fantastic loops. The chicken house had been swept away. I stood by the cabin entrance filled with exasperation at the senseless disorder of the sea. There was, in the white gleam of an enormous wave that flew past without boarding, the slavering grin of a hurried omnipotent maniac. I had a sudden hatred of nature. The cabin stairway was aglow with a faint comforting radiance from the cabin lamp. I stepped over the coaming and went down the curving steps.

In the cabin the captain sat at the cabin table. He sat with his arms laid upon it before him, his eyes fixed upon the fireplace, where a brass stove stood. He was perfectly still, his white head and ruddy face with its white moustache contrasted against the maple panels. The light of the cabin lamp fell upon his immense hands lying on the dark red cloth.

What he thought when he glanced up and saw one of the engineers, who were responsible for the hell he had gone through, I do not know. For him I embodied all the uncontrollable hazards of his calling. As he raised his arm to point to the stairway, the ship plunged, as though sliding down some colossal fissure in the sea. The lamp swung and the rays struck against his face, the face of an old colonel of guards. We remained staring at each other as the deck overhead took the impact of hundreds of tons of water. Down in the cabin it sounded as though great boulders of rock were being hurled upon her. The ship staggered. A pan fell with a ringing crash in the pantry. And then once more we heard the propeller. The captain still pointed. But the familiar beat had reminded him that engineers had their uses. He said quietly:

'What do you want down here? How did you . . .?'

I said I had been washed up on the poop. I said I had been nearly washed overboard. He considered this for a moment, as if he regretted the incompleteness of the disaster.

'Washed up . . .? You must have been born to be hanged,' he said, half to himself. And then, 'You'd better get yourself turned in.'

⚓

THE FLAMING CHARIOT

⚓

THE FLAMING CHARIOT

Guy Gilpatric

⚓ *To attempt to represent life at sea without giving humor its due place would be gross misrepresentation.*

Unfortunately, one story of Guy Gilpatric's merely serves to whet the appetite for more, just as with Mr. Glencannon, one dollop o' Duggan's Dew o' Kirkintillock is inadequate properly to demonstrate its great virtues.

IT WAS an afternoon of lowering skies and leaden seas on which the white-caps gleamed with that unaccountable brightness which presages a storm. A wind that had swept across four hundred miles of Mediterranean since it took its leave of Africa was whisking away these white-caps, turning them into spray, and then sullying the spindrift with clouds of Tyne-coal soot which belched from the funnel of a singularly ugly tramp steamer. This vessel was the *Inchcliffe Castle,* and she was snouting her way Northward past the Balearics towards Marseilles at a spanking clip of seven knots an hour.

Now it happened that this rate of speed, although considerable for her and being, in fact, about twice as fast as a man can walk, was by no means satisfactory to Mr. Montgomery. Therefore, he growled impatiently to himself, strode to the speaking tube, and whistled the engine room. "The bridge'll speak to the Chief," he said. "Oh, are you there, Mr. Glencannon? —Well, I s'y, ay'nt there nothing you can do to choke another knot or so out of 'er? There's a chap out 'ere 'oo's sculling past us in a punt!"

"Ah, noo!" replied a voice in which were combined the tin of the tube and the timber of Aberdeen. "What ye say, Muster Montgomery, is inaccurate on the vurra face o' it! In the feerst place, the poont is a type o' craft unknown in these waters, and the waters is too deep for it anyway. In the second place, I've got the old teapot deleevering her maxeemum, and leaking steam at every pore. And in the theerd place, I'll thank ye to leave the engines to me and mind yere ain domned business." Whereupon, with crushing finality, the tube snapped shut.

"There!" complained Mr. Montgomery to the quartermaster at the wheel. "Bly'me if there ever was a man like 'im!" And returning to the starboard wing of the bridge, he trained his binoculars astern at a three-masted barkentine which, close hauled and with all sails set, was scudding along in swift pursuit.

"Why, I never seen anything like it!" he muttered, in awed and reluctant admiration. "In another 'arf hour, that perishing old windjammer'll be showing us 'er 'eels! I'd better notify the Old Man. . . ."

Shortly, he was joined by Captain Ball, who borrowed his glasses and scanned the barkentine with an expert eye. "Well," he said after a thorough inspection. "He's certainly giving her all she'll take, but he'll jolly well yank her sticks out if he doesn't watch her!"

"Yes, and he'll jolly well pass us if we don't watch 'im!" said Mr. Montgomery. " 'Umiliyting, I calls it, Sir, being trimmed by a ruddy windjammer!"

"H'm," mused Captain Ball, "Sail beating steam . . . it is a narsty idea, at that! I'll just speak to Mr. Glencannon." And he, too, stepped to the tube and had a parlance with the choleric genius who presided below.

When he returned, his face was purple and his mustache was trembling. But soon the clank of furnace-doors and the scrape of coal shovels came up through the skylights—these, and a voice raised in profane exhortation. Then the pulse of the engines throbbed swifter to the stimulus of steam, and the deckplates set up a new vibration as the *Inchcliffe Castle* protestingly increased her gait through the water.

"Ah ha, now we're snorting!" said Captain Ball, glancing at his watch and peering through the glasses at the indicator of the patent log. "I bet Mr. Glencannon'll get a good ten and a quarter out of her."

Mr. Montgomery shook his head dubiously. "I suppose 'e could if anybody could, but just the syme, Captain, I'm afryde that blinking syle boat will shyme us yet!"

The crew, now, were watching the vessel astern. They stood in groups along the *Inchcliffe Castle's* well-deck, marvelling at the other's speed, waxing sarcastic about their own ship, and laying bets as to the time which would elapse before they took the windjammer's wake. For steadily, steadily, she was overhauling them.

Captain Ball beat his fist upon the bridge-rail in helpless exasperation. "Hell's bones!" he groaned. "She's an old-time racing clipper, or the ghost of one, that's what she is! I was fifteen years in sail myself, and I tell you no ordinary tub can travel like that.—No, nor no ordinary skipper, either!"

"I can't myke out 'er nyme—there's no 'eadboards on 'er," said Mr. Montgomery. "My word, Captain, look—'e's planning to shyve us close!"

"Yes—so's he can give us the horse-laugh when he goes by," growled Captain Ball.

High aloft above the barkentine's deck, tiny figures clambered out along the foreyards, while below, groups were hauling in on the main and mizzen sheets until the great sails stretched taut as drum heads. Heeled over until her lee rails hissed whitely through the water, she charged along like a massive pile of gale-driven thunderclouds. Her sails were dirty and frayed and patched; her black hull was streaked and lumpy as the outside of a leaky tar-barrel, and yet, despite it all, she was regal, majestic, beautiful. As she swept alongside the *Inchcliffe Castle,* the roar of water past her bows and the drone of wind through her towering pyramid of hemp and canvas made a hymn to honor the passing of a queen.

"By George, what a sight!" exclaimed Captain Ball. "I say, just ask Mr. Glencannon to step up here. He might as well share our shame."

By the time Mr. Glencannon, in overalls and carpet slippers, had arrived upon the bridge, the two ships were neck and neck. "Foosh!" he said disgustedly, wiping the perspiration from his chin. "So yon's the cause o' all the uproar! Weel, I've seen sail boats monny's the time before. . . ."

"—Yus, and I s'pose you've orften 'ad 'em syle rings around you, too," sneered Mr. Montgomery.

"No, I never ha'," replied Mr. Glencannon with unshaken calm. "And for the vurra gude reason that all the vessels I've sairved on in the past had speed enough to get oot o' their own way. But as lang as ye've seen fit to get pairsonal, Muster Montgomery, I'll just reemind ye that . . ."

He was interrupted by a shout. Down on the *Inchcliffe Castle's* well-deck, the men were pointing excitedly toward the barkentine. "Look, look yon!" exclaimed Mr. Glencannon, following their gaze. "Why, domned if I ever beheld such a spectacle!"

The vessel's decks and rigging were peopled with characters who might have stepped from the pages of the Old Testament. Every man aboard her was clothed completely in black, and had hair that swept his shoulders and a beard that reached his waist! It was a strange and eerie sight. It made one think of the Flying Dutchman, and to expect the Klaboterman himself to clamber gibbering into the shrouds before the ghost-ship should vanish into mist.

"Lunateecks oot for a peekneek!" pronounced Mr. Glencannon, breaking the awed silence.

"Lunatics, and no mistake, but they're great sailors all the same!" grunted Captain Ball. "That's the skipper—the big brute there on the quarter-deck. I say, give the old shell-back a hail, Mister Mate."

"Barkentine a-hoy-y-y!" called Mr. Montgomery. "Wot's yer nyme?"

"What the hell is it to you?" bellowed a voice from between the cupped hands of the bearded skipper, and its accent was distinctly American.

"Haw!" chuckled Mr. Glencannon delightedly. "There's yere answer, Muster Mate! Yon is a master o' reepartee and a mon after my ain heart!" And reaching for the whistle-cord, he applauded the patriarch with three hoarse blasts of the *Inchcliffe Castle's* siren. Then, as the poop of the barkentine slid past the *Castle's* bridge, he removed his cap and waved it politely—a salute which the bearded one acknowledged by thumbing his nose.

Mr. Glencannon, outraged by this gratuitous discourtesy, leaned over the rail and shook his fist. "Why, ye whuskery Yankee goat!" he shouted. "Get 'oot o' our way or we'll run ye doon!"

"In a hawg's eye you will!" scoffed the bearded one, turning on his heel to glance into the binnacle. "Well, so-long, you limping lime-juicers— I'll tell 'em you're coming in Marseels!" He paused just long enough to thumb his nose once more—this time over his left shoulder, and with something of a flourish.

The wind was freshening, and in response to a gust, the barkentine lay over and surged triumphantly ahead.

"Well," sighed Captain Ball mournfully, as her transom hove into view. "That's that! What's her name, anyway?"

"*Flaming Chariot*," read Mr. Glencannon, squinting his eyes. "*Flaming Chariot*, o' Savannah, Georgia."

II

With much coughing and churning, two little French tugs butted the *Inchcliffe Castle* between the granite walls of the Bassin de la Joliette. She ran out her lines and made fast to the wharf. Mr. Montgomery, his labors ended, waved to the bridge from the fo'c'sle head and pointed to a stately three-master berthed in the opposite side of the dock.

"Well, damme if it isn't the *Flaming Chariot!*" exclaimed Captain Ball. The Marseilles harbor pilot, hearing him, nodded, and placing his fore-finger against his temple, agitated it as though scrambling eggs. "*Fou— ils sont fou*—all crez-zee," he declared, indicating the barkentine. "*Crez-zee Americains!*"

"Yes, I fancy they are a bit cracked," agreed Captain Ball, observing that those members of the *Flaming Chariot's* crew who were not engaged in labor were wearing long black robes and smoking corn-cob pipes. "Who are those chaps, anyway?"

"Crez-zee *Americains,*" repeated the pilot, in full and final explanation.

For the next few days the gentlemen of the *Inchcliffe Castle* were too busy to bother about their hirsute neighbors. But one afternoon, when the cargo had been discharged and they were awaiting orders from the agent, Captain Ball yawned, stretched, and said something about paying the barkentine a visit.

"—Me wisit them impudent coves?—Well, orl right if you s'y so, Sir," agreed Mr. Montgomery reluctantly. "But suppose we tyke Mister Glencannon along. After orl, it's 'im we 'ave to thank for our disgryce."

"I'll deem mysel' honored to accompany ye, Captain," said Mr. Glencannon. "I'd like to mak' an inspection aboord yon Yankee zoo. The boorish behavior o' that whuskery skeeper still rankles beeterly."

They strolled down the dock and entered the gate at the opposite side. Over their heads soared the mighty jib-boom of the *Flaming Chariot*—a spar which jutted from her bow out over the traffic to the very center of the Rue Sainte Pauline.

"An old clipper hull—of course—I knew she was a clipper!" declared Captain Ball. "Look at the taper of her; why, she's built like a wedge!"

"Vurra curious," conceded Mr. Glencannon somewhat absently, as he abhorred all sailing ships and this one in particular. "But whoosh, Captain, do ye look at the rust and feelth o' her! 'Tis a wonder the old tub stays afloat!"

"You bet it's a wonder! Why, do you realize, gentlemen, that this craft must be at least sixty years old? Before they re-rigged her as a barkentine, I wouldn't doubt if she'd done seventeen knots or better."

"Only farncy!" remarked Mr. Montgomery, casting a sour glance at Mr. Glencannon. "Seventeen knots and not a h'engineer aboard 'er!— Bly'me, look!" he lowered his voice, "Look there, Captain—the silly blighters are wearing sandals!"

With their flowing black robes tucked up under them, a number of the crew were sitting in the shade of the deck-house, rolling dice. Two or three of them were smoking, and from the condition of the adjacent scupper, it was apparent that the remainder chewed tobacco. They looked, talked and behaved like a conclave of renegade saints.

Aft, beneath the awning, the skipper was engaged in darning a pair of red flannel drawers. Beside his deckchair stood a two-gallon jug and a tin cup, to which he referred frequently and with gusto. It was during such an interval that he spied the delegation from the *Inchcliffe Castle*.

"Well, damned if it ain't the limping limejuicers!" he roared. "Howdy, brethren, howdy! Come aboard and rest your hats!"

"A-weel," murmured Mr. Glencannon. "He seems a bit more ceevil, but I dinna trust him. There's the ladder to yere left, Captain Ball . . . after you, Sir."

They were welcomed on the deck by the bearded skipper, who towered at least six feet seven in his sandalled feet, and was broad and resonant in proportion. "I'm glad you-all dropped in, brothers!" he boomed. "We're clearing with a cargo for Barcelona tomorrer night. Jest unjoint yourselves under this-here awning while I go to my room and break out a fresh jug. Sho', it's the slickest home-made cawn you ever tasted! I can't abide these namby-pamby dago liquors, can you?"

Shortly, he reappeared with a jug and three tin cups. "Aft, the Mates!" he shouted, and then, uncorking the jug, "The Mates is my sons," he explained. "I'd like for you-all to shake hands with 'em."

They were joined by three hairy, bearded huskies who stood fumbling with their robes and digging shyly at the deck-caulking with their horny bare toes.

"Gents," said the skipper, "These here's my sons—Shadrach, Meshach, and Abednego. Tell the comp'ny howdy, boys.—You, Meshach, take your fingers out of your nose!"

"Do you look at yon Meshach," whispered Mr. Glencannon, plucking at Mr. Montgomery's sleeve. "I saw him this morning wiping up the dock wi' five French stevedoors."

"Yes," the skipper was saying, as the trio shuffled away. "They're three good boys and three good mates. And now I'll interduce myself. I'm Ezekiel the Prophet." Quite oblivious to the startled expressions of his visitors he shook hands all around.

"I s'pose I ought to ax pardon for the way I acted, t'other day," mused the Prophet, as he tilted the jug over the crook of his mighty arm. "I'm always kind of short-tempered when I'm at sea. And then, besides, we'd lost the Prophetess only the night before."

"Oh, noo, let me understand ye, Sir," said Mr. Glencannon with ready sympathy. "Do ye mean to say that Mrs. Ezekiel is—er—dead?"

"Yop, you got the idea," nodded the skipper airily. "During the night, Ma heard the Call, so she clumb up to the cross-trees and jumped overboard. It was a mighty slick passing, I'm here to state!"

"Weel, weel, weel, I never!" breathed Mr. Glencannon in amazement.

"Why, sure you never!" beamed the Prophet. "I reckon it all sounds strange to you, brethren, because you don't understand our religion. Well, it's a danged good religion. I'm the boss of it, back in Savannah. I wrote it all myself." And helping himself to a sizeable snifter of corn whisky, he raised his cup, bowed politely, and tossed it off.

"Dawg-gone!" he exclaimed. "That there's the stuff for your bunions! How does it set with you, gents?"

"It's vurra deleecious," said Mr. Glencannon. "It tastes a wee bit like petroleum, only sweeter.—But aboot yere releegion, Sir, ye interest me. I'm a member o' the Kirk in gude standing and a bit o' a theologian mysel', so I wonder wad ye just briefly expoond yere doctrines for my benefeet?"

"Well, they're pretty complicated," said the Prophet, guardedly. "Besides, we don't want no Scotchmen in our religion anyway."

"Oh!" said Mr. Glencannon, gagging as the corn whisky reached his tonsils, and therefore failing to feel the kick which Mr. Montgomery landed in the bulge beneath his deck chair. By the time he had finished his drink and refilled his cup, the Prophet was telling Captain Ball about the ship.

"Why, sho', she's one of the oldest and fastest ships afloat!" he declared. "She was a clipper, built to run the blockade out of Charleston during the War, and . . ."

"The War? Well, that ayn't so long ago," chimed in Mr. Montgomery.

"Aye," agreed Mr. Glencannon, taking his nose out of his cup and feeling to see if his mustache was on fire. "I reecall the War as though it were yesterday!"

"—From 1863 to now ain't long? And you, Mister Scotty—you say you can remember it? Oh, why hell, boys, it's the Civil War I'm talking about —the American War of the Rebellion—not the German War!"

"Oh," said Mr. Montgomery. "A bit of a family brawl, so to s'y. Well, I 'adn't never 'eard of it."

"No, you wouldn't of, you being a limejuicer," said the Prophet, deep pity in his voice. "But I'll tell the world it must of been some war jest the same! Why, if you look sharp along them bulwarks and deckhouses, you can still find cannister shot and minnie balls under the paint and pry 'em out with your knife. Yes, sir," and his eye twinkled strangely, "We've found some mighty funny things aboard this here old ship!"

Mr. Glencannon, engaged in further experimentation with the liquor, had heard comparatively little of this discourse. At about this time, as a matter of fact, he was surprised to find himself floating in a silvery fog through which voices filtered strangely. He peered curiously at the distance-dimmed faces to see if this sudden separation of his astral and physical selves was occasioning comment, but observing that the company was too busy having another drink to bother about such minor psychic phenomena, he banished his fears and joined them. It was really very pleasant, albeit a trifle confusing. . . .

Once, he was conscious of singing *"Scots Wha Hae Wi' Wallace Bled"* through all its several verses. Again, he realized that a whiskery giant was weeping upon his shoulder and that the whiskers tickled his ear.

There was a lapse of time, and then, magically, the scene shifted. He was seated at a table around which were Captain Ball, Mr. Montgomery, and four men with beards so long that the ends were hidden beneath the edge of the table. A Negro, similarly bearded but wearing a gingham apron over his black robe, was serving fried chicken smothered in a creamy white sauce, and pouring a colorless liquid out of a jug. The chicken was delicious. The liquid tasted something like petroleum, only sweeter. . . .

"Yea verily!" boomed a thundering challenge out of nowhere. "We Americans can outsail, outfight, outdrink and outspit any other nation on the face of this earth!"

"A-men!" came a basso response from three black figures seated in a row. "A-men and hallelujah!"

"A hoonderd poonds ye're wrong!" cried somebody, springing to his feet. "Though ye trimmed us at sea, ye domned Yankee, I'll bet ye five hoonderd o' yere ain dollars that ye canna do it again, and you to arrange the details!"

Mr. Glencannon was about to applaud these stalwart sentiments; but then, too late, he realized that the voice was his own, and that, instead of springing to his feet, he had merely fallen into the mashed turnips.

III

Mr. Glencannon was awakened by some one shaking him violently, and he opened his eyes to find himself in his room aboard the *Inchcliffe Castle.* "Come, wyke up!" said a voice which he recognized as that of the Mate. "Wyke up! You 'aven't any time to wyste, you 'aven't."

With difficulty managing to disengage his tongue from the roof of his mouth, "Any time to waste for what?" he inquired thickly. "What is the necessity for a' the roosh and bustle?"

"Why, to get ready for the ryce—the life-boat ryce you challanged the Prophet to larst night!"

"Life-boat race? Why, mon, ye're daft! Whatever are ye talking aboot?" Mr. Glencannon sat bolt upright and then abruptly lay down again.

"Well, it's you who's daft, if ye arsks me," shrugged Mr. Montgomery. "Nobody but a cryzy man would 'ave challenged them gryte 'airy aypes to a rowing ryce and bet a 'undred pounds on it, like you did!"

"A hoonderd poonds?" repeated Mr. Glencannon, weakly. "Ah, noo, noo, Muster Montgomery, let's get this straight. I dinna reecall a word aboot it!"

It appeared, from the Mate's explanation, that the race would be rowed over a course from the basin entrance to the Anse des Catalans light-buoy and back; that Mr. Glencannon and the Prophet Ezekiel would act as coxswains of their respective crews; that the craft used would be two identical life-boats furnished by the *Inchcliffe Castle,* and that the race would start promptly at 2 P.M.

"Yus, and you agreed to it yourself larst night," insisted Mr. Montgomery. "Orl 'ands of both ships 'as been betting on it since morning. It's 'arf arfter twelve now, so you'd jolly well better be picking your crew and getting ready, you 'ad!"

"Whoosh!" said Mr. Glencannon, arising with a Spartan effort. "'Tis vurra plain that with a hoonderd pounds at stake I must summon a' my keenest faculties." And reaching under his bunk, he dragged forth a bottle of Duggan's Dew of Kirkintilloch, filled a tumbler to the brim, and drank it without a flicker of an eyelash.

"There!" he said, smacking his lips. "I shall noo pull on my troosies and set my intellect to work. Meanwhile," and he bowed his head and gnawed thoughtfully at his mustache, "Meanwhile, Muster Montgomery, I'll thank ye to order Number One life-boat lowered into the water richt away, and to have Number Three let doon so's its exoctly opposite the loading door on the poort side. Stand by till I give ye the word to lower it the rest o' the way."

"Right-o!" said Mr. Montgomery, stepping briskly out on deck and blowing his whistle. Then, having given his orders, "Strike me if I don't believe 'e's sunk this time!" he chuckled. "Even that Scotch 'ighw'yman can't swindle his w'y past a boatload of ruddy seven-foot 'Erculeses!"

But later that afternoon as he stood with the cheering crowd upon the pier-head, he changed his mind—yes, and cursed himself for having bet his money on the *Flaming Chariot's* crew. Even though the racing craft were still beyond the Vieux-Port, it was evident that the *Castle's* was well in the lead. Through his glasses, Mr. Montgomery could see that the men were pulling along swiftly, easily, and that Mr. Glencannon, standing in the stern-sheets with the tiller betwen his knees, was fortifying his strength with copious drafts from a quart bottle. Several similar bottles, he observed, were in circulation among the oarsmen.

As the boats approached the finish line, the bearded giants were jaded, weary and sore beset. The Prophet Ezekiel, garbed in his flowing robes, raised voice and arms in futile effort to goad them on. "Row, row, ye shuddering sinners!" he stormed. "You, Shadrach, fer the love o' tunket put some beef into it! Hep! Stroke! Hep!—Wake up, Zeruiah, wake up, gol dang it, before I take this-here tiller and flail the livin' wamus off'n ye!"

But his eloquence was of no avail. Leisurely the *Inchcliffe Castle's* boat crossed the line a dozen lengths in the lead. As it did so, Mr. Glencannon turned, struck an attitude, and with a sweeping gesture thumbed his nose at his vanquished rivals. Then, reacting to the strain of it all, he took a final swig from his bottle and collapsed into the boat.

"Well, I never seen the like, Sir!" said the crestfallen Mr. Montgomery. " 'Ow in the world 'e ever myde that crew o' Liverpool riff-raff row like so many h'Oxford and C'ymbridge h'experts is a fair miracle to me!"

"Yes," chuckled Captain Ball, knowingly. "But you never want to forget, Mister Mate, that when it comes to miracles, Mr. Glencannon's a pretty handy chap to have about!"

"But 'ow did 'e do it, that's orl I arsk—'ow did 'e do it?"

"Huh!" Captain Ball snorted. "Why, when you was up there standing by for his word to lower Number Three into the water, what do you s'pose he was doing through that loading-door—fishing for bloaters?"

"I 'aven't the fyntest notion wot 'e was doing," sulked Mr. Montgomery

"Well," whispered Captain Ball, glancing cautiously about him. "He was lashing a big steel ash-bucket to Number Three's keel, that's what he was doing! Why, it was a regular sea-anchor! It set up a drag in the water under that boat like towing a busted bass drum! . . ."

"Lawks!" gasped Mr. Montgomery! "An arsh-bucket! W'y, a team o' blooming lorry 'orses couldn't myke any speed dragging that!"

"No, nor neither could them whiskery psalm-singers," agreed Captain Ball. "Maybe it'll learn 'em some sea-manners!"

"It's learned me my lesson about Mr. Glencannon, anyw'y," said Mr Montgomery ruefully. "And I 'opes them *Flaming Chariot* billy-goats sinks on their w'y to Barcelonia!"

Next morning bright and early, Mr. Glencannon strolled along the Quai du Port, and turned into the sunshine which flooded the broad Rue Cannebiere. There was a smile on his face and a song in his heart, for in the wallet directly over it reposed a portly packet of American bank notes.

"Weel," he chuckled. "It a' goes to prove ye dinna need whuskers to be sagacious! And it also proves that it's a costly pastime to gae aboot insulting decent people on the high seas. And noo I shall mak' arrangements for sending my winnings hame to Scotland. . . ."

Turning into the banking offices of the Crédit Marseillaise, he made known his wishes and presented his notes at the grilled window.

The cashier moistened his thumb on a sponge and prepared to count the neat stack of tens and twenties. Suddenly he paused, frowned, looked up.

"Monsieur," he announced coldly. "This money is not good!"

"Not good?" repeated Mr. Glencannon, grasping the marble ledge for support. "Ah noo, Mounseer, this is no occasion for humor! I'll thank ye to cease yere leevity and do as ye're bid."

"It is not an affair of the drollery," insisted the cashier. "Have the goodness to regard, Monsieur—why, one can easily see for one's self!" He pushed the bills back to Mr. Glencannon. "Read, Monsieur, read there carefully what is printed."

With trembling fingers, Mr. Glencannon picked up a bill and examined it. Across the top, in large letters, was engraved *"Citizens' Bank of Atlanta, Georgia,"* and then, smaller, on the line below, *"Confederate States of America."*

"Weel, I'll be domned," he murmured weakly. "That old Yankee swundler!" Then into his mind came a vague and tantalizing half-memory, obscured by a strange silvery fog. He tried to summon the rest of it, but it eluded him. He shook his head sadly.

"It's a' vurra peerplexing," he sighed. "Vurra peerplexing indeed. But, yes, I do seem to recall somebody, somewhere, saying something aboot an American Ceevil War. A-weel," and he stuffed the bank-notes into his pocket, and turned toward the door, "I foncy there's nowt to do but gae oot and find a pub where they haven't heard the war news!"

⚓

THE STORM

⚓

THE STORM

H. M. Tomlinson

⚓ *It is important for men to read this kind of writing about the sea. It is the result of a vivid imagination under stern control. While natural phenomena—the picture of the sea, the wind, the dark—are treated with terse but almost poetic imagination, the human and dramatic elements are seen with the clearness of an almost photographic realism which permits of no exaggeration or distortion.*

The combination of these two attitudes produces a tension of dramatic force that is hard to equal.

AT THE saloon mess-table, the guardians of the ship were allusive about her welfare. The set of a current had been adverse; she was seven miles astern of her estimated position. The signs in the heavens induced respectful references to the habits of the Arabian Gulf. The glass was briefly indicated; Colet surmised, while taking another piece of toast, that it was not happy in its divination. The high-pressure cylinder had taken to blowing through its packing; it was wheezy. "Man, yon's a sad waste o' power." And one of the deck-hands was sick. Fever, very likely.

"At Rotterdam," Sinclair baldly hinted.

"Aye, the heat will bring it out," confirmed Gillespie, with luscious gravity. Then he exhibited some startling instances from the store of a long familiarity with sin. He indulged in illustrative cases with composure and fond irrelevance.

"I'll see this man," announced Hale, hastily rising while still the boding symptoms of another exemplary case were unfulfilled. Gillespie shook his pow in appreciative warning over sin.

Colet accompanied the captain on his way to the forecastle, and he noticed, because the master paused to inspect them, that the forehatches were laced over with cordage. The master disappeared within the dark aperture of the forecastle. Colet mounted the ladder to its deck. That was a noble outlook at the beginning of the day. It was dry and red-crusted, weather-stained, isolated as a vantage exposed to an immensity of light. It was solitude. It might have been as old as the sea itself, by the look of it. It was hoar with salt.

And the ship's head was alive. It was massive but buoyant. It seemed to inflate and to mount quickly and easily with enormous intakes of air; then, sighing through its hawse-pipes, it declined into the friendly rollers. If you looked overside and down, the cutwater of the ship was deep and plain in the blue transparency, coming along with unvarying confidence like the brown nose of an exploring monster. When the ship's head plunged over a slope, an acre of blinding foam spread around and swept astern, melting and sibilant.

Companies of flying-fish were surprised by that iron nose, and got up. They skittered obliquely over the bright polish of the inclines, and pumped abruptly into smooth slopes which opposed them. A family of four dolphins were there that morning. They were set in the clear glass just before the cutwater. They did not fly from it. Their bodies but revolved leisurely before it. The crescent valves in their heads could be seen sleepily opening and closing when they touched the surface, with the luxury of life in the cool fathoms. One after another idly they rolled belly up; they were merely revolving without progress, yet the fast-pursuing iron nose never reached them. It was always just behind the family, which wove a lazy and gliding dance before the ship. Artfully leading them on, these familiars of the deep?

It was a fair world into which they were being led. It reposed in an eternal radiant tranquillity. The Indian Ocean was as inviting as its name. There were clouds ahead, but they were fast to the sky line; they were as remote as the ghostly mountains and steeps of a land no man would ever reach. This world of the tropics was but an apparition of splendour. It was there, by the chance of good fortune. It was seen only by the desiring mind. It was like the import of great music, for which there is no word. If you stood looking at it long enough, the bright dream would draw you out of your body.

The ship's head fell sideways into a deeper hollow, and Colet returned without warning to an iron deck. He was swung round on his handhold. The rail he struck was hard. Steady! Solid fountains burst loudly through the hawse-pipes. There was impetuosity in the lift of the ship's head. She got out of the smother in a hurry. By the look of it, more was coming.

Colet saw the shape of the propeller over him and the bright sky through its frame.

The rollers had seemed to be growing heavier. It was getting wet up there. Colet retreated. When he was mounting the ladder amidships a sharp lurch of the ship left him dangling by his hands. The boyish third officer on the deck above respectfully watched him while his feet sought the ladder again.

"A beam sea setting in, Mr. Colet. Makes her roll."

It was making her roll. But it was very agreeable. It shook off the weight of the heat. These were the first seas worth the lively name since the voyage began. It was like the real thing to see the decks getting wet; to be caught at a corner by a dollop of rollicking brine. Hullo, Sinclair! Colet mentioned this novelty as they met by the engine-room entrance. He spoke of it lightly, wiping some spray from his eyes. Sinclair showed amusement, but his gaze was elsewhere. They had to steady themselves, in their pause, by gripping the ironwork. The movements of the ship, to Colet's surprise, were exhilarating. They shifted him from an old centre of thought. The rhythm of the ship's compensations was the measure of easy and solid courage.

"I don't know," mused Colet, "but once, just once, I think I'd like to see all this when it was not play."

"Play?" exclaimed the sailor. "Play? If anybody else had said that, I'd tell him not to be a fool."

Colet made a dramatic appeal to the listening and jealous gods to forget his childish indiscretion. Only his ignorance. The issue of a fathead. It was born of his trust in his company. He reposed in the faith that the *Altair* was a sound old dear.

Sinclair grinned. "Perhaps you didn't catch what the old man was mumbling at breakfast?" He poked his companion in the ribs. "You're coming along, my son. A bit too confident, that's all. When you're a sailor, you'll cross yourself if you hear some one talk as you did."

"I'm sure of it. What was it the captain said at breakfast?"

"Oh, nothing. He's a cautious old boy, I think. Wanted me to believe he doesn't like the look of it. But I can't smell anything in the wind Seems all right. I don't see anything in this."

It was all right, though the draught which was upset by the rocking of the ship was languid, and the breath of an oven.

Night fell; the day was abolished abruptly. There were brief up-glarings of a desperate sun taken by an insurrection of darkness. He was put down. The authority of day was overturned. The ship alone of all the world below held with startled emphasis the memory of a brightness extinguished. For a few moments there was the pale wraith of a deck, vertiginous in its slant, with its fixtures bleak and exposed; and then the only lights were the stars concentrated low in a patch of the southern sky. In the south, the stars were the lights of a city without a name where there could be no land. They could see the frenzied glittering of its lamps. For the show of that city behaved only as would an hallucination in a region that was enthralled by the powers of darkness. Now its level was below them, and now it soared towards the meridian.

"Come now, will you?" said the captain.

Colet was glad of a change from that erratic dinner table, and gestured his readiness. He was to be purser for the evening. He followed the master out of the saloon. As he reached its door the opening uprose, as though to frustrate his intent. He gripped the door-post. Whoa! He waited. The chance came. The deck sloped the other way, and, almost under control, Colet shot through. The far side of the alleyway saved him, though harshly.

"She's lively," said the master. "Here we are." He steadied Colet into his room.

"I thought monsoons were friendly winds," Colet joked.

"There is no wind," he was told. "Not yet. Just a bit of a swell. Sit there. That way you won't feel it so much. There you are, if you would check the manifest for me with the stowage plan." He stood over Colet, and explained the documents. "I was not about when she was loaded, and we have a number of ports. You can help me here. It'll keep you from noticing her capers."

It was not easy to ignore her capers. They raised a number of doubts which jolted one's consideration from the job, yet could not be answered. Get on with the job then. Didn't know enough to answer them. He knew about as much as an ant in its hill under a blundering cow; and the astral cow blundering about now had enormous splay hooves. There was a boom, and an answering panic of crocks in the pantry. His consideration of his job was shifted, and he glanced at Hale, to see whether this was portentous. The attention of the captain, however, rapt as at prayer, was devoted to his desk. Hale but cleared his throat, and turned over a sheet as though it were a token of a rosary.

They worked without a word for a time, and then Colet put a question to the master.

"Eh?" said Hale, turning leisurely. "No, that is probably a slip. Make a mark there."

The master remained, for a spell, thoughtful in that apposition to his amateur purser.

"It's an idea of mine that there's an intention to sell her out East, when we are cleared," he soliloquized. "Chinese owners, I expect. But don't discuss that outside. It's only a guess since I took her over. I go by this and that."

"Surely the owners would have told you?" Colet became bright. He was relieved to hear some cool and intelligent human sounds. It was enjoyable to encourage them.

Hale smiled wanly. "A ship's master is not so important as he used to be. Like the rest of the servants, he's on a length of string, and doesn't always know who is pulling it, nor why. But it's no good complaining of the way the world goes."

His thin hand went over his thin hair. Colet felt stir within him the warmth of a liking for that frail figure. It was insignificant, till its eye met yours. Then you guessed a hidden but constant glim. That man looked as though he had made his humble acceptance, but could not be deceived by the bluff of chance. He met Colet's eye then, and might have guessed that something had quickened in his junior.

"We are apt to make too much of our importance, Colet, when we don't like things, or they don't like us. But, you know, the best we can do is to keep our own doorstep clean. We can always manage that."

As if to try his faith, his own ship then treated him with indignity. She went over, and Hale, nearer her side, sank low, and was huddled into his chair. Colet overlooked the master from a higher position. Hale wrestled patiently with the arm of his seat to escape from his ungraceful posture.

"That was a big one. They racket things so."

The cabin itself was quiet. At times it complained a little, but in undertones. It seemed apart, an illuminated hollow where understandable and well-ordered objects were an assurance of continuity, while all without was dark confusion, besieging it, yet unable to do more than move it, never to disorder it. Its lamp burned steadily. Perhaps it was the master who gave it that air of sanity and composure while anarchy was at its walls. Hale, slight and elderly, with his deliberation which was not unlike weariness, was an augury of grey wisdom and the symbol of conscious control amid the welter of huge and heedless powers. Boom and crash, but the old man took no notice. The portrait of a stout matron, her arm round a little girl, regarded them sedately from a bulkhead. No other ornament was in the cabin, except the faded photograph of a sailing ship over the bunk. Colet's ribs were squeezed, first against one arm of his chair, then the other. That was another distraction; trying to keep still. The deck rose under them, and Colet dizzily wondered how high it intended to go; the grind of the propeller then grew loud in its monody, and even frantic. The cabin trembled. His seat sank under him, and his attention went another way, for the suggestion of empty gulf was sickening, and the propeller moaned in the very deeps. She heaved and tilted. The purser grabbed his escaping papers.

Something avalanched outside, and then continued a noisy career. What

145

was that? Colet again looked at the captain for a sign. There was none. The master sat at his desk, turned from it a little now, scrutinizing a document through his uplifted spectacles. His attention was wholly given to that.

Nothing in it. Don't be a fool. Look after your own doorstep. But a more violent lift, a louder explosion of a breaking sea, would set him calculating, as it began, the probable extent of a movement. How far would this one go? Worse than the last? Sometimes it was. Yet Hale released sheet after sheet, sometimes turning to his desk to make a note; he lit his pipe, and nothing could have been so reassuring as the leisure of its blue smoke. All was well. Colet resumed his clerkship, and half forgot beleaguerment by the unseen in an interval of comparative ease. The seas were lessening.

Certainly. That was only a minor jar; but when Colet would have made the cheerful comment aloud, he saw the captain had lowered his papers and was listening attentively, as though waiting for another cryptic message from the night, gazing at the foot of the door of his cabin over the top of his glasses. Colet watched him for an interpretation. Hale only relaxed and sighed; and then, seeing that the purser was expectant, he spoke.

"Colet, it occurs to me that somewhere about now makes for me forty years of this. Yes. You see that barque there? She was my first, forty years agone this month. This job, when I'm through, will be my last. I was of half a mind not to take it. I've had my share, I think. But that child," Hale indicated the portrait, "she's in for her degree now. I thought I ought to make this trip. A little extra for her."

While he was communing a whispering began on the deck above. It increased to a heavy drumming.

"I thought so," Hale remarked, his ear cocked. "Rain. But no wind, and this swell. A cyclone in the northeast somewhere." He added the conclusion indifferently.

There was a knock at the cabin door. A man out of the dark stood there, a barefooted seaman in his dripping oilskins.

"Mr. Sinclair, sir. He wants you on the bridge."

"Anything wrong, Wilson?"

"I don't know, sir. The steering gear, I think, sir."

"I'm coming."

Hale assembled his papers deftly, stowed them, and opened a cupboard He hauled out oilskins and seaboots. He was buttoning the stiff stuff across his throat, his head thrown back.

"Wait here, Colet," he said. "I thought I heard an unusual thump just now."

The captain, Colet imagined, was diminished by that armour for the weather. His face, framed by the sou'wester, looked womanish, as though he were in the wrong clothes. Hale glanced at the barometer, gave it a closer inspection on whatever it was it told him, and stumped out.

Colet waited. He continued his work, pausing now and then to listen for evidence. There were fewer noises. The ship itself appeared to be making no sound. The waters were nearer, or louder. Anyone would think . . . Had the engines stopped? He opened the door and put his head out. The steward was hurriedly balancing his way along the corridor.

"Anything the matter, steward?"

"Mr. Colet, the rudder's gone."

The steward departed, chary of words, as though he were on his way to get another rudder. He had no time to talk.

The violent rolling of the ship did not relent. That seemed senseless, when she was crippled. She ought to be let off, now she could not steer. Impossible to think, with that rolling.

Colet, to his great annoyance, found that his knees were shaking. He had not told them to. He did not want them to shake. He damned those quivering members of his body, and would have stiffened them, but that he was flung against a bulkhead, and so brought down some of the master's pipes from a rack. Something to do, anyway. He could recover tobacco pipes while others found a rudder. Better men had to look after the ship for those who attended to pipe-racks, while waiting.

They also serve who only look after the tobacco pipes. If there was no wind when he first went into that room, something was howling now all right. It was no good waiting for the captain. Hale was not likely to return till . . . well, he wasn't likely to return. The best thing to do would be to go and find the men at the centre of things, because that cabin had precious little interest now. It was useless to wait there, at that time of night, when for all he knew they soon might be taking to the boats.

He heard a heavy concussion. The cabin shook. The papers on which he had been working fell to the floor. The boats! Colet watched the papers sprawling and scattering. They had lost their meaning. They were just as well where they were. But there would be no boats for the sea which could make that sound. The cabin reversed, and as it did so a tongue of water shot over the carpet straight for the papers. Colet dived for them and snatched them out of its way. Save the stationery!

He straightened them on the desk. With measured deliberation he sought carefully for the sheet on which he had been working. They were all in a mess, these sheets, but so was everything else. At least, the ship's papers could be put in order. No more water seemed to be coming in.

That was only a splash. Not foundering yet. He settled the papers into their sequence, and began again on them at the mark. The captain had said Wait.

It was the only thing to do, but that lad Casabianca deserved a better poem. It would be easy to wait on a deck diminishing in dissolution if one but knew the reason for it. But this was only an idiot joke, dutifully completing a ship's papers when the mysterious reason was trying to turn the ship over. Now the infernal water was under the desk. Reason! No more reason in it than in the hot gas which congealed to a mud ball, on which grew the truth, and crosses and nails for those who dared to mention it. What a joke; and nobody to get a laugh out of it!

Let her roll. He could not stop it. Time for a pipe. Not his affair. Funny, that a man should curse the stars in their courses, when he was beset. Same thing as a rat biting his trap, maybe. Lucky to have a job to do, if only a job of checking packages of pots and pans, when heaven itself was cracking. "We are but little children meek." The tune of this hymn, for some uninvited cause, was running through his head. The movements of the ship kept it going. "Not born in any high estate." Couldn't very well call this estate puffed up. "What can we do for Jesus' sake?" Well, Jesus, I was checking this ship's manifest when I went down. Sorry it's wet.

What was the time? To his surprise, the clock said it was another morning again. The skipper's cabin was in a sorry state. Somebody was attempting the door, but the slant of the ship held it fast. The door rattled, and then Hale entered. He showed no surprise at finding the purser still busy. He took a towel and wiped his face. "I should drop that now," he remarked.

Colet told him he had just finished it. Hale looked at the clock, and thanked him. The purser modestly waited for the master to give a word on the business without, but Hale merely balanced himself patiently to the movements of his room, and sought for something in a drawer.

"By the way, Colet, you could turn in here. It would save you the run to your own place."

But Colet felt a sudden dislike of the suggestion of that isolation.

"Oh, thank you. But I'll make for my own cubby-hole. It'll do me good, to run for it."

That was all. Not a word about the rudder. And perhaps it would be better not to ask questions. Perhaps rudders were indelicate. By Hale's manner, too, it might be only a rather wet night. It would be nobler to assume the night was merely wet.

Hale led on to the head of the companion to the quarter-deck.

"Can't open the lower door," he explained. The master stood there, with his hand on the upper door, as though listening for some one who would let them out. "Now," he muttered, opened it on the instant, and they were both in the night.

The night engulfed them with a roar as though it saw them instantly Colet was separated from Hale. There was no ship. There was but a pealing and a shouting. The darkness was full of driving water. It was hard to breathe. Hale had gone. Colet forgot which was the head and which the stern. A burst of spray raked past. Then he felt a grip on his arm, and a warm mouth sought his ear. Hale was saying something, but his words were torn away.

"What?"

The skipper's voice was at once superior to the chaos:

"We can do it."

Wanted a bit of doing. Like trying to walk a plank you couldn't see which was only there sometimes. It was a wonder it ever came back. My God! she was like a balloon, trying to sail out of it. But the water was up there too. Here was the ladder down to the deck. He had got on to its rungs when the warm mouth came near his ear again:

"Wait. Hold tight."

The thing under their feet heaved, but checked, as if this was too much for it. The night exploded over them and fell in broken thunder. Couldn't go through that.

"Go on," ordered invisible Hale. They reached the deck, and ran. Ran in short lengths. You can't keep running on a slope which changes direction abruptly in the dark. Together they got to the foot of the ladder to the bridge-deck, and Hale pushed Colet at it, the signal to mount quickly; but when he gripped the iron thing it came at him as though loose. He was pulling the ladder out of the ship. Nothing to stand on. Then the ship fell head first into nothing; the purser's face was dragged after the retreating ladder and struck it. Colet could hear the sea in behind him and clambered up; yet hesitated.

"Captain?"

The old man was in that below. No good shouting. The purser got down to the deck again, and groped, with the flood at his knees. He found Hale on his hands and knees, rising, and clutched him.

"Go on, go on," Hale shouted.

The captain came into Colet's cabin with him, and stayed there for a moment. He was smiling.

"You would never have believed that, would you, Colet?"

Colet, a little breathless, held to the edge of his bunk. He hinted that the violence seemed a bit unreasonable.

"No. There's sufficient cause. I've seen it before. We must wait for daylight."

When the master had gone, Colet considered his bunk. No. The settee tonight. No use turning in, when things were happening all the time. But it needed very deliberate control to sit there, waiting for light to come, when the world was falling to pieces. Especially when, the longer you waited, the louder grew the mania of the wind, and the more surprisingly delirious mounted the buoyancy of the ship. Could she stand it? She seemed terrified. Colet remembered a rabbit he had once seen leaping and convulsive in a wire noose. She was desperate, but she was done.

Colet surrendered limply to the anarchy. Once he rose, and vomited. Well . . . the day was about due. The wind did all the moaning that was necessary. That moan outside would do for all creation. No need to add to it. It was the antiphon of doom. And it didn't seem to matter now. Nothing more to do. A sea battered on his door, but Colet did not look up. Might as well rest while waiting.

The port light was a grey round, and the lamp was paled. When Colet noticed that, he wondered how it had come about. He peered out from the port. He could see nothing but wan panic, and a long loose end of rope resting straight on the wind as rigid as an iron bar. This was called day. The deck looked as though no man had been on it for years; but Sinclair came into view, leaning and pulling up against the drive of morning. Coming to him? Colet got at the door to be ready for him. It felt as if it weighed tons. It fought.

"Fuh, Colet," he breathed. "You're not overside, eh?"

He tore his sou'wester off. His hot hair was extinguished and flattened. "What a night!"

Sinclair's appearance was almost that of a stranger. His face was bleached and seamed, his eyes were raw. They blinked sorely as he grinned. He plumped on to the couch and leaned back.

"She has had a time. Two boats look as if elephants had sat in them. The old man was right, after all."

The grin remained on his face. He had forgotten to take it off. He was grinning at the window.

"Look at that rope. Hell! Look at it."

"Is Hale all right?"

"Eh? Yes, he's still up there."

Sinclair was regarding now in childish wonder a wound on his hand "How did that come?" He dismissed his hand.

"The old man? Yes. Well, this ship's got a skipper. Colet, the old man's right, if anyone wants to know."

"How is it now?"

"Don't ask. She's taking it easier, though. Sitting in it like a duck.

Shouldn't have thought it possible, but the old man was sure she would. Been rolling her bridge ends under, too. Glad to see daylight."

Sinclair shut his eyes.

"I say, I think I'll take my ten minutes here. Handy, here."

He sought Colet again, with a grin.

"Nice job for this child presently, when it moderates. Coming with us? The rudder's broken at the couplings. You know that? Must get her under control. There's a boat to be got out. Wires from the steering chains to the rudder. That sort of thing. Fix it up. You'd better make for the bridge-house now, the old man says. Tell him where I am, won't you?"

The chief officer's head fell sideways; this time he was certainly asleep.

The purser adventured for the bridge-house. If you checked yourself from point to point, hand over hand, you were not hurled along. The wind was solid. The purser did not look at the seas, but some heights caught his eye as they fled past. They were aged. It was better not to look at them. Hale turned his head as Colet entered. He grimaced at him humorously. Was the old man enjoying it? A seaman was still at the useless wheel, as if apart, and in a trance, looking to futurity through the glass, and waiting. His jaws moved slightly, now and then, but that was all. Nobody else was there.

"Did you sleep, Colet? No sleep till morn, eh? Well, I think it moderates a bit. We shall be busy, soon. I want you with me in case. The lads are taking a rest now."

The master resumed his vigil. His head was turned to the world beyond. But that world had contracted. One could not see far, but the intimidated eye could see all that it wanted. The sky had closed down on them, and they were circumscribed by a sunless incertitude. In that grey vacancy shadows appeared which were too high to be of water, but those ghosts darkened and emerged as seas which saw the ship at once and came at her in towering velocity. As they shaped, each of them threatened that it was the one which would finish her, but the *Altair* heaved into the sky out of it in time. Yet another was always coming when one had gone. The desolate head of the ship, condemned to dreary unrest, streamed with gauzes of water. Its stanchions and rails were awry and tortured. A length of the bulwarks of the foredeck was ruptured and projected outwards raggedly. The deck ventilators had gone. One lay in the scuppers as if dead, but sometimes turned over and then back in a spasm of unexpected life.

That slight figure of the master, standing in profile, so watchful of vague and immense powers, and so undisturbed by their onrush, was like a token of quiet faith untouched by nightfall and overthrow. There he was. Hale was looking it in the face. He did not move. He was timing the

Indian Ocean, that little man. Colet felt he would as soon be there as elsewhere. Whom did Hale remind him of as he stood there? Somebody. Somebody in a dream? No, good Lord! he was like that dim figure of an old man, when coming up Gallions Reach in an evening long ago; standing just like that, and muttering something of other worlds. Beyond the captain Colet saw a dire spectre loom and bear down on them, its pale head raving with speed and fury. Other worlds! This one? Colet could not help swallowing on a choking chuckle. At that Hale turned on him quickly, and knew what the purser had seen.

"Laughing at it? They do look fairly terrifying, some of them."

The two men had made that signal to each other. Colet lightened, flippantly elate. Chanticleer crowing at spectres, sure of the morning? The steward pranced in with a can of hot coffee and some food. Wonderful fellow. How had he managed all that from the galley? He had saved the grub, but he was like a cat out of a ditch. Coffee was good. Calamity could not even blow off the fragrance of coffee. Stewards could dance through it.

Hour after hour of onset and uplift; screens of white which keened and hid the ship, and passed; vaulting masses which strode over the bows; occasional gusts which careened her, held her over, and hid the sea with wool.

But was it lessening? Had the worst of it gone? One could see farther. The ceiling had lifted. Hale was lighting his pipe when the engine room signalled. The master listened at the black cup, and then put his mouth to it. His mouth and ear dodged about.

"No . . . not yet. . . . We shall try soon. . . . Let you know. . . . Thank your men for me, Gillespie. . . . Not over yet, though. . . . Who? . . . Badly? . . . Where is he? . . . All right . . . I'll do what I can . . . let you know.

"One of the greasers, Colet. Flung into the gear. Very nasty. He must stay there. We dare not bring him up yet."

He walked up and down the enclosure for a spell. He paused, and contemplated the outer world.

"We might," he said to himself. "Colet, would you tell Sinclair I want him?"

A bunch of the people of the ship presently dared the open. They appeared together, in haste, as if they had suddenly agreed to submit no longer. They had come out to rebel. But how could they fight that? They were seen at once, and attacked. They were expunged. When the cataract had gone they were still all there, hurried and desperate. They were minikins in a precarious wild, in a light as hopeless as nullity, their foothold a bare raft of disappearing iron. They could not do it. But they were hauling gear about, refractory stuff in league with the enemy, in an obsession that wires would bind cyclones. Sinclair was there. It was a losing game, but he was playing it. His arm was flung out directing; he toppled over, but his arm continued pointing at the crisis from the deck—no time to get up—and his mouth was open, bawling, though he seemed to make no sound. It was a shadow show. A play of midgets who endeavoured with foolish efforts to frustrate the fate imposed on them by majesty. Well done, Sinclair. Nearly had you then.

They made for a boat as if they meant to use it. That ought to be stopped. That was carrying matters too far. They could not leave the ship. But the boat was manned and swung out—Sinclair, the third officer, the boatswain, and a seaman were leaving them. They were determined about it. They were hanging on board now, uncertain in a threatening void; their adversary was waiting for them below. Sometimes it swept along the topside of the ship, and then retired, for its next leap, to a sudden deep below the ship's wall. For a torturing moment the suspensory boat fell straight to disaster. It checked. It shot up on a roller, afloat. Colet was looking in astonishment straight at the faces of its men. The snoring ship heeled away from them. The boat dropped into a hollow. She sped to a crest higher than the funnel, and was poised for a moment on the foaming summit; she was lost. The seas opened, and she was seen close astern, askew on a slope.

When Colet next saw Sinclair that officer was climbing the ladder amidships, as happy and unexpected a token as an angelic visitor. The purser put his arms round his friend's shoulder.

"All right. Done it, Colet."

She was steering again.

"See that out there?" Sinclair thrust out his arm.

Something was to be seen in the murk. What was it? Smoke?

"Yes. It's a liner. She'll be passing us in an hour."

Colet went to his room in gratitude. He felt as though the sky had gone up to its friendly height. They were let off. They were getting out of it. The violence meant nothing now. His cabin seemed larger, more intimate. He was comforted by even the society of distant but brotherly smoke. They were not alone, either. He was thinking he would go out presently to watch their neighbour pass them when Sinclair entered, and something about Sinclair made him rise as though this were an important meeting.

"The liner's almost abeam. Go up with the old man, Colet. He's going to signal her. There's something not right—Gillespie says the furnace footplates are awash. That and our steering gear together . . . he wants a tow, I expect. I'm going below now to find what I can."

There was light enough to see the signals of the stranger. It was impossible for Colet to make out what was passing between the two ships. The tumbling of their wounded steamer was accentuated, it was sickening, when things were happening, and you did not know what.

"Did you make that out, Lycett?" asked the captain.

"Yes, sir, distinctly. He says he cannot tow. Got the mails. He asks whether you will abandon."

"What, my ship? No. Signal, no."

Young Lycett faintly hesitated; or so Colet imagined. Never before had he watched his fellows so closely. But the lad turned to the rack where rolled flags waited in their pigeon-holes to cue any fate that might come, and went out to his duty. There came another smear of bunting for them on the liner—too late; the light was not good enough. But a star began to wink at her bridge, and they all watched it till it ceased. Lycett returned to them.

"He says he will report us, sir."

The master nodded. "Of course."

That was ended. Nobody spoke. The seaman at the useless wheel was aloof. He had no part in this. He appeared not to have heard anything, not to be interested in what was passing. He was merely waiting for the wheel to show a better spirit, and he could wait forever. He did not even turn his head to look at the departing liner. Only Lycett did that. The master had his hands spread on a desk, and was considering, so it appeared, a diagram before him. He had dismissed the liner. He had forgotten her already? And there she went. Colet, like young Lycett, watched her fade. She was already becoming unsubstantial; the upheavals and the twilight were taking her. Through a side window Colet noticed a stoker below, clutching the bulwarks, his grimy flimsies shuddering in the wind, and he, too, was peering after the ship that was leaving them.

"Take over," said the captain to Lycett, and went out.

The boyish officer at that turned from the place on the seas where the promise of the other ship was dying, as if he had petulantly resolved not to look that way again, and instead stood gazing at the *Altair's* head uneasy in the surge, though not as if he saw it. He was silent. The man at the wheel might not have been there. What were the others doing? There was no sound but that of the swash and parade of the ocean. Lycett became aware of the diagram of the ship before him, and with a new interest began to examine it. He addressed the image at the wheel without lifting his head.

"Wilson, I say, do you think she is a bit by the head?"

"Yes."

"Oh, you have noticed it. How long since you first thought so?"

The image continued its fixed regard of nothing for a while, its jaws moving as though it were making its words. When they were ready, it spoke.

"About an hour."

The youngster bent closer to the diagram, and ended his inspection with a calculation on an old envelope he took from his pocket

"Why, but in that case she won't last till morning!"

Wilson eased his position slightly, and rubbed his mouth with the back of his hand. His voice was so deep and effortless that it sounded like the easy impersonal utterance of the room itself.

"She may. You can't tell."

He might have experienced a full life of such nights and occasions, and so could, if it were worth while, advise youth out of a privy knowledge which was part of the nature of ships and the sea.

"Something may be done," said the man at the wheel.

Colet made as if he were about to leave them.

"Don't go, Mr. Colet," urged the officer in charge. "Wait here, will you, till somebody comes along."

Colet let go the handle of the door, went over to look at the diagram with Lycett, and endured the quiet, while listening to the seas, which were now invisible. The boy began to whistle a tune softly in a hesitating way.

What were the others doing? Sometimes Colet thought he felt the far thumping of human handiwork under their feet. Hale and Sinclair were there, anyhow, and old Gillespie and his men; it was comforting, that certitude. It warmed the world, that secure thought of its good men holding fast. And while his faith was sustained that they could save her, it was not altogether because he himself was there. The ship herself meant something. She had become important. That image at the wheel was admonishing. It was, perchance, the secret familiar of their ship. It was more than human; it spoke out of the ship. Once the steamer plunged head foremost, and something gave in her body. They thrilled to it, as if it were the smothered parting of a piano chord where all was quiet and suspect. Lycett glanced at Colet, and then at the helmsman.

"Was that a bulkhead, Wilson?"

"Couldn't say, sir."

Of course he could not. He was not going to give her away so easily. Colet winked at the boy, and began to pace their little prison, but paused and stretched his arms. No. Stop that. That worried the others. Better have a pipe.

"Are you allowed to smoke, Wilson?"

The seaman only smiled.

"Oh, he chews," said Lycett, and tapped a cigarette on the desk.

Lycett had just struck eight bells when Collins, the second officer, put his head in the door.

"Leave this. You can go below now, the lot of you. When you're wanted you'll know." He disappeared at once.

Colet roamed the deck amidships, accompanied only by the sough of the dark. Their own familiar and confident chant had ceased, that song which used to issue boldly from the open door of the engine-room casing as you passed it. No message but an infrequent clanking came up from below. Her heart had stopped. A flare or two, while he waited for signs, passed deep under the gratings. They were busy, in the depth of her; but doing what?

There was no doubt about it; when one walked aft it was distinctly to walk uphill. Her head was heavy. He tried to convince himself that this was not so. But it was.

There were no stars. There was only the steady drive of the dark. She was responding to it as though she were tired, stumbling and sluggish. Now and then a sea mounted over her foredeck. He looked at the shadows of some bent davits, with the swaying remnants of their falls, and heard a block mewling as it swung. That whining voice was the very triviality of outer desolation. Creak. Whine. The captain's daughter was taking her degree. A bit extra for her. Tonight, who was dining at the "Gridiron"?

Morning came. Colet went out, when his port light had shaped, and saw the crew, for the first time that voyage. The men were assembled on the afterdeck, and they surprised him as much as would a miraculous visitation of quiet and disinterested strangers. Most of them were squatting against the bulwarks, but a few stood gazing seaward, indifferently. It was a scene dim and unreal. The air was warm. Once clanking broke out below again, but did not last long. Neither the captain nor Sinclair was there. He could not see any of the engineers. Perhaps, though, they still hoped to pull her through. The cook appeared at his galley door above, and peremptorily called out that anybody who wanted anything could come for it. There was a cheer from the men, wavering but derisive, and they began to move up to the galley. They might have been ignorant, or they might have known they had plenty of time. The forward deck was level with the water; it could not rise; the head of the ship was a sunken warning. Its lowness prompted Colet at once to appraise the size of the heavy propulsions of the ocean; he looked beyond to see whether a sea higher than the rest was coming.

Not coming yet. But the men were still murmuring about the galley. Nothing was in sight, but one could not see very far. The sun would be there soon. It was warm, but, when he was not thinking of it, he shivered. Yet the sky was rosy along the east. How long to wait?

There came the sun, broad to the ship. It saw them. Their case now was manifest to heaven. A seaman, who was lying as though asleep by the coaming of a hatch below the galley, rose to his feet, stumbled to the side, and began to shout at the sun. The man was in rags. His mates watched him in limp wonder. He raised his bare arms and raved at the bloody day

"To hell with you—you're no good to us."

"Stop that man," commanded a voice. There stood the captain, at the companion aft. Everybody turned that way.

"Stop him," cried Hale, and ran quickly forward. The watchers came to their senses; but the man had scrambled outboard and dropped. One of his mates leaped astride the bulwarks, but Hale got a firm hand on him and looked over. They were all peering over.

"Useless," said Hale, still with his restraining hand on the seaman. "You come down. One's enough."

Colet was overlooking that from the amidships section. Some one's hand heartily slapped his shoulder.

"Nice morning, Colet," said Sinclair, and went pattering down to the main deck and passed through the men. Everyone now listlessly eyed the conference of the master and his lieutenant. Gillespie came hurrying along to join them. While the rest had their eyes on the three, the deck lapsed. There could be no mistake about that jolt.

"Let's get a move on," muttered a seaman. The master did not appear to have noticed it. Then he moved one arm slightly, a gesture of abandonment, and they heard the end of the talk.

"Man, ye can do n'more," from Gillespie.

"The boats, Mr. Sinclair," said the master aloud.

Sinclair took the men's eyes with a glance. He swept his arm with a motion to gather. He strolled to the amidships ladder, and they after him. It was right to show her that they were not in a hurry to leave her. Gillespie briefly inspected his squad, which had gravitated around him, and jerked his head towards Sinclair.

"Job's finished, laddies. Awa' now."

She settled again while they took their stations, but the men kept their own gait. Colet sought the master, who was obscured by the activity at the ship's side.

"Ah, purser, I am just going aft for some things I must have."

"I'll go with you."

"There's time. How good these fellows are!"

The captain, with a japanned dispatch box in his hand, appeared to know exactly where to find all that he wanted; he moved about his room with a

methodical promptitude which gave Colet the impression that the foundering of a ship could be ordered to a common ritual. Hale opened a drawer
of his clothes chest and took out a wrap.

"We must leave her, Colet. It's queer you should have brought her
to this."

There lay Kuan-yin. The master glanced round his cabin; at his desk,
at the barometer, and last at his pictures.

"That's all. Time to go."

One of the two laden boats was waiting for them, close under a boom
which had been rigged out, with a man rope.

"Now, my lad, off with you." The master hesitated. "That greaser who
was killed, Colet. I had meant to bear it in mind. I have a little packet of
his in my cabin. His people might like it. Another minute."

"I'll wait."

"Get in, get in."

"No . . ."

"The boat, sir." Hale flung out his arm.

"Come on," bawled some one from the sea.

The captain paused by the ship's side to con her. Then he called out
seaward.

"Your boat, Collins, keep her away."

Colet eased off along the beam and dropped from his hold as the lifeboat
rose to him. He scrambled up to see what had become of Hale. There was
no sign of him. Gillespie, in the stern of the boat, was angry with alarm.

"There's no time, there's no time." The engineer eagerly half-stood, as
they fell away into a hollow, for a better view of that companion door
within which the captain had vanished. It was unnaturally high and
strangely tilted in a ship whose life seemed poised on a moment of time
and the hesitation of a breath. It remained empty.

"Hale!" shouted Gillespie. "Hale!"

They waited. A sea lifted them swiftly and lightly, and Colet turned his
head in measuring fear from the door aft to the head of the *Altair*. Her
forecastle deck was isolated, a raft of wreckage flush with the swirls and
foam. The seas were pouring solidly across her middle. Her funnel was
bowed over the flood, and each dip of it to the declination of the ocean was,
to the men in the boat, the prelude to the end. But it was her stern which
rose and lowered her head.

"My God! she's going!"

She gave a hollow rumbling groan, and without a check to the silent awe
of the watchers she went down. Colet saw the shape of the propeller over
him and the bright sky through its frame. There was a confusion on the
surface of the waters, which melted as a swell heaved over the place. The
sea was bare.

⚓

TURN ABOUT

⚓

TURN ABOUT

William Faulkner

⚓ *God bless all men in little boats. In punts and wherries and ketches; in scows and dhows and dugouts; in junks, sampans and catamarans; in cutters and skiffs and sloops; in prams and shells and dinghies; in dories, canoes and whaleboats; and even, God, in motorboats. Amen.*

I

THE American—the older one—wore no pink Bedfords. His breeches were of plain whipcord, like the tunic. And the tunic had no long London-cut skirts, so that below the Sam Browne the tail of it stuck straight out like the tunic of a military policeman beneath his holster belt. And he wore simple puttees and the easy shoes of a man of middle age, instead of Savile Row boots, and the shoes and the puttees did not match in shade, and the ordnance belt did not match either of them, and the pilot's wings on his breast were just wings. But the ribbon beneath them was a good ribbon, and the insigne on his shoulders were the twin bars of a captain. He was not tall. His face was thin, a little aquiline; the eyes intelligent and a little tired. He was past twenty-five; looking at him, one thought, not Phi Beta Kappa exactly, but Skull and Bones perhaps, or possibly a Rhodes scholarship.

One of the men who faced him probably could not see him at all. He was being held on his feet by an American military policeman. He was quite drunk, and in contrast with the heavy-jawed policeman who held him erect on his long, slim, boneless legs, he looked like a masquerading girl. He was possibly eighteen, tall, with a pink-and-white face and blue eyes, and a mouth like a girl's mouth. He wore a pea-coat, buttoned awry and stained with recent mud, and upon his blond head, at that unmistakable and rakish swagger which no other people can ever approach or imitate, the cap of a Royal Naval Officer.

"What's this, corporal?" the American captain said. "What's the trouble? He's an Englishman. You'd better let their M.P.'s take care of him."

"I know he is," the policeman said. He spoke heavily, breathing heavily, in the voice of a man under physical strain; for all his girlish delicacy of limb, the English boy was heavier—or more helpless—than he looked. "Stand up!" the policeman said. "They're officers!"

The English boy made an effort then. He pulled himself together, focusing his eyes. He swayed, throwing his arms about the policeman's neck, and with the other hand he saluted, his hand flicking, fingers curled a little, to his right ear, already swaying again and catching himself again. "Cheer-o, sir," he said. "Name's not Beatty, I hope."

"No," the captain said.

"Ah," the English boy said. "Hoped not. My mistake. No offense, what?"

"No offense," the captain said quietly. But he was looking at the policeman. The second American spoke. He was a lieutenant, also a pilot. But he was not twenty-five and he wore the pink breeches, the London boots, and his tunic might have been a British tunic save for the collar.

"It's one of those navy eggs," he said. "They pick them out of the gutters here all night long. You don't come to town often enough."

"Oh," the captain said. "I've heard about them. I remember now." He also remarked now that, though the street was a busy one—it was just outside a popular café—and there were many passers, soldier, civilian, women, yet none of them so much as paused, as though it were a familiar sight. He was looking at the policeman. "Can't you take him to his ship?"

"I thought of that before the captain did," the policeman said. "He says he can't go aboard his ship after dark because he puts the ship away at sundown."

"Puts it away?"

"Stand up, sailor!" the policeman said savagely, jerking at his lax burden. "Maybe the captain can make sense out of it. Damned if I can. He says they keep the boat under the wharf. Run it under the wharf at night, and that they can't get it out again until the tide goes out tomorrow."

"Under the wharf? A boat? What is this?" He was now speaking to the lieutenant. "Do they operate some kind of aquatic motorcycles?"

"Something like that," the lieutenant said. "You've seen them—the boats. Launches, camouflaged and all. Dashing up and down the harbor. You've seen them. They do that all day and sleep in the gutters here all night."

"Oh," the captain said. "I thought those boats were ship commanders' launches. You mean to tell me they use officers just to—"

"I don't know," the lieutenant said. "Maybe they use them to fetch hot water from one ship to another. Or buns. Or maybe to go back and forth fast when they forget napkins or something."

"Nonsense," the captain said. He looked at the English boy again.

"That's what they do," the lieutenant said. "Town's lousy with them all night long. Gutters full, and their M.P.'s carting them away in batches, like nursemaids in a park. Maybe the French give them the launches to get them out of the gutters during the day."

"Oh," the captain said, "I see." But it was clear that he didn't see, wasn't listening, didn't believe what he did hear. He looked at the English boy. "Well, you can't leave him here in that shape," he said.

Again the English boy tried to pull himself together. "Quite all right, 'sure you," he said glassily, his voice pleasant, cheerful almost, quite courteous. "Used to it. Confounded rough *pavé,* though. Should force French do something about it. Visiting lads jolly well deserve decent field to play on, what?"

"And he was jolly well using all of it too," the policeman said savagely. "He must think he's a one-man team, maybe."

At that moment a fifth man came up. He was a British military policeman. "Nah then," he said. "What's this? What's this?" Then he saw the Americans' shoulder bars. He saluted. At the sound of his voice the English boy turned, swaying, peering.

"Oh, hullo, Albert," he said.

"Nah then, Mr. Hope," the British policeman said. He said to the American policeman, over his shoulder: "What is it this time?"

"Likely nothing," the American said. "The way you guys run a war. But I'm a stranger here. Here. Take him."

"What is this, corporal?" the captain said. "What was he doing?"

"He won't call it nothing," the American policeman said, jerking his head at the British policeman. "He'll just call it a thrush or a robin or something. I turn into this street about three blocks back a while ago, and I find it blocked with a line of trucks going up from the docks, and the drivers all hollering ahead what the hell the trouble is. So I come on, and I find it is about three blocks of them, blocking the cross streets too; and I come on to the head of it where the trouble is, and I find about a dozen of the drivers out in front, holding a caucus or something in the middle of the street, and I come up and I say, 'What's going on here?' and they leave me through and I find this egg here laying—"

"Yer talking about one of His Majesty's officers, my man," the British policeman said.

"Watch yourself, corporal," the captain said. "And you found this officer—"

"He had done gone to bed in the middle of the street, with an empty basket for a pillow. Laying there with his hands under his head and his knees crossed, arguing with them about whether he ought to get up and move or not. He said that the trucks could turn back and go around by another street, but that he couldn't use any other street, because this street was his."

"His street?"

The English boy had listened, interested, pleasant. "Billet, you see," he said. "Must have order, even in war emergency. Billet by lot. This street mine; no poaching, eh? Next street Jamie Wutherspoon's. But trucks can go by that street because Jamie not using it yet. Not in bed yet. Insomnia. Knew so. Told them. Trucks go that way. See now?"

"Was that it, corporal?" the captain said.

"He told you. He wouldn't get up. He just laid there, arguing with them. He was telling one of them to go somewhere and bring back a copy of their articles of war—"

"King's Regulations; yes," the captain said.

"—and see if the book said whether he had the right of way, or the trucks. And then I got him up, and then the captain come along. And that's all. And with the captain's permission I'll now hand him over to His Majesty's wet nur—"

"That'll do, corporal," the captain said. "You can go. I'll see to this." The policeman saluted and went on. The British policeman was now supporting the English boy. "Can't you take him home?" the captain said. "Where are their quarters?"

"I don't rightly know, sir, if they have quarters or not. We—I usually see them about the pubs until daylight. They don't seem to use quarters."

"You mean, they really aren't off of ships?"

"Well, sir, they might be ships, in a manner of speaking. But a man would have to be a bit sleepier than him to sleep in one of them."

"I see," the captain said. He looked at the policeman. "What kind of boats are they?"

This time the policeman's voice was immediate, final and completely inflectionless. It was like a closed door. "I don't rightly know, sir."

"Oh," the captain said. "Quite. Well, he's in no shape to stay about pubs until daylight this time."

"Perhaps I can find him a bit of a pub with a back table, where he can sleep," the policeman said. But the captain was not listening. He was looking across the street, where the lights of another café fell across the pavement. The English boy yawned terrifically, like a child does, his mouth pink and frankly gaped as a child's.

The captain turned to the policeman:

"Would you mind stepping across there and asking for Captain Bogard's driver? I'll take care of Mr. Hope."

The policeman departed. The captain now supported the English boy, his hand beneath the other's arm. Again the boy yawned like a weary child. "Steady," the captain said. "The car will be here in a minute."

"Right," the English boy said through the yawn.

II

Once in the car he went to sleep immediately with the peaceful suddenness of babies, sitting between the two Americans. But though the aerodrome was only thirty minutes away, he was awake when they arrived, apparently quite fresh, and asking for whisky. When they entered the mess he appeared quite sober, only blinking a little in the lighted room, in his raked cap and his awry-buttoned pea-jacket and a soiled silk muffler, embroidered with a club insignia which Bogard recognized to have come from a famous preparatory school, twisted about his throat.

"Ah," he said, his voice fresh, clear now, not blurred, quite cheerful, quite loud, so that the others in the room turned and looked at him. "Jolly. Whisky, what?" He went straight as a bird dog to the bar in the corner, the lieutenant following. Bogard had turned and gone on to the other end of the room, where five men sat about a card table.

"What's he admiral of?" one said.

"Of the whole Scotch navy, when I found him," Bogard said.

Another looked up. "Oh, I thought I'd seen him in town." He looked at the guest. "Maybe it's because he was on his feet that I didn't recognize him when he came in. You usually see them lying down in the gutter."

"Oh," the first said. He, too, looked around. "Is he one of those guys?"

"Sure. You've seen them. Sitting on the curb, you know, with a couple of limey M.P.'s hauling at their arms."

"Yes. I've seen them," the other said. They all looked at the English boy. He stood at the bar, talking, his voice loud, cheerful. "They all look like him too," the speaker said. "About seventeen or eighteen. They run those little boats that are always dashing in and out."

"Is that what they do?" a third said. "You mean, there's a male marine auxiliary to the Waacs? Good Lord, I sure made a mistake when I enlisted. But this war never was advertised right."

"I don't know," Bogard said. "I guess they do more than just ride around."

But they were not listening to him. They were looking at the guest.

"They run by clock," the first said. "You can see the condition of one of them after sunset and almost tell what time it is. But what I don't see is, how a man that's in that shape at one o'clock every morning can even see a battleship the next day."

"Maybe when they have a message to send out to a ship," another said, "they just make duplicates and line the launches up and point them toward the ship and give each one a duplicate of the message and let them go. And the ones that miss the ship just cruise around the harbor until they hit a dock somewhere."

"It must be more than that," Bogard said.

He was about to say something else, but at that moment the guest turned from the bar and approached, carrying a glass. He walked steadily enough, but his color was high and his eyes were bright, and he was talking, loud, cheerful, as he came up.

"I say. Won't you chaps join—." He ceased. He seemed to remark something; he was looking at their breasts. "Oh, I say. You fly. All of you. Oh, good gad! Find it jolly, eh?"

"Yes," somebody said. "Jolly."

"But dangerous, what?"

"A little faster than tennis," another said. The guest looked at him, bright, affable, intent.

Another said quickly, "Bogard says you command a vessel."

"Hardly a vessel. Thanks, though. And not command. Ronnie does that. Ranks me a bit. Age."

"Ronnie?"

"Yes. Nice. Good egg. Old, though. Stickler."

"Stickler?"

"Frightful. You'd not believe it. Whenever we sight smoke and I have the glass, he sheers away. Keeps the ship hull down all the while. No beaver then. Had me two down a fortnight yesterday."

The Americans glanced at one another. "No beaver?"

"We play it. With basket masts, you see. See a basket mast. Beaver! One up. The *Ergenstrasse* doesn't count any more, though."

The men about the table looked at one another. Bogard spoke. "I see. When you or Ronnie see a ship with basket masts, you get a beaver on the other. I see. What is the *Ergenstrasse?*"

"She's German. Interned. Tramp steamer. Foremast rigged so it looks something like a basket mast. Booms, cables, I dare say. I didn't think it looked very much like a basket mast, myself. But Ronnie said yes. Called it one day. Then one day they shifted her across the basin and I called her on Ronnie. So we decided to not count her any more. See now, eh?"

"Oh," the one who had made the tennis remark said, "I see. You and

Ronnie run about in the launch, playing beaver. H'm'm. That's nice. Did you ever pl—"

"Jerry," Bogard said. The guest had not moved. He looked down at the speaker, still smiling, his eyes quite wide.

The speaker still looked at the guest. "Has yours and Ronnie's boat got a yellow stern?"

"A yellow stern?" the English boy said. He had quit smiling, but his face was still pleasant.

"I thought that maybe when the boats had two captains, they might paint the stern yellow or something."

"Oh," the guest said. "Burt and Reeves aren't officers."

"Burt and Reeves," the other said, in a musing tone. "So they go, too. Do they play beaver too?"

"Jerry," Bogard said. The other looked at him. Bogard jerked his head a little. "Come over here." The other rose. They went aside. "Lay off of him," Bogard said. "I mean it, now. He's just a kid. When you were that age, how much sense did you have? Just about enough to get to chapel on time."

"My country hadn't been at war going on four years, though," Jerry said. "Here we are, spending our money and getting shot at by the clock, and it's not even our fight, and these limeys that would have been goose-stepping twelve months now if it hadn't been—"

"Shut it," Bogard said. "You sound like a Liberty Loan."

"—taking it like it was a fair or something. 'Jolly.'" His voice was now falsetto, lilting. "'But dangerous, what?'"

"Sh-h-h-h," Bogard said.

"I'd like to catch him and his Ronnie out in the harbor, just once. Any harbor. London's. I wouldn't want anything but a Jenny, either. Jenny? Hell, I'd take a bicycle and a pair of water wings! I'll show him some war."

"Well, you lay off him now. He'll be gone soon."

"What are you going to do with him?"

"I'm going to take him along this morning. Let him have Harper's place out front. He says he can handle a Lewis. Says they have one on the boat. Something he was telling me—about how he once shot out a channel-marker light at seven hundred yards."

"Well, that's your business. Maybe he can beat you."

"Beat me?"

"Playing beaver. And then you can take on Ronnie."

"I'll show him some war, anyway," Bogard said. He looked at the guest. "His people have been in it three years now, and he seems to take it like a sophomore in town for the big game." He looked at Jerry again. "But you lay off him now."

As they approached the table, the guest's voice was loud and cheerful: ". . . if he got the glasses first, he would go in close and look, but when I got them first, he'd sheer off where I couldn't see anything but the smoke. Frightful stickler. Frightful. But *Ergenstrasse* not counting any more. And if you make a mistake and call her, you lose two beaver from your score. If Ronnie were only to forget and call her we'd be even."

III

At two o'clock the English boy was still talking, his voice bright, inno-cent and cheerful. He was telling them how Switzerland had been spoiled by 1914, and instead of the vacation which his father had promised him for his sixteenth birthday, when that birthday came he and his tutor had had to do with Wales. But that he and the tutor had got pretty high and that he dared to say—with all due respect to any present who might have had the advantage of Switzerland, of course—that one could see probably as far from Wales as from Switzerland. "Perspire as much and breathe as hard, anyway," he added. And about him the Americans sat, a little hard-bitten, a little sober, somewhat older, listening to him with a kind of cold astonishment. They had been getting up for some time now and going out and returning in flying clothes, carrying helmets and goggles. An orderly entered with a tray of coffee cups, and the guest realized that for some time now he had been hearing engines in the darkness outside.

At last Bogard rose. "Come along," he said. "We'll get your togs." When they emerged from the mess, the sound of the engines was quite loud—an idling thunder. In alignment along the invisible tarmac was a vague rank of short banks of flickering blue-green fire suspended apparently in mid-air. They crossed the aerodrome to Bogard's quarters, where the lieuten-ant, McGinnis, sat on a cot fastening his flying boots. Bogard reached down a Sidcott suit and threw it across the cot. "Put this on," he said.

"Will I need all this?" the guest said. "Shall we be gone that long?"

"Probably," Bogard said. "Better use it. Cold upstairs."

The guest picked up the suit. "I say," he said. "I say. Ronnie and I have a do ourselves, tomor—today. Do you think Ronnie won't mind if I am a bit late? Might not wait for me."

"We'll be back before teatime," McGinnis said. He seemed quite busy with his boot. "Promise you." The English boy looked at him.

"What time should you be back?" Bogard said.

"Oh, well," the English boy said, "I dare say it will be all right. They let Ronnie say when to go, anyway. He'll wait for me if I should be a bit late."

"He'll wait," Bogard said. "Get your suit on."

"Right," the other said. They helped him into the suit. "Never been up before," he said, chattily, pleasantly. "Dare say you can see farther than from mountains, eh?"

"See more, anyway," McGinnis said. "You'll like it."

"Oh, rather. If Ronnie only waits for me. Lark. But dangerous, isn't it?"

"Go on," McGinnis said. "You're kidding me."

"Shut your trap, Mac," Bogard said. "Come along. Want some more coffee?" He looked at the guest, but McGinnis answered:

"No. Got something better than coffee. Coffee makes such a confounded stain on the wings."

"On the wings?" the English boy said. "Why coffee on the wings?"

"Stow it, I said, Mac," Bogard said. "Come along."

They recrossed the aerodrome, approaching the muttering banks of flame. When they drew near, the guest began to discern the shape, the outlines, of the Handley-Page. It looked like a Pullman coach run upslanted aground into the skeleton of the first floor of an incomplete skyscraper. The guest looked at it quietly.

"It's larger than a cruiser," he said in his bright, interested voice. "I say, you know. This doesn't fly in one lump. You can't pull my leg. Seen them before. It comes in two parts: Captain Bogard and me in one; Mac and 'nother chap in other. What?"

"No," McGinnis said. Bogard had vanished. "It all goes up in one lump. Big lark, eh? Buzzard, what?"

"Buzzard?" the guest murmured. "Oh, I say. A cruiser. Flying. I say, now."

"And listen," McGinnis said. His hand came forth; something cold fumbled against the hand of the English boy—a bottle. "When you feel yourself getting sick, see? Take a pull at it."

"Oh, shall I get sick?"

"Sure. We all do. Part of flying. This will stop it. But if it doesn't. See?"

"What? Quite. What?"

"Not overside. Don't spew it overside."

"Not overside?"

"It'll blow back in Bogy's and my face. Can't see. Bingo. Finished. See?"

"Oh, quite. What shall I do with it?" Their voices were quiet, brief, grave as conspirators.

"Just duck your head and let her go."

"Oh, quite."

Bogard returned. "Show him how to get into the front pit, will you?" he said. McGinnis led the way through the trap. Forward, rising to the slant of the fuselage, the passage narrowed; a man would need to crawl.

"Crawl in there and keep going," McGinnis said.

"It looks like a dog kennel," the guest said.

"Doesn't it, though?" McGinnis agreed cheerfully. "Cut along with you." Stooping, he could hear the other scuttling forward. "You'll find a Lewis gun up there, like as not," he said into the tunnel.

The voice of the guest came back: "Found it."

"The gunnery sergeant will be along in a minute and show you if it is loaded."

"It's loaded," the guest said; almost on the heels of his words the gun fired, a brief staccato burst. There were shouts, the loudest from the ground beneath the nose of the aeroplane. "It's quite all right," the English boy's voice said. "I pointed it west before I let it off. Nothing back there but Marine office and your brigade headquarters. Ronnie and I always do this before we go anywhere. Sorry if I was too soon. Oh, by the way," he added, "my name's Claude. Don't think I mentioned it."

On the ground, Bogard and two other officers stood. They had come up running. "Fired it west," one said. "How in hell does he know which way is west?"

"He's a sailor," the other said. "You forgot that."

"He seems to be a machine gunner too," Bogard said.

"Let's hope he doesn't forget that," the first said.

IV

Nevertheless, Bogard kept an eye on the silhouetted head rising from the round gunpit in the nose ten feet ahead of him. "He did work that gun, though," he said to McGinnis beside him. "He even put the drum on himself, didn't he?"

"Yes," McGinnis said. "If he just doesn't forget and think that that gun is him and his tutor looking around from a Welsh alp."

"Maybe I should not have brought him," Bogard said. McGinnis didn't answer. Bogard jockeyed the wheel a little. Ahead, in the gunner's pit, the guest's head moved this way and that continuously, looking. "We'll get there and unload and haul air for home," Bogard said. "Maybe in the dark— Confound it, it would be a shame for his country to be in this mess for four years and him not even to see a gun pointed in his direction."

"He'll see one tonight if he don't keep his head in," McGinnis said.

But the boy did not do that. Not even when they had reached the objective and McGinnis had crawled down to the bomb toggles. And even when the searchlights found them and Bogard signaled to the other machines and dived, the two engines snarling full speed into and through the bursting shells, he could see the boy's face in the searchlight's glare, leaned far overside, coming sharply out as a spotlighted face on a stage, with an expression upon it of childlike interest and delight. "But he's firing that Lewis," Bogard thought. "Straight too"; nosing the machine farther down, watching the pinpoints swing into the sights, his right hand lifted, waiting to drop into McGinnis' sight. He dropped his hand; above the noise of the engines he seemed to hear the click and whistle of the released bombs as the machine freed of the weight, shot zooming in a long upward bounce that carried it for an instant out of the light. Then he was pretty busy for a time, coming into and through the shells again, shooting athwart another beam that caught and held long enough for him to see the English boy leaning far over the side, looking back and down past the right wing, the undercarriage. "Maybe he's read about it somewhere," Bogard thought, turning, looking back to pick up the rest of the flight.

Then it was all over, the darkness cool and empty and peaceful and almost quiet, with only the steady sound of the engines. McGinnis climbed back into the office, and standing up in his seat, he fired the colored pistol this time and stood for a moment longer, looking backward toward where the searchlights still probed and sabered. He sat down again.

"O.K.," he said. "I counted all four of them. Let's haul air." Then he looked forward. "What's become of the King's Own? You didn't hang him onto a bomb release, did you?" Bogard looked. The forward pit was empty. It was in dim silhouette again now, against the stars, but there was nothing there now save the gun. "No," McGinnis said; "there he is. See? Leaning overside. Dammit, I told him not to spew it! There he comes back!" The guest's head came into view again. But again it sank out of sight.

"He's coming back," Bogard said. "Stop him. Tell him we're going to have every squadron in the Hun Channel group on top of us in thirty minutes."

McGinnis swung himself down and stooped at the entrance to the passage. "Get back!" he shouted. The other was almost out; they squatted so, face to face like two dogs, shouting at another above the noise of the still-unthrottled engines on either side of the fabric walls. The English boy's voice was thin and high.

"Bomb!" he shrieked.

"Yes," McGinnis shouted. "They were bombs! We gave them hell! Get back I tell you! Have every Hun in France on us in ten minutes! Get back to your gun!"

. Again the boy's voice came, high, faint above the noise: "Bomb! All right?"

"Yes! Yes! All right. Back to your gun, damn you!"

McGinnis climbed back into the office. "He went back. Want me to take her awhile?"

"All right," Bogard said. He passed McGinnis the wheel. "Ease her back some. I'd just as soon it was daylight when they come down on us."

"Right," McGinnis said. He moved the wheel suddenly. "What's the matter with that right wing?" he said. "Watch it. . . . See? I'm flying on the right aileron and a little rudder. Feel it."

Bogard took the wheel a moment. "I didn't notice that. Wire somewhere, I guess. I didn't think any of those shells were that close. Watch her. though."

"Right," McGinnis said. "And so you are going with him on his boat tomorrow—today."

"Yes, I promised him. Confound it, you can't hurt a kid, you know."

"Why don't you take Collier along, with his mandolin? Then you could sail around and sing."

"I promised him," Bogard said. "Get that wing up a little."

"Right," McGinnis said.

Thirty minutes later it was beginning to be dawn; the sky was gray. Presently McGinnis said: "Well, here they come. Look at them! They look like mosquitoes in September. I hope he don't get worked up now and think he's playing beaver. If he does he'll just be one down to Ronnie, provided the devil has a beard. . . . Want the wheel?"

V

At eight o'clock the beach, the Channel, was beneath them. Throttled back, the machine drifted down as Bogard ruddered it gently into the Channel wind. His face was strained, a little tired.

McGinnis looked tired, too, and he needed a shave.

"What do you guess he is looking at now?" he said. For again the English boy was leaning over the right side of the cockpit, looking backward and downward past the right wing.

"I don't know," Bogard said. "Maybe bullet holes." He blasted the port engine. "Must have the riggers—"

"He could see some closer than that," McGinnis said. "I'll swear I saw tracer going into his back at one time. Or maybe it's the ocean he's looking at. But he must have seen that when he came over from England." Then Bogard leveled off; the nose rose sharply, the sand, the curling tide edge fled along-side. Yet still the English boy hung far overside, looking backward and downward at something beneath the right wing, his face rapt, with utter and childlike interest. Until the machine was completely stopped he continued to do so. Then he ducked down, and in the abrupt silence of the engines they could hear him crawling in the passage. He emerged just as the two pilots climbed stiffly down from the office, his face bright, eager; his voice high, excited.

"Oh, I say! Oh, good gad! What a chap! What a judge of distance! If Ronnie could only have seen! Oh, good gad! Or maybe they aren't like ours—don't load themselves as soon as the air strikes them."

The Americans looked at him. "What don't what?" McGinnis said.

"The bomb. It was magnificent; I say, I shan't forget it. Oh, I say, you know! It was splendid!"

After a while McGinnis said, "The bomb?" in a fainting voice. Then the two pilots glared at each other; they said in unison: "That right wing!" Then as one they clawed down through the trap and, with the guest at their heels, they ran around the machine and looked beneath the right wing. The bomb, suspended by its tail, hung straight down like a plumb bob beside the right wheel, its tip just touching the sand. And parallel with the wheel track was the long delicate line in the sand where its ultimate tip had dragged. Behind them the English boy's voice was high, clear, childlike:

"Frightened, myself. Tried to tell you. But realized you knew your business better than I. Skill. Marvelous. Oh, I say, I shan't forget it."

VI

A marine with a bayoneted rifle passed Bogard onto the wharf and directed him to the boat. The wharf was empty, and he didn't even see the boat until he approached the edge of the wharf and looked directly down into it and upon the backs of two stooping men in greasy dungarees, who rose and glanced briefly at him and stooped again.

It was about thirty feet long and about three feet wide. It was painted with gray-green camouflage. It was quarter-decked forward, with two blunt, raked exhaust stacks. "Good Lord," Bogard thought, "if all that deck is engine—" Just aft the deck was the control seat; he saw a big wheel, an instrument panel. Rising to a height of about a foot above the freeboard, and running from the stern forward to where the deck began, and continuing on across the after edge of the deck and thence back down the other gunwale to the stern, was a solid screen, also camouflaged, which inclosed the boat save for the width of the stern, which was open. Facing the steerman's seat like an eye was a hole in the screen about eight inches in diameter. And looking down into the long, narrow, still, vicious shape, he saw a machine gun swiveled at the stern, and he looked at the low screen—including which the whole vessel did not sit much more than a yard above water level—with its single empty forward-staring eye, and he thought quietly: "It's steel. It's made of steel." And his face was quite sober, quite thoughtful, and he drew his trench coat about him and buttoned it, as though he were getting cold.

He heard steps behind him and turned. But it was only an orderly from the aerodrome, accompanied by the marine with the rifle. The orderly was carrying a largish bundle wrapped in paper.

"From Lieutenant McGinnis to the captain," the orderly said.

Bogard took the bundle. The orderly and the marine retreated. He opened the bundle. It contained some objects and a scrawled note. The objects were a new yellow silk sofa cushion and a Japanese parasol, obviously borrowed, and a comb and a roll of toilet paper. The note said:

> Couldn't find a camera anywhere and Collier wouldn't let me have his mandolin. But maybe Ronnie can play on the comb.
>
> Mac.

Bogard looked at the objects. But his face was still quite thoughtful, quite grave. He rewrapped the things and carried the bundle on up the wharf a way and dropped it quietly into the water.

As he returned toward the invisible boat he saw two men approaching. He recognized the boy at once—tall, slender, already talking, voluble, his head bent a little toward his shorter companion, who plodded along beside him, hands in pockets, smoking a pipe. The boy still wore the pea-coat beneath a flapping oilskin, but in place of the rakish and casual cap he now wore an infantryman's soiled Balaclava helmet, with, floating behind him as though upon the sound of his voice, a curtainlike piece of cloth almost as long as a burnous.

"Hullo, there!" he cried, still a hundred yards away.

But it was the second man that Bogard was watching, thinking to himself that he had never in his life seen a more curious figure. There was something stolid about the very shape of his hunched shoulders, his slightly down-looking face. He was a head shorter than the other. His face was ruddy, too, but its mold was a profound gravity that was almost dour. It was the face of a man of twenty who has been for a year trying, even while asleep, to look twenty-one. He wore a high-necked sweater and dungaree slacks; above this a leather jacket; and above this a soiled naval officer's warmer that reached almost to his heels and which had one shoulder strap missing and not one remaining button at all. On his head was a plaid fore-and-aft deer stalker's cap, tied on by a narrow scarf brought across and down, hiding his ears, and then wrapped once about his throat and knotted with a hangman's noose beneath his left ear. It was unbelievably soiled, and with his hands elbow-deep in his pockets and his hunched shoulders and his bent head, he looked like someone's grandmother hung, say, for witch. Clamped upside down between his teeth was a short brier pipe.

"Here he is!" the boy cried. "This is Ronnie. Captain Bogard."

"How are you?" Bogard said. He extended his hand. The other said no word, but his hand came forth, limp. It was quite cold, but it was hard, calloused. But he said no word; he just glanced briefly at Bogard and then away. But in that instant Bogard caught something in the look, something strange—a flicker; a kind of covert and curious respect, something like a boy of fifteen looking at a circus trapezist.

But he said no word. He ducked on; Bogard watched him drop from sight over the wharf edge as though he had jumped feet first into the sea. He remarked now that the engines in the invisible boat were running.

"We might get aboard too," the boy said. He started toward the boat, then he stopped. He touched Bogard's arm. "Yonder!" he hissed. "See?" His voice was thin with excitement.

"What?" Bogard also whispered; automatically he looked backward and upward, after old habit. The other was gripping his arm and pointing across the harbor.

"There! Over there. The *Ergenstrasse*. They have shifted her again." Across the harbor lay an ancient, rusting, sway-backed hulk. It was small and nondescript, and, remembering, Bogard saw the foremast was a strange mess of cables and booms, resembling—allowing for a great deal of license or looseness of imagery—a basket mast. Beside him the boy was almost chortling. "Do you think that Ronnie noticed?" he hissed. "Do you?"

"I don't know," Bogard said.

"Oh, good gad! If he should glance up and call her before he notices, we'll be even. Oh, good gad! But come along." He went on; he was still chortling. "Careful," he said. "Frightful ladder."

He descended first, the two men in the boat rising and saluting. Ronnie had disappeared, save for his backside, which now filled a small hatch leading forward beneath the deck. Bogard descended gingerly.

"Good Lord," he said. "Do you have to climb up and down this every day?"

"Frightful, isn't it?" the other said, in his happy voice. "But you know yourself. Try to run a war with makeshifts, then wonder why it takes so long." The narrow hull slid and surged, even with Bogard's added weight. "Sits right on top, you see," the boy said. "Would float on a lawn, in a heavy dew. Goes right over them like a bit of paper."

"It does?" Bogard said.

"Oh, absolutely. That's why, you see." Bogard didn't see, but he was too busy letting himself gingerly down to a sitting posture. There were no thwarts; no seats save a long, thick, cylindrical ridge which ran along the bottom of the boat from the driver's seat to the stern. Ronnie had backed into sight. He now sat behind the wheel, bent over the instrument panel. But when he glanced back over his shoulder he did not speak. His face was merely interrogatory. Across his face there was now a long smudge of grease. The boy's face was empty, too, now.

"Right," he said. He looked forward, where one of the seamen had gone. "Ready forward?" he said.

"Aye, sir," the seaman said.

The other seaman was at the stern line. "Ready aft?"

"Aye, sir."

"Cast off." The boat sheered away, purring, a boiling of water under the stern. The boy looked down at Bogard. "Silly business. Do it shipshape, though. Can't tell when silly fourstriper—" His face changed again, immediate, solicitous. "I say. Will you be warm? I never thought to fetch—"

"I'll be all right," Bogard said. But the other was already taking off his oilskin. "No, no," Bogard said. "I won't take it."

"You'll tell me if you get cold?"

"Yes. Sure." He was looking down at the cylinder on which he sat. It was a half cylinder—that is, like the hot-water tank to some Gargantuan stove, sliced down the middle and bolted, open side down, to the floor plates. It was twenty feet long and more than two feet thick. Its top rose as high as the gunwales and between it and the hull on either side was just room enough for a man to place his feet to walk.

"That's Muriel," the boy said.

"Muriel?"

"Yes. The one before that was Agatha. After my aunt. The first one Ronnie and I had was Alice in Wonderland. Ronnie and I were the White Rabbit. Jolly, eh?"

"Oh, you and Ronnie have had three, have you?"

"Oh, yes," the boy said. He leaned down. "He didn't notice," he whispered. His face was again bright, gleeful. "When we come back," he said. "You watch."

"Oh," Bogard said. "The *Ergenstrasse.*" He looked astern, and then he thought: "Good Lord! We must be going—traveling." He looked out now, broadside, and saw the harbor line fleeing past, and he thought to himself that the boat was well-nigh moving at the speed at which the Handley-Page flew, left the ground. They were beginning to bound now, even in the sheltered water, from one wave crest to the next with a distinct shock. His hand still rested on the cylinder on which he sat. He looked down at it again, following it from where it seemed to emerge beneath Ronnie's seat, to where it beveled into the stern. "It's the air in here, I suppose."

"The what?" the boy said.

"The air. Stored up in here. That makes the boat ride high."

"Oh, yes. I dare say. Very likely. I hadn't thought about it." He came forward, his burnous whipping in the wind, and sat down beside Bogard. Their heads were below the top of the screen.

Astern the harbor fled, diminishing, sinking into the sea. The boat had begun to lift now, swooping forward and down, shocking almost stationary for a moment, then lifting and swooping again; a gout of spray came aboard over the bows like a flung shovelful of shot. "I wish you'd take this coat," the boy said.

Bogard didn't answer. He looked around at the bright face. "We're outside, aren't we?" he said quietly.

"Yes. . . . Do take it, won't you?"

"Thanks, no. I'll be all right. We won't be long, anyway, I guess."

"No. We'll turn soon. It won't be so bad then."

"Yes. I'll be all right when we turn." Then they did turn. The motion became easier. That is, the boat didn't bang head-on, shuddering, into the swells. They came up beneath now, and the boat fled with increased speed, with a long, sickening, yawning motion, first to one side and then the other. But it fled on, and Bogard looked astern with that same soberness with which he had first looked down into the boat. "We're going east now," he said.

"With just a spot of north," the boy said. "Makes her ride a bit better, what?"

"Yes," Bogard said. Astern there was nothing now save empty sea and the delicate needlelike cant of the machine gun against the boiling and slewing wake, and the two seamen crouching quietly in the stern. "Yes. It's easier." Then he said: "How far do we go?"

The boy leaned closer. He moved closer. His voice was happy, confidential, proud, though lowered a little: "It's Ronnie's show. He thought of it. Not that I wouldn't have, in time. Gratitude and all that. But he's the older, you see. Thinks fast. Courtesy, *noblesse oblige*—all that. Thought of it soon as I told him this morning. I said, 'Oh, I say. I've been there. I've seen it'; and he said, 'Not flying?'; and I said, 'Strewth'; and he said 'How far? No lying now'; and I said, 'Oh, far. Tremendous. Gone all night'; and he said, 'Flying all night. That must have been to Berlin'; and I said, 'I don't know. I dare say'; and he thought. I could see him thinking. Because he is the older, you see. More experience in courtesy, right thing. And he said, 'Berlin. No fun to that chap, dashing out and back with us.' And he thought and I waited, and I said, 'But we can't take him to Berlin. Too far. Don't know the way, either'; and he said—fast, like a shot—said, 'But there's Kiel'; and I knew—"

"What?" Bogard said. Without moving, his whole body sprang. "Kiel? In this?"

"Absolutely. Ronnie thought of it. Smart, even if he is a stickler. Said at once 'Zeebrugge no show at all for that chap. Must do best we can for him. Berlin,' Ronnie said. 'My gad! Berlin.'"

"Listen," Bogard said. He had turned now, facing the other, his face quite grave. "What is this boat for?"

"For?"

"What does it do?" Then, knowing beforehand the answer to his own question, he said, putting his hand on the cylinder: "What is this in here? A torpedo, isn't it?"

"I thought you knew," the boy said.

"No," Bogard said. "I didn't know." His voice seemed to reach him from a distance, dry, cricketlike: "How do you fire it?"

"Fire it?"

"How do you get it out of the boat? When that hatch was open a while ago I could see the engines. They were right in front of the end of this tube."

"Oh," the boy said. "You pull a gadget there and the torpedo drops out astern. As soon as the screw touches the water it begins to turn, and then the torpedo is ready, loaded. Then all you have to do is turn the boat quickly and the torpedo goes on."

"You mean—" Bogard said. After a moment his voice obeyed him again. "You mean you aim the torpedo with the boat and release it and it starts moving, and you turn the boat out of the way and the torpedo passes through the same water that the boat just vacated?

"Knew you'd catch on," the boy said. "Told Ronnie so. Airman. Tamer than yours, though. But can't be helped. Best we can do, just on water. But knew you'd catch on."

"Listen," Bogard said. His voice sounded to him quite calm. The boat fled on, yawing over the swells. He sat quite motionless. It seemed to him that he could hear himself talking to himself: "Go on. Ask him. Ask him what? Ask him how close to the ship do you have to be before you fire. . . . Listen," he said, in that calm voice. "Now, you tell Ronnie, you see. You just tell him—just say—" He could feel his voice ratting off on him again, so he stopped it. He sat quite motionless, waiting for it to come back; the boy leaning now, looking at his face. Again the boy's voice was solicitous:

"I say. You're not feeling well. These confounded shallow boats."

"It's not that," Bogard said. "I just— Do your orders say Kiel?"

"Oh, no. They let Ronnie say. Just so we bring the boat back. This is for you. Gratitude. Ronnie's idea. Tame, after flying. But if you'd rather, eh?"

"Yes, some place closer. You see, I—"

"Quite. I see. No vacations in wartime. I'll tell Ronnie." He went for ward. Bogard did not move. The boat fled in long, slewing swoops. Bogard looked quietly astern, at the scudding sea, the sky.

"My God!" he thought. "Can you beat it? Can you beat it?"

The boy came back; Bogard turned to him a face the color of dirty paper. "All right now," the boy said. "Not Kiel. Nearer place, hunting probably just as good. Ronnie says he knows you will understand." He was tugging at his pocket. He brought out a bottle. "Here. Haven't forgot last night. Do the same for you. Good for the stomach, eh?"

Bogard drank, gulping—a big one. He extended the bottle, but the boy refused. "Never touch it on duty," he said. "Not like you chaps. Tame here."

The boat fled on. The sun was already down the west. But Bogard had lost all count of time, of distance. Ahead he could see white seas through the round eye opposite Ronnie's face, and Ronnie's hand on the wheel and the granite-like jut of his profiled jaw and the dead upside-down pipe. The boat fled on.

Then the boy leaned and touched his shoulder. He half rose. The boy was pointing. The sun was reddish; against it, outside them and about two miles away, a vessel—a trawler, it looked like—at anchor swung a tall mast.

"Lightship!" the boy shouted. "Theirs." Ahead Bogard could see a low, flat mole—the entrance to a harbor. "Channel!" the boy shouted. He swept his arm in both directions. "Mines!" His voice swept back on the wind "Place filthy with them. All sides. Beneath us too, Lark, eh?"

VII

Against the mole a fair surf was beating. Running before the seas now, the boat seemed to leap from one roller to the next; in the intervals while the screw was in the air the engine seemed to be trying to tear itself out by the roots. But it did not slow; when it passed the end of the mole the boat seemed to be standing almost erect on its rudder, like a sailfish. The mole was a mile away. From the end of it little faint lights began to flicker like fireflies. The boy leaned. "Down," he said. "Machine guns. Might stop a stray."

"What do I do?" Bogard shouted. "What can I do?"

"Stout fellow! Give them hell, what? Knew you'd like it!"

Crouching, Bogard looked up at the boy, his face wild. "I can handle the machine gun!"

"No need," the boy shouted back. "Give them first innings. Sporting. Visitors, eh?" He was looking forward. "There she is. See?" They were in the harbor now, the basin opening before them. Anchored in the channel was a big freighter. Painted midships of the hull was a huge Argentine flag. "Must get back to stations!" the boy shouted down to him. Then at that moment Ronnie spoke for the first time. The boat was hurtling along now in smoother water. Its speed did not slacken and Ronnie did not turn his head when he spoke. He just swung his jutting jaw and the clamped cold pipe a little, and said from the side of his mouth a single word:

"Beaver."

The boy, stooped over what he had called his gadget, jerked up, his expression astonished and outraged. Bogard also looked forward and saw Ronnie's arm pointing to starboard. It was a light cruiser at anchor a mile away. She had basket masts, and as he looked a gun flashed from her after turret. "Oh, damn!" the boy cried. "Oh, you putt! Oh, confound you, Ronnie! Now I'm three down!" But he had already stooped again over his gadget, his face bright and empty and alert again; not sober; just calm, waiting. Again Bogard looked forward and felt the boat pivot on its rudder and head directly for the freighter at terrific speed. Ronnie now with one hand on the wheel and the other lifted and extended at the height of his head.

But it seemed to Bogard that the hand would never drop. He crouched, not sitting, watching with a kind of quiet horror the painted flag increase like a moving picture of a locomotive taken from between the rails. Again the gun crashed from the cruiser behind them, and the freighter fired point-blank at them from its poop. Bogard heard neither shot.

"Man, man!" he shouted. "For God's sake!"

Ronnie's hand dropped. Again the boat spun on its rudder. Bogard saw the bow rise, pivoting; he expected the hull to slam broadside on into the ship. But it didn't. It shot off on a long tangent. He was waiting for it to make a wide sweep, heading seaward, putting the freighter astern, and he thought of the cruiser again. "Get a broadside, this time, once we clear the freighter," he thought. Then he remembered the freighter, the torpedo, and looked back toward the freighter to watch the torpedo strike, and saw to his horror that the boat was now bearing down on the freighter again, in a skidding turn. Like a man in a dream, he watched himself rush down upon the ship and shoot past under her counter, still skidding, close enough to see the faces on her decks. "They missed and they are going to run down the torpedo and catch it and shoot it again," he thought idiotically.

So the boy had to touch his shoulder before he knew he was behind him. The boy's voice was quite calm: "Under Ronnie's seat there. A bit of a crank handle. If you'll just hand it to me—"

He found the crank. He passed it back; he was thinking dreamily: "Mac would say they had a telephone on board." But he didn't look at once to see what the boy was doing with it, for in that still and peaceful horror he was watching Ronnie, the cold pipe rigid in his jaw, hurling the boat at top speed round and round the freighter, so near that he could see the rivets in the plates. Then he looked aft, his face wild, importunate, and he saw what the boy was doing with the crank. He had fitted it into what was obviously a small windlass low on one flank of the tube near the head. He glanced up and saw Bogard's face. "Didn't go that time!" he shouted cheerfully.

"Go?" Bogard shouted. "It didn't— The torpedo—"

The boy and one of the seamen were quite busy, stooping over the wind-lass and the tube. "No. Clumsy. Always happening. Should think clever chaps like engineers— Happens, though. Draw her in and try her again."

"But the nose, the cap!" Bogard shouted. "It's still in the tube, isn't it? It's all right, isn't it?"

"Absolutely. But it's working now. Loaded. Screw's started turning. Get it back and drop it clear. If we should stop or slow up it would overtake us. Drive back into the tube. Bingo! What?"

Bogard was on his feet now, turned, braced to the terrific merry-go-round of the boat. High above them the freighter seemed to be spinning on her heel like a trick picture in the movies. "Let me have that winch!" he cried.

"Steady!" the boy said. "Mustn't draw her back too fast. Jam her into the head of the tube ourselves. Same bingo! Best let us. Every cobbler to his last, what?"

"Oh, quite," Bogard said. "Oh, absolutely." It was like someone else using his mouth. He leaned, braced, his hands on the cold tube, beside the others. He was hot inside, but his outside was cold. He could feel all his flesh jerking with cold as he watched the blunt, grained hand of the seaman turning the windlass in short, easy, inch-long arcs, while at the head of the tube the boy bent, tapping the cylinder with a spanner, lightly, his head turned with listening delicate and deliberate as a watchmaker. The boat rushed on in those furious, slewing turns. Bogard saw a long, drooping thread loop down from somebody's mouth, between his hands, and he found that the thread came from his own mouth.

He didn't hear the boy speak, nor notice when he stood up. He just felt the boat straighten out, flinging him to his knees beside the tube. The seaman had gone back to the stern and the boy stooped again over his gadget. Bogard knelt now, quite sick. He did not feel the boat when it swung again, nor hear the gun from the cruiser which had not dared to fire and the freighter which had not been able to fire, firing again. He did not feel anything at all when he saw the huge, painted flag directly ahead, and increasing with locomotive speed, and Ronnie's lifted hand drop. But this time he knew that the torpedo was gone; in pivoting and spinning this time the whole boat seemed to leave the water; he saw the bow of the boat shoot skyward like the nose of a pursuit ship going into a wingover. Then his outraged stomach denied him. He saw neither the geyser nor heard the detonation as he sprawled over the tube. He felt only a hand grasp him by the slack of his coat, and the voice of one of the seamen: "Steady all, sir. I've got you."

VIII

A voice roused him, a hand. He was half sitting in the narrow starboard runway, half lying across the tube. He had been there for quite a while; quite a while ago he had felt someone spread a garment over him. But he had not raised his head. "I'm all right," he said, "You keep it."

"Don't need it," the boy said. "Going home now."

"I'm sorry I—" Bogard said.

"Quite. Confounded shallow boats. Turn any stomach until you get used to them. Ronnie and I both, at first. Each time. You wouldn't believe it. Believe human stomach hold so much. Here." It was the bottle. "Good drink. Take enormous one. Good for stomach."

Bogard drank. Soon he did feel better, warmer. When the hand touched him later, he found that he had been asleep.

It was the boy again. The pea-coat was too small for him; shrunken, perhaps. Below the cuffs his long, slender, girl's wrists were blue with cold. Then Bogard realized what the garment was that had been laid over him. But before Bogard could speak, the boy leaned down, whispering; his face was gleeful: "He didn't notice!"

"What?"

"*Ergenstrasse!* He didn't notice that they had shifted her. Gad, I'd be just one down, then." He watched Bogard's face with bright, eager eyes. "Beaver, you know. I say. Feeling better, eh?"

"Yes," Bogard said. "I am."

"He didn't notice at all. Oh, gad! Oh, Jove!"

Bogard rose and sat on the tube. The entrance to the harbor was just ahead; the boat had slowed a little. It was just dusk. He said quietly: "Does this often happen?" The boy looked at him. Bogard touched the tube. "This. Failing to go out."

"Oh, yes. Why they put the windlass on them. That was later. Made first boat; whole thing blew up one day. So put on windlass."

"But it happens sometimes, even now? I mean, sometimes they blow up, even with the windlass?"

"Well, can't say, of course. Boats go out. Not come back. Possible. Not ever know, of course. Not heard of one captured yet, though. Possible. Not to us, though. Not yet."

"Yes," Bogard said. "Yes." They entered the harbor, the boat moving still fast, but throttled now and smooth, across the dusk-filled basin. Again the boy leaned down, his voice gleeful.

"Not a word, now!" he hissed. "Steady all!" He stood up; he raised his. voice: "I say, Ronnie." Ronnie did not turn his head, but Bogard could tell that he was listening. "That Argentine ship was amusing, eh? In there. How do you suppose it got past us here? Might have stopped here as well. French would buy the wheat." He paused, diabolical—Machiavelli with the face of a strayed angel. "I say. How long has it been since we had a strange ship in here? Been months, eh?" Again he leaned, hissing. "Watch, now!" But Bogard could not see Ronnie's head move at all. "He's looking, though!" the boy whispered, breathed. And Ronnie was looking, though his head had not moved at all. Then there came into view, in silhouette against the dusk-filled sky, the vague, basket-like shape of the interned vessel's foremast. At once Ronnie's arm rose, pointing; again he spoke without turning his head, out of the side of his mouth, past the cold, clamped pipe, a single word:

"Beaver."

The boy moved like a released spring, like a heeled dog freed. "Oh, damn you!" he cried. "Oh, you putt! It's the *Ergenstrasse!* Oh, confound you! I'm just one down now!" He had stepped one stride completely over Bogard, and he now leaned down over Ronnie. "What?" The boat was slowing in toward the wharf, the engine idle. "Aren't I, Ronnie? Just one down now?"

The boat drifted in; the seamen had again crawled forward onto the deck. Ronnie spoke for the third and last time. "Right," he said.

IX

"I want," Bogard said, "a case of Scotch. The best we've got. And fix it up good. It's to go to town. And I want a responsible man to deliver it." The responsible man came. "This is for a child," Bogard said, indicating the package. "You'll find him in the Street of the Twelve Hours, somewhere near the Café Twelve Hours. He'll be in the gutter. You'll know him. A child about six feet long. Any English M.P. will show him to you. If he is asleep, don't wake him. Just sit there and wait until he wakes up. Then give him this. Tell him it is from Captain Bogard."

X

About a month later a copy of the English Gazette which had strayed onto an American aerodrome carried the following item in the casualty lists:

MISSING; Torpedo Boat XOOI. Midshipmen R. Boyce Smith and L. C. W. Hope, R. N. R., Boatswain's Mate Burt and Able Seaman Reeves, Channel Fleet, Light Torpedo Division. Failed to return from coast patrol duty.

Shortly after that the American Air Service headquarters also issued a bulletin:

For extraordinary valor over and beyond the routine of duty, Captain H. S. Bogard, with his crew, composed of Second Lieutenant Darrel McGinnis and Aviation Gunners Watts and Harper, on a daylight raid and without scout protection, destroyed with bombs an ammunition depot several miles behind the enemy's lines. From here, beset by enemy aircraft in superior numbers, these men proceeded with what bombs remained to the enemy's corps headquarters at Blank and partially demolished this château, and then returned safely without loss of a man.

And regarding which exploit, it might have been added, had it failed and had Captain Bogard come out of it alive, he would have been immediately and thoroughly court-martialed.

Carrying his remaining two bombs, he had dived the Handley-Page at the château where the generals sat at lunch, until McGinnis, at the toggles below him, began to shout at him, before he ever signaled. He didn't signal until he could discern separately the slate tiles of the roof. Then his hand dropped and he zoomed, and he held the aeroplane so, in its wild snarl, his lips parted, his breath hissing, thinking: "God! God! If they were all there—all the generals, the admirals, the presidents, and the kings—theirs, ours—all of them."

⚓

THE ATTACK

⚓

THE ATTACK

Captain A. F. B. Carpenter, V.C., R.N.

⚓ *In 1918, German submarines had succeeded in a considerable measure in interfering with England's lines of communication and in seriously impairing her trade. Convoying, patroling, mining, had not been adequate to stem the tide. It became necessary to block the submarines at their bases from which they were issuing as fast as they were being sunk.*

On the first attempt to block Zeebrugge, the wind turned southerly thus making the use of artificial fog impossible. On the second attempt the force of the wind and sea was too great for small craft and the attack was abandoned.

The following story told by Captain Carpenter himself describes the third approach and the commencement of the final and successful attack.

The result was that "the canal was blocked and the services of twelve submarines and twenty-three torpedo craft were unavailable for a considerable period."

The editor met Captain Carpenter on board a battleship during the war and merely wishes to say that the British habit of understatement is one of Captain Carpenter's most noticeable characteristics. The reader, therefore, is warned that for true perspective he may safely magnify by several diameters the incidents described.

AFTER zero-time the remaining units kept in close company until such times as each, according to their respective instructions, was deputed to proceed independently to carry out their several duties.

The force was preceded by the Vice-Admiral in *Warwick* with some half a dozen other craft in company ready to fall upon and destroy any

From *The Blockings of Zeebrugge* by Vice Admiral A. F. B. Carpenter V.C., R.N. Copyright, 1922, by Alfred F. B. Carpenter. Reprinted by permission of the author.

enemy patrol vessels which might be encountered. We were now steaming through the German mined areas and were hoping against hope that no mines would be touched to the main detriment of the element of surprise. If any mine had exploded the enemy could not have failed to have their suspicions aroused. The rain gradually increased and the wind became more fitful.

Hot soup was distributed to the men in *Vindictive* at about 10.30 p.m. and a "tot" of rum was served out about an hour later to those who desired it.

About fifty minutes before midnight the hawser with which *Vindictive* was towing *Iris* and *Daffodil* suddenly parted. It was then too late to retake these vessels in tow and, indeed, it would have been a difficult and dangerous task in the rain and inky darkness with so many vessels in close company, to say nothing of the loss of time and the obstacle to accurate navigation. Speed had to be somewhat eased temporarily to allow *Vindictive* to drop back to her original position relative to the other vessels. In accordance with the plan the blockships eased speed for the purpose of arriving at the Mole some twenty minutes after *Vindictive*.

We were momentarily expecting to meet the German patrol vessels and to be discovered from the shore. Suddenly a light-buoy was seen. A hurried bearing laid down on the chart agreed exactly with the reported position of a buoy off Blankenberghe. Incidentally a captured prisoner had recently stated that this buoy had been withdrawn or moved elsewhere, but we had promulgated its original position to all concerned because we suspected that this particular individual was a disciple of Ananias. This agreement between our position by "dead-reckoning" and that of the buoy was decidedly heartening, for we had obtained no "fix" for several miles and were running through a cross tidal stream of doubtful strength.

The difficulties attached to forecasting the movements of tidal streams was borne out in the case of the bombarding monitors, H.M.S. *Erebus* and *Terror*. In addition to being somewhat hampered by the low visibility resulting from the rain, these vessels, on arrival at their firing positions, discovered that the tidal stream was flowing in exactly the opposite direction to that anticipated; this, in turn, caused some delay in opening fire, but, as events subsequently showed, the delay was of no great consequence. The bombardment was carried out without any further hitch. The Germans do not appear to have been able to locate the monitors until the firing was nearly completed. The few German shell which burst in the vicinity of the firing ships were doubtless directed by some means of sound-ranging and direction-finding. On finishing the bombardment the monitors took up their positions for covering the subsequent retirement of the attacking forces.

It may be stated here that, barring the impossibility of aerial attack, the delay in commencing the long-range bombardment and the parting of the towing hawser, there was no hitch of any kind sufficient to alter the general idea of the enterprise. Everything was carried out to schedule time.

Soon after passing the Blankenberghe light-buoy the enemy appeared to suspect that something more than a bombardment was afoot. Star shell were fired to seaward and searchlights were switched on. That was exactly what we had hoped for. If only they would continue to illuminate the atmosphere our navigational difficulties would be enormously reduced. The star shell were extraordinary. They burst with a loud report just overhead and lit up our surroundings to the maximum of the then visibility. Much to our surprise no enemy vessels were encountered or even seen; presumably the enemy set the greater dependence on their mines.

To the southward, namely, between us and the shore, our smoke-screeners had laid down a "peasoup" fog. Nothing was to be seen in that direction except the glare of searchlights and of gun flashes, the latter being presumably directed against the fast motor boats which had run into the anchorage behind the Mole for the purpose of torpedoing vessels secured alongside. At this stage the wind died away completely and the rain was heavier than ever.

In *Vindictive* we took up our action stations. Our battery guns had been instructed not to open fire until it was certain that our individual presence had been discovered. The guns in the fighting-top on our foremast were in readiness to engage. Rocket men had been stationed to fire illuminating flares for the purposes of locating the Mole. The storming parties were under cover awaiting the order to storm the Mole. The cable party were in the forecastle standing by to drop anchor at the foot of the high wall. Other parties with wire hawsers were stationed to assist the *Daffodil* in her important task of pushing *Vindictive* bodily alongside. Crews were standing by the bomb-mortars and flame-throwers for clearing the Mole before sending the stormers over the wall. The Engineering and Stokehold personnel were at their stations below for giving immediate response to all requirements from the conning positions. The first-lieutenant—Lieut. Commander R. R. Rosoman, R.N.—was in the conning tower, from where the ship was being steered by the quartermaster, in readiness to take over the handling of the ship immediately I was rendered *hors de combat*. It was a decidedly tense period, but there were others to follow.

At a given moment by watch-time *Vindictive* altered course towards the Mole—or rather towards the position where it was hoped to find the Mole. Almost immediately we ran into the smoke screen. *The wind had now changed to an off-shore direction,* diametrically opposite to that on which the screening plans had been based. I thought at the time that this smoke screen was the thickest on record—that opinion was changed later.

The visibility at this time can hardly have amounted to a yard—the forecastle was invisible from the bridge. The firing of star shells and guns, and the flashing of searchlights became more frequent. *Vindictive* was being conned from the flame-thrower hut on the port end of the conning tower platform. This position was especially suitable in that it plumbed over the ship's side and thus provided a very good outlook for berthing at the Mole. There was a curious absence of excitement. Even the continued repetition of the question, "Are you all right, sir?" from my first-lieutenant —a prearranged idea to ensure a quick change over of command—became monotonous. Nothing had yet been seen of the Mole from *Vindictive*. This comparatively quiet period was not of long duration.

A few seconds before the schedule time for the last alteration of course— designed to take us alongside the outer wall—the smoke screen, which had been drifting northwards before the new wind, suddenly cleared. Barely 300 yards distant, dead ahead of us, appeared a long low dark object which was immediately recognised as the Mole itself with the light-house at its extremity. We had turned up heading direct for the six-gun battery exactly as arranged in the plan. Those who know aught of navi-gation will realise how far this was a fluke—probably the various errors in compass direction, allowance for tide, etc., had exactly cancelled one another. Course was altered immediately to the southwestward and speed was increased to the utmost.

The Mole battery opened fire at once; our own guns, under the direc-tion of Commander E. O. B. S. Osborne, replied the utmost promptitude. The estimated distances at which we passed the Mole battery was 250 yards off the eastern gun, gradually lessening to 50 yards off the western gun. It was truly a wonderful sight. The noise was terrific and the flashes of the Mole guns seemed to be within arm's length. Of course it was, to all intents and purposes, impossible for the Mole guns to miss their target. They literally poured projectiles into us. In about five minutes we had reached the Mole, but not before the ship had suffered a great amount of damage to both *matériel* and personnel.

Looked at from the view of a naval officer it was little short of criminal, on the part of the Mole battery, that the ship was allowed to reach her destination. Everything was in favour of the defence as soon as we had been sited. Owing to the change of wind our special arrangements for covering the battery with smoke had failed in spite of the magnificent work of our small smoke vessels which, unsupported and regardless of risk, had laid the screen close to the foot of the wall, that is to say right under the muzzles of the guns. From the moment when we were first sighted until arriving alongside the Mole the battery guns had a clear target, illuminated by star shell, of a size equal to half the length of the lighthouse extension itself.

To my mind the chief reasons for our successful running of the gauntlet were twofold, firstly, the fact that we were so close, and secondly, the splendid manner in which our guns' crews stuck to their work. With regard to the former, a longer range would have entailed more deliberate firing, and this in turn would have given time for more deliberate choice of point of aim. A few projectiles penetrating the engine or boiler rooms or holing us at the waterline would have settled the matter. The range being so short one can conjecture that the German gunners, realising that they could not miss, pumped ammunition into us at the utmost speed of which their guns were capable without regard to the particular damage which they were likely to cause. Their loss of serenity, due in the first place to the novel circumstances of the case, must have been considerably augmented by the fact that our own projectiles were hitting the wall near the gun muzzles—it was too much to hope that we should actually obtain any hits on the guns themselves.

The petty officer at one of our 6-inch guns, when asked afterwards what ranges he fired at, said that he reckoned he opened fire at about 200 yards and he continued till close to the Mole. "How close?" he was asked. "Reckoning from the gun muzzle," he replied, "I should say it was about 3 feet!"

One can picture the situation as seen from the Mole itself. A hostile vessel suddenly looming out of the fog at point-blank range, the intense excitement which resulted, the commencement of fire, the bursting of shell on the wall, the ardent desire to hit something as rapidly and as often as possible, the natural inclination to fire at the nearest object, namely, that part of the vessel on their own level, and the realisation that in a few moments the guns would no longer bear on the target. One can imagine the thoughts that were uppermost in their minds, "Hit her, smash her, pump it in, curse those guns of hers, don't lose a second of time, blow her to bits!" One cannot blame those gunners. To use a war-time expression, "They had the wind up." We had counted on that, we had concentrated all our efforts at "putting the wind up." Yet if anybody had seriously suggested that a ship could steam close past a shore battery in these modern days of gunnery he would have been laughed to scorn. Yet it was easy. The reason is not far to seek.

Those who worship *matériel* have followed a false god. The crux of all fighting lies with the personnel—a fact borne out again and again on this particular night just as throughout past history. If the German gunners had been superhuman this tale would not have been told, but human nature, reckoned with by the attackers, was on our side; the initiative was ours.

The material damage was very great, but, though it may sound paradoxical, of not much importance. The upper works and upper deck of the ship received the brunt of it. The most serious matter was the damage to our gangways. Several were shot away and many others damaged beyond further usefulness and, so far as could be observed at the time, only four were left us for the work in hand. Two heavy shell penetrated the ship's side below the upper deck. One passed in just beneath the foremost flame-thrower hut and burst on impact. The other came through within a few feet of the first and wrecked everything in its vicinity. Two other heavy shell came through the screen door to the forecastle and placed one of the howitzer guns out of action. The funnels, ventilators, bridges, charthouse and all such were riddled through and through.

The damage to the personnel was exceedingly serious. Orders had been given that the storming parties should remain below, under cover, until the ship arrived alongside. The number of personnel in exposed positions was to be limited mainly to those manning the guns, rocket apparatus and flame-throwers. The senior officers of the storming parties, however, stationed themselves in the most handy position for leading and directing the assault, with the result that they were exposed to the full blast of the hurricane fire from the Mole battery. Military officers had always acted in a similar manner whatever their instructions might be. One cannot help feeling that in any fighting service, where discipline is based on leadership rather than on mere driving force, officers will do the same thing. Captain Halahan, commanding the naval storming forces, who had repeatedly told me this was to be his last fight, was shot down and killed at the outset. Commander Edwards, standing near him on the gangway deck, was also shot down and completely incapacitated. Colonel Elliot, commanding the Marine storming forces, and his second-in-command, Major Cordner, were killed on the bridge, where they had taken up a commanding position in full view of the gangway deck. Many others were killed or wounded. The death of so many brave men was a terrible blow. Nobody knew better than they the tremendous risk attached to their actions—the pity of it was that they should not have lived to see the success for which they were so largely responsible.

At one minute past midnight the ship actually arrived alongside the Mole, one minute late on schedule time, having steamed alongside at 16 knots speed. The engines were immediately reversed at full speed and the ship bumped the Mole very gently on the specially constructed fender fitted on the port bow.

The conning position in the flame-thrower hut was well chosen, our heads being about 5 feet above the top of the Mole wall. We had previously devoted many hours to studying photographs of the Mole with the idea of recognising objects thereon. Our aerial confrères had photographed every portion of the Mole from almost every conceivable angle with both ordinary and stereo-scopic cameras. We had also had picture post cards and other illustrations at our disposal. Though none of us had ever actually seen the Mole itself we felt pretty sure of being able to recognise any portion of it immediately. In that we were over-confident. The smoke, the intermittent glare and flashes, the alternating darkness and the unceasing rain, added to the dis-turbance of one's attention caused by the noise and the explosion of shell, rendered observation somewhat difficult. As far as we could see we were to the westward of our desired position. The engines were, therefore, kept at full speed astern and the ship, aided by the 3-knot tide running to the eastward, rapidly drifted in that direction. When sufficient sternway had been gathered the engines were put to full speed ahead to check her. A low building was then observed on the Mole abreast the ship, but it was not recognised immediately as the northeastern shed (No. 3), which we had expected to appear much larger. The distance in the uncertain light was also very deceptive, the building in question appearing to be situated within a few feet of the outer wall, whereas it must have been at least 45 yards away.

But time was pressing. Our main diversion had certainly commenced, but at all costs we must have it fully developed before the blockships arrived at twenty minutes past midnight. The order was therefore given to let go the starboard anchor. A voice tube, for this purpose, led from the flame-thrower hut to the cable deck. The order was certainly not given *sotto voce*. But the noise at this time was terrific. I could not be certain whether the order was received as no answer was heard in reply. Certainly the anchor was not let go. Meanwhile the engines were ordered at full speed astern and full speed ahead alternately to keep the ship in position; the manner in which these orders were carried out by the engine-room staff, under the command of Eng. Lieut.-Com. Bury, was admirable. No reply being forth-coming to questions as to the delay in anchoring, Rosoman left the conning tower and went below to investigate. The din had now reached a crescendo. Every gun that would bear appeared to be focused on our upper works, which were being hit every few seconds. Our guns in the fighting-top were pouring out a continuous hail of fire in reply. One could aptly say that we could hardly hear ourselves think.

At last I had news from the cable deck—this was a great relief as I feared that the two heavy shell which burst between decks had killed all the anchoring party. The starboard anchor had jammed somewhere. It had been previously lowered to the water's edge and nothing was holding the cable, but it refused to bulge. The port anchor was, therefore, dropped at the foot of the wall and the ship allowed to drop astern until a hundred yards of cable had been veered. The cable was then secured.

The ship immediately swung bodily out from the Mole. With the helm to starboard she swung in again, but with her bows so tight against the Mole, and her stern so far out, that the foremost gangways just failed to reach the top of the wall. With the helm amidships the ship lay parallel to the wall, but no gangways would reach. With the helm to port the ship again swung away from the Mole. This was an exceedingly trying situation. Everything now depended upon the *Daffodil* (Lieut. H. G. Campbell).

It will be remembered that, as a result of the towing hawser having parted, and in consequence of our increase of speed when running alongside, the *Iris* and *Daffodil* had been left behind. We knew that whatever happened we could absolutely depend on Gibbs and Campbell making short work of any surmountable difficulty, and our trust was not misplaced. They must have cut off a considerable corner to have arrived as early as they did. The *Iris* steamed past us at her utmost speed, which was very slow, and went alongside the Mole about a hundred yards ahead of *Vindictive* exactly as laid down in the Plan.

After we had been struggling against our difficulties alongside for about five minutes *Daffodil* suddenly appeared steaming straight for our foremast in a direction perpendicular to the Mole. Campbell pushed her nose against us, hawsers were passed to his vessel, and he shoved us bodily alongside the Mole, exactly in accordance with the Plan. Really he might have been an old stager at tugmaster's work, pursuing his vocation in one of our own harbours, judging by the cool manner in which he carried out his instructions to the letter.

Immediately the two foremost gangways reached the wall they were lowered until they rested on it. No other gangways were then available. The order was at once passed to "Storm the Mole."

Owing to the light wind of the preceding day we had not expected to find any swell against the wall. The scend of the sea, however, was so heavy and so confused, as each wave rebounded, that the ship was rolling considerably. Every time she rolled over to port there was a heavy jarring bump which was probably caused by the bilge on the port side of the ship crashing down on the step of the Mole some few feet below the surface. The whole ship was shaking violently at each bump and rolling so heavily that we were greatly apprehensive of sustaining vital damage below the water-line.

The Stokes gun batteries had already been bombing the Mole abreast the ship. The flame-throwers should also have helped to clear the way for our storming parties. The order had been given to switch on the foremost flame-thrower. Unfortunately the pipe leading from the containers to the hut had been severed somewhere below by a shell explosion. This was not noticed before the order was obeyed, with the result that many gallons of highly inflammable oil were squirted over the decks. One hesitates to think what would have happened if this oil had become ignited.

Incidentally the actual nozzle of this flame-thrower was shot away just after the order to switch on had been given by the officer in charge, Lieut. A. L. Eastlake, attached R.E., who held the proud position of being the sole representative of the military on board the attacking vessels. Eastlake was the only other occupant of the hut and I don't think he will easily forget the brief period that we experienced in that decidedly uncomfortable erection. Sparks were flying about inside, but somehow, at the time, one didn't connect that pyrotechnic display with the fact that they emanated from the medley of missiles passing through it. Curiously enough neither of us were hit, but our clothing sadly needed repair—an experience which was common enough in shore fighting, but unusual afloat where the missiles are generally rather too large to pass through one's headgear without removing one's head *en route*.

The other flame-thrower fared no better. Commander Brock was in charge. He lit the ignition apparatus and passed down the order to "switch on." The whole outfit of oil ran its course, but unfortunately, at the very commencement, the ignition apparatus was shot away, with the result that the instrument was converted into an oil thrower instead of emitting a flame.

Lieut.-Commander B. F. Adams, leading a party of seamen, stormed the Mole immediately the gangways were placed. The only two gangways which could reach the Mole were, to say the least of it, very unsteady platforms. Their inboard ends were rising and falling several feet as the ship rolled; the outer ends were see-sawing and sliding backwards and forwards on the top of the wall. My own personal impression at the time was that these gangways were alternately lifting off and resting on the wall, but apparently that was not so. The fact remains, however, that the run across these narrow gangways with a 30 feet drop beneath to certain death was not altogether inviting.

The first act of the advance party, in accordance with the instructions, was to secure the ship to the wall by means of the grappling anchors. A great struggle to do this was undertaken. The foremost grappling anchors only just reached the Mole. Some men sat on the top of the wall and endeavored to pull the grapnels over the top as they were lowered from the ship. These grapnels, by virtue of the use for which they were designed, were heavy. That fact, combined with the continuous rolling of the ship, made it exceedingly difficult to control them. Rosoman and a party of men on board joined in the struggle, but a heavy lurch of the ship broke up the davit on which the foremost grappling iron was slung and the latter fell between the ship and the wall.

195

Adams' party were followed out in great style by the remainder of the seamen storming parties led by their surviving officers, and then by the Marines.

As soon as it was clear that the grappling anchors had failed us owing to the heavy swell there was no other alternative than to order *Daffodil* to carry on pushing throughout the proceedings.

A curious incident which has never been explained occurred just previously. Some individual in *Vindictive* had hailed *Daffodil* and called to them to shove off. "By whose orders?" came the response shouted by Campbell from *Daffodil's* bridge. "Captain Halahan's orders," was the reply. As a matter of fact poor gallant Halahan had been killed some ten minutes earlier. "I take my orders from Captain Carpenter," shouted Campbell. "He's dead," was shouted back. "I don't believe it," responded Campbell, and incidentally he was right, though I haven't the faintest idea what he based his belief on. As Mark Twain would have said, "The report of my death was much exaggerated." The incident was certainly curious, but of course (this for the benefit of those who, during the war, saw spies and traitors at every corner) there can only be the explanation that some poor wounded fellow must have been delirious.

Campbell had been shot in the face, but such a trifle as that didn't appear to have worried him, and he continued to push the *Vindictive* alongside from the moment of his arrival until the whole hour and five minutes had elapsed before we felt the Mole. Originally the *Daffodil* had been detailed to secure alongside *Vindictive* as soon as the latter was secured to the Mole and then to disembark her demolition parties for their work on the Mole. That part of the plan could not be carried out, however, though several of his parties climbed over her bows into *Vindictive* on their way to accomplish it.

The demolition charges had been stowed outside the conning tower ready for use; on the passage across we had come to the conclusion that this was a case of risking the success of the whole landing for the furtherance of a secondary object, and the charges had therefore been removed to a safer position. This change of arrangement was indeed fortunate, for the deck on both sides of the conning tower became a regular shambles during the final approach. Yeoman of signals, John Buckley, who had volunteered to take up a position outside the conning tower in readiness to fire illuminating rockets had remained at his post until killed. We found him there at the foot of his rocket tube in the morning, a splendid fellow who had been as helpful in the work of preparation as he was unflinching in the face of almost certain death. All the signalmen except one had been either killed or completely disabled, and almost every soul on the conning tower platform had made the supreme sacrifice.

On the order being given to storm the Mole the storming parties had rushed up every available ladder to the gangway deck. At the top of the foremost ladder the men, in their eagerness to get at the enemy, were stumbling over a body. I had bent down to drag it clear when one of the men shouted: "That's Mr. Walker, sir, he's had his arm shot off." Immediately Walker, who was still conscious, heard this he waved his remaining hand to me and wished me the best of luck. This officer, Lieut. H. T. C. Walker, survived.

The high wall, towering above our upper deck, was now protecting the hull of the ship from gunfire; no vital damage could be sustained in that way so long as we remained alongside. The chief course of danger from which vital damage might accrue before we had completed our work at the Mole was that of the fast German motor boats stationed at Blankenberghe. The latter harbour was barely five minutes' steaming distance away, and, as the enemy would now be fully cognisant of our position, we might reasonably expect a horde of these craft to come to the attack with torpedo. It does not require much naval knowledge to realise that the difficulty of avoiding torpedo fire under such circumstances would be wellnigh insuperable. Where a torpedo craft of that description can suddenly rush in from the outer darkness a large vessel has to depend upon remaining unseen; but of course such tactics were now impossible, and, still further, a torpedo could not be avoided even if seen coming towards the ship. That we were not attacked in that manner was mainly due to the work of certain of our smaller craft specially detailed to deal with the Blankenberghe force; former experience of the latter also led us to believe that the German personnel in those boats had no stomach for a fight.

Our guns in the fighting-top were directing a murderous fire into their special targets. Chief amongst those were the heavy gun battery at the end of the broad part of the Mole and the lighter battery on the lighthouse extension. In neither case could the enemy's guns bear on the ship, and we had the advantage of taking the former battery from the rear and giving the latter a taste of enfilading fire from its western flank. But there was another target of importance. Immediately abreast the ship a German destroyer was berthed alongside the inner wharf of the Mole only 80 yards distant from the ship. We had an uninterrupted view of the greater part of her between the two northern sheds, her bridges showing well above the ground-level of the Mole. Our guns in the fighting-top, in charge of Lieut. Charles N. B. Rigby, R.M.A., riddled that destroyer through and through. We could see the projectiles hitting the Mole floor whenever the gun was temporarily depressed, and then shower upon shower of sparks as they tore through the destroyer's upperworks. The vessel appeared to have sunk, as very little of her upper deck could be seen, although we had such an elevated view-point, but now I think it possible that the wall protected her vitals and that she escaped complete destruction from our gun-fire.

There seems little doubt that our fighting-top was now coming in for the attention of most of the enemy guns. Presently a tremendous crash overhead followed by a cessation of our fire indicated that a heavy shell had made havoc with poor Rigby and his crew of eight men. As a matter of fact, that shell had wrecked the whole fighting-top, killed all the personnel except three gunners who were all severely wounded, and dismounted one of the guns. The only survivor who was not completely disabled—Sergeant Finch, R.M.A.—struggled out from the shambles somehow and, without a thought for his own wounds, examined the remaining gun, found it was still intact, and continued the fight single-handed. Another survivor, Gunner Sutton—who had again been wounded, fired the remaining ammunition when Finch could no longer carry on; finally, a German shell completely destroyed the remains of this gun position. The splendid work of Lieut. Rigby and his gun's crews had been invaluable, and one cannot but attribute the complete success of our diversion very largely to these gallant men. Rigby himself had set a wonderful example; all who knew him had never doubted that he would do so. Finch survived and was afterwards voted the Victoria Cross by the men of the Royal Marines.

As soon as the ship had been securely anchored the howitzer guns manned by the R.M.A., in charge of Captain Reginald Dallas-Brooks, R.M.A., commenced to bombard the targets specially assigned to them. The German batteries on the mainland were shelling our position at the Mole for all they were worth, but their efforts must have been hampered by the continuous fire of our howitzers. The presence of such weapons on board ship was, to say the least of it, most unusual. *Vindictive's* nature had undergone an unusual change as soon as she was secured to the Mole. The direction and range of the enemy's batteries had been worked out beforehand for any position alongside the wall. We were, therefore, in the novel situation of being able to drop heavy howitzer shell upon the enemy's batteries less than a mile away, a decided change from ordinary battleship target practice where ranges of 10 to 15 miles were the order of the day.

The 7.5-inch howitzer gun on the forecastle could not be used. A heavy shell had burst amongst the original gun's crew and had killed or disabled them all. A second crew was sent from one of the naval 6-inch guns in the battery and was just being detailed to work the howitzer when another shell killed, or disabled, all but two men. Soon after opening fire the midship 7.5-inch howitzer was damaged by another shell which killed some of the crew, but the remainder repaired the gun under great difficulty and managed to resume the firing later on. The 11-inch howitzer on the quarterdeck was extremely well handled. This gun fired at a steady rate throughout the proceedings in spite of the darkness, the fumes, the difficulty of manhandling such large projectiles in a cramped-up space and the battering that the ship was receiving around them. The behaviour of the R.M.A. throughout was fine; they worked with a will which may have been equalled elsewhere, but which has certainly never been surpassed; the example set by Captain Brooks was altogether splendid.

Mention must be made of the pyrotechnic party as we called them. Having located and reached the Mole ourselves an early duty was that of indicating its extremity to the approaching blockships. For this purpose a rocket station was rigged up in my cabin below. The rocket apparatus protruded through a port in the stern of the ship and had been placed at an angle calculated to carry the rocket behind the lighthouse before bursting, so that the lighthouse would show clearly against an illuminated background. One of the party was told off for his position, instructed as to the object to be attained, and ordered to carry on according to his own judgment. I believe this man had never previously served afloat and had never been in action, but, like the rest of them, he did his bit without the slightest hesitation and, judging by results, with 100 per cent efficiency. Others of the pyrotechnic brigade landed with the storming parties and worked the portable flame-throwers, special flares, etc., before finally attending the smoke-making apparatus and assisting with the wounded. Lieut. Graham S. Hewett, R.N.V.R., was in command of the pyrotechnic party.

A few minutes after the storming of the Mole had commenced a terrific explosion was seen away to the westward, and we guessed that the submarine party had attacked the viaduct. The explosion presented a wonderful spectacle. The flames shot up to a great height—one mentally considered it at least a mile. Curiously enough the noise of the explosion was not heard.

At about 12:15 a.m. the blockships were expected to be close to the Mole, and a momentary glimpse of them was obtained as they passed close to the lighthouse on their way to the canal entrance. So far so good. We saw nothing more of the blockships and received no further news of them until the operation had been completed. Nevertheless, no news was good news under the circumstances and we felt quite confident that the blockships had not been seriously hampered by the German Mole defences. Our primary object was, therefore, attained; the diversion had been of sufficient magnitude.

⚓

THE BLACK GANG
and
SHORE LEAVE

⚓

THE BLACK GANG
and
SHORE LEAVE
Marcus Goodrich

⚓ *In few places besides the sea, are the fine grained and the coarse grained thrown together in such explosive proximity. The first selection from "Delilah" shows us two sharply delineated characters engaged in this eternal struggle.*

The second selection is equally basic. For as long as there are men cooped up at sea, there will be men bursting loose ashore.

IT IS probable that the early torpedo-boat destroyer, which is practically all raw engine and boilers, was not designed with a view to Sulu Sea operations in the hot season. Even in cold weather, with fire under all four of *Delilah's* boilers and the engines running under maximum steam pressure, it was necessary to wear thick wooden sandals in order to tread the burning expanses of deck over the fire- and engine-rooms. This also was more economical, because it took longer to char away the wooden sandals than it did leather shoes, and the sandals could be sawed out of any thick board as fast as they were needed. Now, even though shod with the thick wood, the men waiting to relieve those below in the fire-rooms climbed off the scorching deck onto every shelf and corner that would hold them. A number even perched on the bronze cables of the railing, a thing normally not permitted because it stretched the cables.

An Ordinary Seaman, a young Texan named Warrington, with nothing on his body but a thin, sleeveless undershirt, dungaree trousers and a pair of wooden sandals, was crouching on the torpedo-tube base, two feet above the deck, waiting for his turn below. He, too, was staring at Poe's agonized face. Three men dragged the Chief Electrician off the After Fire-room Hatch rim, where he had collapsed, and hung him on the railing. Another, who was playing a vigorous stream of salt water on the deck in an attempt to keep the heat down, turned the nozzle on the fainting electrician to revive him. He screamed as the column of cold sea water broke against him. From Poe, the Texan's glance slid down the iron perspective of the deck and encountered the formidable figure of the monk. The association called up in his memory a story of Inquisitional torment . . . the men hung on the bronze wires like black, rotting victims of some ancient torture rack . . . soon he'd have to tackle it again . . . the hour wasn't nearly up, but the other gang seemed to be passing out for good . . . fifteen minutes up . . . fifteen minutes down . . . for an hour . . . then try to rest . . . for an hour . . . like this . . . on an incandescent deck . . . fifteen minutes up . . . fifteen minutes down . . .

As a matter of fact, in this heat very few were able to stick out the full fifteen minutes below, and only the most rugged of the "black gang," the regular coal heavers, were expected to. When a man was on the verge of collapse, he crawled up the ladder and those above hauled him through the hatch onto the deck. Then the man whose turn it was next climbed down in his place. There was no question of anyone being a quitter: the crew knew instinctively and at once when a man was all in, and every one realized that they knew, so there was no shame about giving up and no thought of giving up while there was still strength enough to shovel. Some stuck it out eight minutes, some nine, some ten, some twelve and some thirteen minutes; even Rene, the bulky Chief Machinist's Mate in charge of the resting gang to which Warrington belonged, had stayed the full fifteen minutes only twice.

"Stand by, you guys!" yelled Rene.

His gang had been seriously reduced by the necessary transfer of two members to the other gang as replacements for four men who had suffered permanent collapse; and in the resulting rearrangement of pairs to work below, which now took place, Warrington, the Ordinary Seaman, found himself linked with the one thing in his hated surroundings that he hated most, a thing that infected his consciousness with an unrelaxing dread of terrific power coupled with devastating irresponsibility. This thing was O'Connel. Warrington and O'Connel, the Water-Tender, were the antitheses of each other in everything; even in the quality of their indubitable honesties: the boy's honesty was like that of an old steel blade, the man's like that of the sea. One was seventeen, the other thirty-four. The Texan, who was born in a high, blue room pervaded by the scent of magnolia blossoms, fortified him-

Warrington jammed the handle of the shovel into his stomach for another try.

self with poetry and hunted out his strength from the tunnels of his soul; while the Irishman, who was born in a canal barge, fortified himself with whiskey and sucked up his strength from the magnificent stretches of his great body. The one steered his aggressiveness against the universe and its enemy; the other shattered the faces of every one in the Squadron who was as big as he was. For the youth, this environment was a valley of repellent futility down which he had fled blindly from an intolerable situation in his home; for the man, it was a high place vivid with significant life. The Texan was ever on the verge of annihilating the Irishman on the level of significance; and it always seemed as if O'Connel were about to rend Warrington bone from bone. Both looked life squarely in the face, but they saw there different things.

O'Connel was heavyweight champion of the Squadron, and he was too tough to serve on anything but the black boats. He had been in the Navy twelve years, and his service was a record of turbulence. For much of it, he had been deprived of advancement and pay and slammed in the brig; but for some of it he had gotten the Congressional Medal of Honor and a reputation for being a "hard egg" in the face of things that were likely to smash him as well as in situations where he was the one able to do the smashing. It was for this reason that people looked upon him as a wild man rather than as a bully. It is probable that the function of introspection was but primitively a part of his mental operations, and his test for human authenticity seemed to be a formula involving physical force, elemental simplicity and "guts."

In 1907, when he first went to destroyers, the thing had occurred that gained him the Congressional Medal. A cylinder head blew off at sea while O'Connel and three others were in an engine-room making emergency repairs on the engine. The splattering steel and steam killed one man outright and wounded the other two. The right side of O'Connel's head was crushed in. Nevertheless, he seized the Engineer Officer, who was one of those knocked out, and dragged him up out of the lethal cubicle onto the deck. Then realizing that the scalding steam was intimidating the Rescue Party that had gathered to extricate the men remaining below, he flung himself angrily into the midst of the fat, white death billowing out of the hatchway, and tumbled back down into the engine-room. Those on deck could hear his wild and private curses spouting up with the steam. A moment later, in rapid succession, the limp bodies of the other two men shot up through the steaming hatchway as if they had been hunks of lava flung skyward by the violence of an erupting crater.

When O'Connel had made his raging leap down the hatchway, his intention had been to make his way to the steam manifold and shut off all the steam making its way from the boilers to the engine. But in landing on the steel floor plates he had broken his left leg. It would have taken him so long a time, he had felt, to crawl first to the manifold, hoist himself up and turn off the steam, cracked up as he was, that the lungs of the men he was trying to save would surely have been burnt out by the steam. So he had heaved the men up first; and then afterwards, though the boiled flesh had been peeling from his hairy legs and arms, and his cracked head had assumed something like one of those grotesque shapes usually seen but in the distorting mirrors of a penny arcade, he had rolled and clawed his way to the manifold and shut off the steam. When the rescuers reached him, his slowly relaxing, blood-spattered body was doubled over his broken leg; but his big hands were fiercely gripping a polished engine stanchion after the manner of a wrestler holding to the limb of an opponent, and he was enunciating, more as if in realization than as if in supplication, "Peace, you son of a bitch, peace . . . peace . . . peace . . ."

With his bronze medal on his breast and a silver plate in his skull, he had lain for a long time in hospitals, bunks and champed restlessly in places good for his lungs. But he finally went back to destroyers seemingly cured of everything but a curious, elemental rage at something too far beyond the horizon of his consciousness to assume definite objectivity. When he raised hell, the men said: "You see, he's got a silver plate in his head."

The Irishman hit the floor plates first and stood with his fists on his hips watching the Texan descend the ladder. Through his back the boy felt the wild, blue gaze plunging hostilely at him, and his heavy prescience that this was to be a significant encounter seemed to suffer instant confirmation. He helped the two worn-out men they were relieving up the ladder, slowly lit the taper of his bunker lamp, glanced a little helplessly from the great, iron visage of the boiler that formed the forward wall of the cave in which he found himself to that which formed the after wall, and then, almost shutting his eyes, crawled through the low door into the port coal bunker.

For some seconds O'Connel stared at the bunker hole, where the dim gleams from the Texan's paraffin torch flickered. Finally he stamped over and looked through into the bunker, which, like that on the starboard side of the ship, was a crevice only a little more than two feet wide, but extending the height and depth of the ship. It served the double purpose of carrying fuel and providing a protective belt of coal for the engines and boilers,—the only armour of any sort that stood between these and an enemy's shells. In the depths of this narrow, towering frame, O'Connel saw the Texan leaning for a preparatory instant on the handle of his shovel as if it were a crutch. His eyes, across which there was a sweeping smear of coal dust, were gazing at the deep darkness just above the level of his head, and the squirming light glowed uncertainly amongst the curls of his dull blond hair.

The Irishman lunged back to one of the firebox doors under the after boiler, flung it open and shot in a shovelful of coal from the heap on the floor plates. As he was withdrawing the shovel from before the flaming door, some arresting pattern formed on the stream of consciousness rushing through his great, battered head. He grinned, and the red gush of brilliance from the firebox flashed and shone on the long row of his upper teeth, which were all gold. The sweat pouring down his face was curiously diverted into two deep channels that formed in the flesh on either side of his thick, flat nose as he grinned, and his hair, stiff with coal, seemed to bristle uncannily. His grin burst into a delighted, braying laugh. He banged the shovel on the floor plates with fierce zest as a man might bang out his delight with a spoon on some cabaret table.

The mad banging and laughing penetrated into the bunker and startled the boy. Hanging the bunker lamp to a hook on the bulkhead, he crawled back to the low hole that served for door and peered out into the fire-room. For about as long as O'Connel had stared in at him, he was held by the lurid apparition before the flaming furnace; then he went back in where the coal began and commenced getting it down. After a few shovelfuls, he paused to readjust his grip . . . He was holding the shovel too tight . . . but then if he held it looser the sweat made it slip . . . the heat seemed to be getting him already . . . he'd have to get the coal out fast . . . felt like the air pressure was bursting in his ears . . . blowers turning up too much . . . O'Connel used a lot of coal . . . too much coal they said . . . but the officers weren't watching the smoke on this run . . . deadly hot . . . He moved down to the door and shovelled through it onto the fire-room floor plates the coal he had knocked down. The infranatural laughter bit at him again. His breath stopped for an instant.

The interior of the coal bunker was so narrow that he could maintain himself at any depth in it by the centrifugal pressure of his legs: But now he had shovelled his way to the bottom again, and somewhat farther away from the entrance into the fire-room. He'd fed O'Connel a lot of coal . . . this was about the end . . . as far as he was concerned . . . coal was as hard as a rock . . . wasn't the coal, after all, but the steel side of the ship . . . this would never do . . . couldn't make the shovel go where he wanted it to. In a spurt of irritation he drove the shovel into the lumpy implacability before him. The force of the movement threw him forward into the coal, a section of which, jarred loose, caved in upon him. For a time he lay there in the hot, primordial smother, relaxed, at rest, losing consciousness, much as a snow-beaten man surrenders to the lethal peace of a deep drift. The uninterrupted noises that in the first moments of his recumbency had seemed to have a soothing, lullaby effect upon him, slowly began to wear through their disguises: the malevolent, high-pitched purr of the sea as it slid viciously along the thin skin of the ship, and the pounding struggle of the propellers as they tore and twisted at its waters . . . He began to think or dream or remember: "The sea . . . the sea . . . the unutterably horrible sea . . . an infinite, biological solution in which coiled and gasped monsters and living slime beside which the images of man's diseased obsessions and insane fears become delicate symmetries . . . a festering, amporphous mass pouring over the areas of the earth, licking and pounding in insentient fury at the few rocks up which man has fled . . . a distraught gesture of Creation" . . . Slowly he pulled himself up out of the coal and tried to stand erect. But he could not maintain himself in that position. On all fours he crawled over the hot bunker plates and coal towards the ruddy flicker of the fire-room entrance. His under lip curled out instinctively to catch the dark sweat that poured from about his head. He reached the door. Like a dying animal, covered with black mud, he glared through the hole at O'Connel.

With the heat and the air pressure assaulting the borders of his last province of strength, the Irishman, sweat-drenched and inflamed, was probing the conflagration before him with an enormous, iron slice bar. In proportion to the extent that his body succumbed to tiredness and weakness, he furiously revenged himself upon it by demanding of it heavier and grosser performances. He was left-handed and his right arm had been a little wasted by a series of injuries; but when he found that exhaustion was creeping into his good left arm, he flung it from him as if it had sentient personality; and, in no sense to get relief, but rather to defy his own strength and to humiliate his left arm, he swung angrily about to grip and handle the slice bar with his right hand alone. It was then that he saw Warrington staring at him from the hole.

This confrontation unloosed a considerable emotional and mental convulsion in each of them. The effort to reinstate the image and idea of the boy in his consciousness, which had been intensely monopolized by a quite different problem, and the sudden realization that "the little, white-necked louse was still at it" unpoised the Irishman. He emitted a raucous bleat, such as might come from a gargantuan calf.

"A-a-a-A-a-a! What the hell! Quittin'?" He sneered with both corners of his big mouth.

The instant the boy saw the great creature fighting with the fire, he had succumbed to the torturing obligation of maintaining the authenticity of his difference from him. He *couldn't* quit. The flaming power of his abhorrence of the Irishman and of the idea of admitting any sort of inferiority to him, openly or secretly, concentrated what little physical energy was left in him and strengthened the waning current of his blood. It began to pound unbearably within the sick regions about the back of his head. If his miserable body would only keep up with him . . . see him through . . . Were O'Connel a person like himself there would be no question of keeping on . . . he could say, "I am so tired, help me up the ladder" . . . even sink into the arms of an enemy . . . like himself . . . but this . . . this *thing!* When the Irishman shouted his question at him, the boy, still on all fours, turned about and faced back into the bunker; then he paused there as if endeavouring to marshall before him in the black path, in one convenient obstacle, all the ramifications of the dread necessity for going back.

This manoeuvre confounded O'Connel; so he went over to the hole and gripping Warrington by one of his slim arms dragged him out onto the floor plates of the fire-room. The boy jerked himself free and crawled back into the bunker. Until the thought of his fires called him back to the boilers, O'Connel stood in bewilderment staring at the hole and listening to the spasmodic coughing that began to come through it.

In his first excitement over being down with O'Connel and his fear of not getting out enough coal to meet shovel for shovel the Irishman's effort, Warrington had gotten down, and heaved out into the fire-room considerably more coal than the fires needed; so that the frantic, almost futile efforts that his exhausted body now engaged in, with his eye lids tightly pressed together as if to shut out the feverish dimness that enveloped him, held things back not at all for the moment. To load his shovel from the pile that he knocked down onto the floor of the bunker, hoist it to the level of his knees and then project its load through the hole to O'Connel was demanding more intense mental concentration, attention to bodily balance and physical sacrifice than he ever had been called upon to suffer before. To get a load in the shovel, he felt with its blade for a clear space on the steel near the coal as a blind man searches the way before him with a stick. When he had found such a space, he laid the back of the shovel upon it and then lunged forward on the handle. Such coal as the edge of the shovel encountered slid into the shovel. At this point the terrible phase of his repetitious struggle was upon him. He balanced himself unnaturally on his heels, which he kept wide apart and opposite each other, and rested his back against the bulkhead. Then jamming the end of the shovel handle into his stomach just above the loins, he slid his hands half-way down the handle and slowly began to pull. The force of the lift was taken by his stomach, as a fulcrum, and each shovelful seemed on the verge of sending his straining intestines bursting through the pit of his abdomen. When the shovel hung poised at about the level of his knees, he opened his eyes with an effort, located the red bunker hole, closed his eyes again, and fell toward it. The shovel of coal proceeded through the hole until his body brought up sharply against the steel wall above it. This jerked the coal forward from the shovel. Often he missed the hole, and the coal and shovel clattered tauntingly against the bulkhead.

The Irishman could not get out of his head the idea of this "punk" actually trying to battle it out with him. Every time a shot of coal spat into the fire-room, he turned his head towards the hole. Eventually, the strange manner in which the coal jumped off when the shovel stuck through into the fire-room caught his attention. After watching for the rather long time required by three of these reappearances of the shovel, O'Connel could not resist the temptation to look into the hole. He leapt over, as the shovel was being withdrawn, and peered in. Slowly, as he watched the agony-drenched ritual develop in the reddish haze of the bunker, a crude, eerie revulsion proceeded within him. Some strong attitude, which particular one he had not the faculty to determine on the instant, began to disintegrate. Some handhold to his immediate situation seemed to be giving way. He slumped back uneasily into the centre of the fire-room, where he slung his head from side to side lionesquely, as if seeking to sight something which he could rush upon and smash to reaffirm that all was right with his world. His eyes found the air-pressure gauge. It indicated an excessive pressure of air in the fire-room. His rage, blasting him along the channel provided by this, swept him up the ladder. With his sweating, tightly clenched fist, he crashed open the little, air-tight hatchcover and, like a gleaming wet demon rending up through the earth, projected his coal-blackened upper bulk into the midst of the group clustered on the deck.

"You crummy bastards!" he howled at the ship in general, "watch them blowers!"

The senior Chief Machinist's Mate, Stengle, a small, coffee-coloured man, was jerking about between the two huge nostrils that sucked air down into the fire-room, trying to regulate their speed. The mechanism that controlled them from below had broken down early on the run.

"Keep your shirt on! Keep your shirt on!" he said, shaking a big Stillson wrench at the Irishman as if it had been a forefinger. "I'll have to let 'em run high, or shut 'em down . . . Can't do that."

When O'Connel had dropped back down the hatch, leaving the abrupt banging of its cover as the period to his final, vituperative roar, the men awoke to the fact that the pair below already had survived for thirteen minutes. This was the record so far, for although several individuals had lasted the full quarter of an hour, one or the other of every pair that had gone down up to now had been relieved before the thirteen-minute mark. O'Connel always lasted it out; but no one expected or demanded of Warrington to stay down more than five minutes. As the fourteen-minute mark was approached, the situation took on the aspect of a prize fight in which some "dark horse" was putting up a totally unexpected and wonder arousing show. The men, including the resting gang from the Forward Fire-room, crowded a trifle excitedly around the hatch expecting every second to see it exude the sweat-soaked body of the boy; and the man whose duty it was to relieve him hovered preparatorily about as if made restless by a feeling that he should have been down long ago, but that it was no fault of his that he was not. A red-headed Oiler, named Feenan, who was in the habit of making clumsily sarcastic remarks about the boy's careful and rather over-elegant manner of speaking, stepped to the railing, his unpleasantly freckled face set with primitive primness, spat accurately into the sea, and said:

"He'll never stay down the fifteen minutes."

As if by sudden, unanimous consent, the sporting attitude of the crew gave way to a general feeling of uneasiness.

"Maybe the kid's passed out in the bunker and that wild guy has forgotten all about him."

"What time is it now?" Stengle was asked for the third time.

"Maybe the big harp got sore and smacked him."

Everybody laughed restlessly.

Stengle moved over to the hatch, pulled it open and stuck his dirty, little grey head down into it. O'Connel feeling the pressure of the air jump suddenly from off his chest and ear drums, and perceiving the white fire he was feeding begin to turn red, raised his face questioningly to the hatch. It seemed to Stengle that the Irishman was more all in than he ever had seen him before.

"Time up?" shouted O'Connel.

"Minute to go," Stengle screamed back. His voice barely pierced the barricade of mechanical uproar between them. "How's the kid making out?"

At this question, the alien, about-facing disturbance within O'Connel burst into clear recognition. He flung his two great fists into the air as if they were gonfalons he was bearing into battle, and shouted triumphantly, half-incidentally up to Stengle,

"Going strong!"

Stengle popped his head back out of the hatch and permitted the cover to spring shut.

"Going strong," he repeated to the men around him.

A wave of surprised admiration swept up the deck, and even swirled for a moment about the bridge when "Unc" Blood, the Chief Quartermaster, was summoned there to relieve Ensign Woodbridge at the wheel for a moment.

Blood stationed himself upright behind the wheel, as motionless and set as a carbonized, baroque statue, and fixed his lecherous, little eyes steadily on the Captain in a suggestive fashion, a fashion that often caused the Captain to preface his Wardroom stories about the Chief Quartermaster by saying, "Blood came up bursting with news . . ."

These two had "been together" going on six years, and the Captain never failed to assume what he felt was a discouraging attitude towards the man's propensity to gossip. He assumed this attitude now. For several minutes he would not look in Blood's direction: But when he finally—as he always did—. shot a quick glance at the aging mariner to see if he still was "bursting," Blood's sanguinary glance nailed him. Before the Captain could escape, the point of Blood's blackened beard, which curved to one side in a satyrlike manner, dropped an inch and a half, the bright red cavity of his mouth twitched about his decayed teeth, and the two spikes of his mustachios, which at one moment resembled those of a Western sheriff and at another those of a Chinese gentleman, see-sawed slightly from one side to the other. When the Captain could bear this grin no longer, he said shortly:

"What's the matter?"

Then he stepped quickly over to the binnacle and glanced at the compass in the hope of catching Blood off the course; but, as always in these encounters, the Chief was dead on. In a twanging voice, as if he were saying something slightly vindictive, but really believing himself bathed in a fine, jesting manner, Blood said:

"You know, Cap'n, that new lemon from the Galveston they dumped on us last month at Cavite? . . . He's been down fourteen minutes and is still going strong! . . . Running neck and neck with O'Connel."

"You mean that new youngster?" said the Captain a trifle incredulously; then turning in good-natured and pleased surprise to Ensign Woodbridge (who, arriving back on the bridge in time to overhear Blood's news, already had exclaimed, "Well, I'll be damned") he said: "Woodbridge, that little Ordinary Seaman they gave us is down with O'Connel and sticking it out."

"Well, I'll be damned," said Ensign Woodbridge again, not so much with the feeling of surprise that had first engendered the remark, but with a sense of getting his exclamation in its proper rank and order.

O'Connel no longer was exiled in the depths of fire, coal and steel with a despicable alien. As his stark delight ascended flight after flight of sweet and fierce recognition, he pounded his shovel and shouted, "Guts! Guts! Guts!" He thought: "He's probably Irish after all! . . . Shovel for shovel with me, O'Connel!" He rushed over to the bunker hole to roar in some greeting as if to a well esteemed newcomer.

But the glimpse he got of the Texan down this new perspective brought him up sharply. A veritable incarnation of distress, the boy was struggling with the shovel as if it were some awkward, slippery burden. O'Connel gave a start that seemed to indicate that he was about to leap into the bunker to rescue his wounded comrade.

As he hesitated, Warrington jammed the handle of the shovel into his stomach for another try, and O'Connel realized the other's agony so intimately that his being began to function somewhat as if it were he, himself, fighting there in pain. He dove in to put an end to it.

The boy, sensing the great creature crowding the obscurity before him, glared toward it desperately and emitted a hawking, defiant sound, a sound electric with the sharp anomalous authority that often concentrates in even the meanest man in the throes of physical anguish. It arrested O'Connel and slowly pushed him back into the fire-room again, where he found himself, lost in a wilderness of uncertainty and pity, clumping along a network of unfamiliar mental and emotional trails. "I'm gonna stop this," he told himself truculently, "time must be up . . . them tight bums on the top side holding out till the last second . . . the bastards!" It entered his mind that the thing to do was to "tell the kid the time was up."

"Time up!" he shouted with the relief of having hit upon an actable line of conduct.

The next instant he was at the bunker hole yelling again:

"Time up! Time up! Time up!"

When the boy finally heard him, he sat slowly down cross-legged about his shovel, drifting into the incomparable luxury of oblivion, slowly pulsing away from an acute crisis of high-pitched, kinetic agony.

For a second O'Connel's eyes lingered on the wet haft of the shovel, along which the light from the bunker lamp flickered. It projected upright from the dark mound of the small body like a limb stuck into the cairn marking some isolated and valorous death.

Seeing that his end was gained there, O'Connel swung back into the fire-room, kicked open the door of the coal bunker opposite to that in which Warrington was, and with furious surreptitiousness heaved out nine or ten shovelfuls of coal from that as yet untouched supply. After soundly reclosing this bunker hole door, he fed a shovelful to each of the fires, and then, steadying himself angrily on his slightly swaying legs, he rapidly transferred the remainder of the coal he had gotten out to the diminished pile in front of the Texan's bunker hole. It was a custom that the relieving watch should find a small supply of coal out to start with. As he heaved the last shovelful, he felt the air pressure rise from off of him. He dropped the shovel guiltily. A relieved, victorious feeling surged through him.

"What th' hell!" he yelled up at the open hatch.

The murky bodies of the relief followed one another quickly down the ladder.

The Irishman's figure, assuming a slight exaggeration of its usual arrogant, hard-boiled stance, shuffled over to the bunker hole. He stuck in his head and shouted,

"Hey! Lay off! Time's up!" Then, as he crawled through the hole, he added in loud, incompetent dissimulation, "Hold up, I'll give y' a hand."

Morrow, the relief coal heaver, knelt by the hole and pulled the boy's body through as O'Connel shoved its shoulders within his reach. Morrow and his watch-mate, Whorly, started to carry him towards the ladder; but O'Connel, arising from the bunker hole, snatched the small body from them and climbed up the ladder unassisted, maintaining the boy on his left shoulder and chest with the pressure of his right arm. As the two heads arose from the hatchway, the crowd of men surrounding it, comprising nearly the entire ship's company, let out a triumphal yell. The big bruiser, shaking off all the black hands that shot out to relieve him of his burden, climbed to the deck and stood for a moment glaring in a squinting manner at the slick sea, which the sun, burning the first suggestion of colour for its setting, had raddled a greyish pink.

As he stood there swaying above the crowd of heads with the boy in his arms, he seemed to the monk on the quarterdeck like one of the bulky Pietas, absurd of colour and strangely awkward of workmanship, that the Italian mountaineers bear down the trails to their devotions on feast days.

⚓   ⚓   ⚓

SHORE LEAVE

WHEN *Delilah* steamed past Corregidor Island into Manila Bay, tied up alongside the dock at the Cavite Naval Base and discharged the coffin, a few naval people remarked casually, "I see *Delilah* came in today." Once or twice somebody troubled to make negligent answer to the effect that, "Yes, she's been down south after the body of an Army Officer." *Delilah,* however, in her own view had steamed triumphantly into harbour, surrounded by the aura of a dauntless victory over wounds and ordeal. Her men, when they went ashore on their first liberty, assumed that peculiar, modest manner of men who have behaved very well in a dangerous and exacting crisis. They had unconsciously settled into an emotional arrangement on sighting Corregidor that somehow, as far as it concerned the outside world, was based on the assumption that that outside world knew and felt as much about their long expedition south as they did. They actually would not have been surprised if they had been called upon to parade through streets lined with people cheering approval and admiration: But most of the people they met did not even know that their ship had been south. This vacuum in the attitude of these people where *Delilah's* men, without saying so or thinking about it, had expected a positive plenty, made them vaguely indignant: And the people whom they encountered were irritated, on their part, by this inexplicable quality that tinctured the destroyer's crew. The crew was like a college football player who, falling into the idea that he was in a vital game, had run seventy miraculous yards with a broken rib, only to find, when he staggered up to be helped heroically off the field, that the stands contained not a single person.

A few, such as Cruck, Ferguson and Saunders, found it particularly difficult to adjust their expectancy to what it met, and finally, although they would have been outraged if this had been explained to them, attempted to satisfy this expectancy with public attention earned by new and irrelevant feats. Ashore together on the afternoon of the first liberty party, Cruck, Ferguson and Saunders seemed to sense something disregarding and inhospitable in Cavite's principal street as they strolled along with its trickle of natives, Chinamen, Navy people and dowdy American civilians; and almost as if seeking shelter from this strange bleakness of the angular, sun-baked thoroughfare, the usual mercantile street of little sea ports bequeathed by the Spaniards to tropical countries, they turned into the dusk of a drinking place. They stood for a moment, almost posing, just within the doorway. No one in the crowd there noticed them except an acquaintance of Cruck's, a Machinist's Mate off a submarine, who waved cordially and turned back to the glass of beer on his table. Cruck, speaking loudly to the whole room, but ostensibly addressing Saunders and Ferguson, said something that involved the word, *"Delilah,"* raising and strengthening his enunciation as he pronounced the word. This begot no attention from the crowd in the drinking place. Saunders then replied to him, also using the name, *"Delilah,"* talking in a mumbling manner until he reached the word, which he shouted clearly and distinctly. Not a head turned. For a moment the three stared hard into the long, low-ceilinged room filled with the thin murk of unventilated tobacco smoke, then they swaggered to a table against the middle of the left wall and sat down, talking loudly. They ordered beer. The empty moments before the arrival of the drinks became intolerable in this place that for them was proving as perverse and unsatisfactory as the street. Saunders' gaze, scouting belligerently here and there, caught and held that of a man at the next table. He found himself grinning and asking:

"What ship, sailor?"

"Brooklyn," was the reply. "What ship you off of?"

"Delilah!"

"That's the new transport, ain't it?"

"What the hell navy do you come from?" jeered Cruck angrily.

The tone in which he said this nettled a big Coxswain with the other party. He replied carelessly for his friend:

"What the hell of it?"

Cruck's glare appraised the six or seven men sitting with the big man; then slowly he seemed to dismiss them, and looked down at the glass of beer being set before him. A little beer had slopped over the edge of the glass and formed a puddle about as large as a dollar on the table. Impatiently he flicked at the little puddle with his forefinger. His whole hand got involved with liquid in this gesture. Without thinking he put his wet hand down and gave it a drying stroke across the leg of his white trousers. Such dust and smear as his hand previously had collected, now being dissolved in the beer, wiped off in a long, dark streak on his trouser leg. Looking down and observing this, Cruck put his clenched, uncomfortable hand back upon the table. His coarse nostrils sniffed at the air about him. It was malodorous with that stench peculiar to superficially cleaned bar-rooms in the Orient, of warm matting and stale urine, of Manila tobacco smoke and spilled drink slopped over with crude soap. For Cruck, this always had been a kind of homely fragrance; but now a mysterious feeling of being ridiculous surged through him and brought him to his feet, saying with some fury:

"This place stinks!"

"Aw, sit down," yelled someone from the other side of the room, "you're rockin' the boat!"

A blinding, scorching short-circuit seemed to explode somewhere in the middle of Cruck's body. At one and the same time he was here in this hostile bar-room and back in that boat in the cave being tricked about the tobacco. He kicked the chair over from behind him. At the end of an animal-like, lunging trot, he was behind the big man at the next table who had said, "What the hell of it?" He took a firm grip on the man's black neckerchief with his left hand and swung him around. As the man's face came about, Cruck drove his right fist straight into the centre of it. The man fell to the floor on his back, his knees bent upward like a stricken insect's. The Coxswain's friends stood up and stared down at his face masked by the blood which also was drenching the front of his white jumper. His legs slowly unflexed and straightened out along the damp gritty boards. Then they tried to get at Cruck. He upset their table in front of them. One tripped on a leg of the overturned table and sprawled over it. Saunders, who was now on his feet, kicked him in the throat. People at tables nearby got hastily to their feet and crowded away towards the ends and centre of the room, while those at a distance stood on chairs to see. Ferguson promptly had lunged from his chair to Cruck's side, but he no sooner had arrived there than he had been dropped to his knees by a blow from a man who hurdled the overturned table. In groggy instinctiveness, Ferguson clutched at the flaring ends of the white trouser legs about the ankles planted before him. He jerked them fiercely upward and toward him as he rose again to his feet. The man crashed to the floor in a sitting posture. Ferguson stepped quickly across him, kneeing him accurately on the jaw in the stride of his step. A thin noise was coming through Cruck's teeth as he clung and twisted with his left hand and slugged with his right. This noise was like a wild, steady scream pitched so high that it almost escaped the ear only to slash horribly at nerves buried deep in the body. A kick, then another, drove Cruck to the floor clutching a patch of ripped cloth. He landed nearly on his back in a semi-sitting posture, his fists braced widely on either side of his body, his eyes staring frantically. A beer glass shattered explosively near his right shoulder. A man swung a chair and knocked him flat. Before the chair could land a second time, Saunders had its wielder in a strange-hold. Cruck rolled his body away with a swift, violent movement, and kept rolling in this convulsive fashion between the tables until he brought up, as if he were a log crashing down a hillside, against the legs of the spectators crowded against the tables on the far side of the centre aisle. There he got to his feet and backed along the aisle to the door, where he stood, his uniform covered with dirt and blood, his knees giving spasmodically, staring semi-consciously in the direction of the fight.

Ferguson, jabbing and hooking effectively as he backed away, was himself half-way to the door when he saw Saunders, pressed against the wall near where they had been sitting, slide helplessly to the floor. A man reached down, clutched Saunders by the undershirt where it projected above the V-neck of his white jumper and, as he pulled him up, pounded him in the face. The undershirt gave away. As the man reached down for another hold, Ferguson stopped backing towards the door and charged in again, head down, through the two slugging enemies in front of him. His hurtling, stocky body cleared a tumbled path and felled the man leaning over the disabled Saunders. Two men, one armed with a broken bottle, were making for Cruck, who still stood there unsteadily in the doorway; but now they flung about and leaped for the charging Ferguson. Ferguson kicked at the face of the man he had knocked over, gripped Saunders by the beltline of his trousers and dragged him away along the wall toward the front of the place, upsetting tables behind him as he progressed. His eyes fixed desperately on the doorway as he dragged Saunders along, Ferguson began to shout, at regular intervals, wild, sustained cries of defiant need:

"Delilah!" . . . *"Delilah!"* . . . *"Delilah!"*

This cry ascended from a dirty, remote drinking place, a summons from the cheap murk of a petty brawl; but a brawl, nevertheless, in which Ferguson and his unconscious friend were facing much of what the individual has faced in many a decisive battle of the world. The shout, rising from his bloody lips with all the terrible lilt of cries heard above the frenzy of a Hastings or a Gettysburg, swept up and down the street outside, arrested the two Carey brothers, who just had left the ship, and pulled Orlop, the Chief Gunner's Mate, out of a nearby restaurant onto the sidewalk. As if it took more than one pulse of the cry to launch them, each paused where he stood there in the street until the cry had rung again and again in their ears; then the two Carey brothers, tall, slim, boisterous men from Tennessee who were viciously effective in a fight, began to run. Orlop, walking deliberately, followed them.

The Carey brothers plunged through the door of the drinking place as if they were crashing it in. Their furious ingress knocked Cruck to the floor and brought them, unseeing in the sudden change of light, deep into the interior and up against the crowd trying to keep clear of the fight. The Careys struck out blindly against the bodies in contact with them . . . *"Delilah! Delilah!"* . . . It was behind them there on the other side of the room!

They swung around and leapt toward it, one after the other, like a man and his vivid shadow in a turmoil of obscurity and danger. Now they could make out the struggle against the wall, a crowded tangle of quick, vicious movement.

Cruck's head had cracked hard on the base of the cashier's cage when the Careys had knocked him down. Almost reflexively now, he pulled himself up once more by clawing at the door jamb. He leant there helplessly, just barely able to raise his arms in front of him as one of the nearby spectators, one of those whom the Carey brothers had struck in the first blind moment of their entrance, jumped at him with swinging fists. As the man's first blow landed, Orlop appeared in the doorway. With movements that seemed somehow leisurely and authoritative in all that frantic cruelty and panic, Orlop pulled the man off Cruck, backed him against the opposite door jamb, measured him there for an instant and then hit him accurately on the point of the jaw. This blow, struck so efficiently, so deliberately, and illuminated as if by a spotlight in the rectangular beam of afternoon sunshine that cut the murk just inside the doorway, seemed to concentrate, for the beholders, the deadly, blood-spattering reality of the violence around them. There ran through the crowd trying to keep clear of the fight a murmur of gathering shock that broke here and there into revolted exclamation, into sadistic cheering; then a girl began to scream, the thin, high, chattering scream of a Malay woman in bewilderment and terror.

A waiter, almost on all fours, darted through the door, paused outside for an instant to look wildly up and down the street for the Marine Patrol, and then started running as if goaded by a savage gust of the mad sounds behind him. Other battle cries arose now, cries as enraged and pleading as the *"Delilahs!"* that had summoned Orlop and the Carey brothers.

"Brooklyn!" . . . *"Brooklyn!"* . . . *"Submarines!"* . . . *"Monadnock!"* . . . *"Monadnock!"*

A rapidly increasing crowd had gathered in the street. Struggling vainly to see inside, some pressed close up to the doorway. Others, forced to rely only on their ears, massed before the huge screen of matting that served virtually as the front wall of the semi-open place. They had winced back when the woman's scream issued from behind this matting, back still further before the catastrophic sound of an unseen crash that involved glass. From the dark chaos in there hidden by the screen, a man's voice, exigent and horrible with agony, staggered out into the sunny air of the street:

"O-o-o! . . . O-o-o! . . . My God! . . . n-n-n! . . . n-n-n! . . . n-n-n! . . ."

A barefooted, stocky Tagalog, his sun-blackened face twisted into a truculent mask, leaped forward from the crowd on the sidewalk, reached in and fumbled for a grip on the matting. He gave a fierce jerk. The screen gave a little. He gripped the edge of it with both hands and threw his body back with all his might. The great area of thick matting came completely away with the suddenness of a storm-ripped sail.

The white glare of the sunlight exploded into the smoky dusk of the embattled room as if someone had set off in there a monstrous flashlight cartridge. All motion was arrested instantly, paralysed by the mighty impact of the light. The back of the room seemed to have flashed forward, and the shallow place, cluttered with dirt and blood and rigid, distorted figures, erect or fallen, was for a moment like a gigantic peep-show suddenly exposed to the sun, tawdry, livid, unreal.

"The Patrol! . . . Patrol!" somebody shouted.

Delilah's men hurled themselves out into the street. Before them the crowd out there surged away as from a burst of maniacal danger. The six of them, clawing at each other in frenzied cohesion, clustered briefly on the sidewalk, glaring wildly up and down the sunny ambush between the two rows of shabby, exotic buildings. A Marine Patrol was double-timing up the street from the water-front; another was just rounding a corner in the opposite direction.

"In there," panted Ferguson.

Dragging the almost helpless Saunders with them, they charged from the street into a narrow dry-goods shop. The Chinaman behind the counter closed his eyes at sight of them and dropped to the floor. They brought up, staggering with the inertia of their charge, against the back wall of the store, where their collective breathing sounded like some unnatural boiling in the cool, cloth-scented gloom. The two Carey brothers swung around and faced the front door belligerently. Cruck and Saunders, drunk with blows, swayed against the counter, holding on to one another's arms. Saunders kept sniffing at the blood that blocked his nose. Orlop, his feet slightly spread, stood with bent head and mopped at his handsome, perspiring face with his handkerchief like a man who had been outraged but who also was disgusted because he had lost control of himself. Ferguson, the lips in his round, hard, full face tightly pressed together, was pawing and jabbing at the shadow of the back wall. He gave a tug and then a shove. A shaft of diffused daylight bluely tainted the right half of his body.

"Let's go!" he shouted, and they crowded after him out the rear door.

⚓

THE CRUISE BEGINS, KICK 'EM JINNY
and
CACHACROU HEAD

⚓

THE CRUISE BEGINS, KICK 'EM JINNY
and
CACHACROU HEAD

Frederic A. Fenger

⚓ *"Is it in the nature of all of us, or is it just my own peculiar make-up which brings, when the wind blows, that queer feeling, mingled longing and dread? A thousand invisible fingers seem to be pulling me, trying to draw me away from the four walls where I have every comfort, into the open where I shall have to use my wits and my strength to fool the sea in its treacherous moods, to take advantage of fair winds and to fight when I am fairly caught—for a man is a fool to think he can conquer nature."*

Thus does Fenger open the story of his trip through the Caribbean in a seventeen foot sailing canoe.

There is something particularly dramatic about a man alone in a small boat on the open sea. Man has traditionally banded together to attempt to conquer the sea, partly because he is not generally foolhardy enough to trust himself alone in a boat small enough for one man to handle and because in crises, two are generally better than one. But also partly because it is difficult for man to contemplate facing the sea alone. The element is too big; the human frame too small.

A LAST breakfast with the Captain and Mate—and I was ashore with my trunk and gear. The *Yakaboo*, a mere toy in the clutch of the cargo boom, was yanked swiftly out of the hold and lightly placed on the quay where she was picked up and carried into the customhouse by a horde of

From *Alone in the Caribbean* by Frederic A. Fenger. Copyright, 1917, by George H. Duran Co. By permission of the Author.

yelling blacks. Knowing no man, I stood there for a moment feeling that I had suddenly been dropped into a different world. But it was only a different world because I did not know it and as for knowing no man—I soon found that I had become a member of a community of colonial Englishmen who received me with open arms and put to shame any hospitality I had hitherto experienced. As the nature of my visit became known, I was given all possible aid in preparing for my voyage. A place to tune up the *Yakaboo?* A young doctor who owned the little ginnery on the far side of the *carénage* gave me the key and told me to use it as long as I wished.

I now found that the cruise I had planned was not altogether an easy one. According to the pilot chart for the North Atlantic, by the little blue wind-rose in the region of the lower Antilles, or Windward Islands as they are called, I should find the trade blowing from east to northeast with a force of four, which according to Beaufort's scale means a moderate breeze of twenty-three miles an hour. Imagine my surprise, therefore, when I found that the wind seldom blew less than twenty miles an hour and very often blew a whole gale of sixty-five miles an hour. Moreover, at this season of the year, I found that the "trade" would be inclined to the northward and that my course through the Grenadines—the first seventy miles of my cruise—would be directly into the wind's eye.

I had been counting on that magical figure (30) in the circle of the wind-rose, which means that for every thirty hours out of a hundred one may here expect "calms, light airs, and variables." Not only this, but I was informed that I should encounter a westerly tide current which at times ran as high as six knots an hour. To be sure, this tide current would change every six hours to an easterly set which, though it would be in my favour, would kick up a sea that would shake the wind out of my sails and almost bring my canoe to a stand-still.

Nor was this all. The sea was full of sharks and I was told that if the seas did not get me the sharks would. Seven inches of freeboard is a small obstacle to a fifteen-foot shark. Had the argument stopped with these three I would at this point gladly have presented my canoe to His Excellency the Governor, so that he might plant it on his front lawn and grow geraniums in the cockpit. Three is an evil number if it is against you but a fourth argument came along and the magic triad was broken. If seas, currents, and sharks did not get me, I would be overcome by the heat and be fever-stricken

I slept but lightly that first night on shore. Instead of being lulled to sleep by the squalls which blew down from the mountains, I would find myself leaning far out over the edge of the bed trying to keep from being capsized by an impending comber. Finally my imagination having reached the climax of its fiendish trend, I reasoned calmly to myself. If I would sail from island to island after the manner of the Carib, why not seek out the native and learn the truth from him? The next morning I found my man, with the blood of the Yaribai tribe of Africa in him, who knew the winds, currents, sharks, the heat, and the fever. He brought to me the only Carib on the island, a boy of sixteen who had fled to Grenada after the eruption in Saint Vincent had destroyed his home and family.

From these two I learned the secret of the winds which depend on the phases of the moon. They told me to set sail on the slack of the lee tide and cover my distance before the next lee tide ran strong. They pointed out the fever beaches I should avoid and told me not to bathe during the day, nor to uncover my head—even to wipe my brow. I must never drink my water cold and always put a little rum in it—and a hundred other things which I did not forget. As for the "shyark"—"You no troble him, he no bodder you." "Troble" was used in the sense of tempt and I should therefore never throw food scraps overboard or troll a line astern. I also learned—this from an Englishman who had served in India—that if I wore a red cloth, under my shirt, covering my spine, the actinic rays of the sun would be stopped and I should not be bothered by the heat.

It was with a lighter heart, then, that I set about to rig my canoe—she was yet to be baptized—and to lick my outfit into shape for the long cruise to the northward. I could not have wished for a better place than the cool ginnery which the doctor had put at my disposal. Here with my Man Friday, I worked through the heat of the day—we might have been out of doors for the soft winds from the hills filtered through the open sides, bringing with them the dank odour of the moist earth under shaded cocoa groves. Crowded about the wide-open doors like a flock of strange sea fowl, a group of black boatmen made innumerable comments in their bubbling patois, while their eyes were on my face in continual scrutiny.

And now, while I stop in the middle of the hot afternoon to eat delicious sponge cakes and drink numerous glasses of sorrel that have mysteriously found their way from a little hut near-by, it might not be amiss to contemplate the *Yakaboo* through the sketchy haze of a pipeful of tobacco. She did not look her length of seventeen feet and with her overhangs would scarcely be taken for a boat meant for serious cruising. Upon close examination, however, she showed a powerful midship section that was deceiving and when the natives lifted her off the horses—"O Lard! she light!"—wherein lay the secret of her ability. Her heaviest construction was in the middle third which embodied fully half of her total weight. With her crew and the heavier part of the outfit stowed in this middle third she was surprisingly quick in a seaway. With a breaking sea coming head on, her bow would ride the foamy crest while her stern would drop into the hollow behind, offering little resistance to the rising bow.

She had no rudder, the steering being done entirely by the handling of the main sheet. By a novel construction of the center-board and the well in which the board rolled forward and aft on sets of sheaves, I could place the center of lateral resistance of the canoe's underbody exactly below the center of effort of the sails with the result that on a given course she would sail herself. Small deviations such as those caused by waves throwing her bow to leeward or sudden puffs that tended to make her luff were compensated for by easing off or trimming in the mainsheet. In the absence of the rudder-plane aft, which at times is a considerable drag to a swinging stern, this type of canoe eats her way to windward in every squall, executing a "pilot's luff" without loss of headway, and in puffy weather will actually fetch slightly to windward of her course, having more than overcome her drift.

She was no new or untried freak for I had already cruised more than a thousand miles in her predecessor, the only difference being that the newer boat was nine inches greater in beam. On account of the increased beam it was necessary to use oars instead of the customary double paddle. I made her wider in order to have a stiffer boat and thus lessen the bodily fatigue in sailing the long channel runs

She was divided into three compartments of nearly equal length—the forward hold, the cockpit, and the afterhold. The two end compartments were accessible through watertight hatches within easy reach of the cockpit. The volume of the cockpit was diminished by one half by means of a watertight floor raised above the waterline—like the main-deck of a ship. This floor was fitted with circular metal hatches through which I could stow the heavier parts of my outfit in the hold underneath. The cockpit proper extended for a length of a little over six feet between bulkheads so that when occasion demanded I could sleep in the canoe.

Her rig consisted of two fore and aft sails of the canoe type and a small jib.

An increasing impatience to open the Pandora's Box which was waiting for me, hurried the work of preparation and in two weeks I was ready to start. The Colonial Treasurer gave me a Bill of Health for the *Yakaboo* as for any ship and one night I laid out my sea clothes and packed my trunk to follow me as best it could.

On the morning of February ninth I carried my outfit down to the quay in a drizzle. An inauspicious day for starting on a cruise I thought. My Man Friday, who had evidently read my thoughts, hastened to tell me that this was only a little "cocoa shower." Even as I got the canoe alongside the quay the sun broke through the cloud bank on the hill tops and as the rain ceased the small crowd which had assembled to see me off came out from the protection of doorways as I proceeded to stow the various parts of my nomadic home. Into the forward compartment went the tent like a reluctant green caterpillar, followed by the pegs, sixteen pounds of tropical bacon, my cooking pails and the "butterfly," a powerful little gasoline stove. Into the after compartment disappeared more food, clothes, two cans of fresh water, fuel for the "butterfly," films in sealed tins, developing outfit and chemicals, ammunition, and that most sacred of all things—the ditty bag.

Under the cockpit floor I stowed paint, varnish, and a limited supply of tinned food, all of it heavy and excellent ballast in the right place. My blankets, in a double oiled bag, were used in the cockpit as a seat when rowing. Here I also carried two compasses, an axe, my camera, and a chart-case with my portfolio and log. I had also a high-powered rifle and a Colt's thirty-eight-forty.

With all her load, the *Yakaboo* sat on the water as jaunty as ever. The golden brown of her varnished topsides and deck, her green boot-top and white sails made her as inviting a craft as I had ever stepped into.

I bade good-bye to the men I had come to know as friends and with a shove the canoe and I were clear of the quay. The new clean sails hung from their spars for a moment like the unprinted leaves of a book and then a gentle puff came down from the hills, rippled the glassy waters of the *carénage* and grew into a breeze which caught the canoe and we were sailing northward on the weather tide. I have come into the habit of saying "we," for next to a dog or a horse there is no companionship like that of a small boat. The smaller a boat the more animation she has and as for a canoe, she is not only a thing of life but is a being of whims and has a sense of humour. Have you ever seen a cranky canoe unburden itself of an awkward novice and then roll from side to side in uncontrollable mirth, having shipped only a bare teacupful of water? Even after one has become the master of his craft there is no dogged servility and she will balk and kick up her heels like a skittish colt. I have often "scended" on the face of a mountainous following sea with an exhilaration that made me whoop for joy, only to have the canoe whisk about in the trough and look me in the face as if to say, "You fool, did you want me to go *through* the next one?" Let a canoe feel that you are afraid of her and she will become your master with the same intuition that leads a thoroughbred to take advantage of the tremor he feels through the reins. At every puff she will forget to sail and will heel till her decks are under. Hold her down firmly, speak encouragingly, stroke her smooth sides and she will fly through a squall without giving an inch. We were already acquainted for I had twice had her out on trial spins and we agreed upon friendship as our future status.

It has always been my custom to go slow for the first few days of a cruise, a policy especially advisable in the tropics. After a morning of delightful coasting past the green hills of Grenada, touched here and there with the crimson *flamboyant* like wanton splashes from the brush of an impressionist, and occasional flights over shoals that shone white, brown, yellow and copper through the clear bluish waters, I hauled the *Yakaboo* up on the jetty of the picturesque little coast town of Goyave and here I loafed through the heat of the day in the cool barracks of the native constabulary.

That night I slept on the stiff canvas cot in the Rest Room of the police station—a room which is reserved by the Government for the use of travelling officials, for there are no hotels or lodging houses in these parts. From where I lay, I could look out upon the channel bathed in the strong tropical moonlight. The trade which is supposed to drop at sunset blew fresh throughout the night and by raising my head I could see the gleam of white caps. For the first time I heard that peculiar swish of palm tops which sounds like the pattering of rain. Palmer, a member of the revenue service, who had come into my room in his pajamas, explained to me that the low driving mist which I thought was fog was in reality spindrift carried into the air from the tops of the seas. My thoughts went to the *Yakaboo* bobbing easily at the end of her long line in the open roadstead. All the philosophy of small boat sailing came back to me and I fell asleep with the feeling that she would carry me safely through the boisterous seas of the Grenadine channel.

$$\text{⚓} \quad \text{⚓} \quad \text{⚓}$$

KICK 'EM JINNY

I FIRMLY believe that it was my lucky bug that did the trick, although under ordinary circumstances I would not carry a tarantula for a mascot. It was on my last night at Île-de-Caille, and as I crawled up through the hatch of my upper story abode, something black stood out in the candle flicker against the wall. Before I knew what it was, instinct told me that it was something to look out for and then I noticed the huge hairy legs that proclaimed the tarantula. Of course, I could not have him running around as he pleased so I took the under half of a sixteen gauge cartridge box and covered him before he had time to think of jumping. The box, which measured four and a half inches square, was not too large for I nipped his toes as I pressed the pasteboard against the wall. Then I slid a sheet of paper between him and the wall. It was no trick at all to superimpose the upper half of the pasteboard box, slip out the paper and push the cover down. He was mine. And a good mascot he proved to be although I gave him a rough time of it in the jumble of sea off Kick 'em Jinny

Kick 'em Jinny is the sea-mule of the Grenadines. In a prosaic way the cartographer has marked it "Diamond Rock," and then, as if ashamed of himself, has put the real name in small letters underneath. So "steep-to" that a vessel would strike her bowsprit on its sides before her keel touched bottom, Kick 'em Jinny rises from a diameter of a quarter of a mile to a height of nearly seven hundred feet. Cactus-grown, with no natural resources, one would scarcely expect to find on it any animal life other than a few sea fowl. Yet, besides myriads of screaming gulls, boobies, pelicans and wild pigeons, here are goats, the wild descendants of those left by the Spanish pirates, who used to plant them as a reserve food supply that would take care of itself.

The rock lies a third of a mile to the northward of Isle de Ronde, with the jagged Les Tantes a scant two miles to the eastward. With the trades blowing fresh from the northeast the lee tide runs through the passage between Isle de Ronde and Les Tantes at a rate of three knots an hour, whirling past Kick 'em Jinny in a northwesterly direction—at right angles to the wind and sea. The weather tide in returning runs in almost the opposite direction at the rate of a knot and a half. It must be remembered that the constant northeasterly winds move a surface current of water toward the southwest so that this confluence of wind and current makes a tide rip on the weather side of Kick 'em Jinny, from which its name is derived.

Now you may ask, as I did when I discussed the matter with my friends of St. George's over tall, cool glasses of lime squash—Why not sail under the lee of Kick 'em Jinny? If I sailed under the lee of the rock I should lose much valuable ground to windward while if I fought it out along the back or weather side of Ronde and Kick 'em Jinny and then made a port tack to Les Tantes I should be in the best possible position for my jump to Carriacou. That point settled, it was a question of tides. With the lee tide running to the north-north-west I might not be able to clear the rocky windward shore on my starboard tack, and it would be very difficult to claw off on the port tack, the latter being to eastward and away from shore

With the weather tide, however, I could work my way off shore in case of necessity, but I should be fighting the current as I advanced on the starboard tack. With the weather tide I should encounter the rougher sea, and it was here that the *Yakaboo* would meet her *pons asinorum,* to carry out the idea of the sea-mule.

Many bets had been offered and some had been taken at St. George's that I would not reach Carriacou, which implied that the cruise would come to an end off Kick 'em Jinny. But I put my faith in one—my Man Friday, who had instructed me in the mysteries of "de lee an' wedder toid," and he had shown me how to watch the weather in regard to the changes of the moon. During my stay on Île-de-Caille, I watched the quarters come and go and kept track of the moon in order to note the changing of the tides. I finally selected a day when the second quarter had promised steady winds, with the weather tide beginning to run at nine o'clock in the morning. If there should be any doubt as to the weather for that day, that doubt would be settled by the time the weather tide had started. With everything as much in my favour as possible I would make the attempt

I slept that morning till the sun had climbed well up the back of Caille, for when I awoke the warm day breezes were filtering over me through the mosquito bar. I must have eaten breakfast, but later in the day I was puzzled to remember whether I had or not. My mind was not in the present, nor anywhere near my earthly body—it was living in the next few hours and hovering over that stretch of water to the eastward of Kick 'em Jinny. Bynoe and his crew were also going to sail northward to Cannouan in the

Baltimore, and I remember standing among the rocks of the whale cove bidding good-bye to the rest of the people. The few shillings I gave them seemed a princely gift and tears of gratitude streamed down the black shiny face of the cook when I presented her with a bottle of rheumatism cure.

The tide would turn at seven minutes after the hour and three minutes later the *Yakaboo* was in the water. By the feel of her as she bobbed in the heave of the sea I knew that the fight was on. With long rhythmic strokes the whaleboat swung out of the cove, the canoe moving easily alongside like a *remora.* Cautiously we rowed around the north end of Caille, seeking the currentless waters close to shore. When we reached the windward side of the island we made sail. It did not take many minutes to see that the canoe would be left alone in her fight with Kick 'em Jinny for the whaleboat, with her ballast of "rockstone" and her twelve hundred pounds of live weight to steady her, caught the wind high above the seas with her tall rig and worried her way through the jumble in a way that made me forget, in a moment of admiration, my own sailing.

But I had other business than that of watching the whaleboat. As I hauled in the sheet to lay the canoe on the starboard tack, a sea seemed to come from nowhere and with scant invitation dropped aboard and filled the cockpit. It was like starting up a sleeping horse with an inconsiderate whip lash. The *Yakaboo* shook herself and gathered herself for that first essay of windward work. Try as she would, she could find no ease in the nasty, steep sea, and instead of working well along the shore of Ronde in the wake of the whaleboat, she barely crossed the channel from Caille and fetched up at the southern tip of the island.

On the port tack to sea she did better, although the weather tide running abeam carried us back off Caille. We made perhaps a mile to the eastward and then I decided to try the starboard tack again. The canoe did still better this time—for a while—and then we found ourselves in the toils of Kick 'em Jinny. The tide was now running with full force directly against us and at right angles to the wind. There seemed to be no lateral motion to the seas, they rose and fell as though countless imps were pushing up the surface from below in delirious random. One moment the canoe would be poised on the top of a miniature water column to be dropped the next in a hollow, walled about on all sides by masses of translucent green and blue over which I could see nothing but sky. The stiff wind might not have been blowing at all, it seemed, for the sails were constantly ashake, while the centerboard rattled in its casing like the clapper of a bell. It was not sailing—it was riding a bronco at sea.

Bynoe, who was carrying my extra food supply in the whaleboat, was now making frantic motions for me to turn back. I had already decided,

231

however, that the canoe would worry her way through and I motioned to the whalers to come alongside. With the two boats rising and falling beside one another, as though on some foreshortened see-saw, the stuff was transferred from the whaleboat to the canoe. As the whaleboat rose over me the men dropped my bags into the cockpit with an accuracy and ease of aim acquired from years of life in just such jumping water as this. The canoe sailor must at times not only be ambidextrous, but must also use feet and teeth; in fact, he must be an all around marine acrobat. What wonders we could perform had we but retained the prehensile tail of our animal ancestors! So with the main sheet in my teeth and my legs braced in the cockpit, I caught the bags with one hand and with the other stowed them in the forward end of the well under the deck. A large tin of sea biscuit, a cubical piece of eight-cornered wickedness, which would neither stow under deck nor pass through the hatches, required two hands for catching and stowing and a spare line to lash it in place just forward of my blanket bag. Then they screamed "Good-bye" at me across the waves, while I yelled "Yakaboo," and we parted company. Of that row of six black faces, two I shall never see again for they have since been lost in the very waters where we said "Good-bye."

Taking quick cross-bearings by eye I could detect from time to time changes in the position of the canoe and I knew that there was some advance to the northward. Finally we were so close to Kick 'em Jinny that I could see the chamois-like goats stuck on its sides like blotched rocks. All progress seemed to cease and for three-quarters of an hour I could detect no change of position. No stage racehorse ever made a gamer fight than did the *Yakaboo* against her ocean treadmill. The whaleboat was now a vanishing speck to the northward like a fixed whitecap. I began to wonder whether I should stick in this position till the coming of the lee tide. I remember contemplating a small strip of beach on Les Tantes where, in a pinch, I might land through the breast-high surf with enough food to last till the whalers might see some sign that I could put up on the rocks.

Suddenly a blinding flash brought my attention from Les Tantes to my cockpit. It was the tin of sea biscuit. The water sloshing in the cockpit had softened the glue of the paper covering. Finally, an extra large wave, a grandfather, swept the paper entirely off, leaving the shiny tin exposed to the brilliant sun. With a sweep I cut the line, and the next instant I was mourning the loss of a week's supply of sea biscuit.

The forward compartment now proved to be leaking, through the deck as I discovered later, at just the time, when, if the canoe had any soul at all, she would keep tight for my sake. I shifted my outfit as far aft as possible and sponged the water out by the cupful with one hand ready to slam down the hatch in advance of a boarding sea. It was done—somehow—and as a reward I found the canoe was working her way into easier seas. Then she began to sail and I realised that Kick 'em Jinny was a thing of the past. I lay-to off Les Tantes, having travelled three miles in two hours. We had not conquered Kick 'em Jinny, we had merely slipped by her in one of her lighter moods. But the canoe had stood the test and by this I knew that she would carry me through the rest of the channel to Saint Vincent. What her story would be for the larger openings of from twenty-five to nearly forty miles yet remained to be seen.

With her heels clear of Kick 'em Jinny the *Yakaboo* travelled easily in the freer waters and before the tide could draw me out into the Caribbean I was well under the lee of Carriacou. Another half hour and I should have had to fight for six hours, till the next weather tide would help me back to land.

Late in the afternoon, I stepped out of the canoe on the uninhabited island of Mabouya, which lies off Carriacou. The beach where I landed was typical of the few low-lying cays of the Grenadines. The sand strip, backed by a *cheval de frise* of cactus, curved crescent-like, the horns running into sharp, rocky points which confined the beach. The only break in the cactus was a clump of the dreaded *manchioneel* trees and here I decided to pitch my tent.

Barbot, in relating the second voyage of Columbus, says: "On the shore grow abundance of *mansanilla* trees, not tall, but the wood of them fine, the leaves like those of the pear tree, the fruit a sort of small apples, whence the *Spaniards* gave them the name; of so fine a colour and pleasant a scent, as will easily invite such as are unacquainted to eat them; but containing a mortal poison, against which no antidote has any force. The very leaf of it causes an ulcer, where it touches the flesh, and the dew on it frets off the skin; nay the very shadow of the tree is pernicious, and will cause a man to swell, if he sleeps under it." I thought I would take a chance—perhaps the *manchioneel* had become softer and more civilised since the time of Columbus.

If there were any joy in the feeling of relief as I walked up that lonely beach, I knew it not. Tired as I was, I could only think of the hard work that I had to do before I could lie down to rest. The *Yakaboo* had been leaking steadily all day long and she now lay where I had left her in a foot of water, with my whole outfit except my camera submerged. This did not mean that everything was wet, for my own muslin bags, honestly oiled and dried, would keep their contents dry, but there was the canoe to unload, bail out and drag ashore. There was firewood to collect before dark, and I should have to work sharp before sundown, for there were also the tent to pitch, the supper to cook, and the log to write

For a moment I stopped to look at the glorious sun racing to cool himself in the Caribbean, and I gave thanks for a strong body and a hopeful heart. In two hours I was sitting under the peak of my tent on my blanket roll, watching my supper boil in a little pail over a lively fire of hard charcoals. The *Yakaboo,* bailed out, high and dry on the beach, skulked in the darkness as though ashamed to come near the fire.

It is always easy to say "in two hours I was doing so and so," but to the man who lives out of doors and is constantly using his wits to overcome the little obstacles of nature those "two hours" are often very interesting. As a rule, one is tired from the day's work and if accidents are going to happen they are apt to happen at just this time. The early stages of fatigue bring on carelessness, and to the experienced man the advanced stages of fatigue call for extreme caution. Before unloading the canoe, I should have decided just where I would place my tent and then I should have beached the canoe immediately below the tent if possible. As it was, the *Yakaboo* was sixty yards down the beach and upon returning from one of my trips to her I found that a spark from the fire had ignited my oiled dish bag which was burning with a fierce heat. This had started the bag next to it which contained my ammunition. With one leap I landed on the precious high-power cartridges and began to roll over and over in the sand with the burning bag in my arms. What would have happened had one of my nine-millimeter shells exploded? I had been careless in arranging my outfit upon the sands when I built the fire.

Troubles never come singly—neither do they travel in pairs—they flock. I remember the difficulty I had in starting the fire. The tin in which I carried my matches was absolutely water-tight—I have proved that since by submerging it in a bucket of water for two days and nights. And yet when I came to open the tin I found that the tips of the matches were deliquescent. It was my first experience in tropical cruising and I had not learned that the heat of the sun could draw the moisture out of the wood of the matches, condense this moisture on the inside of the tin, and melt the tips. I found some safety matches tucked away in the middle of my clothes bags and they were dry. This became my method of carrying matches in the future. The natives carry matches in a bamboo joint with a cork for a stopper.

And now that I have taken you into my first camp in the islands I shall tell you briefly of the various parts of my outfit as it was finally shaken down for the cruise.

My tent was of the pyramidal form invented by Comstock, seven feet high with a base seven feet square and having the peak directly over the centre of the forward edge. In back was a two foot wall. It was made of a waterproof mixture of silk and cotton, tinted green, and weighed eight pounds. My mainmast served as a tent pole, and for holding down I used seventeen pegs made of the native cedar, which is a tough, hard wood and not heavy. For my purposes I have found this the most satisfactory tent for varied cruising, as I could use it equally well ashore or rigged over the cockpit of the *Yakaboo* when I slept aboard. Let me here offer a little prayer of thanks to Comstock. You will find some "improvement" upon his idea in almost any outfitter's catalogue and given any name but his— one might as well try to improve it as to alter a Crosby cat.

For sleeping I had two single German blankets, weighing four pounds each. In place of the usual rubber blanket, I used an oiled muslin ground cloth. My blankets were folded in the ground cloth in such a manner that upon drawing them from the blanket bag, I could roll them out on the ground ready for turning in. The blanket bag was made of heavy oiled canvas with the end turned in and strapped so that even when it lay in a cockpit half full of water its contents would still remain dry. One blanket used with pajamas of light duck would have been ample, so far as warmth goes, but for sleeping in the cockpit the second blanket served as a padding for the hard floor.

As for clothes, I started out with a heterogeneous collection of old trousers, shirts and socks, which, according to the law of the survival of favourites, petered out to two pairs of light woollen trousers, two light flannel shirts, and two pairs of thin woollen socks. I indulged myself in half a dozen new sleeveless cotton running shirts, dyed red, B. V. D.'s to correspond, and a dozen red cotton bandana handkerchiefs. For footgear, I carried a pair of heavy oiled tan shoes and pig-skin moccasins. A light Swedish dog-skin coat and a brown felt hat with a fairly wide brim, completed my wardrobe.

For cooking I had the "Ouinnetka" kit, of my own design, consisting of three pails, a frypan, two covers, a cup, and two spoons, all of aluminum, which nested and held a dish cloth and soap. There were no handles, a pair of light tongs serving in their stead. This kit, which was designed for two-man use, weighed a trifle under three pounds.

The rest of my working outfit consisted of a two pound axe, a canoe knife, a small aluminum folding candle lantern, two one-gallon water cans, and a ditty bag, containing a sight compass, parallel rule, dividers, hypodermic outfit, beeswax, and the usual odds and ends which one carries. For sailing I used a two-inch liquid compass. This working outfit totalled forty-three pounds. Had the "butterfly" continued in service, its weight would have added a pound and a half.

My food at the outset brought this weight up to eighty pounds, but as I later on got down to chocolate, erbswurst and the native foods, there was a reduction of from twenty to thirty pounds.

The heaviest single unit of my whole outfit was a quarter-plate Graflex, which, with its developing tank and six tins of films, added twenty-six pounds. A nine millimeter Mannlicher, .22 B.S.A., 38-40 Colt, a deep sea rod and reel, shells, and tackle brought the total up to 120 pounds. I might as well have left out my armament and tackle for when cruising I find little time for shooting or fishing—I would rather travel.

My charts, twelve in number, had first been trimmed to their smallest working size and then cut into eight-inch by ten-inch panels and mounted on muslin with half an inch separating the edges so that they could be folded to show uppermost whatever panel I happened to be sailing on. The charts with my portfolio I kept in a double bag in the aft end of the cockpit.

The various parts of my outfit were in bags having long necks which could be doubled over and securely tied. These were made of unbleached muslin, oiled with a mixture of raw and boiled linseed oil and turpentine. After a wet bit of sailing, when the canoe had at times literally gone through the seas and there was water in every compartment, it was a great comfort to find the entire outfit quite dry.

The weight of the *Yakaboo,* with her rig and outfit aboard, varied from 260 to 290 pounds—not much more than that of an ordinary rowboat.

Nothing is so unalloyed as the joy of pottering over a hot, little fire when the stomach cries out and the body tingles with the healthy fatigue of work in the open. My spirit was at ease, for the canoe had proven herself and even if she did leak, I was getting used to that—as one becomes used to a boil on the neck. To lie on my blankets—no bed was ever so welcome—and to eat and watch the last light fade from the hills of Carriacou made me glad that I had been put on this earth to live. After supper the companionable purr of my faithful pipe made just the conversation to suit my mood. The night was soft and balmy, and as I lay and watched the brilliant constellations of the tropical night the lap-lap of the water on the smooth sands lulled me off to sleep.

⚓   ⚓   ⚓

CACHACROU HEAD

I AWOKE in the morning to find that I had carelessly slipped into the second day of a windy quarter. There was no doubt about it; the trade was blowing strong at six o'clock. I was impatient to be off shore before the surf would be running too high even for the thirty-foot dugout. After gulping down a hasty breakfast and bidding profuse adieux, I reached the beach with my friend just in time to see one of the fishing boats capsize and to watch the natives chase down the shore to pick up her floating gear.

It took nearly the whole male population of the village to turn the dugout and get her bow down to the surf. With a shout and a laugh the people carried the *Yakaboo* and placed her lightly in her nest. Ten of the strongest paddlers were selected and they took their places in the dugout forward and aft of the canoe while I, like the Queen of the Carnival, sat perched high above the rest, in the cockpit. For nearly half an hour —by my watch—we sat and waited. There were thirty men, on the sands, along each gunwale, ready for the word. There was little talking; we all watched the seas that seemed to come in, one after another, with vindictive force.

I was beginning to swear that I was too late when a "soft one" rolled in and we shot from the heave of a hundred and twenty arms plunging our bow into the first sea. Her heel was still on the sand and I feared she wouldn't come up for we shipped two barrels of brine as easily as the *Yakaboo* takes a teacupful. But with the first stroke she was free and with the second she cleared the next sea which broke under her stern.

Once clear of all dangers, eight of the men fell to bailing while the two bow men and the steersman kept her head to it. Then we swung the *Yakaboo* athwartships while I loaded and rigged her. We slid her overboard and I jumped in. The men held her alongside where she tugged like an impatient puppy while I lowered the center-board. "Let 'er go!" I yelled—an expression that seems to be understood in all languages—and I ran up the mizzen, sheeting it not quite home. Then the jib. I shall never forget the sensation as I hauled in on that jib—it seems out of proportion to use the word "haul" for a line scarcely an eighth of an inch in diameter fastened to a sail hardly a yard in area. The wind was strong and the seas were lively.

When that sheeted jib swung the canoe around she did not have time to gather speed, she simply jumped to it. I made fast the jib sheet and prepared to steer by the mizzen when I discovered that the canoe was sailing herself. I looked back toward shore and waved both arms. The day was delirious. A tuna dugout that had been lying into the wind fell away as I started and raced ahead of me, reefed down, her lee rail in the boil and her wild crew to windward. My mainsail was already reefed and I let the canoe have it. By the high-tuned hum of her board I knew that the *Yakaboo* was travelling and the crew of the tuna canoe knew it, too, for we passed them and were off on our wild ride to Dominica.

My channel runs were improving. The sea, the sky, and the clouds were all the same as on the other runs, but the wind was half a gale. What occupied my mind above all, however, was the discovery that the canoe would sail herself under jib and mizzen. I had thought that no boat with so much curve to her bottom could possibly do such a thing—it is not done on paper. The fact remained, however, that the two small sails low down and far apart kept the canoe on her course as well as I could when handling the mainsheet.

I checked this observation by watching my compass which has a two-inch card floating in liquid and is extremely steady. I also learned that I did not have to waste time heading up for the breaking seas, except the very large ones, of course. Sometimes I could roll them under—at other times I let them come right aboard and then I was up to my shoulders in foam. The canoe was tighter than she had ever been and it was only the cockpit that gave trouble. When she began to stagger from weight of water, I would let go the main halyard and she would continue on her course while I bailed. In all the two thousand miles of cruising I had hitherto done, I learned more in this twenty-five mile channel than all the rest put together. Some day—I promised myself—I would build a hull absolutely tight and so strong and of such a form that I could force her through what seas she could not easily ride over. Also, what a foolish notion I had clung to in setting my sails only a few inches above deck; they should be high up so that a foot of water could pass over the deck and not get into the cloth. In this run, if the *Yakaboo* had been absolutely tight and her sails raised and if I had carried a small deck seat to windward, I could have carried full sail and she would have ridden to Dominica on a cloud of brine-smelling steam. As it was, she was travelling much faster than at any time before and I did not know that the most glorious channel run was yet to come.

I laid my course for Cape Cachacrou (Scott's Head), a peculiar hook that runs out to westward of the south end of Dominica. For the first two hours I could not see the Head, then it popped up like an island and began slowly to connect itself with the larger land. The going was excellent and in short time the head was right over our bow, with Dominica rising up four thousand feet to weather. We were not more than half a mile off shore when I took out my watch. I figured out later that our rate had been six miles an hour including slowing up to bail and occasionally coming to a dead stop when riding out a big sea bow on. I could ask no better of a small light craft sailing six points off the wind, logy a part of the time and working in seas that were almost continually breaking

Fate was indulgent, for she waited till I had stowed my watch in its berth to starboard. Then she sent a sea of extra size—it seemed to come right up from below and mouth the *Yakaboo* like a terrier—and before we got over our surprise she gave us the tail end of a squall, like a whip-lash, that broke the mizzen goose-neck and sent the sail a-skying like a crazy kite. I let go all my halyards and pounced after my sails like a frantic washerwoman whose clothes have gone adrift in a backyard gale. The mainsail came first and then the jib. The truant mizzen which had dropped into the sea when I slipped its halyard came out torn and wet and I rolled it up and spanked it and stowed it in the cockpit.

The sea had come up from the sudden shoaling where in a third of a mile the bottom jumps from a hundred and twenty fathoms to twelve, and as for the squall, that was just a frisky bit of trade that was not content with gathering speed around the end of the island but must slide down the side of a mountain to see how much of a rumpus it could raise on the water. I had run unawares—it was my own stupid carelessness that did it—on the shoals that extend to the southeast of Cachacrou Head where the seas jumped with nasty breaking heads that threatened to turn the *Yakaboo* end for end any minute.

With the mizzen out of commission I might as well have stood in pink tights on the back of a balky farm horse and told him to cross his fingers as sail that canoe. I might have hoisted my jib and slowly run off the shoals to the westward, but that would have meant a hard tedious beat back to shore again for a good part of the night. I chose to work directly across the shoals with the oars. But it was no joking matter. My course lay in the trough of the sea and it was a question of keeping her stern to the seas so that I could watch them and making as much as I could between crests.

Most of my difficulty lay in checking her speed when a comber would try to force her along in a mad toboggan ride and from this the palms of my hands became sore and developed a huge blister in each that finally broke and let in the salt water which was about in plenty. For an hour I worked at it, edging in crabwise across the shoals till the seas began to ease up and I pulled around the Head to the quiet waters under its hook. Have you walked about all day in a stiff pair of new shoes and then come home to the exquisite ease of an old pair of bed-room slippers? Then you know how I felt when I could take a straight pull with my fingers crooked on the oars and my raw palms eased from their contact with the handles.

Cachacrou Head is a rock which stands some two hundred and thirty-four feet up from the sea and is connected with the coast of Dominica by a narrow curved peninsula fifty yards across and half a mile in length. There is a small fort on the top of the Head and here on the night of September the seventh, in 1778, the French from Martinique, with a forty-nine gun ship, three frigates and about thirty small sloops filled with all kinds of piratical rabble, captured the fort which was in those days supposed to be impregnable. It was the same old story; there is always a weak point in the armour of one's enemy—thirst being the vulnerable point in this case. The night before the capture some French soldiers who had insinuated themselves into the fort, muddled the heads of the English garrison with wine from Martinique, and spiked the guns. The capture then was easy. By this thin wedge, the French gained control of Dominica and held the island for five years.

Rowing close around the Head, I found a sandy bit of beach just where the peninsula starts for the mainland and with a feeling that here ended a good day's work, hauled the *Yakaboo* up on the smooth hard beach. The sun—it seems that I am continually talking about the sun which is either rising or setting or passing through that ninety degree arc of deadly heat the middle of which is noon (it was now four o'clock)—was far enough on its down path so that the Head above me cast a grateful shade over the beach while the cool wind from the mountains insured the absence of mosquitoes.

The lee coast of Dominica stretching away to the north was in brilliant light. You have probably gathered by this time that the Lesser Antilles are decidedly unsuited for camping and cruising as we like to do it in the North Woods. In a few isolated places on the windward coasts one might live in a tent and be healthy and happy, such as my camp with the Caribs; but to cruise and camp, that is travel and then rest for a day on the beach—this is impossible. In this respect my cruise was a distinct failure.

When I did find a spot such as this, where I could still enjoy a part of the afternoon in comparative comfort, I enjoyed it to the utmost. I did not unload the *Yakaboo* immediately—I merely took those things out of her that I wanted for my present use. *Tabac de Diable,* for instance, and my pipe, and then a change of clothes; but before I put on that change I shed my stiff briny sea outfit and sat down in a little sandy-floored pool in the rocks. There I smoked with my back against a rock while the reflex from the Caribbean rose and fell with delightful intimacy from my haunches to my shoulders.

For some time I rested there, with my hands behind my head to keep the blood out of my throbbing hands and the salt out of my burning palms. Across the bay was the town of Soufrière, not unlike the Soufrière of Saint Lucia, from a distance, while a few miles beyond was Point Michelle and another few miles along was Roseau, the capital town of the island. Away to the north Diablotin rose nearly five thousand feet, within a hundred feet of the Soufrière of Guadeloupe, the highest mountain of the Lesser Antilles.

After a while I got up, like a lazy faun (let us not examine the simile too closely for who would picture a sea faun smoking a Three-B and with a four days' stubble on his chin?) On a flat-topped rock near the canoe I spread out my food bags. Near this I started a fire of hardwood twigs that soon burned down to a hot little bed of coals over which my pot of *erbswurst* was soon boiling. This peameal soup, besides bacon and potatoes, is one of the few foods of which one may eat without tiring, three times a day, day in and day out, when living in the open. It is an excellent campaign food and can be made into a thin or thick soup according to one's fancy. I have eaten it raw and found it to be very sustaining. At home one would quickly tire of the eternal peameal and the salty bacon taste—but I never eat it when I am at home nor do I use in general the foods I take with me when cruising. The two diets are quite distinct.

While the pot was boiling, I betook myself to a cosy angle in the rocks which I softened with my blanket bag, and fell to repairing my mizzen. My eye chanced to wander down the beach—is it chance or instinct?— and finally came to rest on a group of natives who stood watching me. Modesty demanded something in the way of clothes so I put on a clean shirt and trousers and beckoned to them. They were a timid lot and only two of them advanced to within fifty feet of the canoe and then stopped. I talked to them, but it was soon evident that they did not understand a word I said, even the little patois I knew got no word from them. Finally they summoned enough courage to depart and I was left to my mending.

I had finished my sail and was enjoying my pea-soup and biscuits when my eye detected a movement down the beach and I saw a lone figure which advanced without hesitation and walked right into my camp where it smiled down at me from an altitude of three inches over six feet.

"My name ess Pistole Titre, wat you name and frum war you cum?"

I told him that my name was of little importance and that I had just come from Martinique.

"Frum war before dat?"

"Saint Lucia."

"Frum war before dat?"

"Saint Vincent."

"Frum war before dat?"

"Grenada."

"An' you not afraid?"

"Why should I be afraid? The canoe sails well."

"I no mean de sea, I mean jumbie. How you don't know w'en you come to strange ilan de jumbie no take you?"

There might be some truth in this but I answered, "I don't believe in jumbies." This he interpreted into, "I don't believe there are jumbies HERE." The fact that I did not believe in jumbies, the evil spirits of the Africans, was utterly beyond his conception—of course I believed in them, everybody did, but by some occult power I must know their haunts and could avoid them though I had never visited the place before.

"I know jumbies no come here, but how you know? You wonderful man," he concluded.

While this conversation was going on, I was secretly admiring his huge lithe body—such of it as could be seen through an open shirt and by suggestive line of limb; he might have been some bronze Apollo come to animation, except for his face. His face was an expression of good-will, intelligence, and energy that came to me as a refreshing relief from the shiny fulsome visage of the common native.

The jumbies disposed of for the time being, Pistole sat down on a rock and made rapid inroads on a few soda biscuits and some pea-soup which I poured into a calabash. The native can always eat, and the eating of this salty soup with its bacon flavour seemed the very quintessence of gastronomic delight. When he had finished he pointed to a steep upland valley and told me he must go there to milk his cows. As he walked away along the beach, the breeze brought back, "An' he no 'fraid jumbies. O Lard!"

My supper over, I turned the canoe bow toward the water and made up my bed in the cockpit. It would be too fine a night for a tent and I tied my candle light part way up the mizzen mast so that I could lie in my bed and read. At sunset I lit my lamp for the beach under the Head was in darkness. While the short twilight moved up from the sea and hovered for a moment on the highest mountain tops my candle grew from a pale flame to a veritable beacon that cast a sphere of light about the canoe, shutting out night from the tiny rock-hedged beach on which we lay. But Ulysses did not make me drowsy and I blew out my light and lay under that wonderful blue ceiling in which the stars blinked like live diamonds. The Dipper was submerged with its handle sticking out of the sea before me and Polaris hung low, a much easier guide than in the North. Just overhead Orion's belt floated like three lights dropped from a sky rocket. Through the low brush over the peninsula the Southern Cross tilted to westward.

⚓

ROUNDING THE HORN

⚓

ROUNDING THE HORN

Captain Joshua Slocum

⚓ *As the editor writes this, the barometer has been slipping waveringly down, down. Green's Ledge is sounding its mournful twin blasts every 13 seconds. It is a good night to be snugged down in harbor. A good night to take out Captain Slocum's chronicle and turn over the pages by the light of the cabin lamp.*

What testimony to the power of the sea over a man. Not content with a full life as a skipper in all kinds of ships, nor with the life of other men, he must circumnavigate the watery part of the globe—alone.

Further along you will read how the Horn treated Dana's ship. Now read how it feels to round it—alone. No one to relieve you at the wheel, no one to lend a hand shortening sail, no one to spell you when you are sitting astride the borderline between consciousness and unconsciousness, no one to throw you a rope's end if you slip over the side, no one to pass you the half cup of coffee that didn't go into the scuppers, no one to shout at you through the wind, no one to laugh. Forty-six thousand miles alone.

ON JANUARY 26, 1896, the *Spray*, being refitted and well provisioned in every way, sailed from Buenos Aires. There was little wind at the start; the surface of the great river was like a silver disk, and I was glad of a tow from a harbor tug to clear the port entrance. But a gale came up soon after, causing an ugly sea, and instead of being all silver, as before, the river was now all mud. The Plate is a treacherous place for storms. One sailing there should always be on the alert for squalls. I cast anchor before dark in the best lee I could find near the land, but was

From *Around the World in the Sloop Spray* by Captain Joshua Slocum.

tossed miserably all night, heartsore of choppy seas. On the following morning I got the sloop under way, and with reefed sails worked her down the river against a head wind. Standing in that night to the place where pilot Howard joined me for the up-river sail, I took a departure, shaping my course to clear Point Indio on the one hand, and the English Bank on the other.

I had not for many years been south of these regions. I will not say that I expected all fine sailing on the course for Cape Horn direct, but while I worked at the sails and rigging I thought only of onward and forward. It was when I anchored in the lonely places that a feeling of awe crept over me. At the last anchorage on the monotonous and muddy river, weak as it may seem, I gave way to my feelings. I resolved then that I would anchor no more north of the Strait of Magellan.

On the 28th of January the *Spray* was clear of Point Indio, English Bank, and all the other dangers of the River Plate. With a fair wind she then bore away for the Strait of Magellan, under all sail, pressing farther and farther toward the wonderland of the South, till I almost forgot the blessings of our milder North.

My ship passed in safety Bahia Blanca, also the Gulf of St. Matias and the mighty Gulf of St. George, off whose coasts are destructive tide-races, the dread of big craft or little. I gave all the capes a berth of about fifty miles to clear these dangers, for they extend many miles from the land. But where the sloop avoided one danger she encountered another. For, one day, well off this rough coast, while scudding under short sail, a tremendous wave, the culmination, it seemed, of many waves, rolled down upon her in a storm, roaring as it came. I had only a moment to get all sail down and myself up on the peak halliards, out of danger, when I saw the mighty crest towering masthead-high above me. The mountain of water submerged my vessel. She shook in every timber and reeled under the weight of the sea, but rose quickly out of it, and rode grandly over the rollers that followed. It may have been a minute that from my hold in the rigging I could see no part of the *Spray's* hull. Perhaps it was even less time than that, but it seemed a long while, for under great excitement one lives fast, and in a few seconds one may think a great deal of one's past life. Not only did the past, with electric speed, flash before me, but I had time while in my hazardous position for resolutions for the future that would take a long time to fulfil. The first one was, I remember, that if the *Spray* came through this danger I would dedicate my best energies to building a larger ship on her lines, which I hope yet to do. Other promises, less easily kept, I should have made under protest. However, the incident, which filled me with fear, was only one more test of the *Spray's* seaworthiness. It reassured me against rude Cape Horn.

Still further to leeward was a great headland, and I bore off for that.

From the time the great wave swept over the *Spray* until she reached Cape Virgin nothing occurred to move a pulse and set blood in motion. On the contrary, the weather became fine, the sea smooth, and life tranquil. The phenomenon of mirage I witnessed once, and that of looming frequently occurred. I saw, a long way off, the land for which I was steering pictured against the sky in the glistening haze. An albatross sitting on the water one day loomed up like a large ship; two fur-seals asleep on the surface of the sea appeared like great whales, and a bank of haze I could have sworn was high land. The kaleidoscope then changed, and on the following day I sailed in a world where everything seemed small.

On February 11 the *Spray* rounded Cape Virgin and entered the Strait of Magellan. The scene was gloomy; the wind, northeast, and blowing a gale, sent feather-white spume along the coast; such a sea ran as would swamp an ill-appointed ship. As the sloop neared the entrance to the Strait I observed that two great tide-races made ahead, one very close to the point of the land and one farther off-shore. Between the two, in a sort of channel, through combers, went the *Spray* with close-reefed sails. My early experiences in the strong tideway on the Bay of Fundy benefited me now. A rolling sea, however, followed her a long way in, and a fierce head current swept around the cape; but this she stemmed, and was soon chirruping under the lee of Cape Virgin and running every minute into smoother water. Long trailing kelp from sunken rocks waved forebodingly under her keel, and the wreck of a great steamship smashed on the beach abreast gave a gloomy aspect to the scene.

I was not to be let off easy. The Virgin would collect tribute even from the *Spray* passing the promontory. Fitful rain-squalls from the northwest followed the northeast gale. I reefed the sloop's sails, for it was now the blackest of nights all around, except away in the southwest, where the old familiar white arch of a sky clearing for more wind rapidly pushed up by a southwest gale, the terror of Cape Horn. I had only a moment to lower sail and lash all solid when it struck like a shot from a cannon, and for the first half-hour it was something to be remembered by way of a gale. For thirty hours it kept on blowing hard. The sloop could carry no more than a three-reefed mainsail and forestaysail; with these she held on stoutly and was not blown out of the strait. In the height of the squalls in this gale she doused all sail, and this occurred often enough.

Then the wind moderated till she could carry all sail again, and the *Spray,* passing through the narrows without mishap, cast anchor at Sandy Point on February 14, 1896.

Sandy Point (Punta Arenas) is a Chilean coaling-station, and boasts about two thousand inhabitants, of mixed nationality, but mostly Chileans. What with sheep-farming, gold-mining, and hunting, the settlers in this dreary land seemed not the worst off in the world. But the natives, Patagonian and Fuegian, were wretchedly squalid.

The port at the time of my visit was free, but a custom-house was in course of construction. A soldier police guarded the place, aided at times by a sort of vigilante force. Just previous to my arrival the governor had sent a party to foray a Fuegian settlement and wipe out what they could of it on account of the recent massacre of a schooner's crew somewhere else. The port captain, a Chilean naval officer, advised me to ship hands to fight Indians in the strait farther west, and spoke of my stopping until a gun-boat should be going through, which would give me a tow. After canvassing the place, however, I found only one man willing to embark, and he on condition that I should ship another "mon and a doog." But as no one else was willing to come along, and as I drew the line at dogs, I said no more about the matter, but loaded my guns. At this point in my dilemma Captain Pedro Samblich, a good Austrian of large experience, coming along, gave me a bag of carpet-tacks, worth more than all the fighting men and dogs of Tierra del Fuego. I protested that I had no use for carpet-tacks on board. Samblich smiled at my want of experience, and maintained stoutly that I would have use for them. "You must use them with discretion," he said; "that is to say, don't step on them yourself." With this remote hint about the use of the tacks I got on all right, and saw the way to maintain clear decks at night without the care of watching.

Samblich was greatly interested in my voyage, and after giving me the tacks, he put on board bags of biscuits and a large quantity of smoked venison. He declared that my bread, which was ordinary sea-biscuits and easily broken, was not as nutritious as his, which was so hard that I could break it only with a stout blow from a maul. Then he gave me, from his own sloop, a compass which was certainly better than mine, and he offered to unbend her mainsail for me if I would accept it. Last of all, this large-hearted man brought out a bottle of Fuegian gold-dust from a place where it had been *cachéd* and begged me to help myself from it, for use farther along on the voyage. But I felt sure of success without this draft on a friend, and I was right. Samblich's tacks, as it turned out, were of more value than gold.

The port captain finding that I was resolved to go, even alone, since there was no help for it, set up no further objections, but advised me, in case the savages tried to surround me with their canoes, to shoot straight, and begin to do it in time, but to avoid killing them if possible, which I heartily agreed to do. With these simple injunctions the officer gave me my port clearance free of charge, and I sailed on the same day, February 19, 1896. It was not without thoughts of strange and stirring adventure beyond all I had yet encountered that I now sailed into the country and very core of the savage Fuegians.

A fair wind from Sandy Point brought me on the first day to St. Nicholas Bay. Seeing no signs of savages here, I came to anchor in eight fathoms of water, where I lay all night at the foot of a mountain. From this point I had experiences with the terrific squalls, called williwaws, which extended on through the strait to the Pacific. A full-blown williwaw will throw a ship, even without sail on, over on her beam ends; but, like other gales, they cease now and then, if only for a short time.

February 20 was my birthday, and I found myself alone, with hardly so much as a bird in sight, off Cape Froward, the southernmost point of the continent of America. By daylight in the morning I was getting my ship under way for the bout ahead.

Thirty miles farther brought her to Fortescue Bay, and at once among signal-fires of the natives which now blazed up on all sides. At twelve o'clock that night, I gained anchorage under the lee of a little island, and then prepared myself a cup of coffee, of which I was sorely in need; for, to tell the truth, hard beating in the heavy squalls and against the current had told on my strength. The wind had changed from fair to foul early in the evening. Finding that the anchor held, I drank my beverage, and named the place Coffee Island. It lies to the south of Charles Island, with only a narrow channel between.

By daylight the next morning the *Spray* was again under way, beating hard; but she came to in a cove in Charles Island, two and a half miles along on her course. Here she remained undisturbed two days, with both anchors down in a bed of kelp. Indeed, she might have remained undisturbed indefinitely had not the wind moderated; for during these two days it blew so hard, that no boat could venture out on the strait, and the natives being away to other hunting-grounds, the island anchorage was safe. But at the end of the fierce wind-storm fair weather came; then I weighed my anchors, and again sailed out upon the strait.

Canoes manned by savages from Fortescue now came in pursuit. The wind falling light, they gained on me rapidly till coming within hail, when they ceased paddling, and a bow-legged savage stood up and called to me, "Yammerschooner! yammerschooner!" which is their begging term. I said, "No!" Now, I did not wish them to know I was alone, and so I stepped into the cabin, and, passing through the hold, came out at the fore-scuttle, changing my clothes as I went along. That made two men. Then the piece of bowsprit which I had sawed off at Buenos Aires, and which I had still on board, I arranged forward on the lookout, dressed as a seaman, attaching a line by which I could pull it into motion. That made three of us, and we didn't want to "yammerschooner"; but for all that the savages came on faster than before

I saw that besides four at the paddles in the canoe nearest to me, there were others in the bottom, and that they were shifting hands often. At eighty yards I fired a shot across the bows of the nearest canoe, at which they all stopped, but only for a moment. Seeing that they persisted in coming nearer, I fired the second shot so close to the chap who wanted to "yammerschooner" that he changed his mind quickly enough and bellowed in Spanish, "All right! I am going to the island," and sitting down in his canoe, he rubbed one side of his head for some time. I was thinking of the good port captain's advice when I pulled the trigger, and aimed pretty straight; however, a miss was as good as a mile for Mr. "Black Pedro," as he it was, and no other, a leader in several bloody massacres. He made for the island now, and the others followed him. I knew by his Spanish lingo and by his full beard that he was the villain I have named, mongrel, and the worst murderer in Tierra del Fuego. The authorities had been in search of him for two years. The Fuegians are not bearded.

So much for the first day among the savages. I came to anchor at midnight in Three Island Cove, about twenty miles along from Fortescue Bay. I saw on the opposite side of the strait signal-fires, and heard the barking of dogs, but where I lay it was quite deserted by natives. I always took it as a sign that where I found birds sitting about, or seals on the rocks, I should not find savage Indians. Seals are never plentiful in these waters, but in Three Island Cove I saw one on the rocks, and other signs of the absence of savage man.

On the next day the wind was again blowing a gale, and although she was in the lee of the land, the sloop dragged her anchors, so that I had to get her under way and beat farther into the cove, where I came to in a landlocked pool. At another time or place this would have been a rash thing to do, and it was safe now only from the fact that the gale which drove me to shelter would keep the Indians from crossing the strait. This being the case, I went ashore with gun and axe on an island, where I could not in any event be surprised, and there felled trees and split about a cord of fire-wood, which loaded my small boat several times.

While I carried the wood, though I was morally sure there were no savages near, I never once went to or from the skiff without my gun. While I had that and a clear field of over eighty yards about me I felt safe.

The trees on the island, very scattering, were a sort of beech and a stunted cedar, both of which made good fuel. Even the green limbs of the beech, which seemed to possess a resinous quality, burned readily in my great drumstove. In the Strait of Magellan the greatest vigilance was necessary, but I took care against all kinds of surprises, whether by animals or by the elements. In this instance I reasoned that I had all about me the greatest danger of the voyage—the treachery of cunning savages, for which I must be particularly on the alert.

The *Spray* sailed from Three Island Cove in the morning after the gale went down, but was glad to return for shelter from another sudden gale. Sailing again on the following day, she fetched Borgia Bay, a few miles on her course, where vessels had anchored from time to time and had nailed boards on the trees ashore with name and date of harboring carved or painted. Nothing else could I see to indicate that civilized man had ever been there. I had taken a survey of the gloomy place with my spy-glass and was getting my boat out to land and take notes, when the Chilean gun-boat *Huemul* came in, and officers, coming on board, advised me to leave the place at once, a thing that required little eloquence to persuade me to do. I accepted the captain's kind offer of a tow to the next anchorage, at the place called Notch Cove, eight miles farther along, where I should be clear of the worst of the Fuegians.

We made anchorage at the cove about dark that night, while the wind came down in fierce williwaws from the mountains. An instance of Magellan weather was afforded when the *Huemul,* a well-appointed gun-boat of great power, after attempting on the following day to proceed on her voyage, was obliged by sheer force of the wind to return and take up anchorage again and remain till the gale abated, and lucky she was to get back!

Meeting this vessel was a little godsend. She was commanded and officered by high-class sailors and educated gentlemen.

I was left alone the next day, for then the *Huemul* put out on her voyage, the gale having abated. I spent a day taking in wood and water; by the end of that time the weather was fine. Then I sailed from the desolate place.

There is little more to be said concerning the *Spray's* first passage through the strait that would differ from what I have already recorded. She anchored and weighed anchor many times, and beat many days against the current, till finally she gained anchorage and shelter for the night at Port Tamar, with Cape Pillar in sight to the west. Here I felt the throb of the great ocean that lay before me. I knew now that I had put a world behind me, and that I was opening out another world ahead. I had passed the haunts of savages. Great piles of granite mountains of bleak and lifeless aspect were now astern; on some of them not even a speck of moss had ever grown. There was an unfinished newness all about the land now in sight. On the hill back of Port Tamar a small beacon had been thrown up, the only indication that man had ever been there.

Throughout the whole of the strait west of Cape Froward I saw no animals except the dogs of the savages and savages themselves. These I saw often enough, and heard their dogs yelping night and day. Birds were not plentiful. The scream of a wild fowl, which I took for a loon, sometimes startled me with its piercing cry. The steam-boat duck, so called because it propels itself over the sea with its wings, and resembles a miniature side-wheel steamer in its motion, was sometimes seen scurrying ahead. It never flies, but, hitting the water instead of the air with its wings, it moves faster than a row-boat or a canoe. The few fur-seals I saw were very shy; and of fishes I saw next to none at all. I did not catch one; indeed, I seldom or never put a hook over during the whole voyage. Here in the strait I found great abundance of mussels of an excellent quality. I fared sumptuously on them. There was a sort of swan, smaller than a Muscovy duck, which might have been brought down with the gun, but in the loneliness of life about the dreary country I found myself in no mood to make one life less, except in self-defence.

It was the 3d of March when the *Spray* sailed from Port Tamar direct for Cape Pillar, with the wind from the northeast, which I fervently hoped might hold till she cleared the land; but there was no such good luck in store. It soon began to rain and thicken in the northwest, boding no good. The *Spray* neared Cape Pillar rapidly, and, nothing loath, plunged into the Pacific Ocean at once, taking her first bath of it in the gathering storm. There was no turning back even had I wished to do so, for the land was now shut out by the darkness of night. The wind freshened, and I took in a third reef. The sea was confused and treacherous. I saw now only the gleaming crests of the waves. They showed white teeth while the sloop balanced over them. "Everything for an offing," I cried, and I carried on all the sail she would bear.

She ran all night with a free sheet, but on the morning of March 4 the wind shifted to southwest, then back suddenly to northwest, and blew with terrific force. The *Spray,* stripped of her sails, then bore off under bare poles. No ship in the world could have stood up against so violent a gale. Knowing that this storm might continue for many days, and that it would be impossible to work back to the westward along the coast outside of Tierra del Fuego, I had reason to think that I should be obliged to sail east-about after all. The only course for my present safety lay in keeping her before the wind. And so she drove southeast, as though about to round the Horn, while the waves rose and fell and bellowed with never-ending fury; but the Hand that held these held also the *Spray.* She was running now with a reefed forestaysail, the sheets flat amidship. I paid out two long ropes astern to steady her course and to break combing seas, and I lashed the helm amidship. In this trim she ran before it, shipping never a sea. Even while the storm raged at its worst, my ship was wholesome and noble. My mind as to her seaworthiness was put at ease for aye.

When all had been done that I could do for the safety of the vessel, I got to the fore-scuttle, between seas, and prepared a pot of coffee over a wood fire, and made a good Irish stew. Then, as before and afterward on the *Spray,* I insisted on warm meals. In the tide-race off Cape Pillar, however, where the sea was marvellously high, uneven, and crooked, my appetite was slim, and for a time I postponed cooking. (Confidentially, I was sea-sick!)

In no part of the world could a rougher sea be found than at this point, namely, off Cape Pillar, the grim sentinel of the Horn.

Farther offshore, while the sea was majestic, there was less apprehension of danger. There the *Spray* rode, like a bird over the crest of the waves, or sat composedly for a moment deep down in the hollow between seas; and so she drove on. These days passed, as other days, but with always a thrill—yes, of delight.

On the fourth day of the gale, rapidly nearing the pitch of Cape Horn, I inspected my chart and pricked off the course and distance to Port Stanley, in the Falkland Islands, where I might find my way and refit, when I saw through a rift in the clouds a high mountain, about seven leagues away on the port beam. The fierce edge of the gale by this time had blown off, and I had already bent a squaresail on the boom in place of the mainsail, which was torn to rags. I hauled in the trailing ropes, hoisted this awkward sail reefed, the forestaysail being already set, and under this sail brought her at once on the wind, heading for what appeared as an island in the sea. So it turned out to be, though not the one I had supposed.

I was exultant over the prospect of once more entering the Strait of Magellan and beating through again into the Pacific, for it was more than rough on the outside coast of Tierra del Fuego. It was indeed a mountainous sea. Under pressure of the smallest sail I could set the *Spray* made for the land like a racehorse, and steering her over the crests of the waves so that she might not trip was nice work. I stood at the helm now and made the most of it.

Night had already closed when I saw breakers ahead. At this I wore ship and stood offshore, but was immediately startled by the tremendous roaring of breakers again ahead and on the lee bow. This puzzled me, for there should have been no broken water where I supposed myself to be. I kept off a good bit, then wore round, but finding broken water also there, threw her head again offshore. In this way, among dangers, I spent the rest of the night. Hail and sleet in the fierce squalls cut my flesh till the blood trickled over my face; but what of that? When day-light came I found that the sloop was in the midst of the Milky Way of the sea, which is northwest of Cape Horn, and that it was the white breakers of a huge sea over sunken rocks which had threatened to engulf her through the night. It was Fury Island I had sighted and steered for, and what a panorama was before me now and all around! What could I do but fill away among the breakers and find a channel between them, now that it was day? Since she had escaped the rocks through the night, surely she would find her way by daylight. This was the greatest sea adventure of my life. God knows how my vessel escaped.

The sloop at last reached inside of small islands that sheltered her in smooth water. Then I climbed the mast to survey the wild scene outside. The great naturalist Darwin looked over this sea-scape from the deck of the Beagle, and wrote vividly in his journal concerning it.

The *Spray's* good luck followed fast. As she sailed along through a labyrinth of islands, I discovered that she was in Cockburn Channel, which leads into the Strait of Magellan at a point opposite Cape Froward, and that she was already passing Thieves' Bay, suggestively named. And at night, March 8, behold, she was at anchor in a snug cove at the Turn! Every heart-beat on the *Spray* now counted thanks.

Here I pondered on the events of the last few days, and, strangely enough, instead of feeling rested from sitting or lying down, I now began to feel jaded and worn; but a hot meal of venison stew soon put me right, so that I could sleep. As drowsiness came on I sprinkled the deck with tacks, and then I turned in, bearing in mind the advice of my old friend Samblich that I was not to step on them myself. I saw to it carefully that most of them stood point up; for when the *Spray* passed Thieves' Bay two canoes put out and followed in her wake, and there was no disguising the fact any longer that I was alone.

Now, it is well known that one cannot step on a tack without saying something about it. A pretty good Christian will whistle when he steps on the sharp end of a carpet-tack; a savage will howl and claw the air, and that was just what happened that night about twelve o'clock, while I was asleep in the cabin, where the savages thought they had the better of me, sloop and all, but changed their minds when they stepped on deck, for then they thought that I or somebody else had them. I had no need of a dog; they howled like a pack of hounds. I had hardly use for a gun. They jumped pell-mell, some into their canoes and some into the sea, and there was a deal of free language over it as they went. I fired several guns when I came on deck, to let the rascals know that I was at home, and then I turned in again, feeling sure I should not be disturbed any more by people who left in so great a hurry.

The Fuegians, being cruel, are naturally cowards; they regard a rifle with superstitious fear. The only real danger one could see that might come from their quarter would be from allowing them to surround one within bow-shot, or to anchor within range where they might lie in ambush. As for their coming on deck at night, even had I not put tacks about, I could have cleared them off by shots from the cabin and the hold. I always kept a quantity of ammunition within reach in the hold and in the cabin and in the forepeak, so that retreating to any of these places I could hold the situation simply by shooting up through the deck.

Perhaps the greatest danger to be apprehended was from the use of fire. Every canoe carries fire; nothing is thought of that, for it is their custom to communicate by smoke-signals. The harmless brand that lies smouldering in the bottom of one of their canoes might be ablaze in one's cabin if he were not on the alert. The port captain of Sandy Point warned me particularly of this danger. Only a short time before they had fired a Chilean gun-boat by throwing brands in through the stern windows of the cabin. The *Spray* had no openings in the cabin or deck, except two scuttles, and these were guarded by fastenings which could not be undone without waking me if I were asleep.

On the morning of the 9th, after a refreshing rest and a warm breakfast, and after I had swept up the tacks, I got out what spare canvas there was on board, and began to sew the pieces together in the shape of a peak for my squaremainsail, the tarpaulin. The day to all appearances promised fine weather and light winds, but appearances in Tierra del Fuego do not always count. While I was wondering why no trees grew on the slope abreast of the anchorage, half minded to lay by the sail-making and go on shore with my gun and inspect a white bowlder on the beach near the brook, a williwaw came down with such terrific force as to carry the *Spray,* with two anchors down, like a feather out of the cove and away into deep water. No wonder trees did not grow on the side of that hill. Great Boreas! a tree would need to be all roots to hold on against such a furious wind.

From the cove to the nearest land to leeward was a long drift, however, and I had ample time to weigh both anchors before the sloop came near any danger, and so no harm came of it. I saw no more savages that day or the next; they probably had some sign by which they knew of the coming williwaws; at least, they were wise in not being afloat even on the second day, for I had no sooner gotten to work at sail-making again, after the anchor was down, than the wind, as on the day before, picked the sloop up and flung her seaward with a vengeance, anchor and all, as before. This fierce wind, usual to the Magellan country, continued on through the day, and swept the sloop by several miles of steep bluffs and precipices over-hanging a bold shore of unusually wild and uninviting appearance. I was not sorry to get away from it, though in doing so it was no Elysian shore to which I shaped my course. I kept on sailing in hope, since I had no choice but to go on, heading across for St. Nicholas Bay, where I had cast anchor February 19. It was now the 10th of March! Upon reaching the bay the second time I had circumnavigated the wildest part of desolate Tierra del Fuego. The sea was turbulent, and by the merest accident the *Spray* saved her bones from the rocks, coming into the bay. The parting of a staysail-sheet in a williwaw, when she was plunging into the storm, brought me forward to see instantly a dark cliff ahead and breakers so close under the bows that I felt surely lost, and in my thoughts cried, "Is the hand of fate against me, after all, leading me in the end to this dark spot?" I sprang aft again, unheeding the flapping sail, and threw the wheel over, expecting, as the sloop came down into the hollow of a wave, to feel her timbers smash under me on the rocks. But at the touch of her helm she swung clear of the danger, and in the next moment was in the lee of the land.

It was the small island in the middle of the bay for which the sloop had been steering, and which she made with such unerring aim as nearly to run it down. Farther along in the bay was the anchorage, which I managed to reach, but before I could get the anchor down another squall caught the sloop and whirled her round like a top and carried her away, altogether to leeward of the bay. Still farther to leeward was a great headland, and I bore off for that. This was retracing my course toward Sandy Point, for the gale was from the southwest.

I had the sloop soon under good control, however, and in a short time rounded to under the lee of a mountain, where the sea was as smooth as a millpond, and the sails flapped and hung limp while she carried her way close in. Here I thought I would anchor and rest till morning, the depth being eight fathoms very close to the shore. But it was interesting to see, as I let go the anchor, that it did not reach bottom before another williwaw struck down from this mountain and carried the sloop off faster than I could pay out cable. Therefore, instead of resting, I had to heave up the anchor with fifty fathoms of cable hanging up and down in deep water. This was in that part of the strait called Famine Reach. Dismal Famine Reach! On the sloop's crab-windlass I worked the rest of the night.

It was daybreak when the anchor was at the hawse. By this time the wind had gone down, and cat's-paw took the place of williwaws, while the sloop drifted slowly toward Sandy Point. She came within sight of ships at anchor in the roads, and I was more than half minded to put in for new sails, but the wind coming out from the northeast, which was fair for the other direction, I turned the prow of the *Spray* westward once more for the Pacific, to traverse a second time the second half of my first course through the strait.

⚓

ABANDON SHIP

⚓

ABANDON SHIP

John Masefield

⚓ *Cruiser Trewsbury was the second mate of the homeward-bound China Clipper "Blackgauntlet", sailing from Foochow to London. Four other tea ships had left on the same tide in the Season's Race which might bring them the coveted London Prize.*

Captain Duntisbourne, at twenty-seven, was her able but overbearing skipper, consumed by an overwhelming ambition to win. He had driven the "Blackgauntlet" as she had never been driven, but the North East trades had failed them.

As the scene opens the Captain has just berated Cruiser in front of the watch. The flat calm has been broken by a sudden squall . . .

IN A few minutes, after the passing of the squall, the mist gathered again about the ship, so that even the lower topsails were dim to him. It was hot and oppressive again, with the annoyance of gear jangling and drops splashing. Cruiser was filled with fury at the Captain's insolence. What on earth possessed the man to speak like that? However, he knew in his heart the cause of all the trouble. The Captain had had no fit rest for two months, and was like a madman, from the strain, from the days of continual calm and the oppression of the night. Still, it is no consolation to an injured man to be told that his injurer is mad. There would be at least another month with the madman: and the madness would grow worse if the winds still failed, or drew ahead.

'Of all the foul years a man could have at sea,' he thought, 'I think my last year has been the foulest. First in the *Thunderbird*, with a Captain who had plainly been paid to put the ship ashore; then as third mate in the *Natuna,* without pay, with a Captain who was indeed a jovial soul, but usually drunk; and now here with a nervy lunatic whose nerves are all snapping. However, if I can pass for Master at the end of it, I'll be out of it.'

His thoughts went back to the golden time in London more than a year before: a golden time indeed.

Would such a time ever recur, ever be bettered? It did not seem likely. The helmsman behind him struck One Bell, loud voices roused the watch, and presently Frampton and Abbotts were beside him, mustering their men.

"It's pretty thick, Mr. Trewsbury," Abbotts said. "Do you think I ought to rig the foghorn?"

"The Old Man told me to hold on with the foghorn. But the mist is weeping out, it will be blowing in an hour, and blowing hard: something dirty is coming."

He leaned over the rail, called "Relieve the wheel and look-out," and went below to his cabin. The Captain was not in his chair, nor on deck at all, when he left the poop. 'And a very good thing,' he told himself, 'for perhaps he has turned-in at last, to get a real sleep in a bed.'

He himself determined to sleep.

His cabin was on the starboard side of a little alleyway, which ran from the saloon to the break of the poop. His cabin ports opened on to the main deck, and light of a sort entered by bullseyes in the ship's side. On the other side of the alleyway just opposite to his door, was the cabin of the late Mr. Stratton, now not in use. Further aft, to starboard, was the Captain's cabin, and to port, the steward's pantry and cabin, the Captain's bathroom, and a small space known as the Slop-Room. The clipper carried big crews, renewed every three months or so from the destitute of English, Australian and Chinese sea-ports: many slops were needed.

Cruiser on his way to his cabin entered up the rough log, had a look at the glass, which had fallen during the watch, and set it against the next observation. As he passed the Captain's cabin he saw that the door was hooked back wide open. A light burned there in a safety sconce on gimbals: he saw the Captain in his bunk, fully-dressed, ready for a call, with his face to the ship's side, seemingly asleep. 'Well, let him sleep,' he thought. 'If he could sleep for a week, he might be less of an ass with a fellow.'

He was quite sure that wind was coming very soon: a storm was coming up quickly: the warning closeness and thickness was "weeping itself out," and the blast would follow during his watch below. He judged that the first blast would be from some point to the east of south; which would be fair enough. 'There'll be some desperate driving when it does come,' he thought.

As he expected to be called on deck before his watch was out, he took off his shoes, and put them ready to hand inside his bunk. He had rigged a safety candle-sconce inside his bunk, with a little metal tray for matches. He saw that the matches lay to hand there. He hung his coat on a hook; hooked the door wide open, so that all might be clear for a rush on deck; and then turned-in, like the trooper's horse. As always, he thought fervently for two minutes of that lovely girl whose beauty had so moved him: then, wondering what sort of a watch below he would get before the call, he dropped into the sleep of the sailor, which is something unknown ashore.

Deep though his sleep was, he was aware of certain things: he felt a greater uneasiness in the ship's motion, and then the greater steadiness that followed her getting steerage way. He felt the ship beginning to move, and the watch hopping to the braces and singing out. Presently the watch was just over his head, and he knew, though still asleep, that the crojick was being stowed and that the ship was running. "It's come southerly, as I thought," he muttered. "It will shift through south into west."

He knew, in his sleep, that the Captain had gone on deck the instant the wind had filled a sail. Now and then, still in his sleep, he heard the Captain's light nervy tread, which reminded him of a cat's or boxer's. The mizen skysail and royal came in, the main skysail came in and then the wind seemed to increase from the roaring of these flapping kites and the ship's gathering of speed. Then there came the Captain's call, "Get the foretopmast stunsail on her, Mr. Frampton," and the Bosun's answer "Foretopmast stunsail, ay, ay, sir." There was no doubt about the wind now; the storm was coming on fast and they were going like a leaf before it. He wondered how much more of the after sail would be taken off her. The distant cries of the men forward came to him, and the noise of the great sail going up. She felt the new sail and so did he, but the lower stunsail followed to shake her further. The ship was now alive again: she was a racer of the seas again. He heard the Captain (standing, seemingly, right over his head) stamp with his slippered foot, in a way peculiar to him, at something that vexed him (possibly, the gear of the starboard boat). Then he heard the cry of 'Heave the Log', and from the time the lads took to drag the log in, after heaving, he knew, in his sleep, that the ship was doing well. And at this point he heard seven bells and knew that he had only a quarter of an hour more of rest. Still, a quarter of an hour is well worth having, he thought. One can go very deeply into sleep in a quarter of an hour.

He lapsed into the depths and eternities of sleep, glad that the ship was alive and going like a bird again. She was going like a bird of the sea, and the music of her going was a gurgle of water and the tinkling rush of the scuppers running rain. Then all the depths, eternities, noises and tumults of ship, storm, wind and water gathered together and struck in an appalling CRASH, which lifted him in his bunk and flung him to its side.

"Holy sailor," he cried, rousing on the instant. "He's taken the masts out of her."

He knew, as he groped for his shoes and slid them on, that that was not so: from the first crash, which had flung the ship over, there had come partial recovery, followed by an immediate second crash with a rain of gear down from aloft, the thunder of sail slatting loose, cries of men, yells and curses. "She's gone into a derelict," he muttered; "something's hit her."

He slung his coat on and was out of the alleyway and on deck within twenty-five seconds of the blow.

It was, as he noted, eighteen minutes to four.

On deck it was thick wild weather, with a blinding rain; dark as a pocket. Every sail in the ship seemed to be full of seven devils, and things were coming down from aloft right and left. Somewhere on the port side of the poop, sitting in the waterway, the helmsman was whimpering, "I was preak mine head: I was preak mine head." The ship had broached to, and he had probably been flung across the wheelbox.

All hands were to port, shouting into the night.

As he reached the port mizen-rigging, Cruiser saw a vast bulk of blackness loom out a few yards away. There were glimmers of light upon it, and shouts came from it, as it sheered and surged aft into the blinding of the rain. A reek of hot smoke with a smell of engines drove into his face.

"A big steamer," he said, "and she's been into us hard on our port side."

He yelled at the steamer with all his strength. "Stand by us. Stand by us. Don't desert us." But already the black bulk was gone into the storm.

As it was his maxim never to lose one instant of time in an emergency, he leaped down at once on to the main deck.

There, at the main bitts, among some confused and some frightened men, Frampton, the boatswain, already had the watch at work hauling and singing out at the main gear, now banging itself to tatters above them.

"Where did she hit us, Frampton?" he called.

"Just abaft the boudoir and forrard of the croquet ground," said Frampton, not recognizing him. "Lively now with them clue-garnets."

There was no need for Cruiser to go far to look. There in the waist, almost alongside him, the bulwarks were stove-in for a dozen feet, and the forebraces cut through. He knew at once that the ship had had a death-knock. He flung himself down and put his ear to the deck. There was no doubt there: death was pouring in, just below his ear, in a cataract that nothing could stop. A man running aft fell over him and rose up cursing. Cruiser gripped him and swung him round.

"Get to the starboard fo'c's'le," he said, "see that everyone is out. Then go to the round house. Call them up." The man said "Ay, ay, sir," and stumbled forward (he had hurt his knee in the fall), cursing and calling at once, "O, my knee. Rouse out, boys. O, my knee."

"Not so much bloody knee," Frampton called.

Cruiser ran back to the poop, where he found Captain Duntisbourne standing like a statue, looking down on the main deck from the rail.

"Sir," he said, "the ship is sinking. She can't last twenty minutes. Shall I get the boats out?"

The Captain did not answer: perhaps he was stunned by the shock, perhaps overcome by grief for the loss of a ship so dear to him.

"She's sinking, sir," Cruiser called. "Shall I get the boats out?"

The Captain roused suddenly and blew his whistle. "Still there, fore and aft," he shouted. "Mr. Frampton, Mr. Abbott, the port watch and the Idlers . . . clear away the long-boat. Lively now. Mr. Trewsbury and starboard watch; clear away the starboard boat."

"Ay, ay, sir."

"Handsomely now," Cruiser said. "Get the gear back into her. And answer to your names." All were present, except the man Bauer.

"Bauer," the men called, "Bauer."

"Has anybody seen Bauer?" Cruiser called. "Forward there, and see if he's still in the fo'c's'le; or up there, one of you, on to the deckhouse; once before he went there and never got called."

A man ran forward to the darkness of the deckhouse. "If Bauer can sleep through this," a man said, "he'll be able to snooze in hell."

In all this time, a blinding rain was driving, the gear was flogging and thundering, stunsails in long strips were streaming away to leeward, and pennants and bits of gear were crashing from aloft.

"Lord," Cruiser thought, "will no one show a light?"

He had expected to see a great flare rise from the steamer that had hit them. An old maxim surged up in his mind, 'You must do a thing yourself if you want it done.'

He sprang to the gear of the starboard boat in that space where he had stowed it the day before. Among the gear, there was, as he knew, a

265

tin of red lights. He found the tin, wrenched off the lid, took one of the lights and pulled the trigger of the igniter. With a sputter the light lit: at once a red glow wavered about the confusion.

"Take a light there," he called to a man. "Light it at the rail. Perhaps the steamer has lost us."

The second light made the scene lurid as a scene in hell, but no answering flare came from the steamer.

"Have you got Bauer there, yet?" he called

"Hier, sir," Bauer called, "hier, sir."

"What did you think was happening, Bauer, a lullaby?'

"I was asleep on der deckhaus, sir."

"You're awake now, are you?"

"Yes, sir."

"Well, nip into this boat and get the plug in; beat it well home.'

Bauer leaped into the boat and at once burst into curses, English and German.

"What's the matter with you, Bauer?"

"Der paint's all wet, sir."

"You'll be all wet, too, if you don't look alive." He leaned over the boat, holding one of the flares. "There's the plug, man: tomm it well home with the maul, there. Let's have a look at this boat's bread-locker."

"I tink Haussen filled her yesterday, sir."

"You think. Let's see. It isn't filled. You, boy, there, Chedglow; nippy now. Take one of these flares and get to the Captain's pantry. Get what food you can. And see that the steward is out of it. Is Coates there? Coates, you were always a champion at finding food. Go with Chedglow and find some now. Get the water-breaker in, now."

"Just as well, sir," an old seaman, James Fairford, said, "just as well, sir, that we got all this boat's gear overhauled yesterday."

"It would have been well if we'd finished the overhaul," he said. But the bread-locker's empty and the paint's all wet: still, the gear is over hauled."

Up there, on the skids, as he pitched the coil of a fall clear for running, he noticed for the first time that an ugly lop of sea had risen. Lowering a laden boat into such a sea would be ticklish work, as he knew too well Still there might be time to get an oil-bag to work before they lowered.

"Clutterbucke, there," he called to a steady man of his watch, "Clutterbucke."

"Sir."

"You and Nailsworth there, nip forward to the Bosun's locker. Get two of those big colza oil-cans and job two holes in their bottoms with a marler. Then sling one over each bow. You understand what I want? I want oil on the sea before we lower these boats."

"Get an oil-can over each bow, ay, ay, sir," the men repeated. They ran forward to do it.

"Up here, Edgeworth," Cruiser called, "give us a hand to swing her out. You others, starboard watch, aft with you quick and help pass food forward."

With heaving and crying out, they grappled the wet paint of the boat's side and swung her out all clear for lowering. It was a wild scene that they saw, of red and blue flares, men heaving and hauling, scared faces of men hurrying, the cries of men on the tackles, the seas rising up, gleaming in the flares and tossing by, while the wind screamed in the shrouds and the gear flogged. No more beastly time for abandoning ship could have been found by Fate.

"Stay by her, you," Cruiser said. "Don't let anyone get into her before they're ordered. She feels the oil already."

"Yes, sir, she does," Fairford said. "There's nothing like oil." Indeed already the lop of water about the ship was striking with a dead blow instead of savagely.

"We'll get the boats clear with luck," Cruiser said. "That oil is a godsend. Forward there, Edgeworth, and bring us a tin for the boat."

Cruiser swung himself down from the skids by a life-line. He had been up there, swinging out the boat for not more than three minutes. In that time a change had come in the feeling of the ship underfoot. He had said that it was the effect of the oil-bags forward, and had hoped to persuade his men thus, but he knew very well that the main and terrible change was not due to the oil, but to the rapid sinking of the ship.

He had often gone over in his mind some of the emergencies of his profession, with the thought 'What should I do, or what ought I to do, if . . .' He had thought out for himself plans for many emergencies; mast yards and sails going: ship broaching-to, ship brought aback, or caught by the lee in foul weather, the rudder carrying away: cables parting in a road: and collision in storm, fog, dock, port or at sea. He had thought of a smash such as this. Why, only a few nights before, in a middle watch in the Trades, he had thought of this very thing, of getting out the boats in a hurry. He had ever prided himself on having his boats clear for lowering: yet here he was caught in the middle watch with both boats topsy turvy from the painters.

Fresh water was the thing to take in a boat. The boat-breaker was full: where could he get an extra breaker? He ran to the scuttle-boat, usually kept within a permanent coaming on the port side of the deck, under the break of the poop. It was not now there. He remembered at once that it was among the booms by the main-hatch, being cleaned internally with hot ashes from the galley, before being scraped and painted. One of its hoops was to be renewed and its lid was to be repaired by the carpenter.

It should have been finished the day before, but with the light winds and the hands so often at the braces it had been put off till the morrow. Now the morrow had come. He found it lashed to the booms; its top gone, probably to the carpenter's shop, and a mess within it of ashes, sand, canvas, three-cornered scrapers, and ropeyarns. He cut the lashing and tipped the mess on to the deck.

"Here, you, starboard watch," he called. "Stratton, Efans, Jacobson."

"Sir," the voices answered, as the men appeared.

"Heave round on the fresh-water pump here at the bitts. Rinse this butt well out. Fill her, and get her into the starboard boat."

"Ay, ay, sir."

Jacobson at once caught hold of the pump-handle, as the others took hold of the butt. Cruiser could not wait there to see the work done; he remembered the fresh-water buckets always kept standing in a rack at the forward end of the poop. He ran up the ladder and swiftly put five of these into the after well of his boat: each contained about one gallon of rather seedy-looking rainwater: still, rainwater is drink, and drink in an open boat is life. He could think of no other handy tank or water receptacle. There was a small tank built into a locker in the round house, and another, much larger one, built into the fo'c's'le, but it would take half an hour to wrench out either of these. Still, he had filled the boat-breaker the day before; that was nine gallons; the five buckets made fourteen, the scuttle-butt would be another ten: twenty-four gallons. He heard the regular strokes of the fresh-water pump handle as Jacobson pumped, and the splash of the water. Looking across from his place on the skid he could see, in the glare of the flares, the carpenter at work on the port boat, apparently smashing something, perhaps the forward chock. Instantly, he thought of another thing that might be done: he dropped himself down and nipped across the deck to the carpenter.

The carpenter was a little old wizened man with a sad face, a drooping gray moustache, and blue eyes that lit up at a joke or a tale: he was said to have been in a big way once ashore, as the master of works in a cathedral, but that his wife had been a bad one. He was plainly just roused from sleep. He wore unbuttoned trowsers, belted about him, a pair of bluchers, and a coat belonging to one of the bosuns, much too big for his little body. A bag of tools was on the skid at his feet.

"Chips," Cruiser called, "is your shop unlocked? I want some tools for the boat."

Chips looked up gravely and sadly: "You'll want the key, Mr. Trewsbury," he said. Fumbling in his hip pocket he produced a key bright from much rubbing on a metal tobacco box. "You'd better leave it in the door, Mr. Trewsbury," he said. "I think I'll not use it again."

In the uncertain red light, Cruiser thought that there was something wrong with the long-boat's bows. "Anything wrong with her forward there?" he asked.

Chips looked at the deadwood and poked it with his maul. "No, it's nothing gone, sir. It's the mark where the chock came. She's tight," he said, "she's not like one of these liners' boats, all paint and putty."

"Cruiser took the key forward. On his way he looked into the round house, where a light was burning. The sailmaker was there, bent at a locker.

"Sails," he called: "Sails."

The sailmaker, an elderly, pale man, who had once been in the Navy, looked up from his task.

"Ah, Mr. Trewsbury," he said, "I was looking out some sailmaker's stores: a fetch-bag for each boat. I'll bring your bag along, and put it in the boat for you."

"Thank you, Sails. That'll come in very handy. Don't stay too long, Sails."

"I've nearly got the bags ready, sir."

Leaving the round house he went to the Carpenter's shop. He unlocked the door, and as he did so got a full shower of spray across his shoulders from a wave that she ducked to too soon. The gleam of the wave ran aft, lifting and dropping all the freeing ports in succession. Cruiser opened the door, hooked it back and lit a match. As he knew, there was a stub of candle in a sconce above the table. He lit this and looked for some tools. A tin bucket, full of shavings for the Cook, was chocked-off in a corner: he emptied this on to the floor and put into it such tools as he could see, a big heavy hammer, a firmer chisel much gone in the handle, a smaller chisel, a saw, and a couple of pounds' weight of two inch nails. As he turned to go, he noticed a wad of oakum on the deck: he took this. He then remembered that a brace and bits would be precious. He rummaged for them, but could not find. 'Chips must have them all on deck,' he thought. A minute later he saw them in clips on the bulkhead and took them, four assorted bits and a big twist-drill.

Once again he turned to go, when he remembered how lost he might be without a vice. There was a little snatch-block-vice nipped to a ledge in the bulkhead; he released the nip and took that. As he went aft with his load he felt under his feet the strange trembling in the deck in the way of the ship's wound, marking the rush of the torrent into her and the panting out of the air. It was unlike any movement that he had ever before felt.

On his way, quick as he was, he glanced into the round house, to make sure that Sails had gone. He found that he had gone after blowing out the light: the reek of the tallow still filled the place; a dwindling spark was still on the wick. After this Cruiser hurried to the boat and stowed the tools in her. As he swung in his bucket, Sails called to him from below:

"I've put the fetch bag forward, Mr. Trewsbury."

"Thank you, Sails."

"There's everything in it you can need, sir; but I hope you'll not need much."

"We're sure to need some, thank you, Sails. Good luck."

"Good luck, Mr. Trewsbury."

"Starboard watch, there," Cruiser called, "forward three of you and get some blankets into her. Yank them out of the bunks. Oilskins, too Lively with it."

James Fairford was at his elbow. "Mr. Trewsbury, sir," he said, "would we take a few of they rickers?"

"They rickers" were short lengths of light spar, usually the relics of snapped studding sail booms. Captain Duntisbourne always thriftily kept and generally found use for them. They were lashed to the spare spars on deck.

"Three of the light ones," Cruiser said. He stooped and cut the lashings: together they hove out three rickers and got them into the boat. "Get in a coil or so of royal and skysail brace," he said, "I must speak to the Captain."

He went across the poop.

Captain Duntisbourne was standing at the poop rail, burning blue lights for the men on the skids. There was something foul in the upper block of the long-boats's forward fall. A big man, known as Corny, was nipping the davits with his legs, and wrenching at the fall to clear the jam in the sheave. Cruiser noticed the size of the man's smiling toothless mouth: he was smiling, mumbling tobacco and swearing, all at once, while the Boatswain Frampton, at the boat's stern-sheets, lifted in gear handed to him from below.

"Starboard boat all clear for lowering, sir," Cruiser said.

"Very good, Mr. Trewsbury."

"Can I bear a hand here, sir, with my watch?"

"You'll need all your watch, I think, Mr. Trewsbury, to get the gear into your own boat, strewn all over the deck as it has been."

"Shall I take the chronometers, sir?"

"Will you kindly take yourself to hell out of this?"

"I still have hopes of the other place, sir; accompanying you."

The Captain uttered something between a snarl and a grunt, stamped out his now dying flare beneath his foot, and at once ignited another, still staring impassively at the long-boat's forward davit, where Corny still clutched and cursed. Cruiser stepped swiftly to the open companion, put in one hand, took the made-up Red Ensign, stepped to the rail, bent it, toggled it, ran it up to the peak and broke it out there. "We'll go down colours flying," he said. From the feel of the deck beneath him, he judged that that might be at any minute.

The Captain still stood there, his right hand lifted with the flare, his left still steady on the flare-box.

'He'll give no more orders,' Cruiser thought. 'I'll take the chronometers.'

He went into the chart-room, calling, as he entered, "Steward, Steward," and "Puss, Puss," for the two cabin passengers who might still be there. A light was burning in the saloon, which was otherwise deserted: the Steward's cabin was empty. The clock was still ticking at six minutes to four. All that eternity through which he had lived had lasted twelve minutes.

Someone (he supposed it would have been the two lads, Chedglow and Coates) had opened the hatch into the lazarette. It was still open, in the middle of the saloon. A candle was still burning there.

"Chedglow, Coates," he called. "Are you still there?" There was no answer: they had gone. As he looked down into the stores, he was shocked by the roaring wash of the water coming into the after hold. "She's not long for this world," he muttered. He took the chronometers, a North Atlantic chart and the ship's log: going rapidly to his cabin he took his sextant, Raper's Tables, some blank paper pads for working out sights and his box of dividers and protractors. Going out with these, heavily laden, he collided with the two lads, Coates and Chedglow, who were charging down the companion, singing.

He saved the instruments from a fall. "What are you up to?" he asked.

"We're getting food, sir, as you told us."

"On deck with you," he said, "the ship's sinking. Take this sextant, Coates: see you don't drop it. Did you see the cat anywhere?"

"Yes, sir: I caught her once, sir, but she got away on deck."

'We'll probably want the cat for fresh meat before many days are past.' But this thought he kept to himself.

Cruiser swung into the boat and handed in the instruments. There were several boxes there which shewed him that the boys had foraged well. When the chronometers had been stowed, he clambered out. "Coates and Chedglow," he said, "you've been up and down in boats a hundred times. Get in here and tend the life-lines and see no one unhooks the forward fall. These are red lights. Each of you burn one till further orders. Starboard watch. Is the starboard watch all present, Fairford?"

"All present, Mr. Trewsbury."

He saw that the water-breaker was in its place, and shook it, and thanked God that he had filled it the day before.

He went back to the Captain on the poop. "Starboard watch all present, sir. May we bear a hand with the long-boat, sir?"

The Captain slowly turned and surveyed him, without answering, then leaning forward, still holding aloft the flare, he called, "Swing out, there, Mr. Frampton. Get your boat over and your men into her."

The jam, or whatever it had been in the sheaves of the fall, was now gone. Cruiser saw Corny clearing kinks out of the fall, so as to be all clear for lowering. It occurred to Cruiser that in the last five minutes he had heard Corny call seven different things a bastard; the davit, the purchase-block, the sheave, the fall, the gunwale of the boat which had knocked his shin, the belaying-pin welded on the davit which had barked it and now the kinks in the fall, against which he kicked with his naked foot, saying "Ye dam white Manila bastard." The nose of the boat swung out: there seemed to be some hitch in the getting out of the stern; a momentary hitch. Anxious faces shewed in the glare; Cruiser noticed the steward, an old, white-faced man, staring with haggard eyes and mumbling. Cruiser spoke again to the Captain.

"If you don't want the starboard watch, sir, am I to shove off?"

The Captain looked at him, there was a kind of pleasure in his eye; he did not answer. Instead of answering, he took a step away from Cruiser and called "Mr. Frampton, you will leave that boat if you please, and take charge of the starboard boat, and push off in her."

From the after davit of the long-boat there came an unexpected answer from the much-tried Mr. Frampton. "You can shove the starboard boat down your Sunday pants, Captain Duntisbourne. My place is in this port rattle trap, and I'm going in her if I sail to Hull or hell. . . ."

Some men tittered at this; they started to titter before Mr. Frampton had finished what he had to say. But before he could finish, the ship gave a motion of shaking that was plainly a death throe before her plunge. The men at the starboard boat-falls, without waiting for any order, lowered away handsomely: the men about the port skids swarmed up and got into their boat. Captain Duntisbourne turned and walked aft, still holding aloft the flare.

"Captain Duntisbourne," Cruiser said, following him, "will you not get into your boat, sir?"

"Do you command this ship, Mr. Trewsbury?"

"Certainly not, sir."

"Let me at least thank God for that," the Captain said, "my holy topsail, yes."

At this, there were cries from the starboard boat now in the water, of "Mr. Trewsbury, Mr. Trewsbury." Coates, holding a red flare was on the skids calling, "Mr. Trewsbury."

"I'd better get to my boat, sir," he said. "Good luck, sir." He knew that without him, the boat would have no navigator. He walked quickly across the poop and leaped up to the rail. As he did so, the lad Coates slithered down the forward fall. Cruiser caught the life-line and lowered himself down into a boat that was leaping up and dropping away in wild water. The two lads tended the tackles and held their red flares aloft: two men with boat hooks were fending her off and having hard work to do it.

"Get out your oars, there forward," Cruiser called, as he shipped the tiller. "Cast off the after hook, boy. For the Lord's sake, boy, mind how you do it. You'll brain someone. Down port oars and shove her off: back a stroke starboard oars. Cast off, forward, Coates. Mind your heads with the hook there."

The hooks were flung clear as the boat rose up, and in an instant the boat was tossed away, in a spatter of spray. "Back together," Cruiser said, standing in the stern-sheets. He looked at his watch: it was now one minute to four. As the boat rose on the next wave, his head came to the level of the bullseyes of what had been his cabin. He noticed them as dim rounds of light from his still burning candle: he thought that not twenty minutes before he had been asleep in his bunk there.

"Back her clear of the stern," he said. "Back. Back. But easy all. Oars a moment."

They were now dropped astern of the sinking ship. As they rested on their oars, Cruiser put by the tiller, and lit another red flare. Up above them, only a few fathoms away, was the ellipse of the ship's stern, with the black gauntlet carved in high relief over the words

Blackgauntlet.

London.

Ever First.

"She's down by the head already," James Fairford said.

"She's going to dive," Cruiser said. "Give way together. What's wrong with the long-boat?"

The boat's head swung round to port: they pulled under the stern, and saw the run of white water streaking red from the flares. The long-boat, in the light, full of men, was still at the davits.

"My God," Cruiser said, "why don't they lower?"

It may have been that he saw more than they did, as a looker-on will; it may have been that the fall had jammed in the forward sheave again; or that Captain Duntisbourne had had some fancy of his own. Cruiser shouted with all his strength, "Lower away the long-boat falls there."

Even as he shouted, the after end of the long-boat dropped a little, and a man slid down a lifeline into her. On the same instant the ship bowed suddenly forward, as in a big 'scend: a spray lifted high along her rail as she dipped to it. She lifted her bows a few feet, dipped them again in what seemed slow time: and then with horrible speed flung herself over on the lowering boat. The red flares quenched. The men in the starboard boat saw the fabric of the spars lean swiftly and more swiftly with a rattle and splash of falling and flying gear. They heard the masts and yards flog the water as they struck it. As they smote their smack upon the sea, the ship, now sunk, righted a little and plucked them partly upright again, and then went down like a stone, sending up into the night, as she went, a gurgling moan unlike any noise they had ever heard.

⚓

THE FIRST WHALE
and
THE PEQUOD MEETS THE ROSE-BUD

⚓

THE FIRST WHALE
and
THE PEQUOD MEETS THE ROSE-BUD
Herman Melville

⚓ *The publication of this collection of sea stories would be justified if it did no more than republish the two following excerpts. The first is a complete description of a lowering for a whale from the calm preceding the cry of "There she blows!" to the final return to the ship. The second selection is an interlude of salty humor relieving the tension which runs through eight hundred pages of great dramatic writing.*

If you once abandon yourself to the spell of "Moby Dick" you are a lost soul. You will return to it again and again like a ghost to a haunted ship.

Never was there before or has there been since such an Olympic, metaphysical, prophetical, Mosaic and altogether fantastic and satisfying outpouring. And under its ferment of images, its gusto for words, runs a rugged tale of the sea that is without parallel.

I T WAS a cloudy, sultry afternoon; the seamen were lazily lounging about the decks, or vacantly gazing over into the lead-colored waters. Queequeg and I were mildly employed weaving what is called a sword-mat, for an additional lashing to our boat. So still and subdued and yet somehow preluding was all the scene, and such an incantation of revery lurked in the air, that each silent sailor seemed resolved into his own invisible self.

From *Moby Dick* by Herman Melville.

I was the attendant or page of Queequeg, while busy at the mat. As I kept passing and repassing the filling or woof of marline between the long yarns of the warp, using my own hand for the shuttle, and as Queequeg, standing sideways, ever and anon slid his heavy oaken sword between the threads, and idly looking off upon the water, carelessly and unthinkingly drove home every yarn: I say so strange a dreaminess did there then reign all over the ship and all over the sea, only broken by the intermitting dull sound of the sword, that it seemed as if this were the Loom of Time, and I myself were a shuttle mechanically weaving and weaving away at the Fates. There lay the fixed threads of the warp subject to but one single, ever returning, unchanging vibration, and that vibration merely enough to admit of the crosswise interblending of other threads with its own. This warp seemed necessity; and here, thought I, with my own hand I ply my own shuttle and weave my own destiny into these unalterable threads. Meantime, Queequeg's impulsive, indifferent sword, sometimes hitting the woof slantingly, or crookedly, or strongly, or weakly, as the case might be; and by this difference in the concluding blow producing a corresponding contrast in the final aspect of the completed fabric; this savage's sword, thought I, which thus finally shapes and fashions both warp and woof; this easy, indifferent sword must be chance—aye, chance, free will, and necessity—no wise incompatible—all interweavingly working together. The straight warp of necessity, not to be swerved from its ultimate course—its every alternating vibration, indeed, only tending to that; free will still free to ply her shuttle between given threads; and chance, though restrained in its play within the right lines of necessity, and sideways in its motions directed by free will, though thus prescribed to by both, chance by turns rules either, and has the last featuring blow at events.

Thus we were weaving and weaving away when I started at a sound so strange, long drawn, and musically wild and unearthly, that the ball of free will dropped from my hand, and I stood gazing up at the clouds whence that voice dropped like a wing. High aloft in the cross-trees was that mad Gay-Header, Tashtego. His body was reaching eagerly forward, his hand stretched out like a wand, and at brief sudden intervals he continued his cries. To be sure the same sound was that very moment perhaps being heard all over the seas, from hundreds of whalemen's look-outs perched as high in the air; but from few of those lungs could that accustomed old cry have derived such a marvellous cadence as from Tashtego the Indian's.

As he stood hovering over you half suspended in air, so wildly and eagerly peering towards the horizon, you would have thought him some prophet or seer beholding the shadows of Fate, and by those wild cries announcing their coming.

"There she blows! there! there! there! she blows! she blows!"

"Where-away?"

"On the lee-beam, about two miles off! a school of them!"

Instantly all was commotion

The Sperm Whale blows as a clock ticks, with the same undeviating and reliable uniformity. And thereby whalemen distinguish this fish from other tribes of his genus.

"There go flukes!" was now the cry from Tashtego; and the whales disappeared.

"Quick, steward!" cried Ahab. "Time! time!"

Dough-Boy hurried below, glanced at the watch, and reported the exact minute to Ahab.

The ship was now kept away from the wind, and she went gently rolling before it. Tashtego reporting that the whales had gone down heading to leeward, we confidently looked to see them again directly in advance of our bows. For that singular craft at times evinced by the Sperm Whale when, sounding with his head in one direction, he nevertheless, while concealed beneath the surface, mills round, and swiftly swims off in the opposite quarter—this deceitfulness of his could not now be in action; for there was no reason to suppose that the fish seen by Tashtego had been in any way alarmed, or indeed knew at all of our vicinity. One of the men selected for shipkeepers—that is, those not appointed to the boats, by this time relieved the Indian at the main-mast head. The sailors at the fore and mizzen had come down; the line tubs were fixed in their places; the cranes were thrust out; the mainyard was backed, and the three boats swung over the sea like three samphire baskets over high cliffs. Outside of the bulwarks their eager crews with one hand clung to the rail, while one foot was expectantly poised on the gunwale. So look the long line of man-of-war's men about to throw themselves on board an enemy's ship.

But at this critical instant a sudden exclamation was heard that took every eye from the whale. With a start all glared at dark Ahab, who was surrounded by five dusky phantoms that seemed fresh formed out of air.

The phantoms, for so they then seemed, were flitting on the other side of the deck, and, with a noiseless celerity, were casting loose the tackles and bands of the boat which swung there. This boat had always been deemed one of the spare boats, though technically called the captain's, on account of its hanging from the starboard quarter. The figure that now stood by its bows was tall and swart, with one white tooth evilly protruding from its steel-like lips. A rumpled Chinese jacket of black cotton funereally invested him, with wide black trowsers of the same dark stuff. But strangely crowning this ebonness was a glistening white plaited turban, the living hair braided and coiled round and round upon his head. Less swart in aspect, the companions of this figure were of that vivid, tiger-yellow complexion peculiar to some of the aboriginal natives of the Manillas;—a race notorious for a certain diabolism of subtility, and by some honest white mariners supposed to be the paid spies and secret confidential agents on the water of the devil, their lord, whose counting-room they suppose to be elsewhere.

While yet the wondering ship's company were gazing upon these strangers, Ahab cried out to the white-turbaned old man at their head, "All ready there, Fedallah?"

"Ready," was the half-hissed reply.

"Lower away then; d'ye hear?" shouting across the deck. "Lower away there, I say."

Such was the thunder of his voice, that spite of their amazement the men sprang over the rail; the sheaves whirled round in the blocks; with a wallow, the three boats dropped into the sea; while, with a dexterous, off-handed daring, unknown in any other vocation, the sailors, goat-like leaped down the rolling ship's side into the tossed boats below.

Hardly had they pulled out from under the ship's lee, when a fourth keel, coming from the windward side, pulled round under the stern, and showed the five strangers rowing Ahab, who, standing erect in the stern, loudly hailed Starbuck, Stubb, and Flask, to spread themselves widely, so as to cover a large expanse of water. But with all their eyes again riveted upon the swart Fedallah and his crew, the inmates of the other boats obeyed not the command.

"Captain Ahab?—" said Starbuck.

"Spread yourselves," cried Ahab; "give way, all four boats. Thou, Flask, pull out more to leeward!"

"Aye, aye, sir," cheerily cried little King-Post, sweeping round his great steering oar. "Lay back!" addressing his crew. "There!—there!—there again! There she blows right ahead, boys!—lay back!"

"Never heed yonder yellow boys, Archy."

"Oh, I don't mind 'em, sir," said Archy; "I knew it all before now. Didn't I hear 'em in the hold? And didn't I tell Cabaco here of it? What say ye, Cabaco? They are stowaways, Mr. Flask."

"Pull, pull, my fine hearts-alive; pull, my children; pull, my little ones," drawlingly and soothingly sighed Stubb to his crew, some of whom still showed signs of uneasiness. "Why don't you break your backbones, my boys? What is it you stare at? Those chaps in yonder boat? Tut! They are only five more hands come to help us—never mind from where—the more the merrier. Pull, then, do pull; never mind the brimstone—devils are good fellows enough. So, so; there you are now; that's the stroke for a thousand pounds; that's the stroke to sweep the stakes! Hurrah for the gold cup of sperm oil, my heroes! Three cheers, men—all hearts alive! Easy, easy; don't be in a hurry—don't be in a hurry. Why don't you snap your oars, you rascals? Bite something, you dogs! So, so, so, then;—softly, softly! That's it—that's it! long and strong. Give way there, give way! The devil fetch ye, ye ragamuffin rapscallions; ye are all asleep. Stop snoring, ye sleepers, and pull. Pull, will ye? pull, can't ye? pull, won't ye? Why in the name of gudgeons and ginger-cakes don't ye pull?—pull and break something! pull, and start your eyes out! Here!" whipping out the sharp knife from his girdle; "every mother's son of ye draw his knife, and pull with the blade between his teeth. That's it—that's it. Now ye do something; that looks like it, my steel-bits. Start her—start her, my silver-spoons! Start her, marling-spikes!"

Stubb's exordium to his crew is given here at large, because he had rather a peculiar way of talking to them in general, and especially in inculcating the religion of rowing. But you must not suppose from this specimen of his sermonizings that he ever flew into downright passions with his congregation. Not at all; and therein consisted his chief peculiarity. He would say the most terrific things to his crew, in a tone so strangely compounded of fun and fury, and the fury seemed so calculated merely as a spice to the fun, that no oarsman could hear such queer invocations without pulling for dear life, and yet pulling for the mere joke of the thing. Besides he all the time looked so easy and indolent himself, so loungingly managed his steering-oar, and so broadly gaped—open-mouthed at times— that the mere sight of such a yawning commander, by sheer force of contrast, acted like a charm upon the crew. Then again, Stubb was one of those odd sort of humorists, whose jollity is sometimes so curiously ambiguous, as to put all inferiors on their guard in the matter of obeying them.

In obedience to a sign from Ahab, Starbuck was now pulling obliquely across Stubb's bow; and when for a minute or so the two boats were pretty near to each other, Stubb hailed the mate.

"Mr. Starbuck! larboard boat there, ahoy! a word with ye, sir, if ye please!"

"Halloa!" returned Starbuck, turning round not a single inch as he spoke; still earnestly but whisperingly urging his crew; his face set like a flint from Stubb's.

"What think ye of those yellow boys, sir!"

"Smuggled on board, somehow, before the ship sailed. (Strong, strong, boys!") in a whisper to his crew, then speaking out loud again: "A sad business, Mr. Stubb! (seethe her, seethe her, my lads!) but never mind, Mr. Stubb, all for the best. Let all your crew pull strong, come what will. (Spring, my men, spring!) There's hogsheads of sperm ahead, Mr. Stubb, and that's what ye came for. (Pull, my boys!) Sperm, sperm's the play! This at least is duty; duty and profit hand in hand!"

"Aye, aye, I thought as much," soliloquized Stubb, when the boats diverged, "as soon as I clapt eye on 'em, I thought so. Aye, and that's what he went into the after hold for, so often, as Dough-Boy long suspected. They were hidden down there. The White Whale's at the bottom of it. Well, well, so be it! Can't be helped! All right! Give way, men! It ain't the White Whale today! Give way!"

Now the advent of these outlandish strangers at such a critical instant as the lowering of the boats from the deck, this had not unreasonably awakened a sort of superstitious amazement in some of the ship's company; but Archy's fancied discovery having some time previous got abroad among them, though indeed not credited then, this had in some small measure prepared them for the event. It took off the extreme edge of their wonder; and so what with all this and Stubb's confident way of accounting for their appearance, they were for the time freed from superstitious sur-misings; though the affair still left abundant room for all manner of wild conjectures as to dark Ahab's precise agency in the matter from the beginning. For me, I silently recalled the mysterious shadows I had seen creeping on board the Pequod during the dim Nantucket dawn, as well as the enigmatical hintings of the unaccountable Elijah.

Meantime, Ahab, out of hearing of his officers, having sided the furthest to windward, was still ranging ahead of the other boats; a circumstance bespeaking how potent a crew was pulling him. Those tiger-yellow crea-tures of his seemed all steel and whalebone; like five trip-hammers they rose and fell with regular strokes of strength, which periodically started the boat along the water like a horizontal burst boiler out of a Mississippi steamer. As for Fedallah, who was seen pulling the harpooneer oar, he had thrown aside his black jacket, and displayed his naked chest with the whole part of his body above the gunwale, clearly cut against the alternating depressions of the watery horizon; while at the other end of the boat Ahab, with one arm, like a fencer's, thrown half backward into the air, as if to counterbalance any tendency to trip; Ahab was seen steadily managing his steering oar as in a thousand boat lowerings ere the White Whale had torn him. All at once the outstretched arm gave a peculiar motion and then remained fixed, while the boat's five oars were seen simultaneously peaked. Boat and crew sat motionless on the sea. In-stantly the three spread boats in the rear paused on their way. The whales had irregularly settled bodily down into the blue, thus giving no distantly discernible token of the movement, though from his closer vicinity Ahab had observed it.

"Every man look out along his oars!" cried Starbuck. "Thou, Queequeg, stand up!"

Nimbly springing up on the triangular raised box in the bow, the savage stood erect there, and with intensely eager eyes gazed off towards the spot where the chase had last been descried. Likewise upon the extreme stern of the boat where it was also triangularly platformed level with the gunwale, Starbuck himself was seen coolly and adroitly balancing himself to the jerking tossings of his chip of a craft, and silently eyeing the vast blue eye of the sea.

Not very far distant Flask's boat was also lying breathlessly still; its commander recklessly standing upon the top of the loggerhead, a stout sort of post rooted in the keel, and rising some two feet above the level of the stern platform. It is used for catching turns with the whale line. Its top is not more spacious than the palm of a man's hand, and standing upon such a base as that, Flask seemed perched at the mast-head of some ship which had sunk to all but her trucks. But little King-Post was small and short, and at the same time little King-Post was full of a large and tall ambition, so that this loggerhead stand-point of his did by no means satisfy King-Post.

"I can't see three seas off; tip us up an oar there, and let me on to that."

Upon this, Daggoo, with either hand upon the gunwale to steady his way, swiftly slid aft, and then erecting himself volunteered his lofty shoulders for a pedestal.

"Good a mast-head as any, sir. Will you mount?"

"That I will, and thank ye very much, my fine fellow; only I wish you fifty feet taller."

Whereupon planting his feet firmly against two opposite planks of the boat, the gigantic negro, stooping a little, presented his flat palm to Flask's foot, and then putting Flask's hand on his hearse-plumed head and bidding him spring as he himself should toss, with one dexterous fling landed the little man high and dry on his shoulders. And here was Flask now standing, Daggoo with one lifted arm furnishing him with a breastband to lean against and steady himself by.

At any time it is a strange sight to the tyro to see with what wondrous habitude of unconscious skill the whaleman will maintain an erect posture in his boat, even when pitched about by the most riotously perverse and cross-running seas. Still more strange to see him giddily perched upon the loggerhead itself, under such circumstances. But the sight of little Flask mounted upon gigantic Daggoo was yet more curious; for sustaining himself with a cool, indifferent, easy, unthought of, barbaric majesty, the noble negro to every roll of the sea harmoniously rolled his fine form. On his broad back, flaxen-haired Flask seemed a snow-flake. The bearer looked nobler than the rider. Though truly vivacious, tumultuous, ostentatious little Flask would now and then stamp with impatience; but not one added heave did he thereby give to the negro's lordly chest. So have I seen Passion and Vanity stamping the living magnanimous earth, but the earth did not alter her tides and the seasons for that.

Meanwhile Stubb, the third mate, betrayed no such far-gazing solicitudes. The whales might have made one of their regular soundings, not a temporary dive from mere fright; and if that were the case, Stubb, as his wont in such cases, it seems, was resolved to solace the languishing interval with his pipe. He withdrew it from his hatband, where he always wore it aslant like a feather. He loaded it, and rammed home the loading with his thumb-end; but hardly had he ignited his match across the rough sandpaper of his hand, when Tashtego, his harpooneer, whose eyes had been setting to windward like two fixed stars, suddenly dropped like light from his erect attitude to his seat, crying out in a quick phrensy of hurry, "Down, down all, and give way—there they are!"

To a landsman, no whale, nor any sign of a herring, would have been visible at that moment; nothing but a troubled bit of greenish white water, and thin scattered puffs of vapor hovering over it, and suffusingly blowing off to leeward, like the confused scud from white rolling billows. The air around suddenly vibrated and tingled, as it were, like the air over intensely heated plates of iron. Beneath this atmospheric waving and curling, and partially beneath a thin layer of water, also, the whales were swimming. Seen in advance of all the other indications, the puffs of vapor they spouted, seemed their forerunning couriers and detached flying outriders.

All four boats were now in keen pursuit of that one spot of troubled water and air. But it bade far to outstrip them; it flew on and on, as a mass of interblending bubbles borne down a rapid stream from the hills.

"Pull, pull, my good boys," said Starbuck, in the lowest possible but intensest concentrated whisper to his men; while the sharp fixed glance from his eyes darted straight ahead of the bow, almost seemed as two visible needles in two unerring binnacle compasses. He did not say much to his crew, though, nor did his crew say anything to him. Only the silence of the boat was at intervals startlingly pierced by one of his peculiar whispers, now harsh with command, now soft with entreaty.

How different the loud little King-Post. "Sing out and say something, my hearties. Roar and pull, my thunderbolts! Beach me, beach me on their black backs, boys; only do that for me, and I'll sign over to you my Martha's Vineyard plantation, boys; including wife and children, boys. Lay me on—lay me on! O Lord, Lord! but I shall go stark, staring mad:

See! see that white water!" And so shouting, he pulled his hat from his head, and stamped up and down on it; then picking it up, flirted it far off upon the sea; and finally fell to rearing and plunging in the boat's stern like a crazed colt from the prairie.

"Look at that chap now," philosophically drawled Stubb, who, with his unlighted short pipe, mechanically retained between his teeth, at a short distance, followed after—"He's got fits, that Flask has. Fits? yes, give him fits—that's the very word—pitch fits into 'em. Merrily, merrily, hearts-alive. Pudding for supper, you know;—merry's the word. Pull, babes—pull, sucklings—pull, all. But what the devil are you hurrying about? Softly, softly, and steadily, my men. Only pull, and keep pulling; nothing more. Crack all your backbones, and bite your knives in two—that's all. Take it easy—why don't ye take it easy, I say, and burst all your livers and lungs!"

But what it was that inscrutable Ahab said to that tiger-yellow crew of his—these were words best omitted here; for you live under the blessed light of the evangelical land. Only the infidel sharks in the audacious seas may give ear to such words, when, with tornado brow, and eyes of red murder, and foam-glued lips, Ahab leaped after his prey.

Meanwhile, all the boats tore on. The repeated specific allusions of Flask to "that whale," as he called the fictitious monster which he declared to be incessantly tantalizing his boat's bow with its tail—these allusions of his were at times so vivid and lifelike that they would cause some one or two of his men to snatch a fearful look over the shoulder. But this was against all rule; for the oarsmen must put out their eyes, and ram a skewer through their necks; usage pronouncing that they must have no organs but ears, and no limbs but arms, in these critical moments.

It was a sight full of quick wonder and awe! The vast swells of the omnipotent sea; the surging, hollow roar they made, as they rolled along the eight gunwales, like gigantic bowls in a boundless bowling-green; the brief suspended agony of the boat, as it would tip for an instant on the knife-like edge of the sharper waves, that almost seemed threatening to cut it in two; the sudden profound dip into the watery glens and hollows; the keen spurrings and goadings to gain the top of the opposite hill; the headlong, sled-like slide down its other side;—all these, with the first cries of the headsmen and harpooneers, and the shuddering gasps of the oarsmen, with the wondrous sight of the ivory *Pequod* bearing down upon her boats with outstretched sails, like a wild hen after her screaming brood;— all this was thrilling. Not the raw recruit, marching from the bosom of his wife into the fever heat of his first battle; not the dead man's ghost encountering the first unknown phantom in the other world;—neither of these can feel stranger and stronger emotions than that man does, who for the first time finds himself pulling into the charmed, churned circle of the hunted Sperm Whale.

The dancing white water made by the chase was now becoming more and more visible, owing to the increasing darkness of the dun cloud-shadows flung upon the sea. The jets of vapor no longer blended, but tilted everywhere to right and left; the whales seemed separating their wakes. The boats were pulled more apart; Starbuck giving chase to three whales running dead to leeward. Our sail was now set, and, with the still rising wind, we rushed along; the boat going with such madness through the water, that the lee oars could scarcely be worked rapidly enough to escape being torn from the row-locks.

Soon we were running through a suffusing wide veil of mist; neither ship nor boat to be seen.

"Give way, men," whispered Starbuck, drawing still further aft the sheet of his sail; "there is time to kill a fish yet before the squall comes. There's white water again!—close to! Spring!"

Soon after, two cries in quick succession on each side of us denoted that the other boats had got fast; but hardly were they overheard, when with a lightning-like hurtling whisper Starbuck said: "Stand up!" and Queequeg, harpoon in hand, sprang to his feet.

Though not one of the oarsmen was then facing the life and death peril so close to them ahead, yet with their eyes on the intense countenance of the mate in the stern of the boat, they knew that the imminent instant had come; they heard, too, an enormous wallowing sound as of fifty elephants stirring in their litter. Meanwhile the boat was still booming through the mist, the waves curling and hissing around us like the erected crests of enraged serpents.

"That's his hump. *There, there,* give it to him!" whispered Starbuck.

A short rushing sound leaped out of the boat; it was the darted iron of Queequeg. Then all in one welded commotion came an invisible push from astern, while forward the boat seemed striking on a ledge; the sail collapsed and exploded; a gush of scalding vapor shot up near by; something rolled and tumbled like an earthquake beneath us. The whole crew were half suffocated as they were tossed helter-skelter into the white curdling cream of the squall. Squall, whale, and harpoon had all blended together; and the whale, merely grazed by the iron, escaped.

Though completely swamped, the boat was nearly unharmed. Swimming round it we picked up the floating oars, and lashing them across the gunwale, tumbled back to our places. There we sat up to our knees in the sea, the water covering every rib and plank, so that to our downward gazing eyes the suspended craft seemed a coral boat grown up to us from the bottom of the ocean.

The wind increased to a howl; the waves dashed their bucklers together; the whole squall roared, forked, and crackled around us like a white fire upon the prairie, in which, unconsumed, we were burning; immortal in these jaws of death! In vain we hailed the other boats; as well roar to the live coals down the chimney of a flaming furnace as hail those boats in that storm. Meanwhile the driving scud, rack, and mist, grew darker with the shadows of night; no sign of the ship could be seen. The rising sea forbade all attempts to bale out the boat. The oars were useless as propellers, performing now the office of life-preservers. So, cutting the lashing of the waterproof match keg, after many failures Starbuck contrived to ignite the lamp in the lantern; then stretching it on a waif pole, handed it to Queequeg as the standard-bearer of this forlorn hope. There, then, he sat, holding up that imbecile candle in the heart of that almighty forlornness. There, then, he sat, the sign and symbol of a man without faith, hopelessly holding up hope in the midst of despair.

Wet, drenched through, and shivering cold, despairing of ship or boat, we lifted up our eyes as the dawn came on. The mist still spread over the sea, the empty lantern lay crushed in the bottom of the boat. Suddenly Queequeg started to his feet, hollowing his hand to his ear. We all heard a faint creaking, as of ropes and yards hitherto muffled by the storm. The sound came nearer and nearer; the thick mists were dimly parted by a huge, vague form. Affrighted, we all sprang into the sea as the ship at last loomed into view, bearing right down upon us within a distance of not much more than its length.

Floating on the waves we saw the abandoned boat, as for one instant it tossed and gaped beneath the ship's bows like a chip at the base of a cataract; and then the vast hull rolled over it, and it was seen no more till it came up weltering astern. Again we swam for it, were dashed against it by the seas, and were at last taken up and safely landed on board. Ere the squall came close to, the other boats had cut loose from their fish and returned to the ship in good time. The ship had given us up, but was still cruising, if haply it might light upon some token of our perishing,—an oar or a lance pole.

⚓   ⚓   ⚓

THE PEQUOD MEETS THE ROSE-BUD

"In vain it was to rake for Ambergriese in the paunch of this Leviathan, insufferable fetor denying not inquiry." *Sir T. Browne, V.E.*

IT WAS a week or two after the last whaling scene recounted, and when we were slowly sailing over a sleepy, vapory, mid-day sea, that the many noses on the *Pequod's* deck proved more vigilant discoverers than the three pairs of eyes aloft. A peculiar and not very pleasant smell was smelt in the sea.

"I will bet something now," said Stubb, "that somewhere hereabouts are some of those drugged whales we tickled the other day. I thought they would keel up before long."

Presently, the vapors in advance slid aside; and there in the distance lay a ship, whose furled sails betokened that some sort of whale must be alongside. As we glided nearer, the stranger showed French colors from his peak; and by the eddying 'cloud of vulture sea-fowl that circled, and hovered, and swooped around him, it was plain that the whale alongside must be what the fishermen called a blasted whale, that is, a whale that has died unmolested on the sea, and so floated an unappropriated corpse. It may well be conceived, what an unsavory odor such a mass must exhale; worse than an Assyrian city in the plague, when the living are incompetent to bury the departed. So intolerable indeed is it regarded by some, that no cupidity could persuade them to moor alongside of it. Yet are there those who will still do it; notwithstanding the fact that the oil obtained from such subjects is of a very inferior quality, and by no means of the nature of attar-of-rose.

Coming still nearer with the expiring breeze, we saw that the Frenchman had a second whale alongside; and this second whale seemed even more of a nosegay than the first. In truth, it turned out to be one of those problematical whales that seem to dry up and die with a sort of prodigious

288

dyspepsia, or indigestion; leaving their defunct bodies almost entirely bankrupt of anything like oil. Nevertheless, in the proper place we shall see that no knowing fisherman will ever turn up his nose at such a whale as this, however much he may shun blasted whales in general.

The *Pequod* had now swept so nigh to the stranger, that Stubb vowed he recognised his cutting spade-pole entangled in the lines that were knotted round the tail of one of these whales.

"There's a pretty fellow, now," he banteringly laughed, standing in the ship's bows, "there's a jackal for ye! I well know that these Crappoes of Frenchmen are but poor devils in the fishery; sometimes lowering their boats for breakers, mistaking them for Sperm Whale spouts; yes, and sometimes sailing from their port with their hold full of boxes of tallow candles, and cases of snuffers, foreseeing that all the oil they will get won't be enough to dip the Captain's wick into; aye, we all know these things; but look ye, here's a Crappo that is content with our leavings, the drugged whale there, I mean; aye, and is content too with scraping the dry bones of that other precious fish he has there. Poor devil! I say, pass round a hat, someone, and let's make him a present of a little oil for dear charity's sake. For what oil he'll get from that drugged whale there, wouldn't be fit to burn in a jail; no, not in a condemned cell. And as for the other whale, why, I'll agree to get more oil by chopping up and trying out these three masts of ours, than he'll get from that bundle of bones; though, now that I think of it, it may contain something worth a good deal more than oil; yes, ambergris. I wonder now if our old man has thought of that. It's worth trying. Yes, I'm in for it"; and so saying he started for the quarter-deck.

By this time the faint air had become a complete calm; so that whether or no, the *Pequod* was now fairly entrapped in the smell, with no hope of escaping except by its breezing up again. Issuing from the cabin, Stubb now called his boat's crew, and pulled off for the stranger. Drawing across her bow, he perceived that in accordance with the fanciful French taste, the upper part of her stem-piece was carved in the likeness of a huge drooping stalk, was painted green, and for thorns had copper spikes projecting from it here and there; the whole terminating in a symmetrical folded bulb of a bright red color. Upon her head boards, in large gilt letters, he read *"Bouton-de-Rose,"*—Rose-button, or Rose-bud; and this was the romantic name of this aromatic ship.

Though Stubb did not understand the *Bouton* part of the inscription, yet the word *rose,* and the bulbous figure-head put together, sufficiently explained the whole to him.

"A wooden rose-bud, eh?" he cried with his hand to his nose, "that will do very well; but how like all creation it smells!"

Now in order to hold direct communication with the people on deck, he had to pull round the bows to the starboard side, and thus come close to the blasted whale; and so talk over it.

Arrived then at this spot, with one hand still to his nose, he bawled—"*Bouton-de-Rose,* ahoy! are there any of you Bouton-de-Roses that speak English?"

"Yes," rejoined a Guernsey-man from the bulwarks, who turned out to be the chief-mate.

"Well, then, my Bouton-de-Rose-bud, have you seen the White Whale?"

"*What* whale?"

"The *White* Whale—a Sperm Whale—Moby Dick, have ye seen him?"

"Never heard of such a whale. Cachalot Blanche! White Whale—no."

"Very good, then; good bye now, and I'll call again in a minute."

Then rapidly pulling back towards the *Pequod,* and seeing Ahab leaning over the quarter-deck rail awaiting his report, he moulded his two hands into a trumpet and shouted—"No, Sir! No!" Upon which Ahab retired, and Stubb returned to the Frenchman.

He now perceived that the Guernsey-man, who had just got into the chains, and was using a cutting-spade, had slung his nose in a sort of bag.

"What's the matter with your nose, there?" said Stubb. "Broke it?"

"I wish it was broken, or that I didn't have any nose at all!" answered the Guernsey-man, who did not seem to relish the job he was at very much. "But what are you holding *yours* for?"

"Oh, nothing! It's a wax nose; I have to hold it on. Fine day, aint it? Air rather gardenny, I should say; throw us a bunch of posies, will ye, *Bouton-de-Rose?*"

"What in the devil's name do you want here?" roared the Guernsey-man, flying into a sudden passion.

"Oh! keep cool—cool? yes, that's the word; why don't you pack those whales in ice while you're working at 'em? But joking aside, though; do you know, Rose-bud, that it's all nonsense trying to get any oil out of such whales? As for that dried up one, there, he hasn't a gill in his whole carcase."

"I know that well enough; but, d'ye see, the captain here won't believe it; this is his first voyage; he was a Cologne manufacturer before. But come aboard, and mayhap he'll believe you, if he won't me; and so I'll get out of this dirty scrape."

"Anything to oblige ye, my sweet and pleasant fellow," rejoined Stubb, and with that he soon mounted to the deck. There a queer scene presented itself. The sailors, in tasselled caps of red worsted, were getting the heavy tackles in readiness for the whales. But they worked rather slow and talked very fast, and seemed in anything but a good humor. All their noses upwardly projected from their faces like so many jib-booms. Now and then pairs of them would drop their work, and run up to the mast-head to get some fresh air. Some thinking they would catch the plague, dipped oakum in coal-tar, and at intervals held it to their nostrils. Others having broken the stems of their pipes almost short off at the bowl, were vigorously puffing tobacco-smoke, so that it constantly filled their olfactories.

Stubb was struck by a shower of outcries and anathemas proceeding from the captain's round-house abaft; and looking in that direction saw a fiery face thrust from behind the door, which was held ajar from within. This was the tormented surgeon, who, after in vain remonstrating against the proceedings of the day, had betaken himself to the captain's round-house (*cabinet* he called it) to avoid the pest; but still, could not help yelling out his entreaties and indignations at times.

Marking all this, Stubb argued well for his scheme, and turning to the Guernsey-man had a little chat with him, during which the stranger mate expressed his detestation of his captain as a conceited ignoramus, who had brought them all into so unsavory and unprofitable a pickle. Sounding him carefully, Stubb further perceived that the Guernsey-man had not the slightest suspicion concerning the ambergris. He therefore held his peace on that head, but otherwise was quite frank and confidential with him, so that the two quickly concocted a little plan for both circumventing and satirizing the captain, without his at all dreaming of distrusting their sincerity. According to this little plan of theirs, the Guernsey-man, under cover of an interpreter's office, was to tell the captain what he pleased, but as coming from Stubb; and as for Stubb, he was to utter any nonsense that should come uppermost in him during the interview.

By this time their destined victim appeared from his cabin. He was a small and dark, but rather delicate looking man for a sea-captain, with large whiskers and moustache, however; and wore a red cotton velvet vest with watch-seals at his side. To this gentleman, Stubb was now politely introduced by the Guernsey-man, who at once ostentatiously put on the aspect of interpreting between them.

"What shall I say to him first?" said he.

"Why," said Stubb, eyeing the velvet vest and the watch and seals, "you may as well begin by telling him that he looks a sort of babyish to me, though I don't pretend to be a judge."

"He says, Monsieur," said the Guernsey-man, in French, turning to his captain, "that only yesterday his ship spoke a vessel, whose captain and chief-mate, with six sailors, had all died of a fever caught from a blasted whale they had brought alongside."

Upon this the captain started, and eagerly desired to know more.

"What now?" said the Guernsey-man to Stubb.

"Why, since he takes it so easy, tell him that now I have eyed him care-fully, I'm quite certain that he's no more fit to command a whale-ship than a St. Jago monkey. In fact, tell him from me he's a baboon."

"He vows and declares, Monsieur, that the other whale, the dried one, is far more deadly than the blasted one; in fine, Monsieur, he conjures us, as we value our lives, to cut loose from these fish."

Instantly the captain ran forward, and in a loud voice commanded his crew to desist from hoisting the cutting-tackles, and at once cast loose the cable and chains confining the whales to the ship.

"What now?" said the Guernsey-man, when the captain had returned to them.

"Why, let me see; yes, you may as well tell him now that—that—in fact, tell him I've diddled him, and (aside to himself) perhaps somebody else."

"He says, Monsieur, that he's very happy to have been of any service to us."

Hearing this, the captain vowed that they were the grateful parties (mean-ing himself and mate) and concluded by inviting Stubb down into his cabin to drink a bottle of Bordeaux.

"He wants you to take a glass of wine with him," said the interpreter.

"Thank him heartily; but tell him it's against my principles to drink with the man I've diddled. In fact, tell him I must go."

"He says, Monsieur, that his principles won't admit of his drinking; but that if Monsieur wants to live another day to drink, then Monsieur had best drop all four boats, and pull the ship away from these whales, for it's so calm they won't drift."

By this time Stubb was over the side, and getting into his boat, hailed the Guernsey-man to this effect,—that having a long towline in his boat, he would do what he could to help them, by pulling out the lighter whale of the two from the ship's side. While the Frenchman's boats, then, were engaged in towing the ship one way, Stubb benevolently towed away at his whale the other way, ostentatiously slacking out a most unusually long tow-line.

Presently a breeze sprang up; Stubb feigned to cast off from the whale; hoisting his boats, the Frenchman soon increased his distance, while the *Pequod* slid in between him and Stubb's whale. Whereupon Stubb quickly pulled to the floating body, and hailing the *Pequod* to give notice of his intentions, at once proceeded to reap the fruit of his unrighteous cunning. Seizing his sharp boat-spade, he commenced an excavation in the body, a little behind the side fin. You would almost have thought he was digging a cellar there in the sea; and when at length his spade struck against the gaunt ribs, it was like turning up old Roman tiles and pottery buried in fat English loam. His boat's crew were all in high excitement, eagerly helping their chief and looking as anxious as gold-hunters.

And all the time numberless fowls were diving, and ducking, and screaming, and yelling, and fighting around them. Stubb was beginning to look disappointed, especially as the horrible nosegay increased, when suddenly from out the very heart of this plague, there stole a faint stream of perfume, which flowed through the tide of bad smells without being absorbed by it, as one river will flow into and then along with another, without at all blending with it for a time.

"I have it, I have it," cried Stubb, with delight, striking something in the subterranean regions, "a purse! a purse!"

Dropping his spade, he thrust both hands in, and drew out handfuls of something that looked like ripe Windsor soap, or rich mottled old cheese; very unctuous and savory withal. You might easily dent it with your thumb; it is of a hue between yellow and ash color. And this, good friends, is ambergris, worth a gold guinea an ounce to any druggist. Some six handfuls were obtained; but more was unavoidably lost in the sea, and still more, perhaps, might have been secured were it not for impatient Ahab's loud command to Stubb to desist, and come on board, else the ship would bid them good bye.

⚓

THE GALE

⚓

THE GALE

Joseph Conrad

⚓ *Whenever we see, or hear, or read a genuine work of art we may be sure that the artist's concept of his relation to his art outstrips the single manifestation we are enjoying. We are fortunate, therefore, in Conrad's preface to "The Nigger of the Narcissus" to have his own attempt to put this creed into words. He says in part, "All art, therefore, appeals primarily to the senses, and the artistic aim when expressing itself in written words must also make its appeal through the senses, if its high desire is to reach the secret spring of responsive emotions. It must strenuously aspire to the plasticity of sculpture, to the colour of painting, and to the magic suggestiveness of music—which is the art of arts. And it is only through complete, unswerving devotion to the perfect blending of form and substance; it is only through an unremitting never-discouraged care for the shape and ring of sentences that an approach can be made to plasticity, to colour, and that the light of magic suggestiveness may be brought to play for an evanescent instant over the commonplace surface of words: of the old, old words, worn thin, defaced by ages of careless usage."*

And of "The Nigger of the Narcissus," the third Chapter of which follows, Conrad says, "It is the book by which, not as a novelist, perhaps, but as an artist striving for the utmost sincerity of expression, I am willing to stand or fall."

MEANTIME the *Narcissus*, with square yards, ran out of the fair monsoon. She drifted slowly, swinging round and round the compass, through a few days of baffling light airs. Under the patter of short warm showers, grumbling men whirled the heavy yards from side to side;

they caught hold of the soaked ropes with groans and sighs, while their officers, sulky and dripping with rain water, unceasingly ordered them about in wearied voices. During the short respites they looked with disgust into the smarting palms of their stiff hands, and asked one another bitterly: "Who would be a sailor if he could be a farmer?" All the tempers were spoilt, and no man cared what he said. One black night, when the watch, panting in the heat and half-drowned with the rain, had been through four mortal hours hunted from brace to brace, Belfast declared that he would "chuck going to sea forever and go in a steamer." This was excessive, no doubt. Captain Allistoun, with great self-control, would mutter sadly to Mr. Baker: "It is not so bad—not so bad," when he had managed to shove, and dodge, and maneuver his smart ship through sixty miles in twenty-four hours. From the doorstep of the little cabin, Jimmy, chin in hand, watched our distasteful labors with insolent and melancholy eyes. We spoke to him gently—and out of his sight exchanged sour smiles.

Then, again, with a fair wind and under a clear sky, the ship went on piling up the South Latitude. She passed outside Madagascar and Mauritius without a glimpse of the land. Extra lashings were put on the spare spars. Hatches were looked to. The steward in his leisure moments and with a worried air tried to fit washboards to the cabin doors. Stout canvas was bent with care. Anxious eyes looked to the westward, towards the cape of storms. The ship began to dip into a southwest swell, and the softly luminous sky of low latitudes took on a harder sheen from day to day above our heads: it arched high above the ship, vibrating and pale, like an immense dome of steel, resonant with the deep voice of freshening gales. The sunshine gleamed cold on the white curls of black waves. Before the strong breath of westerly squalls the ship, with reduced sail, lay slowly over, obstinate and yielding. She drove to and fro in the unceasing endeavor to fight her way through the invisible violence of the winds; she pitched headlong into dark smooth hollows; she struggled upwards over the snowy ridges of great running seas; she rolled, restless, from side to side, like a thing in pain. Enduring and valiant, she answered to the call of men; and her slim spars waving forever in abrupt semicircles, seemed to beckon in vain for help towards the stormy sky.

It was a bad winter off the Cape that year. The relieved helmsmen came off flapping their arms, or ran stamping hard and blowing into swollen, red fingers. The watch on deck dodged the sting of cold sprays or, crouching in sheltered corners, watched dismally the high and merciless seas boarding the ship time after time in unappeasable fury. Water tumbled in cataracts over the forecastle doors. You had to dash through a waterfall to get into your damp bed. The men turned in wet and turned out stiff to face the redeeming and ruthless exactions of their glorious and obscure fate. Far aft, and peering watchfully to windward, the officers could be seen through the mist of squalls. They stood by the weather rail, holding on grimly, straight and glistening in their long coats; then, at times, in the disordered plunges of the hard-driven ship, they appeared high up, attentive, tossing violently above the gray line of a clouded horizon, and in motionless attitudes.

They watched the weather and the ship as men on shore watch the momentous chances of fortune. Captain Allistoun never left the deck, as though he had been part of the ship's fittings. Now and then the steward, shivering, but always in shirtsleeves, would struggle towards him with some hot coffee, half of which the gale blew out of the cup before it reached the master's lips. He drank what was left gravely in one long gulp, while heavy sprays pattered loudly on his oilskin coat, the seas swishing broke about his high boots; and he never took his eyes off the ship. He watched her every motion; he kept his gaze riveted upon her as a loving man who watches the unselfish toil of a delicate woman upon the slender thread of whose existence is hung the whole meaning and joy of the world. We all watched her. She was beautiful and had a weakness. We loved her no less for that. We admired her qualities aloud, we boasted of them to one another, as though they had been our own, and the consciousness of her only fault we kept buried in the silence of our profound affection. She was born in the thundering peal of hammers beating upon iron, in black eddies of smoke, under a gray sky, on the banks of the Clyde. The clamorous and somber stream gives birth to things of beauty that float away into the sunshine of the world to be loved by men. The *Narcissus* was one of that perfect brood. Less perfect than many perhaps, but she was ours, and, consequently, incomparable. We were proud of her. In Bombay, ignorant landlubbers alluded to her as that "pretty gray ship." Pretty! A scurvy meed of commendation! We knew she was the most magnificent sea boat ever launched. We tried to forget that, like many good sea boats, she was at times rather crank. She was exacting. She wanted care in loading and handling, and no one knew exactly how much care would be enough. Such are the imperfections of mere men! The ship knew, and sometimes would correct the presumptuous human ignorance by the wholesome discipline of fear. We had heard ominous stories about past voyages. The cook (technically a seaman, but in reality no sailor)—the cook, when unstrung by some misfortune, such as the rolling over of a saucepan, would mutter gloomily while he wiped the floor: "There! Look at what she has done! Some voy'ge she will drown all hands! You'll see if she won't." To which the steward, snatching in the galley a moment to draw breath in the hurry of his worried life, would remark philosophically: "Those that see won't tell, anyhow. I don't want to see it." We derided those fears. Our hearts went out to the old man when he pressed her hard so as to make her hold her own, hold to every inch gained to windward; when he made her, under reefed sails, leap obliquely at enormous waves. The men, knitted together aft into a ready group by the first sharp order of an officer coming to take charge of the deck in bad weather: "Keep handy the watch," stood admiring her valiance. Their eyes blinked in the wind; their dark faces were wet with drops of water more salt and bitter than human tears; beards and mustaches, soaked, hung straight and dripping like fine seaweed. They were fantastically misshapen; in high boots, in hats like helmets, and swaying clumsily, stiff and bulky in glistening oilskins, they resembled men strangely equipped for some fabulous adventure. Whenever she rose easily to a towering green sea, elbows dug ribs, faces brightened, lips murmured: "Didn't she do it cleverly," and all the heads turning like one watched with sardonic grins the foiled wave go roaring to leeward, white with the foam of a monstrous rage. But when she had not been quick enough and, struck heavily, lay over trembling under the blow, we clutched at ropes, and looking up at the narrow bands of drenched and strained sails waving desperately aloft, we thought in our hearts: "No wonder. Poor thing!"

The thirty-second day out of Bombay began inauspiciously. In the morning a sea smashed one of the galley doors. We dashed in through lots of steam and found the cook very wet and indignant with the ship: She's getting worse every day. She's trying to drown me in front of my own stove!" He was very angry. We pacified him, and the carpenter, though washed away twice from there, managed to repair the door. Through that accident our dinner was not ready till late, but it didn't matter in the end because Knowles, who went to fetch it, got knocked down by a sea and the dinner went over the side. Captain Allistoun, looking more hard and thin-lipped than ever, hung on to full topsails and foresail, and would not notice that the ship, asked to do too much, appeared to lose heart altogether for the first time since we knew her. She refused to rise, and bored her way sullenly through the seas. Twice running, as though she had been blind or weary of life, she put her nose deliberately into a big wave and swept the decks from end to end. As the boatswain observed with marked annoyance, while we were splashing about in a body to try and save a worthless washtub: "Every blooming thing in the ship is going overboard this afternoon." Venerable Singleton broke his habitual silence and said with a glance aloft: "The old man's in a temper with the weather, but it's no good bein' angry with the winds of heaven." Jimmy had shut his door, of course. We knew he was dry and comfortable within his little cabin, and in our absurd way were pleased one moment, exasperated the next, by that certitude. Donkin skulked shamelessly, uneasy and miserable. He grumbled: "I'm perishin' with cold houtside in bloomin' wet rags, an' that 'ere black sojer sits dry on a blamed chest full of bloomin' clothes; blank his black soul!" We took no notice of him; we hardly gave a thought to Jimmy and his bosom friend. There was no leisure for idle probing of hearts. Sails blew adrift. Things broke loose. Cold and wet, we were washed about the deck while trying to repair damages. The ship tossed about, shaken furiously, like a toy in the hand of a lunatic. Just at sunset there was a rush to shorten sail before the menace of a somber hail cloud. The hard gust of wind came brutal like the blow of a fist. The ship relieved of her canvas in time received it pluckily: she yielded reluctantly to the violent onset; then, coming up with a stately and irresistible motion, brought her spars to windward in the teeth of the screeching squall. Out of the abysmal darkness of the black cloud overhead white hail streamed on her, rattled on the rigging, leaped in handfuls off the yards, rebounded on the deck—round and gleaming in the murky turmoil like a shower of pearls. It passed away. For a moment a livid sun shot horizontally the last rays of sinister light between the hills of steep, rolling waves. Then a wild night rushed in—stamped out in a great howl that dismal remnant of a stormy day.

There was no sleep on board that night. Most seamen remember in their life one or two such nights of a culminating gale. Nothing seems left of the whole universe but darkness, clamor, fury—and the ship. And like the last vestage of a shattered creation she drifts, bearing an anguished remnant of sinful mankind, through the distress, tumult, and pain of an avenging terror. No one slept in the forecastle. The tin oil lamp suspended on a long string, smoking, described wide circles; wet clothing made dark heaps on the glistening floor; a thin layer of water rushed to and fro. In the bed-places men lay booted, resting on elbows and with open eyes. Hung-up suits of oilskin swung out and in, lively and disquieting like reckless ghosts of decapitated seamen dancing in a tempest. No one spoke and all listened. Outside the night moaned and sobbed to the accompaniment of a continuous loud tremor as of innumerable drums beating far off. Shrieks passed through the air. Tremendous dull blows made the ship tremble while she rolled under the weight of the seas toppling on her deck. At times she soared up swiftly as if to leave this earth forever, then during interminable moments fell through a void with all the hearts on board of her standing still, till a frightful shock, expected and sudden, started them off again with a big thump. After every dislocating jerk of the ship, Wamibo, stretched full length, his face on the pillow, groaned slightly with the pain of his tormented universe. Now and then, for the fraction of an intolerable second, the ship, in the fiercer burst of a terrible uproar, remained on her side, vibrating and still, with a stillness more appalling than the wildest motion. Then upon all those prone bodies a stir would pass, a shiver of suspense. A man would protrude his anxious head and a pair of eyes glistened in the sway of light glaring wildly. Some moved their legs a little as if making ready to jump out. But several, motionless on their backs and with one hand gripping hard the edge of the bunk, smoked nervously with quick puffs, staring upwards; immobilized in a great craving for peace.

At midnight, orders were given to furl the fore and mizzen topsails. With immense efforts men crawled aloft through a merciless buffeting, saved the canvas, and crawled down almost exhausted, to bear in panting silence the cruel battering of the seas. Perhaps for the first time in the history of the merchant service the watch, told to go below, did not leave the deck, as if compelled to remain there by the fascination of a venomous violence. At every heavy gust men, huddled together, whispered to one another: "It can blow no harder," and presently the gale would give them the lie with a piercing shriek, and drive their breath back into their throats. A fierce squall seemed to burst asunder the thick mass of sooty vapors; and above the wrack of torn clouds glimpses could be caught of the high moon rushing backwards with frightful speed over the sky, right into the wind's eye. Many hung their heads, muttering that it "turned their inwards out" to look at it. Soon the clouds closed up, and the world again became a raging, blind darkness that howled, flinging at the lonely ship salt sprays and sleet.

About half-past seven the pitchy obscurity round us turned a ghastly gray, and we knew that the sun had risen. This unnatural and threatening daylight, in which we could see one another's wild eyes and drawn faces, was only an added tax on our endurance. The horizon seemed to have come on all sides within arm's length of the ship. Into that narrowed circle furious seas leaped in, struck, and leaped out. A rain of salt, heavy drops flew aslant like mist. The main-topsail had to be goosewinged, and with stolid resignation everyone prepared to go aloft once more; but the officers yelled, pushed back, and at last we understood that no more men would be allowed to go on the yard than were absolutely necessary for the work. As at any moment the masts were likely to be jumped out or blown overboard, we concluded that the captain didn't want to see all his crowd go over the side at once. That was reasonable. The watch then on duty, led by Mr Creighton, began to struggle up the rigging. The wind flattened them against the ratlines; then, easing a little, would let them ascend a couple of steps; and again, with a sudden gust, pin all up the shrouds the whole crawling line in attitudes of crucifixion. The other watch plunged down on the main deck to haul up the sail. Men's heads bobbed up as the water flung them irresistibly from side to side. Mr. Baker grunted encouragingly in our midst, spluttering and blowing amongst the tangled rope like an energetic porpoise. Favored by an ominous and untrustworthy lull, the work was done without anyone being lost either off the deck or from the yard. For the moment the gale seemed to take off, and the ship, as if grateful for our efforts, plucked up heart and made better weather of it.

At eight the men off duty, watching their chance, ran forward over the flooded deck to get some rest. The other half of the crew remained aft for their turn of "seeing her through her trouble," as they expressed it. The two mates urged the master to go below. Mr. Baker grunted in his ear: "Ough! surely now . . . Ough! . . . confidence in us . . . nothing more to do . . . she must lay it out or go. Ough! Ough!" Tall young Mr. Creighton smiled down at him cheerfully: ". . . She's right as a trivet! Take a spell, sir." He looked at them stonily with bloodshot, sleepless eyes. The rims of his eyelids were scarlet, and he moved his jaw unceasingly with a slow effort, as though he had been masticating a lump of indiarubber. He shook his head. He repeated: "Never mind me. I must see it out—I must see it out," but he consented to sit down for a moment on the skylight, with his hard face turned unflinchingly to windward. The sea spat at it—and, stoical, it streamed with water as though he had been weeping. On the weather side of the poop the watch, hanging on to the mizzen rigging and to one another, tried to exchange encouraging words. Singleton, at the wheel, yelled out: "Look out for yourselves!" His voice reached them in a warning whisper. They were startled.

A big, foaming sea came out of the mist; it made for the ship, roaring wildly, and in its rush it looked as mischievous and discomposing as a madman with an axe. One or two, shouting, scrambled up the rigging; most, with a convulsive catch of the breath, held on where they stood. Singleton dug his knees under the wheel box, and carefully eased the helm to the headlong pitch of the ship, but without taking his eyes off the coming wave. It towered close-to and high, like a wall of green glass topped with snow. The ship rose to it as though she had soared on wings, and for a moment rested poised upon the foaming crest as if she had been a great sea bird. Before we could draw breath a heavy gust struck her, another roller took her unfairly under the weather bow, she gave a toppling lurch, and filled her decks. Captain Allistoun leaped up, and fell; Archie rolled over him, screaming: "She will rise!" She gave another lurch to leeward; the lower deadeyes dipped heavily; the men's feet flew from under them, and they hung kicking above the slanting poop. They could see the ship putting her side in the water, and shouted all together: "She's going!" Forward the forecastle doors flew open, and the watch below were seen leaping out one after another, throwing their arms up; and, falling on hands and knees, scrambled aft on all fours along the high side of the deck, sloping more than the roof of a house. From leeward the seas rose, pursuing them; they looked wretched in a hopeless struggle, like vermin fleeing before a flood; they fought up the weather ladder of the poop one after another, half naked and staring wildly; and as soon as they got up they shot to leeward in clusters, with closed eyes, till they brought up heavily with their ribs against the iron stanchions of the rail; then, groaning, they rolled in a confused mass. The immense volume of water thrown forward by the last scend of the ship had burst the lee door of the forecastle. They could see their chests, pillows, blankets, clothing, come out floating upon the sea. While they struggled back to windward they looked in dismay. The straw beds swam high, the blankets, spread out, undulated; while the chests, waterlogged and with a heavy list, pitched heavily, like dismasted hulks, before they sank; Archie's big coat passed with outspread arms, resembling a drowned seaman floating with his head under water. Men were slipping down while trying to dig their fingers into the planks; others, jammed in corners, rolled enormous eyes. They all yelled unceasingly: "The masts! Cut! Cut! . . ." A black squall howled low over the ship, that lay on her side with the weather yardarms pointing to the clouds; while the tall masts, inclined nearly to the horizon, seemed to be of an unmeasurable length. The carpenter let go his hold, rolled against the skylight, and began to crawl to the cabin entrance, where a big axe was kept ready for just such an emergency. At that moment the topsail sheet parted, the end of the heavy chain racketed aloft, and sparks of red fire streamed down through the flying sprays. The sail flapped once with a jerk that seemed to tear our hearts out through our teeth, and instantly changed into a bunch of fluttering narrow ribbons that tied themselves into knots and became quiet along the yard. Captain Allistoun struggled, managed to stand up with his face near the deck, upon which men swung on the ends of ropes, like nest robbers upon a cliff. One of his feet was on somebody's chest; his face was purple; his lips moved. He yelled also; he yelled, bending down: "No! No!" Mr. Baker, one leg over the binnacle-stand, roared out: "Did you say no? Not cut?" He shook his head madly. "No! No!" Between his legs the crawling carpenter heard, collapsed at once, and lay full length in the angle of the skylight. Voices took up the shout—"No! No!" Then all became still. They waited for the ship to turn over altogether, and shake them out into the sea; and upon the terrific noise of wind and sea not a murmur of remonstrance came out from those men, who each would have given ever so many years of life to see "them damned sticks go overboard!" They all believed it their only chance; but a little hard-faced man shook his gray head and shouted "No!" without giving them as much as a glance. They were silent, and gasped. They gripped rails, they had wound ropes'-ends under their arms; they clutched ringbolts, they crawled in heaps where there was foothold; they held on with both arms, hooked themselves to anything to windward with elbows, with chins, almost with their teeth; and some, unable to crawl away from where they had been flung, felt the sea leap up, striking against their backs as they struggled upwards. Singleton had stuck to the wheel. His hair flew out in the wind; the gale seemed to take its life-long adversary by the beard and shake his old head. He wouldn't let go, and, with his knees forced between the spokes, flew up and down like a man on a bough. As Death appeared unready, they began to look about. Donkin, caught by one foot in a loop of some rope, hung, head down, below us, and yelled, with his face to the deck: "Cut! Cut!" Two men lowered themselves cautiously to him; others hauled on the rope. They caught him up, shoved him into a safer place, held him. He shouted curses at the master, shook his fist at him with horrible blasphemies, called upon us in filthy words to "Cut! Don't mind that murdering fool! Cut, some of you!" One of his rescuers struck him a backhanded blow over the mouth; his head banged on the deck, and he became suddenly very quiet, with a white face, breathing hard, and with a few drops of blood trickling from his cut lip. On the lee side another man could be seen stretched out as if stunned; only the washboard prevented him from going over the side. It was the steward. We had to sling him up like a bale, for he was paralyzed with fright. He had rushed up out of the pantry when he felt the ship go over, and had rolled down helplessly, clutching a china mug. It was not broken. With difficulty we tore it from him, and when he saw it in our hands he was amazed. "Where did you get that thing?" he kept on asking, in a trembling voice. His shirt was blown to shreds; the ripped sleeves flapped like wings. Two men made him fast, and, doubled over the rope that held him, he resembled a bundle of wet rags. Mr. Baker crawled along the line of men, asking: "Are you all there?" and looking them over. Some blinked vacantly, others shook convulsively; Wamibo's head hung over his breast; and in painful attitudes, cut by lashings, exhausted with clutching, screwed up in corners, they breathed heavily. Their lips twitched, and at every sickening heave of the overturned ship they opened them wide as if to shout. The cook, embracing a wooden stanchion, unconsciously repeated a prayer. In every short interval of the fiendish noises around he could be heard there, without cap or slippers, imploring in that storm the Master of our lives not to lead him into temptation. Soon he also became silent. In all that crowd of cold and hungry men, waiting wearily for a violent death, not a voice was heard; they were mute, and in somber thoughtfulness listened to the horrible imprecations of the gale.

Hours passed. They were sheltered by the heavy inclination of the ship from the wind that rushed in one long unbroken moan above their heads, but cold rain showers fell at times into the uneasy calm of their refuge.

Under the torment of that new infliction a pair of shoulders would writhe a little. Teeth chattered. The sky was clearing, and bright sunshine gleamed over the ship. After every burst of battering seas, vivid and fleeting rainbows arched over the drifting hull in the flick of sprays. The gale was ending in a clear blow, which gleamed and cut like a knife. Between two bearded shellbacks Charley, fastened with somebody's long muffler to a deck ring-bolt, wept quietly, with rare tears wrung out by bewilderment, cold, hunger, and general misery. One of his neighbors punched him in the ribs, asking roughly: "What's the matter with your cheek? In fine weather there's no holding you, youngster." Turning about with prudence he worked himself out of his coat and threw it over the boy. The other man closed up, muttering: "'Twill make a bloomin' man of you, sonny." They flung their arms over and pressed against him. Charley drew his feet up and his eyelids dropped. Sighs were heard, as men, perceiving that they were not to be "drowned in a hurry," tried easier positions. Mr. Creighton, who had hurt his leg, lay amongst us with compressed lips. Some fellows belonging to his watch set about securing him better. Without a word or a glance he lifted his arms one after another to facilitate the operation, and not a muscle moved in his stern, young face. They asked him with solicitude: "Easier now, sir?" He answered with a curt: "That'll do." He was a hard young officer, but many of his watch used to say they liked him well enough because he had "such a gentlemanly way of damning us up and down the deck." Others, unable to discern such fine shades of refinement, respected him for his smartness. For the first time since the ship had gone on her beam ends Captain Allistoun gave a short glance down at his men. He was almost upright—one foot against the side of the skylight, one knee on the deck; and with the end of the vang round his waist swung back and forth with his gaze fixed ahead, watchful, like a man looking out for a sign. Before his eyes the ship, with half her deck below water, rose and fell on heavy seas that rushed from under her flashing in the cold sunshine. We began to think she was wonderfully buoyant—considering. Confident voices were heard shouting: "She'll do, boys!" Belfast exclaimed with fervor: "I would giv' a month's pay for a draw at a pipe!" One or two, passing dry tongues on their salt lips, muttered something about a "drink of water." The cook, as if inspired, scrambled up with his breast against the poop water cask and looked in. There was a little at the bottom. He yelled, waving his arms, and two men began to crawl backwards and forwards with the mug. We had a good mouthful all round. The master shook his head impatiently, refusing. When it came to Charley one of his neighbors shouted: "That bloomin' boy's asleep." He slept as though he had been dosed with narcotics. They let him be. Singleton held to the wheel with one hand while he drank, bending down to shelter his lips from the wind. Wamibo had to be poked and yelled at before he saw the mug held before his eyes. Knowles said sagaciously: "It's better'n a tot o' rum." Mr. Baker grunted: "Thank ye." Mr. Creighton drank and nodded. Donkin gulped greedily, glaring over the rim. Belfast made us laugh when with grimacing mouth he shouted: "Pass it this way. We're all taytottlers here." The master, presented with the mug again by a crouching man, who screamed up at him: "We all had a drink, captain," groped for it without ceasing to look ahead, and handed it back stiffly as though he could not spare half a glance away from the ship. Faces brightened. We shouted to the cook: "Well done, doctor!" He sat to leeward, propped by the water cask and yelled back abundantly, but the seas were breaking in thunder just then, and we only caught snatches that sounded like: "Providence" and "born again." He was at his old game of preaching. We made friendly but derisive gestures at him and from below he lifted one arm, holding on with the other, moved his lips; he beamed up to us, straining his voice—earnest, and ducking his head before the sprays.

Suddenly someone cried: "Where's Jimmy?" and we were appalled once more. On the end of the row the boatswain shouted hoarsely: "Has anyone seed him come out?" Voices exclaimed dismally: "Drowned—is he? . . . No! In his cabin! . . . Good Lord! . . . Caught like a bloomin' rat in a trap. . . . Couldn't open his door . . . Aye! She went over too quick and the water jammed it. . . . Poor beggar! . . . No help for 'im. . . . Let's go and see . . ." "Damn him, who could go?" screamed Donkin. "Nobody expects you to," growled the man next to him; "you're only a thing." "Is there half a chance to get at 'im?" inquired two or three men together. Belfast untied himself with blind impetuosity, and all at once shot down to leeward quicker than a flash of lightning. We shouted all together with dismay; but with his legs overboard he held and yelled for a rope. In our extremity nothing could be terrible; so we judged him funny kicking there, and with his scared face. Someone began to laugh, and, as if hysterically infected with screaming merriment, all those haggard men went off laughing, wild-eyed, like a lot of maniacs tied up on a wall. Mr. Baker swung off the binnacle-stand and tendered him one leg. He scrambled up rather scared, and consigning us with abominable words to the "divvle." "You are . . . Ough! You're a foul-mouthed beggar, Craik," grunted Mr. Baker. He answered, stuttering with indignation: "Look at 'em, sorr. The bloomin' dirty images! Laughing at a chum going overboard. Call themselves men, too." But from the break of the poop the boatswain called out: "Come along," and Belfast crawled away in a hurry to join him. The five men, poised and gazing over the edge of the poop, looked for the best way to get forward. They seemed to hesitate. The others, twisting in their lashings, turned painfully, stared with open lips. Captain Allistoun saw nothing; he seemed with his eyes to hold the ship up in a superhuman concentration of effort. The wind screamed loud in sunshine; columns of spray rose straight up; and in the glitter of rainbows bursting over the trembling hull the men went over cautiously, disappearing from sight with deliberate movements.

They went swinging from belaying pin to cleat above the seas that beat the half-submerged deck. Their toes scraped the planks. Lumps of green cold water toppled over the bulwark and on their heads. They hung for a moment on strained arms, with the breath knocked out of them, and with closed eyes—then, letting go with one hand, balanced with lolling heads, trying to grab some rope or stanchion further forward. The long-armed and athletic boatswain swung quickly, gripping things with a fist hard as iron, and remembering suddenly snatches of the last letter from his "old woman." Little Belfast scrambled rageously, muttering "cursed nigger." Wamibo's tongue hung out with excitement; and Archie, intrepid and calm, watched his chance to move with intelligent coolness.

When above the side of the house, they let go one after another, and falling heavily, sprawled, pressing their palms to the smooth teakwood. Round them the backwash of waves seethed white and hissing. All the doors had become trap doors of course. The first was the galley door. The galley extended from side to side, and they could hear the sea splashing with hollow noises in there. The next door was that of the carpenter's shop. They lifted it, and looked down. The room seemed to have been devastated by an earthquake. Everything in it had tumbled on the bulkhead facing the door, and on the other side of that bulkhead there was Jimmy, dead or alive. The bench, a half-finished meat-safe, saws, chisels, wire rods, axes, crowbars lay in a heap besprinkled with loose nails. A sharp adz stuck up with a shining edge that gleamed dangerously down there like a wicked smile. The men clung to one another peering. A sickening, sly lurch of the ship nearly sent them overboard in a body. Belfast howled "Here goes!" and leaped down. Archie followed cannily, catching at shelves that gave way with him, and eased himself in a great crash of ripped wood. There was hardly room for three men to move. And in the sunshiny blue square of the door, the boatswain's face, bearded and dark, Wamibo's face, wild and pale, hung over—watching.

Together they shouted: "Jimmy! Jim!" From above the boatswain contributed a deep growl: "You. . . . Wait!" In a pause, Belfast entreated: Jimmy, darlin', are ye aloive?" The boatswain said: "Again! All together, boys!" All yelled exictedly. Wamibo made noises resembling loud barks. Belfast drummed on the side of the bulkhead with a piece of iron. All ceased suddenly. The sound of screaming and hammering went on thin and distinct—like a solo after a chorus. He was alive. He was screaming and knocking below us with the hurry of a man prematurely shut up in a coffin. We went to work. We attacked with desperation the abominable heap of things heavy, of things sharp, of things clumsy to handle. The boatswain crawled away to find somewhere a flying end of a rope; and Wamibo, held back by shouts: "Don't jump! . . . Don't come in here, muddlehead!"—remained glaring above us—all shining eyes, gleaming fangs, tumbled hair; resembling an amazed and half-witted fiend gloating over the extraordinary agitation of the damned. The boatswain adjured us to "bear a hand," and a rope descended. We made things fast to it and they went up spinning, never to be seen by man again. A rage to fling things overboard possessed us. We worked fiercely, cutting our hands, and speaking brutally to one another. Jimmy kept up a distracting row; he screamed piercingly, without drawing breath, like a tortured woman; he banged with hands and feet. The agony of his fear wrung our hearts so terribly that we longed to abandon him, to get out of that place deep as a well and swaying like a tree, to get out of his hearing, back on the poop where we could wait passively for death in incomparable repose. We shouted to him to "shut up, for God's sake." He redoubled his cries. He must have fancied we could not hear him. Probably he heard his own clamor but faintly. We could picture him crouching on the edge of the upper berth, letting out with both fists at the wood, in the dark, and with his mouth wide open for that unceasing cry. Those were loathsome moments. A cloud driving across the sun would darken the doorway menacingly. Every movement of the ship was pain. We scrambled about with no room to breathe, and felt frightfully sick. The boatswain yelled down at us: Bear a hand! Bear a hand! We two will be washed away from here directly if you ain't quick!" Three times a sea leaped over the high side and flung bucketfuls of water on our heads. Then Jimmy, startled by the shock, would stop his noise for a moment—waiting for the ship to sink, perhaps—and began again, distressingly loud, as if invigorated by the gust of fear. At the bottom the nails lay in a layer several inches thick. It was ghastly. Every nail in the world, not driven in firmly somewhere, seemed to have found its way into that carpenter's shop. There they were, of all kinds, the remnants of stores from seven voyages. Tin-tacks, copper tacks (sharp as needles), pump nails, with big heads, like tiny iron mushrooms; nails without any heads (horrible); French nails polished and slim. They lay in a solid mass more inabordable than a hedgehog. We hesitated, yearning for a shovel, while Jimmy below us yelled as though he had been flayed. Groaning, we dug our fingers in, and very much hurt, shook our hands, scattering nails and drops of blood. We passed up our hats full of assorted nails to the boatswain, who, as if performing a mysterious and appeasing rite, cast them wide upon a raging sea.

We got to the bulkhead at last. Those were stout planks. She was a ship, well finished in every detail—the *Narcissus* was. They were the stoutest planks ever put into a ship's bulkhead—we thought—and then we perceived that, in our hurry, we had sent all the tools overboard. Absurd little Belfast wanted to break it down with his own weight, and with both feet leaped straight up like a springbok, cursing the Clyde shipwrights for not scamping their work. Incidentally he reviled all North Britain, the rest of the earth, the sea—and all his companions. He swore, as he alighted heavily on heels, that he would never, never anymore associate with any fool that "hadn't savvy enough to know his knee from his elbow." He managed by his thumping to scare the last remnant of wits out of Jimmy. We could hear the object of our exasperated solicitude darting to and fro under the planks. He had cracked his voice at last, and could only squeak miserably. His back or else his head rubbed the planks, now here, now there, in a puzzling manner. He squeaked as he dodged the invisible blows. It was more heartrending even than his yells. Suddenly Archie produced a crowbar. He had kept it back; also a small hatchet. We howled with satisfaction. He struck a mighty blow and small chips flew at our eyes. The boatswain above shouted: "Look out! Look out there. Don't kill the man. Easy does it!" Wamibo, maddened with excitement, hung head down and insanely urged us: "Hoo! Strook 'im! Hoo! Hoo!" We were afraid he would fall in and kill one of us and, hurriedly we entreated the boatswain to "shove the blamed Finn overboard." Then, all together, we yelled down at the planks: "Stand from under! Get forward," and listened. We only heard the deep hum and moan of the wind above us, the mingled roar and hiss of the seas. The ship, as if overcome with despair, wallowed lifelessly, and our heads swam with that unnatural motion. Belfast clamored: "For the love of God, Jimmy, where are ye? . . . Knock! Jimmy darlint! . . . Knock! You bloody black beast! Knock!" He was as quiet as a dead man inside a grave; and, like men standing above a grave, we were on the verge of tears—but with vexation, the strain, the fatigue; with the great longing to be done with it, to get away, and lay down to rest. somewhere where we could see our danger and breathe. Archie shouted: "Gi'e me room!" We crouched behind him, guarding our heads, and he struck time after time in the joint of planks. They cracked. Suddenly the crowbar went halfway in through a splintered oblong hole. It must have missed Jimmy's head by less than an inch. Archie withdrew it quickly, and that infamous nigger rushed at the hole, put his lips to it, and whispered "Help" in an almost extinct voice; he pressed his head to it, trying madly to get out through that opening one inch wide and three inches long. In our disturbed state we were absolutely paralyzed by his incredible action. It seemed impossible to drive him away. Even Archie at last lost his composure. "If ye don't clear oot I'll drive the crowbar thro' your head," he shouted in a determined voice. He meant what he said, and his earnestness seemed to make an impression on Jimmy. He disappeared suddenly, and we set to prizing and tearing at the planks with the eagerness of men trying to get at a mortal enemy, and spurred by the desire to tear him limb from limb. The wood split, cracked, gave way. Belfast plunged in head and shoulders and groped viciously. "I've got 'im! Got 'im," he shouted. "Oh! There! . . . He's gone; I've got 'im! . . . Pull at my legs! . . . Pull!" Wamibo hooted unceasingly. The boatswain shouted directions: "Catch hold of his hair, Belfast; pull straight up, you two! . . . Pull fair!" We pulled fair. We pulled Belfast out with a jerk, and dropped him with disgust. In a sitting posture, purple-faced, he sobbed despairingly: "How can I hold on to 'is blooming short wool?" Suddenly Jimmy's head and shoulders appeared. He stuck halfway, and with rolling eyes foamed at our feet. We flew at him with brutal impatience, we tore the shirt off his back, we tugged at his ears, we panted over him; and all at once he came away in our hands as though somebody had let go his legs. With the same movement, without a pause, we swung him up. His breath whistled, he kicked our upturned faces, he grasped two pairs of arms above his head, and he squirmed up with such precipitation that he seemed positively to escape from our hands like a bladder full of gas. Streaming with perspiration, we swarmed up the rope, and, coming into the blast of cold wind, gasped like men plunged into icy water. With burning faces we shivered to the very marrow of our bones. Never before had the gale seemed to us more furious, the sea more mad, the sunshine more merciless and mocking, and the position of the ship more hopeless and appalling. Every movement of her was ominous of the end of her agony and of the beginning of ours. We staggered away from the door, and, alarmed by a sudden roll, fell down in a bunch. It appeared to us that the side of the house was more smooth than glass and more slippery than ice. There was nothing to hang on to but a long brass hook used sometimes to keep back an open door. Wamibo held on to it and we held on to Wamibo, clutching our Jimmy. He had completely collapsed now. He did not seem to have the strength to close his hand. We stuck to him blindly in our fear. We were not afraid of Wamibo letting go (we remembered that the brute was stronger than any three men in the ship), but we were afraid of the hook giving way, and we also believed that the ship had made up her mind to turn over at last. But she didn't. A sea swept over us. The boatswain spluttered: "Up and away. There's a lull. Away aft with you, or we will all go to the devil here." We stood up surrounding Jimmy. We begged him to hold up, to hold on, at least. He glared with his bulging eyes, mute as a fish, and with all the stiffening knocked out of him. He wouldn't stand; he wouldn't even as much as clutch at our necks; he was only a cold black skin loosely stuffed with soft cotton wool; his arms and legs swung jointless and pliable; his head rolled about; the lower lip hung down, enormous and heavy. We pressed round him, bothered and dismayed; sheltering him we swung here and there in a body; and on the very brink of eternity we tottered all together with concealing and absurd gestures, like a lot of drunken men embarrassed with a stolen corpse.

Something had to be done. We had to get him aft. A rope was tied slack under his armpits, and, reaching up at the risk of our lives, we hung him on the foresheet cleat. He emitted no sound; he looked as ridiculously lamentable as a doll that had lost half its sawdust, and we started on our perilous journey over the main deck, dragging along with care that pitiful, that limp, that hateful burden. He was not very heavy, but had he weighed a ton he could not have been more awkward to handle. We literally passed him from hand to hand. Now and then we had to hang him up on a handy belaying pin, to draw a breath and reform the line. Had the pin broken he would have irretrievably gone into the Southern Ocean, but he had to take his chance of that; and after a little while, becoming apparently aware of it, he groaned slightly, and with a great effort whispered a few words. We listened eagerly. He was reproaching us with our carelessness in letting him run such risks: "Now, after I got myself out from there," he breathed out weakly. "There" was his cabin. And he got himself out. We had nothing to do with it apparently! . . . No matter. . . . We went on and let him take his chances, simply because we could not help it; for though at that time we hated him more than ever—more than anything under heaven—we did not want to lose him. We had so far saved him; and it had become a personal matter between us and the sea. We meant to stick to him. Had we (by an incredible hypothesis) undergone similar toil and trouble for an empty cask, that cask would have become as precious to us as Jimmy was. More precious, in fact, because we would have had no reason to hate the cask. And we hated James Wait. We could not get rid of the monstrous suspicion that this astounding black man was shamming sick, had been malingering heartlessly in the face of our toil, of our scorn, of our patience—and now was malingering in the face of our devotion—in the face of death. Our vague and imperfect morality rose with disgust at his unmanly lie. But he stuck to it manfully—amazingly. No! It couldn't be. He was at all extremity. His cantankerous temper was only the result of the provoking invincibleness of that death he felt by his side. Any man may be angry with such a masterful chum. But, then, what kind of men were we—with our thoughts! Indignation and doubt grappled within us in a scuffle that trampled upon the finest of our feelings. And we hated him because of the suspicion; we detested him because of the doubt. We could not scorn him safely—neither could we pity him without risk of our dignity. So we hated him, and passed him carefully from hand to hand. We cried, "Got him?" "Yes. All right. Let go." And he swung from one enemy to another, showing about as much life as an old bolster would do. His eyes made two narrow white slits in the black face. He breathed slowly, and the air escaped through his lips with a noise like the sound of bellows. We reached the poop ladder at last, and it being a comparatively safe place, we lay for a moment in an exhausted heap to rest a little. He began to mutter. We were always incurably anxious to hear what he had to say. This time he mumbled peevishly, "It took you some time to come. I began to think the whole smart lot of you had been washed overboard. What kept you back? Hey? Funk?" we said nothing. With sighs we started again to drag him up. The secret and ardent desire of our hearts was the desire to beat him viciously with our fists about the head: and we handled him as tenderly as though he had been made of glass. . . .

The return on the poop was like the return of wanderers after many years amongst people marked by the desolation of time. Eyes were turned slowly in their sockets glancing at us. Faint murmurs were heard, "Have you got 'im after all?" The well-known faces looked strange and familiar; they seemed faded and grimy; they had a mingled expression of fatigue and eagerness. They seemed to have become much thinner during our absence, as if all these men had been starving for a long time in their abandoned attitudes. The captain, with a round turn of a rope on his wrist, and kneeling on one knee, swung with a face cold and stiff; but with living eyes he was still holding the ship up, heeding no one, as if lost in the unearthly effort of that endeavor. We fastened up James Wait in a safe place. Mr. Baker scrambled along to lend a hand. Mr. Creighton, on his back, and very pale, muttered, "Well done," and gave us, Jimmy and the sky, a scornful glance, then closed his eyes slowly. Here and there a man stirred a little, but most remained apathetic, in cramped positions, muttering between shivers. The sun was setting. A sun enormous, unclouded and red, declining low as if bending down to look into their faces. The wind whistled across long sunbeams that, resplendent and cold, struck full on the dilated pupils of staring eyes without making them wink. The wisps of hair and the tangled beards were gray with the salt of the sea. The faces were earthly, and the dark patches under the eyes extended to the ears, smudged into the hollows of sunken cheeks. The lips were livid and thin, and when they moved it was with difficulty, as though they had been glued to the teeth. Some grinned sadly in the sunlight, shaking with cold. Others were sad and still.

Charley, subdued by the sudden disclosure of the insignificance of his youth, darted fearful glances. The two smooth-faced Norwegians resembled decrepit children, staring stupidly. To leeward, on the edge of the horizon, black seas leaped up towards the glowing sun. It sank slowly, round and blazing, and the crests of waves splashed on the edge of the luminous circle. One of the Norwegians appeared to catch sight of it, and, after giving a violent start, began to speak. His voice, startling the others, made them stir. They moved their heads stiffly, or turning with difficulty, looked at him with surprise, with fear, or in grave silence. He chattered at the setting sun, nodding his head, while the big seas began to roll across the crimson disc; and over miles of turbulent waters the shadows of high waves swept with a running darkness the faces of men. A crested roller broke with a loud hissing roar, and the sun, as if put out, disappeared. The chattering voice faltered, went out together with the light. There were sighs. In the sudden lull that follows the crash of a broken sea a man said wearily, "Here's that blooming Dutchman gone off his chump." A seaman, lashed by the middle, tapped the deck with his open hand with unceasing quick flaps. In the gathering grayness of twilight a bulky form was seen rising aft, and began marching on all fours with the movements of some big cautious beast. It was Mr. Baker passing along the line of men. He grunted encouragingly over everyone, felt their fastenings. Some, with half-open eyes, puffed like men oppressed by heat; others mechanically and in dreamy voices answered him, "Aye! aye! sir!" He went from one to another grunting, "Ough! . . . See her through it yet"; and unexpectedly, with loud angry outbursts, blew up Knowles for cutting off a long piece from the fall of the relieving tackle. "Ough!—Ashamed of yourself—Relieving tackle—Don't you know better!—Ough!—Able seaman! Ough!" The lame man was crushed. He muttered, "Get som'think for a lashing for myself, sir." "Ough! Lashing—yourself. Are you a tinker or a sailor—What? Ough!—May want that tackle directly—Ough!—More use to the ship than your lame carcass. Ough!—Keep it!—Keep it, now you've done it." He crawled away slowly, muttering to himself about some men being "worse than children." It had been a comforting row. Low exclamations were heard: "Hallo . . . Hallo." . . . Those who had been painfully dozing asked with convulsive starts, "What's up? . . . What is it?" The answers came with unexpected cheerfulness: "The mate is going bald-headed for lame Jack about something or other." "No!" . . . "What 'as he done?" Someone even chuckled. It was like a whiff of hope, like a reminder of safe days. Donkin who had been stupefied with fear, revived suddenly and began to shout: " 'Ear 'im; that's the way they tawlk to hus. Vy donch 'ee 'it 'im—one ov yer? 'It 'im. 'It 'im! Comin' the mate hover hus. We are as good men as 'ee! We're hall goin' to 'ell now. We 'ave been starved in this rotten ship, an' now we're goin' to be drowned for them black-'earted bullies! 'It 'im!" He shrieked in the deepening gloom, he blubbered and sobbed, screaming: "'It 'im! 'It 'im!" The rage and fear of his disregarded right to live tried the steadfastness of hearts more than the menacing shadows of the night that advanced through the unceasing clamor of the gale. From aft Mr. Baker was heard: "Is one of you men going to stop him—must I come along?" "Shut up!" . . . "Keep quiet!" cried various voices, exasperated, trembling with cold. "You'll get one across the mug from me directly," said an invisible seaman, in a weary tone, "I won't let the mate have the trouble." He ceased and lay still with the silence of despair. On the black sky the stars, coming out, gleamed over an inky sea that, speckled with foam, flashed back at them the evanescent and pale light of a dazzling whiteness born from the black turmoil of the waves. Remote in the eternal calm they glittered hard and cold above the uproar of the earth; they surrounded the vanquished and tormented ship on all sides: more pitiless than the eyes of a triumphant mob, and as unapproachable as the hearts of men.

The icy south wind howled exultingly under the somber splendor of the sky. The cold shook the men with a resistless violence as though it had tried to shake them to pieces. Short moans were swept unheard off the stiff lips. Some complained in mutters of "not feeling themselves below the waist"; while those who had closed their eyes, imagined they had a block of ice on their chests. Others, alarmed at not feeling any pain in their fingers, beat the deck feebly with their hands—obstinate and exhausted. Wamibo stared vacant and dreamy. The Scandinavians kept on a meaningless muttering through chattering teeth. The spare Scotchmen, with determined efforts, kept their lower jaws still. The West-country men lay big and stolid in an invulnerable surliness. A man yawned and swore in turns. Another breathed with a rattle in his throat. Two elderly hard-weather shellbacks, fast side by side, whispered dismally to one another about the landlady of a boarding-house in Sunderland, whom they both knew. They extolled her motherliness and her liberality; they tried to talk about the joint of beef and the big fire in the downstairs kitchen. The words dying faintly on their lips, ended in light sighs. A sudden voice cried into the cold night, "Oh Lord!" No one changed his position or took any notice of the cry. One or two passed, with a repeated and vague gesture, their hand over their faces, but most of them kept very still. In the benumbed immobility of their bodies they were excessively wearied by their thoughts, that rushed with the rapidity and vividness of dreams. Now and then, by an abrupt and startling exclamation, they answered the weird hail of some illusion; then, again, in silence contemplated the vision of known faces and familiar things. They recalled the aspect of forgotten shipmates and heard the voice of dead and gone skippers. They

315

remembered the noise of gaslit streets, the steamy heat of taprooms, or the scorching sunshine of calm days at sea.

Mr. Baker left his insecure place, and crawled, with stoppages, along the poop. In the dark and on all fours he resembled some carnivorous animal prowling amongst corpses. At the break, propped to windward of a stanchion, he looked down on the main deck. It seemed to him that the ship had a tendency to stand up a little more. The wind has eased a little, he thought, but the sea ran as high as ever. The waves foamed viciously, and the lee side of the deck disappeared under a hissing whiteness as of boiling milk, while the rigging sang steadily with a deep vibrating note, and, at every upward swing of the ship, the wind rushed with a long-drawn clamor amongst the spars. Mr. Baker watched very still. A man near him began to make a blabbing noise with his lips, all at once and very loud, as though the cold had broken brutally through him. He went on: —"Ba—ba—ba—brr—brr—ba—ba." "Stop that!" cried Mr. Baker, groping in the dark. "Stop it!" He went on shaking the leg he found under his hand. "What is it, sir?" called out Belfast, in the tone of a man awakened suddenly; "we are looking after that 'ere Jimmy." "Are you? Ough! Don't make that row then. Who's that near you?" "It's me—the boatswain, sir," growled the West-country man; "we are trying to keep life in that poor devil." "Aye, aye!" said Mr. Baker. "Do it quietly, can't you." "He wants us to hold him up above the rail," went on the boatswain, with irritation, "says he can't breathe here under our jackets." "If we lift 'im, we drop 'im overboard," said another voice, "we can't feel our hands with cold." "I don't care. I am choking!" exclaimed James Wait in a clear tone. "Oh, no, my son," said the boatswain, desperately, "you don't go till we all go on this fine night." "You will see yet many a worse," said Mr. Baker, cheerfully. "It's no child's play, sir!" answered the boatswain. "Some of us further aft, here, are in a pretty bad way." "If the blamed sticks had been cut out of her she would be running along on her bottom now like any decent ship, an' giv' us all a chance," said someone, with a sigh. "The old man wouldn't have it . . . much he cares for us," whispered another. "Care for you!" exclaimed Mr. Baker, angrily. "Why should he care for you? Are you a lot of women passengers to be taken care of? We are here to take care of the ship —and some of you ain't up to that. Ough! . . . What have you done so very smart to be taken care of? Ough! . . . Some of you can't stand a bit of a breeze without crying over it." "Come, sorr. We ain't so bad," protested Belfast, in a voice shaken by shivers; "we ain't . . . brrr. . . ." "Again," shouted the mate, grabbing at the shadowy form; "again! . . . Why, you're in your shirt! What have you done?" "I've put my oilskin and jacket over that half-dead nayggur—and he says he chokes," said Belfast, complainingly. "You wouldn't call me nigger if I wasn't half dead, you Irish beggar!" boomed James Wait, vigorously. "You . . . brrr. . . . You wouldn't be white if you were ever so well . . . I will fight you . . . brrrr . . . in fine weather . . . brrr . . . with one hand tied behind my back . . . brrrrrr. . . ." "I don't want your rags—I want air," gasped out the other faintly, as if suddenly exhausted.

The sprays swept over whistling and pattering. Men disturbed in their peaceful torpor by the pain of quarrelsome shouts, moaned, muttering curses. Mr. Baker crawled off a little way to leeward where a water cask loomed up big, with something white against it. "Is it you, Podmore?" asked Mr. Baker. He had to repeat the question twice before the cook turned, coughing feebly. "Yes, sir. I've been praying in my mind for a quick deliverance; for I am prepared for any call. . . . I—" "Look here, cook," interrupted Mr. Baker, "the men are perishing with cold." "Cold!" said the cook, mournfully; "they will be warm enough before long." "What?" asked Mr. Baker, looking along the deck into the faint sheen of frothing water. "They are a wicked lot," continued the cook solemnly, but in an unsteady voice, "about as wicked as any ship's company in this sinful world! Now, I"—he trembled so that he could hardly speak; his was an exposed place, and in a cotton shirt, a thin pair of trousers, and with his knees under his nose, he received, quaking, the flicks of stinging, salt drops; his voice sounded exhausted—"now, I—any time. . . . My eldest youngster, Mr. Baker . . . a clever boy . . . last Sunday on shore before this voyage he wouldn't go to church, sir. Says I, 'You go and clean yourself, or I'll know the reason why!' What does he do? . . . Pond, Mr. Baker—fell into the pond in his best rig, sir! . . . Accident? . . . 'Nothing will save you, fine scholar though you are!' says I. . . . Accident! . . . I whopped him, sir, till I couldn't lift my arm. . . ." His voice faltered. "I whopped 'im!" he repeated, rattling his teeth; then, after a while, let out a mournful sound that was half a groan, half a snore. Mr. Baker shook him by the shoulders. "Hey! Cook! Hold up, Podmore! Tell me—is there any fresh water in the galley tank? The ship is lying along less, I think; I would try to get forward. A little water would do them good. Hallo! Look out! Look out!" The cook struggled. "Not you, sir—not you!" He began to scramble to windward. "Galley! . . . my business!" he shouted. "Cook's going crazy now," said several voices. He yelled: "Crazy, am I? I am more ready to die than any of you, officers incloosive—there! As long as she swims I will cook! I will get you coffee." "Cook, ye are a gentleman!" cried Belfast. But the cook was already going over the weather ladder. He stopped for a moment to shout back on the poop: "As long as she swims I will cook!" and disappeared as though he had gone overboard. The men who had heard sent after him a cheer that sounded like a wail of sick children. An hour or more afterwards someone said distinctly: "He's gone for good." "Very likely," assented the boatswain; "even in fine weather he was as smart about the deck as a milch cow on her first voyage. We ought to go and see." Nobody moved. As the hours dragged slowly through the darkness Mr. Baker crawled back and forth along the poop several times. Some men fancied they had heard him exchange murmurs with the master, but at that time the memories were incomparably more vivid than anything actual, and they were not certain whether the murmurs were heard now or many years ago. They did not try to find out. A mutter more or less did not matter. It was too cold for curiosity, and almost for hope. They could not spare a moment or a thought from the great mental occupation of wishing to live. And the desire of life kept them alive, apathetic and enduring, under the cruel persistence of wind and cold; while the bestarred black dome of the sky revolved slowly above the ship, that drifted, bearing their patience and their suffering, through the stormy solitude of the sea.

Huddled close to one another, they fancied themselves utterly alone. They heard sustained loud noises, and again bore the pain of existence through long hours of profound silence. In the night they saw sunshine, felt warmth, and suddenly, with a start, thought that the sun would never rise upon a freezing world. Some heard laughter, listened to songs; others, near the end of the poop, could hear loud human shrieks, and, opening their eyes, were surprised to hear them still, though very faint, and far away. The boatswain said: "Why, it's the cook, hailing from forward, I think." He hardly believed his own words or recognized his own voice. It was a long time before the man next to him gave a sign of life. He punched hard his other neighbor and said: "The cook's shouting!" Many did not understand, others did not care; the majority further aft did not believe. But the boatswain and another man had the pluck to crawl away forward to see. They seemed to have been gone for hours, and were very soon forgotten. Then suddenly men that had been plunged in a hopeless resignation became as if possessed with a desire to hurt. They belabored one another with fists. In the darkness they struck persistently anything soft they could feel near, and, with a greater effort than for a shout, whispered excitedly: "They've got some hot coffee. . . . Bosun got it. . . ." "No!" . . . "Where?" . . . "It's coming! Cook made it." James Wait moaned. Donkin scrambled viciously, caring not where he kicked, and anxious that the officers should have none of it. It came in a pot, and they drank in turns. It was hot, and while it blistered the greedy palates, it seemed incredible. The men sighed out parting with the mug: "How 'as he done it?" Some cried weakly: "Bully for you, doctor!"

He had done it somehow. Afterwards Archie declared that the thing was "meeraculous." For many days we wondered, and it was the one ever-interesting subject of conversation to the end of the voyage. We asked the cook, in fine weather, how he felt when he saw his stove "reared up on end." We inquired, in the northeast trade and on serene evenings, whether he had to stand on his head to put things right somewhat. We suggested he had used his bread board for a raft, and from there comfortably had stoked his grate; and we did our best to conceal our admiration under the wit of fine irony. He affirmed not to know anything about it, rebuked our levity, declared himself, with solemn animation, to have been the object of a special mercy for the saving of our unholy lives. Fundamentally he was right, no doubt; but he need not have been so offensively positive about it—he need not have hinted so often that it would have gone hard with us had he not been there, meritorious and pure, to receive the inspiration and the strength for the work of grace. Had we been saved by his recklessness or his agility, we could have at length become reconciled to the fact; but to admit our obligation to anybody's virtue and holiness alone was as difficult for us as for any other handful of mankind. Like many benefactors of humanity, the cook took himself too seriously, and reaped the reward of irreverence. We were not ungrateful, however. He remained heroic. His saying—*the* saying of his life— became proverbial in the mouth of men as are the sayings of conquerors or sages. Later on, whenever one of us was puzzled by a task and advised to relinquish it, he would express his determination to persevere and to succeed by the words: "As long as she swims I will cook!"

The hot drink helped us through the bleak hours that precede the dawn. The sky low by the horizon took on the delicate tints of pink and yellow like the inside of a rare shell. And higher, where it glowed with a pearly sheen, a small black cloud appeared, like a forgotten fragment of the night set in a border of dazzling gold. The beams of light skipped on the crests of waves. The eyes of men turned to the eastward. The sunlight flooded their weary faces. They were giving themselves up to fatigue as though they had done forever with their work. On Singleton's black oilskin coat the dried salt glistened like hoar frost. He hung on by the wheel, with open and lifeless eyes. Captain Allistoun, unblinking, faced the rising sun. His lips stirred, opened for the first time in twenty-four hours, and with a fresh firm voice he cried, "Wear ship!"

The commanding sharp tones made all these torpid men start like a sudden flick of a whip. Then again, motionless where they lay, the force of habit made some of them repeat the order in hardly audible murmurs. Captain Allistoun glanced down at his crew, and several, with fumbling fingers and hopeless movements, tried to cast themselves adrift. He repeated impatiently, "Wear ship. Now then, Mr. Baker, get the men along. What's the matter with them?" "Wear ship. Do you hear there? Wear ship!" thundered out the boatswain suddenly. His voice seemed to break through a deadly spell. Men began to stir and crawl. "I want the fore topmast staysail run up smartly," said the master, very loudly; "if you can't manage it standing up you must do it lying down—that's all. Bear a hand!" "Come along! Let's give the old girl a chance," urged the boatswain. "Aye! aye! Wear ship!"

exclaimed quavering voices. The forecastle men, with reluctant faces, prepared to go forward. Mr. Baker pushed ahead grunting on all fours to show the way, and they followed him over the break. The others lay still with a vile hope in their hearts of not being required to move till they got saved or drowned in peace.

After some time they could be seen forward appearing on the forecastle head, one by one in unsafe attitudes; hanging on to the rails; clambering over the anchors; embracing the crosshead of the windlass or hugging the forecapstan. They were restless with strange exertions, waved their arms, knelt, lay flat down, staggered up, seemed to strive their hardest to go overboard. Suddenly a small white piece of canvas fluttered amongst them, grew larger, beating. Its narrow head rose in jerks—and at last it stood distended and triangular in the sunshine. "They have done it!" cried the voices aft. Captain Allistoun let go the rope he had round his wrist and rolled to leeward headlong. He could be seen casting the lee main braces off the pins while the backwash of waves splashed over him. "Square the main yard!" he shouted up to us—who stared at him in wonder. We hesitated to stir. "The main brace, men. Haul! haul anyhow! Lay on your backs and haul!" he screeched, half drowned down there. We did not believe we could move the main yard, but the strongest and the less discouraged tried to execute the order. Others assisted halfheartedly. Singleton's eyes blazed suddenly as he took a fresh grip of the spokes. Captain Allistoun fought his way up to windward. "Haul, men! Try to move it! Haul, and help the ship." His hard face worked suffused and furious. "Is she going off, Singleton?" he cried. "Not a move yet, sir," croaked the old seaman in a horribly hoarse voice. "Watch the helm, Singleton," spluttered the master. "Haul, men! Have you no more strength than rats? Haul, and earn your salt." Mr. Creighton, on his back, with a swollen leg and a face as white as a piece of paper, blinked his eyes; his bluish lips twitched. In the wild scramble men grabbed at him, crawled over his hurt leg, knelt on his chest. He kept perfectly still, setting his teeth without a moan, without a sigh. The master's ardor, the cries of that silent man inspired us. We hauled and hung in bunches on the rope. We heard him say with violence to Donkin, who sprawled abjectly on his stomach, "I will brain you with this belaying pin if you don't catch hold of the brace," and that victim of men's injustice, cowardly and cheeky, whimpered: "Are you goin' ter murder hus now," while with sudden desperation he gripped the rope. Men sighed, shouted, hissed meaningless words, groaned. The yards moved, came slowly square against the wind, that hummed loudly on the yardarms. "Going off, sir," shouted Singleton, "she's just started." "Catch a turn with that brace. Catch a turn!" clamored the master. Mr. Creighton, nearly suffocated and unable to move, made a mighty effort, and with his left hand managed to nip the rope. "All fast!" cried someone. He closed his eyes as if going off into a swoon, while huddled together about the brace we watched with scared looks what the ship would do now.

She went off slowly as though she had been weary and disheartened like the men she carried. She paid off very gradually, making us hold our breath till we choked, and as soon as she had brought the wind abaft the beam she started to move, and fluttered our hearts. It was awful to see her, nearly overturned, begin to gather way and drag her submerged side through the water. The deadeyes of the rigging churned the breaking seas. The lower half of the deck was full of mad whirlpools and eddies; and the long line of the lee rail could be seen showing black now and then in the swirls of a field of foam as dazzling and white as a field of snow. The wind sang shrilly amongst the spars; and at every slight lurch we expected her to slip to the bottom sideways from under our backs. When dead before it she made the first distinct attempt to stand up, and we encouraged her with a feeble and discordant howl. A great sea came running up aft and hung for a moment over us with a curling top; then crashed down under the counter and spread out on both sides into a great sheet of bursting froth. Above its fierce hiss we heard Singleton's croak: "She is steering!" He had both his feet now planted firmly on the grating, and the wheel spun fast as he eased the helm. "Bring the wind on the port quarter and steady her!" called out the master, staggering to his feet, the first man up from amongst our prostrate heap. One or two screamed with excitement: "She rises!" Far away forward, Mr. Baker and three others were seen erect and black on the clear sky, lifting their arms, and with open mouths as though they had been shouting all together. The ship trembled, trying to lift her side, lurched back, seemed to give up with a nerveless dip, and suddenly with an unexpected jerk swung violently to windward, as though she had torn herself out from a deadly grasp. The whole immense volume of water, lifted by her deck, was thrown bodily across to starboard. Loud cracks were heard. Iron ports breaking open thundered with ringing blows. The water topped over the starboard rail with the rush of a river falling over a dam. The sea on deck, and the seas on every side of her, mingled together in a deafening roar. She rolled violently. We got up and were helplessly run or flung about from side to side. Men, rolling over and over, yelled, "The house will go!" "She clears herself!" Lifted by a towering sea she ran along with it for a moment, spouting thick streams of water through every opening of her wounded sides. The lee braces having been carried away or washed off the pins, all the ponderous yards on the fore swung from side to side and with appalling rapidity at every roll. The men forward were seen crouching here and there with fearful glances upwards at the enormous spars that whirled about over their heads. The torn canvas and the ends of broken gear streamed in the wind like wisps of hair. Through the clear sunshine, over the flashing turmoil and uproar of the seas, the ship ran blindly, disheveled and headlong, as if fleeing for her life; and on the poop we spun, we tottered about, distracted and noisy. We all spoke at once in a thin babble; we had the aspect of invalids and the gestures of maniacs. Eyes shone, large and haggard, in smiling, meager faces that seemed to have been dusted over with powdered chalk. We stamped, clapped our hands, feeling ready to jump and do anything; but in reality hardly able to keep on our feet. Captain Allistoun, hard and slim, gesticulated madly from the poop at Mr. Baker: "Steady these foreyards! Steady them the best you can!" On the main deck, men excited by his cries, splashed, dashing aimlessly here and there with the foam swirling up to their waists. Apart, far aft, and alone by the helm, old Singleton had deliberately tucked his white beard under the top button of his glistening coat. Swaying upon the din and tumult of the seas, with the whole battered length of the ship launched forward in a rolling rush before his steady old eyes, he stood rigidly still, forgotten by all, and with an attentive face. In front of his erect figure only the two arms moved crosswise with a swift and sudden readiness, to check or urge again the rapid stir of circling spokes. He steered with care.

⚓

THE HORN

⚓

THE HORN

Richard H. Dana, Jr.

⚓ *"Two Years Before The Mast" will always be among the favorite books of the sea—and deservedly so. It has the merit, as Dana himself points out, of having been written by a man who has actually been to sea in the humble position of seaman. Dana was a happy combination—an educated man, a man who, though well-born, could mix with the toughest characters of the seaman's trade and hold their respect, a man who was a born writer, and a man with a mission. Given all these factors, it is little wonder that a work of lasting merit was produced.*

The act of rounding the Horn is one of sailing's classics and has been chosen from "Two Years Before The Mast" as a classic within a classic.

THERE began now to be a decided change in the appearance of things. The days became shorter and shorter; the sun running lower in its course each day, and giving less and less heat; and the nights so cold as to prevent our sleeping on deck; the Magellan Clouds in sight, of a clear night; the skies looking cold and angry; and, at times, a long, heavy, ugly sea, setting in from the southward, told us what we were coming to. Still, however, we had a fine, strong breeze, and kept on our way, under as much sail as our ship would bear. Toward the middle of the week, the wind hauled to the southward, which brought us upon a taught bowline, made the ship meet, nearly head on, the heavy swell which rolled from that direction; and there was something not at all encouraging in the manner in which she met it. Being so deep and heavy, she wanted

From *Two Years Before the Mast* by Richard H. Dana, Jr.

the buoyancy which should have carried her over the seas, and she dropped heavily into them, the water washing over the decks; and every now and then, when an unusually large sea met her fairly upon the bows, she struck it with a sound as dead and heavy as that with which a sledge-hammer falls upon the pile, and took the whole of it in upon the fore-castle, and rising, carried it aft in the scuppers, washing the rigging off the pins, and carrying along with it everything which was loose on deck. She had been acting in this way all of our forenoon watch below; as we could tell by the washing of the water over our heads, and the heavy breaking of the seas against her bows (with a sound as though she were striking against a rock), only the thickness of the plank from our heads, as we lay in our berths, which are directly against the bows. At eight bells, the watch was called, and we came on deck, one hand going aft to take the wheel, and another going to the galley to get the *grub* for dinner. I stood on the forecastle, looking at the seas, which were rolling high, as far as the eye could reach, their tops white with foam, and the body of them of a deep indigo blue, reflecting the bright rays of the sun. Our ship rose slowly over a few of the largest of them, until one immense fellow came rolling on, threatening to cover her, and which I was sailor enough to know, by "the feeling of her" under my feet, she would not rise over. I sprang upon the knight-heads, and seizing hold of the forestay with my hands, drew myself up upon it. My feet were just off the stanchion, when she struck fairly into the middle of the sea, and it washed her fore and aft, burying her in the water. As soon as she rose out of it, I looked aft, and everything forward of the main-mast, except the long-boat, which was griped and double-lashed down to the ring-bolts, was swept off clear. The galley, the pig-sty, the hen-coop, and a large sheep-pen which had been built upon the forehatch, were all gone, in the twinkling of an eye—leaving the deck as clean as a chin new-reaped—and not a stick left, to show where they had stood. In the scuppers lay the galley, bottom up, and a few boards floating about, the wreck of the sheep-pen,—and half a dozen miserable sheep floating among them, wet through, and not a little frightened at the sudden change that had come upon them. As soon as the sea had washed by, all hands sprung up out of the forecastle to see what had become of the ship; and in a few moments the cook and Old Bill crawled out from under the galley, where they had been lying in the water, nearly smothered, with the galley over them. Fortunately, it rested against the bulwarks, or it would have broken some of their bones. When the water ran off, we picked the sheep up, and put them in the long-boat, got the galley back in its place, and set things a little to rights; but, had not our ship had uncommonly high bulwarks and rail, everything must have been washed overboard, not excepting Old

It was a place well suited to stand at the junction of the two oceans.

Bill and the cook. Bill had been standing at the galley-door, with the kid of beef in his hand for the forecastle mess, when, away he went, kid, beef, and all. He held on to the kid till the last, like a good fellow, but the beef was gone, and when the water had run off, we saw it lying high and dry, like a rock at low tide—nothing could hurt *that*. We took the loss of our beef very easily, consoling ourselves with the recollection that the cabin had more to lose than we; and chuckled not a little at seeing the remains of the chicken-pie and pan-cakes floating in the scuppers. "This will never do!" was what some said, and every one felt. Here we were, not yet within a thousand miles of the latitude of Cape Horn, and our decks swept by a sea, not one half so high as we must expect to find there. Some blamed the captain for loading his ship so deep, when he knew what he must expect; while others said that the wind was always southwest, off the Cape, in the winter; and that, running before it, we should not mind the seas so much. When we got down into the fore-castle, Old Bill, who was somewhat of a croaker,—having met with a great many accidents at sea—said that if that was the way she was going to act, we might as well make our wills, and balance the books at once, and put on a clean shirt. "'Vast there, you bloody old owl! you're always hanging out blue lights! You're frightened by the ducking you got in the scuppers, and can't take a joke! What's the use in being always on the look-out for Davy Jones?" "Stand by!" says another, "and we'll get an afternoon watch below, by this scrape;" but in this they were disappointed, for at two bells, all hands were called and set to work, getting lashings upon everything on deck; and the captain talked of sending down the long topgallant masts; but, as the sea went down toward night, and the wind hauled abeam, we left them standing, and set the studding sails.

The next day, all hands were turned-to upon unbending the old sails, and getting up the new ones; for a ship, unlike people on shore, puts on her best suit in bad weather. The old sails were sent down, and three new topsails, and new fore and main courses, jib, and fore-topmast staysail, which were made on the coast, and never had been used, were bent, with a complete set of new earings, robands and reef-points; and reef-tackles were rove to the courses, and spilling-lines to the topsails. These, with new braces and clewlines, fore and aft, gave us a good suit of running rigging.

The wind continued westerly, and the weather and sea less rough since the day on which we shipped the heavy sea, and we were making great progress under studding-sails, with our light sails all set, keeping a little to the eastward of south; for the captain, depending upon westerly winds off the Cape, had kept so far to the westward, that, though we were within about five hundred miles of the latitude of Cape Horn, we were nearly seventeen hundred miles to the westward of it. Through the rest of the week, we continued on with a fair wind, gradually, as we got more to the southward, keeping a more easterly course, and bringing the wind on our larboard quarter, until—

Sunday, June 26th, when, having a fine, clear day, the captain got a lunar observation, as well as his meridian altitude, which made us in lat. 47° 50′ S., long. 113° 49′ W.; Cape Horn bearing, according to my calculation, E. S. E. ½ E., and distant eighteen hundred miles.

Monday, June 27th. During the first part of this day, the wind continued fair, and, as we were going before it, it did not feel very cold, so that we kept at work on deck, in our common clothes and round jackets. Our watch had an afternoon watch below, for the first time since leaving San Diego, and having inquired of the third mate what the latitude was at noon, and made our usual guesses as to the time she would need, to be up with the Horn, we turned-in, for a nap. We were sleeping away "at the rate of knots," when three knocks on the scuttle, and "All hands, ahoy!" started us from our berths. What could be the matter? It did not appear to be blowing hard, and looking up through the scuttle, we could see that it was a clear day, overhead; yet the watch were taking in sail. We thought there must be a sail in sight, and that we were about to heave-to and speak her; and were just congratulating ourselves upon it— for we had seen neither sail nor land since we had left port—when we heard the mate's voice on deck, (he turned-in "all standing," and was always on deck the moment he was called,) singing out to the men who were taking in the studding-sails, and asking where his watch were. We did not wait for a second call, but tumbled up the ladder; and there, on the starboard bow, was a bank of mist, covering sea and sky, and driving directly for us. I had seen the same before, in my passage round in the Pilgrim, and knew what it meant, and that there was no time to be lost. We had nothing on but thin clothes, yet there was not a moment to spare, and at it we went.

The boys of the other watch were in the tops, taking in the top-gallant studding-sails, and the lower and topmast studding-sails were coming down by the run. It was nothing but "haul down and clew up," until we got all the studding-sails in, and the royals, flying-jib, and mizen top-gallant sail furled, and the ship kept off a little, to take the squall. The fore and main top-gallant sails were still on her, for the "old man" did not mean to be frightened in broad daylight, and was determined to carry sail till the last minute. We all stood waiting for its coming, when the first blast showed us that it was not to be trifled with. Rain, sleet, snow, and wind, enough to take our breath from us, and make the toughest turn his back to windward! The ship lay nearly over upon her beam-ends;

the spars and rigging snapped and cracked; and her top-gallant masts bent like whip-sticks. "Clew up the fore and main top-gallant sails!" shouted the captain, and all hands sprang to the clewlines. The decks were standing nearly at an angle of forty-five degrees, and the ship going like a mad steed through the water, the whole forward part of her in a smother of foam. The halyards were let go and the yard clewed down, and the sheets started, and in a few minutes the sails smothered and kept in by clewlines and buntlines.—"Furl 'em, sir?" asked the mate.—"Let go the topsail halyards, fore and aft!" shouted the captain, in answer, at the top of his voice. Down came the topsail yards, the reef-tackles were manned and hauled out, and we climbed up to windward, and sprang into the weather rigging. The violence of the wind, and the hail and sleet, driving nearly horizontally across the ocean, seemed actually to pin us down to the rigging. It was hard work making head against them. One after another, we got out upon the yards. And here we had work to do; for our new sails, which had hardly been bent long enough to get the starch out of them, were as stiff as boards, and the new earings and reef-points, stiffened with the sleet, knotted like pieces of iron wire. Having only our round jackets and straw hats on, we were soon wet through, and it was every moment growing colder. Our hands were soon stiffened and numbed, which, added to the stiffness of everything else, kept us a good while on the yard. After we had got the sail hauled upon the yard, we had to wait a long time for the weather earing to be passed; but there was no fault to be found, for French John was at the earing, and a better sailor never laid out on a yard; so we leaned over the yard, and beat our hands upon the sail to keep them from freezing. At length the word came—"Haul out to leeward,"—and we seized the reef-points and hauled the band taught for the lee earing. "Taught band—Knot away," and we got the first reef fast, and were just going to lay down, when— "Two reefs—two reefs!" shouted the mate, and we had a second reef to take, in the same way. When this was fast, we laid down on deck, manned the halyards to leeward, nearly up to our knees in water, set the topsail, and then laid aloft on the main topsail yard, and reefed that sail in the same manner; for, as I have before stated, we were a good deal reduced in numbers, and, to make it worse, the carpenter, only two days before, cut his leg with an axe, so that he could not go aloft. This weakened us so that we could not well manage more than one topsail at a time, in such weather as this, and, of course, our labor was doubled. From the main topsail yard, we went upon the main yard, and took a reef in the mainsail. No sooner had we got on deck, than—"Lay aloft there, mizen-topmen, and close-reef the mizen topsail!" This called me; and being nearest to the rigging, I got first aloft, and out to the weather

329

earing. English Ben was on the yard just after me, and took the lee earing, and the rest of our gang were soon on the yard, and began to fist the sail, when the mate considerately sent up the cook and steward, to help us. I could now account for the long time it took to pass the other earings, for, to do my best, with a strong hand to help me at the dog's ear, I could not get it passed until I heard them beginning to complain in the bunt. One reef after another we took in, until the sail was close-reefed, when we went down and hoisted away at the halyards. In the meantime, the jib had been furled and the staysail set, and the ship, under her reduced sail, had got more upright and was under management; but the two top-gallant sails were still hanging in the buntlines, and slatting and jerking as though they would take the masts out of her. We gave a look aloft, and knew that our work was not done yet; and sure enough, no sooner did the mate see that we were on deck, than— "Lay aloft there, four of you, and furl the top-gallant sails!" This called me again, and two of us went aloft, up the fore rigging, and two more up the main, upon the top-gallant yards. The shrouds were now iced over, the sleet having formed a crust or cake round all the standing rigging, and on the weather side of the masts and yards. When we got upon the yard, my hands were so numb that I could not have cast off the knot of the gasket to have saved my life. We both lay over the yard for a few seconds, beating our hands upon the sail, until we started the blood into our fingers' ends, and at the next moment our hands were in a burning heat. My companion on the yard was a lad, who came out in the ship a weak, puny boy, from one of the Boston schools,—"no larger than a spritsail sheet knot," nor "heavier than a paper of lamp-black," and "not strong enough to haul a shad off a gridiron," but who was now "as long as a spare topmast, strong enough to knock down an ox, and hearty enough to eat him." We fisted the sail together, and after six or eight minutes of hard hauling and pulling and beating down the sail, which was as stiff as sheet iron, we managed to get it furled; and snugly furled it must be, for we knew the mate well enough to be certain that if it got adrift again, we should be called up from our watch below, at any hour of the night, to furl it.

I had been on the look-out for a moment to jump below and clap on a thick jacket and south-wester; but when we got on deck we found that eight bells had been struck, and the other watch gone below, so that there were two hours of dog watch for us, and a plenty of work to do. It had now set in for a steady gale from the south-west; but we were not yet far enough to the southward to make a fair wind of it, for we must give Terra del Fuego a wide berth. The decks were covered with snow, and there was a constant driving of sleet. In fact, Cape Horn had set in with good earnest. In the midst of all this, and before it became dark, we had all the studding-sails to make up and stow away, and then to lay aloft and rig in all the booms, fore and aft, and coil away the tacks, sheets, and halyards. This was pretty tough work for four or five hands, in the face of a gale which almost took us off the yards, and with ropes so stiff with ice that it was almost impossible to bend them. I was nearly half an hour out on the end of the fore yard, trying to coil away and stop down the topmast studding-sail tack and lower halyards. It was after dark when we got through, and we were not a little pleased to hear four bells struck, which sent us below for two hours, and gave us each a pot of hot tea with our cold beef and bread, and, what was better yet, a suit of thick, dry clothing, fitted for the weather, in place of our thin clothes, which were wet through and now frozen stiff.

This sudden turn, for which we were so little prepared, was as unacceptable to me as to any of the rest; for I had been troubled for several days with a slight tooth-ache, and this cold weather, and wetting and freezing, were not the best things in the world for it. I soon found that it was getting strong hold, and running over all parts of my face; and before the watch was out I went aft to the mate, who had charge of the medicine-chest, to get something for it. But the chest showed like the end of a long voyage, for there was nothing that would answer but a few drops of laudanum, which must be saved for any emergency; so I had only to bear the pain as well as I could.

When we went on deck at eight bells, it had stopped snowing, and there were a few stars out, but the clouds were still black, and it was blowing a steady gale. Just before midnight, I went aloft and sent down the mizen royal yard, and had the good luck to do it to the satisfaction of the mate, who said it was done "out of hand and shipshape." The next four hours below were but little relief to me, for I lay awake in my berth, the whole time, from the pain in my face, and heard every bell strike, and, at four o'clock, turned out with the watch, feeling little spirit for the hard duties of the day. Bad weather and hard work at sea can be borne up against very well, if one only has spirit and health; but there is nothing brings a man down, at such a time, like bodily pain and want of sleep. There was, however, too much to do to allow time to think; for the gale of yesterday, and the heavy seas we met with a few days before, while we had yet ten degrees more southing to make, had convinced the captain that we had something before us which was not to be trifled with, and orders were given to send down the long top-gallant masts. The top-gallant and royal yards were accordingly struck, the flying jibboom rigged in, and the top-gallant masts sent down on deck, and all lashed together by the side of the long-boat. The rigging was then sent down and coiled away below, and everything made snug aloft. There was not a sailor in the ship who was not rejoiced to see these sticks come down; for, so long as the yards were aloft, on the least sign of a lull, the top-gallant sails were loosed, and then we had to furl them again in a snow-squall, and *shin* up and down single ropes caked with ice, and send royal yards down in the teeth of a gale coming right from the south pole. It was an interesting sight, too, to see our noble ship, dismantled of all her top-hamper of long tapering masts and yards, and boom pointed with spear-head, which ornamented her in port; and all that canvas, which a few days before had covered her like a cloud, from the truck to the water's edge, spreading far out beyond her hull on either side, now gone; and she, stripped, like a wrestler for the fight. It corresponded, too, with the desolate character of her situation;—alone, as she was, battling with storms, wind, and ice, at this extremity of the globe, and in almost constant night.

Friday, July 1st. We were now nearly up to the latitude of Cape Horn, and having over forty degrees of easting to make, we squared away the yards before a strong westerly gale, shook a reef out of the fore-topsail, and stood on our way, east-by-south, with the prospect of being up with the Cape in a week or ten days. As for myself, I had had no sleep for forty-eight hours; and the want of rest, together with constant wet and cold, had increased the swelling, so that my face was nearly as large as two, and I found it impossible to get my mouth open wide enough to eat. In this state, the steward applied to the captain for some rice to boil for me, but he only got a—"No! d— you! Tell him to eat salt junk and hard bread, like the rest of them." For this, of course, I was much obliged to him, and in truth it was just what I expected. However, I did not starve, for the mate, who was a man as well as a sailor, and had always been a good friend to me, smuggled a pan of rice into the galley, and told the cook to boil it for me, and not let the "old man" see it. Had it been fine weather, or in port, I should have gone below and lain by until my face got well; but in such weather as this, and short-handed as we were, it was not for me to desert my post; so I kept on deck, and stood my watch and did my duty as well as I could.

Saturday, July 2d. This day the sun rose fair, but it ran too low in the heavens to give any heat, or thaw out our sails and rigging; yet the sight of it was pleasant; and we had a steady "reef topsail breeze" from the westward. The atmosphere, which had previously been clear and cold, for the last few hours grew damp, and had a disagreeable, wet chilliness in it; and the man who came from the wheel said he heard the captain tell "the passenger" that the thermometer had fallen several degrees since morning, which he could not account for in any other way than by supposing that there must be ice near us; though such a thing had never been heard of in this latitude, at this season of the year. At twelve o'clock we went below, and had just got through dinner, when the cook put his head down the scuttle and told us to come on deck and see the finest sight that we had ever seen. "Where away, cook?" asked the first man who was up. "On the larboard bow." And there lay, floating in the ocean, several miles off, an immense, irregular mass, its top and points covered with snow, and its center of a deep indigo color. This was an iceberg, and of the largest size, as one of our men said who had been in the Northern ocean. As far as the eye could reach, the sea in every direction was of a deep blue color, the waves running high and fresh, and sparkling in the light, and in the midst lay this immense mountain-island, its cavities and valleys thrown into deep shade, and its points and pinnacles glittering in the sun. All hands were soon on deck, looking at it, and admiring in various ways its beauty and grandeur. But no description can give any idea of the strangeness, splendor, and, really, the sublimity, of the sight. Its great size;—for it must have been from two to three miles in circumference, and several hundred feet in height;—its slow motion, as its base rose and sank in the water, and its high points nodded against the clouds; the dashing of the waves upon it, which, breaking high with foam, lined its base with a white crust; and the thundering sound of the cracking of the mass, and the breaking and tumbling down of huge pieces; together with its nearness and approach, which added a slight element of fear,—all combined to give to it the character of true sublimity. The main body of the mass was, as I have said, of an indigo color, its base crusted with frozen foam; and as it grew thin and transparent toward the edges and top, its color shaded off from a deep blue to the whiteness of snow. It seemed to be drifting slowly toward the north, so that we kept away and avoided it. It was in sight all the afternoon; and when we got to leeward of it, the wind died away, so that we lay-to quite near it for a greater part of the night. Unfortunately, there was no moon, but it was a clear night, and we could plainly mark the long, regular heaving of the stupendous mass, as its edges moved slowly against the stars. Several times in our watch loud cracks were heard, which sounded as though they must have run through the whole length of the iceberg, and several pieces fell down with a thundering crash, plunging heavily into the sea. Toward morning, a strong breeze sprang up, and we filled away, and left it astern, and at daylight it was out of sight. The next day, which was

Sunday, July 3d, the breeze continued strong, the air exceedingly chilly, and the thermometer low. In the course of the day we saw several icebergs, of different sizes, but none so near as the one which we saw the day before. Some of them, as well as we could judge, at the distance at which we were, must have been as large as that, if not larger. At noon we were in latitude 55° 12′ south, and supposed longitude 89° 5′ west.

Toward night the wind hauled to the southward, and headed us off our course a little, and blew a tremendous gale; but this we did not mind, as there was no rain nor snow, and we were already under close sail.

Monday, July 4th. This was "independent day" in Boston. What firing of guns, and ringing of bells, and rejoicings of all sorts, in every part of our country! The ladies (who have not gone down to Nahant, for a breath of cool air, and sight of the ocean) walking the streets with parasols over their heads, and the dandies in their white pantaloons and silk stockings! What quantities of ice-cream have been eaten, and what quantities of ice brought into the city from a distance, and sold out by the lump and the pound! The smallest of the islands which we saw today would have made the fortune of poor Jack, if he had had it in Boston; and I dare say he would have had no objection to being there with it. This, to be sure, was no place to keep the fourth of July. To keep ourselves warm, and the ship out of the ice, was as much as we could do. Yet no one forgot the day; and many were the wishes, and conjectures, and comparisons, both serious and ludicrous, which were made among all hands. The sun shone bright as long as it was up, only that a scud of black clouds was ever and anon driving across it. At noon we were in lat. 54° 27′ S., and long. 85° 5′ W., having made a good deal of easting, but having lost in our latitude by the heading of the wind. Between daylight and dark—that is, between nine o'clock and three— we saw thirty-four ice islands, of various sizes; some no bigger than the hull of our vessel, and others apparently nearly as large as the one that we first saw; though, as we went on, the islands became smaller and more numerous; and, at sundown of this day, a man at the mast-head saw large fields of floating ice called "field-ice" at the south-east. This kind of ice is much more dangerous than the large islands, for those can be seen at a distance, and kept away from; but the field-ice, floating in great quantities, and covering the ocean for miles and miles, in pieces of every size—large, flat, and broken cakes, with here and there an island rising twenty and thirty feet, and as large as the ship's hull;—this, it is very difficult to sheer clear of. A constant look-out was necessary; for any of these pieces, coming with the heave of the sea, were large enough to have knocked a hole in the ship, and that would have been the end of us; for no boat (even if we could have got one out) could have lived in such a sea; and no man could have lived in a boat in such weather. To make our condition still worse, the wind came out due east, just after sundown, and it blew a gale dead ahead, with hail and sleet, and a thick fog, so that we could not see half the length of the ship. Our chief reliance, the prevailing westerly gales, was thus cut off; and here we were, nearly seven hundred miles to the westward of the Cape, with a gale dead from the eastward, and the weather so thick that we could not see the ice with which we were surrounded, until it was directly under our bows. At four, P.M. (it was then quite dark) all hands were called, and sent aloft in a violent squall of hail and rain, to take in sail. We had now all got on our "Cape Horn rig"—thick boots, south-westers coming down over our neck and ears, thick trowsers and jackets, and some with oil-cloth suits over all. Mittens, too, we wore on deck, but it would not do to go aloft with them on, for it was impossible to work with them, and, being wet and stiff, they might let a man slip overboard, for all the hold he could get upon a rope; so, we were obliged to work with bare hands, which, as well as our faces, were often cut with the hail-stones, which fell thick and large. Our ship was now all cased with ice,—hull, spars, and standing rigging;—and the running rigging so stiff that we could hardly bend it so as to belay it, or, still worse, take a knot with it; and the sails nearly as stiff as sheet iron. One at a time, (for it was a long piece of work and required many hands,) we furled the courses, mizen topsail, and fore-topmast staysail, and close-reefed the fore and main topsails, and hove the ship to under the fore, with the main hauled up by the clewlines and buntlines, and ready to be sheeted home, if we found it necessary to make sail to get to windward of an island. A regular look-out was then set, and kept by each watch in turn, until the morning. It was a tedious and anxious night. It blew hard the whole time, and there was an almost constant driving of either rain, hail, or snow. In addition to this, it was "as thick as muck," and the ice was all about us. The captain was on deck nearly the whole night, and kept the cook in the galley, with a roaring fire, to make coffee for him, which he took every few hours, and once or twice gave a little to his officers; but not a drop of anything was there for the crew. The captain, who sleeps all the daytime, and comes and goes at night as he chooses, can have his brandy and water in the cabin, and his hot coffee at the galley; while Jack, who has to stand through everything, and work in wet and cold, can have nothing to wet his lips or warm his stomach. This was a "temperance ship," and, like too many such ships, the temperance was all in the forecastle. The sailor, who only takes his one glass as it is dealt out to him, is in danger of being drunk; while the captain, who has all under his hand, and can drink as much as he chooses, and upon whose self-possession and cool judgment the lives of all depend, may be trusted with any amount, to drink at his will. Sailors will never be convinced that rum is a dangerous thing, by taking it away from them, and giving it to the officers; nor that, that temperance is their friend, which takes from them what they have always had, and gives them nothing in the place of it. By seeing it allowed to their officers, they will not be convinced that it is taken from them for their good; and by receiving nothing in its place, they will not believe that it is done in kindness. On the contrary, many of them look upon the change as a new instrument of tyranny. Not that they prefer rum. I never knew a sailor, in my life, who would not prefer a pot of hot coffee or chocolate, in a cold night, to all the rum afloat. They all say that rum only warms them for a time; yet, if they can get nothing better, they will miss what they have lost. The momentary warmth and glow from drinking it; the break and change which is made in a long, dreary watch by the mere calling all hands aft and serving of it out; and the simply having some event to look forward to, and to talk about; give it an importance and a use which no one can appreciate who has not stood his watch before the mast. On my passage round Cape Horn before, the vessel that I was in was not under temperance articles, and grog was served out every middle and morning watch, and after every reefing of topsails; and though I had never drank rum before, and never intend to again, I took my allowance then at the capstan, as the rest did, merely for the momentary warmth it gave the system, and the change in our feelings and aspect of our duties on the watch. At the same time, as I have stated, there was not a man on board who would not have pitched the rum to the dogs, (I have heard them say so, a dozen times) for a pot of coffee or chocolate; or even for our common beverage—"water bewitched, and tea begrudged," as it was.* The temperance reform is the best thing that ever was undertaken for the sailor; but when the grog is taken from him, he ought to have something in its place. As it is now, in most vessels, it is a mere saving to the owners; and this accounts for the sudden increase of temperance ships, which surprised even the best friends of the cause. If every merchant, when he struck grog from the list of the expenses of his ship, had been obliged to substitute as much coffee, or chocolate, as would give each man a pot-full when he came off the topsail yard, on a stormy-night;— I fear Jack might have gone to ruin on the old road.*

But this is not doubling Cape Horn. Eight hours of the night, our watch

* The proportions of the ingredients of the tea that was made for us, (and ours, as I have before stated, was a favorable specimen of American merchantmen) were, a pint of tea, and a pint and a half of molasses, to about three gallons of water. These are all boiled down together in the "coppers," and before serving it out, the mess is stirred up with a stick, so as to give each man his fair share of sweetening and tea-leaves. The tea for the cabin is, of course, made in the usual way, in a tea-pot, and drank with sugar.

* I do not wish these remarks, so far as they relate to the saving of expense in the outfit, to be applied to the owners of our ship, for she was supplied with an abundance of stores, of the best kind that are given to seamen; though the dispensing of them is necessarily left to the captain. Indeed, so high was the reputation of "the employ" among men and officers, for the character and outfit of their vessels, and for their liberality in conducting their voyages, that when it was known that they had a ship fitting out for a long voyage, and that hands were to be shipped at a certain time,—a half hour before the time, as one of the crew told me, numbers of sailors were steering down the wharf, hopping over the barrels, like flocks of sheep.

was on deck, and during the whole of that time we kept a bright look-out: one man on each bow, another in the bunt of the fore yard, the third mate on the scuttle, one on each quarter, and a man always standing by the wheel. The chief mate was everywhere, and commanded the ship when the captain was below. When a large piece of ice was seen in our way, or drifting near us, the word was passed along, and the ship's head turned one way and another; and sometimes the yards squared or braced up. There was little else to do than to look out; and we had the sharpest eyes in the ship on the forecastle. The only variety was the monotonous voice of the look-out forward—"Another island!"—"Ice ahead!"—"Ice on the lee bow!"—"Hard up the helm!"—"Keep her off a little!"—"Stead-y!"

In the meantime, the wet and cold had brought my face into such a state that I could neither eat nor sleep; and though I stood it out all night, yet, when it became light, I was in such a state, that all hands told me I must go below, and lie-by for a day or two, or I should be laid up for a long time, and perhaps have the lock-jaw. When the watch was changed I went into the steerage, and took off my hat and comforter, and showed my face to the mate, who told me to go below at once, and stay in my berth until the swelling went down, and gave the cook orders to make a poultice for me, and said he would speak to the captain.

I went below and turned-in, covering myself over with blankets and jackets, and lay in my berth nearly twenty-four hours, half asleep and half awake, stupid, from the dull pain. I heard the watch called, and the men going up and down, and sometimes a noise on deck, and a cry of "ice," but I gave little attention to anything. At the end of twenty-four hours the pain went down, and I had a long sleep, which brought me back to my proper state; yet my face was so swollen and tender, that I was obliged to keep to my berth for two or three days longer. During the two days I had been below, the weather was much the same that it had been, head winds, and snow and rain; or, if the wind came fair, too foggy, and the ice too thick, to run. At the end of the third day the ice was very thick; a complete fog-bank covered the ship. It blew a tremendous gale from the eastward, with sleet and snow, and there was every promise of a dangerous and fatiguing night. At dark, the captain called all hands aft, and told them that not a man was to leave the deck that night; that the ship was in the greatest danger; any cake of ice might knock a hole in her, or she might run on an island and go to pieces. No one could tell whether she would be a ship the next morning. The lookouts were then set, and every man was put in his station. When I heard what was the state of things, I began to put on my clothes to stand it out with the rest of them, when the mate came below, and looking at my face, ordered me back to my berth, saying that if we went down, we should all go down together, but if I went on deck I might lay myself up for life. This was the first word I had heard from aft; for the captain had done nothing, nor inquired how I was, since I went below.

In obedience to the mate's orders, I went back to my berth; but a more miserable night I never wish to spend. I never felt the curse of sickness so keenly in my life. If I could only have been on deck with the rest, where something was to be done, and seen, and heard; where there were fellow-beings for companions in duty and danger—but to be cooped up alone in a black hole, in equal danger, but without the power to do, was the hardest trial. Several times, in the course of the night, I got up, determined to go on deck; but the silence which showed that there was nothing doing, and the knowledge that I might make myself seriously ill, for nothing, kept me back. It was not easy to sleep, lying, as I did, with my head directly against the bows, which might be dashed in by an island of ice, brought down by the very next sea that struck her. This was the only time I had been ill since I left Boston, and it was the worst time it could have happened. I felt almost willing to bear the plagues of Egypt for the rest of the voyage, if I could but be well and strong for that one night. Yet it was a dreadful night for those on deck. A watch of eighteen hours, with wet, and cold, and constant anxiety, nearly wore them out; and when they came below at nine o'clock for breakfast, they almost dropped asleep on their chests, and some of them were so stiff that they could with difficulty sit down. Not a drop of anything had been given them during the whole time, (though the captain, as on the night that I was on deck, had his coffee every four hours,) except that the mate stole a potfull of coffee for two men to drink behind the galley, while he kept a look-out for the captain. Every man had his station, and was not allowed to leave it; and nothing happened to break the monotony of the night, except once setting the main topsails to run clear of a large island to leeward, which they were drifting fast upon. Some of the boys got so sleepy and stupified, that they actually fell asleep at their posts; and the young third mate, whose station was the exposed one of standing on the fore scuttle, was so stiff, when he was relieved, that he could not bend his knees to get down. By a constant look-out, and a quick shifting of the helm, as the islands and pieces came in sight, the ship went clear of everything but a few small pieces, though daylight showed the ocean covered for miles. At daybreak it fell a dead calm, and with the sun, the fog cleared a little, and a breeze sprung up from the westward, which soon grew into a gale. We had now a fair wind, daylight, and comparatively clear weather; yet, to the surprise of every one, the ship continued hove-to. Why does not he run? What is the captain about? was asked by every one; and from questions, it soon grew into complaints and murmurings. When the daylight was so short, it was too bad to lose it, and a fair wind, too, which every one had been praying for. As hour followed hour, and the captain showed no sign of making sail, the crew became impatient, and there was a good deal of talking and consultation together, on the forecastle. They had been beaten out with the exposure and hardship, and impatient to get out of it, and this unaccountable delay was more than they could bear in quietness, in their excited and restless state. Some said that the captain was frightened,—completely cowed, by the dangers and difficulties that surrounded us, and was afraid to make sail; while others said that in his anxiety and suspense he had made a free use of brandy and opium, and was unfit for his duty. The carpenter, who was an intelligent man, and a thorough seaman, and had great influence with the crew, came down into the forecastle, and tried to induce the crew to go aft and ask the captain why he did not run, or request him, in the name of all hands, to make sail. This appeared to be a very reasonable request, and the crew agreed that if he did not make sail before noon, they would go aft. Noon came, and no sail was made. A consultation was held again, and it was proposed to take the ship from the captain and give the command of her to the mate, who had been heard to say that, if he could have his way, the ship would have been half the distance to the Cape before night,—ice or no ice. And so irritated and impatient had the crew become, that even this proposition, which was open mutiny, punishable with state prison, was entertained, and the carpenter went to his berth, leaving it tacitly understood that something serious would be done, if things remained as they were many hours longer. When the carpenter left, we talked it all over, and I gave my advice strongly against it. Another of the men, too, who had known something of the kind attempted in another ship by a crew who were dissatisfied with their captain, and which was followed with serious consequences, was opposed to it. S—, who soon came down, joined us, and we determined to have nothing to do with it. By these means, they were soon induced to give it up, for the present, though they said they would not lie where they were much longer without knowing the reason.

The affair remained in this state until four o'clock, when an order came forward for all hands to come aft upon the quarter-deck. In about ten minutes they came forward again, and the whole affair had been blown. The carpenter, very prematurely, and without any authority from the crew, had sounded the mate as to whether he would take command of the ship, and intimated an intention to displace the captain; and the mate, as in duty bound, had told the whole to the captain, who immediately sent for all hands aft. Instead of violent measures, or, at least, an outbreak of quarter-deck bravado, threats, and abuse, which they had every reason to expect, a sense of common danger and common suffering seemed to have tamed his spirit, and begotten something like a humane fellow-feeling; for he received the crew in a manner quiet, and even almost kind. He told them what he had heard, and said that he did not believe that they would try to do any such thing as was intimated; that they had always been good men,—obedient, and knew their duty, and he had no fault to find with them; and asked them what they had to complain of—said that no one could say that he was slow to carry sail, (which was true enough;) and that, as soon as he thought it was safe and proper, he should make sail. He added a few words about their duty in their present situation, and sent them forward, saying that he should take no further notice of the matter; but, at the same time, told the carpenter to recollect whose power he was in, and that if he heard another word from him he would have cause to remember him to the day of his death.

This language of the captain had a very good effect upon the crew, and they returned quietly to their duty.

For two days more the wind blew from the southward and eastward; or in the short intervals when it was fair, the ice was too thick to run; yet the weather was not so dreadfully bad, and the crew had watch and watch. I still remained in my berth, fast recovering, yet still not well enough to go safely on deck. And I should have been perfectly useless; for, from having eaten nothing for nearly a week, except a little rice, which I forced into my mouth the last day or two, I was as weak as an infant. To be sick in a forecastle is miserable indeed. It is the worst part of a dog's life; especially in bad weather. The forecastle, shut up tight to keep out the water and cold air;— the watch either on deck, or asleep in their berths;—no one to speak to;—the pale light of the single lamp, swinging to and fro from the beam, so dim that one can scarcely see, much less read by it;—the water dropping from the beams and carlines, and running down the sides; and the forecastle so wet, and dark, and cheerless, and so lumbered up with chests and wet clothes, that sitting up is worse than lying in the berth! These are some of the evils. Fortunately, I needed no help from any one, and no medicine; and if I had needed help, I don't know where I should have found it. Sailors are willing enough, but it is true, as is often said—No one ships for nurse on board a vessel. Our merchant ships are always undermanned, and if one man is lost by sickness, they cannot spare another to take care of him. A sailor is always presumed to be well, and if he's sick, he's a poor dog. One has to stand his wheel, and another his lookout, and the sooner he gets on deck again, the better.

Accordingly, as soon as I could possibly go back to my duty, I put on my thick clothes and boots and south-wester, and made my appearance on deck. Though I had been but a few days below, yet everything looked strangely enough. The ship was cased in ice,—decks, sides, masts, yards, and rigging. Two close-reefed top-sails were all the sail she had on, and every sail and rope was frozen so stiff in its place, that it seemed as though it would be impossible to start anything. Reduced, too, to her topmasts, she had altogether a most forlorn and crippled appearance. The sun had come up brightly; the snow was swept off the decks, and ashes thrown upon them, so that we could walk, for they had been as slippery as glass. It was, of course, too cold to carry on any ship's work, and we had only to walk the deck and keep ourselves warm. The wind was still ahead, and the whole ocean, to the eastward, covered with islands and field-ice. At four bells the order was given to square away the yards; and the man who came from the helm said that the captain had kept her off to N. N. E. What could this mean? Some said that he was going to put into Valparaiso, and winter, and others that he was going to run out of the ice and cross the Pacific, and go home round the Cape of Good Hope. Soon, however, it leaked out, and we found that we were running for the straits of Magellan. The news soon spread through the ship, and all tongues were at work, talking about it. No one on board had been through the straits, but I had in my chest an account of the passage of the ship A. J. Donelson, of New York, through those straits, a few years before. The account was given by the captain, and the representation was as favorable as possible. It was soon read by every one on board, and various opinions pronounced. The determination of our captain had at least this good effect; it gave every one something to think and talk about, made a break in our life, and diverted our minds from the monotonous dreariness of the prospect before us. Having made a fair wind of it, we were going off at a good rate, and leaving the thickest of the ice behind us. This, at least, was something.

Having been long enough below to get my hands well warmed and softened, the first handling of the ropes was rather tough; but a few days hardened them, and as soon as I got my mouth open wide enough to take in a piece of salt beef and hard bread, I was all right again.

Sunday, July 10th. Lat. 54° 10′, long. 79° 07′. This was our position at noon. The sun was out bright; the ice was all left behind, and things had quite a cheering appearance. We brought our wet pea-jackets and trowsers on deck, and hung them up in the rigging, that the breeze and the few hours of sun might dry them a little; and, by the permission of the cook, the galley was nearly filled with stockings and mittens, hung round to be dried. Boots, too, were brought up; and having got a little tar and slush from below, we gave them a thick coat. After dinner, all hands were turned-to, to get the anchors over the bows, bend on the chains, etc. The fish-tackle was got up, fish-davit rigged out, and after two or three hours of hard and cold work, both the anchors were ready for instant use, a couple of kedges got up, a hawser coiled away upon the fore-hatch, and the deep-sea-lead-line overhauled and got ready. Our spirits returned with having something to do; and when the tackle was manned to bowse the anchor home, notwithstanding the desolation of the scene, we struck up "Cheerily ho!" in full chorus. This pleased the mate, who rubbed his hands and cried out—"That's right, my boys; never say die! That sounds like the old crew!" and the captain came up, on hearing the song, and said to the passenger, within hearing of the man at the wheel,—"That sounds like a lively crew. They'll have their song so long as there're enough left for a chorus!"

This preparation of the cable and anchors was for the passage of the straits; for, being very crooked, and with a variety of currents, it is necessary to come frequently to anchor. This was not, by any means, a pleasant prospect, for, of all the work that a sailor is called upon to do in cold weather, there is none so bad as working the ground-tackle. The heavy chain cables to be hauled and pulled about decks with bare hands; wet hawsers, slip-ropes, and buoy-ropes to be hauled aboard, dripping in water, which is running up your sleeves, and freezing; clearing hawse under the bows; getting under weigh and coming-to, at all hours of the night and day, and a constant look-out for rocks and sands and turns of tides;—these are some of the disagreeables of such a navigation to a common sailor. Fair or foul, he wants to have nothing to do with the ground-tackle between port and port. One of our hands, too, had unluckily fallen upon a half of an old newspaper which contained an account of the passage, through the straits, of a Boston brig, called, I think, the *Peruvian,* in which she lost every cable and anchor she had, got aground twice, and arrived at Valparaiso in distress. This was set off against the account of the A. J. Donelson, and led us to look forward with less confidence to the passage, especially as no one on board had ever been through, and the captain had no very perfect charts. However, we were spared any further experience on the point; for the next day, when we must have been near the Cape of Pillars, which is the south-west point of the mouth of the straits, a gale set in from the eastward, with a heavy fog, so that we could not see half of the ship's length ahead. This, of course, put an end to the project, for the present; for a thick fog and a gale blowing dead ahead are not the most favorable circumstances for the passage of difficult and dangerous straits. This weather, too, seemed likely to last for some time, and we could not think of beating about the mouth of the straits for a week or two, waiting for a favorable opportunity; so we braced up on the larboard tack, put the ship's head due south, and struck her off for Cape Horn again.

II

In our first attempt to double the Cape, when we came up to the latitude of it, we were nearly seventeen hundred miles to the westward, but, in running for the straits of Magellan, we stood so far to the eastward, that we made our second attempt at a distance of not more than four or five hundred miles; and we had great hopes, by this means, to run clear of the ice; thinking that the easterly gales, which had prevailed for a long time, would have driven it to the westward. With the wind about two points free, the yards braced in a little, and two close-reefed topsails and a reefed foresail on the ship, we made great way toward the southward; and, almost every watch, when we came on deck, the air seemed to grow colder, and the sea to run higher. Still, we saw no ice, and had great hopes of going clear of it altogether, when, one afternoon, about three o'clock, while we were taking a *siesta* during our watch below, "All hands!" was called in a loud and fearful voice. "Tumble up here, men!—tumble up!—don't stop for your clothes—before we're upon it!" We sprang out of our berths and hurried upon deck. The loud, sharp voice of the captain was heard giving orders, as though for life or death, and we ran aft to the braces, not waiting to look ahead, for not a moment was to be lost. The helm was hard up, the after yards shaking, and the ship in the act of wearing. Slowly, with the stiff ropes and iced rigging, we swung the yards round, everything coming hard, and with a creaking and rending sound, like pulling up a plank which has been frozen into the ice. The ship wore round fairly, the yards were steadied, and we stood off on the other tack, leaving behind us, directly under our larboard quarter, a large ice island, peering out of the mist, and reaching high above our tops, while astern; and on either side of the island, large tracts of field-ice were dimly seen, heaving and rolling in the sea. We were now safe, and standing to the northward; but, in a few minutes more, had it not been for the sharp look-out of the watch, we should have been fairly upon the ice, and left our ship's old bones adrift in the Southern ocean. After standing to the northward a few hours, we wore ship, and, the wind having hauled, we stood to the southward and eastward. All night long, a bright look-out was kept from every part of the deck; and whenever ice was seen on the one bow or the other, the helm was shifted and the yards braced, and by quick working of the ship she was kept clear. The accustomed cry of "Ice ahead!"—"Ice on the lee bow!"—"Another island!" in the same tones, and with the same orders following them, seemed to bring us directly back to our old position of the week before. During our watch on deck, which was from twelve to four, the wind came out ahead, with a pelting storm of hail and sleet, and we lay hove-to, under a close-reefed main topsail, the whole watch. During the next watch it fell calm, with a drenching rain, until daybreak, when the wind came out to the westward, and the weather cleared up, and showed us the whole ocean, in the course which we should have steered, had it not been for the head wind and calm, completely blocked up with ice. Here then our progress was stopped, and we wore ship, and once more stood to the northward and eastward; not for the straits of Magellan, but to make another attempt to double the Cape, still farther to the eastward; for the captain was determined to get round if perseverance could do it; and the third time, he said, never failed.

With a fair wind we soon ran clear of the field-ice, and by noon had only the stray islands floating far and near upon the ocean. The sun was out bright, the sea of a deep blue, fringed with the white foam of the waves which ran high before a strong south-wester; our solitary ship tore on through the water, as though glad to be out of her confinement; and the ice islands lay scattered upon the ocean here and there, of various sizes and shapes, reflecting the bright rays of the sun, and drifting slowly northward before the gale. It was a contrast to much that we had lately seen, and a spectacle not only of beauty, but of life; for it required but little fancy to imagine these islands to be animate masses which had broken loose from the "thrilling regions of thick-ribbed ice," and were working their way, by wind and current, some alone, and some in fleets, to milder climes. No pencil has ever yet given anything like the true effect of an iceberg. In a picture, they are huge, uncouth masses, stuck in the sea, while their chief beauty and grandeur, —their slow, stately motion; the whirling of the snow about their summits, and the fearful groaning and cracking of their parts,—the picture cannot give. This is the large iceberg; while the small and distant islands, floating on the smooth sea, in the light of a clear day, look like little floating fairy isles of sapphire.

From a north-east course we gradually hauled to the eastward, and after sailing about two hundred miles, which brought us as near to the western coast of Terra del Fuego as was safe, and having lost sight of the ice altogether,—for the third time we put the ship's head to the southward, to try the passage of the Cape. The weather continued clear and cold, with a strong gale from the westward, and we were fast getting up with the latitude of the Cape, with a prospect of soon being round. One fine afternoon, a man who had gone into the fore-top to shift the rolling tackles, sung out, at the top of his voice, and with evident glee,—"Sail ho!" Neither land nor sail had we seen since leaving San Diego; and any one who has traversed the length of a whole ocean alone, can imagine what an excitement such an announcement produced on board. "Sail ho!" shouted the cook, jumping out of his galley; "Sail ho!" shouted a man, throwing back the slide of the scuttle, to the watch below, who were soon out of their berths and on deck; and "Sail ho!" shouted the captain down the companionway to the passenger in the cabin. Beside the pleasure of seeing a ship and human beings in so desolate a place, it was important for us to speak a vessel, to learn whether there was ice to the eastward, and to ascertain the longitude; for we had no chronometer, and had been drifting about so long that we had nearly lost our reckoning, and opportunities for lunar observations are not frequent or sure in such a place as Cape Horn. For these various reasons, the excitement in our little community was running high, and conjectures were made, and everything thought of for which the captain would hail, when the man aloft sung out—"Another sail, large on the weather bow!" This was a little odd, but so much the better, and did not shake our faith in their being sails. At length the man in the top hailed, and said he believed it was land, after all. "Land in your eye!" said the mate, who was looking through the telescope; "they are ice islands, if I can see a hole through a ladder;" and a few moments showed the mate to be right; and all our expectations fled; and instead of what we most wished to see, we had what we most dreaded, and what we hoped we had seen the last of. We soon, however, left these astern, having passed within about two miles of them; and at sundown the horizon was clear in all directions.

Having a fine wind, we were soon up with and passed the latitude of the Cape, and having stood far enough to the southward to give it a wide berth, we began to stand to the eastward, with a good prospect of being round and steering to the northward on the other side, in a very few days. But ill luck seemed to have lighted upon us. Not four hours had we been standing on in this course, before it fell dead calm; and in half an hour it clouded up; a few straggling blasts, with spits of snow and sleet, came from the eastward; and in an hour more, we lay hove-to under a close-reefed main topsail, drifting bodily off to leeward before the fiercest storm that we had yet felt, blowing dead ahead, from the eastward. It seemed as though the genius of the place had been roused at finding that we had nearly slipped through his fingers, and had come down upon us with tenfold fury. The sailors said that every blast, as it shook the shrouds, and whistled through the rigging, said to the old ship, "No you don't!"—"No, you don't!"

For eight days we lay drifting about in this manner. Sometimes,—generally towards noon,—it fell calm; once or twice a round copper ball showed itself for a few moments in the place where the sun ought to have been; and a puff or two came from the westward, giving some hope that a fair wind had come at last. During the first two days, we made sail for these puffs, shaking the reefs out of the topsails and boarding the tacks of the courses; but finding that it only made work for us when the gale set in again, it was soon given up, and we lay-to under our close-reefs. We had less snow and hail than when we were farther to the westward, but we had an abundance of what is worse to a sailor in cold weather—drenching rain. Snow is blinding, and very bad when coming upon a coast, but, for genuine discomfort, give me rain with freezing weather. A snow-storm is exciting, and it does not wet through the clothes (which is important to a sailor); but a constant rain there is no escaping from. It wets to the skin, and makes all protection vain. We had long ago run through all our dry clothes, and as sailors have no other way of drying them than by the sun, we had nothing to do but to put on those which were the least wet. At the end of each watch, when we came below, we took off our clothes and wrung them out; two taking hold of a pair of trowsers,—one at each end,—and jackets in the same way. Stockings, mittens, and all, were wrung out also and then hung up to drain and chafe dry against the bulkheads. Then, feeling of all our clothes, we picked out those which were the least wet, and put them on, so as to be ready for a call, and turned-in, covered ourselves up with blankets, and slept until three knocks on the scuttle and the dismal sound of "All starbowlines ahoy! Eight bells, there below! Do you hear the news?" drawled out from on deck, and the sulky answer of "Aye, aye!" from below, sent us up again.

On deck, all was as dark as a pocket, and either a dead calm, with the rain pouring steadily down, or, more generally, a violent gale dead ahead, with rain pelting horizontally, and occasional variations of hail and sleet;—decks afloat with water swashing from side to side, and constantly wet feet; for boots could not be wrung out like drawers, and no composition could stand the constant soaking. In fact, wet and cold feet are inevitable in such weather, and are not the least of those little items which go to make up the grand total of the discomforts of a winter passage round the Cape. Few words were spoken between the watches as they shifted, the wheel was relieved, the mate took his place on the quarter-deck, the look-outs in the bows; and each man had his narrow space to walk fore and aft in, or, rather, to swing himself forward and back in, from one belaying pin to another,—for the decks were too slippery with ice and water to allow of much walking. To make a walk, which is absolutely necessary to pass away the time, one of us hit upon the expedient of sanding the deck; and afterwards, whenever the rain was not so violent as to wash it off, the weatherside of the quarter-deck, and a part of the waist and forecastle were sprinkled with the sand which we had on board for holystoning; and thus we made a good promenade, where we walked fore and aft, two and two, hour after hour, in our long, dull and comfortless watches. The bells seemed to be an hour or two apart, instead of half an hour, and an age to elapse before the welcome sound of eight bells. The sole object was to make the time pass on. Any change was sought for, which would break the monotony of the time; and even the two hours' trick at the wheel, which came round to each of us, in turn, once in every other watch, was looked upon as a relief. Even the never-failing resource of long yarns, which eke out many a watch, seemed to have failed us now; for we had been so long together that we had heard each other's stories told over and over again, till we had them by heart; each one knew the whole history of each of the others, and we were fairly and literally talked out. Singing and joking, we were in no humor for, and, in fact, any sound of mirth or laughter would have struck strangely upon our ears, and would not have been tolerated, any more than whistling, or a wind instrument. The last resort, that of speculating upon the future, seemed now to fail us, for our discouraging situation, and the danger we were really in, (as we expected every day to find ourselves drifted back among the ice) "clapped a stopper" upon all that.

From saying—"*when* we get home"—we began insensibly to alter it to—"*if* we get home"—and at last the subject was dropped by a tacit consent.

In this state of things, a new light was struck out, and a new field opened, by a change in the watch. One of our watch was laid up for two or three days by a bad hand, (for in cold weather the least cut or bruise ripens into a sore,) and his place was supplied by the carpenter. This was a windfall, and there was quite a contest, who should have the carpenter to walk with him. As "Chips" was a man of some little education, and he and I had had a good deal of intercourse with each other, he fell in with me in my walk. He was a Fin, but spoke English very well, and gave me long accounts of his country; —the customs, the trade, the towns, what little he knew of the government, (I found he was no friend of Russia,) his voyages, his first arrival in America, his marriage and courtship;—he had married a countrywoman of his, a dress-maker, whom he met with in Boston. I had very little to tell him of my quiet, sedentary life at home; and, in spite of our best efforts, which had protracted these yarns through five or six watches, we fairly talked one another out, and I turned him over to another man in the watch, and put myself upon my own resources.

I commenced a deliberate system of time-killing, which united some profit with a cheering up of the heavy hours. As soon as I came on deck, and took my place and regular walk, I began with repeating over to myself a string of matters which I had in my memory, in regular order. First, the multiplication table and the tables of weights and measures; then the states of the Union, with their capitals; the counties of England, with their shire towns; the kings of England in their order; and a large part of the peerage, which I committed from an almanac that we had on board; and then the Kanaka numerals. This carried me through my facts, and, being repeated deliberately, with long intervals, often eked out the two first bells. Then came the ten commandments; the thirty-ninth chapter of Job, and a few other passages from Scripture. The next in the order, that I never varied from, came Cowper's Castaway, which was a great favorite with me; the solemn measure and gloomy character of which, as well as the incident that it was founded upon, made it well suited to a lonely watch at sea. Then his lines to Mary, his address to the jackdaw, and a short extract from Table Talk; (I abounded in Cowper, for I happened to have a volume of his poems in my chest;) "Ille et nefasto" from Horace, and Goethe's "Erl King." After I had got through these, I allowed myself a more general range among everything that I could remember, both in prose and verse. In this way, with an occasional break by relieving the wheel, heaving the log, and going to the scuttlebutt for a drink of water, the longest watch was passed away; and I was so regular in my silent recitations, that if there was no interruption by ship's duty, I could tell very nearly the number of bells by my progress.

Our watches below were no more varied than the watch on deck. All washing, sewing, and reading was given up; and we did nothing but eat, sleep, and stand our watch, leading what might be called a Cape Horn life. The forecastle was too uncomfortable to sit up in; and whenever we were below, we were in our berths. To prevent the rain, and the sea-water which broke over the bows, from washing down, we were obliged to keep the scuttle closed, so that the forecastle was nearly air-tight. In this little, wet, leaky hole, we were all quartered, in an atmosphere so bad that our lamp, which swung in the middle from the beams, sometimes actually burned blue, with a large circle of foul air about it. Still, I was never in better health than after three weeks of this life. I gained a great deal of flesh, and we all ate like horses. At every watch, when we came below, before turning-in, the bread barge and beef kid were overhauled. Each man drank his quart of hot tea night and morning; and glad enough we were to get it, for no nectar and ambrosia were sweeter to the lazy immortals, than was a pot of hot tea, a hard biscuit, and a slice of cold salt beef, to us after a watch on deck. To be sure, we were mere animals, and had this life lasted a year instead of a month, we should have been little better than the ropes in the ship. Not a razor, nor a brush, nor a drop of water, except the rain and the spray, had come near us all the time; for we were on an allowance of fresh water; and who would strip and wash himself in salt water on deck, in the snow and ice, with the thermometer at zero?

After about eight days of constant easterly gales, the wind hauled occasionally a little to the southward, and blew hard, which, as we were well to the southward, allowed us to brace in a little and stand on, under all the sail we could carry. These turns lasted but a short while, and sooner or later it set in again from the old quarter; yet at each time we made something, and were gradually edging along to the eastward. One night, after one of these shifts of the wind, and when all hands had been up a great part of the time, our watch was left on deck, with the mainsail hanging in the buntlines, ready to be set if necessary. It came on to blow worse and worse, with hail and snow beating like so many furies upon the ship, it being as dark and thick as night could make it. The mainsail was blowing and slatting with a noise like thunder, when the captain came on deck, and ordered it to be furled. The mate was about to call all hands, when the captain stopped him, and said that the men would be beaten out if they were called up so often; that as our watch must stay on deck, it might as well be doing that as anything else. Accordingly, we went upon the yard; and never shall I forget that piece of work. Our watch had been so reduced by sickness, and by some having been left in California, that, with one man at the wheel, we had only the third mate and three beside myself to go aloft; so that, at most, we could only attempt to furl one yard-arm at a time. We manned the weather yard-arm, and set to work to make a furl of it. Our lower masts being short, and our yards very square, the sail had a head of nearly fifty feet, and a short leach, made still shorter by the deep reef which was in it, which brought the clue away out on the quarters of the yard, and made a bunt nearly as square as the mizen royal-yard. Beside this difficulty, the yard over which we lay was cased with ice, the gaskets and rope of the foot and leach of the sail as stiff and hard as a piece of suction-hose, and the sail itself about as pliable as though it had been made of sheets of sheathing copper. It blew a perfect hurricane, with alternate blasts of snow, hail, and rain. We had to *fist* the sail with bare hands. No one could trust himself to mittens, for if he slipped, he was a gone man. All the boats were hoisted in on deck, and there was nothing to be lowered for him. We had need of every finger God had given us. Several times we got the sail upon the yard, but it blew away again before we could secure it. It required men to lie over the yard to pass each turn of the gaskets, and when they were passed, it was almost impossible to knot them so that they would hold. Frequently we were obliged to leave off altogether and take to beating our hands upon the sail, to keep them from freezing. After some time,—which seemed forever,—we got the weather side stowed after a fashion, and went over to leeward for another trial. This was still worse, for the body of the sail had been blown over to leeward, and as the yard was a-cock-bill by the lying over of the vessel, we had to light it all up to windward. When the yard-arms were furled, the bunt was all adrift again, which made more work for us. We got all secure at last, but we had been nearly an hour and a half upon the yard, and it seemed an age. It had just struck five bells when we went up, and eight were struck soon after we came down. This may seem slow work, but considering the state of everything, and that we had only five men to a sail with just half as many square yards of canvas in it as the mainsail of the Independence, sixty-gun ship, which musters seven hundred men at her quarters, it is not wonderful that we were no quicker about it. We were glad enough to get on deck, and still more, to go below. The oldest sailor in the watch said, as he went down,—"I shall never forget that main yard;—it beats all my going a fishing. Fun is fun, but furling one yard-arm of a course, at a time, off Cape Horn, is no better than man-killing."

During the greater part of the next two days, the wind was pretty steady from the southward. We had evidently made great progress, and had good hope of being soon up with the Cape, if we were not there already. We could put but little confidence in our reckoning, as there had been no opportunities for an observation, and we had drifted too much to allow of our dead reckoning being anywhere near the mark. If it would clear off enough to give a chance for an observation, or if we could make land, we should know where we were; and upon these, and the chances of falling in with a sail from the eastward, we depended almost entirely.

Friday, July 22d. This day we had a steady gale from the southward, and stood on under close sail, with the yards eased a little by the weather braces, the clouds lifting a little, and showing signs of breaking away. In the afternoon, I was below with Mr. H—, the third mate, and two others, filling the bread locker in the steerage from the casks, when a bright gleam of sunshine broke out and shone down the companionway and through the sky-light, lighting up everything below, and sending a warm glow through the heart of every one. It was a sight we had not seen for weeks,—an omen, a god-send. Even the roughest and hardest face acknowledged its influence. Just at that moment we heard a loud shout from all parts of the deck, and the mate called out down the companionway to the captain, who was sitting in the cabin. What he said, we could not distinguish, but the captain kicked over his chair, and was on deck at one jump. We could not tell what it was; and, anxious as we were to know, the discipline of the ship would not allow of our leaving our places. Yet, as we were not called, we knew there was no danger. We hurried to get through with our job, when, seeing the steward's black face peering out of the pantry, Mr. H— hailed him, to know what was the matter. "Lan' o, to be sure, sir! No you hear 'em sing out, 'Lan' o?' De cap'em say 'im Cape Horn!"

This gave us a new start, and we were soon through our work, and on deck; and there lay the land, fair upon the larboard beam, and slowly edging away upon the quarter. All hands were busy looking at it,—the captain and mates from the quarter-deck, the cook from his galley, and the sailors from the forecastle; and even Mr. N., the passenger, who had kept in his shell for nearly a month, and hardly been seen by anybody, and who we had almost forgotten was on board, came out like a butterfly, and was hopping round as bright as a bird.

The land was the island of Staten Land, just to the eastward of Cape Horn; and a more desolate-looking spot I never wish to set eyes upon;— bare, broken, and girt with rocks and ice, with here and there, between the rocks and broken hillocks, a little stunted vegetation of shrubs. It was a place well suited to stand at the junction of the two oceans, beyond the reach of human cultivation, and encounter the blasts and snows of a perpetual winter. Yet, dismal as it was, it was a pleasant sight to us; not only as being the first land we had seen, but because it told us that we had passed the Cape,—were in the Atlantic,—and that, with twenty-four hours of this breeze, might bid defiance to the Southern ocean. It told us, too, our latitude and longitude better than any observation; and the captain now knew where we were, as well as if we were off the end of Long wharf.

In the general joy, Mr. N. said he should like to go ashore upon the island

and examine a spot which probably no human being had ever set foot upon; but the captain intimated that he would see the island—specimens and all,—in—another place, before he would get out a boat or delay the ship one moment for him.

We left the land gradually astern; and at sundown had the Atlantic ocean clear before us.

⚓

THE LYDIA AND THE NATIVIDAD

⚓

THE LYDIA AND THE NATIVIDAD

C. S. Forester

⚓ *Of all the Hornblower series, it seems to me that the parts in which he appears as a Captain commanding his own ship, most nearly satisfy the average reader's craving for action. Here the interest is self-contained. It is ship against ship, without the distraction of hierarchy in a fleet or diplomacy in high places. The fight is between the "Lydia" and the "Natividad," between Hornblower and Crespo.*

FROM the *Lydia's* masthead, in the clear daylight of the Pacific, a ship might be seen at a distance of as much as twenty miles, perhaps. A circle of twenty miles' radius, therefore, covered the extent of sea over which she had observation. It kept Hornblower occupied, during the remaining hours of darkness, to calculate the size of the circle in which the *Natividad* would necessarily be found next morning. She might be close at hand; she might be as much as a hundred and fifty miles away. That meant that if pure chance dictated the positions of the ships at dawn, it was almost exactly fifty to one against the *Natividad* being in sight; fifty to one on the ruin of Hornblower's professional reputation and only his professional abilities to counterbalance those odds. Only if he had guessed his enemy's plans correctly would he stand justified, and his officers knew it as well as he. Hornblower was conscious that Gerard was looking at him with interest through the darkness, and that consciousness caused him to hold himself rigid and immobile on the deck, neither walking up and down nor fidgeting, even though he could feel his heart beating faster each time he realised that dawn was approaching.

The blackness turned to grey. Now the outlines of the ship could be ascertained. The main topsail could be seen clearly. So could the fore topsail.

Astern of them now the faintest hint of pink began to show in the greyness of the sky. Now the bulk of the grey waves overside could be seen as well as their white edges. Overhead by now the stars were invisible. The accustomed eye could pierce the greyness for a mile about the ship. And then astern, to the eastward, as the *Lydia* lifted on a wave, a grain of gold showed over the horizon, vanished, returned, and grew. Soon it became a great slice of the sun, sucking up greedily the faint mist which hung over the sea. Then the whole disc lifted clear, and the miracle of the dawn was accomplished.

"Sail ho!" came pealing down from the masthead; Hornblower had calculated aright.

Dead ahead, and ten miles distant, she was wallowing along, her appearance oddly at contrast with the one she had presented yesterday morning. Something had been done to give her a jury rig. A stumpy topmast had been erected where her foremast had stood, raked far back in clumsy fashion; her main topmast had been replaced by a slight spar—a royal mast, presumably —and on this jury rig she carried a queer collection of jibs and foresails and spritsails all badly set—"Like old Mother Brown's washing on the line," said Bush—to enable her to keep away from the wind with main course and mizzen topsail and driver set.

At sight of the *Lydia* she put her helm over and came round until her masts were in line, heading away from the frigate.

"Making a stern chase of it," said Gerard, his glass to his eye. "He had enough yesterday, I fancy."

Hornblower heard the remark. He could understand Crespo's psychology better than that. If it were profitable to him to postpone action, and it undoubtedly was, he was quite right to continue doing so, even at the eleventh hour. At sea nothing was certain. Something might prevent the *Lydia's* coming into action; a squall of wind, the accidental carrying away of a spar, an opportune descent of mist—any one of the myriad things which might happen at sea. There was still a chance that the *Natividad* might get clear away, and Crespo was exploiting that chance to the last of his ability. That was logical though unheroic, exactly as one might expect of Crespo.

It was Hornblower's duty to see that the chance did not occur. He examined the *Natividad* closely, ran his eyes over the *Lydia's* sails to see that every one was drawing, and bethought himself of his crew.

"Send the hands to breakfast," he said—every captain of a King's ship took his men into action with full bellies if possible.

He remained, pacing up and down the quarterdeck, unable to keep himself still any longer. The *Natividad* might be running away, but he knew well that she would fight hard enough when he caught her up. Those smashing twenty-four-pounders which she carried on her lower deck were heavy metal against which to oppose the frail timbers of a frigate. They had wrought enough damage yesterday—he could hear the melancholy clanking of the pumps keeping down the water which leaked through the holes they had made; that clanking sound had continued without a break since yesterday. With a jury mizzenmast, and leaking like a sieve despite the sail under her bottom, with sixty four of her attenuated crew hors de combat, the *Lydia* was in no condition to fight a severe battle. Defeat for her and death for him might be awaiting them across that strip of blue sea.

Polwheal suddenly appeared beside him on the quarterdeck, a tray in his hand.

"Your breakfast, sir," he said, "seeing as how we'll be in action when your usual time comes."

As he proffered the tray Hornblower suddenly realised how much he wanted that steaming cup of coffee. He took it eagerly and drank thirstily before he remembered that he must not display human weakness of appetite before his servant.

"Thank you, Polwheal," he said, sipping discreetly.

"An' 'er la'ship's compliments, sir, an' please may she stay where she is in the orlop when the action is renooed."

"Ha—h'm," said Hornblower, staring at him, thrown out of his stride by this unexpected question. All through the night he had been trying to forget the problem of Lady Barbara, as a man tries to forget an aching tooth. The orlop meant that Lady Barbara would be next to the wounded, separated from them only by a canvas screen—no place for a woman. But for that matter neither was the cable tier. The obvious truth was that there was no place for a woman in a frigate about to fight a battle.

"Put her wherever you like as long as she is out of reach of shot," he said, irritably.

"Aye aye, sir. An' 'er la'ship told me to say that she wished you the best of good fortune today, sir, an'—an'—she was confident that you would meet with the success you—you deserve, sir."

Polwheal stumbled over this long speech in a manner which revealed that he had not been quite as successful in learning it fluently as he wished.

"Thank you, Polwheal," said Hornblower, gravely. He remembered Lady Barbara's face as she looked up at him from the main deck yesterday. It was clean cut and eager—like a sword, was the absurd simile which came up in his mind.

"Ha—h'm," said Hornblower angrily. He was aware that his expression had softened, and he feared lest Polwheal should have noticed it, at a moment when he knew about whom he was thinking. "Get below and see that her ladyship is comfortable."

The hands were pouring up from breakfast now; the pumps were clanking with a faster rhythm now that a fresh crew was at work upon them. The guns' crews were gathered about their guns, and the few idlers were crowded on the forecastle eagerly watching the progress of the chase.

"Do you think the wind's going to hold, sir?" asked Bush, coming onto the quarterdeck like a bird of ill omen. "Seems to me as if the sun's swallowing it."

There was no doubting the fact that as the sun climbed higher in the sky the wind was diminishing in force. The sea was still short, steep, and rough, but the *Lydia's* motion over it was no longer light and graceful. She was pitching and jerking inelegantly, deprived of the steady pressure of a good sailing wind. The sky overhead was fast becoming of a hard metallic blue.

"We're overhauling 'em fast," said Hornblower, staring fixedly at the chase so as to ignore these portents of the elements.

"Three hours and we're up to 'em," said Bush. "If the wind only holds."

It was fast growing hot. The heat which the sun was pouring down on them was intensified by its contrast with the comparative coolness of the night before. The crew had begun to seek the strips of shade under the gangways, and were lying there wearily. The steady clanging of the pumps seemed to sound louder now that the wind was losing its force. Hornblower suddenly realised that he would feel intensely weary if he permitted himself to think about it. He stood stubborn on the quarterdeck with the sun beating on his back, every few moments raising his telescope to stare at the *Natividad,* while Bush fussed about the trimming of the sails as the breeze began to waver.

"Steer small, blast you," he growled at the quartermaster at the wheel as the ship's head fell away in the trough of a wave.

"I can't sir, begging your pardon," was the reply. "There aren't enough wind."

It was true enough. The wind had died away so that the *Lydia* could not maintain the two knot speed which was sufficient to give her rudder power to act.

"We'll have to wet the sail. Mr. Bush, see to it, if you please," said Hornblower.

One division of one watch was roused up to this duty. A soaking wet sail will hold air which would escape if it were dry. Whips were rove through the blocks on the yards, and sea water hoisted up and poured over the canvas. So hot was the sun and so rapid the evaporation that the buckets had to be kept continually in action. To the clanging of the pumps was now added the shrilling of the sheaves in the blocks. The *Lydia* crept, still plunging madly, over the tossing sea and under the glaring sky.

"She's boxing the compass now," said Bush with a jerk of his thumb at the distant *Natividad*. "She can't compare with this beauty. She won't find that new rig of hers any help, neither."

The *Natividad* was turning idly backwards and forwards on the waves, showing sometimes her broadside and sometimes her three masts in line, unable to steer any course in the light air prevailing. Bush looked complacently up at his new mizzenmast, a pyramid of canvas, and then across at the swaying *Natividad,* less than five miles away. The minutes crept by, their passage marked only by the monotonous noises of the ship. Hornblower stood in the scorching sunlight, fingering his telescope.

"Here comes the wind again, by God!" said Bush, suddenly. It was sufficient wind to make the ship heel a little, and to summon a faint harping from the rigging. " 'Vast heaving with those buckets, there.' "

The *Lydia* crept steadily forward, heaving and plunging to the music of the water under her bows, while the *Natividad* grew perceptibly nearer.

"It will reach him quickly enough. There! What did I say?"

The *Natividad's* sails filled as the breeze came down to her. She straightened upon her course.

" 'Twon't help him as much as it helps us. God, if it only holds!" commented Bush.

The breeze wavered and then renewed itself. The *Natividad* was hull-up now across the water when a wave lifted her. Another hour—less than an hour—and she would be in range.

"We'll be trying long shots at her soon," said Bush.

"Mr. Bush," said Hornblower, spitefully, "I can judge of the situation without the assistance of your comments, profound though they be."

"I beg your pardon, sir," said Bush, hurt. He flushed angrily for a moment until he noticed the anxiety in Hornblower's tired eyes, and then stumped away to the opposite rail to forget his rage.

As if by way of comment the big main-course flapped loudly, once, like a gun. The breeze was dying away as motivelessly as it had begun. And the *Natividad* still held it; she was holding her course steadily, drawing away once more, helped by the fluky wind. Here in the tropical Pacific one ship can have a fair wind while another two miles away lies becalmed, just as the heavy sea in which they were rolling indicated that last night's gale was still blowing, over the horizon, at the farther side of the Gulf of Tehuantepec. Hornblower stirred uneasily in the blazing sun. He feared lest he should see the *Natividad* sail clean away from him; the wind had died away so much that there was no point in wetting the sails, and the *Lydia* was rolling and sagging about aimlessly now to the send of the waves. Ten minutes passed before he was reassured by the sight of the *Natividad's* similar behaviour.

There was not a breath of wind now. The *Lydia* rolled wildly, to the accompaniment of a spasmodic creaking of woodwork, flapping of sails, and clattering of blocks. Only the clangour of the pumps sounded steadily through the hot air. The *Natividad* was four miles away now—a mile and a half beyond the farthest range of any of the *Lydia's* guns.

"Mr. Bush," said Hornblower. "We will tow with the boats. Have the launch and the cutter hoisted out."

Bush looked doubtful for a moment. He feared that two could play at that game. But he realised—as Hornblower had realised before him—that the *Lydia's* graceful hull would be more amenable to towing than the *Natividad's* ungainly bulk, even without counting the possibility that yesterday's action might have left her with no boat left that would swim. It was Hornblower's duty to try every course that might bring his ship into action with the enemy.

"Boats away!" roared Harrison. "Cutter's crew, launch's crew."

The pipes of his mates endorsed the orders. The hands tailed on to the tackles, and each boat in turn was swayed up into the air, and lowered outboard, the boats' crews fending off as the *Lydia* rolled in the swell.

There began for the boats' crews a period of the most exhausting and exasperating labour. They would tug and strain at the oars, moving the ponderous boats over the heaving waves, until the tow ropes tightened with a jerk as the strain came upon them. Then, tug as they would, they would seem to make no progress at all, the oar blades foaming impotently through the blue water, until the *Lydia* consented to crawl forward a little and the whole operation could be repeated. The heaving waves were a hindrance to them—sometimes every man on one side of a boat would catch a simultaneous crab so that the boat would spin round and become a nuisance to the other one—and the *Lydia,* so graceful and willing when under sail, was a perfect bitch when being towed.

She yawed and she sagged, falling away in the trough on occasions so much that the launch and the cutter were dragged, with much splashing from the oars, stern first after her wavering bows, and then changing her mind and heaving forward so fast after the two ropes that the men, flinging their weight upon the oar looms in expectation of a profitless pull, were precipitated backwards with the ease of progression while in imminent danger of being run down.

They sat naked on the thwarts while the sweat ran in streams down their faces and chests, unable—unlike their comrades at the pumps—to forget their fatigues in the numbness of monotonous work when every moment called for vigilance and attention, tugging painfully away, their agonies of thirst hardly relieved by the allowance of water doled out to them by the petty officers in the sternsheets, tugging away until even hands calloused by years of pulling and hauling cracked and blistered so that the oars were agony to touch.

Hornblower knew well enough the hardship they were undergoing. He went forward and looked down at the toiling seamen, knowing perfectly well that his own body would not be able to endure that labour for more than half an hour at most. He gave orders for an hourly relief at the oars, and he did his best to cheer the men on. He felt an uneasy sympathy for them—three quarters of them had never been sailors until this commission, and had no desire to be sailors either, but had been swept up by the all-embracing press seven months ago. Hornblower was always able (rather against his will) to do what most of his officers failed to do—he saw his crew not as topmen or hands, but as what they had been before the press caught them, stevedores, wherry men, porters.

He had waggoners and potters—he had even two draper's assistants and a printer among his crew; men snatched without notice from their families and their employment and forced into this sort of labour, on wretched food, in hideous working conditions, haunted always by the fear of the cat or of Harrison's rattan, and with the chance of death by drowning or by hostile action to seal the bargain. So imaginative an individualist as Hornblower was bound to feel sympathy with them even when he felt he ought not, especially as he (in common with a few other liberals) found himself growing more and more liberal minded with the progress of years. But to counterbalance this weakness of his there was his restless nervous anxiety to finish off well any task he had set himself to do. With the *Natividad* in sight he could not rest until he had engaged her, and when a captain of a ship cannot rest his crew certainly cannot—aching backs or bleeding hands notwithstanding.

By careful measurement with his sextant of the subtended angles he was able to say with certainty at the end of an hour that the efforts of the boats' crews had dragged the *Lydia* a little nearer to the *Natividad,* and Bush, who had taken the same measurements, was in agreement. The sun rose higher and the *Lydia* crept inch by inch towards her enemy.

"*Natividad's* hoisting out a boat, sir," hailed Knyvett from the foretop.

"How many oars?"

"Twelve, sir, I think. They're taking the ship in tow."

"And they're welcome," scoffed Bush. "Twelve oars won't move that old tub of a *Natividad* very far."

Hornblower glared at him and Bush retired to his own side of the quarter-deck again; he had forgotten his captain was in this unconversational mood. Hornblower was fretting himself into a fever. He stood in the glaring sun while the heat was reflected up into his face from the deck under his feet. His shirt chafed him where he sweated. He felt caged, like a captive beast, within the limitations of practical details. The endless clanking of the pumps, the rolling of the ship, the rattle of the rigging, the noise of the oars in the rowlocks, were driving him mad, as though he could scream (or weep) at the slightest additional provocation.

At noon he changed the men at the oars and pumps, and sent the crew to dinner—he remembered bitterly that he had already made them breakfast in anticipation of immediate action. At two bells he began to wonder whether the *Natividad* might be within extreme long range, but the mere fact of wondering told him that it was not the case—he knew his own sanguine temperament too well, and he fought down the temptation to waste powder and shot. And then, as he looked for the thousandth time through his telescope, he suddenly saw a disc of white appear on the high stern of the *Natividad*. The disc spread and expanded into a thin cloud, and six seconds after its first appearance the dull thud of the shot reached his ears. The *Natividad* was evidently willing to try the range.

"*Natividad* carries two long eighteens aft on the quarterdeck," said Gerard to Bush in Hornblower's hearing. "Heavy metal for stern chasers."

Hornblower knew it already. He would have to run the gauntlet of those two guns for an hour, possibly, before he could bring the brass nine-pounder on his forecastle into action. Another puff of smoke from the *Natividad,* and this time Hornblower saw a spout of water rise from the breast of a wave half a mile ahead. But at that long range and on that tossing sea it did not mean that the *Lydia* was still half a mile beyond the *Natividad's* reach. Hornblower heard the next shot arrive, and saw a brief fountain of water rise no more than fifty yards from the *Lydia's* starboard quarter.

"Mr. Gerard," said Hornblower. "Send for Mr. Marsh and see what he can do with the long nine forward."

It would cheer the men up to have a gun banging away occasionally instead of being merely shot at without making any reply. Marsh came waddling up from the darkness of the magazine, and blinked in the blinding sunshine. He shook his head doubtfully as he eyed the distance between the ships, but he had the gun cleared away, and he loaded it with his own hand, lovingly. He measured out the powder charge on the fullest scale, and he spent several seconds selecting the roundest and truest shot from the locker. He trained the gun with care, and then stood aside, lanyard in hand, watching the heave of the ship and the send of the bows, while a dozen telescopes were trained on the *Natividad* and every eye watched for the fall of the shot. Suddenly he jerked the lanyard and the cannon roared out, its report sounding flat in the heated motionless air.

"Two cables' lengths astern of her!" yelled Knyvett from the foretop. Hornblower had missed the splash—another proof, to his mind, of his own incompetence, but he concealed the fact under a mask of imperturbability.

"Try again, Mr. Marsh," he said.

The *Natividad* was firing both stern chasers together now. As Hornblower spoke there came a crash forward as one of the eighteen-pounder balls struck home close above the water line. Hornblower could hear young Savage, down in the launch, hurling shrill blasphemies at the men at the oars to urge them on—that shot must have passed just over his head. Marsh stroked his beard and addressed himself to the task of reloading the long nine-pounder. While he was so engaged, Hornblower was deep in the calculation of the chances of battle.

That long nine, although of smaller calibre, was of longer range than his shorter main deck guns, while the carronades which comprised half of the *Lydia's* armament were useless at anything longer than close range. The *Lydia* would have to draw up close to her enemy before she could attack her with effect. There would be a long and damaging interval between the moment when the *Natividad* should be able to bring all her guns into action and the moment when the *Lydia* could hit back at her. There would be casualties, guns dismounted perhaps, serious losses. Hornblower balanced the arguments for and against continuing to try and close with the enemy while Mr. Marsh was squinting along the sights of the nine-pounder. Then Hornblower scowled to himself, and ceased tugging at his chin, his mind made up. He had started the action; he would go through it to the end, cost what it might. His flexibility of mind could crystallise into sullen obstinacy.

The nine-pounder went off as though to signal this decision.

"Just alongside her!" screamed Knyvett triumphantly from the foretop.

"Well done, Mr. Marsh," said Hornblower, and Marsh wagged his beard complacently.

The *Natividad* was firing faster now. Three times a splintering crash told of a shot which had been aimed true. Then suddenly a thrust as if from an invisible hand made Hornblower reel on the quarterdeck, and his ears were filled with a brief rending noise. A skimming shot had ploughed a channel along the planking of the quarterdeck. A marine was sitting near the taffrail stupidly contemplating his left leg, which no longer had a foot on the end of it; another marine dropped his musket with a clatter and clapped his hands to his face, which a splinter had torn open, with blood spouting between his fingers.

"Are you hurt, sir?" cried Bush, leaping across to Hornblower.

"No."

Hornblower turned back to stare through his glass at the *Natividad* while the wounded were being dragged away. He saw a dark dot appear alongside the *Natividad,* and lengthen and diverge. It was the boat with which they had been trying to tow—perhaps they were giving up the attempt. But the boat was not being hoisted in. For a second Hornblower was puzzled. The *Natividad's* stumpy foremast and mainmast came into view. The boat was pulling the ship laboriously round so that her whole broadside would bear. Not two, but twenty-five guns would soon be opening their fire on the *Lydia*.

Hornblower felt his breath come a little quicker, unexpectedly, so that he had to swallow in order to regulate things again. His pulse was faster, too.

He made himself keep the glass to his eye until he was certain of the enemy's manoeuvre, and then walked forward leisurely to the gangway. He was compelling himself to appear lighthearted and carefree; he knew that the fools of men whom he commanded would fight more diligently for a captain like that.

"They're waiting for us now, lads," he said. "We shall have some pebbles about our ears before long. Let's show 'em that Englishmen don't care."

They cheered him for that, as he expected and hoped they would do. He looked through his glass again at the *Natividad*. She was still turning, very slowly—it was a lengthy process to turn a clumsy two-decker in a dead calm. But her three masts were fully separate from each other now, and he could see a hint of the broad white stripes which ornamented her side.

"Ha—h'm," he said.

Forward he could hear the oars grinding away as the men in the boats laboured to drag the *Lydia* to grips with her enemy. Across the deck a little group of officers—Bush and Crystal among them—were academically discussing what percentage of hits might be expected from a Spanish broadside at a range of a mile. They were coldblooded about it in a fashion he could never hope to imitate with sincerity. He did not fear death so much—not nearly as much—as defeat and the pitying contempt of his colleagues. The chiefest dread at the back of his mind was the fear of mutilation. An ex-naval officer stumping about on two wooden legs might be an object of condolence, might receive lip service as one of Britain's heroic defenders, but he was a figure of fun nevertheless. Hornblower dreaded the thought of being a figure of fun. He might lose his nose or his cheek and be so mutilated that people would not be able to bear to look at him. It was a horrible thought which set him shuddering while he looked through the telescope, so horrible that he did not stop to think of the associated details, of the agonies he would have to bear down there in the dark cockpit at the mercy of Laurie's incompetence.

The *Natividad* was suddenly engulfed in smoke, and some seconds later the air and the water around the *Lydia,* and the ship herself, were torn by the hurtling broadside.

"Not more than two hits," said Bush, gleefully.

"Just what I said," said Crystal. "That captain of theirs ought to go round and train every gun himself."

"How do you know he did not?" argued Bush.

As punctuation the nine-pounder forward banged out its defiance. Hornblower fancied that his straining eyes saw splinters fly amidships of the *Natividad,* unlikely though it was at that distance.

"Well aimed, Mr. Marsh!" he called. "You hit him squarely."

Another broadside came from the *Natividad,* and another followed it, and another after that. Time after time the *Lydia's* decks were swept from end to end with shot. There were dead men laid out again on the deck, and the groaning wounded were dragged below.

"It is obvious to anyone of a mathematical turn of mind," said Crystal, "that those guns are all laid by different hands. The shots are too scattered for it to be otherwise."

"Nonsense!" maintained Bush sturdily. "See how long it is between broadsides. Time enough for one man to train each gun. What would they be doing in that time otherwise?"

"A Dago crew—" began Crystal, but a sudden shriek of cannon balls over his head silenced him for a moment.

"Mr. Galbraith!" shouted Bush. "Have that main t'gallant stay spliced directly." Then he turned triumphantly on Crystal. "Did you notice," he asked, "how every shot from that broadside went high? How does the mathematical mind explain that?"

"They fired on the upward roll, Mr. Bush. Really, Mr. Bush, I think that after Trafalgar—"

Hornblower longed to order them to cease the argument which was lacerating his nerves, but he could not be such a tyrant as that.

In the still air the smoke from the *Natividad's* firing had banked up round her so that she showed ghostly through the cloud, her solitary mizzen topmast protruding above it into the clear air.

"Mr. Bush," he asked, "at what distance do you think she is now?"

Bush gauged the distance carefully.

"Three parts of a mile, I should say, sir."

"Two thirds, more likely, sir," said Crystal.

"Your opinion was not asked, Mr. Crystal," snapped Hornblower.

At three quarters of a mile, even at two thirds, the *Lydia's* carronades would be ineffective. She must continue running the gauntlet. Bush was evidently of the same opinion, to judge by his next orders.

"Time for the men at the oars to be relieved," he said, and went forward to attend to it. Hornblower heard him bustling the new crews down into the boats, anxious that the pulling should be resumed before the *Lydia* had time to lose what little way she carried.

It was terribly hot under the blazing sun, even though it was now long past noon. The smell of the blood which had been spilt on the decks mingled with the smell of the hot deck seams and of the powder smoke from the nine-pounder with which Marsh was still steadily bombarding the enemy. Hornblower felt sick—so sick that he began to fear lest he should disgrace himself eternally by vomiting in full view of his men. When fatigue and anxiety had weakened him thus he was far more conscious of the pitching and rolling of the ship under his feet. The men at the guns were silent now, he noticed—

for long they had laughed and joked at their posts, but now they were beginning to sulk under the punishment. That was a bad sign.

"Pass the word for Sullivan and his fiddle," he ordered.

The red-haired Irish madman came aft, and knuckled his forehead, his fiddle and bow under his arm.

"Give us a tune, Sullivan," he ordered. "Hey there, men, who is there among you who dances the best hornpipe?"

There was a difference of opinion about that apparently.

"Benskin, sir," said some voices.

"Hall, sir," said others.

"No, MacEvoy, sir."

"Then we'll have a tournament," said Hornblower. "Here, Benskin, Hall, MacEvoy. A hornpipe from each of you, and a guinea for the man who does it best."

In later years it was a tale told and retold, how the *Lydia* towed into action with hornpipes being danced on her main deck. It was quoted as an example of Hornblower's cool courage, and only Hornblower knew how little truth there was in the attribution. It kept the men happy, which was why he did it. No one guessed how nearly he came to vomiting when a shot came in through a forward gunport and spattered Hall with a seaman's brains without causing him to miss a step.

Then later in that dreadful afternoon there came a crash from forward, followed by a chorus of shouts and screams overside.

"Launch sunk, sir!" hailed Galbraith from the forecastle, but Hornblower was there as soon as he had uttered the words.

A round shot had dashed the launch practically into its component planks, and the men were scrambling in the water, leaping up for the bobstay or struggling to climb into the cutter, all of them who survived wild with the fear of sharks.

"The Dagoes have saved us the trouble of hoisting her in," he said, loudly. "We're close enough now for them to feel our teeth."

The men who heard him cheered.

"Mr. Hooker!" he called to the midshipman in the cutter. "When you have picked up those men, kindly starboard your helm. We are going to open fire."

He came aft to the quarterdeck again.

"Hard-a-starboard," he growled at the quartermaster. "Mr. Gerard, you may open fire when your guns bear."

Very slowly the *Lydia* swung round. Another broadside from the *Natividad* came crashing into her before she had completed the turn, but Hornblower actually did not notice it. The period of inaction was over now. He had brought his ship within four hundred yards of the enemy, and all his duty now was to walk the deck as an example to his men. There were no more decisions to make.

"Cock your locks!" shouted Gerard in the waist.

"Easy, Mr. Hooker. Way enough!" roared Hornblower.

The *Lydia* turned, inch by inch, with Gerard squinting along one of the starboard guns to judge of the moment when it would first bear.

"Take your aim!" he yelled, and stood back, timing the roll of the ship in the heavy swell. "Fire!"

The smoke billowed out amid the thunder of the discharge, and the *Lydia* heaved to the recoil of the guns.

"Give him another, lads!" shouted Hornblower through the din. Now that action was joined he found himself exalted and happy, the dreadful fears of mutilation forgotten. In thirty seconds the guns were reloaded, run out, and fired. Again and again and again, with Gerard watching the roll of the ship and giving the word. Counting back in his mind, Hornblower reckoned five broadsides from the *Lydia,* and he could only remember two from the *Natividad* in that time. At that rate of firing the *Natividad's* superiority in numbers of guns and weight of metal would be more than counterbalanced. At the sixth broadside a gun went off prematurely, a second before Gerard gave the word. Hornblower sprang forward to detect the guilty crew—it was easy enough from their furtive look and suspicious appearance of busyness. He shook his finger at them.

"Steady, there!" he shouted. I'll flog the next man who fires out of turn."

It was very necessary to keep the men in hand while the range was as long as at present, because in the heat and excitement of the action the gun captains could not be trusted to judge the motion of the ship while preoccupied with loading and laying.

"Good old Horny!" piped up some unknown voice forward, and there was a burst of laughter and cheering, cut short by Gerard's next order to fire.

The smoke was banked thick about the ship already—as thick as a London fog, so that from the quarterdeck it was impossible to see individuals on the forecastle, and in the unnatural darkness which it brought with it one could see the long orange flashes of the guns despite the vivid sunshine outside. Of the *Natividad* all that could be seen was her high smoke cloud and the single topmast jutting out from it. The thick smoke, trailing about the ship in greasy wreaths, made the eyes smart and irritated the lungs, and affected the skin like thundery weather until it pricked uncomfortably.

Hornblower found Bush beside him.

"*Natividad's* feeling our fire, sir," he roared through the racket. "She's firing very wildly. Look at that, sir."

Of the broadside fired only one or two shots struck home. Half a dozen plunged together into the sea astern of the *Lydia* so that the spray from the fountains which they struck up splashed round them on the quarterdeck. Hornblower nodded happily. This was his justification for closing to that range and for running the risks involved in the approach. To maintain a rapid fire, well aimed, amid the din and the smoke and the losses and the confusion of a naval battle called for discipline and practice of a sort that he knew the *Natividad's* crew could not boast.

He looked down through the smoke at the *Lydia's* main deck. The inexperienced eye, observing the hurry and bustle of the boys with the cartridge buckets, the mad efforts of the gun crews, the dead and the wounded, the darkness and the din, might well think it a scene of confusion, but Hornblower knew better. Everything that was being done there, every single action, was part of the scheme worked out by Hornblower seven months before when he commissioned the *Lydia,* and grained into the minds of all on board during the long and painful drills since. He could see Gerard standing by the mainmast, looking almost saintly in his ecstasy—gunnery was as much Gerard's ruling passion as women; he could see the midshipmen and other warrant officers each by his sub-division of guns, each looking to Gerard for his orders and keeping his guns working rhythmically, the loaders with their rammers, the cleaners with their sponges, the gun captains crouching over the breeches, right hands raised.

The port-side battery was already depleted of most of its men; there were only two men to a gun there, standing idle yet ready to spring into action if a shift of the fight should bring their guns to bear. The remainder were on duty round the ship—replacing casualties on the starboard side, manning the pumps whose doleful clanking continued steadily through the fearful din, resting on their oars in the cutter, hard at work aloft repairing damages. Hornblower found time to be thankful that he had been granted seven months in which to bring his crew into its present state of training and discipline.

Something—the concussion of the guns, a faint breath of air, or the send of the sea—was causing the *Lydia* to turn away a trifle from her enemy. Hornblower could see that the guns were having to be trained round farther and farther so that the rate of firing was being slowed down. He raced forward, running out along the bowsprit until he was over the cutter where Hooker and his men sat staring at the fight.

"Mr. Hooker, bring her head round two points to starboard."

"Aye aye, sir."

The men bent to their oars and headed their boat towards the *Natividad;* the towrope tightened while another badly aimed broadside tore the water all round them into foam. Tugging and straining at the oars they would work the ship round in time. Hornblower left them and ran back to the quarterdeck. There was a white-faced ship's boy seeking him there.

"Mr. Howell sent me, sir. Starboard side chain pump's knocked all to pieces."

"Yes?" Hornblower knew that Howell the ship's carpenter would not merely send a message of despair.

"He's rigging another one, sir, but it will be an hour before it works, sir. He told me to tell you the water's gaining a little, sir."

"Ha—h'm," said Hornblower. The infant addressing him grew round-eyed and confidential now that the first strangeness of speaking to his captain had worn off.

"There was fourteen men all knocked into smash at the pump, sir. 'Orrible, sir."

"Very good. Run back to Mr. Howell and tell him the captain is sure he will do his best to get the new pump rigged."

"Aye aye, sir."

The boy dived down to the main deck, and Hornblower watched him running forward, dodging the hurrying individuals in the crowded space there. He had to explain himself to the marine sentry at the fore hatchway—no one could go below without being able to show that it was his duty which was calling him there. Hornblower felt as if the message Howell had sent did not matter at all. It called for no decision on his part. All there was to do was to go on fighting, whether the ship was sinking under their feet or not. There was a comfort in being free of all responsibility in this way.

"One hour and a half already," said Bush, coming up rubbing his hands. "Glorious, sir. Glorious."

It might have been no more than ten minutes for all Hornblower could tell, but Bush had in duty bound been watching the sand glass by the binnacle.

"I've never known Dagoes stick to their guns like this before," commented Bush. "Their aim's poor, but they're firing as fast as ever. And it's my belief we've hit them hard, sir."

He tried to look through the eddying smoke, even fanning ridiculously with his hands in the attempt—a gesture which, by showing that he was not quite as calm as he appeared to be, gave Hornblower an absurd pleasure. Crystal came up as well as he spoke.

"The smoke's thinning a little, sir. It's my belief that there's a light air of wind blowing."

He held up a wetted finger.

"There is indeed, sir. A trifle of breeze over the port quarter. Ah!"

There came a stronger puff as he spoke, which rolled away the smoke in a solid mass over the starboard bow and revealed the scene as if a theatre curtain had been raised. There was the *Natividad*, looking like a wreck. Her jury foremast had gone the way of its predecessor, and her mainmast had followed it. Only her mizzenmast stood now, and she was rolling wildly in the swell with a huge tangle of rigging trailing over her disengaged side. Abreast her foremast three ports had been battered into one; the gap looked like a missing tooth.

"She's low in the water," said Bush, but on the instant a fresh broadside vomited smoke from her battered side, and this time by some chance every shot told in the *Lydia,* as the crash below well indicated. The smoke billowed round the *Natividad,* and as it cleared the watchers saw her swinging round head to wind, helpless in the light air. The *Lydia* had felt the breeze. Hornblower could tell by the feel of her that she had steerage way again; the quartermaster at the wheel was twirling the spokes to hold her steady. He saw his chance on the instant.

"Starboard a point," he ordered. "Forward, there! Cast off the cutter."

The *Lydia* steadied across her enemy's bows and raked her with thunder and flame.

"Back the main tops'l," ordered Hornblower.

The men were cheering again on the main deck through the roar of the guns. Astern the red sun was dipping to the water's edge in a glory of scarlet and gold. Soon it would be night.

"She must strike soon. Christ! Why don't she strike?" Bush was saying, as at close range the broadsides tore into the helpless enemy, raking her from bow to stern. Hornblower knew better. No ship under Crespo's command and flying El Supremo's flag would strike her colours. He could see the golden star on a blue ground fluttering through the smoke.

"Pound him, lads, pound him!" shouted Gerard.

With the shortening range he could rely on his gun captains to fire independently now. Every gun's crew was loading and firing as rapidly as possible. So hot were the guns that at each discharge they leaped high in their carriages, and the dripping sponges thrust down their bores sizzled and steamed at the touch of the scorching hot metal. It was growing darker, too. The flashes of the guns could be seen again now, leaping in long orange tongues from the gun muzzles. High above the fast fading sunset could be seen the first star, shining out brilliantly.

The *Natividad's* bowsprit was gone, splintered and broken and hanging under her forefoot, and then in the dwindling light the mizzenmast fell as well, cut through by shots which had ripped their way down the whole length of the ship.

"She must strike now, by God!" said Bush.

At Trafalgar Bush had been sent as prizemaster into a captured Spanish ship, and his mind was full of busy memories of what a beaten ship looked like—the dismounted guns, the dead and wounded heaped on the deck and rolling back and forth as the dismasted ship rolled on the swell, the misery, the pain, the helplessness. As if in reply to him there came a sudden flash and report from the *Natividad's* bows. Some devoted souls with tackles and handspikes had contrived to slew a gun round so that it would bear right forward, and were firing into the looming bulk of the *Lydia*.

"Pound him, lads, pound him!" screamed Gerard, half mad with fatigue and strain.

The *Lydia* by virtue of her top hamper was going down to leeward fast upon the rolling hulk. At every second the range was shortening. Through the darkness, when their eyes were not blinded with gun flashes, Hornblower and Bush could see figures moving about on the *Natividad's* deck. They were firing muskets now, as well. The flashes pricked the darkness and Hornblower heard a bullet thud into the rail beside him. He did not care. He was conscious now of his overmastering weariness.

The wind was fluky, coming in sudden puffs and veering unexpectedly. It was hard, especially in the darkness, to judge exactly how the two ships were nearing each other.

"The closer we are, the quicker we'll finish it," said Bush.

"Yes, but we'll run on board of her soon," said Hornblower.

He roused himself for a further effort.

"Call the hands to stand by to repel boarders," he said, and he walked across to where the two starboard-side quarterdeck carronades were thundering away. So intent were their crews on their work, so hypnotised by the monotony of loading and firing, that it took him several seconds to attract their notice. Then they stood still, sweating, while Hornblower gave his orders. The two carronades were loaded with canister brought from the reserve locker beside the taffrail. They waited, crouching beside the guns, while the two ships drifted closer and closer together, the *Lydia's* main deck guns still blazing away. There were shouts and yells of defiance from the *Natividad*, and the musket flashes from her bows showed a dark mass of men crowding there waiting for the ships to come together. Yet the actual contact was unexpected, as a sudden combination of wind and sea closed the gap with a rush. The *Natividad's* bow hit the *Lydia* amidships, just forward of the mizzenmast, with a jarring crash. There was a pandemonium of yells from the *Natividad* as they swarmed forward to board, and the captains of the carronades sprang to their lanyards.

"Wait!" shouted Hornblower.

His mind was like a calculating machine, judging wind and sea, time and distance, as the *Lydia* slowly swung round. With hand spikes and the brute strength of the men he trained one carronade round and the other followed his example, while the mob on the *Natividad's* forecastle surged along the bulwarks waiting for the moment to board. The two carronades came right up against them.

"Fire!"

A thousand musket balls were vomited from the carronades straight into the packed crowd. There was a moment of silence, and then the pandemonium of shouts and cheers was replaced by a thin chorus of screams and cries—the blast of musket balls had swept the *Natividad's* forecastle clear from side to side.

For a space the two ships clung together in this position; the *Lydia* still had a dozen guns that would bear, and these pounded away with their muzzles almost touching the *Natividad's* bow. Then wind and sea parted them again, the *Lydia* to leeward now, drifting away from the rolling hulk; in the English ship every gun was in action, while from the *Natividad* came not a gun, not even a musket shot.

Hornblower fought off his weariness again.

"Cease firing," he shouted to Gerard on the main deck, and the guns fell silent.

Hornblower stared through the darkness at the vague mass of the *Natividad,* wallowing in the waves.

"Surrender!" he shouted.

"Never!" came the reply—Crespo's voice, he could have sworn to it, thin and high-pitched. It added two or three words of obscene insult.

Hornblower could afford to smile at that, even through his weariness. He had fought his battle and won it.

"You have done all that brave men could do," he shouted.

"Not all, yet, Captain," wailed the voice in the darkness.

Then something caught Hornblower's eye—a wavering glow of red round about the *Natividad's* vague bows.

"Crespo, you fool!" he shouted. "Your ship's on fire! Surrender, while you can."

"Never!"

The *Lydia's* guns, hard against the *Natividad's* side, had flung their flaming wads in amongst the splintered timbers. The tinder-dry wood of the old ship had taken fire from them, and the fire was spreading fast. It was brighter already than when Hornblower had noticed it; the ship would be a mass of flames soon. Hornblower's first duty was to his own ship—when the fire should reach the powder charges on the *Natividad's* decks, or when it should attain the magazine, the ship would become a volcano of flaming fragments, imperilling the *Lydia*.

"We must haul off from her, Mr. Bush," said Hornblower, speaking formally to conceal the tremor in his voice. "Man the braces, there."

The *Lydia* swung away, close-hauled, clawing her way up to windward of the flaming wreck. Bush and Hornblower gazed back at her. There were bright flames now to be seen, spouting from the shattered bows—the red glow was reflected in the heaving sea around her. And then, as they looked, they saw the flames vanish abruptly, like an extinguished candle. There was nothing to be seen at all, nothing save darkness and the faint glimmer of the wave crests. The sea had swallowed the *Natividad* before the flames could destroy her.

"Sunk, by God!" exclaimed Bush, leaning out over the rail.

TRAFALGAR

⚓

TRAFALGAR

Robert Southey

⚓ *Robert Southey wrote "The Life of Nelson" in 1813, the same year in which he was made poet laureate. This was just eight years after the Battle of Trafalgar. All the controversies that gather round the head of a popular figure like Nelson were still current, his frailties were gossip, most of the details of his great achievements were common knowledge. It was against this background that the following account was written, striking in its simplicity when one might have expected the flowery writing that was usual at that period.*

THE station which Nelson had chosen was some fifty or sixty miles to the west of Cadiz, near Cape St. Mary's. At this distance he hoped to decoy the enemy out, while he guarded against the danger of being caught with a westerly wind near Cadiz, and driven within the Straits. The blockade of the port was rigorously enforced, in hopes that the Combined fleet might be forced to sea by want. The Danish vessels, therefore, which were carrying provisions from the French ports in the bay, under the name of Danish property, to all the little ports from Ayamonte to Algeziras, from whence they were conveyed in coasting boats to Cadiz, were seized. Without this proper exertion of power, the blockade would have been rendered nugatory, by the advantage thus taken of the neutral flag. The supplies from France were thus effectually cut off. There was now every indication that the enemy would speedily venture out: officers and men were in the highest spirits at the prospect of giving them a decisive blow; such, indeed, as would put an end to all further contest upon the seas. Theatrical amusements were per-

From *The Life Of Nelson*, by Robert Southey.

formed every evening in most of the ships: and "God Save the King" was the hymn with which the sports concluded. "I verily believe," said Nelson, writing on the 6th of October, "that the country will soon be put to some expense on my account; either a monument or a new pension and honours; for I have not the smallest doubt but that a very few days, almost hours, will put us in battle. The success no man can insure; but for the fighting them, if they can be got at, I pledge myself. The sooner the better: I don't like to have these things upon my mind."

At this time he was not without some cause of anxiety; he was in want of frigates—the eyes of the fleet, as he always called them: to the want of which the enemy before were indebted for their escape, and Bonaparte for his arrival in Egypt. He had only twenty-three ships—others were on the way—but they might come too late; and, though Nelson never doubted of victory, mere victory was not what he looked to, he wanted to annihilate the enemy's fleet. The Carthagena squadron might effect a junction with this fleet on the one side; and, on the other, it was to be expected that a similar attempt would be made by the French from Brest; in either case a formidable contingency to be apprehended by the blockading force. The Rochefort squadron did push out, and had nearly caught the *Agamemnon* and *L'Aimable* in their way to reinforce the British Admiral. Yet Nelson at this time weakened his own fleet. He had the unpleasant task to perform of sending home Sir Robert Calder, whose conduct was to be made the subject of a court-martial, in consequence of the general dissatisfaction which had been felt and expressed at his imperfect victory. Sir Robert Calder, and Sir John Orde, Nelson believed to be the only two enemies whom he had ever had in his profession; and, from that sensitive delicacy which distinguished him, this made him the more scrupulously anxious to show every possible mark of respect and kindness to Sir Robert. He wished to detain him till after the expected action; when the services which he might perform, and the triumphant joy which would be excited, would leave nothing to be apprehended from an inquiry into the previous engagement. Sir Robert, however, whose situation was very painful, did not choose to delay a trial, from the result of which he confidently expected a complete justification: and Nelson, instead of sending him home in a frigate, insisted on his returning in his own ninety-gun ship; ill as such a ship could at that time be spared. Nothing could be more honourable than the feeling by which Nelson was influenced; but, at such a crisis, it ought not to have been indulged.

On the 9th, Nelson sent Collingwood what he called, in his Diary, the *Nelson-touch*. "I send you," said he, "my plan of attack, as far as a man dare venture to guess at the very uncertain position the enemy may be found in: but it is to place you perfectly at ease respecting my intentions, and to give full scope to your judgment for carrying them into effect. We can, my dear

Coll., have no little jealousies. We have only one great object in view, that of annihilating our enemies, and getting a glorious peace for our country. No man has more confidence in another than I have in you; and no man will render your services more justice than your very old friend—Nelson and Bronte." The order of sailing was to be the order of battle; the fleet in two lines, with an advanced squadron of eight of the fastest-sailing two-deckers. The second in command, having the entire direction of his line, was to break through the enemy, about the twelfth ship from their rear; he would lead through the centre, and the advanced squadron was to cut off three or four ahead of the centre. This plan was to be adapted to the strength of the enemy, so that they should always be one-fourth superior to those whom they cut off. Nelson said, "That his Admirals and captains, knowing his precise object to be that of a close and decisive action, would supply any deficiency of signals, and act accordingly. In case signals cannot be seen or clearly understood, no captain can do wrong if he places his ship alongside that of an enemy." One of the last orders of this admirable man was, that the name and family of every officer, seaman, and marine, who might be killed or wounded in action, should be, as soon as possible, returned to him, in order to be transmitted to the Chairman of the Patriotic Fund, that the case might be taken into consideration, for the benefit of the sufferer or his family.

About half-past nine in the morning of the 19th, the *Mars,* being the nearest to the fleet of the ships which formed the line of communication with the frigates in-shore, repeated the signal, that the enemy were coming out of port. The wind was at this time very light, with partial breezes, mostly from the S.S.W. Nelson ordered the signal to be made for a chase in the south-east quarter. About two, the repeating-ships announced that the enemy were at sea. All night the British fleet continued under all sail, steering to the south-east. At daybreak they were in the entrance of the Straits, but the enemy were not in sight. About seven, one of the frigates made signal that the enemy were bearing north. Upon this the *Victory* hove-to; and shortly afterwards Nelson made sail again to the northward. In the afternoon the wind blew fresh from the south-west, and the English began to fear that the foe might be forced to return to port. A little before sunset, however, Blackwood, in the *Euryalus,* telegraphed that they appeared determined to go to the westward. "And that," said the Admiral in his Diary, "they shall not do, if it is in the power of Nelson and Bronte to prevent them." Nelson had signified to Blackwood that he depended upon him to keep sight of the enemy. They were observed so well, that all their motions were made known to him; and, as they wore twice, he inferred that they were aiming to keep the port of Cadiz open, and would retreat there as soon as they saw the British fleet; for this reason he was very careful not to approach near enough to be seen by them during the night. At daybreak the Combined fleets were distinctly seen from the *Victory's* deck, formed in a close line of battle ahead, on the starboard tack, about twelve miles to leeward, and standing to the south. Our fleet consisted of twenty-seven sail of the line and four frigates; theirs of thirty-three and seven large frigates. Their superiority was greater in size and weight of metal than in numbers. They had four thousand troops on board; and the best riflemen who could be procured, many of them Tyrolese, were dispersed through the ships. Little did the Tyrolese, and little did the Spaniards, at that day, imagine what horrors the wicked tyrant whom they served was preparing for their country.

Soon after daylight Nelson came upon deck. The 21st of October was a festival in his family, because on that day his uncle, Captain Suckling, in the *Dreadnought,* with two other line-of-battle ships, had beaten off a French squadron of four sail of the line and three frigates. Nelson, with that sort of superstition from which few persons are entirely exempt, had more than once expressed his persuasion that this was to be the day of his battle also; and he was well pleased at seeing his prediction about to be verified. The wind was now from the west, light breezes, with a long heavy swell. Signal was made to bear down upon the enemy in two lines; and the fleet set all sail. Colling-wood, in the *Royal Sovereign,* led the lee line of thirteen ships; the *Victory* led the weather line of fourteen. Having seen that all was as it should be, Nelson retired to his cabin, and wrote the following prayer:—

"May the great God, whom I worship, grant to my country, and for the benefit of Europe in general, a great and glorious victory; and may no misconduct in any one tarnish it! and may humanity after victory be the predominant feature in the British fleet! For myself individually, I commit my life to Him that made me; and may His blessing alight on my endeavours for serving my country faithfully! To Him I resign myself, and the just cause which is entrusted to me to defend. Amen, Amen, Amen."

Having thus discharged his devotional duties, he annexed, in the same Diary, the following remarkable writing:—

"October 21st, 1805.—Then in sight of the Combined fleets of France and Spain, distant about ten miles.

"Whereas the eminent services of Emma Hamilton, widow of the Right Honourable Sir William Hamilton, have been of the very greatest service to my King and my country, to my knowledge, without ever receiving any reward from either our King or country.

First: That she obtained the King of Spain's letter in 1796, to his brother, the King of Naples, acquainting him of his intention to declare war against England; from which letter the ministry sent out orders to the then Sir John Jervis, to strike a stroke, if opportunity offered, against either the arsenals of Spain or her fleets. That neither of these was done is not the fault of Lady Hamilton; the opportunity might have been offered.

"Secondly: The British fleet under my command could never have returned the second time to Egypt, had not Lady Hamilton's influence with the Queen of Naples caused letters to be wrote to the Governor of Syracuse, that he was to encourage the fleet's being supplied with everything, should they put into any port in Sicily. We put into Syracuse, and received every supply; went to Egypt, and destroyed the French fleet.

"Could I have rewarded these services, I would not now call upon my country; but as that has not been in my power, I leave Emma Lady Hamilton therefore a legacy to my King and country, that they will give her an ample provision to maintain her rank in life.

"I also leave to the beneficence of my country my adopted daughter, Horatia Nelson Thompson; and I desire she will use in future the name of Nelson only.

"These are the only favours I ask of my King and country, at this moment when I am going to fight their battle. May God bless my King and country, and all those I hold dear! My relations it is needless to mention: they will, of course, be amply provided for.

"NELSON AND BRONTE

"Witness $\begin{cases} \text{HENRY BLACKWOOD.} \\ \text{T. M. HARDY."} \end{cases}$

The child of whom this writing speaks was believed to be his daughter, and so, indeed, he called her the last time that he pronounced her name. She was then about five years old, living at Merton, under Lady Hamilton's care. The last minutes which Nelson passed at Merton were employed in praying over this child, as she lay sleeping. A portrait of Lady Hamilton hung in his cabin; and no Catholic ever beheld the picture of his patron saint with devouter reverence. The undisguised and romantic passion with which he regarded it amounted almost to superstition; and when the portrait was now taken down, in clearing for action, he desired the men who removed it to "take care of his guardian angel." In this manner he frequently spoke of it, as if he believed there were a virture in the image. He wore a miniature of her, also, next his heart.

Blackwood went on board the *Victory* about six. He found him in good spirits, but very calm; not in that exhilaration which he had felt upon entering into battle at Aboukir and Copenhagen: he knew that his own life would be particularly aimed at, and seems to have looked for death with almost as sure an expectation as for victory. His whole attention was fixed upon the enemy. They attacked to the northward, and formed their line on the larboard tack; thus bringing the shoals of Trafalgar and St. Pedro under the lee of the British, keeping the port of Cadiz open for themselves. This was judiciously done; and Nelson, aware of all the advantages which it gave them, made signal to prepare to anchor.

Villeneuve was a skilful seaman; worthy of serving a better master, and a better cause. His plan of defence was as well conceived, and as original, as the plan of attack. He formed the fleet in a double line; every alternate ship being about a cable's length to windward of her second ahead and astern. Nelson, certain of a triumphant issue to the day, asked Blackwood what he should consider as a victory. That officer answered, that, considering the handsome way in which battle was offered by the enemy, their apparent determination for a fair trial of strength, and the situation of the land, he thought it would be a glorious result if fourteen were captured. He replied: "I shall not be satisfied with less than twenty." Soon afterwards he asked him, if he did not think there was a signal wanting. Captain Blackwood made answer, that he thought the whole fleet seemed very clearly to understand what they were about. These words were scarcely spoken before that signal was made, which will be remembered as long as the language, or even the memory, of England shall endure—Nelson's last signal:—"England expects every Man will do his Duty!" It was received throughout the fleet with a shout of answering acclamation, made sublime by the spirit which it breathed, and the feeling which it expressed. "Now," said Lord Nelson, "I can do no more. We must trust to the great Disposer of all events, and the justice of our cause. I thank God for this great opportunity of doing my duty."

He wore that day, as usual, his Admiral's frockcoat, bearing on the left breast four stars, of the different orders with which he was invested. Ornaments which rendered him so conspicuous a mark for the enemy were beheld with ominous apprehensions by his officers. It was known that there were riflemen on board the French ships; and it could not be doubted but that his life would be particularly aimed at. They communicated their fears to each other; and the surgeon, Mr. Beatty, spoke to the chaplain, Dr. Scott, and to Mr. Scott, the public secretary, desiring that some person would entreat him to change his dress, or cover the stars; but they knew that such a request would highly displease him. "In honour I gained them," he had said, when such a thing had been hinted to him formerly, "and in honour I will die with them." Mr. Beatty, however, would not have been deterred by any fear of exciting displeasure, from speaking to him himself upon a subject in which the weal of England, as well as the life of Nelson, was concerned—but he was ordered from the deck before he could find an opportunity. This was a point upon which Nelson's officers knew that it was hopeless to remonstrate or reason with him; but both Blackwood and his own captain, Hardy, represented to him how advantageous to the fleet it would be for him to keep out of action as long as possible; and he consented at last to let the *Leviathan* and the *Téméraire,* which were sailing abreast of the *Victory,* be ordered to pass ahead. Yet even here the last infirmity of this noble mind was indulged; for these ships could not pass ahead if the *Victory* continued to carry all her sail; and so far was Nelson from shortening sail, that it was evident he took pleasure in pressing on, and rendering it impossible for them to obey his own orders. A long swell was setting into the Bay of Cadiz: our ships, crowding all sail, moved majestically before it, with light winds from the southwest. The sun shone on the sails of the enemy; and their well-formed line, with their numerous three-deckers, made an appearance which any other assailants would have thought formidable; but the British sailors only admired the beauty and the splendour of the spectacle; and, in full confidence of winning what they saw, remarked to each other, what a fine sight yonder ships would make at Spithead!

The French Admiral, from the *Bucentaure,* beheld the new manner in which his enemy was advancing—Nelson and Collingwood each leading his line; and pointing them out to his officers, he is said to have exclaimed, that such conduct could not fail to be successful. Yet Villeneuve had made his own dispositions with the utmost skill, and the fleets under his command waited for the attack with perfect coolness. Ten minutes before twelve they opened their fire. Eight or nine of the ships immediately ahead of the *Victory* and across her bows, fired single guns at her, to ascertain whether she was yet within their range. As soon as Nelson perceived that their shot passed over him, he desired Blackwood, and Captain Prowse, of the *Sirius,* to repair to their respective frigates; and, on their way, to tell all the captains of the line-of-battle ships that he depended on their exertions; and that, if by the prescribed mode of attack they found it impracticable to get into action immediately, they might adopt whatever they thought best, provided it led them quickly and closely alongside an enemy. As they were standing on the front poop, Blackwood took him by the hand, saying, he hoped soon to return and find him in possession of twenty prizes. He replied, "God bless you, Blackwood; I shall never see you again!"

Nelson's column was steered about two points more to the north than Collingwood's, in order to cut off the enemy's escape into Cadiz: the lee line, therefore, was first engaged. "See," cried Nelson, pointing to the *Royal Sovereign,* as she steered right for the centre of the enemy's line, cut through it astern of the *Santa Ana,* three-decker, and engaged her at the muzzle of her guns on the starboard side; "see how that noble fellow, Collingwood, carries his ship into action!" Collingwood, delighted at being first in the heat of the fire, and knowing the feelings of his Commander and old friend, turned to his captain, and exclaimed: "Rotherham, what would Nelson give to be here?" Both these brave officers, perhaps, at this moment, thought of Nelson with gratitude, for a circumstance which had occurred on the preceding day. Admiral Collingwood, with some of the captains, having gone on board the *Victory* to receive instructions, Nelson inquired of him where his captain was: and was told, in reply, that they were not upon good terms with each other. "Terms!" said Nelson, "good terms with each other!" Immediately he sent a boat for Captain Rotherham; led him, as soon as he arrived, to Collingwood, and saying: "Look; yonder are the enemy!" bade them shake hands like Englishmen.

The enemy continued to fire a gun at a time at the *Victory,* till they saw that a shot had passed through her main-top-gallant sail; then they opened their broadsides, aiming chiefly at her rigging, in the hope of disabling her before she could close with them. Nelson, as usual, had hoisted several flags, lest one should be shot away. The enemy showed no colours till late in the action, when they began to feel the necessity of having them to strike. For this reason, the *Santissima Trinidad,* Nelson's old acquaintance, as he used to call her, was distinguishable only by her four decks; and to the bow of this opponent he ordered the *Victory* to be steered. Meantime, an incessant raking fire was kept up upon the *Victory.* The Admiral's secretary was one of the first who fell; he was killed by a cannon-shot while conversing with Hardy. Captain Adair of the marines, with the help of a sailor, endeavoured to remove the body from Nelson's sight, who had a great regard for Mr. Scott; but he anxiously asked, "Is that poor Scott that's gone?" and being informed that it was indeed so, exclaimed, "Poor fellow!" Presently, a double-headed shot struck a party of marines, who were drawn up on the poop, and killed eight of them: upon which Nelson immediately desired Captain Adair to disperse his men round the ship, that they might not suffer so much from being together. A few minutes afterwards a shot struck the fore-brace bits on the quarter-deck, and passed between Nelson and Hardy, a splinter from the bit tearing off Hard's buckle, and bruising his foot. Both stopped, and looked anxiously at each other: each supposed the other to be wounded. Nelson then smiled, and said: "This is too warm work, Hardy, to last long."

The *Victory* had not yet returned a single gun; fifty of her men had been by this time killed or wounded, and her main-top-mast with all her studding-sails and their booms shot away. Nelson declared, that, in all his battles, he had seen nothing which surpassed the cool courage of his crew on this occasion. At four minutes after twelve, she opened her fire from both sides of her deck. It was not possible to break the enemy's line without running on board one of their ships; Hardy informed him of this, and asked him which he would prefer. Nelson replied: "Take your choice, Hardy, it does signify much." The master was ordered to put the helm to port, and the *Victory* ran on board the *Redoutable,* just as her tiller ropes were shot away. The French ship received her with a broadside: then instantly let down her lower-deck ports, for fear of being boarded through them, and never afterwards fired a great gun during the action. Her tops, like those of all the enemy's ships, were filled with riflemen. Nelson never placed musketry in his tops; he had a strong dislike to the practice: not merely because it endangers setting fire to the sails, but also because it is a murderous sort of warfare, by which individuals may suffer, and a commander now and then be picked off, but which never can decide the fate of a general engagement.

Captain Harvey, in the *Téméraire,* fell on board the *Redoutable* on the other side. Another enemy was in like manner on board the *Téméraire,* so that these four ships formed as compact a tier as if they had been moored together, their heads lying all the same way. The lieutenants of the *Victory,* seeing this, depressed their guns of the middle and lower decks, and fired with a diminished charge, lest the shot should pass through and injure the *Téméraire.* And because there was danger that the *Redoutable* might take fire from the lower-deck guns, the muzzles of which touched her side when they were run out, the fireman of each gun stood ready with a bucket of water; which, as soon as the gun was discharged, he dashed into the hole made by the shot. An incessant fire was kept up from the *Victory* from both sides; her larboard guns playing upon the *Bucentaure,* and the huge *Santissima Trinidad.*

It had been part of Nelson's prayer, that the British fleet might be distinguished by humanity in the victory he expected. Setting an example himself, he twice gave orders to cease firing upon the *Redoutable,* supposing that she had struck, because her great guns were silent; for, as she carried no flag, there was no means of instantly ascertaining the fact. From this ship, which he had thus twice spared, he received his death. A ball fired from her mizzen-top, which, in the then situation of the two vessels, was not more than fifteen yards from that part of the deck where he was standing, struck the epaulette on his left shoulder, about a quarter after one, just in the heat of action. He fell upon his face, on the spot which was covered with his poor secretary's blood. Hardy, who was a few steps from him, turning round, saw three men raising him up. "They have done for me at last, Hardy!" said he. "I hope not!" cried Hardy. "Yes," he replied; "my backbone is shot through!" Yet even now, not for a moment losing his presence of mind, he observed, as they were carrying him down the ladder, that the tiller-ropes, which had been shot away, were not yet replaced, and ordered that new ones should be rove immediately. Then, that he might not be seen by the crew, he took out his handkerchief, and covered his face and his stars. Had he but concealed these badges of honour from the enemy, England, perhaps, would not have had cause to receive with sorrow the news of the battle of Trafalgar. The cockpit was crowded with wounded and dying men; over whose bodies he was with some difficulty conveyed, and laid upon a pallet in the midshipmen's berth. It was soon perceived, upon examination, that the wound was mortal. This, however, was concealed from all except Captain Hardy, the chaplain, and the medical attendants. He himself being certain, from the sensation in his back, and the gush of blood he felt momently within his breast, that no human care could avail him, insisted that the surgeon should leave him, and attend to those to whom he might be useful. "For," said he, "you can do nothing for me." All that could be done was to fan him with paper and frequently to give him lemonade to alleviate his intense thirst. He was in great pain, and expressed much anxiety for the event of the action, which now began to declare itself. As often as a ship struck, the crew of the *Victory* hurrahed; and at every hurrah, a visible expression of joy gleamed in the eyes, and marked the countenance, of the dying hero. But he became impatient to see Captain Hardy; and as that officer, though often sent for, could not leave the deck, Nelson feared that some fatal cause prevented him, and repeatedly cried: "Will no one bring Hardy to me? He must be killed! He is surely dead!" An hour and ten minutes elapsed from the time when Nelson received his wound, before Hardy could come to him. They shook hands in silence; Hardy in vain struggling to suppress the feelings of that most painful and yet sublimest moment. "Well, Hardy," said Nelson; "how goes the day with us?" "Very well," replied Hardy; "ten ships have struck, but five of the van have tacked, and show an intention to bear down upon the *Victory*. I have called two or three or our fresh ships round, and have no doubt of giving them a drubbing." "I hope," said Nelson, "none of our ships have struck?" Hardy answered, "There was no fear of that." Then, and not till then, Nelson spoke of himself. "I am a dead man, Hardy," said he: "I am going fast; it will be all over with me soon. Come nearer to me. Let my dear Lady Hamilton have my hair, and all other things belonging to me." Hardy observed, that he hoped Mr. Beatty could yet hold out some prospect of life. "Oh no!" he replied; "it is impossible; my back is shot through. Beatty will tell you so." Captain Hardy then, once more, shook hands with him; and with a heart almost bursting, hastened upon deck.

By this time all feeling below the breast was gone; and Nelson, having made the surgeon ascertain this, said to him: "You know I am gone. I know it. I feel something rising in my breast" (putting his hand on his left side) "which tells me so." And upon Beatty's inquiring whether his pain was very great? he replied, "So great that he wished he was dead. Yet," said he, in a lower voice, "one would like to live a little longer too!" And after a few minutes, in the same undertone, he added: "What would become of poor

Lady Hamilton if she knew my situation!" Next to his country, she occupied his thoughts. Captain Hardy, some fifty minutes after he had left the cockpit, returned, and again taking the hand of his dying friend and Commander, congratulated him on having gained a complete victory. How many of the enemy were taken he did not know, as it was impossible to perceive them distinctly, but fourteen or fifteen at least. "That's well!" cried Nelson; "but I bargained for twenty." And then, in a stronger voice, he said: "Anchor, Hardy; anchor." Hardy, upon this, hinted that Admiral Collingwood would take upon himself the direction of affairs. "Not while I live, Hardy," said the dying Nelson, ineffectually endeavouring to raise himself from the bed; "do you anchor." His previous order for preparing to anchor had shown how clearly he foresaw the necessity of this. Presently, calling Hardy back, he said to him, in a low voice: "Don't throw me overboard;" and he desired that he might be buried by his parents, unless it should please the King to order otherwise. Then reverting to private feelings,—"Take care of my dear Lady Hamilton, Hardy; take care of poor Lady Hamilton. Kiss me, Hardy," said he. Hardy knelt down and kissed his cheek; and Nelson said: "Now I am satisfied. Thank God, I have done my duty!" Hardy stood over him in silence for a moment or two, then knelt again, and kissed his forehead. "Who is that?" said Nelson; and being informed, he replied: "God bless you, Hardy!" And Hardy then left him, for ever.

Nelson now desired to be turned upon his right side, and said: "I wish I had not left the deck; for I shall soon be gone." Death was, indeed, rapidly approaching. He said to the chaplain: "Doctor, I have *not* been a *great* sinner;" and after a short pause, "Remember that I leave Lady Hamilton, and my daughter Horatia as a legacy to my country." His articulation now became difficult; but he was distinctly heard to say: "Thank God, I have done my duty!" These words he repeatedly pronounced; and they were the last words which he uttered. He expired at thirty minutes after four, three hours and a quarter after he had received his wound.

⚓

A NARRATIVE OF
THE MUTINY ON BOARD
HIS MAJESTY'S SHIP BOUNTY

⚓

A NARRATIVE OF
THE MUTINY ON BOARD
HIS MAJESTY'S SHIP BOUNTY

Lieutenant William Bligh

⚓ *The copy of the "Narrative of the Bounty" from which the following pages are taken was lent the editor by Rockwell Kent. It was the original account published in London in 1790, the same year in which Bligh returned to England. The cleanness of the copy, the clearness of the engraving of charts and elevations of the boat, the firmness of the paper make it difficult to believe that the intervening years have been telescoped in so startling a fashion.*

This is the account of the mutiny and the succeeding trip to Tofoa, from which nineteen men made their unequaled voyage of 3,618 miles.

I SAILED from Otaheite on the 4th of April 1789, having on board 1015 fine bread-fruit plants, besides many other valuable fruits of that country, which, with unremitting attention, we had been collecting for three and twenty weeks, and which were now in the highest state of perfection.

On the 11th of April, I discovered an island in latitude 18° 52′ S. and longitude 200° 19′ E. by the natives called Whytootackee. On the 24th we anchored at Annamooka, one of the Friendly Islands; from which, after completing our wood and water, I sailed on the 27th, having every reason to expect, from the fine condition of the plants, that they would continue healthy.

On the evening of the 28th, owing to light winds, we were not clear of the islands, and at night I directed my course towards Tofoa. The master had the first watch; the gunner the middle watch; and Mr. Christian, one of the mates, the morning watch. This was the turn of duty for the night.

Just before sun-rising, Mr. Christian, with the master at arms, gunner's mate, and Thomas Burket, seaman, came into my cabin while I was asleep, and seizing me, tied my hands with a cord behind my back, and threatened me with instant death, if I spoke or made the least noise: I, however, called so loud as to alarm every one; but they had already secured the officers who were not of their party, by placing sentinels at their doors. There were three men at my cabin door, besides the four within; Christian had only a cutlass in his hand, the others had muskets and bayonets. I was hauled out of bed, and forced on deck in my shirt, suffering great pain from the tightness with which they had tied my hands. I demanded the reason of such violence, but received no other answer than threats of instant death, if I did not hold my tongue. Mr. Elphinston, the master's mate, was kept in his berth; Mr. Nelson, botanist, Mr. Peckover, gunner, Mr. Ledward, surgeon, and the master, were confined to their cabins; and also the clerk, Mr. Samuel, but he soon obtained leave to come on deck. The fore hatchway was guarded by sentinels; the boatswain and carpenter were, however, allowed to come on deck, where they saw me standing abaft the mizen-mast, with my hands tied behind my back, under a guard, with Christian at their head.

The boatswain was now ordered to hoist the launch out, with a threat, if he did not do it instantly, to take care of himself.

The boat being out, Mr. Hayward and Mr. Hallet, midshipmen, and Mr. Samuel, were ordered into it; upon which I demanded the cause of such an order, and endeavoured to persuade some one to a sense of duty; but it was to no effect: "Hold your tongue, Sir, or you are dead this instant," was constantly repeated to me.

The master, by this time, had sent to be allowed to come on deck, which was permitted; but he was soon ordered back again to his cabin.

I continued my endeavours to turn the tide of affairs, when Christian changed the cutlass he had in his hand for a bayonet, that was brought to him, and, holding me with a strong gripe by the cord that tied my hands, he with many oaths threatened to kill me immediately if I would not be quiet: the villains round me had their pieces cocked and bayonets fixed. Particular people were now called on to go into the boat, and were hurried over the side: whence I concluded that with these people I was to be set adrift.

I therefore made another effort to bring about a change, but with no other effect than to be threatened with having my brains blown out.

The boatswain and seamen, who were to go in the boat, were allowed to collect twine, canvas, lines, sails, cordage, an eight and twenty gallon cask of water, and the carpenter to take his tool chest. Mr. Samuel got 150 lbs. of bread, with a small quantity of rum and wine. He also got a quadrant and

With a moderate easterly breeze which sprung up we were able to sail.

compass into the boat; but was forbidden, on pain of death, to touch either map, ephemeris, book of astronomical observations, sextant, timekeeper, or any of my surveys or drawings.

The mutineers now hurried those they meant to get rid of into the boat. When most of them were in, Christian directed a dram to be served to each of his own crew. I now unhappily saw that nothing could be done to effect the recovery of the ship: there was no one to assist me, and every endeavour on my part was answered with threats of death.

The officers were called, and forced over the side into the boat, while I was kept apart from every one, abaft the mizen-mast; Christian, armed with a bayonet, holding me by the bandage that secured my hands. The guard round me had their pieces cocked, but, on my daring the ungrateful wretches to fire, they uncocked them.

Isaac Martin, one of the guard over me, I saw, had an inclination to assist me, and, as he fed me with shaddock, (my lips being quite parched with my endeavours to bring about a change) we explained our wishes to each other by our looks; but this being observed, Martin was instantly removed from me; his inclination then was to leave the ship, for which purpose he got into the boat; but with many threats they obliged him to return.

The armourer, Joseph Coleman, and the two carpenters, McIntosh and Norman, were also kept contrary to their inclination; and they begged of me, after I was astern in the boat, to remember that they declared they had no hand in the transaction. Michael Byrne, I am told, likewise wanted to leave the ship.

It is of no moment for me to recount my endeavours to bring back the offenders to a sense of their duty: all I could do was by speaking to them in general; but my endeavours were of no avail, for I was kept securely bound, and no one but the guard suffered to come near me.

To Mr. Samuel I am indebted for securing my journals and commission, with some material ship papers. Without these I had nothing to certify what I had done, and my honour and character might have been suspected, without my possessing a proper document to have defended them. All this he did with great resolution, though guarded and strictly watched. He attempted to save the time-keeper, and a box with all my surveys, drawings, and remarks for fifteen years past, which were numerous; when he was hurried away, with "Damn your eyes, you are well off to get what you have."

It appeared to me, that Christian was some time in doubt whether he should keep the carpenter, or his mates; at length he determined on the latter, and the carpenter was ordered into the boat. He was permitted, but not without some opposition, to take his tool chest.

Much altercation took place among the mutinous crew during the whole business: some swore "I'll be damned if he does not find his way home, if he gets any thing with him," (meaning me); others, when the carpenter's chest was carrying away, "Damn my eyes, he will have a vessel built in a month." While others laughed at the helpless situation of the boat, being very deep, and so little room for those who were in her. As for Christian, he seemed meditating instant destruction on himself and every one.

I asked for arms, but they laughed at me, and said I was well acquainted with the people where I was going, and therefore did not want them; four cutlasses, however, were thrown into the boat, after we were veered astern.

When the officers and men, with whom I was suffered to have no communication, were put into the boat, they only waited for me, and the master at arms informed Christian of it; who then said—"Come, captain Bligh, your officers and men are now in the boat, and you must go with them; if you attempt to make the least resistance you will instantly be put to death:" and, without any farther ceremony, holding me by the cord that tied my hands, with a tribe of armed ruffians about me, I was forced over the side, where they untied my hands. Being in the boat we were veered astern by a rope. A few pieces of pork were then thrown to us, and some cloaths, also the cutlasses I have already mentioned; and it was now that the armourer and carpenters called out to me to remember that they had no hand in the transaction. After having undergone a great deal of ridicule, and been kept some time to make sport for these unfeeling wretches, we were at length cast adrift in the open ocean.

Having little or no wind, we rowed pretty fast towards Tofoa, which bore NE. about 10 leagues from us. While the ship was in sight she steered to the WNW., but I considered this only as a feint; for when we were sent away—"Huzza for Otaheite," was frequently heard among the mutineers.

Christian, the captain of the gang, is of a respectable family in the north of England. This was the third voyage he had made with me; and, as I found it necessary to keep my ship's company at three watches, I gave him an order to take charge of the third, his abilities being thoroughly equal to the task; and by this means my master and gunner were not at watch and watch.

Haywood is also of a respectable family in the north of England, and a young man of abilities, as well as Christian. These two were objects of my particular regard and attention, and I took great pains to instruct them, for they really promised, as professional men, to be a credit to their country.

Young was well recommended, and appeared to me an able stout seaman; therefore I was glad to take him: he, however, fell short of what his appearance promised.

Stewart was a young man of creditable parents, in the Orkneys; at which place, on the return of the Resolution from the South Seas, in 1780, we received so many civilities, that, on that account only, I should gladly have taken him with me: but, independent of this recommendation, he was a seaman, and had always borne a good character.

Notwithstanding the roughness with which I was treated, the remembrance of past kindnesses produced some signs of remorse in Christian. When they were forcing me out of the ship, I asked him, if this treatment was a proper return for the many instances he had received of my friendship? he appeared disturbed at my question, and answered, with much emotion, "That,—captain Bligh,—that is the thing;—I am in hell—I am in hell."

As soon as I had time to reflect, I felt an inward satisfaction, which prevented any depression of my spirits: conscious of my integrity, and anxious solicitude for the good of the service in which I was engaged, I found my mind wonderfully supported, and I began to conceive hopes, notwithstanding so heavy a calamity, that I should one day be able to account to my King and country for the misfortune. —A few hours before, my situation had been peculiarly flattering. I had a ship in the most perfect order, and well stored with every necessary both for service and health: by early attention to those particulars I had, as much as lay in my power, provided against any accident, in case I could not get through Endeavour Straits, as well as against what might befall me in them; add to this, the plants had been successfully preserved in the most flourishing state: so that, upon the whole, the voyage was two thirds completed, and the remaining part in a very promising way; every person on board being in perfect health, to establish which was ever amongst the principal objects of my attention.

It will very naturally be asked, what could be the reason for such a revolt? in answer to which, I can only conjecture that the mutineers had assured themselves of a more happy life among the Otaheiteans, than they could possibly have in England; which, joined to some female connections, have most probably been the principal cause of the whole transaction.

The women at Otaheite are handsome, mild and cheerful in their manners and conversation, possessed of great sensibility, and have sufficient delicacy to make them admired and beloved. The chiefs were so much attached to our people, that they rather encouraged their stay among them than otherwise, and even made them promises of large possessions. Under these, and many other attendant circumstances, equally desirable, it is now perhaps not so much to be wondered at, though scarcely possible to have been foreseen, that a set of sailors, most of them void of connections, should be led away; especially when, in addition to such powerful inducements, they imagined it in their power to fix themselves in the midst of plenty, on the finest island in the world, where they need not labour, and where the allurements of dissipation are beyond any thing that can be conceived. The utmost, however, that any commander could have supposed to have happened is, that some of the people would have been tempted to desert. But if it should be asserted, that a commander is to guard against an act of mutiny and piracy in his own ship, more than by the common rules of service, it is as much as to say that he must sleep locked up, and when awake, be girded with pistols.

Desertions have happened, more or less, from many of the ships that have been at the Society Islands; but it ever has been in the commanders' power to make the chiefs return their people: the knowledge, therefore, that it was unsafe to desert, perhaps, first led mine to consider with what ease so small a ship might be surprised, and that so favourable an opportunity would never offer to them again.

The secrecy of this mutiny is beyond all conception. Thirteen of the party, who were with me, had always lived forward among the people; yet neither they, nor the mess-mates of Christian, Stewart, Haywood, and Young, had ever observed any circumstance to give them suspicion of what was going on. With such close-planned acts of villainy, and my mind free from any suspicion, it is not wonderful that I have been got the better of. Perhaps, if I had had marines, a sentinel at my cabin-door might have prevented it; for I slept with the door always open, that the officer of the watch might have access to me on all occasions. The possibility of such a conspiracy was ever the farthest from my thoughts. Had their mutiny been occasioned by any grievances, either real or imaginary, I must have discovered symptoms of their discontent, which would have put me on my guard: but the case was far otherwise. Christian, in particular, I was on the most friendly terms with; that very day he was engaged to have dined with me; and the preceding night he excused himself from supping with me, on pretence of being unwell; for which I felt concerned, having no suspicions of his integrity and honour.

It now remained with me to consider what was best to be done. My first determination was to seek a supply of bread-fruit and water at Tofoa, and afterwards to sail for Tongataboo, and there risk a solicitation to Poulaho, the king, to equip my boat, and grant a supply of water and provisions, so as to enable us to reach the East Indies.

The quantity of provisions I found in the boat was 150 lb. of bread, 16 pieces of pork, each piece weighing 2 lb. 6 quarts of rum, 6 bottles of wine, with 28 gallons of water, and four empty barrecoes.

Wednesday, April 29th. Happily the afternoon kept calm, until about 4 o'clock, when we were so far to windward, that, with a moderate easterly breeze which sprung up, we were able to sail. It was nevertheless dark when we got to Tofoa, where I expected to land; but the shore proved to be so steep and rocky, that I was obliged to give up all thoughts of it, and keep the boat under the lee of the island with two oars; for there was no anchorage. Having fixed on this mode of proceeding for the night, I served to every person half a pint of grog, and each took to his rest as well as our unhappy situation would allow.

In the morning, at dawn of day, we set off along shore in search of landing, and about ten o'clock we discovered a stony cove at the NW. part of the island, where I dropt the grapnel within 20 yards of the rocks. A great deal of surf ran on the shore; but, as I was unwilling to diminish our stock of provisions, I landed Mr. Samuel, and some others, who climbed the cliffs, and got into the country to search for supplies. The rest of us remained at the cove, not discovering any way to get into the country, but that by which Mr. Samuel had proceeded. It was great consolation to me to find, that the spirits of my people did not sink, notwithstanding our miserable and almost hopeless situation. Towards noon Mr. Samuel returned, with a few quarts of water, which he had found in holes; but he had met with no spring, or any prospect of a sufficient supply in that particular, and had only seen signs of inhabitants. As it was impossible to know how much we might be in want, I only issued a morsel of bread, and a glass of wine, to each person for dinner.

I observed the latitude of this cove to be 19° 41′ S.

This is the NW. part of Tofoa, the north-westernmost of the Friendly Islands.

Thursday, April 30th. Fair weather, but the wind blew so violently from the ESE. that I could not venture to sea. Our detention therefore made it absolutely necessary to see what we could do more for our support; for I determined, if possible, to keep my first stock entire: I therefore weighed, and rowed along shore, to see if any thing could be got; and at last discovered some cocoa-nut trees, but they were on the top of high precipices, and the surf made it dangerous landing; both one and the other we, however, got the better of. Some, with much difficulty, climbed the cliffs, and got about 20 cocoa-nuts, and others slung them to ropes, by which we hauled them through the surf into the boat. This was all that could be done here; and, as I found no place so eligible as the one we had left to spend the night at, I returned to the cove, and, having served a cocoa-nut to each person, we went to rest again in the boat.

At dawn of day I attempted to get to sea; but the wind and weather proved so bad, that I was glad to return to my former station; where, after issuing a morsel of bread and a spoonful of rum to each person, we landed, and I went off with Mr. Nelson, Mr. Samuel, and some others, into the country, having hauled ourselves up the precipice by long vines, which were fixed there by the natives for that purpose; this being the only way into the country.

We found a few deserted huts, and a small plantain walk, but little taken care of; from which we could only collect three small bunches of plantains. After passing this place, we came to a deep gully that led towards a mountain, near a volcano; and, as I conceived that in the rainy season very great torrents of water must pass through it, we hoped to find sufficient for our use remaining in some holes of the rocks; but, after all our search, the whole that we found was only nine gallons, in the course of the day. We advanced within two miles of the foot of the highest mountain in the island, on which is the volcano that is almost constantly burning. The country near it is all covered with lava, and has a most dreary appearance. As we had not been fortunate in our discoveries, and saw but little to alleviate our distresses, we filled our cocoa-nut shells with the water we found, and returned exceedingly fatigued and faint. When I came to the precipice whence we were to descend into the cove, I was seized with such a dizziness in my head, that I thought it scarce possible to effect it; however, by the assistance of Mr. Nelson and others, they at last got me down, in a weak condition. Every person being returned by noon, I gave about an ounce of pork and two plantains to each, with half a glass of wine. I again observed the latitude of this place 19° 41′ south. The people who remained by the boat I had directed to look for fish, or what they could pick up about the rocks; but nothing eatable could be found: so that, upon the whole, we considered ourselves on as miserable a spot of land as could well be imagined.

I could not say positively, from the former knowledge I had of this island, whether it was inhabited or not; but I knew it was considered inferior to the other islands, and I was not certain but that the Indians only resorted to it at particular times. I was very anxious to ascertain this point; for, in case there had only been a few people here, and those could have furnished us with but very moderate supplies, the remaining in this spot to have made preparations for our voyage, would have been preferable to the risk of going amongst multitudes, where perhaps we might lose every thing. A party, therefore, sufficiently strong, I determined should go another route, as soon as the sun became lower; and they cheerfully undertook it.

Friday, May the 1st: stormy weather, wind ESE. and SE. About two o'clock in the afternoon the party set out; but, after suffering much fatigue, they returned in the evening, without any kind of success.

At the head of the cove, about 150 yards from the water-side, was a cave; across the stony beach was about 100 yards, and the only way from the country into the cove was that which I have already described. The situation secured us from the danger of being surprised, and I determined to remain on shore for the night, with a part of my people, that the others might have more room to rest in the boat, with the master; whom I directed to lie at a grapnel, and be watchful, in case we should be attacked. I ordered one plantain for each person to be boiled; and, having supped on this scanty allowance, with a quarter of a pint of grog, and fixed the watches for the night, those whose turn it was, laid down to sleep in the cave; before which we kept up a good fire, yet notwithstanding we were much troubled with flies and mosquitoes.

At dawn of day the party set out again in a different route, to see what they could find; in the course of which they suffered greatly for want of water: they, however, met with two men, a woman, and a child; the men came with them to the cove, and brought two cocoa-nut shells of water. I immediately made friends with these people, and sent them away for bread-fruit, plantains, and water. Soon after other natives came to us; and by noon I had 30 of them about me, trading with the articles we were in want of: but I could only afford one ounce of pork, and a quarter of a bread-fruit, to each man for dinner, with half a pint of water; for I was fixed in not using any of the bread or water in the boat.

No particular chief was yet among the natives: they were, notwithstanding, tractable, and behaved honestly, giving the provisions they brought for a few buttons and beads. The party who had been out, informed me of having discovered several neat plantations; so that it became no longer a doubt of there being settled inhabitants on the island; and for that reason I determined to get what I could, and sail the first moment the wind and weather would allow me to put to sea.

Saturday, May the 2d: stormy weather, wind ESE. It had hitherto been a weighty consideration with me, how I was to account to the natives for the loss of my ship: I knew they had too much sense to be amused with a story that the ship was to join me, when she was not in sight from the hills. I was at first doubtful whether I should tell the real fact, or say that the ship had overset and sunk, and that only we were saved: the latter appeared to me to be the most proper and advantageous to us, and I accordingly instructed my people, that we might all agree in one story. As I expected, enquiries were made after the ship, and they seemed readily satisfied with our account; but there did not appear the least symptom of joy or sorrow in their faces, although I fancied I discovered some marks of surprise. Some of the natives were coming and going the whole afternoon, and we got enough of bread-fruit, plantains, and cocoa-nuts for another day; but water they only brought us about five pints. A canoe also came in with four men, and brought a few cocoa-nuts and bread-fruit, which I bought as I had done the rest. Nails were much enquired after, but I would not suffer one to be shewn, as I wanted them for the use of the boat.

Towards evening I had the satisfaction to find our stock of provisions somewhat increased: but the natives did not appear to have much to spare. What they brought was in such small quantities, that I had no reason to hope we should be able to procure from them sufficient to stock us for our voyage. At sunset all the natives left us in quiet possession of the cove. I thought this a good sign, and made no doubt that they would come again the next day with a larger proportion of food and water, with which I hoped to sail without farther delay: for if, in attempting to get to Tongataboo, we should be blown away from the islands altogether, there would be a larger quantity of provisions to support us against such a misfortune.

At night I served a quarter of a bread-fruit and a cocoa-nut to each person for supper; and, a good fire being made, all but the watch went to sleep.

At day-break I was happy to find every one's spirits a little revived, and that they no longer regarded me with those anxious looks, which had constantly been directed towards me since we lost sight of the ship: every countenance appeared to have a degree of cheerfulness, and they all seemed determined to do their best.

As I doubted of water being brought by the natives, I sent a party among the gullies in the mountains, with empty shells, to see what they could get. In their absence the natives came about us, as I expected, but more numerous; also two canoes came in from round the north side of the island. In one of them was an elderly chief, called Maccaackavow. Soon after some of our foraging party returned, and with them came a good-looking chief, called Eegijeefow, or perhaps more properly Eefow, Egij or Eghee, signifying a chief. To both these men I made a present of an old shirt and a knife, and I soon found they either had seen me, or had heard of my being at Annamooka. They knew I had been with captain Cook, who they enquired after, and also captain Clerk. They were very inquisitive to know in what manner I had lost my ship. During this conversation a young man appeared, whom I remembered to have seen at Annamooka, called Nageete: he expressed much pleasure at seeing me. I now enquired after Poulaho and Feenow, who, they said, were at Tongataboo; and Eefow agreed to accompany me thither, if I would wait till the weather moderated. The readiness and affability of this man gave me much satisfaction.

This, however, was but of short duration, for the natives began to increase in number, and I observed some symptoms of a design against us; soon after they attempted to haul the boat on shore, when I threatened Eefow with a cutlass, to induce him to make them desist; which they did, and every thing became quiet again. My people, who had been in the mountains, now returned with about three gallons of water. I kept buying up the little bread-fruit that was brought to us, and likewise some spears to arm my men with, having only four cutlasses, two of which were in the boat. As we had no means of improving our situation, I told our people I would wait until sun-set, by which time, perhaps, something might happen in our favour: that if we attempted to go at present, we must fight our way through, which we could do more advantageously at night; and that in the meantime we would endeavour to get off to the boat what we had bought. The beach was now lined with the natives, and we heard nothing but the knocking of stones together, which they had in each hand. I knew very well this was the sign of an attack. It being now noon, I served a cocoa-nut and a bread-fruit to each person for dinner, and gave some to the chiefs, with whom I continued to appear intimate and friendly. They frequently importuned me to sit down, but I as constantly refused; for it occured both to Mr. Nelson and myself, that they intended to seize hold of me, if I gave them such an opportunity. Keeping, therefore, constantly on our guard, we were suffered to eat our uncomfortable meal in some quietness.

Sunday, 3rd May, fresh gales at SE. and ESE., varying to the NE. in the latter part, with a storm of wind.

After dinner we began by little and little to get our things into the boat, which was a troublesome business, on account of the surf. I carefully watched the motions of the natives, who still increased in number, and found that, instead of their intention being to leave us, fires were made, and places fixed on for their stay during the night. Consultations were also held among them, and every thing assured me we should be attacked. I sent orders to the master, that when he saw us coming down, he should keep the boat close to the shore, that we might the more readily embark.

I had my journal on shore with me, writing the occurrences in the cave, and in sending it down to the boat it was nearly snatched away, but for the timely assistance of the gunner.

The sun was near setting when I gave the word, on which every person, who was on shore with me, boldly took up his proportion of things, and carried them to the boat. The chiefs asked me if I would not stay with them all night, I said, "No, I never sleep out of my boat; but in the morning we will again trade with you, and I shall remain until the weather is moderate, that we may go, as we have agreed, to see Poulaho, at Tongataboo." Maccaackavow then got up, and said, "You will not sleep on shore? then Mattie," (which directly signifies we will kill you) and left me. The onset was now preparing; every one, as I have described before, kept knocking stones together, and Eefow quitted me. We had now all but two or three things in the boat, when I took Nageete by the hand, and we walked down the beach, every one in a silent kind of horror.

When I came to the boat, and was seeing the people embark, Nageete wanted me to stay to speak to Eefow; but I found he was encouraging them to the attack, and I determined, had it then begun, to have killed him for his treacherous behaviour. I ordered the carpenter not to quit me until the other people were in the boat. Nageete, finding I would not stay, loosed himself from my hold and went off, and we all got into the boat except one man, who, while I was getting on board, quitted it, and ran up the beach to cast the stern fast off, notwithstanding the master and others called to him to return, while they were hauling me out of the water.

I was no sooner in the boat than the attack began by about 200 men; the unfortunate poor man who had run up the beach was knocked down, and the stones flew like a shower of shot. Many Indians got hold of the stern rope, and were near hauling us on shore, and would certainly have done it if I had not had a knife in my pocket, with which I cut the rope. We then hauled off to the grapnel, every one being more or less hurt. At this time I saw five of the natives about the poor man they had killed, and two of them were beating him about the head with stones in their hands.

We had no time to reflect, before, to my surprise, they filled their canoes with stones, and twelve men came off after us to renew the attack, which they did so effectually as nearly to disable all of us. Our grapnel was foul, but Providence here assisted us; the fluke broke, and we got to our oars, and pulled to sea. They, however, could paddle round us, so that we were obliged to sustain the attack without being able to return it except with such stones as lodged in the boat, and in this I found we were very inferior to them. We could not close, because our boat was lumbered and heavy, and that they knew very well: I therefore adopted the expedient of throwing overboard some cloaths, which they lost time in picking up; and, as it was now almost dark, they gave over the attack, and returned towards the shore, leaving us to reflect on our unhappy situation.

The poor man I lost was John Norton: this was his second voyage with me as a quarter-master, and his worthy character made me lament his loss very much. He left an aged parent, I am told, whom he supported.

I once before sustained an attack of a similar nature, with a smaller number of Europeans, against a multitude of Indians; it was after the death of captain Cook, on the Morai at Owhyhee, where I was left by lieutenant King: yet, notwithstanding, I did not conceive that the power of a man's arm could throw stones, from two to eight pounds weight, with such force and exactness as these people did. Here unhappily I was without arms, and the Indians knew it; but it was a fortunate circumstance that they did not begin to attack us in the cave: in that case our destruction must have been inevitable, and we should have had nothing left for it but to die as bravely as we could, fighting close together; in which I found every one cheerfully disposed to join me. This appearance of resolution deterred them, supposing they could effect their purpose without risk after we were in the boat.

Taking this as a sample of the dispositions of the Indians, there was little reason to expect much benefit if I persevered in my intention of visiting Poulaho; for I considered their good behaviour hitherto to proceed from a dread of our fire-arms, which, now knowing us destitute of, would cease; and, even supposing our lives not in danger, the boat and every thing we had would most probably be taken from us, and thereby all hopes precluded of ever being able to return to our native country.

We were now sailing along the west side of the island Tofoa, and my mind was employed in considering what was best to be done, when I was solicited by all hands to take them towards home: and, when I told them no hopes of relief for us remained, but what I might find at New Holland, until I came to Timor, a distance of full 1200 leagues, where was a Dutch settlement, but in what part of the island I knew not, they all agreed to live on one ounce of bread, and a quarter of a pint of water, per day. Therefore, after examining our stock of provisions, and recommending this as a sacred promise for ever to their memory, we bore away across a sea, where the navigation is but little known, in a small boat, twenty-three feet long from stem to stern, deep laden with eighteen men; without a chart, and nothing but my own recollection and general knowledge of the situation of places, assisted by a book of latitudes and longitudes, to guide us. I was happy, however, to see every one better satisfied with our situation in this particular than myself.

Our stock of provisions consisted of about one hundred and fifty pounds of bread, twenty-eight gallons of water, twenty pounds of pork, three bottles of wine, and five quarts of rum. The difference between this and the quantity we had on leaving the ship, was principally owing to loss in the bustle and confusion of the attack. A few cocoa-nuts were in the boat, and some bread-fruit, but the latter was trampled to pieces.

It was about eight o'clock at night when I bore away under a reefed lug fore-sail: and, having divided the people into watches, and got the boat in a little order, we returned God thanks for our miraculous preservation, and, fully confident of his gracious support, I found my mind more at ease than for some time past.

⚓

STRIKING THE JOLLY ROGER

⚓

STRIKING THE JOLLY ROGER

Robert Louis Stevenson

⚓ *There is probably not a single reader of this book who has not, at one time or another, read "Treasure Island". It may be well, however, briefly to describe the action which takes place just prior to the following episode.*

The "Hispaniola", in search of buried treasure, has reached the island, and the mutineers are now in control of her. They have left a watch aboard and have gone ashore to carouse. The owner and captain and the loyal hands of the crew have fortified themselves behind a stockade on the island.

Young Jim Hawkins, who is telling the story, has just stolen out of the stockade where his friends are nursing the wounds they have received in the attack made on them by the mutineers.

He has gone in search of the little boat made by Ben Gunn, the marooned sailor, and has found it carefully hidden away near the shore . . .

THE coracle—as I had ample reason to know before I was done with her —was a very safe boat for a person of my height and weight, both buoyant and clever in a seaway; but she was the most cross-grained lop-sided craft to manage. Do as you pleased, she always made more leeway than anything else, and turning round and round was the manoeuvre she was best at. Even Ben Gunn himself has admitted that she was "queer to handle till you knew her way."

Certainly I did not know her way. She turned in every direction but the one I was bound to go; the most part of the time we were broadside on, and I am very sure I never should have made the ship at all but for the tide.

From *Treasure Island* by Robert Louis Stevenson. Copyright, 1911, by Charles Scribner's Sons.

407

By good fortune, paddle as I pleased, the tide was still sweeping me down; and there lay the *Hispaniola* right in the fairway, hardly to be missed.

First she loomed before me like a blot of something yet blacker than darkness, then her spars and hull began to take shape, and the next moment, as it seemed (for, the further I went, the brisker grew the current of the ebb), I was alongside of her hawser, and had laid hold.

The hawser was as taut as a bowstring, and the current so strong she pulled upon her anchor. All round the hull, in the blackness, the rippling current bubbled and chattered like a little mountain stream. One cut with my sea-gully, and the *Hispaniola* would go humming down the tide.

So far so good; but it next occurred to my recollection that a taut hawser, suddenly cut, is a thing as dangerous as a kicking horse. Ten to one, if I were so foolhardy as to cut the *Hispaniola* from her anchor, I and the coracle would be knocked clean out of the water.

This brought me to a full stop, and if fortune had not again particularly favoured me, I should have had to abandon my design. But the light airs which had begun blowing from the south-east and south had hauled round after nightfall into the south-west. Just while I was meditating, a puff came, caught the *Hispaniola,* and forced her up into the current; and to my great joy, I felt the hawser slacken in my grasp, and the hand by which I held it dip for a second under water.

With that I made my mind up, took out my gully, opened it with my teeth, and cut one strand after another, till the vessel swung only by two. Then I lay quiet, waiting to sever these last when the strain should be once more lightened by a breath of wind.

All this time I had heard the sound of loud voices from the cabin; but, to say truth, my mind had been so entirely taken up with other thoughts that I had scarcely given ear. Now, however, when I had nothing else to do, I began to pay more heed.

One I recognised for the coxswain's, Israel Hands, that had been Flint's gunner in former days. The other was, of course, my friend of the red nightcap. Both men were plainly the worse for drink, and they were still drinking; for, even while I was listening, one of them, with a drunken cry, opened the stern window and threw out something, which I divined to be an empty bottle. But they were not only tipsy; it was plain that they were furiously angry. Oaths flew like hailstones, and every now and then there came forth such an explosion as I thought was sure to end in blows. But each time the quarrel passed off, and the voices grumbled lower for awhile, until the next crisis came, and, in its turn, passed away without result.

On shore, I could see the glow of the great camp fire burning warmly through the shore-side trees. Some one was singing, a dull, old droning

I felt the hawser slacken once more, and with a good, tough effort, cut the last fibres through.

sailor's song, with a droop and a quaver at the end of every verse, and seemingly no end to it at all but the patience of the singer. I had heard it on the voyage more than once, and remembered these words:

> "But one man of her crew alive,
> What put to sea with seventy-five."

And I thought it was a ditty rather too dolefully appropriate for a company that had met such cruel losses in the morning. But, indeed, from what I saw, all these buccaneers were as callous as the sea they sailed on.

At last the breeze came; the schooner sidled and drew nearer in the dark; I felt the hawser slacken once more, and with a good, tough effort, cut the last fibres through.

The breeze had but little action on the coracle, and I was almost instantly swept against the bows of the *Hispaniola*. At the same time the schooner began to turn upon her heel, spinning slowly, end for end, across the current.

I wrought like a fiend, for I expected every moment to be swamped; and since I found I could not push the coracle directly off, I now shoved straight astern. At length I was clear of my dangerous neighbour; and just as I gave the last impulsion, my hands came across a light cord that was trailing overboard across the stern bulwark. Instantly I grasped it.

Why I should have done so I can hardly say. It was at first mere instinct; but once I had it in my hands and found it fast, curiosity began to get the upper hand, and I determined I should have one look through the cabin window.

I pulled in hand over hand on the cord, and, when I judged myself near enough, rose at infinite risk to about half my height, and thus commanded the roof and a slice of the interior of the cabin.

By this time the schooner and her little consort were gliding pretty swiftly through the water; indeed, we had already fetched up level with the camp fire. The ship was talking, as sailors say, loudly, treading the innumerable ripples with an incessant weltering splash; and until I got my eye above the window-sill I could not comprehend why the watchmen had taken no alarm. One glance, however, was sufficient; and it was only one glance that I durst take from that unsteady skiff. It showed me Hands and his companion locked together in deadly wrestle, each with a hand upon the other's throat.

I dropped upon the thwart again, none too soon, for I was near overboard. I could see nothing for a moment, but these two furious, encrimsoned faces, swaying together under the smoky lamp; and I shut my eyes to let them grow once more familiar with the darkness.

The endless ballad had come to an end at last, and the whole diminished company about the camp fire had broken into the chorus I had heard so often:

> "Fifteen men on the dead man's chest—
> Yo-ho-ho, and a bottle of rum!
> Drink and the devil had done for the rest—
> Yo-ho-ho, and a bottle of rum!"

I was just thinking how busy drink and the devil were at that very moment in the cabin of the *Hispaniola,* when I was surprised by a sudden lurch of the coracle. At the same moment she yawed sharply and seemed to change her course. The speed in the meantime had strangely increased.

I opened my eyes at once. All round me were little ripples, combing over with a sharp, bristling sound and slightly phosphorescent. The *Hispaniola* herself, a few yards in whose wake I was still being whirled along, seemed to stagger in her course, and I saw her spars toss a little against the blackness of the night; nay, as I looked longer, I made sure she also was wheeling to the southward.

I glanced over my shoulder, and my heart jumped against my ribs. There, right behind me, was the glow of the camp fire. The current had turned at right angles, sweeping round along with it the tall schooner and the little dancing coracle; ever quickening, ever bubbling higher, ever muttering louder, it went spinning through the narrows for the open sea.

Suddenly the schooner in front of me gave a violent yaw, turning, perhaps, through twenty degrees; and almost at the same moment one shout followed another from on board; I could hear feet pounding on the companion ladder; and I knew that the two drunkards had at last been interrupted in their quarrel and awakened to a sense of their disaster.

I lay down flat in the bottom of that wretched skiff, and devoutly recommended my spirit to its Maker. At the end of the straits, I made sure we must fall into some bar of raging breakers, where all my troubles would be ended speedily; and though I could, perhaps, bear to die, I could not bear to look upon my fate as it approached.

So I must have lain for hours, continually beaten to and fro upon the billows, now and again wetted with flying sprays, and never ceasing to expect death at the next plunge. Gradually weariness grew upon me; a numbness, an occasional stupor, fell upon my mind even in the midst of my terrors; until sleep at last supervened, and in my sea-tossed coracle I lay and dreamed of home and the old "Admiral Benbow."

It was broad day when I awoke, and found myself tossing at the southwest end of Treasure Island. The sun was up, but was still hid from me behind the great bulk of the Spy-glass, which on this side descended almost to the sea in formidable cliffs.

Haulbowline Head and Mizzen-mast Hill were at my elbow; the hill bare and dark, the head bound with cliffs forty or fifty feet high, and fringed with great masses of fallen rock. I was scarce a quarter of a mile to seaward, and it was my first thought to paddle in and land.

That notion was soon given over. Among the fallen rocks the breakers spouted and bellowed; loud reverberations, heavy sprays flying and falling, succeeded one another from second to second; and I saw myself, if I ventured nearer, dashed to death upon the rough shore, or spending my strength in vain to scale the beetling crags.

Nor was that all; for crawling together on flat tables of rock, or letting themselves drop into the sea with loud reports, I beheld huge slimy monsters —soft snails, as it were, of incredible bigness—two or three score of them together, making the rocks to echo with their barkings.

I have understood since that they were sea lions, and entirely harmless. But the look of them, added to the difficulty of the shore and the high running of the surf, was more than enough to disgust me of that landing-place. I felt willing rather to starve at sea than to confront such perils.

In the meantime I had a better chance, as I supposed, before me. North of Haulbowline Head, the land runs in a long way, leaving, at low tide, a long stretch of yellow sand. To the north of that, again, there comes another cape—Cape of the Woods, as it was marked upon the chart—buried in tall green pines, which descended to the margin of the sea.

I remembered what Silver had said about the current that sets northward along the whole west coast of Treasure Island; and seeing from my position that I was already under its influence, I preferred to leave Haulbowline Head behind me, and reserve my strength for an attempt to land upon the kindlier-looking Cape of the Woods.

There was a great, smooth swell upon the sea. The wind blowing steady and gentle from the south, there was no contrariety between that and the current, and the billows rose and fell unbroken.

Had it been otherwise, I must long ago have perished; but as it was, it is surprising how easily and securely my little and light boat could ride. Often, as I still lay at the bottom, and kept no more than an eye above the gunwale, I would see a big blue summit heaving close above me; yet the coracle would but bounce a little, dance as if on springs, and subside on the other side into the trough as lightly as a bird.

I began after a little to grow very bold, and sat up to try my skill at paddling. But even a small change in the disposition of the weight will produce violent changes in the behaviour of a coracle. And I had hardly moved before the boat, giving up at once her gentle dancing movement, ran straight down a slope of water so steep that it made me giddy, and struck her nose, with a spout of spray, deep into the side of the next wave.

I was drenched and terrified, and fell instantly back into my old position, whereupon the coracle seemed to find her head again, and led me as softly as before among the billows. It was plain she was not to be interfered with, and at that rate, since I could in no way influence her course, what hope had I left of reaching land?

I began to be horribly frightened, but I kept my head, for all that. First, moving with all care, I gradually baled out the coracle with my sea-cap; then getting my eye once more above the gunwale, I set myself to study how it was she managed to slip so quietly through the rollers.

I found each wave, instead of the big, smooth glossy mountain it looks from shore, or from a vessel's deck, was for all the world like any range of hills on the dry land, full of peaks and smooth places and valleys. The coracle, left to herself, turning from side to side, threaded, so to speak, her way through these lower parts, and avoided the steep slopes and higher, toppling summits of the wave.

"Well, now," thought I to myself, "it is plain I must lie where I am, and not disturb the balance; but it is plain, also, that I can put the paddle over the side, and from time to time, in smooth places, give her a shove or two towards land." No sooner thought upon than done. There I lay on my elbows, in the most trying attitude, and every now and again gave a weak stroke or two to turn her head to shore.

It was very tiring, and slow work, yet I did visibly gain ground; and, as we drew near the Cape of the Woods, though I saw I must infallibly miss that point, I had still made some hundred yards of easting. I was, indeed, close in. I could see the cool, green tree-tops swaying together in the breeze, and I felt sure I should make the next promontory without fail.

It was high time, for I now began to be tortured with thirst. The glow of the sun from above, its thousand-fold reflection from the waves, the sea-water that fell and dried upon me, caking my very lips with salt, combined to make my throat burn and my brain ache. The sight of the trees so near at hand had almost made me sick with longing; but the current had soon carried me past the point; and, as the next reach of sea opened out, I beheld a sight that changed the nature of my thoughts.

Right in front of me, not half a mile away, I beheld the *Hispaniola* under sail. I made sure, of course, that I should be taken; but I was so distressed for want of water, that I scarce knew whether to be glad or sorry at the thought; and, long before I had come to a conclusion, surprise had taken possession of my mind, and I could do nothing but stare and wonder.

The *Hispaniola* was under her main-sail and two jibs, and the beautiful white canvas shone in the sun like snow or silver. When I first sighted her, all her sails were drawing; she was laying a course about north-west; and I presumed the men on board were going round the island on their way back to the anchorage. Presently she began to fetch more and more to the westward, so that I thought they had sighted me and were going about in chase. At last, however, she fell right into the wind's eye, was taken dead aback, and stood there awhile helpless, with her sails shivering.

"Clumsy fellows," said I; "they must still be drunk as owls." And I thought how Captain Smollett would have set them skipping.

Meanwhile, the schooner gradually fell off, and filled again upon another tack, sailed swiftly for a minute or so, and brought up once more dead in the wind's eye. Again and again was this repeated. To and fro, up and down, north, south, east, and west, the *Hispaniola* sailed by swoops and dashes, and at each repetition ended as she had begun, with idly flapping canvas. It became plain to me that nobody was steering. And, if so, where were the men? Either they were dead drunk, or had deserted her, I thought, and perhaps if I could get on board, I might return the vessel to her captain.

The current was bearing coracle and schooner southward at an equal rate. As for the latter's sailing, it was so wild and intermittent, and she hung each time so long in irons, that she certainly gained nothing, if she did not even lose. If only I dared to sit up and paddle, I made sure that I could overhaul her. The scheme had an air of adventure that inspired me, and the thought of the water breaker beside the fore companion doubled my growing courage.

Up I got, was welcomed almost instantly by another cloud of spray, but this time stuck to my purpose; and set myself, with all my strength and caution, to paddle after the unsteered *Hispaniola*. Once I shipped a sea so heavy that I had to stop and bail, with my heart fluttering like a bird; but gradually I got into the way of the thing, and guided my coracle among the waves, with only now and then a blow upon her bows and a dash of foam in my face.

I was now gaining rapidly on the schooner; I could see the brass glisten on the tiller as it banged about; and still no soul appeared upon her decks. I could not choose but suppose she was deserted. If not, the men were lying drunk below, where I might batten them down, perhaps, and do what I chose with the ship.

For some time she had been doing the worst thing possible for me—standing still. She headed nearly due south, yawing, of course, all the time. Each time she fell off her sails partly filled, and these brought her, in a moment, right to the wind again. I have said this was the worst thing possible for me; for helpless as she looked in this situation, with the canvas cracking like cannon, and the blocks trundling and banging on the deck, she still continued to run away from me, not only with the speed of the current, but by the whole amount of her leeway, which was naturally great.

But now, at last, I had my chance. The breeze fell, for some seconds, very low, and the current gradually turning her, the *Hispaniola* revolved slowly round her centre, and at last presented me her stern, with the cabin window still gaping open, and the lamp over the table still burning on into the day. The main-sail hung drooped like a banner. She was stock-still, but for the current.

For the last little while I had even lost; but now, redoubling my efforts, I began once more to overhaul the chase.

I was not a hundred yards from her when the wind came again in a clap; she filled on the port tack, and was off again, stooping and skimming like a swallow.

My first impulse was one of despair, but my second was towards joy. Round she came, till she was broad-side on to me—round still till she had covered a half, and then two-thirds, and then three-quarters of the distance that separated us. I could see the waves boiling white under her forefoot. Immensely tall she looked to me from my low station in the coracle.

And then, of a sudden, I began to comprehend. I had scarce time to think— scarce time to act and save myself. I was on the summit of one swell when the schooner came stooping over the next. The bowsprit was over my head. I sprang to my feet, and leaped, stamping the coracle under water. With one hand I caught the jib-boom, while my foot was lodged between the stay and the brace; and as I still clung there panting, a dull blow told me that the schooner had charged down upon and struck the coracle, and that I was left without retreat on the *Hispaniola*.

I had scarce gained a position on the bowsprit, when the flying jib flapped and filled upon the other tack, with a report like a gun. The schooner trembled to her keel under the reverse; but next moment, the other sails still drawing, the jib flapped back again, and hung idle.

This had nearly tossed me off into the sea; and now I lost no time, crawled back along the bowsprit, and tumbled head-foremost on the deck.

I was on the lee side of the forecastle, and the main-sail, which was still drawing, concealed from me a certain portion of the after-deck. Not a soul was to be seen. The planks, which had not been swabbed since the mutiny, bore the print of many feet; and an empty bottle, broken by the neck, tumbled to and fro like a live thing in the scuppers.

Suddenly the *Hispaniola* came right into the wind. The jibs behind me cracked aloud; the rudder slammed to; the whole ship gave a sickening heave and shudder, and at the same moment the main-boom swung inboard, the sheet groaning in the blocks, and showed me the lee after-deck.

There were the two watchmen, sure enough: red-cap on his back, as stiff as a handspike, with his arms stretched out like those of a crucifix, and his teeth showing his open lips; Israel Hands propped against the bulwarks, his chin on his chest, his hands lying open before him on the deck, his face as white, under its tan, as a tallow candle.

For awhile the ship kept bucking and sidling like a vicious horse, the sails filling, now on one tack, now on another, and the boom swinging to and fro till the mast groaned aloud under the strain. Now and again, too, there would come a cloud of light sprays over the bulwark, and a heavy blow of the ship's bows against the swell: so much heavier weather was made of it by this great rigged ship than by my home-made, lop-sided coracle, now gone to the bottom of the sea.

At every jump of the schooner, red-cap slipped to and fro; but—what was ghastly to behold—neither his attitude nor his fixed teeth-disclosing grin was anyway disturbed by this rough usage. At every jump, too, Hands appeared still more to sink into himself and settle down upon the deck, his feet sliding ever the farther out, and the whole body canting towards the stern, so that his face became, little by little, hid from me; and at last I could see nothing beyond his ear and the frayed ringlet of one whisker.

At the same time, I observed, around both of them, splashes of dark blood upon the planks, and began to feel sure that they had killed each other in their drunken wrath.

While I was thus looking and wondering, in a calm moment, when the ship was still, Israel Hands turned partly round, and, with a low moan, writhed himself back to the position in which I had seen him first. The moan, which told of pain and deadly weakness, and the way in which his jaw hung open, went right to my heart. But when I remembered the talk I had overheard from the apple barrel, all pity left me.

I walked aft until I reached the main-mast.

"Come aboard, Mr. Hands," I said, ironically.

He rolled his eyes round heavily; but he was too far gone to express surprise. All he could do was to utter one word, "Brandy."

It occurred to me there was no time to lose; and, dodging the boom as it once more lurched across the deck, I slipped aft, and down the companion stairs into the cabin.

It was such a scene of confusion as you can hardly fancy. All the lockfast places had been broken open in quest of the chart. The floor was thick with mud, where ruffians had sat down to drink or consult after wading in the marshes round their camp. The bulkheads, all painted in clear white, and beaded round with gilt, bore a pattern of dirty hands. Dozens of empty bottles clinked together in corners to the rolling of the ship. One of the doctor's medical books lay open on the table, half of the leaves gutted out, I suppose, for pipelights. In the midst of all this the lamp still cast a smoky glow, obscure and brown as umber.

I went into the cellar; all the barrels were gone, and of the bottles a most surprising number had been drunk out and thrown away. Certainly, since the mutiny began, not a man of them could ever have been sober.

Foraging about, I found a bottle with some brandy left, for Hands; and for myself I routed out some biscuit, some pickled fruits, a great bunch of raisins, and a piece of cheese. With these I came on deck, put down my own stock behind the rudder head, and well out of the coxswain's reach, went forward to the water-breaker, and had a good, deep drink of water, and then, and not till then, gave Hands the brandy.

He must have drunk a gill before he took the bottle from his mouth.

"Aye," said he, "by thunder, but I wanted some o' that!"

I had sat down already in my own corner and begun to eat.

"Much hurt?" I asked him.

He grunted, or, rather, I might say, he barked.

"If that doctor was aboard," he said, "I'd be right enough in a couple of turns; but I don't have no manner of luck, you see, and that's what's the matter with me. As for that swab, he's good and dead, he is," he added, indicating the man with the red cap. "He warn't no seaman, anyhow. And where mought you have come from?"

"Well," said I, "I've come aboard to take possession of this ship, Mr. Hands; and you'll please regard me as your captain until further notice."

He looked at me sourly enough, but said nothing. Some of the colour had come back into his cheeks, though he still looked very sick, and still continued to slip out and settle down as the ship banged about.

"By-the-by," I continued, "I can't have these colours, Mr. Hands; and, by your leave, I'll strike 'em. Better none than these."

And, again dodging the boom, I ran to the colour lines, handed down their cursed black flag, and chucked it overboard.

"God save the king!" said I, waving my cap; "and there's an end to Captain Silver!"

He watched me keenly and slyly, his chin all the while on his breast.

"I reckon," he said at last—"I reckon, Cap'n Hawkins, you'll kind of want to get ashore, now. S'pose we talks."

"Why, yes," says I, "with all my heart, Mr. Hands. Say on." And I went back to my meal with a good appetite.

"This man," he began, nodding feebly at the corpse—"O'Brien were his name—a rank Irelander—this man and me got the canvas on her, meaning for to sail her back. Well, *he's* dead now, he is—as dead as bilge; and who's to sail this ship, I don't see. Without I gives you a hint, you ain't that man, as far's I can tell. Now, look here, you gives me food and drink, and a old scarf or ankecher to tie my wound up, you do; and I'll tell you how to sail her; and that's about square all round, I take it."

"I'll tell you one thing," says I: "I'm not going back to Captain Kidd's anchorage. I mean to get into North Inlet, and beach her quietly there."

"To be sure you did," he cried. "Why, I ain't sich an infernal lubber, after all. I can see, can't I? I've tried my fling, I have, and I've lost, and it's you has the wind of me? North Inlet? Why, I haven't no ch'ice, not I! I'd help you sail her up to Execution Dock, by thunder; so I would."

Well, as it seemed to me, there was some sense in this. We struck our bargain on the spot. In three minutes I had the *Hispaniola* sailing easily before the wind along the coast of Treasure Island, with good hopes of turning the northern point ere noon, and beating down again as far as North Inlet before high water, when we might beach her safely, and wait till the subsiding tide permitted us to land.

Then I lashed the tiller and went below to my own chest, where I got a soft silk handkerchief of my mother's. With this, and with my aid, Hands bound up the great bleeding stab he had received in the thigh, and after he had eaten a little and had a swallow or two more of the brandy, he began to pick up visibly, sat straighter up, spoke louder and clearer, and looked in every way another man.

The breeze served us admirably. We skimmed before it like a bird, the coast of the island flashing by, and the view changing every minute. Soon we were past the high lands and bowling beside low, sandy country, sparsely dotted with dwarf pines, and soon we were beyond that again, and had turned the corner of the rocky hill that ends the island on the north.

I was greatly elated with my new command, and pleased with the bright, sunshiny weather and these different prospects of the coast. I had now plenty of water and good things to eat, and my conscience, which had smitten me hard for my desertion, was quieted by the great conquest I had made. I should, I think, have had nothing left me to desire but for the eyes of the coxswain as they followed me derisively about the deck, and the odd smile that appeared continually on his face. It was a smile that had in it something both of pain and weakness—a haggard, old man's smile; but there was, besides that, a grain of derision, a shadow of treachery in his expression as he craftily watched, and watched, and watched me at my work.

The wind, serving us to a desire, now hauled into the west. We could run so much the easier from the northeast corner of the island to the mouth of the North Inlet. Only, as we had no power to anchor, and dared not beach her till the tide had flowed a good deal farther, time hung on our hands. The coxswain told me how to lay the ship to; after a good many trials I succeeded, and we both sat in silence, over another meal.

417

"Cap'n," said he, at length, with that same uncomfortable smile, "here's my old shipmate, O'Brien; s'pose you was to heave him overboard. I ain't partic'lar as a rule, and I don't take no blame for settling his hash; but I don't reckon him ornamental, now, do you?"

"I'm not strong enough, and I don't like the job; and there he lies for me," said I.

"This here's an unlucky ship—this *Hispaniola,* Jim," he went on, blinking. "There's a power of men been killed in this *Hispaniola*—a sight o' poor seamen dead and gone since you and me took ship to Bristol. I never seen sich dirty luck, not I. There was this here O'Brien, now—he's dead, ain't he? Well, now, I'm no scholar, and you're a lad as can read and figure; and, to put it straight, do you take it as a dead man is dead for good, or do he come alive again?"

"You can kill the body, Mr. Hands, but not the spirit; you must know that already," I replied. "O'Brien there is in another world, and maybe watching us."

"Ah!" says he. "Well, that's unfort'nate—appears as if killing parties was a waste of time. Howsomever, sperrits don't reckon for much, by what I've seen. I'll chance it with the sperrits, Jim. And now, you've spoke up free, and I'll take it kind if you'd step down into that there cabin and get me a—well, a—shiver my timbers! I can't hit the name on 't; well, you get me a bottle of wine, Jim—this here brandy's too strong for my head."

Now, the coxswain's hesitation seemed to be unnatural; and as for the notion of his preferring wine to brandy, I entirely disbelieved it. The whole story was a pretext. He wanted me to leave the deck—so much was plain; but with what purpose I could in no way imagine. His eyes never met mine; they kept wandering to and fro, up and down, now with a look to the sky, now with a flitting glance upon the dead O'Brien. All the time he kept smiling, and putting his tongue out in the most guilty, embarrassed manner, so that a child could have told that he was bent on some deception. I was prompt with my answer, however, for I saw where my advantage lay; and that with a fellow so densely stupid I could easily conceal my suspicions to the end.

"Some wine?" said I. "Far better. Will you have white or red?"

"Well, I reckon it's about the blessed same to me, shipmate," he replied; "so it's strong, and plenty of it, what's the odds?"

"All right," I answered. "I'll bring you port, Mr. Hands. But I'll have to dig for it."

With that I scuttled down the companion with all the noise I could, slipped off my shoes, ran quietly along the sparred gallery, mounted the forecastle ladder, and popped my head out of the fore companion. I knew he would not expect to see me there; yet I took every precaution possible; and certainly the worst of my suspicions proved too true.

He had risen from his position to his hands and knees; and, though his leg obviously hurt him pretty sharply when he moved—for I could hear him stifle a groan—yet it was at a good, rattling rate that he trailed himself across the deck. In half a minute he had reached the port scuppers, and picked, out of a coil of rope, a long knife, or rather a short dirk, discoloured to the hilt with blood. He looked upon it for a moment, thrusting forth his under jaw, tried the point upon his hand, and then, hastily concealing it in the bosom of his jacket, trundled back again into his old place against the bulwark.

This was all that I required to know. Israel could move about; he was now armed; and if he had been at so much trouble to get rid of me, it was plain that I was meant to be the victim. What he would do afterwards—whether he would try to crawl right across the island from North Inlet to the camp among the swamps, or whether he would fire Long Tom, trusting that his own comrades might come first to help him, was, of course, more than I could say.

Yet I felt sure that I could trust him in one point, since in that our interests jumped together, and that was in the disposition of the schooner. We both desired to have her stranded safe enough, in a sheltered place, and so that, when the time came, she could be got off again with as little labour and danger as might be; and until that was done I considered that my life would certainly be spared.

While I was thus turning the business over in my mind, I had not been idle with my body. I had stolen back to the cabin, slipped once more into my shoes, and laid my hand at random on a bottle of wine, and now, with this for an excuse, I made my reappearance on the deck.

Hands lay as I had left him, all fallen together in a bundle, and with his eyelids lowered, as though he were too weak to bear the light. He looked up, however, at my coming, knocked the neck off the bottle, like a man who had done the same thing often, and took a good swig, with his favourite toast of "Here's luck!" Then he lay quiet for a little, and then, pulling out a stick of tobacco, begged me to cut him a quid.

"Cut me a junk o' that," says he, "for I haven't no knife, and hardly strength enough, so be as I had. Ah, Jim, Jim, I reckon I've missed stays! Cut me a quid, as'll likely be the last, lad; for I'm for my long home, and no mistake."

"Well," said I, "I'll cut you some tobacco; but if I was you and thought myself so badly, I would go to my prayers, like a Christian man."

"Why?" said he. "Now, you tell me why."

"Why?" I cried. "You were asking me just now about the dead. You've broken your trust; you've lived in sin and lies and blood; there's a man you killed lying at your feet this moment; and you ask me why! For God's mercy, Mr. Hands, that's why."

I spoke with a little heat, thinking of the bloody dirk he had hidden in his pocket, and designed, in his ill thoughts, to end me with. He, for his part, took a great draught of the wine, and spoke with the most unusual solemnity.

"For thirty years," he said, "I've sailed the seas, and seen good and bad, better and worse, fair weather and foul, provisions running out, knives going, and what not. Well, now I tell you, I never seen good come o' goodness yet. Him as strikes first is my fancy; dead men don't bite; them's my views—amen, so be it. And now, you look here," he added, suddenly changing his tone, "we've had about enough of this foolery. The tide's made good enough by now. You just take my orders, Cap'n Hawkins, and we'll sail slap in and be done with it."

All told, we had scarce two miles to run; but the navigation was delicate, the entrance to this northern anchorage was not only narrow and shoal, but lay east and west, so that the schooner must be nicely handled to be got in. I think I was a good, prompt subaltern, and I am very sure that Hands was an excellent pilot; for we went about and about, and dodged in, shaving the banks, with a certainty and a neatness that were a pleasure to behold.

Scarcely had we passed the heads before the land closed around us. The shores of North Inlet were as thickly wooded as those of the southern anchorage; but the space was longer and narrower, and more like, what in truth it was, the estuary of a river. Right before us, at the southern end, we saw the wreck of a ship in the last stages of dilapidation. It had been a great vessel of three masts, but had lain so long exposed to the injuries of the weather, that it was hung about with great webs of dripping seaweed, and on the deck of it shore bushes had taken root, and now flourished thick with flowers. It was a sad sight, but it showed us that the anchorage was calm.

"Now," said Hands, "look there; there's a pet bit for to beach a ship in. Fine flat sand, never a catspaw, trees all around of it, and flowers a-blowing like a garding on that old ship."

"And once beached," I inquired, "how shall we get her off again?"

"Why, so," he replied: "you take a line ashore there on the other side at low water: take a turn about one o' them big pines; bring it back, take a turn around the capstan, and lie-to for the tide. Come high water, all hands take a pull upon the line, and off she comes as sweet as natur'. And now, boy, you stand by. We're near the bit now, and she's too much way on her. Starboard a little—so—steady—starboard—larboard a little—steady—steady!"

So he issued his commands, which I breathlessly obeyed; till, all of a sudden, he cried, "Now, my hearty, luff!" And I put the helm hard up, and the *Hispaniola* swung round rapidly, and ran stem on for the low wooded shore.

The excitement of these last manoeuvres had somewhat interfered with the watch I had kept hitherto, sharply enough, upon the coxswain. Even then I was still so much interested, waiting for the ship to touch, that I had quite forgot the peril that hung over my head, and stood craning over the starboard bulwarks and watching the ripples spreading wide before the bows. I might have fallen without a struggle for my life, had not a sudden disquietude seized upon me, and made me turn my head. Perhaps I had heard a creak, or seen his shadow moving with the tail of my eye; perhaps it was an instinct like a cat's; but, sure enough, when I looked round, there was Hands, already half-way towards me, with the dirk in his right hand.

We must both have cried out aloud when our eyes met; but while mine was the shrill cry of terror, his was a roar of fury like a charging bull's. At the same instant he threw himself forward, and I leaped sideways towards the bows. As I did so, I let go of the tiller, which sprang sharp to leeward; and I think this saved my life, for it struck Hands across the chest, and stopped him, for the moment, dead.

Before he could recover, I was safe out of the corner where he had me trapped, with all the deck to dodge about. Just forward of the main-mast I stopped, drew a pistol from my pocket, took a cool aim, though he had already turned and was once more coming directly after me, and drew the trigger. The hammer fell, but there followed neither flash nor sound; the priming was useless with sea-water. I cursed myself for my neglect. Why had not I, long before, reprimed and reloaded my only weapons? Then I should not have been as now, a mere fleeing sheep before this butcher.

Wounded as he was, it was wonderful how fast he could move, his grizzled hair tumbling over his face, and his face itself as red as a red ensign with his haste and fury. I had no time to try my other pistol, nor, indeed, much inclination, for I was sure it would be useless. One thing I saw plainly: I must not simply retreat before him, or he would speedily hold me boxed into the bows, as a moment since he had so nearly boxed me in the stern. Once so caught, and nine or ten inches of the blood-stained dirk would be my last experience on this side of eternity. I placed my palms against the main-mast, which was of a goodish bigness, and waited, every nerve upon the stretch.

Seeing that I meant to dodge, he also paused; and a moment or two passed in feints on his part, and corresponding movements upon mine.

It was such a game as I had often played at home about the rocks of Black Hill Cove; but never before, you may be sure, with such a wildly beating heart as now. Still, as I say, it was a boy's game, and I thought I could hold my own at it, against an elderly seaman with a wounded thigh. Indeed, my courage had begun to rise so high, that I allowed myself a few darting thoughts on what would be the end of the affair; and while I saw certainly that I could spin it out for long, I saw no hope of any ultimate escape.

Well, while things stood thus, suddenly the *Hispaniola* struck, staggered, ground for an instant in the sand, and then, swift as a blow, canted over to the port side, till the deck stood at an angle of forty-five degrees, and about a puncheon of water splashed into the scupper holes, and lay, in a pool, between the deck and bulwark.

We were both of us capsized in a second, and both of us rolled, almost together, into the scuppers; the dead red-cap, with his arms still spread out, tumbling stiffly after us. So near were we, indeed, that my head came against the coxswain's foot with a crack that made my teeth rattle. Blow and all, I was the first afoot again; for Hands had got involved with the dead body. The sudden canting of the ship had made the deck no place for running on; I had to find some new way of escape, and that upon the instant, for my foe was almost touching me. Quick as thought, I sprang into the mizzen shrouds, rattled up hand over hand, and did not draw a breath till I was seated on the cross-trees.

I had been saved by being prompt; the dirk had struck not half a foot below me, as I pursued my upward flight; and there stood Israel Hands with his mouth open and his face upturned to mine, a perfect statue of surprise and disappointment.

Now that I had a moment to myself, I lost no time in changing the priming of my pistol, and then, having one ready for service, and to make assurance doubly sure, I proceeded to draw the load of the other, and recharge it afresh from the beginning.

My new employment struck Hands all of a heap; he began to see the dice going against him; and, after an obvious hesitation, he also hauled himself heavily into the shrouds, and, with the dirk in his teeth, began slowly and painfully to mount. It cost him no end of time and groans to haul his wounded leg behind him; and I had quietly finished my arrangements before he was much more than a third of the way up. Then, with a pistol in either hand, I addressed him.

"One more step, Mr. Hands," said I, "and I'll blow your brains out! Dead men don't bite, you know," I added, with a chuckle.

He stopped instantly. I could see by the working of his face that he was trying to think, and the process was so slow and laborious that, in my newfound security, I laughed aloud. At last, with a swallow or two, he spoke, his face still wearing the same expression of extreme perplexity. In order to speak he had to take the dagger from his mouth, but, in all else, he remained unmoved.

"Jim," says he, "I reckon we're fouled, you and me, and we'll have to sign articles. I'd have had you but for that there lurch: but I don't have no luck, not I; and I reckon I'll have to strike, which comes hard, you see, for a master mariner to a ship's younker like you, Jim."

I was drinking in his words and smiling away, as conceited as a cock upon a wall, when, all in a breath, back went his right hand over his shoulder. Something sang like an arrow through the air; I felt a blow and then a sharp pang, and there I was pinned by the shoulder to the mast. In the horrid pain and surprise of the moment—I scarce can say it was by my own volition, and I am sure it was without a conscious aim—both my pistols went off, and both escaped out of my hands. They did not fall alone; with a choked cry, the coxswain loosed his grasp upon the shrouds, and plunged head first into the water.

Owing to the cant of the vessel, the masts hung far out over the water, and from my perch on the cross-trees I had nothing below me but the surface of the bay. Hands, who was not so far up, was, in consequence, nearer to the ship, and fell between me and the bulwarks. He rose once to the surface in a lather of foam and blood, and then sank again for good. As the water settled, I could see him lying huddled together on the clean, bright sand in the shadow of the vessel's sides. A fish or two whipped past his body. Sometimes, by the quivering of the water, he appeared to move a little, as if he were trying to rise. But he was dead enough, for all that, being both shot and drowned, and was food for fish in the very place where he had designed my slaughter.

I was no sooner certain of this than I began to feel sick, faint, and terrified. The hot blood was running over my back and chest. The dirk, where it had pinned my shoulder to the mast, seemed to burn like a hot iron; yet it was not so much these real sufferings that distressed me, for these, it seemed to me, I could bear without a murmur; it was the horror I had upon my mind of falling from the cross-trees into that still green water beside the body of the coxswain.

I clung with both hands till my nails ached, and I shut my eyes as if to cover up the peril. Gradually my mind came back again, my pulses quieted down to a more natural time, and I was once more in possession of myself.

It was my first thought to pluck forth the dirk; but either it stuck too hard or my nerve failed me; and I desisted with a violent shudder. Oddly enough, that very shudder did the business. The knife, in fact, had come the nearest in the world to missing me altogether; it held me by a mere pinch of skin, and this the shudder tore away. The blood ran down the faster, to be sure; but I was my own master again, and only tacked to the mast by my coat and shirt.

These last I broke through with a sudden jerk, and then regained the deck by the starboard shrouds. For nothing in the world would I have again ventured, shaken as I was, upon the overhanging port shrouds, from which Israel had so lately fallen.

I went below, and did what I could for my wound; it pained me a good deal, and still bled freely; but it was neither deep nor dangerous, nor did it greatly gall me when I used my arm. Then I looked around me, and as the ship was now, in a sense, my own, I began to think of clearing it from its last passenger—the dead man, O'Brien.

He had pitched, as I have said, against the bulwarks, where he lay like some horrible, ungainly sort of puppet; life-size, indeed, but how different from life's colour or life's comeliness! In that position, I could easily have my way with him; and as the habit of tragical adventures had worn off almost all my terror for the dead, I took him by the waist as if he had been a sack of bran, and, with one good heave, tumbled him overboard. He went in with a sounding plunge; the red cap came off, and remained floating on the surface; and as soon as the splash subsided, I could see him and Israel lying side by side, both wavering with the tremulous movement of the water. O'Brien, though still quite a young man, was very bald. There he lay, with that bald head across the knees of the man who had killed him, and the quick fishes steering to and fro over both.

I was now alone upon the ship; the tide had just turned. The sun was within so few degrees of setting that already the shadow of the pines upon the western shore began to reach right across the anchorage, and fall in patterns on the deck. The evening breeze had sprung up, and though it was well warded off by the hill with the two peaks upon the east, the cordage had begun to sing a little softly to itself and the idle sails to rattle to and fro.

I began to see a danger to the ship. The jibs I speedily doused and brought tumbling to the deck; but the main-sail was a harder matter. Of course, when the schooner canted over, the boom had swung out-board, and the cap of it and a foot or two of sail hung even under water. I thought this made it still more dangerous; yet the strain was so heavy that I half feared to meddle. At last, I got my knife and cut the halyards. The peak dropped instantly, a great belly of loose canvas floated broad upon the water; and since, pull as I liked, I could not budge the downhall, that was the extent of what I could accomplish. For the rest, the *Hispaniola* must trust to luck, like myself.

By this time the whole anchorage had fallen into shadow—the last rays, I remember, falling through a glade of the wood, and shining, bright as jewels, on the flowery mantle of the wreck. It began to be chill; the tide was rapidly fleeting seaward, the schooner settling more and more on her beam-ends.

I scrambled forward and looked over. It seemed shallow enough, and holding the cut hawser in both hands for a last security, I let myself drop softly overboard. The water scarcely reached my waist; the sand was firm and covered with ripple marks, and I waded ashore in great spirits, leaving the *Hispaniola* on her side, with her main-sail trailing wide upon the surface of the bay. About the same time the sun went fairly down, and the breeze whistled low in the dusk among the tossing pines.

At least, and at last, I was off the sea, nor had I returned thence empty handed. There lay the schooner, clear at last from buccaneers and ready for our own men to board and get to sea again. I had nothing nearer my fancy than to get home to the stockade and boast of my achievements. Possibly I might be blamed a bit for my truantry, but the recapture of the *Hispaniola* was a clenching answer, and I hoped that even Captain Smollett would confess I had not lost my time.

So thinking, and in famous spirits, I began to set my face homeward for the block-house and my companions. I remembered that the most easterly of the rivers which drain into Captain Kidd's anchorage ran from the two-peaked hill upon my left; and I bent my course in that direction that I might pass the stream while it was small. The wood was pretty open, and keeping along the lower spurs, I had soon turned the corner of that hill, and not long after waded to the mid-calf across the water-course.

This brought me near to where I had encountered Ben Gunn, the maroon; and I walked more circumspectly, keeping an eye on every side. The dusk had come nigh hand completely, and, as I opened out the cleft between the two peaks, I became aware of a wavering glow against the sky, where, as I judged, the man of the island was cooking his supper before a roaring fire. And yet I wondered, in my heart, that he should show himself so careless. For if I could see this radiance, might it not reach the eyes of Silver himself where he camped upon the shore among the marshes?

Gradually the night fell blacker; it was all I could do to guide myself even roughly towards my destination; the double hill behind me and the Spy-glass on my right hand loomed faint and fainter; the stars were few and pale; and in the low ground where I wandered I kept tripping among bushes and rolling into sandy pits.

Suddenly a kind of brightness fell about me. I looked up; a pale glimmer of moonbeams had alighted on the summit of the Spy-glass, and soon after I saw something broad and silvery moving low down behind the trees, and knew the moon had risen.

With this to help me, I passed rapidly over what remained to me of my journey; and, sometimes walking, sometimes running, impatiently drew near to the stockade. Yet, as I began to thread the grove that lies before it, I was not so thoughtless that I slacked my pace and went a trifle warily. It would have been a poor end of my adventures to get shot down by my own party in mistake.

The moon was climbing higher and higher; its light began to fall here and there in masses through the more open districts of the wood; and right in front of me a glow of a different colour appeared among the trees. It was red and hot, and now and again it was a little darkened—as it were the embers of a bonfire smouldering.

For the life of me, I could not think what it might be.

At last I came right down upon the borders of the clearing. The western end was already steeped in moonshine; the rest, and the block-house itself, still lay in a black shadow, chequered with long, silvery streaks of light. On the other side of the house an immense fire had burned itself into clear embers and shed a steady, red reverberation, contrasted strongly with the mellow paleness of the moon. There was not a soul stirring, nor a sound beside the noises of the breeze.

I stopped, with much wonder in my heart, and perhaps a little terror also. It had not been our way to build great fires; we were, indeed, by the captain's orders, somewhat niggardly of firewood; and I began to fear that something had gone wrong while I was absent.

I stole round by the eastern end, keeping close in shadow, and at a convenient place, where the darkness was thickest, crossed the palisade.

To make assurance surer, I got upon my hands and knees, and crawled, without a sound, towards the corner of the house. As I drew nearer, my heart was suddenly and greatly lightened. It is not a pleasant noise in itself, and I have often complained of it at other times; but just then it was like music to hear my friends snoring together so loud and peaceful in their sleep. The sea-cry of the watch, that beautiful "All's well," never fell more reassuringly on my ear.

In the meantime, there was no doubt of one thing: they kept an infamous bad watch. If it had been Silver and his lads that were now creeping in on them, not a soul would have seen daybreak. That was what it was, thought I, to have the captain wounded; and again I blamed myself sharply for leaving them in that danger with so few to mount guard.

By this time I had got to the door and stood up. All was dark within, so that I could distinguish nothing by the eye. As for sounds, there was the steady drone of the snorers, and a small occasional noise, a flickering or pecking that I could in no way account for.

With my arms before me I walked steadily in. I should lie down in my own place (I thought, with a silent chuckle) and enjoy their faces when they found me in the morning.

My foot struck something yielding—it was a sleeper's leg; and he turned and groaned, but without awakening.

And then, all of a sudden, a shrill voice broke forth out of the darkness: "Pieces of eight! pieces of eight! pieces of eight! pieces of eight! pieces of eight!" and so forth, without pause or change, like the clacking of a tiny mill.

Silver's green parrot, Captain Flint! It was she whom I had heard pecking at a piece of bark; it was she, keeping better watch than any human being, who thus announced my arrival with her wearisome refrain.

I had no time left me to recover. At the sharp, clipping tone of the parrot, the sleepers awoke and sprang up; and with a mighty oath, the voice of Silver cried:

"Who goes?"

I turned to run, struck violently against one person, recoiled, and ran full into the arms of a second, who, for his part, closed upon and held me tight.

"Bring a torch, Dick," said Silver, when my capture was thus assured.

And one of the men left the log-house, and presently returned with a lighted brand.

⚓

AGROUND
and
CAPTAIN COOK'S DEATH

⚓

AGROUND

and

CAPTAIN COOK'S DEATH

Alexander Kippis

⚓ *Two selections have been made from Captain Cook's remarkable voyages. The first describes how the ship became lodged on a reef and the Alger-like deeds performed by a young midshipman to save it; the second recounts the untimely death of Captain Cook.*

I N NAVIGATING the coast of New South Wales, where the sea in all parts conceals shoals which suddenly project from the shore, and rocks that rise abruptly like a pyramid from the bottom, our commander had hitherto conducted his vessel in safety for an extent of two and twenty degrees of latitude, being more than one thousand three hundred miles. But on the 10th of June, as he was pursuing his course from a bay to which he had given the name of Trinity Bay, the *Endeavour* fell into a situation as critical and dangerous as any that is recorded in the history of navigation, a history which abounds with perilous adventures and almost miraculous escapes. Our voyagers were now near the latitude assigned to the islands that were discovered by Quiros, and which, without sufficient reason, some geographers have thought proper to join to this land. The ship had the advantage of a fine breeze and a clear moonlight night, and in standing off from six till near nine o'clock, she had deepened her water from fourteen to twenty-one fathom. But while our navigators were at supper it suddenly shoaled, and they fell into twelve, ten, and eight fathom within the compass of a few minutes. Mr. Cook immediately ordered every man to his station, and all was ready to put about and come to an anchor, when deep water being met with again at the next cast of the

From *Captain Cook's Voyages*, by Alexander Kippis.

lead, it was concluded that the vessel had gone over the tail of the shoals which had been seen at sunset, and that the danger was now over. The idea of security was now confirmed by the water's continuing to deepen to twenty and twenty-one fathom, so that the gentlemen left the deck in great tranquillity, and went to bed. However, a little before eleven, the water shoaled at once from twenty to seventeen fathom, and before the lead could be cast again the ship struck, and remained immovable, excepting so far as she was influenced by the heaving of the surge, that beat her against the crags of the rock upon which she lay. A few moments brought every person upon deck, with countenances suited to the horrors of the situation. As our people knew, from the breeze which they had in the evening, that they could not be very near the shore, there was too much reason to conclude that they were on a rock of coral, which, on account of the sharpness of its points and the roughness of its surface, is more fatal than any other. On examining the depth of water round the ship, it was speedily discovered that the misfortune of our voyagers was equal to their apprehensions. The vessel had been lifted over a ledge of the rock and lay in a hollow within it, in some places of which hollow there were from three to four fathom, and in others not so many feet of water. To complete the scene of distress, it appeared from the light of the moon that the sheathing boards from the bottom of the ship were floating away all round her, and at last her false keel, so that every moment was making way for the whole company's being swallowed up by the rushing in of the sea. There was now no chance but to lighten her, and the opportunity had unhappily been lost of doing it to the best advantage; for as the *Endeavour* had gone ashore just at high water, and by this time it had considerably fallen, she would when lightened be but in the same situation as at first. The only alleviation of this circumstance was, that as the tide ebbed the vessel settled to the rocks, and was not beaten against them with so much violence. Our people had, indeed, some hope from the next tide, though it was doubtful whether the ship would hold together so long, especially as the rock kept grating part of her bottom with such force as to be heard in the fore store-room. No effort, however, was remitted from despair of success. That no time might be lost, the water was immediately started in the hold and pumped up; six guns, being all that were upon the deck, a quantity of iron and stone ballast, casks, hoop-staves, oil jars, decayed stores, and a variety of things besides, were thrown overboard with the utmost expedition. Every one exerted himself not only without murmuring and discontent, but even with an alacrity which almost approached to cheerfulness. So sensible, at the same time, were the men of the awfulness of their situation, that not an oath was heard among them, the detestable habit of profane swearing being instantly subdued by the dread of incurring guilt when a speedy death was in view.

When Lieutenant Cook and all the people about him were thus employed, the opening of the morning of the 11th of June presented them with a fuller prospect of their danger. The land was seen by them at about eight leagues' distance, without any island in the intermediate space, upon which, if the ship had gone to pieces, they might have been set ashore by the boats, and carried thence by different turns to the main. Gradually, however, the wind died away, and, early in the forenoon, it became a dead calm: a circumstance this, peculiarly happy in the order of Divine Providence; for if it had blown hard, the vessel must inevitably have been destroyed. High water being expected at eleven in the morning, and everything being made ready to heave her off if she should float; to the inexpressible surprise and concern of our navigators, so much did the day tide fall short of that of the night, that though they had lightened the ship nearly fifty ton, she did not float by a foot and a half. Hence it became necessary to lighten her still more, and everything was thrown overboard that could possibly be spared. Hitherto the Endeavour had not admitted much water; but as the tide fell, it rushed in so fast, that she could scarely be kept free, though two pumps were incessantly worked. There were now no hopes but from the tide at midnight; to prepare for taking the advantage of which the most vigorous efforts were exerted. About five o'clock in the afternoon the tide began to rise, but, at the same time, the leak increased to a most alarming degree. Two more pumps, therefore, were manned, one of which unhappily would not work. Three pumps, however, were kept going, and at nine o'clock the ship righted. Nevertheless, the leak had gained so considerably upon her, that it was imagined that she must go to the bottom, as soon as she ceased to be supported by the rock. It was, indeed, a dreadful circumstance to our commander and his people, that they were obliged to anticipate the floating of the vessel, not as an earnest of their deliverance, but as an event which probably would precipitate their destruction. They knew that their boats were not capable of carrying the whole of them on shore, and that when the dreadful crisis should arrive, all command and subordination being at an end, a contest for preference might be expected, which would increase even the horrors of shipwreck, and turn their rage against each other. Some of them were sensible that if they should escape to the mainland, they were likely to suffer more upon the whole, than those who would be left on board to perish in the waves. The latter would only be exposed to instant death; whereas the former, when they got on shore, would have no lasting or effectual defence against the natives, in a part of the country where even nets and fire-arms could scarcely furnish them with food. But supposing that they should find the means of subsistence; how horrible must be their state, to be condemned to languish out the remainder of their lives in a desolate wilderness without the possession or hope of domestic comfort; and to be cut off from all commerce with mankind, excepting that

433

of the naked savages, who prowl the desert, and who perhaps are some of the most rude and uncivilized inhabitants of the earth.

The dreadful moment which was to determine the fate of our voyagers now drew on; and every one saw, in the countenances of his companions, the picture of his own sensations. Not, however, giving way to despair, the lieutenant ordered the capstan and windlass to be manned with as many hands as could be spared from the pumps, and the ship having floated about twenty minutes after ten o'clock, the grand effort was made, and she heaved into deep water. It was no small consolation to find, that she did not now admit of more water than she had done when upon the rock. By the gaining, indeed, of the leak upon the pumps, three feet and nine inches of water were in the hold; not withstanding which, the men did not relinquish their labour. Thus they held the water as it were at bay: but having endured excessive fatigue of body, and agitation of mind, for more than twenty-four hours, and all this being attended with little hope of final success, they began, at length, to flag. None of them could work at the pump above five or six minutes together, after which, being totally exhausted, they threw themselves down upon the deck, though a stream of water, between three or four inches deep, was running over it from the pumps. When those who succeeded them had worked their time, and in their turn were exhausted, they threw themselves down in the same manner, and the others started up again, to renew their labour. While thus they were employed in relieving each other, an accident was very nearly putting an immediate end to all their efforts. The planking which lines the ship's bottom is called the ceiling, between which and the outside planking there is a space of about eighteen inches. From this ceiling only, the man who had hitherto attended the well had taken the depth of the water, and had given the measure accordingly. But, upon his being relieved, the person who came in his room reckoned the depth to the outside planking, which had the appearance of the leak's having gained upon the pumps eighteen inches in a few minutes. The mistake, however, was soon detected; and the accident, which in its commencement was very formidable to them, became, in fact, highly advantageous. Such was the joy which every man felt, at finding his situation better than his fears had suggested, that it operated with wonderful energy, and seemed to possess him with a strong persuasion that scarcely any real danger remained. New confidence and new hope inspired fresh vigour; and the efforts of the men were exerted with so much alacrity and spirit, that before eight o'clock in the morning the pumps had gained considerably upon the leak. All the conversation now turned upon carrying the ship into some harbour, as a thing not to be doubted; and as hands could be spared from the pumps, they were employed in getting up the anchors. It being found impossible to save the little bower anchor, it was cut away at a whole cable, and the cable of the stream anchor was lost among the rocks; but, in the situation of our people, these were trifles which scarcely attracted their notice. The fore-topmast and fore-yard were next erected, and there being a breeze from the sea, the *Endeavour,* at eleven o'clock, got once more under sail, and stood for the land.

Notwithstanding these favourable circumstances, our voyagers were still very far from being in a state of safety. It was not possible long to continue the labour by which the pumps had been made to gain upon the leak; and as the exact place of it could not be discovered, there was no hope of stopping it within. At this crisis, Mr. Monkhouse, one of the midshipmen, came to Lieutenant Cook, and proposed an expedient he had once seen used on board a merchant ship, which had sprung a leak that admitted more than four feet water in an hour, and which by this means had been safely brought from Virginia to London. To Mr. Monkhouse, therefore, the care of the expedient, which is called fothering the ship, was, with proper assistance, committed; and his method of proceeding was as follows. He took a lower studding sail, and having mixed together a large quantity of oakum and wool, he stitched it down as lightly as possible, in handfuls upon the sail, and spread over it the dung of the sheep of the vessel, and other filth. The sail being thus prepared, it was hauled under the ship's bottom by ropes, which kept it extended. When it came under the leak, the suction that carried in the water, carried in with it the oakum and wool from the surface of the sail. In other parts the water was not sufficiently agitated to wash off the oakum and the wool. The success of the expedient was answerable to the warmest expectations; for hereby the leak was so far reduced, that, instead of gaining upon three pumps, it was easily kept under with one. Here was such a new source of confidence and comfort, that our people could scarcely have expressed more joy, if they had been already in port. It had lately been the utmost object of their hope, to run the ship ashore in some harbour, either of an island or the main, and to build a vessel out of her materials, to carry them to the East Indies. Nothing, however, was now thought of but to range along the coast in search of a convenient place to repair the damage the Endeavour had sustained, and then to prosecute the voyage upon the same plan as if no impediment had happened. In justice and gratitude to the ship's company, and the gentlemen on board, Mr. Cook has recorded, that although in the midst of their distress all of them seemed to have a just sense of their danger, no man gave way to passionate exclamations, or frantic gestures. "Every one appeared to have the perfect possession of his mind, and every one exerted himself to the utmost, with a quiet and patient perseverance, equally distant from the tumultuous violence of terror, and the gloomy inactivity of despair." Though the lieutenant hath said nothing of himself, it is well known that his own composure, fortitude, and activity, were equal to the greatness of the occasion.

To complete the history of this wonderful preservation, it is necessary to bring forward a circumstance which could not be discovered till the ship was laid down to be repaired. It was then found that one of her holes, which was large enough to have sunk our navigators, if they had had eight pumps instead of four, and had been able to keep them incessantly going, was in a great measure filled up by a fragment of the rock, upon which the Endeavour had struck. To this singular event, therefore, it was owing that the water did not pour in with a violence, which must speedily have involved the *Endeavour* and all her company in inevitable destruction.

Hitherto none of the names by which our commander had distinguished the several parts of the country seen by him, were memorials of distress. But the anxiety and danger which he and his people had now experienced induced him to call the point in sight, which lay to the northward, Cape Tribulation.

The next object after this event was to look out for a harbour where the defects of the ship might be repaired, and the vessel put into proper order for future navigation. On the 14th a small harbour was happily discovered, which was excellently adapted to the purpose. It was, indeed, remarkable, that during the whole course of the voyage our people had seen no place which, in their present circumstances, could have afforded them the same relief. They could not, however, immediately get into it; and in the midst of all their joy for their unexpected deliverance, they had not forgotten that there was nothing but a lock of wool between them and destruction.

⚓   ⚓   ⚓

CAPTAIN COOK'S DEATH

"The next day, February the 12th, the ships were put under a taboo, by the chiefs: a solemnity, it seems, that was requisite to be observed before Kariopoo, the king, paid his first visit to Captain Cook, after his return. He waited upon him the same day, on board the *Resolution,* attended by a large train, some of which bore the presents designed for Captain Cook, who received him in his usual friendly manner, and gave him several articles in return. This amicable ceremony being settled, the taboo was dissolved; matters went on in the usual train; and the next day, February the 13th, we were visited by the natives in great numbers; the *Resolution's* mast was landed, and the astronomical observatories erected on their former situation. I landed, with another gentleman, at the town of Kavaroah, where we found a great number of canoes, just arrived from different parts of the island, and the Indians busy in constructing temporary huts on the beach for their residence during the stay of the ships. On our return on board the *Discovery,* we learned that an Indian had been detected in stealing the armourer's tongs from the forge, for which he received a pretty severe flogging, and was sent out of the ship. Notwithstanding the example made of this man, in the afternoon another had the audacity to snatch the tongs and a chisel from the same place, with which he jumped overboard and swam for the shore. The master and a midshipman were instantly despatched after him, in the small cutter. The Indian, seeing himself pursued, made for a canoe; his countrymen took him on board, and paddled as swift as they could towards the shore. We fired several muskets at them, but to no effect, for they soon got out of the reach of our shot. Pareah, one of the chiefs, who was at that time on board the *Discovery,* understanding what had happened, immediately went ashore, promising to bring back the stolen goods. Our boat was so far distanced, in chasing the canoe which had taken the thief on board, that he had time to make his escape into the country. Captain Cook, who was then ashore, endeavoured to intercept his landing; but it seems that he was led out of the way by some of

437

the natives, who had officiously intruded themselves as guides. As the master was approaching near the landing-place, he was met by some of the Indians in a canoe. They had brought back the tongs and chisel, together with another article that we had not missed, which happened to be the lid of the water-cask. Having recovered these things, he was returning on board, when he was met by the *Resolution's* pinnace with five men in her, who, without any orders, had come from the observatories to his assistance. Being thus unexpectedly reinforced, he thought himself strong enough to insist upon having the thief, or the canoe which took him in, delivered up as reprisals. With that view he turned back; and having found the canoe on the beach, he was preparing to launch it into the water when Pareah made his appearance, and insisted upon his not taking it away, as it was his property. The officer not regarding him, the chief seized upon him, pinioned his arms behind, and held him by the hair of his head; on which one of the sailors struck him with an oar. Pareah instantly quitted the officer, snatched the oar out of the man's hand, and snapped it in two across his knee. At length the multitude began to attack our people with stones. They made some resistance, but were soon overpowered, and obliged to swim for safety to the small cutter, which lay farther out than the pinnace. The officers, not being expert swimmers, retreated to a small rock in the water, where they were closely pursued by the Indians. One man darted a broken oar at the master; but his foot slipping at the time, he missed him, which fortunately saved that officer's life. At last Pareah interfered and put an end to their violence. The gentlemen, knowing that his presence was their only defence against the fury of the natives, entreated him to stay with them till they could get off in the boats; but that he refused, and left them. The master went to seek assistance from the party at the observatories; but the midshipman chose to remain in the pinnace. He was very rudely treated by the mob, who plundered the boat of everything that was loose on board, and then began to knock her to pieces for the sake of the iron-work; but Pareah fortunately returned in time to prevent her destruction. He had met the other gentleman on his way to the observatories, and, suspecting his errand, had forced him to return. He dispersed the crowd again, and desired the gentlemen to return on board: they represented that all the oars had been taken out of the boat; on which he brought some of them back, and the gentlemen were glad to get off without farther molestation. They had not proceeded far, before they were overtaken by Pareah, in a canoe: he delivered the midshipman's cap, which had been taken from him in the scuffle, joined noses with them, in token of reconciliation, and was anxious to know if Captain Cook would kill him for what had happened. They assured him of the contrary, and made signs of friendship to him in return. He then left them and paddled over to the town of Kavaroah, and that was the last time we ever saw him. Captain Cook returned on board soon after, much displeased with the whole of this disagreeable business, and the same night sent a lieutenant on board the *Discovery* to learn the particulars of it, as it had originated in that ship.

"To widen the breach between us, some of the Indians in the night took away the *Discovery's* large cutter, which lay swamped at the buoy of one of her anchors: they had carried her off so quietly that we did not miss her till the morning, Sunday, February the 14th. Captain Clerke lost no time in waiting upon Captain Cook to acquaint him with the accident: he returned on board with orders for the launch and small cutter to go, under the command of the second lieutenant, and lie off the east point of the bay, in order to intercept all canoes that might attempt to get out; and, if he found it necessary, to fire upon them. At the same time the third lieutenant of the Resolution, with the launch and small cutter, was sent on the same service to the opposite point of the bay; and the master was despatched in the large cutter in pursuit of a double canoe, already under sail, making the best of her way out of the harbour. He soon came up with her, and by firing a few muskets drove her on shore, and the Indians left her: this happened to be the canoe of Omea, a man who bore the title of Orono. He was on board himself, and it would have been fortunate if our people had secured him, for his person was held as sacred as that of the king. During this time Captain Cook was preparing to go ashore himself, at the town of Kavaroah, in order to secure the person of Kariopoo, before he should have time to withdraw himself to another part of the island, out of our reach. This appeared the most effectual step that could be taken, on the present occasion, for the recovery of the boat. It was the measure he had invariably pursued, in similar cases, at other islands in these seas, and it had always been attended with the desired success: in fact, it would be difficult to point out any other mode of proceeding on these emergencies likely to attain the object in view: we had reason to suppose that the king and his attendants had fled when the alarm was first given: in that case, it was Captain Cook's intention to secure the large canoes which were hauled up on the beach. He left the ship about seven o'clock, attended by the lieutenant of marines, a sergeant, corporal, and seven private men: the pinnace's crew were also armed, and under the command of Mr. Roberts. As they rowed towards the shore, Captain Cook ordered the launch to leave her station at the west point of the bay, in order to assist his own boat. This is a circumstance worthy of notice; for it clearly shows that he was not unapprehensive of meeting with resistance from the natives, or unmindful of the necessary preparation for the safety of himself and his people. I will venture to say that, from the appearance of things just at that time, there was not one beside himself who judged that such precaution was absolutely requisite: so little did his conduct on the occasion bear the marks of rashness, or a precipitate self-confidence! He landed, with the marines, at the upper end of the town of Kavaroah: the Indians immediately flocked round, as usual, and showed him the customary marks of respect, by prostrating themselves before him.—There were no signs of hostilities, or much alarm among them. Captain Cook, however, did not seem willing to trust to appearances; but was particularly attentive to the disposition of the marines, and to have them kept clear of the crowd. He first inquired for the king's sons, two youths who were much attached to him, and generally his companions on board. Messengers being sent for them, they soon came to him, and informing him that their father was asleep at a house not far from them, he accompanied them thither, and took the marines along with them. As he passed along the natives everywhere prostrated themselves before him, and seemed to have lost no part of that respect they had always shown to his person. He was joined by several chiefs, among whom was Kanynah, and his brother Koohowrooah. They kept the crowd in order, according to their usual custom; and, being ignorant of his intention in coming on shore, frequently asked him if he wanted any hogs, or other provisions: he told them that he did not, and that his business was to see the king. When he arrived at the house, he ordered some of the Indians to go in and inform Kariopoo that he waited without to speak with him. They came out two or three times, and instead of returning any answer from the king, presented some pieces of red cloth to him, which made Captain Cook suspect that he was not in the house; he therefore desired the lieutenant of marines to go in. The lieutenant found the old man just awaked from sleep, and seemingly alarmed at the message; but he came out without hesitation. Captain Cook took him by the hand, and in a friendly manner asked him to go on board to which he very readily consented. Thus far matters appeared in a favourable train, and the natives did not seem much alarmed or apprehensive of hostility on our side: at which Captain Cook expressed himself a little surprised, saying that as the inhabitants of the town appeared innocent of stealing the cutter, he should not molest them, but that he must get the king on board. Kariopoo sat down before his door, and was surrounded by a great crowd: Kanynah and his brother were both very active in keeping order among them. In a little time, however, the Indians were observed arming themselves with long spears, clubs, and daggers, and putting on thick mats, which they use as armour. This hostile appearance increased, and became more alarming on the arrival of two men in a canoe from the opposite side of the bay, with the news of a chief called Kareemoo having been killed by one of the *Discovery's* boats. In their passage across they had also delivered this account to each of the ships. Upon that information the women, who were sitting upon the beach at their breakfasts, and conversing familiarly with our people in the boats, retired, and a confused murmur spread through the crowd. An old priest came to Captain Cook, with a cocoanut in his hand, which he held out to him as a present, at the same time singing very loud. He was often desired to be silent, but in vain: he continued importunate and troublesome, and there was no such thing as getting rid of him or his noise: it seemed as if he meant to divert their attention from his countrymen, who were growing more tumultuous, and arming themselves in every quarter. Captain Cook, being at the same time surrounded by a great crowd, thought his situation rather hazardous: he therefore ordered the lieutenant of marines to march his small party to the waterside, where the boats lay within a few yards of the shore: the Indians readily made a lane for them to pass, and did not offer to interrupt them. The distance they had to go might be about fifty or sixty yards; Captain Cook followed, having hold of Kariopoo's hand, who accompanied him very willingly: he was attended by his wife, two sons, and several chiefs. The troublesome old priest followed, making the same savage noise. Keowa, the youngest son, went directly into the pinnace, expecting his father to follow; but just as he arrived at the waterside, his wife threw her arms about his neck, and, with the assistance of two chiefs, forced him to sit down by the side of a double canoe. Captain Cook expostulated with them, but to no purpose: they would not suffer the king to proceed, telling him that he would be put to death if he went on board the ship. Kariopoo, whose conduct seemed entirely resigned to the will of others, hung down his head, and appeared much distressed.

"While the king was in this situation, a chief, well known to us, of the name of Coho, was observed lurking near with an iron dagger, partly concealed under his cloak, seemingly with the intention of stabbing Captain Cook or the lieutenant of marines. The latter proposed to fire at him, but Captain Cook would not permit it. Coho closing upon them obliged the officer to strike him with his piece, which made him retire. Another Indian laid hold of the sergeant's musket and endeavoured to wrench it from him, but was prevented by the lieutenant's making a blow at him. Captain Cook, seeing the tumult increase and the Indians growing more daring and resolute, observed that if he were to take the king off by force he could not do it without sacrificing the lives of many of his people. He then paused a little, and was on the point of giving his orders to re-embark, when a man threw a stone at him; which he returned with a discharge of small shot (with which one barrel of his double piece was loaded). The man, having a thick mat before him, received little or no hurt: he brandished his spear and threatened to dart it at Captain Cook, who, being still unwilling to take away his life, instead of firing with ball knocked him down with his musket. He expostulated strongly with the most forward of the crowd upon their turbulent behaviour. He had given up all thoughts of getting the king on board, as it appeared impracticable; and his care was then only to act on the defensive, and to secure a safe embarkation for his small party, which was closely pressed by a body of several thousand people. Keowa, the king's son, who was in the pinnace, being alarmed on hearing the first firing, was, at his own entreaty, put on shore again; for even at that time Mr. Roberts, who commanded her, did not apprehend that Captain Cook's person was in any danger: otherwise he would have detained the prince, which, no doubt, would have been a great check on the Indians. One man was observed behind a double canoe, in the action of darting his spear at Captain Cook, who was forced to fire at him in his own defence, but happened to kill another close to him, equally forward in the tumult: the sergeant observing that he had missed the man he aimed at received orders to fire at him, which he did, and killed him. By this time the impetuosity of the Indians was somewhat repressed; they fell back in a body and seemed staggered: but being pushed on by those behind, they returned to the charge and poured a volley of stones among the marines, who, without waiting for orders, returned it with a general discharge of musketry, which was instantly followed by a fire from the boats. At this Captain Cook was heard to express his astonishment: he waved his hand to the boats, called to them to cease firing, and to come nearer in to receive the marines. Mr. Roberts immediately brought the pinnace as close to the shore as he could, without grounding, notwithstanding the shower of stones that fell among the people: but——, the lieutenant, who commanded in the launch, instead of pulling in to the assistance of Captain Cook, withdrew his boat farther off, at the moment that everything seems to have depended upon the timely exertions of those in the boats. By his own account he mistook the signal: but be that as it may, this circumstance appears to me to have decided the fatal turn of the affair, and to have removed every chance which remained with Captain Cook of escaping with his life. The business of saving the marines out of the water, in consequence of that, fell altogether upon the pinnace; which thereby became so much crowded that the crew were, in a great measure, prevented from using their fire-arms, or giving what assistance they otherwise might have done to Captain Cook; so that he seems, at the most critical point of time, to have wanted the assistance of both boats, owing to the removal of the launch. For notwithstanding that they kept up a fire on the crowd, from the situation to which they removed in that boat, the fatal confusion which ensued on her being withdrawn, to say the least of it, must have prevented the full effect that the prompt cooperation of the two boats, according to Captain Cook's orders, must have had towards the preservation of himself and his people.[1] At that time it was to the boats alone that Captain Cook had to look for his safety; for when the marines had fired, the Indians rushed among them and forced them into the water, where four of them were killed: their lieutenant was wounded, but fortunately escaped and

[1] I have been informed on the best authority that, in the opinion of Captain Philips, who commanded the marines, and whose judgment must be of the greatest weight, it is extremely doubtful whether anything could successfully have been done to preserve the life of Captain Cook, even if no mistake had been committed on the part of the launch.

was taken up by the pinnace. Captain Cook was then the only one remaining on the rock: he was observed making for the pinnace, holding his left hand against the back of his head, to guard it from the stones, and carrying his musket under the other arm. An Indian was seen following him, but with caution and timidity; for he stopped once or twice, as if undetermined to proceed. At last he advanced upon him unawares, and with a large club, or common stake, gave him a blow on the back of the head, and then precipitately retreated. The stroke seemed to have stunned Captain Cook: he staggered a few paces, then fell on his hand and one knee, and dropped his musket. As he was rising, and before he could recover his feet, another Indian stabbed him in the back of the neck with an iron dagger. He then fell into a bit of water about knee deep, where others crowded upon him and endeavoured to keep him under: but struggling very strongly with them he got his head up, and casting his look towards the pinnace, seemed to solicit assistance. Though the boat was not above five or six yards distant from him, yet from the crowded and confused state of the crew, it seems it was not in their power to save him. The Indians got him under again, but in deeper water: he was, however, able to get his head up once more, and being almost spent in the struggle, he naturally turned to the rock, and was endeavouring to support himself by it, when a savage gave him a blow with a club, and he was seen alive no more. They hauled him up lifeless on the rocks, where they seemed to take a savage pleasure in using every barbarity to his dead body, snatching the daggers out of each other's hands, to have the horrid satisfaction of piercing the fallen victim of their barbarous rage.

"I need make no reflection on the great loss we suffered on this occasion, or attempt to describe what we felt. It is enough to say that no man was ever more beloved or admired: and it is truly painful to reflect that he seems to have fallen a sacrifice merely for want of being properly supported; a fate singularly to be lamented as having fallen to his lot, who had ever been conspicuous for his care of those under his command, and who seemed, to the last, to pay as much attention to their preservation as to that of his own life.

"If anything could have added to the shame and indignation universally felt on this occasion, it was to find that his remains had been deserted, and left exposed on the beach, although they might have been brought off. It appears, from the information of four or five midshipmen, who arrived on the spot at the conclusion of the fatal business, that the beach was then almost entirely deserted by the Indians, who at length had given way to the fire of the boats, and dispersed through the town: so that there seemed no great obstacle to prevent the recovery of Captain Cook's body; but the lieutenant returned on board without making the attempt. It is unnecessary to dwell longer on this painful subject, and to relate the complaints and censures that fell on the conduct of the lieutenant. It will be sufficient to observe that they were so loud as to oblige Captain Clerke publicly to notice them, and to take the depositions of his accusers down in writing. The captain's bad state of health and approaching dissolution, it is supposed, induced him to destroy these papers a short time before his death.

"It is a painful task to be obliged to notice circumstances which seem to reflect upon the character of any man. A strict regard to truth, however, compelled me to the insertion of these facts, which I have offered merely as facts, without presuming to connect with them any comment of my own: esteeming it the part of a faithful historian, 'to extenuate nothing, nor set down aught in malice.'

"The fatal accident happened at eight o'clock in the morning, about an hour after Captain Cook landed. It did not seem that the king, or his sons, were witnesses to it: but it is supposed that they withdrew in the midst of the tumult. The principal actors were the other chiefs, many of them the king's relations and attendants: the man who stabbed him with the dagger was called Nooah. I happened to be the only one who recollected his person, from having on a former occasion mentioned his name in the journal I kept. I was induced to take particular notice of him, more from his personal appearance than any other consideration, though he was of high rank, and a near relation of the king: he was stout and tall, with a fierce look and demeanour, and one who united in his figure the two qualities of strength and agility, in a greater degree than ever I remembered to have seen before in any other man. His age might be about thirty, and by the white scurf on his skin, and his sore eyes, he appeared to be a hard drinker of kava. He was a constant companion of the king, with whom I first saw him, when he paid a visit to Captain Clerke. The chief who first struck Captain Cook with the club was called Karimano, craha, but I did not know him by his name. These circumstances I learned of honest Kaireekea, the priest; who added, that they were both held in great esteem on account of that action: neither of them came near us afterward. When the boats left the shore, the Indians carried away the dead body of Captain Cook and those of the marines, to the rising ground at the back of the town, where we could plainly see them with our glasses from the ships.

"This most melancholy accident appears to have been altogether unexpected and unforeseen, as well on the part of the natives as ourselves. I never saw sufficient reason to induce me to believe that there was anything of design, or a preconcerted plan on their side, or that they purposely sought to quarrel with us: thieving, which gave rise to the whole, they were equally guilty of in our first and second visits. It was the cause of every misunderstanding that happened between us: their petty thefts were generally overlooked, but sometimes slightly punished; the boat which they at last ventured to take away was an object of no small magnitude to people in our situation, who could not possibly replace her, and therefore not slightly to be given up. We had no other chance of recovering her but by getting the person of the king into our possession: on our attempting to do that the natives became alarmed for his safety, and naturally opposed those whom they deemed his enemies. In the sudden conflict that ensued, we had the unspeakable misfortune of losing our excellent commander, in the manner already related. It is in this light the affair has always appeared to me, as entirely accidental, and not in the least owing to any previous offence received, or jealousy of our second visit entertained by the natives.

"Pareah seems to have been the principal instrument in bringing about this fatal disaster. We learned afterward that it was he who had employed some people to steal the boat: the king did not seem to be privy to it, or even apprized of what had happened, till Captain Cook landed.

"It was generally remarked that at first the Indians showed great resolution in facing our fire-arms; but it was entirely owing to ignorance of their effect. They thought that their thick mats would defend them from a ball as well as from a stone; but being soon convinced of their error, yet still at a loss to account how such execution was done among them, they had recourse to a stratagem which, though it answered no other purpose, served to show their ingenuity and quickness of invention. Observing the flashes of the muskets, they naturally concluded that water would counteract their effect, and therefore very sagaciously dipped their mats, or armour, in the sea, just as they came on to face our people: but finding this last resource to fail them, they soon dispersed, and left the beach entirely clear. It was an object they never neglected, even at the greatest hazard, to carry off their slain; a custom probably owing to the barbarity with which they treat the dead body of an enemy, and the trophies they make of his bones."

In consequence of this barbarity of disposition, the whole remains of Captain Cook could not be recovered. For though every exertion was made for that purpose, though negotiations and threatenings were alternately employed, little more than the principal part of his bones (and that with great difficulty) could be procured. By the possession of them, our navigators were enabled to perform the last offices to their eminent and unfortunate commander. The bones having been put into a coffin, and the service being read over them, were committed to the deep, on the 21st, with the usual military honours. What were the feelings of the companies of both the ships, on this occasion, must be left to the world to conceive; for those who were present know that it is not in the power of any pen to express them.

⚓

THE VOYAGE TO AMERICA

⚓

THE VOYAGE TO AMERICA

Christopher Columbus

⚓ *It is difficult for us to realize today the almost insurmountable problems that faced Columbus in his great enterprise. We can understand
the labor involved in the search for a patron and the justification to this
patron of the sizable investment. But the attitude of the seamen who
were embarking on this adventure, the superstitions that governed
them, the terror of the unknown, robbed Columbus of the faith in his
men which is one of the prerequisites of a successful voyage. His statement, "sailed this day nineteen leagues, and determined to count less
than the true number, that the crew might not be dismayed if the voyage
should prove long," is testimony to the lengths to which he had to resort
to bolster the courage of his men.*

*Thanks to the mariner's custom of keeping a log, we have this valu-
able historical document by which we can follow day by day his progress across an uncharted ocean.*

I LEFT the city of Granada on Saturday the twelfth day of May, 1492, and
proceeded to Palos, a seaport, where I armed three vessels, very fit for such
an enterprise; and, having provided myself with abundance of stores and
seamen, I set sail from the port on Friday the third of August, half an hour
before sunrise, and steered for the Canary Islands of your Highnesses which
are in the said ocean; thence to take my departure and proceed till I arrived
at the Indies and perform the embassy of your Highnesses to the Princes
there, and discharge the orders given me. For this purpose I determined to
keep an account of the voyage, and to write down punctually every thing
we performed or saw from day to day, as will hereafter appear. Moreover,

Translated by Samuel Kettell.

Sovereign Princes, besides describing every night the occurrences of the day, and every day those of the preceding night, I intend to draw up a nautical chart, which shall contain the several parts of the ocean and land in their proper situations; and also to compose a book to represent the whole by picture with latitudes and longitudes; on all which accounts it behooves me to abstain from my sleep, and make many trials in navigation, which things will demand much labour.

Friday, Aug. 3d. Set sail from the bar of Saltes at 8 o'clock, and proceeded with a strong breeze till sunset, sixty miles or fifteen leagues S., afterwards S.W. and S. by W., which is the direction of the Canaries.

Saturday, Aug. 4th. Steered S.W. by S.

Sunday, Aug. 5th. Sailed day and night more than forty leagues.

Monday, Aug. 6th. The rudder of the caravel *Pinta* became loose, being broken or unshipped. It was believed that this happened by the contrivance of Gomez Rascon and Christopher Quintero, who were on board the caravel, because they disliked the voyage. The Admiral says he had found them in an unfavourable disposition before setting out. He was in much anxiety at not being able to afford any assistance in this case, but says that it somewhat quieted his apprehensions to know that Martin Alonzo Pinzon, Captain of the *Pinta,* was man of courage and capacity. Made a progress, day and night of twenty-nine leagues.

Tuesday, Aug. 7th. The *Pinta's* rudder again broke loose; secured it, and made for the island of Lanzarote, one of the Canaries. Sailed, day and night, twenty-five leagues.

Wednesday, Aug. 8th. There were divers opinions among the pilots of the three vessels, as to their true situation, and it was found that the Admiral was the most correct. His object was to reach the island of Grand Canary, and leave there the *Pinta,* she being leaky, besides having her rudder out of order, and take another vessel there, if any one could be had. They were unable to reach the island that day.

Thursday, Aug. 9th. The Admiral did not succeed in reaching the island of Gomera till Sunday night. Martin Alonzo remained at Grand Canary by command of the Admiral, he being unable to keep the other vessels company.

The Admiral afterwards returned to Grand Canary, and there with much labor repaired the *Pinta,* being assisted by Martin Alonzo and the others; finally they sailed to Gomera. They saw a great eruption of flames from the Peak of Teneriffe, which is a lofty mountain. The *Pinta,* which before had carried lateen sails, they altered and made her square-rigged. Returned to Gomera, Sunday, Sept. 2d., with the *Pinta* repaired.

The Admiral says that he was assured by many respectable Spaniards, inhabitants of the island of Ferro, who were at Gomera with Doña Inez Peraza, mother of Guillen Peraza, afterwards first Count of Gomera, that

Sailed this day nineteen leagues, and determined to count less than true numbers, that the crew might not be dismayed if the voyage should prove long.

they every year saw land to the west of the Canaries; and others of Gomera affirmed the same with the like assurances. The Admiral here says that he remembers, while he was in Portugal, in 1484, there came a person to the King from the island of Madeira, soliciting for a vessel to go in quest of land, which he affirmed he saw every year, and always of the same appearance. He also says that he remembers the same was said by the inhabitants of the Azores and described as in a similar direction, and of the same shape and size. Having taken in wood, water, meat, and other provisions which had been provided by the men which he left ashore on departing for Grand Canary to repair the *Pinta,* the Admiral took his final departure from Gomera with the three vessels on Thursday, Sept. 6th.

Thursday, Sept. 6th. Set sail from the harbour of Gomera this morning and shaped their course for the voyage. The Admiral learnt by a vessel from the island of Ferro that there were three Portuguese caravels cruising about there in search of him. This circumstance probably originated in the envy of the King of Portugal, as the Admiral had left him to resort to Castile. It was calm the whole day and night; in the morning they found themselves between Gomera and Teneriffe.

Friday, Sept. 7th. Calm all Friday, and till three o'clock P. M. on Saturday.

Saturday, Sept. 8th. At three in the afternoon the wind rose from the N.E. Steered their course W., encountered a strong head sea, which impeded their progress. Sailed, day and night, nine leagues.

Sunday, Sept. 9th. Sailed this day nineteen leagues, and determined to count less than the true number, that the crew might not be dismayed if the voyage should prove long. In the night sailed one hundred and twenty miles, at the rate of ten miles an hour, which make thirty leagues. The sailors steered badly, causing the vessels to fall to leeward toward the Northeast, for which the Admiral reprimanded them repeatedly.

Monday, Sept. 10th. This day and night sailed sixty leagues, at the rate of ten miles an hour, which are two leagues and a half. Reckoned only forty-eight leagues, that the men might not be terrified if they should be long upon the voyage.

Tuesday, Sept. 11th. Steered their course W. and sailed above twenty leagues; saw a large fragment of the mast of a vessel, apparently of a hundred and twenty tons, but could not pick it up. In the night sailed about twenty leagues, and reckoned only sixteen, for the cause above stated.

Wednesday, Sept. 12th. This day steering their course, sailed day and night thirty-three leagues, and reckoned less, for the same cause.

Thursday, Sept. 13th. This day and night sailed W. thirty-three leagues, and reckoned three or four less. The currents were against them. At the first of the evening this day, the needles varied to the N.W. and the next morning about as much in the same direction.

Friday, Sept. 14th. Steered this day and night W. twenty leagues; reckoned somewhat less. The crew of the *Nina* stated that they had seen a *grajao,* and a tropic bird, or water-wagtail, which birds never go farther than twenty-five leagues from the land.

Saturday, Sept. 15th. Sailed day and night, W. twenty-seven leagues and more. In the beginning of the night saw a remarkable bolt of fire fall into the sea at the distance of four or five leagues.

Sunday, Sept. 16th. Sailed day and night. W. thirty-nine leagues, and reckoned only thirty-six. Some clouds arose and it drizzled. The Admiral here says that from this time they experienced very pleasant weather, and that the mornings were most delightful, wanting nothing but the melody of the nightingales. He compares the weather to that of Andalusia in April. Here they began to meet with large patches of weeds very green, and which appeared to have been recently washed away from the land; on which account they all judged themselves to be near some island, though not a continent, according to the opinion of the Admiral, who says, the continent we shall find further ahead.

Monday, Sept. 17th. Steered W. and sailed, day and night, above fifty leagues; wrote down only forty-seven; the current favoured them. They saw a great deal of weed which proved to be rockweed. It came from the W. and they met with it very frequently. They were of opinion that land was near. The pilots took the sun's amplitude, and found that the needles varied to the N.W. a whole point of the compass; the seamen were terrified and dismayed without saying why. The Admiral discovered the cause, and ordered them to take the amplitude again the next morning, when they found that the needles were true; the cause was that the star moved from its place while the needles remained stationary. At dawn they saw many more weeds, apparently river weeds, and among them a live crab which the Admiral kept, and says that these are sure signs of land, being never found eighty leagues out at sea. They found the sea-water less salt since they left the Canaries, and the air more mild. They were all very cheerful, and strove which vessel should outsail the others, and be the first to discover land; they saw many tunnies, and the crew of the *Nina* killed one. The Admiral here says that these signs were from the west, 'where I hope that high God in whose hand is all victory will speedily direct us to land.' This morning he says he saw a white bird called the water-wagtail, or tropic bird, which does not sleep at sea.

Tuesday, Sept. 18th. Continued their course, and sailed day and night more than fifty-five leagues; wrote down only forty-eight. All this time they had experienced fair weather, and sailed as they would have done upon the river at Seville. This day Martin Alonzo in the *Pinta,* which was a swift sailer, ran ahead of the other vessels, he having informed the Admiral that he had seen great flocks of birds towards the W. and that he expected that night to reach land; for this reason he kept on head of the others. A great mass of dark, heavy clouds appeared in the north, which is a sign of being near the land.

Wednesday, Sept. 19th. Continued on, and sailed, day and night, twenty-five leagues, experiencing a calm. Wrote down twenty-two. This day at ten o'clock a pelican came on board, and in the evening another; these birds are not accustomed to go twenty leagues from land. It drizzled without wind, which is a sure sign of land. The Admiral was unwilling to remain here, beating about in search of land, but he held it for certain that there were islands to the North and South, which in fact was the case and he was sailing in the midst of them. His wish was to proceed on to the Indies, having such fair weather, for if it please God, as the Admiral says, we shall examine these parts upon our return. Here the pilots found their places upon the chart: the reckoning of the *Nina* made her four hundred and forty leagues distant from the Canaries, that of the *Pinta* four hundred and twenty, that of the Admiral four hundred.

Thursday, Sept. 20th. Steered W. by N., varying with alternate changes of the wind and calms; made seven or eight leagues' progress. Two pelicans came on board, and afterwards another—a sign of the neighbourhood of land. Saw large quantities of weeds to-day, though none was observed yesterday. Caught a bird similar to a *grajao;* it was a river and not a marine bird, with feet like those of a gull. Towards night two or three land birds came to the ship, singing; they disappeared before sunrise. Afterwards saw a pelican coming from W.N.W. and flying to the S.W.; an evidence of land to the westward, as these birds sleep on shore, and go to sea in the morning in search of food, never proceeding twenty leagues from the land.

Friday, Sept. 21st. Most of the day calm, afterwards a little wind. Steered their course day and night, sailing less than thirteen leagues. In the morning found such abundance of weeds that the ocean seemed to be covered with them; they came from the west. Saw a pelican; the sea smooth as a river, and the finest air in the world. Saw a whale, an indication of land, as they always keep near the coast.

Saturday, Sept. 22d. Steered about W.N.W. varying their course, and making thirty leagues' progress. Saw few weeds. Some *pardelas* were seen, and another bird. The Admiral here says: 'This head wind was very necessary to me, for my crew had grown much alarmed, dreading that they never should meet in these seas with a fair wind to return to Spain.' Part of the day saw no weed, afterwards great plenty of it.

Sunday, Sept. 23d. Sailed N.W. and N.W. by N. and at times W. nearly twenty-two leagues. Saw a turtle dove, a pelican, a river bird, and other white fowl; weeds in abundance with crabs among them. The sea being smooth and tranquil, the sailors murmured, saying that they had got into smooth water, where it would never blow to carry them back to Spain; but afterwards the sea rose without wind, which astonished them. The Admiral says on this occasion: 'The rising of the sea was very favourable to me, as it happened formerly to Moses when he led the Jews from Egypt.'

Monday, Sept. 24th. Continued their course W. and sailed day and night fourteen leagues and a half; reckoned twelve; a pelican came to the ship, and they saw many *pardelas*.

Tuesday, Sept. 25th. Very calm this day; afterwards the wind rose. Continued their course W. till night. The Admiral held a conversation with Martin Alonzo Pinzon, captain of the *Pinta,* respecting a chart which the Admiral had sent him three days before, in which it appears he had marked down certain islands in that sea. Martin Alonzo was of opinion that they were in their neighbourhood, and the Admiral replied that he thought the same, but as they had not met with them, it must have been owing to the currents which had carried them to the N.E. and that they had not made such progress as the pilots stated. The Admiral directed him to return the chart, when he traced their course upon it in presence of the pilot and sailors.

At sunset Martin Alonzo called out with great joy from his vessel that he saw land, and demanded of the Admiral a reward for his intelligence. The Admiral says, when he heard him declare this, he fell on his knees and returned to God, and Martin Alonzo with his crew repeated *Gloria in excelsis Deo,* as did the crew of the Admiral. Those on board the *Nina* ascended the rigging, and all declared they saw land. The Admiral also thought it was land, and about twenty-five leagues distant. They remained all night repeating these affirmations, and the Admiral ordered their course to be shifted from W. to S.W. where the land appeared to lie. They sailed that day four leagues and a half W. and in the night seventeen leagues S.W., in all twenty-one and a half; told the crew thirteen leagues, making it a point to keep them from knowing how far they had sailed. In this manner two reckonings were kept, the shorter one falsified and the other being the true account. The sea was very smooth and many of the sailors went in it to bathe, saw many dories and other fish.

Wednesday, Sept. 26th. Continued their course W. till the afternoon, then S.W. and discovered that what they had taken for land was nothing but clouds. Sailed, day and night, thirty-one leagues; reckoned to the crew twenty-four. The sea was like a river, the air soft and mild.

Thursday, Sept. 27th. Continued their course W. and sailed, day and night, twenty-four leagues, reckoned to the crew twenty. Saw many dories and killed one. Saw a tropic bird.

Friday, Sept. 28th. Continued their course West, and sailed, day and night with calms, fourteen leagues, reckoned thirteen; met with a few weeds; caught two dories, and the other vessels more.

Saturday, Sept. 29th. Continued their course W. and sailed twenty-four leagues; reckoned to the crew twenty-one. On account of calms made little progress this day. Saw a bird called *rabihorcado,* which forces the pelicans to disgorge what they have swallowed, and then devours it; this is its only way of providing food. It is a marine bird, but never alights at sea, nor goes twenty leagues from land; there are many of them in the Cape Verde islands. Afterwards there came two pelicans. The air was soft and refreshing, and the Admiral says nothing was wanting but the singing of the nightingale; the sea smooth as a river. Three times they saw three pelicans, and a *rabihorcado.* Many weeds appeared.

Sunday, Sept. 30th. Continued their course W. and sailed day and night in calms, fourteen leagues; reckoned eleven. Four tropic birds came to the ship, which is a very clear sign of land, for so many birds of one sort together show that they are not straying about, having lost themselves. Twice, saw two pelicans; many weeds. The constellation called *Las Guardias,* which at evening appeared in a westerly [northerly?] direction, was seen in the N.E. the next morning, making no more progress in a night of nine hours. This was the case every night, as says the Admiral. At night the needles varied a point towards the N.W., in the morning they were true, by which it appears that the polar star moves, like the others, and the needles are always right.

Monday, Oct. 1st. Continued their course W. and sailed twenty-five leagues; reckoned to the crew twenty. Experienced a heavy shower. The pilot of the Admiral began to fear this morning that they were five hundred and seventy-eight leagues West of the island of Ferro. The short reckoning which the Admiral showed his crew gave five hundred and eighty-four, but the true one which he kept to himself was seven hundred and seven leagues.

Tuesday, Oct. 2d. Continued their course W. day and night, thirty-nine leagues; reckoned to the crew thirty; the sea ever smooth and favourable. 'Many thanks be to God,' says the Admiral here. Weed came from the E. towards the W., the contrary to what they had before observed. Saw many fish and took one. A white bird, which appeared to be a gull, was seen.

Wednesday, Oct. 3d. Continued their accustomed course, and sailed fortyseven leagues; reckoned to the crew forty. Many *pardelas* appeared, and great quantities of weed, some of it old, and some very fresh, which appeared to contain fruit. Saw no other birds. The Admiral believed they had passed the islands contained in his chart. Here the Admiral says that he was unwilling to stay beating up and down as the week before, when the had so many signs of land, though he knew there were islands in that quarter, because his wish was to proceed onward to the Indies, and to linger on the way he thought would be unwise.

Thursday, Oct. 4th. Continued their course W. Sailed day and night, sixtythree leagues, and reckoned to the crew forty-six. There came to the ship above forty *pardelas* in a flock, with two pelicans; a boy on board the caravel hit one of them with a stone. A *rabihorcado* came to the ship, and a white bird like a gull.

Friday, Oct. 5th. Continued their course and sailed eleven miles an hour day and night; fifty-seven leagues, the wind abating in the night, reckoned to the crew forty-five. Fine weather and the sea smooth. 'Many thanks to God,' says the Admiral. The air soft and temperate; no weeds; many *pardelas* were seen, and swallow-fishes in great numbers came on board.

Saturday, Oct. 6th. Continued their course W. and sailed forty leagues day and night; reckoned to the crew thirty-three. This night Martin Alonzo gave it as his opinion that they had better steer from W. to S.W. The Admiral thought from this that Martin Alonzo did not wish to proceed onward to Cipango; but he considered it best to keep on his course, as he should probably reach the land sooner in that direction, preferring to visit the continent first, and then the islands.

Sunday, Oct. 7th. Continued their course W. and sailed twelve miles an hour, for two hours, then eight miles an hour. Sailed till an hour after sunrise, twenty-three leagues; reckoned to the crew eighteen. At sunrise the caravel *Nina*—which kept ahead on account of her swiftness in sailing, while all the vessels were striving to outsail one another and gain the reward promised by the King and Queen by first discovering land—hoisted a flag at her mast head, and fired a *lombarda* as a signal that she had discovered land, for the Admiral had given orders to that effect. He had also ordered that the ships should keep in close company at sunrise and sunset, as the air was more favourable at those times for seeing at a distance. Towards evening, seeing nothing of the land which the *Nina* had made signals for, and observing large flocks of birds coming from the N. and making for the S.W., whereby it was rendered probable that they were either going to land to pass the night or abandoning the countries of the North on account of the approaching winter, he determined to alter his course, knowing also that the Portuguese had discovered most of the islands they possessed by attending to the flight of birds. The Admiral accordingly shifted his course from W. to W.S.W. with a resolution to continue two days in that direction. This was done about an hour after sunset. Sailed in the night nearly five leagues, and twenty-three in the day. In all twenty-eight.

Monday, Oct. 8th. Steered W.S.W. and sailed day and night eleven or twelve leagues; at times during the night, fifteen miles an hour, if the account can be depended upon. Found the sea like the river at Seville, 'thanks to God,' says the Admiral. The air soft as that of Seville in April, and so fragrant that it was delicious to breathe it. The weeds appeared very fresh. Many land birds, one of which they took, flying towards the S.W.; also *grajaos*, ducks, and a pelican were seen.

Tuesday, Oct. 9th. Sailed S.W. five leagues, when the wind changed, and they stood W. by N. four leagues. Sailed in the whole day and night, twenty leagues and a half; reckoned to the crew seventeen. All night heard birds passing.

Wednesday, Oct. 10th. Steered W.S.W. and sailed at times ten miles an hour, at others twelve, and at others seven; day and night made fifty-nine leagues' progress; reckoned to the crew but forty-four. Here the men lost all patience, and complained of the length of the voyage, but the Admiral encouraged them in the best manner he could, representing the profits they were about to acquire, and adding that it was to no purpose to complain, having come so far; they had nothing to do but continue on to the Indies till with the help of our Lord they should arrive there.

Thursday, Oct. 11th. Steered W.S.W.; and encountered a heavier sea than they had met with before in the whole voyage. Saw *pardelas* and a green rush near the vessel. The crew of the *Pinta* saw a cane and a log; they also picked up a stick which appeared to have been carved with an iron tool, a piece of cane, a plant which grows on land, and a board. The crew of the *Nina* saw other signs of land, and a stalk loaded with roseberries. These signs encouraged them, and they all grew cheerful. Sailed this day till sunset, twenty-seven leagues.

After sunset steered their original course W. and sailed twelve miles an hour till two hours after midnight, going ninety miles, which are twenty-two leagues and a half; and as the *Pinta* was the swiftest sailer, and kept ahead of the Admiral, she discovered land and made the signals which had been ordered. The land was first seen by a sailor called Rodrigo de Triana, although the Admiral at ten o'clock that evening standing on the quarter-deck saw a light, but so small a body that he could not affirm it to be land; calling to Pero Gutierrez, groom of the King's wardrobe, he told him he saw a light, and bid him look that way, which he did and saw it; he did the same to Rodrigo Sanchez of Segovia, whom the King and Queen had sent with the squadron as comptroller, but he was unable to see it from his situation. The Admiral again perceived it once or twice, appearing like the light of a wax candle moving up and down, which some thought an indication of land. But the Admiral held it for certain that land was near; for which reason, after they had said the *Salve* which the seamen are accustomed to repeat and chant after their fashion, the Admiral directed them to keep a strict watch upon the forecastle and look out diligently for land, and to him who should first discover it he promised a silken jacket, besides the reward which the King and Queen had offered, which was an annuity of ten thousand maravedis. At two o'clock in the morning the land was discovered, at two leagues' distance; they took in sail and remained under the square-sail lying to till day, which was Friday, when they found themselves near a small island, one of the Lucayos, called in the Indian language Guanahani. Presently they descried people, naked, and the Admiral landed in the boat, which was armed, along with Martin Alonzo Pinzon, and Vincent Yanez his brother, captain of the *Nina*. The Admiral bore the royal standard, and the two captains each a banner of the Green Cross, which all the ships had carried; this contained the initials of the names of the King and Queen each side of the cross, and a crown over each lettter. Arrived on shore, they saw trees very green, many streams of water, and diverse sorts of fruits. The Admiral called upon the two Captains, and the rest of the crew who landed, as also to Rodrigo de Escovedo, notary of the fleet, and Rodrigo Sanchez, of Segovia, to bear witness that he before all others took possession (as in fact he did) of that island for the King and Queen his sovereigns.

⚓

HOW ÆOLUS, KING OF THE WINDS, SENT FORTH A STORM AGAINST ÆNEAS

⚓

HOW ÆOLUS, KING OF THE WINDS, SENT FORTH A STORM AGAINST ÆNEAS

Virgil

⚓ *Man's destiny is inevitably bound up in the sea, for on it man has ventured forth in daring voyages of discovery and pioneers have launched their ships to settle the newly discovered land. If we can see beyond the quaintness of language of Virgil's translator, we can discover how real to the ancient Trojan was the overwhelming force of wind and sea. It is little wonder that he personified them and that they became titanic struggles between Gods who served the wills of other Gods as capricious as himself.*

SCARCELY had the Trojans, losing sight of Sicily, with joy launched out into the deep, and were ploughing the foaming billows with their brazen prows, when Juno, harbouring everlasting rancour in her breast, thus with herself:

"Shall I then, baffled, desist from my purpose, nor have it in my power to turn away the Trojan king from Italy, because I am restrained by fate? Was Pallas able to burn the Grecian ships, and bury them in the ocean, for the offence of one, and the frenzy of Ajax, Oileus' son? She herself, hurling from the clouds Jove's rapid fire, both scattered their ships, and upturned the sea with the winds; him too she snatched away in a whirlwind, breathing flames from his transfixed breast, and dashed him against the pointed rock. But I, who move majestic, the queen of heaven, both sister and wife of Jove, must maintain a series of wars with one single race for so many years. And who will henceforth adore Juno's divinity, or humbly offer sacrifice on her altars?"

The goddess by herself revolving such thoughts in her inflamed breast, repairs to Æolia, the native land of storms, regions pregnant with boisterous

From C. Davidson's translation of *The Æneid* (1866).

winds. Here, in a vast cave, King Æolus controls with imperial sway the reluctant winds and sounding tempests, and confines them with chains in prison. They roar indignant round their barriers, filling the mountain with loud murmurs. Æolus is seated on a lofty throne, wielding a sceptre, and assuages their fury, and moderates their rage. For, unless he did so, they, in their rapid career, would bear away sea and earth, and the deep heaven, and sweep them through the air. But the almighty Sire, guarding against this, hath pent them in gloomy caves, and thrown over them the ponderous weight of mountains and appointed them a king, who, by fixed laws, and at command, knows both to curb them, and when to relax their reins; whom Juno then in suppliant words thus addressed:

"Æolus, (for the sire of gods and the king of men hath given thee power both to smooth the waves and raise them with the wind,) a race by me detested sails the Tuscan Sea, transporting Ilium, and its conquered gods, into Italy. Strike force into thy winds, overset and sink the ships; or drive them different ways, and strew the ocean with carcasses. I have twice seven lovely nymphs, the fairest of whom, Deïopeia, I will join to thee in firm wedlock, and assign to be thine own for ever, that with thee she may spend all her years for this service, and make thee father of a beautiful offspring."

To whom Æolus replies:

" 'Tis thy task, O Queen, to consider what you would have done: on me it is incumbent to execute your commands. You conciliate to me whatever of power I have, my sceptre, and Jove. You grant me to sit at the tables of the Gods; and you make me lord of storms and tempests."

Thus having said, whirling the point of his spear, he struck the hollow mountain's side: and the winds, as in a formed battalion, rush forth at every vent, and scour over the lands in a hurricane. They press upon the ocean, and at once, east, and south, and stormy south-west, plough up the whole deep from its lowest bottom, and roll vast billows to the shores. The cries of the seamen succeed, and the cracking of the cordage. In an instant clouds snatch the heavens and day from the eyes of the Trojans, sable night sits brooding on the sea, thunder roars from pole to pole, the sky glares with repeated flashes, and all nature threatens them with immediate death. Forthwith Æneas' limbs are relaxed with cold shuddering fear. He groans, and, spreading out both his hands to heaven, thus expostulates:

"O thrice and four times happy they, who had the good fortune to die before their parents' eyes, under the high ramparts of Troy! O thou, the bravest of the Grecian race, great Tydeus' son, why was I not destined to fall on the Trojan plains, and pour out this soul by thy right hand? where stern Hector lies prostrate by the sword of Achilles; where mighty Sarpedon lies; where Simois rolls along so many shields, and helmets, and bodies of heroes snatched away beneath its waters."

While uttering such words a tempest, roaring from the north, strikes across the sail, and heaves the billows to the stars. The oars are shattered: then the prow turns away, and exposes the side to the waves. A steep mountain of waters follows in a heap. These hang on the towering surge; to whose eyes the wide-yawning deep discloses the earth between two waves; the whirling tide rages with mingled sand. Three other ships the south wind, hurrying away, throws on hidden rocks; rocks in the midst of the ocean, which the Italians call Altars, a vast ridge rising to the surface of the sea. Three from the deep the east wind drives on shoals and flats, a piteous spectacle! and dashing on the shelves, it encloses them with mounds of sand. Before the eyes of Æneas himself, a mighty billow, falling from the height, dashes against the stern of one which bore the Lycian crew, and faithful Orontes: the pilot is tossed out and rolled headlong, prone into the waves: but her the driving surge thrice whirls around in the same place, and the rapid eddy swallows up in the deep. Then floating here and there on the vast abyss, are seen men, their arms, and planks, and the Trojan wealth, among the waves. Now the storm overpowered the stout vessel of Ilioneus, now that of brave Achates, and that in which Abas sailed, and that in which old Alethes; all, at their loosened and disjointed sides, receive the hostile stream, and gape with chinks.

Meanwhile Neptune perceived that the sea was in great uproar and confusion, a storm sent forth, and the depths overturned from their lowest channels. He, in violent commotion, and looking forth from the deep, reared his serene countenance above the waves; sees Æneas' fleet scattered over the ocean, the Trojans oppressed with the waves and the ruin from above. Nor were Juno's wiles and hate unknown to her brother. He calls to him the east and west winds; then thus addresses them:

"And do you thus presume upon your birth? Dare you, winds! without my sovereign leave, to embroil heaven and earth, and raise such mountains? Whom I——But first it is right to assuage the tumultuous waves. A chastisement of another nature from me awaits your next offence. Fly apace, and bear this message to your king: That not to him the empire of the sea, and the awful trident, but to me by lot are given: his dominions are the mighty rocks, your proper mansions, Eurus: in that palace let King Æolus proudly boast and reign in the close prison of the winds."

So he speaks, and, more swiftly than his speech, smooths the swelling seas, disperses the collected clouds, and brings back the day. With him Cymothoë, and Triton with exerted might, heave the ships from the pointed rock. He himself raised them with his trident; lays open the vast sandbanks, and calms the sea; and in his light chariot glides along the surface of the waves. And as when a sedition has perchance arisen among a mighty multitude, and the minds of the ignoble vulgar rage; now firebrands, now stones fly; fury supplies them with arms: if then, by chance, they espy a man revered in piety and worth, they are hushed, and stand with ears erect; he, by eloquence, rules their passions and calms their breasts. Thus all the raging tumult of the ocean subsides, as soon as the sire, surveying the seas, and wafted through the open sky, guides his steeds, and flying, gives the reins to his easy chariot.

The weary Trojans direct their course towards the nearest shores, and make the coast of Libya. In a long recess, a station lies; an island forms it into a harbour by its jutting sides, against which every wave from the ocean is broken, and divides itself into receding curves. On either side vast cliffs, and two twin-like rocks, threaten the sky; under whose summit the waters all around are calm and still. Above is a sylvan scene with waving woods, and a dark grove with awful shade hangs over. Under the opposite front a cave is of pendant rocks, within which are fresh springs, and seats of living stone, the recess of nymphs. Here neither cables hold, nor anchors with crooked fluke moor the weather-beaten ships. To this retreat Æneas brings seven ships, collected from all his fleet; and the Trojans, longing much for land, disembarking, enjoy the wished-for shore, and stretch their brine-drenched limbs upon the beach.